SALT IN THE SEAS

KARYNE NORTON

SALT IN THE SEAS

THE HALF-LIGHT CHRONICLES

BOOK TWO

FIRST LIGHT
PUBLISHING

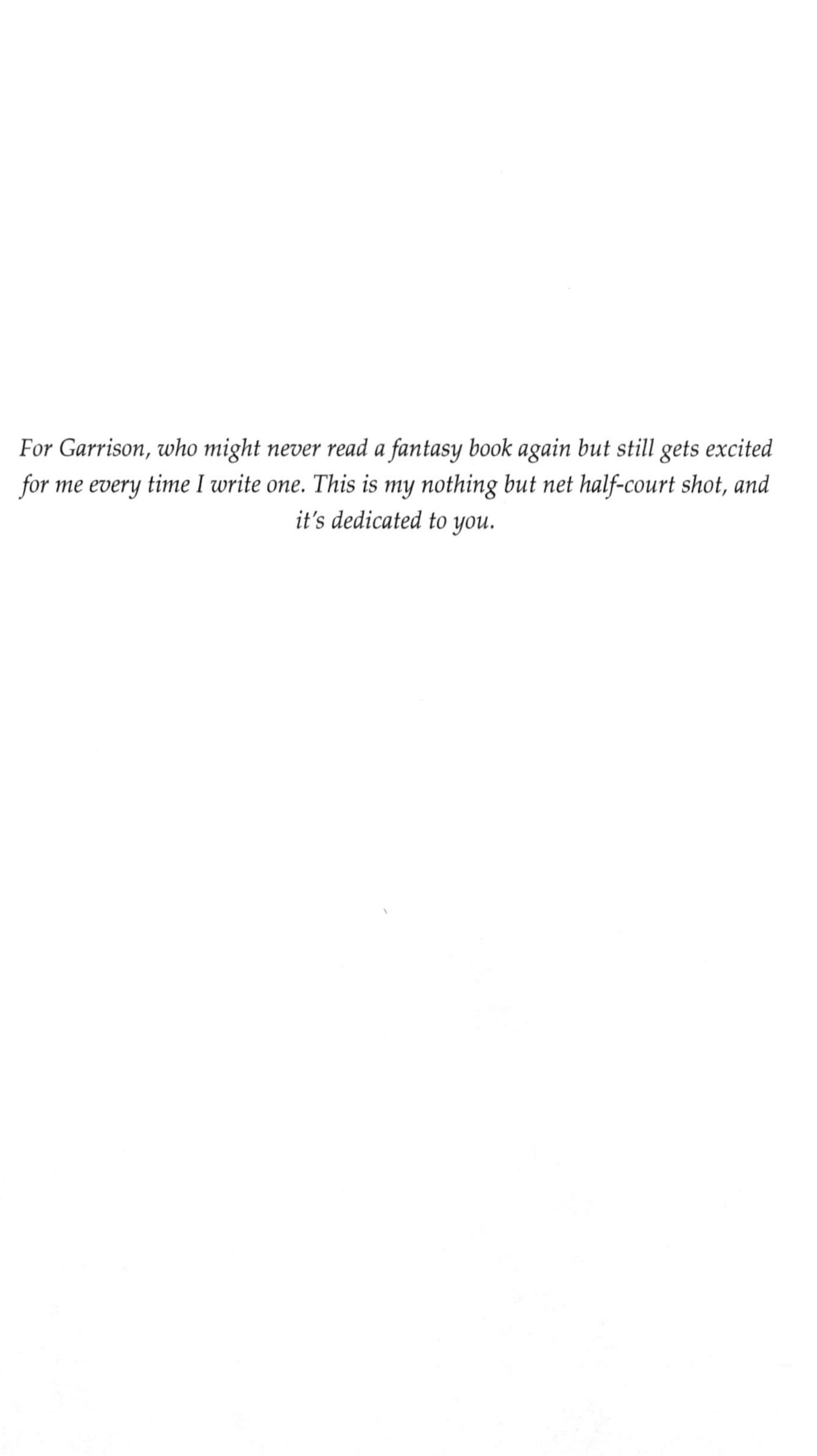

For Garrison, who might never read a fantasy book again but still gets excited for me every time I write one. This is my nothing but net half-court shot, and it's dedicated to you.

ILIONA
LAST CHANCE
SERENDELLAN
STARHAVEN
LUHMEN MOUNTAIN
MAHLIC
GAHLDRIC VALLEY
VELSPETZ
ELANESSE
WEST HARBOR
LORVANDAS
BOLSPA
RYKARN
FAIRMOOR
ISLA
DARKWOOD
DAHLVAS
BAMBOO ISLAND
SAYHLA PORT
VALORIAN
SEER'S SANCTUARY
ANDE
TIDEHOLM
SAYHLA ISLAND

AHMRANAS
HEART'S HOPE
ALLEY
ANDRA
LAND'S END
SELAHSTRA
MAHRAGLEN
THE LANDS OF
RHYSTAHN
ORTHPOINT
MYNDREN
DRAGON'S ROOST
VENDARAS
SUNSHROUD
WINDMERE INLET
WYVERN WATCH
CELANOFT
GALGOTTA
EASTHAVEN
DEHVLON
BURROWER BEACH
SEAGLASS PORT
IRONSPIRE
ASHENWOOD

ELANESSE
RYKARN
MT. VESCA
ISLARA
DAHLVAS
BAMBOO ISLAND
LOVERS' FALLS
VALORIAN
ANDEL
THE CONTINENT OF
VENDARAS

THE NORTHERN SEA
RTHPOINT
HLRIC
SERT
MYNDREN
MYNDREN MOUNTAINS
SUNSHROUD
WINDMERE INLET
CELANOFT
DEHVLON
EAGLASS
PORT
THE DARKWATER
CURRENTS

SUNSPARK
ATOLL
SEER'S
SANCTUARY
SEER'S
SCHOOL
WATER'S
EDGE
WHELK
BAY
WAVECREST
PAELEN'S

THE SUNKISSED SANDS OF
SAYHLA ISLAND
THE MYSTIC REEF
CORALCREST
YHLEEN SHORE
TIDEHOLM
SALTWIND COVE
OPALINE LAGOON
WATERS

THE WHEEL OF MAGIC

THE WHEEL OF MAGIC

The Wheel of Magic is made up of a hub, six spokes, and a rim.

Hub: The simplest form of magic that only requires movement of energy to manipulate things. It manifests during adolescence, but fades if not developed.

Spokes: Once a progeny earns their starlock during their Awakening, they can progress in developing their magic from the hub out to a spoke. There are three sets of spokes (somatic, noetic, pneumatic) each with a constructive and destructive side. Typically progenies develop a specific skill along one spoke, which they can sometimes mirror on the opposite (constructive or destructive) side.

Rim: Advanced progenies can develop additional skills along their spoke, but the most advanced develop skills along a second neighboring spoke. This then gives them access to the elemental magic found on the rim between their two developed spokes. Rim magic can also be accessed through blood magic.

Somatic: Progenies who adjust the body (heal, harm, disguise, etc)

Noetic: Progenies who tune into the mind (thoughts, memories, emotions etc)

Pneumatic: Progenies who sift through the soul (motives, past, future, etc)

For other terms please see glossary in back of book.

SALT IN THE SEAS

CHAPTER 1

Aeliana hurried down the empty hall of the fortress, counting the doors as she followed along on her scribbled map. When she reached the eighth door, she prayed her mother's memory had been accurate as she pulled the heavy oak door open with a creak. An old servant's room lay before her, the hall windows revealing dust and derelict objects.

She glanced down the abandoned hall once more, then breathed a sigh of relief as she let the door click shut behind her in the room.

Tucking the parchment in her skirt pocket, she held out her hands and let her starlock burn warm against her chest. Its energy joined with that in her blood, then spread to her hands, where a small light sputtered and flickered. She frowned, unsure why her magic seemed to be fading even though Sylmar still required her to train on a daily basis. Shoving the concern aside, she held her palms out to shed light on the rest of the room, ignoring the remains of whoever had stayed there last, likely decades before.

Instead, she tapped on the stone walls and looked for unnatural seams in the grout. Her mother had been certain this was one of Mayvus' hiding spots.

Sure enough, the third wall made a hollow sound, and Aeliana slid her fingers along the grout until she felt one stone give way. She pressed harder until it released a spring mechanism that brought the hidden door open.

"You were right, Mother," she whispered with a grin. Before she could examine the contents of the closet, footsteps and voices carried down the hall.

"Why is Sylmar so bent on cleaning all the rooms when the outer walls still need to be rebuilt?" Kendalyhn's complaint carried through the thick oak door as if she stood directly beside it. The bitter young woman already had it out for Aeliana; she was the last person Aeliana wanted finding her here.

She pulled the hidden stone wall door open wider, then wedged herself inside the tight space, her back pressed up against a shelf.

"He has soldiers working on the wall, love." Iris' soft maternal tone gave Aeliana some comfort. The older woman had been her mother's maidservant for years, and while Aeliana still didn't want to be caught, Iris would at least understand Aeliana's desire to help her mother. "With Mayvus gone, there's no rush. He's determined to use these rooms to provide refuge for the families left without husbands and fathers from the battle. At least until things turn around for everyone."

Aeliana pulled the stone door back just as the latch on the oak door clicked. She closed her eyes, praying they wouldn't notice the inconsistency of the wall. She was too scared to shut it all the way in case she couldn't get it back open.

"Ugh," Kendalyhn groaned. "I don't even think Mayvus used these rooms."

"Salvage what you can," Iris said. "But don't be afraid to toss anything that's beyond repair. After we get through this hall, we can bring families in to help us clear out more."

An itch started on Aeliana's leg, one that felt suspiciously like a spider crawling up under her skirt. She batted at it while gritting her teeth to keep herself from screaming, but then her heel bumped the shelf behind her, and something glass clinked to the floor. She froze, holding her breath.

"Did you hear that?" Kendalyhn asked.

"That tinkling? It sounded like the winex laughing again," Iris said.

"We should probably block this hall while we're working; otherwise, they'll try to help, which is more harmful during this early phase of the moon."

Their voices faded as Kendalyhn bemoaned the number of rooms down the hall, and after several moments Aeliana felt confident they'd shut the door behind them and moved on. She let out her breath and allowed the light to flow back into her palms.

When she tugged her skirt up, she found a large spider bite swelling on her thigh. With no sign of the spider, she shuddered, wondering if it was still tangled in her skirts. But then her gaze caught the glint of glass, and she bent to find a vial of blood at her feet, along with dozens more on the shelf.

She bit her lip in indecision. She was already going to be late for her training session with Sylmar. What harm was a few more moments? She pulled out the parchment, then used the back side of the map to make a careful list of all the labels on the vials, name after name, along with where their magic landed on the spokes and rim of the Wheel of Magic. All people that Mayvus had either branded or planned to brand by fusing their blood to her body, essentially making them puppets she could control—taking their magic for her own.

After each one had been documented, she stuffed all the vials in her skirt pockets, wincing when they clinked together as she stepped from the closet. She pressed them against her thighs to immobilize them while she opened the oak door and peered down the hall.

"What are you doing?" Kendalyhn whispered at her back.

Aeliana let out a yelp before turning around.

The other woman was a few years older than Aeliana, but her petite build, impish grin, and short black hair made her look far younger. Right now, her smile held more of a smirk, and her eyebrows rose. "Were you spying on Iris and me?"

"No, I—" Aeliana paused, trying to think of what she could say to a woman who could sift her soul and pick apart her past motives. "I'm avoiding Sylmar."

Kendalyhn snorted. "Aren't we all?" She eyed Aeliana disdainfully. "But in your case, he still has a lot to teach you, and you'd be foolish not to learn from him."

"You already think I'm foolish," Aeliana muttered, then pushed past Kendalyhn before the other woman could agree. She concentrated on keeping the vials of blood silent against her legs, despite knowing her walk would appear stiff and awkward.

Sylmar was going to have her hide, but she still had to dispose of the blood; otherwise, he might think she was delving into blood magic again. She grimaced when she realized she only had time to dispose of them in one of the privies. Sequestering herself away, she broke the vials one by one and dumped them down the chute into the cesspit. She gagged as the metallic scent mixed with feces and urine, permeating the confined space, but she felt a sense of accomplishment when she was able to mark off forty-two vials having been destroyed.

Her mother would be proud.

She smiled and tucked the parchment back in her pocket before exiting the privy and rushing down the hall to the training room. She was sniffing the sleeves of her blouse, hoping no one else could smell the blood on her, when she rounded the corner and skidded into the training room.

Velden grinned at her from the space they'd cleared for sparring. The tattoos dancing across his skin and the fish hooks dangling from his ears made him look more like the pirates she watched for every day, but his webbed hands were proof that he belonged in the water, not floating on it. Holm, his opponent, turned to follow his gaze, then gave Aeliana a small wave. Velden's lanky form was no match for Holm's height and bulk, so he used the other man's distraction to get in a blow.

Sylmar cleared his throat from where he stood in the room's center. He leaned on his staff to glare at her. "Well, what happened this time?" His guttural voice matched the harsh scars lining his face.

"I'm sorry. I lost track of time." She hurried to stand before him, smoothing down her skirt. She held back a grimace when she found a drop of blood on it, then caught sight of a cut on her palm. How had she not noticed one of the vials had cut her? She tucked it in the folds of her skirt while picturing the broken skin mending, willing her star-lock to heal the wound. Except that part of her magic seemed to be failing lately too.

Sylmar placed a hand on Aeliana's shoulder. "What were you doing that had you so distracted?"

"It was my turn to help Iris with the winex after lunch. You know how needy they are these days. It took longer than I anticipated." The first part had been the truth.

His eyes narrowed, and he gripped her shoulder tighter. "Why are you lying?"

She went still, but her heart beat faster. Why had she let him touch her? Sifting the truth of her words was his secondary spoke and something he could only do with a point of contact. She'd been foolish to let her guard down.

"Give her a break, Sylmar," Velden called from the sparring ring. "You were young once. Or have you forgotten? At her age, I had plenty of secrets and private affairs I didn't want to share with my elders or mentors. Nothing nefarious, just the normal reckless life of a youth. Let her live a little."

Velden winked at her, then grunted when Holm jabbed him in the stomach with his fist. The two resumed their wrestling, while Aeliana turned to Sylmar with a sheepish smile, her face too hot and likely red.

Sylmar placed his hand back on his staff and hummed his disapproval, but then directed Aeliana to a chair, apparently willing to let it drop for now. A flutter of relief rushed through Aeliana. Her secret errands for her mother hadn't been discovered. Until they had solid evidence, Sylmar wouldn't be willing to listen to her mother's theory that Mayvus was alive. Not when Mayvus' assumed death gave everyone else comfort.

"Today I want you to try connecting with Durriken," Sylmar said.

Her anxiety returned. She ran a hand over the detestable mark on her right hand. "I don't want to bother him. He lost his freedom for years, then I severed his paw. I think the last dragon alive deserves to be left in peace."

"I'm not asking you to control him through your brand, but as long as you have it, you can see if you can tell where he left Mayvus' body." The eagerness that rolled off Sylmar made Aeliana hesitate.

At one time, Sylmar had been Mayvus' bondmate. He'd been willing to use blood magic to brand people, taking over their will and replacing it with his own. Such evil was the reason Aeliana had never wanted to brand Durriken in the first place, but desperation had overruled her desires. It had been the only way to weaken Mayvus.

She shook her head to dispel the suspicion. Sylmar was faithful to the Recreants' cause. He simply wanted to find Mayvus' body to reassure everyone she was no longer a threat. Aeliana didn't always like his methods, but she could trust him with information.

"All right." She'd only caught glimpses of Durriken's location or hints of his thoughts in the past. As long as she refused to impose her will on him, maybe it wasn't as intrusive as it seemed.

She closed her eyes and pressed on the brand mark, focusing on the massive dragon as she'd last seen him, his azure and amethyst scales fading into the night sky as he flew off with his prize: Mayvus.

CHAPTER 2

Sharp pain stabbed through Aeliana's—no, Durriken's—wing. They flew over a charred city, the sting of an arrow piercing his nearly translucent blue wing. He dove for the barren ground, not bothering to see where the arrow had come from. It was nothing compared to the phantom pain she—no, he—constantly sensed in his severed paw.

The clarity within his mind was overwhelming, but her own mind felt fuzzy, like she only half existed while connected to him. Or maybe she was simply experiencing his memory. She still didn't understand the brand that joined them.

An irritated rumble in her chest showed that Durriken was equally aware of the invasion in his mind. So, then, not a memory.

He ignored the men camped outside the city's ruins. Instead, he crossed the wall dividing forest from destruction and landed in a sprawling courtyard, his gait unsteady with his change in balance. He limped across the broken stones that had once held a market with shops and patrons, his remaining paws crushing the scattered wares.

Only it wasn't just wares.

Brittle bones and ashes flattened beneath his feet, the sense of the souls they'd held weighing him down further. When he reached the courtyard's center, he spun once, letting his tail curl in until he settled in a ball, his nose nestled beneath the curve of his scales. Aeliana felt the Sun on his back, spreading its warmth through to the tips of his paws.

For a moment it seemed as if he'd returned to Islara just to nap in the wake of his destruction, and Aeliana would be forced to remain curled up in his mind while he did so. Hundreds, if not thousands, of lives had been taken from the city by the fire of his breath mere weeks earlier. He'd annihilated Islara and its residents in the span of a day, and now he wanted to sleep in their remains?

But Aeliana sensed an alertness within him, a new kind of pain that grew to surpass that in his foreleg.

Could a dragon feel sorrow? Remorse?

Durriken growled his irritation. He didn't want her here for this moment. He didn't want her sensing the way he mourned the people he'd killed.

She didn't feel right about it either. Not when he didn't want her there. She focused on his external surroundings instead, letting her magic flow across their connection and through to the other side, but it wasn't something she could control. Daisies grew by his snout, but he let out a frustrated huff of hot air that wilted them into the ground.

She stretched the limits of her autonomy, attempting to divide his will from her own. If she could make him understand she didn't want this forced connection, maybe he would willingly exchange information. They could remain the equals they'd been when they'd parted. But the moment she sensed his will separate from her own, a new urgency emerged—a desire to impose her own will on his.

She fought against its pull while trying to remember what information Sylmar sought, what she was supposed to ask. The questions remained out of reach, just beyond the haze left in the wake of her need to command him. The effort to resist was too reminiscent of her past struggles against blood magic.

Blood magic. Mayvus. *That* had been her question.

The desire to know where he'd taken Mayvus after the battle flooded her mind, and Durriken stiffened as if it flooded his too.

A growl started deep in his belly, and he lifted his head, every muscle taut as if he was on high alert. When nothing more happened, he settled his head back on his paws. Aeliana felt his lips lift in a satisfied smirk as he pushed a memory on her. Blood and torn flesh filled his mouth, leaving her nauseous, but she fought to let the memory continue. The descent over a small peak in the Myndren Mountains, the desire for revenge, the throb of a freshly lost paw. He'd circled to land in a cave, where he'd settled to gnaw on his prize.

The memory cut off too abruptly. Had he eaten Mayvus? Left her to die? She wanted to be certain, and the urge to force his cooperation tugged at her belly. It was what the brand had been designed to do, to control him, and yet it went against everything Aeliana believed in. She refused to command him to give her more.

The tether between them snapped with an audible crack that reverberated through Aeliana's head, and her eyes flew open as she gasped.

Sylmar bent before her, his perpetual frown filling her vision. Behind him, Holm jabbed at a hay bag in the corner, but Velden must have left the training room. Because she was in the training room in the fortress of the Myndren Mountains. Not Islara. And not even in the cave where Durriken had deposited Mayvus.

"Well?" Sylmar asked.

Aeliana blinked, her heart pounding a rhythm faster than the thud of Holm's fists. "Um, what?"

A sound between a bark and a cough escaped Sylmar as he straightened. "Did you sense Durriken?"

The vision of Islara's ruins came back to her, the memory she'd received from Durriken sending a shudder through her spine. "I did."

"And?"

"He's in Islara." She tugged on her braid, bringing the brown ends that hung at her waist up to her chin, letting the edges brush her skin while she debated what that might mean. Did Durriken return just to mourn the people he'd killed? He'd ignored the people outside the city's walls, but she had no idea if they were fellow Recreants or if they were Loyalists who served the Vendaran crown. At least they weren't the Zealots who'd followed Mayvus. Those who'd been loyal to the evil high priestess had scattered when she'd disappeared, and those who'd been freed from the brands forcing them to serve her had sworn fealty to Aeliana's mother, Emeris, instead.

There had been a loneliness inside Durriken that still echoed within

Aeliana's chest. A feeling of not belonging. Despite his scales and fangs and fire, it made sense for the last known dragon to hold such a hollow sensation. But it also resonated with Aeliana in ways she didn't want to admit as she attempted to settle amidst the Vendarans despite having grown up in Lorvandas.

Sylmar leaned on his staff, his brow furrowed in thought. "Any sign of Mayvus' body?"

"He took her to a cave. I might be able to find the right peak to adjust our search. He seemed… pleased. But I couldn't tell if Mayvus was alive in his memory."

Sylmar rubbed at his short greying beard. "We know she's dead. We just need to find her remains. Put the people at ease."

Aeliana bit back her argument. Ever since Durriken had flown off with Mayvus in his grasp, they'd sent out daily scouts, and every day for the last six weeks, the scouts had returned without answers. Most everyone found this reassuring. It meant Durriken had likely disposed of Mayvus in his own gruesome way before moving on to new territory. Two enemies no longer a threat.

But Emeris kept insisting that Mayvus was alive.

She also insisted they were in Celanoft, not the Myndren Mountains, most days. Her lingering confusion after being branded for so long meant Aeliana was the only one who believed her about Mayvus.

Screeches and tinkling laughter filled the air, resounding from the hall in a crescendo that stunned the training room's occupants.

Sylmar let out a deflated grunt, then hobbled to the wall, flattening himself against its stone surface. A moment later, a horde of silver creatures galloped into the room like playful puppies tripping and tumbling over their oversized feet. They weren't much bigger than toddlers, but their limbs were longer, their dual rows of teeth sharper. Wide eyes filled their faces and sunlight from the open windows gleamed off their hairless heads.

Aeliana grinned, then kneeled down, arms wide as she let the winex at the front of the pack lunge at her. The force knocked her back, and the black tear-shaped mark on his cheek filled her vision before at least half of the others swarmed her.

"Felk." Her voice came out muffled beneath their squirming forms. "Call them off. I concede. I'll get your dinner."

At the mention of food, the pack retreated, whispering amongst themselves about which meal she might have for them. They sat on their heels, wriggling with anticipation.

"It's late," Felk whined, pulling her back up to her knees so they were eye to eye.

Lilik scooted next to him, laying her head on his shoulder in solidarity. Despite cycling lives with the moon, the two remained inseparable. It was as if their fight to find and protect their eggs in their past life left them bonded in ways their life cycle couldn't break. Now their children had been born alongside their own rebirths these last two new moons.

Taking care of Felk as a newborn had been difficult. A dozen winex had been pure chaos.

"Iris is making soup down in the kitchen." Aeliana stood, brushing off her blouse and skirt.

Half of the winex cheered while the others grumbled. "We always have soup," one mumbled.

"I can take them," Holm said. He loomed over the winex, and several of them shrank back from his height and girth even though they were quickly learning he was soft inside. A few had figured out he was the easiest one to convince to sneak them treats from the kitchens since he was often doing the same.

Holm's face held a red hue, maybe from his effort at beating the hay bag into submission, but more likely over his eagerness to find his bondmate in the kitchen. He and Iris were the only couple Aeliana knew who were happily bonded. Considering she'd had less than a year in Vendaras, where bonding both symbolized and strengthened marriage ties, that wasn't saying much.

She rubbed the dark red bond mark on her left palm, still not sure what to think of being tied to Lukai in such a permanent way. She compared it to the ugly black brand bubbled up on her right palm. A bond was meant to connect people in a way that allowed them to protect each other. It went both ways to aid both bondmates. But a brand went one way, allowing the one who performed the branding ceremony to control the other.

They still seemed too similar to Aeliana.

"I should watch for Lukai anyway," Sylmar said, finally leaving his sanctuary at the room's edge when the last of the winex had followed Holm from the room. "He and the others are due back from scouting soon. In the morning you can try to show them the peak where Durriken took Mayvus."

"All right. I'll go check on my mother." A wave of anticipation rippled through Aeliana. After years without family, every moment she could spend with her mother was precious.

Sylmar nodded. "I wouldn't tell her about Durriken's memory. She'll find a way to convince herself it means Mayvus is alive, feeding her delusions."

Aeliana stiffened. "I doubt she'd believe Mayvus was dead even if we presented her sister's body to her."

"Which is what made her such a wise leader. Illusions and memories are too easily crafted to take the first thing you see or hear as truth." He limped through the doorway, throwing his final words over his shoulder. "But no one could survive Durriken's vengeful jaws."

"She still *is* a wise leader," Aeliana muttered to the empty room. "And she's right. Mayvus is alive." Sylmar was usually the mistrusting one, but with Mayvus, it was almost like he needed the closure too much to see the truth.

It didn't matter if Aeliana was the only one who believed her mother. They'd prove it to the others soon enough.

The training room was at the center of the fortress, directly above the kitchens. It had probably been a dining room in more affluent times, but now it was empty save the weapons and armor they'd brought in for sparring. Aeliana left it behind for the hall to the eastern wing, passing several soldiers who touched their fingers to their foreheads while inclining their heads in her direction.

She'd given up on deterring the strange custom, deciding to view it as their cultural way of respecting her mother, the high priestess—the woman many of them wanted to be their queen. But it still made her uncomfortable. If Sylmar and the others continued writing Emeris off as a mere figurehead, it wouldn't be long before they expected Aeliana to fill that role instead.

A glance out the hall window revealed the precarious northern keep where they'd confronted Mayvus. They'd removed all the bodies and blocked off the battlements surrounding it, uncertain when its deteriorating structure would eventually give. Since then, Orra had quietly claimed it, escaping there for days at a time when she wasn't scouring the mountains for the stone starbridge she was so desperate to find, either unconvinced or unconcerned about the keep's inevitable fall.

Sometimes Aeliana feared her mother's mind was like the northern keep. One wrong step could shift the balance and bring the whole thing down.

When she reached her mother's chambers, the door was already open, Sunlight streaming in through the windows. That was a good sign. Sure enough, she found her mother sitting on the settee instead of lying in bed, her short walnut hair intricately braided. Iris, her mother's loyal maidservant from years ago, must have been here to help before she made it to the kitchen.

"Aeliana." Her mother breathed the word out as if it cost her, but her smile seemed sincere.

The starlock hanging from the leather cord around Aeliana's neck grew warm against her chest, practically begging her to push some of her energy through to ease her mother's pain. When she did, her mother's tense posture relaxed ever so slightly.

"You're looking well." Aeliana bent down to embrace her mother, taking careful note of her pallor and the dark skin under her eyes. Still, her words were true. Her mother looked better than the day before.

"Yes, unfortunately."

Aeliana laughed lightly as she settled next to her mother. "Usually people find that to be a good thing."

"Not if it means she's getting stronger too."

Aeliana grimaced. "Durriken gave me a memory today. He showed me the cave where he took her body. I think I might be able to find the right peak for the soldiers to search."

Her mother patted her hair, her face troubled. "They won't find her.

She's been healing just like me. If Mayvus were dead, I would be too because of the curse. I told your father the same thing after the dragon took Mayvus."

Aeliana's heart sank. Gaeren, Riveran, and Cyrus had traveled across the barrier to look for her father weeks ago. No one had seen him for years, not since the day he'd taken Aeliana across the barrier for her safety just to be overpowered by two of Mayvus' Zealots.

She understood why the others didn't trust anything Emeris said about Mayvus to be true when she had these moments of confusion.

"If my father's alive, he's on the other side of the Lorvandan barrier." The gentle reminder made Emeris furrow her brow.

"Oh, that's right," her mother said. "I hope the others find him before Mayvus returns."

"You still think she used the stone starbridge to cross the barrier to Ahmranas?" Aeliana asked as she pulled the piece of parchment from her pocket.

"If the people can't find the starbridge or her body, it's the only thing that makes sense. She wasn't dead that night, but she was weak. She couldn't have made it far."

Aeliana nodded, hating her mother's logic because it meant Mayvus was out of their reach, growing stronger. Orra had denied the possibility, claiming she would have sensed it because of her strange connection to the four starbridges. After the Great Divide, when all of Rhystahn had been broken into five lands and separated by water and barriers, the Sun had forged four objects to take people across the barriers: a golden arrow, an onyx stone, a silver fish, and an iron cutlass. Each one connected a different land to Vendaras.

When Aeliana had touched the arrow that took her from Lorvandas to Vendaras, Orra had sensed it. But the strangely powerful woman also begrudgingly admitted she'd been weak the night of their battle. Perhaps too weak to sense Mayvus using the onyx stone to go from Vendaras to Ahmranas.

"What's this?" Emeris asked, reaching for Aeliana's parchment.

"I found more vials of blood in that passageway you suggested I search." She flattened the parchment against her lap, pointing out a spot on the crude map she'd made of the fortress. "That makes eight stores we've found and destroyed."

"Good work!" Emeris beamed at Aeliana, which sent an unfamiliar rush of pride through her.

"Do you think there are more?" Aeliana asked.

"Of course. We haven't found her stash of my blood yet. Or Durriken's."

It was the only reason Aeliana had kept the brand on Durriken. Sylmar wanted her to use it to gain information, but that felt too much like something Mayvus would have done. If Mayvus had truly been dead, Aeliana would have cut out the brand herself. Durriken deserved to be free. But if Mayvus had a stash of his blood, he could easily be branded by her evil aunt once more. Keeping the brand was a form of protection for Durriken, even if it felt invasive.

"We need to find them all before she returns—keep her powerless," Emeris muttered, bending over the parchment.

"What about the eastern gardens?" Aeliana asked. "I haven't looked there because it's where the winex nest."

Emeris shook her head. "She spent more time in the western wing." She pointed at a spot on the parchment. "You should try this turret. And maybe this hallway. I think there's a servants' passage that hasn't been used for years."

Aeliana took the parchment back and made a note on it.

"When Holm's not out searching the caves," her mother said, "he's been clearing out the Sungazer for me. I'd like to start praying with people a few times a day. Iris thinks I'm strong enough now."

Aeliana smiled. "That sounds good for you."

"You're welcome to join me. The people are eager to welcome you in as my daughter."

"I might be able to come." Aeliana squirmed at what was likely a lie. Praying would be strange enough. She'd grown up around humans in Lorvandas learning to worship the Stars, while the Vendarans gave praise to the Sun. But that was just one small sobering reminder of how little Aeliana understood about Vendaran culture and how unfit she was to follow in her mother's footsteps.

Until this year, she'd hated the magic that lived and bred in her starblood. Now she was here among other half-lights, descendants of both humans and Stars. She'd finally come to terms with the magic in her blood, but she still had so much to learn.

Emeris held out an arm, beckoning Aeliana to lean against her. When Aeliana did, her mother settled her chin on Aeliana's head. "Holm found several of Mayvus' journals in there. It would be good for us to go through them. Maybe find evidence of the curse so Sylmar will finally believe me and rebuild a defense."

Aeliana's heart picked up its pace. Her mother had insisted some curse connected her to Mayvus, tying their life forces together in ways beyond even blood magic. It was magic no one had heard of, so the others all filed it under the category of "things Emeris was confused about." But Aeliana had seen Emeris' confidence the night they fought Mayvus—the way she'd been willing to sacrifice herself because it would mean killing Mayvus.

It was the reason Aeliana believed her when no one else did.

"Have you started reading them?" Aeliana asked.

"I've tried, but reading makes my head ache. So far I've only seen recent notes about her tests on the winex."

Aeliana shuddered, not sure she wanted to know what horrible things her aunt had done. She sat back up to face her mother. "The night of the battle, Lilik told me she was breeding them and testing their blood in the dungeons. She probably stored more there."

Emeris narrowed her eyes. "Then we should check the dungeons next."

CHAPTER 3

GAEREN HANDED the tavern owner a slip of paper. "Any chance you've come across a traveler named Rildan? Looks a bit like this."

The owner squinted at the drawing. The new priestess-in-training in Gahldric Valley's Stargazer had drawn it after Gaeren had shared his memory with her. It wasn't perfect because he wasn't as skilled at giving memories as he was at receiving them, but it was good enough.

"Can't say I have." The owner passed the drawing back, then resumed wiping down the bar. The entire dining area was empty save for one man slumped at a stool, lost in his drink far too early in the day.

"If you hear of him," Gaeren pressed, "could you send word to Gahldric Valley's Stargazer? Or maybe tell him his daughter's looking for him there?"

The tavern owner frowned. "I'm no messenger."

Gaeren sighed, reached into the pouch at his belt, then threw some coin on the counter.

The owner snatched it up fast enough to prove he'd been waiting for it. "I might be able to remember that if a man named Rilban shows up."

Gaeren stiffened, then added a final coin to the bar. "Ril-*dan*," he emphasized.

The owner grinned and palmed it. "Yes, that."

The door behind them swung open, filling the darkness with the Sun's light. Riveran stepped in, scanning the room until his gaze landed on Gaeren. "We'd better get going."

The tavern owner grumbled something about bird poop under his breath as he eyed the brown and white hawk sitting on Riveran's shoulder. Gullet squawked right back at him, and Gaeren pursed his lips to hold back a grin. For once, the bird hated someone else more than him.

"Gahldric Valley's Stargazer. Rildan." Gaeren backed away from the tavern owner, trying to gauge if the man would actually remember.

"It might be easier to remember if you buy a drink," the owner said.

"I gave you enough for five." Gaeren was tempted to pull the man's memories of the conversation and feed it back into his mind, but most of the humans in Lorvandas had been too frightened by his half-light magic for that to be useful. It gave Gaeren a new appreciation for how Aeliana had grown up here. She'd spoken about her kidnappers forcing her to do unspeakable things with her magic, but she hadn't even mentioned the constant need to hide who she was.

The tavern owner waved him away. "I'll remember. Just get that smelly pet out of here before he sullies the room."

Riveran opened his mouth to argue, but Gaeren tugged on the sleeve of his tunic and pulled him through the open door before all Gaeren's hard work came undone.

"That pub wasn't clean enough for Gullet to nest in," Riveran mumbled, getting a gentle nip on his ear from the hawk. He pulled off his hat, then used a small cloth to wipe the sweat off his nearly shaved head.

The motion drew Gaeren's eyes to the black X marked on his friend's forehead, the symbol of the lowest of criminals back in Vendaras. The Lorvandans here might not know what it stood for, but it still made them uneasy. Guilt pricked at Gaeren's conscience. That mark was there because Riveran had helped him. Riveran plopped the hat back on, hiding the mark once more.

"Let's get out of this place," Gaeren said. "No one here seems keen on giving up information." He led the way to the edge of town, where they'd agreed to meet Cyrus.

While they walked, several of the people eyed them strangely, their gazes lingering on Gaeren's short brown hair and the weapons they carried. Pants and long sleeves hid most of the deep tan of Gaeren's and Riveran's skin, but when people drew close enough, it was unmistakable. The people didn't trust them because of the differences they saw. How would the people react if they knew of their starblood? If they knew Gaeren and Riveran hailed from Vendaras?

They passed through the small city's gate, eager to leave it behind.

"There you are," Cyrus called, scrambling up from his place at the base of a tree. His face broke out into a grin, shifting all his freckles into a new constellation. "I'm dying for the apple pie I know is waiting back home."

Riveran elbowed him. "You sure you're not dying to see the young priestess who made it?"

Cyrus rolled his eyes. "I wouldn't marry a woman just because she makes a good pie."

Riveran snorted. "She would marry you just to make you more pie."

Cyrus' face turned red, but he merely shoved Riveran aside and twisted his hair into a knot while they walked. The slightly younger man still kept his red hair long like the way of a Lorvandan priest, but lately he'd taken to tying it up, claiming the summer heat was taking its toll.

After two moons of traveling around Lorvandas, they still weren't any closer to finding Rildan. They'd sent letters to Stargazers in the far corners of the country but made personal visits to those within riding distance from Cyrus' home. The excitement of being across the barrier and seeing a new part of the world had faded as their goal seemed more impossible. Daisy's kidnappers had claimed Rildan was dead. What if they hadn't been lying?

"How many cities do we have left?" Gaeren asked.

"Dozens," Cyrus admitted, brushing off his brown priest's robes, which he'd taken to wearing again after returning home. "We've only hit the northeastern regions, which is where Aeliana said she spent most of her life, but they traveled all over. And if Rildan didn't know where they were, he likely traveled just as much if not more."

"We should split up," Gaeren said. "Cover more ground." He avoided looking at Riveran, who had refused this idea every time Gaeren brought it up.

"I was actually wondering if one of us should return to Vendaras," Cyrus said. "I don't want them to worry. It would be good to give them an update and to get one in return."

"What if the starbridge drops us off at Bamboo Island again?" Gaeren asked.

The only way across the barrier dividing Lorvandas from Vendaras was by using the golden arrow starbridge. Gaeren still didn't understand how it worked, but when Aeliana had used it several moons ago, it had brought her from Gahldric Valley in Lorvandas to Bamboo Island in Vendaras. And when he, Cyrus, and Rildan had used it last moon, it had taken them from the Myndren Mountains to an island on the east coast of Lorvandas.

"It would take weeks to reach the Myndren Mountains," Gaeren added. "If Rildan shows up here, we'd be stuck waiting for someone to return just to make the trek all over again."

Cyrus grimaced. "Maybe we take Gullet? He could send word?"

"That would be a difficult distance for him," Riveran said. "Possible, but not ideal."

"It would be good to get an update though," Gaeren conceded. "Cyrus and I could stay behind and split up to cover twice the number of cities while you and Gullet check on the Recreants. If you think it's too far for Gullet, you can travel south to Andel. They'll have dozens of ships heading north along the east coast, and you won't have to worry about running into anyone from Elanesse."

Even saying the name of his family, the name shared by the capital city of Vendaras, gave him an odd mix of nostalgia and pain. As the prince and second in line to the throne, he'd been set up to be his sister's throne warden. After all he'd seen, he knew his family shouldn't be on the throne, but he wasn't sure what the right solution was. And he still loved his sister, despite the fact that he and Riveran had last left Elanesse as traitors to the crown.

Even if he wanted to return home, he couldn't.

"Splitting up seems dangerous," Riveran said. "What if we both return home, then send a new delegation to check in with Cyrus? If Rildan shows up, he can stay with Cyrus at the Stargazer until we return."

This time Cyrus argued, unwilling to miss his chance to return to Vendaras. They spent the remainder of the journey north to Gahldric Valley going in circles with their arguments. When the Stargazer's grounds came into view at the edge of the hill overlooking Gahldric Valley, Gaeren felt a pang of homesickness. He wasn't a stranger to the plains and valleys making up most of Lorvandas, but he missed the humid marshland he'd grown up in. As they stepped through the Stargazer's gates and made their way toward the buildings surrounding the tower, they were no closer to a decision, but the scent of cooked apples wafted through the kitchen windows.

"A piece of pie will help us all think more clearly," Cyrus announced, and while Gaeren didn't agree, he wasn't about to turn down pie.

Gullet took off for the orchard to find his own dinner, and Bartholem greeted them in the kitchens, his slow gait keeping him from meeting worshipers at the entrance. According to Cyrus, his grandfather had aged significantly in the six moons Cyrus had been gone. He was old enough that it could have been natural degeneration, but Gaeren suspected it was brought on by the loss of his wife, who'd been killed by Aeliana's captors.

"Did you have any luck today?" The shy priestess looked everywhere but at Cyrus as she handed him a heaping plate of apple pie.

"One man thought the picture looked familiar," Cyrus said as the three of them sat at a table.

Gaeren's ears perked up. Why hadn't Cyrus said anything on the road?

"But then he showed me his son and said I was welcome to take the boy off his hands."

Bartholem laughed and patted Cyrus on the shoulder. "Tomorrow is another day."

Cyrus dug into his pie, but Gaeren and Riveran waited for the priestess to bring bowls of stew and plates of bread. When they'd first arrived, Gaeren had thought it was a Lorvandan tradition to eat dessert before dinner, but he'd soon learned that was unique to Cyrus. Or maybe just when his smitten priestess was baking.

Bartholem joined them, taking in half a bowl of stew and part of a slice of bread. His long white hair and beard only added to his frailness, but his face held the wrinkles of wisdom and his eyes the depths of experience.

"Bartholem, how would you go about searching for Rildan?" Gaeren asked. "If you were in our place, would you split up to cover more ground? Send someone home for aid? Continue traveling together to each city?"

Riveran leaned back, waiting for the answer.

"Splitting up might get you answers faster," Bartholem mused, "but I would consider offering a reward. You could return to Vendaras for aid, whether it be for more people or more finances. While you're gone, the people of Lorvandas will search for you, eager for the reward. The resources you would have spent searching could be put toward payment for information instead."

All three men stared at each other, considering this new option.

"Are we draining the Stargazer's resources?" Cyrus' gaze took on a troubled look, but it didn't stop him from pushing aside his empty dessert plate and reaching for his bowl of stew.

Bartholem chuckled. "You've all helped out enough here to earn your keep. But after Harvest Day, there will be little work to do and fewer resources to share."

"I'm not sure we'll find more in Vendaras," Gaeren admitted. "I'm guessing Sylmar's struggling to support the remaining army, and it's not like I'm on good enough terms to ask my parents for anything."

Bartholem stood, leaning on the table for support. "I had an idea about that." He shuffled to a covered basket near the door, and they all watched as he brought it back. "I was cleaning out the storage closet, and the label on this long-forgotten basket seemed familiar. If I understood your stories of Vendaras correctly, these ought to be valuable."

He lifted the cloth to reveal its contents.

Dozens of tiny trinkets glinted up at them, all in varying shapes and sizes. Some looked like miniature weapons, others like figures or food. Gaeren and Riveran both gasped and leaned away, but Cyrus ran his hands through the basket as if shopping for wares. "Are these what I think they are?"

Bartholem's eyes took on a twinkle, and he sent a knowing glance Gaeren and Riveran's way.

"The label said 'starlocks.'"

CHAPTER 4

"How do you have starlocks?" Gaeren asked.

"They've been collecting dust in our stores for centuries," Bartholem admitted. "No one realized what kind of treasure they were. But now I suspect you'll find a purpose for them."

"You want us to sell them in Vendaras?" Riveran's eyes widened in horror, his hand slipping to the X on his forehead. "That would seal my death."

Bartholem's face fell. "Are they not valuable?"

"Priceless," Gaeren breathed out, placing a protective hand over the lump under his shirt, where his own tear-shaped starlock rested against his skin. "Inside each one there's a lock of hair, freely given by a Star to enhance a progeny's magic. But they're only given to half-lights chosen by the Sun. Supposedly people used to pass the starlocks down in their families, but corruption made that unpredictable. Now, when a progeny dies, their starlock and body are retrieved by the Star who blessed them. Starlocks left behind like these are ancient and rare. They would only be available in black market trade."

"Would they even work for someone not chosen by the Stars?" Cyrus asked.

"It's the Sun who does the choosing." Gaeren flicked an apologetic glance at Bartholem. The old man tolerated Gaeren and Riveran's worship of the Sun quite well for a Lorvandan priest, but talk of their differences always reminded the priest of the death of his wife. "And yes, they would work, but not with the same intensity. Selling these on the black market could fund an entire war, but it could also be putting power in the hands of our enemies."

"Perhaps we should keep them here, then. Out of the half-lights' reach." Bartholem covered them with the linen and set them back by the door. "The Stars will provide other resources."

"Even so, the reward is a good idea," Gaeren said, and Cyrus and Riveran hummed their assent. "After sending out letters, Riveran and I can return to Vendaras. Then, after updating the other Recreants, we'll return to collect both Cyrus and Rildan."

Cyrus frowned, but this time he didn't argue. After dinner, he pulled out maps of Lorvandas, and the three men huddled in the chancery, writing letters and marking off all the cities they needed to contact, well into the night. It would likely take a week just to get all the letters sent out, and even that delay left Gaeren on edge.

A tense quiet sat between them as they worked. Cyrus seemed to support the plan, but Gaeren sensed he still didn't care for it. It made the most sense for Cyrus to stay behind. He knew the area best. But was this one of those moments where Gaeren was supposed to set aside the authority he took for granted and let other people make decisions? Were they supposed to vote like he'd seen the Lorvandans doing? Like the Recreants back home wanted in their democracy?

If Larkos, his first mate, were here, he'd have plenty to say about it.

They continued their strained silence until Riveran yawned and stretched, wishing them a good rest of their night. Cyrus and Gaeren sealed the last of the letters and blew out their candles before dropping them off in the kitchen.

Instead of going to bed, Cyrus stepped into the Stargazer to perform his nightly ritual of worship. Like always, Gaeren followed him, mostly to observe the customs of the Lorvandans. He didn't understand why they worshiped the Stars, who were created by the Sun just like people.

"Which Star are you praying to tonight?" Gaeren asked the question softly so as not to disturb the other worshipers.

"Andreas," Cyrus said without turning his eyes from the heavens.

The Stargazer was designed exactly like the Vendaran Sungazers—a tall tower with an open roof, allowing worshipers to see the Stars above. Except in Vendaras, worship was done during the day when the Sun was out.

"And he's a leader among the Stars, correct?" Gaeren asked.

"Yes. If there were ever a hierarchy among the Stars, he would be among the top five."

"And his role is typically to oversee disputes among the people?"

Cyrus nodded and turned to Gaeren. "You have a good memory."

"What do you suppose his role is now that the Stars have been so silent?" Gaeren liked needling Cyrus, partly because it was a challenge to fluster the other man's faith and partly because he truly wanted the answers.

"Perhaps they've found other ways to influence us without being physically present."

Gaeren hummed his skepticism. "And why do you choose to pray to him tonight?"

Cyrus hesitated. "We've agreed that some of us should remain behind and some of us should go back to Vendaras. I'm asking him to make it clear who should go and who should stay so it doesn't turn into another fight."

Gaeren raised his eyebrows. He thought the decision had already been made. Besides, their bickering didn't seem worthy of a deity's intervention. It wasn't as if their actions would have an impact on the world at large. That was one of the biggest differences he'd noticed between their faiths. The human Lorvandans worshiped the Stars but saw them as friends. Vendaran half-lights worshiped the Sun, but their worship held more fear and respect than love.

"Well, then, I hope he answers your prayer."

This time Cyrus smiled and tipped his face back to the sky.

Gaeren followed suit, running through the names of the Stars Cyrus had mentioned in the past. "Which one would you pray to for direction in your life's purpose?"

"I already know my life's purpose." Cyrus' frown gave less weight to his confident words. "I'm meant to challenge people to grow in their faith."

"But if you didn't—" Gaeren scratched the back of his neck and avoided Cyrus' eyes. "If you thought you had one purpose for your whole life only to discover you never wanted that in the first place, which one would you ask to help you find your new purpose?"

"I suppose Bryton," Cyrus said. "His role is to reveal truth. He's one people are often reluctant to pray to, because sometimes the truth isn't what we want it to be."

Gaeren let out a bitter laugh. "Well said."

Cyrus grinned. "It's said you should always pray to Sheen when you pray to Bryton. He brings truth and she brings mercy. One without the other is unbalanced."

Gaeren frowned and tapped his lips. "What else did you say Sheen did?"

Cyrus shook his head. "I don't think we've talked about her before."

Gaeren felt certain they had, but he couldn't place when he'd heard her name.

"If I could only have one," Cyrus said, "I'd pray for truth. I'd rather get the truth even if I didn't like it." He kneeled in the dirt and bent forward until his nose touched the ground.

Gaeren kneeled beside him. "Sort of like how you'll come around to admitting the Stars are subject to the Sun just like we are?"

Cyrus' voice came out muffled from where he bent forward. "Exactly. If that's the truth, I want to know it."

"Well, then, maybe I'll ask the Sun to have Bryton shed some light on my purpose." Gaeren winced at the vulnerability of his confession. But this sort of admission happened often with Cyrus. If he didn't tell the priest-in-training now, he'd tell him eventually. "I'm no longer a prince and Aeliana no longer needs my protection, so there must be something the Sun wants me to do. I'd like to figure that out."

Cyrus sat up, his gaze back on the Stars, and Gaeren thought he'd leave the conversation there. It was unusual for Cyrus, who always had an answer or a question for everything.

"Sometimes I think the harder thing is the timing of the truth," Cyrus finally said.

"What do you mean?" Gaeren asked.

"Sometimes the Stars give us the truth, but not when we're expecting it. So we either latch on to a lie while we're waiting, or we miss it completely." Cyrus smiled. "Maybe the Stars, or the Sun, want you to take some time figuring out your next purpose. Maybe that's part of your purpose."

Gaeren frowned. He didn't like that at all. How would he know when he had the right purpose?

"Sometimes we're too eager to act when we need to sit still and listen. Like how the people were so determined to go to war. When they didn't stop to listen, the Stars were forced to intervene, to divide the lands by waters and barriers for our protection."

"You mean the Sun," Gaeren murmured. "And it was a punishment."

But his mind was traveling back, calling up the memory he'd misplaced, and he found himself back in the hammock of his hideout, poring through a book detailing the Great Divide.

"It was Sheen," Gaeren said. "She was the Star who thought she was supposed to split the people."

Cyrus' gaze turned wary. "According to your book, *The Sins of the Stars*." He spit out the name like the words were painful.

Gaeren stood, his mind racing. "I know, but if that book is right, the Stars divided the lands in the Great Divide, not the Sun, just like you've said." His words came out too loud, and a few worshipers cast him strange looks.

Cyrus rose, pulling Gaeren to the side of the Stargazer and out from the atrium. Cool air kissed their skin, a warning that Harvest Day and winter were around the corner.

"The Stars *did* divide the lands," Cyrus said, "but your book claims the Stars were wrong to do that, and the Stars can't be wrong." His words didn't hold any conviction.

"It also claims Sheen was punished for her actions. She was grounded to the earth. So she wouldn't be up there for us to pray to." Gaeren gestured to the sky. "Perhaps praying for her mercy is futile."

Cyrus frowned. "That's a lot of claims. If there's a Star roaming the earth, where has she been all this time?"

"Can't you think of someone who has unexplainable power and

wisdom, someone who exudes mercy and seems ageless? Someone who claims she's not a Star because she doesn't take to the skies?"

Understanding made Cyrus' features go slack. "Orra," he breathed out.

"She never even lied about it. She just kept redirecting our questions." Gaeren laughed and ran a hand through his hair. Then his smile faded, and he shook his head. "Even if it happens to be true, it doesn't change anything. Not really."

"What do you mean?" Cyrus tugged on his robes in agitation. "It changes everything. She could tell us if the Sun created the Stars or if it's just a place that holds the Stars' power. She could tell us what really happened in the Great Divide."

"But her power has dwindled to that of a half-light's. She still needs our help finding the starbridges."

"And we will help her." Cyrus straightened. "For now, you and Riveran can head back. See if they found the stone starbridge, see if Emeris and Orra are stronger. See what they need."

Gaeren raised his eyebrows. "I thought you wanted to go."

Cyrus glanced at the sky. "I think Andreas has given me my answer. I'm more useful here, for now. I'll find Rildan."

Gaeren narrowed his eyes, studying the priest-in-training. "You're afraid of what truth Orra might tell you. After all your talk about wanting it even if it hurts."

A nervous twitch started in Cyrus' eye, and he rubbed at it. "Or maybe I'm trusting the timing of it."

Gaeren snorted. "Fine. But when she tells you I'm right, I'm going to say 'I told you so,' both about the Sun and about you being too scared to hear the truth."

A faint smile crossed Cyrus' face. "I would expect nothing less from you."

CHAPTER 5

Aeliana's breakfast threatened to surface as the stench coming from behind the dungeon's gate hit her nose. A whimper sounded from behind her, but she wasn't sure if it was Felk or Lilik. With the full moon approaching, they were both fully grown, but they huddled together, whether subconsciously remembering this place as dangerous or simply imagining the horrors that had occurred here.

"No one thought to clean up this place." Lukai pulled a handkerchief from his pocket and handed it to Aeliana before pulling his shirt up over his upturned nose. His lamp's light brought a shine to the golden hair curving around his ears and curling up just above his collar.

"I don't think anyone intends to use it unless Mayvus shows up alive," Aeliana said.

Lukai tensed beside her, a reaction she was getting used to whenever she backed up her mother's claims.

She was grateful he didn't argue, even though it was because he was trying to make up for past wrongs. It was the same reason he'd agreed to sneak down here with her while Emeris sent Sylmar and the others on a goose chase. Supposedly she'd suddenly remembered Mayvus utilizing a certain part of the Myndren Mountains for Durriken's dragon nest and felt certain that must be where they'd find the onyx stone.

"What do you hope to find here besides winex feces and urine?" Lukai asked as they peered through the bars and took in the dismal state of the first room. Deep scratches marred the overturned tables and chairs, and the few blankets were torn to shreds.

"She was studying their blood. I want to find her research. I want to know what she hoped to learn or gain. How it might relate to the connection between her and my mother."

One of the winex whimpered again. "Blood." This time Felk latched on to Aeliana's elbow, pulling her back toward him and away from Lukai. He pointed toward a second chamber. "Do you smell it?"

Aeliana shook her head. "I don't need to. I trust you." She wasn't about to stop breathing through her mouth even if she felt paranoid that she could taste the winex waste.

"It's all over that room. Winex blood." Felk cowered as he said the words, and Lilik shivered beside him.

"Do you want to go back up to the fortress?" Aeliana asked.

Felk hesitated but shook his head. "I want to know what she did."

Lukai swung open the gate for the room Felk had indicated, letting its hinges squeak. In his lantern's light, various chains and tables came into view, dried pools of grey dotting every stone and wood surface.

This was the reason they'd gotten the winex to help them fight against Mayvus. She'd been taking them and breeding them for her own purposes. Hundreds if not thousands of them had been hatched and grown in the vicinity of the fortress so she could conduct her research without having to hunt them down. But what exactly had she been researching?

A quick study of the room revealed a crude lab set up in the corner, with ampules of silver blood and piles of papers with notes. Despite Aeliana's efforts to hold off the stench, the metallic bite of that much blood made its way through as she approached the table. Several broken glasses had spread the sticky substance across the papers, fusing them together in illegible stacks. She pulled them apart, looking for some semblance of order.

"Are these—?" Lukai cut off his question, but Aeliana turned, catching sight of several lumps all bundled together.

Lilik let out a cry, placing hands over winex eggs. "You said we got them all." Her voice rose in panic.

"You did," Aeliana said. "You were held in this exact dungeon, so you would have come back for these eggs if they—if you thought they were viable." She swallowed hard. That truth wasn't necessarily any more reassuring.

The winex's cries grew louder, and Felk pulled her from the eggs, huddling around her smaller form as if to block out their surroundings. He glanced around warily. "The winex way is better. These are memories I would never want back."

Aeliana winced. "Hard memories can still teach us good things." She ran a finger along the scars left by Arvid and Vera, evidence of all the times her captors had drawn her blood and used it for evil. The scars were reminders that she would never go down that path.

But maybe that wasn't true for everyone. Marnok's face swam before her eyes. He'd had no memories, just like the winex. He'd taught her to heal and had been a good friend. When her mother had recognized Marnok and had given him the memories he'd lost, he'd left. Whatever she'd shown him had made it impossible for him to face his friends. Or maybe it had required him to face something else.

Aeliana hoped they'd see him soon, especially since he'd always been a gentler teacher than Sylmar. She'd hardly progressed in learning to heal since Marnok had left.

Felk and Lilik sniffed at the eggs, placing their ears against the shells and turning them over. Perhaps they held hope that some could be hatched, or maybe this was their way of grieving the loss.

She gave them their space and turned back to the papers, skimming through the summaries while studying the tables and lists. "The Zealot soldiers were right," she murmured.

"About what?" Lukai's voice startled her when it came from over her left shoulder.

"She was testing the blood on wounds," she said, handing him the papers she'd just studied. She grabbed several more. "Sort of like the blood magic Arvid did to heal over my cuts, but winex don't have star-blood. There's some other property in their blood she was trying to define or maybe extract."

"Why would she want to do that?" Lukai asked. "If she can use brands or blood magic to heal, why would she need something else?"

Aeliana flipped through more pages. "Maybe so her supply of magic wouldn't dwindle so quickly?" She rounded the table, putting Lilik and Felk back in her line of sight. Lilik tucked an egg under each arm and slinked out of the room, followed by Felk holding three more. Aeliana nearly called after them but decided to let it go.

She pulled at a fresh set of papers in front of her, these ones unmarred by the spilled blood. This time the subjects had side effects, some growing sick and others hemorrhaging to death. "She tried mixing their blood with half-lights' blood." Aeliana's stomach churned as she took in their symptoms, the ways they'd died slow painful deaths.

"To what end?" Disgust leaked from Lukai's words, but he kept perusing the research with her.

"The winex blood healed the subjects quickly," Aeliana said. "Winex's bodies function at an accelerated rate compared to ours. It's why they age so much faster. But it also makes them heal faster."

"Which is why they're so dangerous."

Aeliana shot Lukai an irritated glance, but Lilik and Felk hadn't returned, and he remained invested in his set of papers.

"I don't think she actually wanted their healing properties." Lukai frowned, then held his papers out for Aeliana. "Look. Whoever was conducting this research for her was trying to divide the healing properties out—not to use them—but to remove them."

Aeliana scanned the messy script, following Lukai's line of thought. "The side effects—she thought her subjects were aging too quickly because of the same property that healed them."

"It makes sense." Lukai picked up another stack. "But that means there was something else she wanted from their blood."

Aeliana watched as Lilik and Felk came back in, silently retrieving another half-dozen eggs. Tears glinted on Lilik's cheeks in the lantern light. Had those been her eggs? What had kept them from hatching? And what had kept Lilik from coming back for them after the battle? She had to have known they were there. Why hadn't she removed them then?

Aeliana turned back to the papers, only able to handle one mystery at a time. What could Mayvus have wanted from the winex's blood if not their faster than average healing properties? Winex held no magic. Most people felt they had below average intelligence. Their only gift was their ability to be reborn. As long as they never died, they were practically immortal creatures.

"Immortality," Aeliana breathed out. The room spun as it all came together in her mind, and she gripped the edge of the table.

"Hmm?" Lukai asked, more focused on his set of papers than her revelation.

It wasn't difficult to imagine Mayvus wanting immortality, testing winex after winex on the slim chance she might discover what exactly allowed them to be reborn. But she wouldn't want to also age so quickly. So that element would have to be extracted.

Aeliana moved closer to the eggs, placing a hand over one's smooth surface. It was cold and lifeless, something Felk and Lilik had likely sensed from the start. A shell that entombed the creature that could have been. Except…there.

She let her finger wiggle in through a tiny crack in the shell, more like a hole that had once held some sort of apparatus. Maybe it was something Mayvus had inserted into the eggs. Had she poisoned them?

"Does any of her research talk about the eggs?" Aeliana asked.

"Not yet," Lukai said.

A hiss erupted from Aeliana's left, and she stepped back as Lilik returned, pulling the egg from Aeliana's grasp. Lilik bared her teeth at Aeliana, reminding Aeliana what Lilik had been like before Felk had found her, before Aeliana had raised the winex to be allies instead of enemies.

"I'm sorry," Aeliana whispered. "I'm just trying to understand."

Lilik turned her back on Aeliana and grabbed a second egg, scampering out of the dungeon with a growl.

Felk frowned, glancing between Aeliana and the door. "She's hurting."

Aeliana nodded.

"The unborn winex are all dead. Mayvus murdered them." His normally bright eyes clouded over with pain.

"How can you tell?"

"Winex eggs always hatch. I just know that. Like I know my name. Instinct."

Aeliana hesitated, not wanting to further his grief. "Could something have been inserted in the egg to kill it?"

He gave her a sharp look, then loped over to study one of the eggs, letting his long fingers slide over the same gaps she'd found. His lips curled with a snarl. "She drained them."

Aeliana stilled. "Drained them?"

"They're lighter." He picked up the egg as if weighing it. "I thought it was because they decayed. But it's the fluid. It's all gone."

"Aeliana?" Lukai called, his voice strained. "I think this is what you're looking for."

She turned back to the lab table. Lukai's face looked pale in the lantern light.

"Felk's right," he said. "She drained the fluid, then bottled it up, testing it for its regeneration properties."

A memory clicked in her mind. When they'd met up with Felk to join forces against Mayvus, he'd said there were rumors among the soldiers of the blood holding regenerative properties. It had sounded unbelievable at the time, but now it seemed eerily possible. When the blood hadn't worked, she must have tested the fluid from the eggs. Had that worked?

Aeliana took the papers Lukai offered, skimming through the various trials Mayvus had done. "She revived animals with it?"

Lukai nodded, then shuddered. "It didn't work on people, but not because she didn't try. It did, however, bring some of them back from the brink of death."

Aeliana's mouth grew dry. "We need to tell Sylmar."

"You're bleeding." Lukai took the papers from her hand, turning her palm over to reveal a cut dripping blood.

"Oh, I guess the glass must have gotten me." She took the handkerchief he'd given her for the stench and used it to staunch the flow.

Lukai grimaced. "I hope you didn't get any of that winex blood in there. Let me heal you." His hands were gentle as he ran his fingers over her palm. He closed his pale blue eyes and leaned closer, his breath hitting her cheek. His proximity heightened Aeliana's awareness of how alone they were.

They still hadn't talked much about the bond that connected them. Aeliana's parents had bonded her to Lukai as an infant, an old tradition now only held by royalty as a precursor to betrothals and marriages. Supposedly it had been for her protection, but now it left them connected in ways Aeliana wasn't sure she wanted, even though they'd agreed to just focus on building a friendship for now.

With the bond, they could each sense if the other was in danger, and at times, it made them put the other's needs before their own. But Lukai had used that connection to justify taking Aeliana's blood without her permission. For her protection. They hadn't talked about *that* much either. She scowled and pulled her hand away before he finished.

"That's good enough. Thank you."

His eyebrows rose at her sharp tone, but he let his hands drop and stepped away, the nervous shuffle of his feet making her think he too had suddenly become aware of just how alone they were. Except his gaze kept dropping to her lips, and she suspected his discomfort was for far different reasons than hers.

"Aeliana, maybe we should—"

"Yes. Let's go see if Sylmar's back." She grabbed the papers from the table and spun around, eager to leave both Lukai and the stench of death and torture behind.

CHAPTER 6

"WE HEARD RUMORS OF THIS." Sylmar set the papers down on the table in the training room, his tone far too relaxed. "I don't understand your surprise. Mayvus was intrigued by immortality long before she tested the winex. The fact that she continued to study it up to the battle gives me reassurance that she never found answers." His gaze strayed to Lukai, who picked up a sword and approached Kendalyhn while gesturing to the sparring ring.

"But what if by the time we got here, she was no longer researching immortality but building up stores of what she needed?" Aeliana twisted her hands together, unwilling to sit in the chair next to Sylmar's with her nerves so taut.

Sylmar sat back, frowning. "You heard what Holm found at the cave Durriken showed you?"

Aeliana held back a groan. "Yes. The ground was full of blood and flesh."

"Let's say Mayvus discovered something that could revive her from the brink of death—then what? Who could have aided her up in Durriken's lair? Mayvus is dead."

His scars puckered with pain Aeliana would never understand. The loss he felt over a bond he'd grown to hate seemed contradictory, but she supposed that was what made it so painful.

"It's time for us to all move on," he added. As if bolstered by his own words, he set his jaw and turned back to Lukai and Kendalyhn.

Aeliana crossed her arms over her chest, irritated at the way their sparring match held his attention far more than her revelation. A sheen of sweat formed on each of the combatants' foreheads, and they grinned at each other before Lukai made another lunge.

In the back of her mind, a need to protect him niggled at her, as if ready to surface should Kendalyhn's advances become more than just practice. The bond was designed for protection, but sometimes it felt too similar to the brand Aeliana had imposed on Durriken, the brand Mayvus had briefly forced on her.

The brand Mayvus had also used to keep Aeliana's mother prisoner for over a dozen years.

"We didn't find all of her supporters," she said. "Just because we cut the brand marks off all those left behind and just because they swore fealty to my mother doesn't mean the ones we should be worried about aren't still out there giving Mayvus what she needs."

"Brogdon let us keep his mark as a test," Sylmar pointed out. "Insisted we lock him up so we could know the moment she regained power. If she were alive, we would know. He would know. Go talk to him if you need that reassurance. He could use the company."

Aeliana bit her lip. She hadn't been able to go to Jasperus' son. She knew the guilt he felt over his father's death that night held him prisoner far more than the room they'd put him in. She even knew it wasn't his fault. But she also still felt guilt over the ways her blood had been used to steal and murder in the past. How could she reassure him that he wasn't to blame when that same guilt sat deep in her soul?

Lukai pinned Kendalyhn to the ground, his practice sword pointed at her chest. Instead of conceding, Kendalyhn kicked her feet out underneath his, tripping him so that he fell on top of her. The move wasn't something that could have been done in a real battle, but they both laughed, leaving Aeliana with a strange twinge inside her chest. Untangling themselves certainly didn't need to take that long.

Her bond mark itched, and Lukai's gaze shot to hers before he stepped away from Kendalyhn while scratching at the matching mark on his left palm.

"Again!" Sylmar called out. "That risky move would have been more likely to kill you, Kendalyhn. If you do it in practice, you'll wind up doing it in real battle."

Lukai and Kendalyhn rolled their eyes, but resumed their standoff.

"I don't think you're taking this seriously enough," Aeliana said. "My mother insists something connects her to Mayvus. That if Mayvus was dead, she would be too. No one believes her because they all think she's gone crazy."

"You have to admit her mind is broken." Sylmar said the words gently, but they still stung. "Living in her memories was the thing that kept her sane, and yet using magic in that way—living in the past instead of the present—well, that brings on a different sort of insanity. I'm not saying it can't be fixed, but it will probably take time. In another year, she might agree her claims were preposterous. Her ideas can't be trusted right now."

"But they can at least be considered. Respected." Aeliana raised her eyebrows, waiting for Sylmar to agree.

"I'm glad you have this time with your mother." He patted her arm in a rare show of affection. "It's good for both of you after so many years apart. But I'm concerned at how much influence she's having over you. You're obsessed with this idea. Even if she's right, what would you have us do differently? We continue to search the mountains every day. It's true we're spending more effort looking for the onyx stone, but our eyes are still open for any sign of Mayvus. What else can we do?"

"We should be building a defense. Destroying all the blood she collected. Did you know she had stores of it hidden throughout the fortress? What if she has more in the mountains? We need to make sure she can't control anyone again." Aeliana glared at him. "General Nels has been letting soldiers go home, and everyone left has been hunting for a black rock that she might have already used to take herself across the barrier."

Sylmar glared right back at her. "We can't afford to feed all the soldiers. And they have their own families to feed. Rebuilding here will take time—time we can afford because Mayvus is gone. You have to let this go." His last words were spoken with a finality that left no room for Aeliana to argue.

This time she was the first to turn and watch Lukai and Kendalyhn. They were an even match, both trained from a young age to protect Aeliana and her mother. Kendalyhn's entire family had been killed when she was young, most likely because her mother had been a good friend of Aeliana's mother. Would she and Kendalyhn have been friends if Aeliana hadn't been kidnapped and if Kendalyhn's mother hadn't died? Maybe more like sisters? The thought was laughable when Kendalyhn had nothing but glares for Aeliana.

Though…she had plenty of smiles for Lukai right now.

The pair headed their way, each reaching for the pitcher of water and glasses laid out.

"I think it's time we increase Aeliana's training." Sylmar pushed against the table to stand, then picked up his staff from where it leaned against the wall. "If she's making trips down to the dungeons, she has too much time on her hands. And with the threat of Mayvus out of the way"—he gave Aeliana a pointed look—"it's time she studied Vendaran culture as well as history and warfare. Anyone could teach her the basics, but a woman would be able to give her the finer points of hair and clothing."

Aeliana's hand shot up to her braid. Iris had tried convincing her to cut it. Would Sylmar make her?

He rubbed at his short grey beard. "It will have to be someone familiar with the previous generation's expectations as well as current trends."

"Iris might be the only one with the patience for that task," Kendalyhn said, earning a frown from Lukai that oddly made Aeliana feel slightly better.

"No." Sylmar grunted. "Iris has more than she can handle with feeding the winex on top of the soldiers, so this task is best left to you, Kendalyhn."

Kendalyhn and Aeliana exchanged horrified looks.

"She's not teachable, Sylmar," Kendalyhn said.

"You saw what happened the last time she was involved in my training," Aeliana added.

"Look at that. You're already agreeing on something." Sylmar made his way toward the door. "I think this combination might be the most motivating for progress. I'll expect the equivalent of a Vendaran princess when you tell me she's ready to be tested."

Kendalyhn snorted as he rounded the corner. Lukai failed to hide his smirk, but Aeliana couldn't tell which of them he was laughing at.

She'd come here expecting Sylmar's vigilance and paranoia to confirm her fears. She'd thought he'd support her urge to investigate her mother's claims now that there was evidence Mayvus' research could have kept her alive. Without Sylmar's vested interest, she'd have to keep hunting for the truth in secret, something that would become even harder now that he knew she'd been looking. She and her mother would be on their own to find the last of Mayvus' stores of blood to cripple the evil priestess' resources in preparation for her return.

It would take so much longer, especially if Aeliana also had to play tea party with Kendalyhn.

If her mother was right and Mayvus was growing stronger, they might not have much time.

She bit her lip, glancing at the closest thing she had to an enemy among friends. Kendalyhn glared back at her.

"Come on, princess." The other woman spat out the word. "Let's get this over with."

CHAPTER 7

GAEREN, Cyrus, and Riveran spent more than a week writing and sending out more letters. When they had only a single batch of letters left, Gaeren woke with his stomach as nauseous as that of a landlubber at sea. After delivering them, it would be time to return to Vendaras.

After they ate porridge cooked and sweetened by Cyrus' admirer, they gathered up the last of the letters and bound them in burlap sacks. Before the second bell, they had their horses loaded.

"Who's that?" Riveran asked. Gullet squawked from his shoulder as Cyrus and Gaeren turned to take in a lone figure crossing over the gate's threshold.

"I'm not sure," Cyrus said. "Probably just a worshiper if the guards let them in."

Gaeren huffed. "Your priests and priestesses let anyone in if they say they're there to worship the Stars. Which makes no sense this time of day." He gestured toward the clear blue sky, void of Stars.

"What would you rather we did?" Cyrus asked.

Gaeren didn't bother answering. The humans in Lorvandas weren't under the same stresses of politics and war. They weren't as wary of strangers, which was both refreshing and dangerous. Gaeren turned back to their horses, checking over their hooves and tack.

"Stars' greetings!" a voice called out.

They turned once more and found the stranger headed their way.

"Stars' blessings in return," Cyrus said. "Can we help you with something?"

"I was told there were some men here looking for me."

Gaeren started, then took in the familiar eyes and nose on the unfamiliar face. A scar pocked the man's forehead and another ran down his cheek. Long dark hair grew to his shoulders, and weathered skin spoke of a hard life.

"Rildan?" Gaeren whispered.

The man's lips twisted in a scowl, but before anyone could guess what might have upset him, he pulled out a dagger and lunged at Gaeren.

Despite the surprise attack, Gaeren dodged the stranger easily, and with help from Riveran and Cyrus, he quickly got the older man on the ground, smothering his face in the grass. Riveran gripped the man's wrists so tightly they turned red and puffy, and the stranger sputtered out a mouth full of soil.

"Who are you?" Cyrus asked.

"A fool," the man muttered.

"Why did you attack me?" Gaeren asked.

"I was told you were looking for me. And that you had my daughter." He spat the last word out while attempting to jerk his hands from Riveran's grip.

Gaeren stilled. "We're looking for you on behalf of your daughter, but we aren't holding her."

All the tension eased from the stranger's limbs. "Then where is she?"

"Across the barrier," Gaeren said.

"How?"

"She found the golden arrow," Cyrus said. "It was held here in the Stargazer for years, just like you asked."

Rildan sighed, letting his cheek rest against the grass. Riveran tentatively released his grip, but Rildan made no move to attack.

"When Aeliana came for the arrow, her kidnappers were with her," Cyrus continued. "They took her across the barrier. I went, too, and that's where we met up with Sylmar and Velden."

Rildan turned over and sat up, grass stains covering his clothes and dirt smudged on his cheeks. But the lost expression on his face was far more pitiful.

"I take it Sylmar's conversion was genuine?" Rildan asked.

Gaeren frowned. "He's been leading a faction of Recreants for years, but I suppose he'd just left Mayvus when you last saw him."

Rildan nodded. "I didn't trust him, but Emeris did. She was always better at reading people. Her pneumatic skills gave her an unfair advantage." The features of his face smoothed out as the hint of a smile crept across his lips. "She'll be sure to inform me she was right if I ever see her again."

"Good," Gaeren said. "I'll enjoy watching her rub that in."

Rildan's neck cracked as he glanced sharply up at Gaeren. "Are you saying—can we cross the barrier?"

Gaeren reached in his pocket and pulled out the humming golden arrow as an answer.

Rildan's eyes closed, and his entire body slumped. A whispered word came out on a sigh, but Gaeren couldn't catch it. The vulnerability gave Gaeren courage to voice his own questions.

"Do you remember me?" Gaeren asked. "From when I was a child?"

Rildan's eyes fluttered open, then narrowed.

"You look far different than I remember," Gaeren said, "but I suppose I've changed as well. I've grown a few feet."

"Henri?" Rildan's jaw went slack.

Gaeren winced. "Yes, I guess that's the lie you would remember as well."

A guttural noise escaped Rildan's throat. Nothing like the light-hearted laugh Gaeren remembered from his youth.

"Yet one more instance in which Emeris was right," Rildan said. "She suspected your identity was false. But was she right about you being the prince?"

Gaeren shrugged sheepishly. "One and the same." He reached out a hand toward Rildan, and after a moment's hesitation, Rildan grasped it, allowing Gaeren to pull him to his feet.

Rildan turned to Cyrus and Riveran, his gaze lingering on Gullet. "How exactly did you all end up here?"

"I'm from Gahldric Valley. Name's Cyrus." Cyrus stuck out a hand, and Rildan grasped his forearm. "But I intend to go back to help Aeliana. And to study the Vendaran faith more." He brushed a hand over his priest's robes.

"And I've been searching for Daisy ever since you all disappeared," Gaeren said.

"Daisy." Rildan's eyes lit up at the nickname, making Gaeren realize he'd let it slip after weeks of using her given name. "You two were thick as thieves."

"Yes, well, I didn't anticipate finding out she was part of the Wyndren family."

Rildan grimaced. "I suppose that put a damper on your desire to find an old friend."

"Not exactly." Gaeren grinned. "My first mate has been slowly converting me to a Recreant for the last five or six years. I'm not eager for my family to be in danger, but I can't ignore their corruption."

Rildan's brow raised, but he turned to Riveran instead. "Are you his first mate?"

"No. My name's Riveran. I'm just an old friend along for the ride." Riveran held out his hands as if to prove he had nothing to hide even though his cap still covered the X on his forehead. "I'm not really sure how Gaeren always tangles me up in his adventures."

"How did you get separated from Dai-Aeliana?" Gaeren asked. "Or better yet, how did you survive? I saw them stab you before you used the arrow."

Rildan winced. "We landed on Lorvandas' eastern shore. I threw the arrow into the woods, hoping they'd go after it, but they took Aeliana with them, leaving me for dead."

"I'm surprised they didn't take Aeliana and the arrow," Gaeren said.

"They probably would have, except it takes time for a starbridge to recharge in the Sun's light. After being used, they could have stepped on it and never found it because it held no hum. So instead, they ran. A healer found me and patched me up. By the time I was ready for travel, their trail had gone cold, but at least I found the starbridge. I wasn't willing to bring it near Arvid and Vera in case they took

Aeliana back without me. So I left it with a priestess named Della and tried hunting them down."

Cyrus blinked and fiddled with his horse's bridle. "Gams." He shook his head. "I still can't believe she kept that secret all that time."

"So why are you looking for me?" Rildan asked. "Why didn't Aeliana come? Or Emeris?"

"They're both fine," Gaeren was quick to say, then he winced. "Well, Emeris was injured in our fight against Mayvus, but Aeliana and another healer are taking care of her."

A mix of emotions crossed Rildan's face. "Aeliana's a progeny, then?"

Cyrus grinned. "One of the most powerful."

Rildan's face paled. "Which is why Mayvus wanted her. Even as a child. What happened?"

The others exchanged glances.

"You've missed a lot," Gaeren said. "Why don't you come inside, and we can tell you everything."

After they got the horses settled back in the stable and dumped their sacks of letters back in the chancery, it took far longer than Gaeren wanted for Cyrus to catch Rildan up on Aeliana's trek across Vendaras with Sylmar and the Recreants. Every bone in Gaeren's body itched to use the golden arrow and return home, but he sensed the other man needed answers before he was willing to go with them.

"Do you want me to show you the rest?" Gaeren asked, holding out his hands.

Rildan raised his eyebrows. "You have Emeris' gifting?"

"It's my opposite spoke, so it won't be like the memories you've gotten from her, but it'll do the job."

Rildan hesitated, but there was a gleam in his eye that made Gaeren think the older man missed this form of his wife's magic.

"Yes." Rildan placed his hands in Gaeren's. "Show me."

Gaeren closed his eyes, and instead of tuning in to Rildan's memories, he picked through his own, starting with the memory of how they'd all met in the Islaran ruins, including how Aeliana had saved Durriken. He nudged them in Rildan's direction, knowing they'd grow clouded and blurry with Gaeren's unrefined skill. He rushed through their journey toward the Myndren Mountains before tuning in to the details of Emeris' rescue and their messy success in getting Aeliana's blood back from Mayvus, knowing those elements were what would matter to Rildan the most.

When he pulled back from the memory, Rildan's face seemed older, graver, but he nodded with satisfaction.

"And you're certain Mayvus is dead?" Rildan dropped Gaeren's hands but picked up the last of his bread, tearing off a small piece to nibble on.

Gaeren flinched. "I don't see how anyone could've survived that."

"What needs to be done here before we can leave?" Rildan asked.

Gaeren's heart beat a little faster. "Nothing."

"I'd like to wait to say goodbye to Gamps," Cyrus said. "The last time I left, I wasn't able to, and then he watched Gams die. I can't leave without saying goodbye."

"Of course." Gaeren was quick to agree. It was the least they could do after all the ways Bartholem had helped them.

"He won't be up for a few hours." Cyrus' voice rang with an apology.

"That gives us time to plan," Rildan said.

Gaeren nodded his assent with the others, but it was a half-truth. He'd already been planning their next move for the last two moons.

By the time Bartholem woke, Gaeren had equipped each of them with weapons he'd stashed in his rooms. They had sacks of food from the new priestess-in-training, who blushed as she handed Cyrus additional sweets. In order to avoid onlookers, Bartholem temporarily closed off the Stargazer, only allowing the priests and priestesses to remain to witness such a holy event.

Holy or not, Gaeren agreed it was an exciting thing to watch.

Tears filled Bartholem's eyes as he hugged Cyrus goodbye. He spoke a blessing over the four of them, then sat back on one of the Stargazer's benches, his eyes wide with wonder.

Gaeren handed the golden arrow to Cyrus. "I still don't know how to say the words."

Cyrus grinned. "It's nice to finally be necessary to something all you magical people are doing." He gripped the arrow in his right hand, then held Riveran's hand in his left. The rest of them continued linking arms, and Gaeren braced himself for the disorienting experience of using a starbridge to travel across the barrier.

As Cyrus uttered the foreign words, the expected hum of the arrow intensified and passed through them all like a crack of thunder. The room filled with light, and Bartholem's awed face faded from view. A weightlessness took over Gaeren's body, and his anchor to the earth dissipated. He tried to blink away the brightness but only saw it more on the backs of his lids. When his feet once more hit dirt, he stumbled, catching himself on bamboo shoots dotting the soil. A salty sea scent met his nose, and thick air coated his skin. He sucked in a deep breath, relishing the way the salt always reminded him of Aeliana as a child— as Daisy.

A small sob escaped Rildan's throat from beside him. "I'm back," the older man whispered. He fell to his knees and dropped his face to the ground, inhaling deeply.

The heartfelt moment was broken by Riveran turning to the side and puking.

Gaeren laughed and patted him on the back a little too hard. "Never thought you would be one to get sick from travel. You always seemed hardy enough on the sea." He'd teased his friend mercilessly after the last time they'd used the arrow and Riveran had thrown up all over the first group of people they'd found.

Riveran glared up at him and wiped his mouth with the back of his hand. "Just you wait; one of these days we'll find your weakness, and I'll be sure to exploit it."

Cyrus pulled Rildan to his feet, then they all spun to take in the view of the wild jungle canopies on one side and the view of the sea on the other. A gap in the trees revealed the scorched remains of Bamboo Island, the surface desolated by Durriken moons prior. New growth attempted to hide the destruction, but it mostly looked unchanged from the last time Gaeren had seen it.

"It's exactly where it dropped us before." Cyrus said the words in awe but shuddered, likely remembering his previous experience—with Arvid and Vera present—far differently.

"This is where it dropped me the first time I used it, too," Rildan said. "I never thought the dusty golden arrow on a Stargazer's shelf could take me to Vendaras or that I'd live among half-lights. I was only here a handful of years, but I've been chasing that feeling of 'home' ever since."

"It already feels like we're so much closer," Gaeren said.

"We are." Riveran's face still held a greenish tint. "Several hundred miles closer."

They all grinned at each other as if they'd accomplished that task with their own skill, but then movement caught Gaeren's attention. The crow's nest of an unfamiliar black ship rose from the ocean to the right, its dark mast and bow coming into full view as it rounded the shoreline and nearly ran aground.

Before he could warn the others to duck out of sight, a shout came from the ship.

"Maybe they didn't see us," Cyrus said as they all drew back within the foliage.

"Four men ashore!" A distant call confirmed the opposite.

Rildan grimaced. "Maybe they're friendly."

A strangled cackle drifted across the water. "Bring 'em in!"

CHAPTER 8

"You could at least wear trousers around your room to get used to them." Kendalyhn's words came out with a sneer as she entered Aeliana's dressing chamber. Everything the other woman had taught her so far had come with bite. It was like they were back on the road from Valorian to Islara and Aeliana had lost any ground gained with her since then.

"Why can't I be Vendaran and wear skirts? Orra wears them."

Kendalyhn rolled her eyes. "Orra also senses the starbridges being used. And she survived a Star collecting Jasper's body when it should have burned her up. There's something off about all the magic she can do." She shuddered as she swept past Aeliana, then patted the chair sitting before the dressing mirror. It was one of their forced tutoring times, and Sylmar's prediction that they'd be motivated for quick progress had been proven false over the last eleven days.

Especially since Aeliana kept sneaking away to question Mayvus' former soldiers about her research.

Now she reluctantly sat, eyeing Kendalyhn's hands for hidden scissors.

"If you're not going to cut your hair, you at least need to learn different braids to hide its length." Kendalyhn glared at Aeliana through the mirror. With Aeliana sitting, Kendalyhn was a head or two taller than her and seemed to relish the change.

"That's... actually a really good idea." The admission was immediately followed by a wince as Kendalyhn yanked a brush through Aeliana's hair.

As Kendalyhn's fingers moved deftly through Aeliana's locks, she gave curt instructions, and Aeliana did her best to replicate the intricate knots while mentally running through which soldiers she still needed to question. None of them had been close enough to Mayvus to really have good information. Those in her tight ring of knowledge had either been killed or had run off.

"You're doing it wrong." Kendalyhn pulled the braid from Aeliana's distracted fingers and took over. A frown marred her soft brown skin and broke up her perfectly symmetrical and delicate features. "It's probably better for you to watch it done right."

Aeliana tried to rein in her focus. The sooner they got through all these lessons, the less time Sylmar would make her spend with Kendalyhn and the more time she could look for blood stores and get to the bottom of Mayvus' endgame so they'd be prepared when she returned.

"My mother taught me all sorts of braids." The more Kendalyhn's fingers worked, the more her tongue loosened. "We did them over and over while reciting scripture. She told me they were the only crown a priestess should ever take. Even then she was warning me of Mayvus' plans." Her brow pinched, and she tugged a section of hair tighter.

Questions sat on the tip of Aeliana's tongue, but it was rare for Kendalyhn to open up, so she listened, taking in whatever the bitter woman was willing to share.

"When I was older, she let me grow my hair just enough to be scandalous for a priestess, then required me to braid it daily, except she taught me to braid tiny daggers into it."

Aeliana squinted at the mirror, trying to catch the glint of metal in the knots forming a crown on Kendalyhn's head.

"I don't wear them anymore," Kendalyhn snapped. "There's no need when I can strap a dozen better ones in plain sight." Her scowl slowly smoothed out as she continued working Aeliana's hair, twisting it over and around itself to hide the length. "The hilts were delicate butterflies or finely crafted flowers, but they hid the one weapon my parents hoped I might get past Mayvus' soldiers."

"Were you…?" Aeliana sat up straighter. "Did they intend for you to kill her?"

Kendalyhn shoved one final pin in Aeliana's hair, scraping her scalp in a way that was sure to draw blood. "I was raised to be an assassin. To infiltrate the high priestess' trainees. But I never even had the chance to apply."

Aeliana's mind raced. Sylmar had told her Kendalyhn's parents were killed by Mayvus, but he hadn't explained all this.

"We should take this one out and have you do it again," Kendalyhn said. "I'm not about to act like your maidservant and come to your room each morning to do your hair."

Aeliana hesitated. "I don't mind learning braids, but something tells me that's not all Sylmar wanted you teaching me."

Kendalyhn crossed her arms over her chest. "What do you think I should be teaching you?"

"You've only been talking about clothing and hair and how mine's a disaster. He wants me to know how to present myself as a Vendaran. As the daughter of a respected priestess. Something you have experience with."

"Fine." Kendalyhn huffed as she sat in the chair next to Aeliana, her crossed leg swinging impatiently. "Where should we start? Do I need to help you unlearn your ridiculous notion that the Stars are our creators instead of the Sun? Or can we skip to blessing rituals and prayers?"

Aeliana fought to keep her voice even. "Maybe you can explain the priesthood hierarchy. In Vendaras, there are priests and priestesses at every Stargazer. All have autonomy to run their Stargazers how they choose, so long as they abide by scripture. They're held accountable by the Council of Priests, which is essentially the seventeen most experienced priests and priestesses in the country, who vote on how to handle religious affairs."

Kendalyhn's frown smoothed out and her foot stilled as she listened. "There's no one who has final say over them all?"

Aeliana shook her head. "I suspect that's why they don't have people like Mayvus working their way to the top, but maybe I misunderstood."

Kendalyhn sighed. "Before Mayvus kidnapped your mother, the two of them were the two highest priestesses, each having spiritual authority over half the nation alongside the Elanesse's monarchy. Mayvus tore down half the Sungazers in the eastern province to secure her place." Her jaw tightened.

"And they intentionally gained that power because they felt they were rightful heirs to the throne instead of the Elanesse?" Aeliana tried piecing their history together, remembering the story Orra had shared about the Wyndren sisters being descendants of one side of the Elanesse and Gaeren and Enla being descendants of another.

"I suspect that was Mayvus' motivation, but your mother just wanted to lead the people to worship the Sun. It was what made my parents—" Kendalyhn cut off, then busied herself gathering up Aeliana's brush and pins just to lay them back out in a more organized fashion.

"It's what made your parents sacrifice themselves for her?" Aeliana finished softly.

Kendalyhn's hands stilled. "Who told you that?"

"Sylmar gave me the basics."

Kendalyhn's eyes narrowed, but, apparently unable to find a way to make that Aeliana's fault, she continued talking. "According to the official records, my parents desecrated their Sungazer. If by 'desecrating it' Mayvus meant they used it to actually worship the Sun instead of a woman rising to power, then yes, they were guilty." Her lips pursed, but her eyes held a vulnerable hint of pain that Aeliana had rarely ever seen on the other woman's features. "Their convictions were strong because they'd been inspired by your mother."

"So you blame her for their deaths," Aeliana murmured, "which is why you hate me."

Kendalyhn stepped behind Aeliana and began ripping pins from Aeliana's hair. "I don't hate you because of my parents."

Aeliana raised her eyebrows, watching Kendalyhn through the mirror. "But you do hate me?"

Kendalyhn frowned, her fingers taking on a new urgency to pull Aeliana's hair from the braid. "It seems like you understand the hierarchy of the priesthood well enough. Should we move on to the blessings and rituals?"

"Why can't you just answer my question? You get along well enough with Lukai and the others, but you have some sort of secret grudge against me. It makes no sense."

Kendalyhn's face reddened, and she backed away, her hands on her hips. "Secrets? You're the one who's been avoiding our lessons and giving evasive answers. You hardly even look at Lukai, and now he's worried you're going to break your bond—"

"Our bond? What does Lukai and our bond have to do with anything?"

"I've followed you." Kendalyhn jabbed a finger in Aeliana's shoulder. "Watched you sneak off with soldiers."

This time it was Aeliana's face that heated. "I'm questioning them," she blurted out, then immediately regretted it. "But you can't tell Sylmar."

Kendalyhn snorted, then wrapped her fingers around Aeliana's shoulders, her eyes glazing over as she attempted to sift Aeliana's soul.

Aeliana wrenched away with a snarl. Her starlock heated in automatic self-defense and light sparked from her hands, but it sputtered out before it could form a functional light shield.

Kendalyhn's eyebrows rose. "Does Sylmar know you're losing your touch because you're out of practice?"

Aeliana scowled, then held out her hand. "Go ahead; sift my soul. I'm telling the truth. I'm questioning the soldiers for information about Mayvus."

Kendalyhn grasped her hand, and her eyes went blank once more before the tension in her shoulders dissipated. "You're asking them about her research on the winex?"

Aeliana sighed. "Among other things. My mother's right. Mayvus is alive. We're destroying her stores of blood and studying her research, trying to figure out how we can weaken her when she returns."

Kendalyhn backed away, her relief shifting to a smirk as she tossed the pins on the table and crossed her arms over her chest. "You're actually doing something behind Sylmar's back?"

Aeliana winced, then nodded, unsure if she'd just given her almost enemy fuel or gained some of her respect.

"All right, princess." Kendalyhn sat back down and crossed one leg over the other, her brow furrowed. "Your mother might be crazy, but at least you're not sitting around on your backside waiting for everyone to hand you everything like I thought."

"I'm not a princess. And my mother isn't—"

A knock on the door interrupted Aeliana, and Iris used her wide hips to prop the door open while she peered around a stack of blankets. "Your mother sent me, love. Felk and the others are asking for you."

Kendalyhn wasted no time standing. "That's clearly you and not me. I was hoping to get some sparring in this morning anyway." Her smirk returned. "Have fun talking to... *Felk.*" She laughed as she scooted past Iris.

The older woman frowned at her back before muttering to Aeliana, "I wish Sylmar had told you to come to me for these things."

"I think everyone would have been happier with that arrangement," Aeliana agreed, but for the first time since the battle, she felt like she might have gained some ground with Kendalyhn, and a tiny seed of hope sprouted within her and her lips lifted. Maybe it shouldn't have been a big deal, but the other woman was the closest to Aeliana in age, and a small part of her longed for a female friend amongst all these men.

Iris tugged her into the hallway and passed her half the load of blankets. "What are you smiling about, then?"

"Maybe Sylmar had the right idea, even if it didn't seem like it. He's got some wisdom hiding behind his scowl."

Iris made a disgusted sound in the back of her throat before leading the way. "Don't let him hear you say that."

CHAPTER 9

By the time they reached the door to the eastern garden, Aeliana's arms ached from holding the blankets. Murmurs and sighs escaped from the courtyard where the winex had settled.

"Your mother's already in there," Iris said. "These next two days will feel long."

"Saying goodbye to thirty winex will be much harder than just saying goodbye to Felk," Aeliana agreed.

"I meant because they're all whining about being in pain. Then tomorrow they'll all be crying like newborns." Iris used her elbow to push down the handle and balance it open, once more with her hip.

The sound of Emeris' lullaby mixed with the whimpers, then replaced them as the winex all settled down. When Iris and Aeliana peeked their heads over the blankets, most of the winex had their eyes closed with soft smiles on their lips. The shimmery silver of their skin had dulled to a dry grey, and many of the creatures had labored breathing. Still, Aeliana had learned not to fear for their early death. Nothing that ailed them ever took them earlier than their lunar cycle. They would all still be here tomorrow, when they returned to their infant state.

Aeliana's gaze focused more on her mother, uncertain if the lullaby was familiar from a real memory of it being sung to her as a child or one her mother had shared. The few memories she had from before she was kidnapped were fragments that couldn't tell a complete story. She'd received others to fill in the gaps, but they were from her mother's perspective, and they felt fabricated because of it.

After tucking her blankets around the winex who didn't have them, she settled next to Felk, whose eyes fluttered open.

"We set aside extra stores of food the last few days," he murmured. "Iris knows where, so don't let her fool you into thinking she's working extra hard to provide it. It should last us until we're strong enough to help again."

"Is that what you would do out in the forest?"

He nodded. "We should probably head out and do that again the next cycle. There will be too many of us for the fortress."

She frowned, then smoothed the wrinkled skin between his eyes.

"Any sign of your friend?" He took her free hand in his and let his eyes close once more.

"Not yet. I expect I'll see Gullet arrive before any of the men." Even though the hawk could arrive first, she still watched for the sailors on the edge of the cliffs. There was only one lookout where she could see the water. If they came from the southeast, she imagined seeing the tip of a ship rising from the waves.

"He'll come back soon," Felk reassured her.

Aeliana's face heated. "I'm just eager for him to give you your memories. By the time he's here, you'll be reborn again. My mother can only give you memories of the cycles you've had here. You're missing so much."

"It's our way," Felk said quietly. "I don't mind it."

Aeliana squeezed his hand. "I know. I just want you to remember all the history we have together." She bit her lip, trying to explain the difference without hurting his feelings. "Your kind is able to love deeply in a short period of time, but for us, love grows over time and adds layers. I want you to see those layers even if you don't need them, because they're important to me."

Felk shrugged, and Aeliana let it lie. Asking him to want something different too closely resembled the expectations of the Recreants around her. Some, like Gaeren's sailors, wanted a democracy, but most from the eastern province still wanted a leader. They'd fought for

Aeliana's mother to have that role. And with her mother's decline and Aeliana's role in removing Mayvus, many of them expected Aeliana to be next in line.

But what did she truly have to offer? She'd been shoved aside for fourteen years and bled for the magic deep in her marrow. Her kidnappers had used her power for heinous crimes, things she still didn't share details about. Despite knowing she was innocent of what they'd done with her blood, she still felt tainted by it.

"Aeliana?" her mother whispered, startling her. "I think they're all asleep now."

Sure enough, Felk's hand lay limp in her grasp. She set it back on his chest, and he turned on his side with a small sigh. Hopefully they'd sleep most of the day and night and wake as infants, hale and hearty.

She followed her mother from the courtyard, then let the door shut behind her with a soft click.

"I thought if I sent for you, you could blame me for not finishing your training. Now you're free to do a bit more hunting or interrogating." Her mother hooked her arm through Aeliana's and steered her back toward the main hall. Those they passed stopped to give their customary signal and bow, some even with tears in their eyes. Her mother had only begun saying prayers with people in the Sungazer a few days ago, and people were starved to receive blessings from their high priestess.

"I feel like we've found all the blood stores in the fortress," Aeliana admitted. "I wonder if she kept key people's blood, like yours and Durriken's, somewhere else. Somewhere safer."

"If she did, only a select few would know where. Maybe even just her," Emeris mused, pulling a sheet of parchment from her pocket. It was filled with names, some crossed out, others with question marks.

"What's that?" Aeliana asked, trying to read it without running into other people in the hall.

"It's a list of the soldiers I remember from the hazy time I was branded." She circled a few names, then passed the parchment to Aeliana. "If you haven't questioned these men, start with them. They were among Mayvus' trusted ten."

Aeliana frowned. Her aunt had built an army on lies and brands.

Several of the soldiers had woken up from their confusion with blood on their hands and weapons in their grip. They'd slain comrades and fought for a cause they didn't believe in.

The only name she recognized was Brogdon, Jasperus' son, whom she wasn't ready to visit. Even so, her mother's line of thinking brought up new questions and possibilities.

"Do you know how Mayvus' brand worked? Did she… ask you questions? Or just go through your mind when she needed information?"

Her mother paled and her pace slowed, but she didn't hesitate. "When we were together, which wasn't often, she would ask, knowing I'd be compelled to answer." Her voice trailed off and her eyes glazed over, a look Aeliana was coming to recognize as her mother getting lost in her memories of the past. It was a strategy she'd used to protect herself when branded, and it was a difficult habit to break. It was also the reason for much of her confusion.

"Mother?" She gently tapped her mother's arm, forcing her back to the present.

Emeris' eyes widened and cleared. "Yes? Oh, um…" She placed a hand to her forehead and paused in the hall.

"You were telling me how your brand worked."

"That's right." She resumed walking, her face pinched. "She'd ask me things knowing I'd be compelled to answer. But when she left me locked up, I'd sense her in my mind, finding out what she wanted to know."

"Could she ever ask something across your connection? Could you answer?"

"She never asked; she commanded, and I had to answer, but she usually sensed it much faster. Especially after the brand had been in place for so long." Her mother shivered, and her eyes clouded over, a sign that their conversation needed to pivot.

"I think it's Velden's day off from searching the grounds," Aeliana said as they approached the door to the main hall.

Her mother's eyes lit up. "I love his stories."

"You remember you can't believe half of them?"

Her mother chuckled. "That's why I love them."

Aeliana opened the door, and sure enough, Velden stood by the cold fireplace, juggling balls of water with his webbed hands before a small crowd of soldiers. "Looks like he might have more than just stories today."

"Are you not coming?" her mother asked. "I thought we could spend some time together."

The child-like plea left Aeliana waffling. "I thought you wanted me to question the soldiers."

"Oh, that's right." Emeris' hand returned to her forehead as she joined the crowd, where no fewer than half a dozen soldiers offered her their seats as they all gave their customary bow. She'd be well taken care of.

Aeliana slipped back into the hallway, quickening her pace as she headed for her chambers. She would question more of the soldiers eventually, but first she wanted to reach out to another one of Mayvus' brands. One who might have a different perspective.

She lay down on her bed and closed her eyes, focusing inward for the tiny thread she'd found that connected her to Durriken. Each time she looked, she seemed to find it more easily, though she wasn't sure how to feel about that. This time her grasp on it seemed more solid, and instead of landing in Durriken's mind in a state of confusion, she sensed the transition as smoothly as if she'd jumped into a pool of water.

The heaviness of Durriken's form left her anchored, the light mattress under her body back in the Myndren Mountains no longer palpable. The physical sensation was immediately followed by the irritated internal grunt of Durriken sensing her presence.

I'm sorry. She attempted the words, not knowing if they'd cross over but hoping they would.

Whether or not he was aware or cared, he took flight, drawing Aeliana's attention to the forest growing smaller beneath him. The remains of Islara shrank to their right before being replaced by trees as they flew south. Just as Aeliana gained her bearings, the dragon angled down, circling as he lowered, as if hunting for the perfect clearing.

Durriken's anticipation fluttered through Aeliana, crossing over the thread that connected them, but she couldn't say what he looked forward to.

I have no wish to control you. She tried communicating again, suspecting Durriken could hear her but was unwilling to respond unless it benefitted him. *But if you're willing to share information, I could use your help.*

Her stomach jolted as he dropped, apparently finding the exact spot he wished to land. The motion almost made her lose her hold, and for a heartbeat she felt the sheets against her skin, the coolness of her chambers back in Myndren.

Durriken let out a satisfied harrumph.

Did Mayvus have any stores of blood in the mountains? Anyplace she had you take her that only she knew of?

Durriken landed in the clearing, his paws touching down on the grass with a gentleness she hadn't expected. His weight shifted as his front paw stepped more inline. His limp was no longer pronounced as he compensated for the missing fourth leg.

He lay down, resting his head over his stump, and let out a smoky breath. It seemed no answer would come, and Aeliana's confidence that he'd heard her, that he could understand, waned. Perhaps the brand wasn't like her mother's because Durriken was a dragon. And yet he'd spoken in her mind when she'd first branded him. He'd heard her respond. She had to hope it was possible even across this distance.

Eventually Durriken's ears perked at the flutter of leaves, the crack of snapping twigs. He held unnaturally still though his heart raced.

Aeliana internally winced, wondering if she would be forced to watch him catch his prey. Perhaps it was time for her to release her hold on their brand.

Yes.

She sensed his purr of agreement cut short as he realized his mistake. So... he *could* understand her in this strange state.

Please, Durriken.

He hesitated, shaking his withers as if he might shake off her hold.

She tried again. *When Mayvus returns, I don't want her to brand you again. You or anyone else.*

He stilled, finally sensing her desperation enough to respond. *Mayvus is dead.*

The flicker of memories returned at double speed, blood and torn flesh, the cave in the mountain's peak. A ripple of disgust ran through him. Despite Mayvus' status as the enemy, he took no pleasure in the taste of starblood, and when her body felt lifeless, he deposited it on the cave floor and flew away.

Before she could ask more questions, a small figure broke through the trees, interrupting the memories he'd shown her.

"You came back." A young boy breathed out the words, his eyes lit up in wonder.

Panic engulfed Aeliana, but Durriken made no move to attack. Instead, he peered beyond the boy.

"I couldn't bring Adella today. Grandpa wants her to sleep more."

Durriken's rumble of disappointment flooded through Aeliana, but the true shock came when the boy stepped closer and rubbed the dragon's nose. His stance held trust instead of fear, and his lips lifted in a smile.

"You're slimy," he said with a laugh.

Durriken let a huff of air out through his nostrils, sending the boy to his backside in a gust of wind. But the boy giggled and leaped to his feet.

"Again!"

Everything inside Aeliana drooped with relief as the boy and dragon resumed their game. She'd always wanted to believe the best of Durriken. All the atrocities he'd done had been when he was under Mayvus' brand and authority, but that alone wasn't enough for her to be certain. What if he wasn't any better than the beast Mayvus had made him become? What if he'd simply wanted freedom to do a different kind of evil?

But that fear had been unfounded.

Durriken circled the clearing, tucking in the sharp edges of his scales as he let the boy chase—and even catch—his tail.

Now that she'd seen him this way, she could never see him any other way. She couldn't go back to remembering him the way Mayvus had made him, even if that was all the others could see.

She sensed a wetness on her cheeks. It pulled her from her hold on the thread binding them, and she let it go willingly.

She sucked in a breath, taking in the familiar stone ceiling above her before rolling to her side. She wiped at the tears still staining her cheeks. She hadn't gotten the answer she needed. In many ways, her effort to reach Durriken had been a failure.

Even so, she smiled.

CHAPTER 10

GAEREN DEBATED RUNNING across the center of Bamboo Island. They'd have enough of a head start to lose the ship's crew, but eventually they'd hit the other coastline, and without a ship of their own, they'd be trapped by the open water. Their best bet was to face the crew head-on and find some other way to get the upper hand.

"They still have to row in. Let's find a better vantage point." He led Riveran, Cyrus, and Rildan down the slope to the rocky beach, exchanging dark soil for brown sand and swapping moss and bamboo for seashells and seaweed. They crouched behind several large boulders to assess the possible enemy.

The black ship loomed over them from where it had dropped anchor a few hundred feet away, and a small boat rode inland. Voices drifted across the water with a confident carelessness that left Gaeren on edge. He made a mental note never to travel without his spyglass again.

"Can we get to the cave?" Cyrus asked.

"What cave?" Gaeren wracked his brain for all the times he'd stopped on Bamboo Island, but there had never been a cave.

"There's a cave hidden down the shore." Cyrus pointed north, but Riveran slapped his hand back down behind the boulders.

They all shrank back as laughter rose from the beach.

"Sorry," Cyrus whispered, "but it's where Sylmar took Aeliana and me. There's an underground passage that leads to the mainland."

"Impossible," Riveran muttered.

"No, he's right," Rildan said. "It's how I first crossed over from Lorvandas to Vendaras and met Emeris. Sylmar must have hidden the passage years ago, then waited in it for my return."

"There were only four of them," Gaeren said. "They probably assume we headed inland. We have the element of surprise."

He peered around the boulders. Two of the boat's passengers nocked arrows and pointed them in the men's direction.

"Or not," Gaeren muttered.

"Don't make this difficult!" The familiar voice made Gaeren go still.

He squinted, scanning the men at the water's edge until a bald head full of tattoos gleamed in the Sun's light.

"Larkos? Sun's fire, it's Larkos!" Gaeren stepped out, hands raised.

The older man stood and waved, but the other sailors didn't lower their weapons.

"Who's that with you?" Larkos called out.

"All friends," Gaeren said.

The sailors set down their weapons and hopped from the boat, dragging it in until the hull scraped against sand. Gaeren went to meet them, looking beyond the small boat to the ship bobbing in the sea. Familiar parts stood out to him: the curve of the bow, the height of the stern. The main mast was the right height, but the sail looked far too worn and weathered. The ominous black made his heart sink, but the practical side of him won out.

It had to be done. His ship could never be *Starspeed* again.

"How do you like the look of *To the Deep and Back*?" Larkos asked.

A grin tugged at Gaeren's lips at the name, but the sight of the changes was still too fresh, his pain too raw. "She'll do."

"She'll do?" Larkos snorted as he approached. "You'd better have something nicer to say when you board, both for the sailors, who spent hours disguising her, and for her own pride. She's been testy ever since we traded down her sails."

"I can't blame her," Gaeren said. "It's like giving a princess rags to wear. You could've chosen something a little less threadbare."

Riveran greeted the other men with slaps and punches, and Gullet squawked from his shoulder, flapping his wings now and then. It was anyone's guess if he was happy to see the sailors or irritated at all the commotion. Gaeren introduced Cyrus and Rildan, and before long they were all squished aboard the tiny rowboat.

"We weren't expecting so many," Larkos said.

"Why not?" Gaeren asked. "You knew we went looking for Rildan."

Larkos gave a sheepish shrug, his tattoos rolling as his muscles bunched with each row. "No one seemed confident you'd be successful. And we thought the other Lorvandan would stay behind."

Rildan grimaced. "It's nice to meet you, too."

Larkos' chuckle came from deep in his belly.

"How's Fay like the eye patch?" Gaeren nudged Thallahan, who sat in front of him, as he picked up an oar to aid in the rowing. Riveran grabbed a second, and they each matched the strokes of the sailor in front of them.

"She likes it more than I do." Thallahan turned back with a sly grin. "Says she only has to work to look half as beautiful." He'd lost his eye in their battle with Mayvus, when they'd been trapped in the northern keep with dozens of soldiers, but at least that was all he'd lost. Breeve had lost his life.

"Did you bring her with you?" Taking a woman on board was never any sailor's first choice, but they'd discussed the option, knowing Thallahan's connection to Gaeren might put Fay in danger.

Thallahan shook his head. "But we picked up Breeve's ma and siblings, plus Erech."

The pain from the loss of Breeve warred with Gaeren's eagerness to see Erech. Eventually he grinned when the thought of the stableboy back on his ship won out. The boy was a hard worker, eager to please.

"Oh." Thallahan turned to Riveran. "We picked up your wife and boy, too."

Riveran's hand slipped and he missed a stroke. "How's Bayla?"

The familiar twinge of anger stirred in Gaeren's chest, but it was a remembered response. Now that he knew Riveran hadn't really left his sister for the other woman, that the marriage had been a lie, it hurt less. If anything, a new sense of righteous anger replaced the old igno-rant frustration. His parents had forced Riveran to fake a loveless arrangement just to hide the fact that the future queen had been bonded to a man with no magic.

"She's doing well," Thallahan said. "And Rox was starting to walk a bit last I saw. We left them with Breeve's ma in a town just north of Rykarn. Far enough away from the seedier parts, but close enough for the amenities. The women are all set to start over and take care of each other."

Riveran's shoulders relaxed, and he resumed rowing.

Thallahan used his good eye to study Riveran. "That baby isn't yours, is he?"

Riveran glanced at Gaeren as though asking permission for the admission. "Not by blood."

"And Bayla?" Thallahan pressed.

"She's more like a sister," Riveran admitted.

"Why didn't you bring Fay?" Gaeren asked Thallahan, taking the attention off his friend's discomfort.

"With our wedding planned for Winter Solstice, her parents felt it best to continue preparations."

Gaeren let his oar rest on his knees. "They had no problem with you sailing off on a ship bound for the Recreants?"

Larkos glanced back from his place at the bow, his scowl far too serious. "We have a lot to catch you up on."

By the time they got settled aboard *To the Deep and Back*, Gaeren was anxious for Larkos to explain himself. The two of them settled in Gaeren's old quarters, which, thankfully, remained the way he'd left them.

"It appears you're welcome back in Elanesse." Larkos leaned back in his chair and let his boots rest up on Gaeren's desk.

Gaeren grimaced. The older man had gotten far too comfortable in the captain's quarters while Gaeren had been gone. He shoved the sailor's boots off the desk and half sat, half leaned there instead. "How is that possible? When I left, they knew it would be to aid the Recreants. They had just given Mayvus a crown, and I went up against her. My actions were clearly treasonous."

"It's not like I get to talk to the king and queen or get regular updates from your sister."

"Then how do you know I'm welcome back?"

Larkos grinned. "Your sister sent letters to Bayla for you and Riveran. She must have sifted your future and seen you'd be coming this way."

Gaeren rolled his eyes. "And I suppose you opened them."

"It's my duty to make sure your ship stays safe in your absence."

"Well, what did they say?"

His voice deepened as he quoted the missive. "Enla has heard of your valiant efforts to defend our nation's honor by exposing the dark deeds of Mayvus. Because of your heroic acts, you are both welcome to return, Gaeren as the throne warden and Riveran as his advisor." He opened a drawer and pulled out two letters, sliding them over in Gaeren's direction.

Gaeren's eyebrows rose as he grabbed them. "Riveran can return as well? And what will she do about the X on his forehead?"

Larkos shrugged. "The message wasn't that detailed."

Gaeren frowned, pulling out the unusually formal letter. "It feels more like a trap."

Larkos rubbed the scruff of his beard in thought. "Maybe, but I have to admit it seems genuine. Even before we arrived with our black ship, there were rumors that the king and queen had denounced their connection with Mayvus. I don't think they'd go so far as to align with the Recreants, but it was still a surprising move."

"So a genuine attempt to save face, but not exactly a real desire to do the right thing." Gaeren had thought he couldn't be more disappointed in his parents, but they still managed to find ways. For most of his childhood, Enla had shielded him from the depth of their oppression, but now that he'd fought alongside the Recreants and seen the ways his parents chose their own safety and comfort over the needs of the Vendarans, he couldn't go back to being ignorant.

Larkos leaned forward, his elbows on his knees. "You seem even more bitter toward your family than the last time I saw you."

Gaeren sighed. "I'm not sure I can go back to Elanesse. I don't trust my family to look out for the best interests of the people."

They stared at each other for a long moment. It was the response Larkos had likely wanted for the last five years while he needled Gaeren with talk of Recreants wanting a democracy, but now that Larkos was getting it, he didn't seem as satisfied as Gaeren had anticipated.

"You can still love your family, even if you don't love their choices." The older man's voice sounded foreign with its softness.

"It makes it harder though," Gaeren admitted. And he wasn't even factoring in all the ways his parents had favored Enla over the years, or how his father had used his destructive somatic skills as disciplinary measures on both him and Enla. His parents might not want to align themselves with Mayvus, but that didn't suddenly make them benevolent rulers.

"That it does." Larkos gave him a sad smile, one more reminiscent of Calia, his wife and bondmate. She would have patted Gaeren on the head and offered him some sweets to go with the sympathy, and his throat tightened with the thought. He was more homesick for Larkos and Calia's home than his own.

But it was the palace he was being summoned to.

"Is it a command?" Gaeren murmured as he reread the letter. "Or an offer?"

"Probably a little of both," Larkos said. "We weren't planning on staying long anyway, but we hightailed it out of there because we didn't want anyone to connect *To the Deep and Back* with you. Thought we should wait and see if you wanted the connection or if you wanted to remain anonymous."

"What was it Aeliana called me?" Gaeren asked. "Braggart Brownbeard?"

Larkos snorted. "I'm sure these men could come up with more formidable names if you're looking to go the pirate route."

Gaeren picked up the second letter, but it was sealed. "Riveran's message was too private to read, but mine was fair game?"

Larkos' grin turned sly. "I'm not acting captain over Riveran's ship."

Gaeren clenched his jaw, staring out the porthole at Bamboo Island's shoreline. He'd thought they'd need to sail around the southern tip of Vendaras to avoid Elanesse. The trip would have taken at least a moon, but they could shave off more than a week if they went by Elanesse instead.

Except his sister would try to change everything.

He'd told Cyrus he didn't know what his purpose was anymore, and while that was true, he'd come to terms with the idea that his purpose no longer included being a prince or throne warden. He didn't want to take those titles on again. Not after experiencing freedom from them.

But what if being welcomed back was the only way he could save Enla? He still wasn't sure which deal the sprite had taken back at Lovers' Falls. The conniving creature initially agreed to help Gaeren get across the barriers in order to protect Aeliana, but when it suggested Enla would be the one to pay the price for his deal, Gaeren had tried to make another, trading his own life for hers. Riveran had then killed the sprite, so who knew which deal, if any, had been made? Guilt swirled through him as he weighed his options.

"We'll make for Elanesse. Make a point of accepting Enla's forgiveness, but then take Rildan home. I can't avoid my sister forever, but I can't serve her anymore, either."

"Denying allegiance to the family of Elanesse could lose you more than your title," Larkos warned him.

Losing his title sounded more like a win, but Gaeren took the older man's words to heart, thinking of the sister he still loved, the people he still desired to do right by, the palace he'd grown up in with all its safety and security.

Gaeren nodded. "I'll tread carefully. Hopefully she won't make me choose." He wanted to protect Enla, but there were others he'd made promises to as well. He pictured Aeliana, the light billowing off her skin like she was a Star herself, then the people they'd traveled with and the purpose he'd felt when fighting alongside them. "The cost could be high, but the reward will be far greater."

CHAPTER 11

ORRA SAT on the balcony of the north tower watching the Sun rise higher in the sky. The smoky scent of cooked meat clung to the air even though the kitchen was far below. She stroked the blond braid at her wrist, letting her mind drift through the years, seeing flashes of history instead of the soldiers roaming the courtyard. Even though she currently had none of the starbridges in her possession, somehow this still felt like the closest she'd come to righting her wrongs.

The world was changing around her like it had before the Great Divide. Except this time, she sensed the Sun was orchestrating the changes. The Sun was throwing stones and letting the ripples affect everyone else. If only she'd let the Sun direct those changes the first time around.

"I'm going to make things right," she murmured, dropping a kiss against the braid. Her short dark hair swung against her cheek and eyes, a reminder of the choices that had brought her to this point. "But not on my own."

"Breakfast is ready in the kitchen." Aeliana spoke from behind her.

Orra didn't turn. "Sylmar doesn't want you up here." The tower wouldn't fall, but the others didn't trust it. Which was part of the reason Orra had made it her own little sanctuary. When she wasn't out searching for the onyx stone, she was here, contemplating her options, soaking up the Sun's light, growing stronger.

"Well, Sylmar also asked me to get you to eat more."

A smile tickled Orra's lips. "I don't get my energy from food."

"And yet I've seen you eat. At least come down so Iris doesn't think you hate her cooking."

Orra rose and hooked her arm in Aeliana's, allowing the younger woman to lead her through the tower. It no longer held bodies, but it still had the dank and foreboding feel of a tomb.

"You don't get your energy from food," Aeliana said, "and your magic is different from the rest of ours. You don't even have a starlock."

Orra hummed her agreement. "Neither does Marnok." No one had seen their mysterious friend since the battle. He'd received memories from Emeris about his past, things he needed to deal with somewhere else. Yet one more mystery still unsolved, though Orra had her suspicions.

"Yes," Aeliana agreed. "But… it still seems different. His is limited to healing. He's clearly on the somatic spoke. You heal and you seem to sift the future."

"Surely Sylmar has taught you about secondary spokes."

Orra kept her grip on Aeliana's arm but moved her free hand to the railing of the stairs. The stone steps were her least favorite part of the tower. It was as if they still held the souls of the soldiers she'd killed in the wake of her magic.

"Even Sylmar has discernment skills on the pneumatic spoke," Orra continued. "He just prefers to let Kendalyhn do that chore for him."

Aeliana laughed. "Yes, but the constructive somatic spoke and the constructive pneumatic spoke aren't adjacent. Secondary spokes are always adjacent."

A small smile threatened to bloom on Orra's face. "He's taught you very well."

"And you showed up on the other side of the barrier looking like a ghost. How did you do that?"

Orra hesitated. "Sometimes I'm not sure. Every time I push myself to the rim of the Wheel, I wonder if it will be my last time." They reached the bottom step, and she held out her hand, examining how it shook.

"I thought the rim was elementals," Aeliana said as they crossed the threshold from inside the tower to the battlement.

"It's an advanced branch of magic that generally focuses on an elemental, yes," Orra said. "But it's so much more than that for me." She closed her eyes and tilted her face up to the Sun.

"So then… are you a Star?" Aeliana whispered.

Orra considered the question. At one time she could have said yes, but it had been so long since she'd felt worthy of the title. She'd thrown it away along with so many other blessings from the Sun. She sighed and opened her eyes. "What do you know of Stars?"

"Very little," Aeliana admitted as they resumed walking. "No one's seen them on land in a thousand years—since the Great Divide. They no longer commune with us because it's safer that way."

"The Lorvandan view," Orra said. "Vendarans would say the Stars abandoned the people as a punishment for their sins. But either way, you're right—they've been gone. What else?"

Aeliana shrugged. "I've heard they look human when they come to our world, but in the skies they're like balls of light. Others say they're a literal glittering star." She pulled out her starlock and held up the small shape as if Orra needed the example.

Orra bent forward and pinched the charm between her thumb and forefinger. Her eyes widened as she sensed the lock of hair from within. "Andreas," she murmured.

"What?" Aeliana asked.

Orra dropped the charm like a hot coal and picked up her pace as they left the Sun's light on the battlement for the cold halls of the fortress. "They're more like balls of light yes, but they're merely a reflection of the Sun. They absorb the Sun's power just like the blood of a half-light. Except they can hold so much more." Her pitch rose and she let go of Aeliana's arm so her hands could move with her words. "They constantly reflect it, which makes them bright against the night sky. They become less like Stars and more like the Sun. They constantly absorb its power, meaning their own power is limitless."

"So the Vendarans are right? The Sun is our maker and source of power?"

Orra smiled and let her hands drop. "They're right about some things. I suspect no one has it exactly right. But my point is that the beings I'm describing have power beyond this world. I may have more power than you, but is my power limitless?"

Aeliana hesitated. "If a Star chose to abandon the sky, then its power would no longer be limitless. It could only absorb more from the Sun during the day, like half-lights."

Orra grew still as Aeliana nearly touched on the truth. They would realize it soon enough. Better that they hear it from Orra than someone else.

"No Star would choose to be grounded," Orra said softly. "I was grounded as a consequence of my actions. And I'll remain grounded until I reverse what I've done."

Aeliana's breath hitched. "But you are a Star?"

"I was at one time. I'm not sure that's what I could be called now." Orra briefly closed her eyes, all her regrets weighing her down with shame. She pushed them aside, bringing the topic back to Aeliana and the things she needed to hear. "We're all products of our life experiences. Your blood may say that you're a half-light, and Cyrus' might say he's a human, but the two of you have more in common than you have with many of these Vendarans."

Aeliana smiled ruefully.

"And after all this, you'll both have even less in common with the Lorvandans back across the barrier. You're not Vendaran or Lorvandan. Just like you, I'm not any one thing. All of us need to take the time to figure out who we are."

Aeliana's brow furrowed. "Sylmar wants me to be more Vendaran. They all do."

Orra hummed her understanding but said nothing more. That was for Aeliana to figure out on her own.

They rounded a corner, and the clink of dishes and murmur of chatter drifted into the hall.

"Still no sign of the starbridge?" Aeliana asked.

Orra shook her head. "No. And I hear Sylmar no longer wants you digging through Mayvus' research."

"He has me training with Kendalyhn." Aeliana made a face. "Even if he thinks my mother's wrong about a curse, he has to see we're missing something. Mayvus had stores of blood hidden away, and she was researching winex blood and the fluid in their eggs. There's something here we need to find. Something other than an onyx stone or Mayvus' body."

Orra reined in the fragments of power attempting to slither out to test the future. She couldn't search for every little answer. Not when her power was so limited. "Your mother's mind might be broken in some ways, but don't forget that she is a gifted progeny. Her spoke's strength lies in her memory. She may not be able to communicate it to you perfectly, but the answers you're looking for could be locked up in there somewhere. And she's not the only one with secrets to unlock. When everyone holds back part of the riddle, it's impossible to see the solution."

Aeliana stopped outside the kitchen door, giving distracted waves and hugs to the young winex filing past her. It still left Orra in awe that Aeliana had managed to befriend creatures long overlooked as unintelligent enemies. How had she been grounded for a thousand years without ever considering such a thing?

"What do you mean?" Aeliana asked.

"Hmm?" Orra pulled her gaze from the line of the winex.

"Who else has secrets they're holding back?"

Orra's focus blurred as dozens of faces passed through her mind. "Who isn't holding back secrets?"

She pursed her lips as the blurred faces converged, leaving the image of an onyx stone. One she'd last seen in the palm of an Ahmranan pirate. No, a thief. A murderer. He'd been too terrible to be given the docile label of a pirate.

"Those who are hiding secrets are usually trying to get to the bottom of everyone else's," Orra murmured as an afterthought. She turned on her heel and strode toward the main hall. She'd spend another day searching the grounds, sensing for the place she'd last felt the stone's power. It was all she could do at this point.

"Orra?" Aeliana's words met Orra's ears as if muffled by water. "Won't you at least eat breakfast first?"

"No, thank you. The winex need it more than I do. Besides, Holm appreciates Iris' cooking enough for the both of us." Orra rounded the corner, ignoring Aeliana's protests.

She'd meant what she'd told Aeliana. She could no longer consider herself a Star after being grounded for so many years. But that didn't mean she couldn't act like one. She could still reflect the Sun.

She ran a finger over the braid on her wrist then pressed it to her lips. "Perhaps today will be the day," she whispered. "Don't give up on me yet."

CHAPTER 12

A ELIANA FROWNED AFTER ORRA, trying to decide if it was the most she'd learned from Orra at one time or the most Orra had confused her. She wasn't exactly surprised the woman was a grounded Star, but the confirmation only brought out dozens more questions, questions Orra would likely never answer.

And the secrets Orra spoke of…

Who else knew as much about Mayvus as her mother? Sylmar. But he hadn't been around her for years. His knowledge was outdated.

One of Mayvus' former soldiers passed by Aeliana on his way into the kitchen, giving her the three-fingered salute, his bow and lowered eyes almost more shameful on his end than respectful of her. Her stomach flipped as she nodded in return. He probably knew more about Mayvus. He may have been compelled to follow her, but he'd still followed her.

She'd interviewed most of the men on her mother's list, but they'd all been dead ends, the men's memories too hazy thanks to Mayvus' control over her brands. Or maybe because her mother's memory was too hazy, and the names she'd given Aeliana weren't really men in Mayvus' trusted circle.

Aeliana stepped into the kitchen and bit her lip as she surveyed the various men sitting at tables as far away from the boisterous winex as possible. Were there others here who had known Mayvus the best? Would she have to interrogate everyone?

"Here, love," Iris said, passing Aeliana a plate with biscuits and smoked meat. The portion was noticeably smaller than the week prior, making Aeliana wonder how sustainable their fortress was. Several of the soldiers had headed to their various homes, eager to start life fresh once more. But even more had stayed, hoping to reestablish the Wyndren family's right to the throne—Aeliana's mother's right. Not to mention the families who'd lost husbands and fathers, arriving to take Sylmar up on his offer for refuge.

"Thank you, Iris." Aeliana smiled at the older woman, but her thoughts still lingered on questioning soldiers and ferreting out secrets.

"You're taking it to your room again, aren't you?" Iris' voice held disapproval, but she sighed and set an extra biscuit on the plate. "Don't be late for your training again. Kendalyhn gets just as testy as Sylmar when that happens."

"Sorry." Aeliana ducked away from Iris' swat, then headed down the hall. Once in her room, she set her plate down and flipped through pages in one of Mayvus' journals, nibbling on a biscuit while she searched.

She'd never been a great student—not that Arvid and Vera had allowed her much schooling—and Mayvus' handwriting was going to be the death of her. For the millionth time, she wished Cyrus were there. He would have read the papers without any problem and likely explained them all to Aeliana far quicker than she could read.

Three names kept popping up: Tychus and Piorre—two men she'd never heard of who likely hadn't survived—and Brogdon. She bit her lip again, knowing she probably had to go see him. The soldier had been quiet in his self-assigned prison, which seemed like a waste when his voice could ring with the same authority that Jasperus' had. She swallowed past the lump in her throat, hating the way her mind so easily recalled the way Brogdon had killed his own father at Mayvus' command. She couldn't fully blame him when he was under Mayvus' control as her brand, but he'd also taken the brand willingly.

"I wondered if you might be in here," Velden said.

Aeliana turned in her chair to find him leaning against the door-frame, arms crossed over his loose vest and bare chest. With his exposed arms and shaved head, she felt cold just looking at him.

"Is it time for my training already?" Aeliana rubbed at her eyes, which still seemed to focus a handsbreadth in front of her.

Velden shook his head and pushed off the frame. "Not yet." He pulled up another chair from the small table and spun it around so he could sit backward and lean over it to face her. "I just thought I should check on you."

She raised her eyebrows and leaned back. "Usually it's Iris trying to mother me."

Velden chuckled. "Until Emeris grows stronger, we all need to mother you a bit. What are you looking for in here?" Velden pulled some of the books on the table closer to him, studying their titles before flipping through the pages. "Is this Mayvus'? I thought Sylmar told you to stop all this research."

She ignored his fake shocked expression. "My mother swears there's a curse on her, not just blood magic done by Mayvus but maybe something done by someone else. Orra gave me some cryptic comment about everyone having secrets. I'm trying to find out who might know something, but they're all too scared to talk."

Velden grinned and set the journal down. "I happen to agree with Orra on that one."

"You're an open book," Aeliana scoffed. "You don't have any secrets."

His smile fell and his gaze grew distant. "You'd be surprised."

Orra's warning came back to Aeliana, but this time it held more clarity. Somehow Velden's secrets didn't hold much threat. Probably because, like Orra had said, Velden wasn't desperate to discover everyone else's secrets.

"Mayvus stored a lot of blood throughout the fortress," Aeliana said. "Her notes are at least helping us find and destroy most of that. I doubt we'll catch it all."

"Do we really need to if she's dead?" Velden cocked his head.

Aeliana's face heated. "I suppose not."

"I heard you didn't quite believe the evidence in Durriken's cave."

Velden rubbed his hands together, flicking water on his lap as he leaned in conspiratorially. "Tell me more."

A spark of hope gave her courage. "Would you help me talk to Brogdon? He might be able to tell both of us more."

Velden's brow furrowed. "Why do you need help? He's as soft as Holm even if he's as loud as Jasperus."

"I want to ask him about Mayvus' research, but I haven't gone to see him yet. It's starting to feel like I waited too long." She twisted her hands together. "I'm not sure he'll want to tell me at this point."

Velden rubbed his neck, leaving water that trailed down the back of his shirt. "I know Sylmar already questioned him a lot." A sly grin spread across his lips. "But he's much more likely to tell a pretty young woman what she wants to know than a scary old man."

Aeliana let out a groan. "You always think people can be charmed into cooperation."

"It hasn't failed me yet." His teeth practically sparkled with his triumph.

She narrowed her eyes. "Something tells me you didn't just come here to check on me or even solve my problems. What are you trying to charm me into right now?"

Velden's grin turned sheepish. "I mostly came to avoid Sylmar. He's trying to get me to train Felk's little army."

Aeliana chuckled. "They're like puppies right now. Practically harmless."

His face scrunched up. "They're a little more eager than I like. I usually come away with several bites and scratches." He rubbed at his arms as if sensing them now.

Aeliana set her book on the table and tugged Velden back to his feet.

"Seriously?" he groaned. "I thought you out of everyone would be the one to let me slide by training."

Aeliana tugged harder on his arm, pulling him out into the hall. "You forget how much I like Felk."

"More than you like me?" Velden asked.

"Today you're lucky," she said. "Today I want you to come with me to see Brogdon. Usually it depends on who you're spraying with water."

He shot the liquid from his hands into her face as if to prove her point, then wriggled out of her grip and ran down the hall laughing. She shook her head but didn't give chase. He was old enough to be her father, but he often acted more like a child. When she caught up to Velden outside Brogdon's room, the guard standing outside the door gave both of them somber pause.

"Can we see Brogdon?" Aeliana asked.

The guard bowed and pressed three fingers to his forehead before stepping aside. After a knock, Brogdon called for them to enter.

His room seemed more like a workshop, full of wood furniture in various stages of completion with a bed hidden somewhere beneath the table he was constructing. The petite man sat in a chair, huddled over a table leg that he continued sanding.

"Sorry about the mess." His voice boomed out across the room, making Aeliana jump, more so because it was an exact copy of Jasperus', which she hadn't heard for a few moons now.

"I didn't realize you enjoyed woodworking," she said.

His gaze remained on his work. "It's more that I want to be useful, and this was the best way how."

"I think you've been plenty useful by giving us confidence that Mayvus no longer has access to her brands." Aeliana tried to smile, but her words came out strained.

Brogdon's hands stilled. "I'm glad you came."

"I'm sorry I didn't come sooner," she said softly.

"I understand."

For a while, the only sound in the room was the hush of his plane and scraper on the wood.

Velden cleared his throat. "Aeliana wants to ask you about Mayvus' research."

Aeliana glared at him, but the older man beamed as if he'd done exactly what she'd asked. She turned back to Brogdon apologetically. "I wanted to see if you knew anything about her research on the winex. Your name was mentioned among those conducting the studies."

Brogdon winced, then slowly nodded. "She wanted a way to recreate their ability to be reborn. Instead she found ways to quickly heal people, but the side effects outweighed the benefits. As far as I know, that's as much as she got from it all."

"What about Tychus and Piorre?"

His gaze flicked up to hers in surprise. "They came back?" Then his mouth clamped shut, and he turned back to the table leg, resuming his vigorous sanding. "I mean, I thought they'd died. Maybe there was something to her research after all."

Aeliana's heart picked up its pace, the throb echoing in her ears. She didn't have Sylmar or Kendalyhn's ability to sift the truth of someone's words, but something about Brogdon felt off. Maybe she'd never be able to trust him. Maybe that wasn't fair.

"I don't remember any soldiers by those names," Velden said. "But I haven't met them all."

"No." Aeliana kept her gaze on Brogdon. "They were in her research notes. I haven't met them either. Maybe they are dead. But they were the two she trusted with the winex, besides Brogdon. They all knew the most."

Brogdon's laugh came out forced. "They were a strange pair, talking more in grunts than words. They liked the cold dungeon. If they lived and if you find them, you probably won't get anything out of them anyway."

Something about his casual manner, the perfect way the words could be true even if they weren't, didn't sit right with Aeliana. She stepped closer before removing the table leg from his hands.

Brogdon looked up at her but couldn't hold her gaze for long. She flipped his hand over, running a finger along his brand. She felt sick looking at the black circle, the way it reflected Mayvus' experience in doing brands, how she could get it so perfectly shaped. Aeliana's own brand mark on her right palm throbbed, and she swore she sensed Durriken's own distaste, like bitter herbs in the back of her throat.

"Who comes to check your brand these days? To verify that it's no longer active?"

Brogdon licked his lips, his gaze flicking to Velden.

"It was me," Velden admitted. "I sifted for the truth of the present, but he was always honest. He hadn't sensed Mayvus at all."

"But you don't do it anymore?" Aeliana let Brogdon's hand drop and turned back to Velden, who shrugged.

"We found her remains in the cave. There was no need."

Aeliana gritted her teeth. "Can you please sift him now?" The request burned, partly because she hated the way they were all so content to believe what they wanted, but mostly because she disliked this kind of invasive magic.

"I haven't felt her presence since the dragon took her," Brogdon said. "He's welcome to test me, but I know she's gone. I'm just not ready to face people. Not after what I've done."

The guilt in his words resonated with her, and she almost called Velden off. But she hesitated, afraid they might all miss the tiniest of clues. "It's just a formality, Brogdon. If you don't sense her, there's nothing to fear."

She stepped aside, allowing Velden to grasp Brogdon's hand. It would only take a moment to be sure. Knowing they were safe was worth temporarily invading Brogdon's thoughts, right? Especially since he'd allowed it.

The moment Velden's fingers touched Brogdon's, Brogdon brought his head against Velden's with a sickening crack. As Velden crumpled to the floor, Brogdon turned to Aeliana. Her starlock warmed against her skin, and the light exploded around her without a second thought, forming a shield to block him.

The thinness of it shocked her, and in the back of her mind she registered that Sylmar would be gravely disappointed.

Shouts from the corridor made it clear she wouldn't be fighting this battle alone for long. If she could just hold him off long enough, if they could just get enough people in here to tie him down and cut out the brand mark…

Her light flickered when Brogdon backed away and crouched, bringing a carving tool up to Velden's neck. He dragged her poor unconscious friend closer, and while neither of them were overly large, it was clear he was using magic when he pulled Velden up like a doll.

What was his spoke? She wracked her brain, trying to remember if he was somatic or if he might be using blood magic. Did it even matter at this point? The risk to Velden was the same, and the solution still required cutting out Brogdon's brand mark.

"Guess you should've had him keep checking my brand, huh?" Brogdon's eyes drifted wildly between the door to his chambers and Aeliana.

"How long?" Aeliana asked. "When was she strong enough to control you?"

"Long enough. And it won't be much longer for you." Brogdon pulled Velden closer, but when the tip of his tool dug into Velden's neck, Velden's eyes flew open. Water gushed from his hands, momentarily enveloping Brogdon's face. As Brogdon sputtered and shook Velden off, a blast of air swept through the room, taking the water out the window with it.

It brought back memories of the wind Mayvus had used to push Aeliana across the balcony, wind she'd likely stolen from Brogdon through his brand.

Aeliana shook off the memory, but by now the men were locked in chokeholds, both their faces turning purple as they rolled around the room. Other soldiers flooded in from the hall, and despite the bursts of wind knocking them down, their numbers were too great for Brogdon to get the upper hand.

He screeched as Velden used a dagger to cut out his brand, and Aeliana winced both at the sight and the scent of blood. It no longer called to her the way it once had, but it was a constant reminder of the pull it could have. Her mind even strayed to the way it had done good when she'd branded Durriken. Enslaving one beast had freed hundreds of people.

She shoved the thought aside.

Velden pulled seaweed from his pouch, letting water from his hands soak it until he could wrap it around Brogdon's hand. The other man wept, curling into a ball, his entire body shaking. Velden's voice grew low as he bent closer, but Brogdon flinched when Velden's hand patted his back.

Most of the other soldiers shifted uncomfortably, eyeing the door before slowly making their exits.

"Send for Sylmar," Aeliana whispered to one before he could leave.

With the room less crowded, she made her way to Brogdon's side, his whimpers now becoming more intelligible.

"I should have known. I should have..." He rocked and groaned again. "Kill me now. It's safer. Please."

Aeliana kneeled down but didn't touch Brogdon. "You're safe now. Velden cut out your brand. Now you're like me. You're free." She held up her scarred right palm. The lines from Arvid and Vera stood out, but there was also a jagged pockmark above Durriken's brand, the remnant of the brand mark Mayvus had placed on her, cut out by Gaeren. It felt like ages ago, but as she relived it now with Brogdon, it could have been hours.

"Never free..." he moaned again, but this time his shuddering ceased.

"Please, Brogdon. I know it's a lot, but I need you to tell me what you know."

"She's alive."

The words were cold, absent of feeling, and they stirred up all sorts of terror in Aeliana's chest.

"What more do you need to know? Mayvus is alive, and she'll come for us all."

Footsteps pounded from the hall, and Aeliana stood, more than willing to let Sylmar finish the interrogation. Because Brogdon was right. What else mattered besides the terrifying truth that Mayvus was alive?

CHAPTER 13

As they pulled *To the Deep and Back* into Elanesse's harbor, Gaeren grew more antsy. He no longer feared Enla's invitation was a trap. Too many of the sailors had confirmed Larkos' theory. Even Erech, from his time as a stableboy, had said the royal family had publicly declared they were no longer tied with Mayvus.

If anything, that only gave Gaeren more questions for Enla.

"I think that boy's already a better cook than Breeve." Riveran patted his belly as they weaved their way through the docks.

"I'd rather have Breeve's burned food curdling in my stomach." They'd stopped to see Breeve's family on their way north. It'd been one of the hardest visits, telling a mother firsthand how her son had braved death and lost. She'd already heard the details from Larkos but seemed to want them again. Gaeren hadn't been there for the boy's last moments, so instead he told her all the ways the young man had faithfully served on his ship. The way he'd been a solid fourth-generation sailor who would have made his father proud.

"I can take Erech off cooking duties and make him swab decks again," Riveran said. "Maybe stick Thallahan behind the stove?"

Gaeren snorted. "If you want to be poisoned."

Their banter faded the farther they got into town. Despite being welcome at the palace, Gaeren and Riveran opted to quietly take horses to his family's sprawling estate. They could have announced their arrival in advance with Gullet and had Enla and maybe even his parents out to parade their heartfelt reunion. But Gaeren still saw the hatred in Enla's eyes from when they'd last said goodbye. A heartfelt reunion was more likely to turn into a yelling match that fed the kind of rumors his parents despised.

So Gullet stayed back with Cyrus, Rildan, and Larkos, while the other sailors were given two days leave. Rather than pass the horses over to the palace stableboys and effectively announce their arrival, they stopped a mile or so outside the palace walls. Riveran tied their horses to a tree near a stream and promised them he'd return soon. Thanks to Riveran's strange connection to animals, they stood eerily still, ducking their heads to accept his nose rubs.

"Come on," Gaeren urged. "You've already said goodbye ten times, and they're not even our horses."

"I don't know if I should be present for this," Riveran admitted, glancing toward the towers rising in the distance.

"I need you there as a buffer," Gaeren said. "My sister won't kill me if you're here."

Riveran's laugh came out uneasy. "She might just kill us both instead."

Instead of walking through the main entrance and halls, they snuck through a gap in the hedge Gaeren had made years before, which placed them in the family gardens. Gaeren gave his mocking bow to the statue of the first Queen of Elanesse, then paused and frowned, trying to figure out what seemed different about her. He gave up, then led Riveran through a side door, questioning the guards about which meeting room Enla might be in. Before they could reach it, she rushed out, her cheeks flushed and the chain holding her heart-shaped starlock on her forehead knocked askew.

"Gaeren." Tears filled her blue eyes as she breathed out his name, and suddenly she was throwing her arms around his neck, her short blonde hair tickling his cheek. She squeezed him tight like she'd done when they were children, and a memory flooded his mind of a time he'd forced her to swing with him across the hay in the barn. It held a mix of fear and elation, with a strange sense of protection: the first time he'd instinctively understood his role as a throne warden. When the rope had snapped and they'd fallen, he'd twisted to make sure she landed on him instead of the other way around, breaking his ankle instead of hers. His starlock heated against his skin, drawing him back to the present, making the images dissipate into reality.

That same ankle twinged as he squeezed Enla back.

"I take it you don't completely hate me," he said.

She pulled back and smacked his shoulder. "I hate you with every fiber of my being." But the words were counteracted by her smile. She turned to Riveran and grew flustered, wiping the tears that had spilled down her cheeks. "It's good to see you too, Riveran."

Gaeren warred between frustration with his old friend and his sister. For the last two years, he'd hated Riveran because his parents had led him to believe the other man had slighted his sister—breaking their bond and marrying another woman. But after learning it had all been a farce to cover up the fact that Riveran had never received a starlock or developed magic, Gaeren's anger had shifted to his sister. Somehow the conflicting feelings canceled each other out and a sadness swept over him instead.

"I wish you'd told me about Riveran from the start."

Enla nodded, glancing between both men. "I wish I had, too."

"But that's not what we came to talk about."

Enla nodded again, then glanced over her shoulder at the body-guards who'd followed her into the hall. "Cancel the rest of my meetings for today. And schedule a dinner with our parents."

"Change the dinner to breakfast," Gaeren said. "Or maybe mid-morning tea. Or even dinner tomorrow."

Enla raised her eyebrows. "Fine. We have time for tea between council meetings in the morning." She linked her hand through Gaeren's, but before she could lead the way, Riveran reached out and snatched her hand. The guards drew weapons, and Gaeren even tensed at the forward action, but Enla showed no surprise.

"With my parents' health declining"—her words came out soft and halted—"we decided the wedding couldn't wait." A gold ring with a ridiculous number of gems sparkled on her hand, and Riveran dropped it like a hot coal, his face pained.

Gaeren's jaw dropped. For some reason, he hadn't thought she'd actually go through with it. Not when she knew Riveran still loved her. Not when he suspected she still loved him.

The silence that followed made Gaeren uncomfortable. He cleared his throat. "It's a nice ring."

It was an old tradition, not often used, especially by those who had bonds to mark their loyalties, but the royal family took any opportunity to show off their wealth. When Riveran and Enla continued avoiding each other's gazes, Gaeren tugged Enla down the hall and tried to shift the topic from the more obvious and awkward one lingering in the air.

"Mother and Father have gotten worse, then?"

Enla shrugged. "Better in some ways, worse in others."

Riveran caught up to them, a strange expression crossing his face. "You didn't mention the wedding in your letter."

So much for avoiding the awkwardness.

Enla glanced nervously at Gaeren. "It only took place last week. I didn't have a chance to write you again."

Gaeren frowned. She shouldn't be writing her old bond at any time. In fact, what would Croft think of her offering to reinstate Riveran as an advisor? He hadn't thought much of the letter Riveran had received, but now he wished he'd asked about it.

"Well," Gaeren said, "I appreciate you getting the pompous celebration over with before I reached town. It's bad enough that Thallahan wants me to come back for his wedding on Winter Solstice."

Enla stopped short, and the guards' armor clanked behind them as they stopped too. "Come back? Why in Rhystahn would you leave again?"

Riveran and Gaeren exchanged glances before Gaeren replied, "That's actually what we came to talk about."

Enla scoffed and resumed walking, her pace suddenly more like a sprint. "I should have known you weren't really back. I had hoped... I saw dozens of paths with you staying. Even some where you married Lenda."

"Lenda?" Gaeren practically choked on his bondmate's name.

"There were only a few with you leaving, so I thought..." She trailed off, her face taking on a dark hue. "I should have known. Now I'll have to search those all over again."

"Or you could just let the future unfold. It's not good for you to search so much."

"It's a constantly moving target. Even worse when you're involved. It's like you're so unpredictable even the future can't settle on your options."

He grinned. He actually liked the sound of that, but it probably wasn't something he should say out loud.

"If you're trying to reform Gaeren," Riveran said, "I don't think it's working."

She glanced up, and Gaeren attempted to drop his smile, unsure what expression he finally landed on.

Enla let out an unladylike snort. "It was easier when the two of you weren't getting along." She linked her other arm through Riveran's. "Come on. I've only told you a fraction of what's gone on since you left, and I'm guessing you could say the same to me."

"Mother and Father were branded by Mayvus?" Gaeren sat back in his chair, stunned. Out of all the things he'd expected Enla to say, that hadn't been one of them. Even Riveran's mouth swung open in surprise, which meant that news hadn't been in his letter either.

Enla sat prim and proper at the tea table where they'd been served an array of sandwiches, fruit, and cheese. The servants had even left pudding pies, suggesting the conversation they were about to have would be a long one. Once she'd made sure they would have enough to eat, she'd dismissed all the servants and guards.

"One morning, they woke up with renewed minds and clear focus. I thought something the healers had done made them feel better, but Mother took off her gloves and screamed. Father found his brand mark as well. We cut them out before we even knew where they'd come from, but as news from the east trickled our way, we quickly put it together." She frowned at her tea cup as if it were to blame. "Some of the notes Mother had lying around made it clear she'd been wooing influential leaders across the country to stand behind Mayvus as well, though she doesn't remember it."

Gaeren rubbed his palms over his face, trying to imagine when that had happened—*how* it had happened. Mayvus would have needed some of their blood to brand them. Had the dignitaries procured a sample? Had Mayvus done it herself the last time they'd seen her? She'd probably had dozens of opportunities over the years. If she'd stored it like she'd stored Durriken's, she probably had more of it in the fortress. The thought left him anxious to return to Myndren and scour the fortress for himself.

"That explains their behavior before I left," Gaeren said. "I mean, they've always been…"

"They put the needs of the nation before their family." Enla's words were careful and tinted with warning.

It wasn't how he would describe how their father had used his destructive somatic skills for discipline. "I thought Mother was losing her mind, but really, it was being controlled by someone else."

Enla nodded, her face pale. "So far, we've been able to keep this amongst ourselves. Only the highest of council members are aware. Those who had been questioning their decisions lately."

"What about Father Fernandus?"

"We told the priest," she admitted.

"Did any of the healers figure it out?"

She shook her head. "We had to tell Tobias, but none of the other healers know."

The elderly progeny was often found by his parents' side—almost as often as his uncle Danton, who was charged with protecting the king as the throne warden. Gaeren had known Tobias as long as he'd known Father Fernandus, and he was the most trustworthy of the healers. "And they just accept their miraculous healing without question?"

"We let them think their efforts were successful, just like we'd origi-nally thought. A few of them are still trying to figure out what initial malady struck them." A wry smile flitted across her face. "But most of them are moving on to deal with Father and Mother's other symptoms."

"What's wrong with them now?" Gaeren asked.

Frowning, she toyed with the bread from her sandwich. "I can't know for sure. It's like they're aging quickly. Father Fernandus thinks their shame over their actions is taking its toll. For a while, we were receiving missives every other day that reminded them of the poor choices they'd made. Families from Islara requesting assistance or justice. Dignitaries from the southern provinces asking us to recant our support or they would threaten war. Most of the fires have been put out by myself and the council members, but I know they're feeling guilt over all that occurred under their rule. Mother has so much anxiety that Tobias often gives her calming tinctures. Father is ready to step down and give me full authority, but I've asked him to wait a little longer."

Gaeren chewed on the inside of his cheek, trying to decide how to ask his question without pushing Enla the wrong direction. "I know we both assumed we'd be far older before that happened, but is it possible that's best in this scenario? You've been making most of the decisions for the last few years anyway."

Enla leaned forward. "Don't you see? I've been making the decisions, and these things have still happened. Maybe I'm the problem."

Gaeren placed his hand over his sister's, stopping her fingers from shredding the bread. "You can't possibly believe that. You're the only thing that's held our family together." Even as he said the words, guilt threaded through him. She'd held their family together, but not their nation. What if they all stepped down? What if they made efforts to shift from a monarchy to a democracy? If it was their choice, could the bloody end to the monarchy be a peaceful transition instead?

"I can't sift the past to know which wrong decisions were mine and which were overruled by Father. But when I sift the future, I still see difficult decisions ahead. Decisions I don't want to have to make." Her eyes glazed over in that way he hated. "There is pain that can't be avoided in every path."

He shook her hand to bring her focus back on him. "You need to stop searching the future. Live in the moment. Make the best decision you can with the information you have right now."

Her smile wavered as if she might cry. "This is why I wanted you here as my throne warden." She sat back, pulling her hands from his. "But I can't hold you to that anymore. When you broke your bond with Lenda, that ship sailed right along with you."

Gaeren eyed Riveran, who gave a slight shake to his head before glancing down at Gaeren's hand. Gaeren flipped it over to study the bond mark on his palm. The dark red mark had faded around the edges since the fight against Mayvus, as if his temporary connection to Aeliana had threatened the health of his bond. But it was still there.

"I…didn't break my bond with Lenda."

Her gaze rose to his, the confusion on her face painful to watch. "You did. I remember Lenda coming to me and crying…" She frowned, her eyes losing focus once more. "Wait, no… that was only one of the possibilities." She bit her lip. "Wasn't it?"

Alarm shot through Gaeren. "I mean it, Enla. You need to stop sifting the future. Have your mentors been holding you accountable? Are you marking the options so you can keep track of reality?" It was a strategy he'd come up with back when Riveran had left and Enla's sanity had gone with him. She'd gotten so twisted in all the "what ifs" that she'd had trouble hanging on to reality. Every day he'd made her write down branches showing future possibilities. And every day he'd made her mark which direction things had gone, while crossing out all the things that hadn't happened.

"My skills have advanced beyond most of my mentors," she murmured. "A few still come to help me work on projecting emotion, but… well, there hasn't been much need for that. There's been far more need for me to assess our options for the future."

"What about Croft?" Riveran asked, his jaw tight as he studied the tablecloth a little too closely. "Is he holding you accountable? Does he even know the limits you need to stick to?"

Enla's face turned pink. "Croft takes good care of me."

"He doesn't even know you," Riveran muttered.

Enla picked up her tea cup and took a lengthy draw, like it was water in a desert.

The awkward moment lengthened until Gaeren no longer remembered how it had started. Hadn't they been worried about Enla overusing her magic?

"You *should* have broken your bond," Enla finally said.

Ah, that was where it had started. "You said that the last time I was here. But the time before that, you insisted I lean into the bond." He couldn't help the dry tone at this point.

"Well, after you didn't lean into it, it became necessary to get rid of it."

"Then why doesn't Lenda do it?"

This time Riveran huffed his annoyance. "If Lenda breaks it, it would be considered treason. That's why even the perception of me breaking ours made me lose everything."

The strained silence returned and Gaeren avoided looking at the X on Riveran's forehead.

"If you do it," Enla said, "Lenda will be cast as the spurned lover by a spoiled prince. Others will swoop in to rescue her."

"Why don't you want me to marry her?" Gaeren ground out. "Wouldn't that be the best scenario?"

"You've never wanted to marry her."

"But we're bonded." He shoved his palm at her, as if she hadn't ever seen the mark plaguing his skin. "I may not love her, but I don't want to hurt her. Not after watching—" He glanced at Riveran, but the damage was already done. The other man's throat bobbed as he swallowed, and he stood, mumbling some excuse about needing to take care of personal matters.

Enla flinched as the door shut behind Riveran, and she closed her eyes. "It's not the same, Gaeren."

"What do you mean it's not the same?" He leaned forward with a heated whisper. "Breaking bonds is always painful. It nearly killed you. I felt it when I tried to take your memories."

She sighed. "I didn't realize how much that stayed with you, but I suppose with the way you hold on to memories…"

He blinked and sat back. Was she saying it wouldn't hurt him? That it wouldn't hurt Lenda?

"I can't know for sure, but I suspect that the pain of breaking a bond is directly related to the strength of the bond." She grabbed his palm and traced the mark. "Yours even looks smaller than I remember. Like you've been ignoring it. You could let it fade over your entire lifetime, but neither one of you would feel free to move on unless you chose to break it. It would be a horrible existence. Free yourself. Free Lenda."

She flipped over his other palm, and he winced as she took in the sight of his pink and white puckered skin: the mark that he'd used blood magic to brand Aeliana. It was something he'd done temporarily to save her. Even though they'd cut it out after Durriken took Mayvus, it was something he'd never be able to hide.

"I wondered which choice you'd make," she whispered.

He tensed, waiting for her to berate him, to call him out on reaching new lows. He already expected his parents to disown him for it, but he'd hoped Enla might hear him out.

She traced the skin, her gaze losing focus again. "You know, if you can't stomach the thought of cutting out your bond mark, maybe you should find a woman to help you break it the old-fashioned way."

His mind reeled at the flip-flop of topics. "Break it the—" His face heated, and he pulled his hand away. "Stop sifting my future. We promised we wouldn't use our magic to invade each other's privacy."

Her focus returned as she smiled and crossed her arms. "I wasn't even using my magic. I was simply making a suggestion. If you were willing to do blood magic for this woman, maybe you're willing to break a bond for her." Her eyebrows rose so high that Gaeren responded the only way he knew how.

He smashed an entire pudding pie in her face.

CHAPTER 14

"I DIDN'T EXPECT to find you here." The quiet, almost faded, voice brought a smile to Gaeren's face.

He turned to the Sungazer's entrance to find Fernandus, their family's ancient priest. The old man puttered at the edge of the room, adjusting a book here and moving a candle there. He was clearly allowing Gaeren the opportunity to finish worshiping while making himself available.

"I didn't expect to find myself here either." Gaeren supposed his time with Cyrus was rubbing off on him, but he wasn't sure if that would please Fernandus, considering Cyrus worshiped the Stars. Not that Gaeren had ever sensed displeasure from the doting priest. Despite warning Gaeren and Enla of the Sun's judgment, Fernandus had never been one to make them feel guilty for their actions, not even when he called them out on their wrong choices.

Gaeren stood and dusted off the knees of his trousers, which were clean because, unlike most Sungazers, theirs had polished floors and cushions for the royal family to be comfortable while worshiping.

"Those are the best times for worship. If you didn't expect it, then the Sun likely led you here." Fernandus smiled and tottered closer to Gaeren, holding out his hand, palm up. It was an older greeting that few priests still did, but it was exactly what Gaeren expected from the man.

He placed his hands in the priest's and kneeled, allowing the priest to then bring his hands to Gaeren's forehead for a blessing.

"May the Sun's light give you guidance in whatever troubles you this morning. May its light dawn bright with understanding and peace. May you never lose its light. Even when it sleeps, may the Stars reflect its glory for your guidance." The rumble of the priest's voice swept over Gaeren, and the papery feel of his palms against Gaeren's skin brought back hundreds of childhood memories.

He hadn't always enjoyed their family's times of worship, but Fernandus had always been a bright spot in the Sungazer. The old man had a way of challenging Gaeren to be better without making him feel so much pain over his mistakes. If his parents had had half of Fernandus' compassion, their family dynamic might have been more tolerable.

Gaeren winced as Fernandus kneeled with him. The old man's knees popped and a small groan escaped his lips. Surely the Sun would understand if the priest no longer kneeled at this stage of life. But even if the Sun understood, Gaeren knew Fernandus would never approach the Sun with anything less than what was expected of a priest.

"I'm meeting with my parents this morning," Gaeren said. Fernandus hadn't asked what troubled him, but it was the way their conversations went, something he'd always taken for granted.

The old man made a clucking noise on the roof of his mouth. "Sometimes those we love are the hardest to speak the plain truth to."

Gaeren frowned, unsure he could call what he felt for his parents "love," but figured it wasn't worth mincing words during the little time he had with Fernandus. "I don't expect the conversation to go well," Gaeren admitted. "They'll want me to settle down as throne warden."

Fernandus tilted his head, squinting one eye at Gaeren in consideration. "You've always been a wanderer. I can't imagine they'll be surprised if you resist that."

"It might not surprise them, but it will upset them."

Fernandus' lips tilted up. "Well, yes, that's true. But I suspect after all they've been through, they'll leave the decision up to Enla. When you have the itch to leave again, she's the one you'll need to worry about."

Gaeren sat back on his heels and glanced toward the door, imagining his sister rising from bed and preparing for a long day of meetings. After catching up yesterday, she knew his plans, but she was hoping the sight of his parents would change his mind, that their weaknesses would move him to take his place as throne warden and settle in. She might be harder to convince than his parents, and yet she'd continued to encourage him to break his bond. He couldn't understand it.

"You performed my bonding ceremony, right?" Gaeren asked.

Fernandus smiled, his eyes taking on a faraway look. "Yes, you and Lenda were just babes in your mothers' arms. Oh, how you cried when I pricked your palm. Enla came over and shushed you." The smile fell away from his face. "She took to mothering you at a very young age."

His unspoken words made Gaeren squirm. The closest the queen had come to mothering him was to send him out to sea because she thought he was too soft for the horrors of court. As Enla took on more responsibilities, she continued the tradition, more to protect him from their parents—who clearly favored her—than to manipulate him. Regardless of motive, his time at sea had left him naive and vulnerable to influence by the Recreants, things that Enla likely saw as flaws, but he saw as bonuses.

Now that he was practically a Recreant himself, she could never fully win him back, even if she could never completely lose his love and loyalty as a sibling. He shook away the thoughts. He wasn't here to ask Fernandus about politics.

"Did anything go wrong during the bonding ceremony?" he asked.

Fernandus' brow furrowed. "Wrong? Not that I can remember. Why?"

Gaeren flipped his hand over and rubbed the mark on his palm. "I don't feel like our bond took the same way others do."

Fernandus hummed his understanding. "Bonding at such a young age is a tricky thing. It's far less about love and far more about protection. You may not be in love with her, but you desire to protect her."

"I'm not sure she's ever been in danger enough for me to feel that pull. She's a destructive somatic. She can take care of herself, and she usually does."

Fernandus smiled. "I think if she were in danger, you would find the pull is there, but that's not something we truly need to test. I imagine Enla and Croft's quick wedding has prompted this discussion. Are you hesitant to seal the bond with marriage?"

Gaeren paused. It would be easy to agree to that and move on, but he wanted answers. "Actually," he admitted, "Enla has encouraged me to break my bond."

Fernandus' smile faded. "Why would she do that?"

Gaeren shrugged. "I don't understand it. She wants me to stay and settle down as throne warden, yet she wants me to be free of commitments like Lenda. Sometimes I wonder if her visions of the future are so muddled that she can't give me good advice."

Fernandus sighed. "I do wish that she would spend less time sifting the future, but that is between her and her mentors."

"Is it a sin to break my bond?" The directness of his own question made Gaeren realize he was truly considering it. His stomach churned with the realization that he was thinking about doing the very thing he'd despised for the last few years. But so much had changed. He had changed.

Fernandus hummed again, clasping his hands in his lap. "I've done hundreds of bonding ceremonies and sealed many more in marriage. A bond is a sacred thing that should not be taken lightly. Most of the time when a bond is broken, it is done because of lust or retaliation or anger. In those instances, yes, I would say it's a sin. Is it possible for a bond to be broken for good reason? Maybe."

Gaeren frowned at the evasive answer. "What about when my parents forced Riveran and Enla to break their bond? Was that a sin?"

Fernandus closed his eyes tight, the wrinkles deepening and making Gaeren wonder if he was in pain.

"I have always regretted my role in that," Fernandus murmured. "I feel as if I gave your parents permission to do something that was not in Enla's or Riveran's best interest. But Enla was in favor of it for the sake of the nation, and I saw the benefits they spoke of. I do not envy the decision they had to make, and I fear my acceptance of their potential solution was seen as permission. Which is why I hesitate to give you an answer now with the certainty you seek."

Gaeren sighed. "I suppose I am looking for permission. But unlike Enla, I'm not sure if it's what I want. Mostly because I know I'll feel guilty."

"Breaking a marriage bond is different from breaking other bonds," Fernandus said slowly. "And while yours was intended for marriage, it hasn't yet happened. In this case, I feel like so much relies on the intention behind your action. We tend to look to the outcome of our choice to determine if it's right or wrong. But oftentimes there are two right choices or two wrong choices, and we should be looking at whether or not our actions reflect the Sun regardless of the outcome."

Gaeren frowned, trying to parse out the priest's meaning.

"Is it what Lenda wants?" Fernandus asked.

"I guess I should ask her. Enla makes it sound like Lenda wants it but that I should do it so she's not seen as a traitor."

"Well, then, I suggest you make time to speak with Lenda as well as your parents before you head east."

Gaeren started. "I never said I was leaving."

Fernandus smiled again, then placed all his weight on Gaeren's shoulders as he groaned and stood. "And yet you're leaving. It was only a matter of time. I've heard of all that took place in the Myndren Mountains, and I understand your desire to see all that through. I think even Enla understands it, though she may not like it. Returning to those you fought beside might be one of the first times I see you do what's truly right for you. Remember what I said about choices?"

Gaeren hesitated, still not sure he understood even though he could recall the words. "I should strive to reflect the Sun instead of focusing on which choice has the better outcome?"

Fernandus beamed. "Exactly. Staying here as throne warden is good, but fighting alongside those who need someone to fight for them is also good. Which one will allow you to reflect the Sun's glory more?"

The priest gave him one last farewell blessing before tottering back to the Sungazer's entrance, leaving Gaeren with far more questions than answers.

Later that morning, Gaeren stood outside the council room, hesitating long enough that the guards eyed each other. He could have gone to see his parents in their rooms last night. It probably would have been the appropriate thing for a son to do. But after their last encounter, after they'd told him they supported Mayvus, he no longer felt like their son. Meeting them in the council room for this tea appointment with Enla felt far more appropriate.

He tried to remember that they'd been branded, but that still didn't excuse the way they'd manipulated him during his childhood. Enla would always be their favorite, and he would always be the wayward prince who couldn't settle down long enough to obey their commands. At least now he was old enough to fight back if his father used his destructive somatic skills to "teach him a lesson."

Not that the guards would let him defend himself.

It might have been a childish rebellion at one time, but now he came to their door understanding the Recreants and their desire for democracy or, at the very least, a just and kind ruler. Things his parents could never be. Maybe there was hope for Enla, but he doubted the Recreants would wait long enough to find out.

The door swung inward, revealing Enla in a flowing blue gown that matched the shade of her eyes. She cocked her head and gave him a knowing smile. "There wasn't a single path in which you opened the door. I hope I gave you long enough to think through what you wanted to say."

Gaeren elbowed past her and rolled his eyes.

He'd feared the council room might be full, but thankfully his parents had cleared the room. Outside of the few guards at the door, only Tobias and Gaeren's uncle Danton remained. Tobias kept a watchful eye on the queen, reminding Gaeren of Enla's words from the night before about their mother's anxiety. As the king's throne warden, Danton stood off to the side, aware of everything transpiring without participating in it. It was a stark reminder of what Gaeren's future was meant to be and how he wanted no part of it.

Instead of sitting at the head of the council's table, his parents were seated in a corner settee with tea and cookies already on the small table. It would be easier to face them this way—without an audience. He didn't expect their reaction to be any better in private. In fact, it would probably be worse, but at least he could say what he needed without far-reaching repercussions.

He strode forward, and his parents stood to greet him. He bent low to kiss his mother's hand, then allowed her to pull him in for a stiff hug. "Forgive me, Gaeren," she murmured in his ear. Her voice broke enough that he reconsidered his resolve to hold them at a distance, but then his father's scowl reminded him there was still too much history to forgive and forget.

He shook hands with the king, bracing himself for whatever judgment was coming.

"You couldn't come home in time for your sister's wedding, could you?"

And there it was.

"I was in Lorvandas. I had no way of knowing she was getting married." He turned back to Enla, who smiled sweetly.

"It's all right, Father. When people heard he was across the barrier, that left a far better impression on them than his surly presence would have."

His father grunted but didn't disagree, something that maybe should have bothered Gaeren far more than it did. They all sat, backs straight, waiting for someone else to speak. Enla poured tea in all their cups, and the silence stretched to an uncomfortable length.

When his mother reached for her cup, Gaeren saw the stark white of the scar on her palm, and he winced. His mother quickly hid it behind her cup, then took a sip and glanced at the king.

"We were fools to trust her," his father said.

"Does that mean you gave her your blood?" Gaeren asked.

"Gaeren!" Enla admonished. "Of course they wouldn't do that."

Gaeren could have disagreed but opted to keep the peace.

After a heavy sigh, his father responded, "We suspect she took it a few years back when she came to visit and your mother was ill. Mayvus brought healers from the eastern province, and they bled your mother, supposedly purging her of the foul elements that were leaving her ill. They convinced us that having the blood of her bondmate would make her better, so I gave mine as well."

For the first time, Gaeren noticed a softness to his father's face as he reached for the queen's hand. Regardless of the things he'd done, he truly did care about her. At least *that* action had been motivated by love, even if it had resulted in the horrors that had come with them being branded by Mayvus.

"Because your mother grew better after their care, we thought nothing more of it. It was about six moons ago that we started wearing gloves to hide our brand marks, and that's when our memories get fuzzy, so we suspect she hung on to it all that time."

Gaeren frowned, stirring his tea with a spoon. After watching Aeliana be forced to do Mayvus' bidding under her brand, he couldn't help but feel sorry for anyone who had been under that woman's control. It didn't make up for everything, but it made it harder to hate his parents.

"We've asked Enla to step into her role," his mother said. "It's time we retired, considering our poor judgment has left people in a state of mistrust of the crown."

"But she needs her throne warden," his father added.

Gaeren had known this was where the conversation was headed. He'd thought it would be easy to refuse. But his parents' remorse somehow made it harder.

"I've promised to reunite Rildan with his family back in Myndren. I have commitments I need to follow through on first." He hoped that angle might make his father reconsider, since his father had always wanted him to show more initiative and responsibility.

His father scoffed. "Someone else can deliver things for you. I hear Riveran has been assisting you. Perhaps he could." His father practically choked on his friend's name.

"Well, now that you've brought him up," Gaeren said, "what *is* your plan for him? He holds the mark of a traitor, and yet he's been invited to be one of Enla's advisors."

A pink hue spread across Enla's face and neck. But she lowered her eyes, leaving the king to answer.

"We invited him to be one of *your* advisors," his father corrected.

"Riveran has proved his loyalty in his service to you. We'd even be willing to have our healers remove the mark on his forehead to aid people's trust in him."

"And what will you tell people of my mark?" Gaeren held up his hand, the evidence of his blood magic making his mother's face grow pale.

Tobias rushed forward, letting a few drops fall from a vial into the queen's tea. Gaeren frowned, both at the interruption and the uneasy feeling that his mother shouldn't accept unknown tinctures from anyone, no matter how long they'd been in the royal family's service.

"You were a victim, just like us," his father said, holding out his own palm and matching scar.

Gaeren let out a bitter laugh. "This was my choice, and I don't regret it. It saved a life. A life that then saved thousands."

His father's lips pursed. "Even if that's true, that's not the story we'll tell the people. We'll find something that fits with Riveran's story when we remove his mark."

Gaeren sat back, crossing his right foot over his left knee, attempting to hide his irritation behind a slouch. "I can't speak for him, but I wonder if he would prefer to leave it—if he would prefer to have the people see that you were willing to trust someone who had been in such high disregard. It might give others hope that they could rise from their lowly positions."

His father's face darkened, and creases formed between his eyebrows. "His situation is rare. I don't expect to find many others I would absolve of their crimes."

"What about all the sailors who joined me in aiding the Recreants in the eastern province?" Gaeren leaned forward, truly eager to hear his father's answer. "Several of them have the same mark on their foreheads. They were all just as willing to put their lives in danger to save our nation from Mayvus' power. They might not have been serving the crown, but they were serving the people. Their goals aligned with ours because we serve the people first and foremost, right?"

The uncomfortable silence returned.

"I fear Larkos may have filled your head with too many ideals," his mother said, placing her cup back on its saucer.

"It does sound idyllic, doesn't it?" Gaeren asked. "A nation where people can make decisions for themselves, where they can work hard and be rewarded for their efforts, where they can be given equal opportunities regardless of what family they're born into or how much money or starblood they have."

His father snorted and his face grew more red. Danton shifted, as if warning Gaeren he was going too far.

But Gaeren couldn't stop. "These people are going to bring a war to your door if you don't change something. If you don't find a way to put things in their favor, they will find a way to turn it around themselves."

His father's eyebrows rose. "Are you threatening us?"

A laugh bubbled up in Gaeren's throat. "I'm warning you of a threat that's already there. I don't want to see anyone in our family hurt, but I also don't want to see the people hurting. I will never aid them in battle against you. But I won't stand by as their rights continue to be stripped away."

This time, Enla's face paled as the conversation touched on topics they had yet to discuss. Perhaps she hadn't sifted the future for his thoughts on politics because she assumed he was far more concerned about his bond and sailing.

"I'm leaving tomorrow for Myndren. I will reunite Rildan with his family. Depending on what's happened in my absence, it might be best for me to stay there and aid them. I think my talents would be wasted here."

"Talents," his father scoffed. "You were raised to be a throne warden, but you're too entitled to take on that role. I thought you were too soft, but now I suspect that you're too immature. You're still trying to prove yourself, and the easiest way for you to do that is to go against us. If I tell you to go right, you go left. It's the way it's always been. But for some reason, I thought that when things got hard, your sister would be able to count on you. I thought your bond as siblings would at least give you enough scruples for that."

The anger that had been building in Gaeren halted as he took in the tears clinging to Enla's lashes. Was that what she thought too?

Tobias rushed forward again, but Enla waved away whatever soothing tincture he offered for her tea.

Gaeren cleared his throat. "My decision to leave has nothing to do with my care for Enla. She is my sister, and that will never change. I would gladly give my life for her. But unless she changes the way our family is leading the Vendaran people, I don't know that she can be my queen." His words rang through the room with a finality that shocked even him. He hadn't meant to say something so definitive, so treasonous. He'd expected that time and distance would make them realize that was likely how he felt, but he knew the blunt words stung far more than a distant realization would.

Enla's face grew blotchy.

"I'm surprised you didn't sift that," he muttered.

Her lips trembled, and she gave a slight shake of her head. "I did, and it hurts just as much to hear it the second time around."

This time *he* felt the sting, and he knew it was time for him to go. He never should have come in the first place. He should have ignored Enla's letter and let everyone assume he was irresponsible rather than reveal the truth that he really was the traitor they'd called him the last time he'd left. He stood, brushing off the crumbs that had fallen on his lap.

Danton's hand drifted to the pommel of his sword, his wary eyes watching Gaeren's every move. Gaeren ignored the implied threat.

"I don't expect to be welcome here again, but if the Recreants do bring war to your door, know that I will welcome you aboard my ship or wherever my home ends up being. I will still call you family." He looked at his parents' stricken faces and realized he meant the words. "Even you, Father." He turned on his heel and walked out of the council room with a lump in his throat.

He hadn't meant to burn bridges. How could he protect Enla now?

Even so, he couldn't regret any of his words.

Maybe Larkos could be ready to sail tonight.

CHAPTER 15

AELIANA REACHED out to steady her mother's elbow as they climbed over another large rock. "Are you all right?"

Emeris nodded with a faint smile, but her face grew pale and her breathing remained labored.

Aeliana glanced around at the others who'd volunteered to check Durriken's cave with them. Only two remained behind them—Iris, because she'd never leave Emeris' side, and Brogdon, because he'd only come at Sylmar's insistence in the first place.

It had been a week since Velden had cut out Brogdon's brand mark. Aeliana could still picture the way Sylmar's face had paled as Brogdon spilled the little information he'd retained without his brand: Mayvus had survived. She'd been growing stronger in the cave where Durriken had left her by reaching out to her brands and finding the stragglers who still supported her. She'd used them to get a sense of what the Recreants were up to and how she might once again gain the upper hand.

Brogdon hadn't been sure what had allowed her to survive in the first place.

Sylmar had shifted all their efforts to reinforcing the outer walls and building up their defenses, but now it was time to chase Mayvus down while she was still potentially incapacitated. Or, at the very least, get a clue to her whereabouts and plans.

"I think we're almost there." Aeliana left her hand at Emeris' elbow to guide her, wishing her mother, in her weakened state, had stayed behind. Felk and his clan of nearly full-grown winex ran ahead, loping back and forth to check and make sure everyone was accounted for. Holm corrected their course now and then since he was the only one in their party who had been to the cave. His pace gave Aeliana the impression he was desperate for proof one way or another since he'd been the one to previously see Mayvus' remains.

Kendalyhn and Lukai followed, easily keeping up while half-heartedly arguing over whether his somatic magic was more powerful than her pneumatic skills. He'd likely come out of a need to protect Aeliana, and Kendalyhn wouldn't miss the chance for a fight. Occasionally he glanced back at Aeliana, his smile fading to a pinched frown, but she didn't care if he spent his time with Kendalyhn. She still needed space after the way he'd stolen her blood under the guise of protecting her.

Orra, Velden, and Sylmar fell in the middle of the line, each wanting to see the cave for themselves for their own mysterious reasons.

Emeris tripped, nearly taking Aeliana down with her.

"If Mayvus is there, you're in no condition to fight her," Aeliana pointed out.

"She won't be there." Emeris huffed out.

"How can you be so sure?"

"I know the way her mind works. If she lost Sylmar as a brand, she wouldn't stick around to be found."

Aeliana tensed. "You mean Brogdon?"

Her mother's eyes clouded over. "She lost Sylmar as a bondmate, didn't she?"

"Yes, but that was years ago, and you said—"

Her mother's face grew more vacant.

"Never mind." Aeliana patted her mother's arm. "I still think she could be there if she's too weak to move."

"She's as strong as I am." Emeris smiled wryly. Even though her physical strength had been slow to return, her confidence had increased. Proof that Mayvus was alive equated to proof that her talk of curses wasn't completely ridiculous.

Sylmar grunted, showing he was listening from several paces ahead. He'd still shown disdain for Emeris' curse theory, latching on instead to what he already felt certain of: Mayvus was after immortality. It was the next level of power she had to reach since she'd mastered the entire Wheel of Magic through her brands. Although hopefully she'd been set back with the brands they'd cut out and the blood they'd destroyed. He still felt confident she hadn't found what she needed. Not if she'd been studying the winex when they'd arrived.

As the path all but disappeared, they had to rely on Holm's memory and instructions, along with the winex's instincts. A howl erupted from ahead, followed by several others in response. Aeliana and her mother exchanged a glance, and several others drew weapons.

Felk came running back to Aeliana, his excitement palpable. "We found it. No one's there, but they used to be."

He tugged on her arm, pulling her away from Emeris and around the bend, where the maw of a cave stretched before them. Bones and animal carcasses littered the opening—more likely evidence that Durriken had been here than Mayvus or her followers. But as they stepped in farther, it became clear that fires had been situated throughout the cave. Not the kind made by Durriken's snout, but ones strategically placed for warmth or food, evidence of more than just Mayvus having been here.

"There was flesh"—Holm reached out to an empty spot on the ground—"just here. And over there…" He pointed in a corner, but faded off, either unwilling to describe the horror he'd seen or too confused by the inconsistency.

Iris patted his arm. "We've all been under stress, love. If she still has some brands available to her, that sort of illusion would be simple. Especially since you had no way of sifting it for truth."

He frowned and pulled away, uncharacteristically rejecting his wife's comfort. "I know what I saw."

They spread out, examining the ground for any clues, nudging at the embers with their swords.

"It looks like whoever was here left a week or so ago," Kendalyhn said.

Aeliana glanced at Brogdon, whose grim face left her wishing they'd let him stay behind. Obviously, cutting out his brand had initiated Mayvus' departure.

"I thought maybe she'd escaped using the stone starbridge," her mother murmured, "but clearly she was here. And now she's strong enough to leave, but not strong enough for a confrontation. She expected we would come." Her mother almost sounded pleased, even though this meant there was another dead end. She kneeled down and placed her hands on the coals, then shook her head. "I wish I'd been strong enough to come right away. We can't learn anything from being here."

Still, the others continued searching while the winex dropped to all fours and sniffed their way through the cave.

"How can she even be alive after Durriken..." Lukai shuddered, not bothering to finish his question.

"I don't know how it works, but I think she used fluid from the winex eggs," Aeliana said.

A round of whimpers started from the winex, echoing through the chamber and making everyone wince.

"Maybe that helped her heal faster," Emeris said, "but it was the curse that kept her alive."

Sylmar grunted. "How exactly are the two of you cursed? I've only ever seen witches use their magic with that purpose. You keep saying you'd be dead if she were dead, but that's not how bonds and brands work. I don't even think there's blood magic that can connect people in that way."

Emeris hesitated. "It's possible the witches did something. But I also wonder about our parents. We were split up as children. Never told about the other. Not until our mother died and Mayvus came to live with our father and me. Then Mayvus had a lot of questions. Questions about magic and witches. Our father never answered them."

Hearing this family history left an uneasy feeling sliding through Aeliana's gut. Her family was even more broken than she'd realized. But was any of this even true? Or was it more of her mother's confusion?

"We were drawn to each other," Emeris continued. "I thought it was some sort of sister bond, whether manufactured by magic or forged by the Sun. We were two parts of a whole. There were times when I felt her pain. When I was slapped, her cheek turned red." She placed a hand over her cheek as if recalling the memory.

Aeliana expected Sylmar to scoff, but a strange look of understanding came over his face.

"The bond we felt as sisters faded quickly in favor of Mayvus' obsession with power. I wish I could go back to those years right after she came home. Perhaps I could have kept her from turning to such darkness."

"There was something strange between you," Sylmar admitted. "But nothing that could keep her from dying. At least not back then. Maybe she did something to enhance it with her blood magic. She's always been obsessed with immortality—was it possible, could she manufacture it—those were the kinds of questions that kept her up at night. She was never very concerned about growing followers. She just sort of assumed that would come with the territory once she found a way to give us the longevity of the Stars."

"Obtaining immortality and being under a curse aren't mutually exclusive," Orra murmured, but no one else seemed to hear her.

Aeliana leaned in. "What?"

Orra tugged on the braid at her wrist but didn't raise her voice. "One might argue they're one and the same."

"Either way," Sylmar said, "we know she's alive and growing stronger."

The air grew thick with the silence of fear until Velden awkwardly broke it.

"Well, the good news is that Durriken hasn't been here either."

"He's been down in Islara for the last few weeks," Aeliana said, "mourning over those he killed." She left off the friendship he'd been forming with the little boy, still not sure what to think of this new side of the dragon.

"Mourning?" Kendalyhn's voice held disbelief.

"He was branded just like me," Brogdon said. "If I can mourn the things I did under her control, why can't he?"

Aeliana's heart swelled with gratefulness that anyone would defend the dragon she was beginning to admire. Perhaps she could come to a point where she admired or at least understood Brogdon as well.

"So now what?" Lukai asked. "We finish fortifying and hunt for Mayvus instead of the stone starbridge?"

"No." Brogdon's disagreement was so abrupt that several turned their heads his way. "She's looking for the starbridge too. We need to find it first."

"Mayvus is looking for the stone? Why?" Aeliana asked.

Brogdon glanced at Sylmar as if seeking permission.

"This group is safe enough," Sylmar said. "Especially in this location away from prying ears. You might as well share everything you told me that first night." He sat on a rock near one of the piles of cold coal and laid his staff across his knees as though settling in for stories around a campfire.

It made Aeliana think of Jasperus and all the tales he would tell in the evenings. Except he was no longer here and the things they were about to share would probably not be as pleasant. Still, everyone found a spot, including the winex, who curled up by the cave entrance in a protective ring. Holm and Iris scrunched together on a rock while Orra and Emeris leaned back against the cave wall. Aeliana sat near Lukai, their arms brushing, and Kendalyhn and Brogdon sat across from them. The other woman stared moodily into the embers.

But Velden remained standing, practically hovering over Sylmar. "Who are you concerned about overhearing us in the fortress?"

"I'm not certain of it," Sylmar admitted, "but I suspect some could still be branded and planted among us. I wonder if some are even using illusions to mask their marks."

Cold washed over Aeliana, and she couldn't help the shiver that ran through her. Lukai placed an arm around her shoulder, drawing her close. But she stiffened, and he dropped his arm.

Everyone's eyes shifted to Brogdon, who kept his own closed, as if that posture gave him the courage to confess everything. "It's difficult to piece things together from the time I was branded. Mayvus had a way of feeding us information that we needed to know and removing our understanding of why."

Emeris hummed her agreement, giving credence to his words.

"Before you all came, I knew Mayvus was recruiting soldiers. That's all I could remember during the brief time she lost control of all her brands. But she wasn't as careful this time, and I remember more. She needs the stone because she's been using it to bring soldiers from Ahmranas."

Aeliana's chest constricted as the others' faces reflected her shock. She placed her hands on her temples as that strange detail they'd never grasped fit in the puzzle with perfect ease. Mayvus hadn't found supporters in Vendaras. She'd created them by bringing over Ahmranans.

Except Sylmar looked unsurprised, his frown bunching up his scars with renewed determination. Even Orra placed her hands over her face and bent forward with a whispered, "Not again."

"I should have known," Emeris murmured. "Several of the others would whisper about life near glacial lakes and mountains and family being beyond their reach. They sounded hopeful when they talked of the land Mayvus promised them that would be free of the ice caps."

Brogdon snorted. "She was referring to the desert that lies between Elanesse and Myndren. It's no more inhabitable than their mountains."

Emeris shook her head, clucking her tongue. "I'm not surprised, but I do find it interesting that they believed her."

"They believed her because it's happened before." Orra's quiet reply drew every eye. "In Pirate Redwood's day, pirates crossed the barrier and brought sailors over. They've probably been waiting for someone to cross the barrier with an offer just like Mayvus'. She would have been like a prophecy come true. A hero of old." She wrapped her fingers around the braid at her wrist. "I should have sensed her using it to build an army, but I didn't. I was either too far away or my power was too weak."

It made Aeliana sick to her stomach to think of these people being fooled by her aunt. "If she used it to bring over soldiers, how did she lose it?"

"Maybe it was in a pocket when she was carried off by Durriken?" Brogdon suggested. "All I know is that she's waiting to find it or waiting for us to find it so she can steal it."

"Where are the soldiers now?" Aeliana asked. "How have we not heard of this since we cut out everyone's brands?"

"With how she kept information compartmentalized, I would guess that only the Ahmranans themselves were aware of it. And they're likely among the soldiers who fled."

"Tychus and Piorre," Aeliana muttered.

Velden cleared his throat. "So we're looking for a black rock that transports people across the barrier, Mayvus, and the"—he stood on tiptoe and craned his neck over everyone's heads as if counting the various fire pits—"dozen or so Ahmranans who've been keeping her alive?"

"She could have double that or more," Orra pointed out. "And if she finds the onyx stone, she'll use it again. She'll be out of our reach— or worse, she'll bring back more Ahmranans."

"Even if we find the stone and keep it from her," Aeliana said, "we need to understand this curse."

Kendalyhn and Lukai exchanged skeptical glances.

"Or whatever it is that's binding their life force," Aeliana amended. "Whenever we face her again, we need to be sure she can't survive and that it won't affect my mother." It baffled her that they still doubted Emeris after everything that had happened in the last week, but at least they should be able to agree to this, curse or no curse.

Sylmar nodded. "I think there's merit to your efforts to go through Mayvus' research and destroy her blood stores. I'll make sure everyone takes shifts in aiding with that, but it will need to be kept quiet. We don't know who we can trust outside this group."

It was the closest thing she was going to get to an apology.

"And if any sort of"—Sylmar turned a thoughtful gaze on Emeris— "connection is found between the two sisters, we'll reevaluate our plans."

"Witches, blood magic, a bargain made with the sprites," Emeris mused. "Maybe it's a combination of them all."

"I hope the witches weren't involved." Iris shuddered, tightening her hold on Holm's arm.

"Are the sprites any better?" Aeliana asked.

Emeris shrugged. "Maybe it was none of those things. It could be some sort of prophecy, foretold by the Stars."

Orra hesitated, her eyes clouding over before she shook her head, as if she'd caught and stopped herself from sifting the future.

"The point is that nothing should be discounted, no matter how ridiculous it sounds." Emeris' chin rose a fraction.

Aeliana caught a glimpse of the high priestess and potential queen everyone had been bowing to, and she couldn't help grinning while checking Sylmar's reaction.

Except he was already studying Aeliana, his eyes troubled as he hesitated. Whatever he considered saying got tucked away as he turned back to her mother. "We'll all keep an open mind."

"So, again," Velden said, "we're looking for a black rock that transports people across the barrier and clues about a curse or experiment gone wrong." He linked his webbed fingers and stretched them out, letting his knuckles crack with a satisfying ripple. "All while keeping it under wraps so any secret brands back at the fortress remain unaware of our efforts. It's cake compared to what we've all been through."

Sylmar grimaced. "And we hope that the curse doesn't work the way Emeris thinks it does."

Aeliana tensed as everyone turned sad eyes on her mother.

In that moment, the reality of what a curse would mean hit Aeliana in the chest with such force that her starlock warmed in preparation for a defense. But there was no defense for this truth: if the curse was real and it worked the way her mother said, it didn't matter how much they all loved the priestess. Every single one of these people would be willing to sacrifice her in order to get rid of Mayvus.

Fear slithered through Aeliana's gut, bringing her back to the night on the balcony when her mother had asked to be killed. Was it so different from when Aeliana had asked Gaeren to kill her before she could be branded by Mayvus? But what if her mother's request came from a place of confusion rather than sacrifice?

Stems unfurled at Aeliana's feet with unnatural speed, the daisies already looking wilted and diseased as her fear tainted the magic growing them. She finally understood why Sylmar looked so haunted every time talk of a curse came up. It wasn't just because he thought

Emeris was losing her sanity; it was because he expected her to die if the curse truly existed.

They'd rescued their high priestess from the fortress not just because they cared for her, but because they thought she knew how to defeat Mayvus. Except her own sacrifice was the solution Emeris had been guarding all these years. It was the price she'd been willing to pay that night on the balcony, and it was a price she'd be willing to pay all over again.

Only Aeliana wasn't willing to pay it. She set her jaw and smashed the daisies down with her boot. She needed to be the one to uncover whatever curse or magic had kept Mayvus alive, because she also needed to find a way around it.

CHAPTER 16

EVEN THOUGH THE days grew shorter, the time spent combing the mountains for the stone starbridge grew longer. Aeliana tried to go out with the others as much as possible, but there were just as many hiding spots left to explore within the fortress along with all the research they'd found tucked away with Mayvus' blood stores. Now that Sylmar was on board, she found several more stockpiles, including one with some of Emeris' blood, giving them hope Mayvus wouldn't be able to brand Emeris again.

They even found a map marking out every brand Mayvus had had on the Wheel of Magic, including each point of the spokes she'd managed to control. The number was horrifying, but Sylmar was more distraught over the names on the list. He'd known almost all of them, and while they'd buried at least a dozen, there were still almost fifty more unaccounted for. Perhaps they were dead, perhaps they were with Mayvus, or perhaps Mayvus had already found the starbridge and they were with her on the other side of the barrier.

That was the option Aeliana feared the most—that they were searching for two things impossibly out of their reach—which was why she focused more of her energy on finding the source of the possible curse. But whenever it all seemed impossible, Sylmar insisted she head back out to hunt for the starbridge to at least burn off her nervous energy.

After two more weeks with no sign of Mayvus, the onyx stone, or a clue about the curse, he sent her out more often than he let her stay in. But today she sat in the chancery, poring over more of Mayvus' notes.

"Find anything new today?" Sylmar hobbled into the room and bent over her papers.

"Not really." Aeliana rubbed her palms over her eyes as all the words blended together. "Just more experiments. This time on someone named Anara."

"Can you show me?" He settled heavily into the chair next to her, laying his staff on the table.

His lips moved silently as he read through the papers she'd passed him, and his face grew pale.

"Did you know her?"

"I knew of her. She was young when I left. No results?" He flipped the papers around, frowning at their blank backs.

"No. I can't decide if that's a good or bad thing. Same for this man. Ermen?" She passed him another set of papers.

Sylmar clucked his tongue. "He was older than me. I can't imagine he survived the experiments."

"Both took tonics from the stores of winex fluid once a week for nearly a month, so they survived longer than any of the others she experimented on. Maybe they're both still alive?"

He hummed noncommittally and continued studying the papers, his brow furrowed.

"I don't suppose anyone's returned from the mountains yet for the day?" For a moment she let hope build within her. If Sylmar sought her out now, maybe someone had returned early because they'd found something.

"No sign of the stone." He set the papers down. "Or Mayvus. We did find another secret stash of blood near the eastern garden. We destroyed them and cross-checked them with her map of the Wheel of Magic. I'd like to add the names to your master list, too. It's time we made the list more public."

"Why?"

"If you were on that list, wouldn't you want to know?" Sylmar asked.

Aeliana winced. "Honestly, I'm not sure I would."

Sylmar shrugged. "At the very least, we should let the people decide if they want to know. They could come and ask if their name was on the list if they'd like. If she has their blood here, she probably has it somewhere else too."

Aeliana grimaced. "Hopefully not." She passed over the map of Mayvus' brands, but Sylmar hardly glanced at it.

"You can hope all you want, but Brogdon's blood was in this room, and it was also in one of the first stores you found. She's ruthless and bordering on insanity, but she's also cautious and calculating. The blood we've found is evidence of her meticulous preparation."

Aeliana frowned. She hadn't reached out to Durriken since she'd last seen him playing with the little boy. She hadn't felt right bothering him since he'd clearly disliked her meddling in the past. But maybe he would want this information.

Or…maybe he would return with vengeance and destroy the entire fortress to ensure no more of his blood was available, especially now that Mayvus was alive.

She supposed she should tell him that bit of news too. Her frown deepened as she ran her finger along the groove at the table's edge.

Sylmar held Aeliana's list up to Mayvus' diagram for comparison. "Have you found anything about a connection between her and your mother? Or maybe her research on immortality?"

Aeliana shook her head. "I shouldn't be surprised. I don't know why I thought we'd suddenly come across something. Why would she lay out her weaknesses for someone to find? Knowing she had some sort of secret she guarded doesn't make it magically appear."

Sylmar grunted, but he squinted at the two papers, leaving Aeliana unsure if he'd even heard her.

"Do you think she created some sort of connection after you left her? Could she have branded my mother twice? Or bonded her on top of branding her?"

Sylmar's eyes never left the lists. "I suppose anything is possible. She always wanted more magic. No matter the cost." Regret passed over his features before his face settled back into his customary grim scowl. "But that still doesn't explain the connection they had when they were younger." He set her papers on the desk before tucking his own back in his tunic pocket.

Aeliana's eyes narrowed. Had he just taken some of the papers detailing the experiments on Anara and Ermen? "I think you took the wrong—"

"I didn't just come here for an update," he interrupted. "A ship's been spotted."

Aeliana sat up straighter, her gaze flicking to the open window showing blue skies beyond. "Gaeren? Why didn't you lead with that?"

Sylmar studied her too closely. "We're not sure if it's him. None of us have seen his ship, but this one is black as night. It doesn't seem like something he would sail. And Gullet hasn't shown up."

His pessimism didn't deter her hope. "They planned to disguise his ship, so I don't think its color should indicate anything."

"Which is why I came to tell you. I figured you would want to go check for yourself." He scratched his beard, and the lines and scars on his face seemed less harsh as he angled his head toward the doorway. "Go on. I'll clean up this mess."

It was an uncharacteristic offer. Too often, he was her mentor, her teacher, her judge. He seemed determined to train her to be just like him one moment, then determined for her to rise above his failings the next. Sometimes she saw it as overbearing, but in moments like this, she suspected deep down he cared a little too much, except he didn't know how to show it.

"Thank you, Sylmar." She stood, then on a whim she bent and kissed the thinning hair on the crown of his head. She ignored his grumbling as she ran from the room.

The windows on this side of the fortress wouldn't give her a view of the water, so she didn't bother stopping to look for the ship. Instead, she ran for the east wing, calling out for Felk.

It was the last two days of his cycle, so he was slow to respond. "Mama?" The silver gleam of his hairless head poked out from the doorway of his quarters.

"Gaeren's back," she said breathlessly, tugging on his elbow as she ran past.

He let out a whoop that echoed through the hall and loped after her, not as quick to overtake her as he'd been in his younger days.

She laughed as he passed by, knowing he would bring back word if he saw any confirmation of the ship. Soldiers parted for her as she ran to the stables, and no one questioned when she saddled an extra horse. She would bring twenty if she could, knowing the sailors would be exhausted from their travels, but at least this way she could get Gaeren back quickly to give a report to Sylmar.

At least, that was the reason she gave herself for readying a second horse.

Felk ran beside her, still not interested in riding horses when he was so much faster on his own. With the Sun high in the sky, they would reach the beach and return long before the Sun's sleep. Hopefully Sylmar would think to tell Iris to prepare more food.

She rode her horse hard even though the wind chilled her to the bone. Summer this far north was short, and the leaves were already starting to change colors. She wrapped her cloak tighter around her, fastening it high at her neck. For a moment, she let herself hope that her father would be with Gaeren, that he would be the one needing the extra horse.

After so long without him—after Arvid and Vera had claimed they'd killed him—it was unlikely.

As they rounded a bend, the Sun glinted off the water, giving her an initial peek at the black ship anchored in the bay. Her heart soared at its polished beauty, the gleaming onyx more like obsidian glass. The sails had been lowered to keep it moored, and small figures could be seen milling at the base of the mast. She squinted, but it was impossible to make out any individuals.

"Come on, let's get closer," she said.

Felk didn't need to be told twice. He took off, eager to meet the man she'd told him about. They hadn't always been friends in Felk's past lives, but Gaeren was the only one who could restore Felk's past memories, and Aeliana wanted that for him. Selfishly, she wanted it for herself. She wanted Felk to remember the ways he'd protected her like she now protected him.

Still, as they reached the forest's edge, she called him back. "Not all of those men had good experiences with winex on Summer Solstice. Let me go out first and tell them you're with me."

His face fell. She hadn't told him the details of that night, the way he'd brought an army of winex to fight and how halfway through they'd gone rogue, attacking friend and foe alike. He wasn't responsible for choices made by the other winex, and he didn't need that guilt hanging over him.

"What if they aren't your friends?" His voice came out in a protective growl.

Aeliana smiled. "Then I'll scream, and you'll be welcome to come out and attack."

"I'm slow these days. It might take me too long," he grumbled as she dismounted, but he stayed with the horses anyway.

As she approached the beach, several men pulled a boat ashore, their chatter seeming friendly enough. It wasn't until she caught glimpse of a shaved head with an X on its forehead that she knew for certain she had the right group. She ran forward, her boots slipping in the sand and her skirt and hair getting tangled in the wind. A laugh bred from disbelief and relief bubbled to the surface.

The closer she got, the more she recognized the men—Thallahan with his new eye patch and Larkos with his pirate tattoos. She found their rough exteriors amusing after seeing their loyal hearts. At the head of a rowboat, a man remained bent at the waist, tying a rope around a rock, his Sun-streaked brown hair falling in his eyes.

Aeliana's chest constricted, making her aware of just how much she'd feared for their safety. When he stood, his gaze caught hers, and a smile split his face.

"Daisy!"

Something inside her warmed at the sound of the word on his lips. She'd once hated the nickname, finding it too familiar for a stranger, but now it was like a soft blanket enveloping her.

He closed the distance between them and wrapped her in a bear hug that was tight enough to be painful, but she squeezed him back. When he stepped away to study her, a strange look crossed his face. At first there was a sadness that made her think he had hard news to share, but then his lips tilted into his mischievous smile, and she knew.

"You found him," she breathed the words out and peered past Gaeren, unsure of what her father might look like but eager to recognize him among the crew.

"It's more like he found us," he said.

Three other boats still rode in from the larger ship, too far away for her to identify the men, though one held a man with long red hair tied back. Cyrus. He'd come back, too. She should be frustrated that he hadn't stayed where it was safe, but instead her heart leaped, and she raised an arm in greeting. She grinned as he stood to wave back, knocking the boat off-balance and getting yanked back down by the crew.

Several of the men came to greet her, quickly separating her from Gaeren and their brief reunion. Riveran gave her an equally exuberant hug, making Gullet squawk and take flight, but she was distracted by her single-minded purpose as she scanned the men disembarking each of the boats.

Which one was her father?

A hand gripped her arm, and suddenly Gaeren was back at her side. "Look who I found."

She looked past him but only saw Cyrus, who nearly tackled her now that he was free of his boat. "You'll never believe all the things we've seen." The intensity on his freckled face reminded her of how much she loved his zeal for life.

But then his face shifted as her vision swam. She reached to grip him back, to steady herself, but it was like everything around her disappeared, even the ground beneath her feet. Panic overtook her, as the sensation was reminiscent of traveling across the barrier. Had Cyrus or Gaeren been holding the golden arrow? Had they somehow activated it?

But when her feet found solid ground and her vision settled, there was still a lack of clarity. Was this one of Gaeren's memories? It was almost like the person controlling it was slowing it down and speeding it up without rhyme or reason. She watched as a stranger approached, introducing himself as Rildan. Then the memory flowed through different areas of Gahldric's Stargazer and through their travel across the barrier, where they'd met up with Larkos and the sailors. The memories were disjointed and uncomfortable, carrying a sense of frightening eternality. Like she might never escape.

She spent weeks sailing: working the rigging, searching for seashells, cooking down in the galley. She spoke and dined with men she knew by name when moments ago, on the beach, they had all been strangers.

Was that moments ago? Or weeks ago?

With a sharp tug that shifted to a slice through her entire body, Aeliana was pulled from the memories. Cyrus and Gaeren once again stood before her, questioning looks in their eyes.

"Are you all right?"

"I'm not—I don't know." Aeliana took a step back from them, pressing her hand against her temple. An ache spread behind her eyes and her starlock felt hot, as if it worked to bring her back from her state of confusion. How had she seen all that? It obviously couldn't have been Cyrus. But it had felt more controlled the last time Gaeren had given her memories of their past. And he'd asked permission then. Had he done it on accident this time in his eagerness to see her?

The others still milled around the beach, pulling supplies from the boats and securing them on the shore, as if she'd never left, but exhaustion swept through her as though she'd just finished the journey along with them. As if she'd just experienced the last eight weeks with Gaeren, Riveran, and Cyrus.

And her father.

"Aeliana?"

She turned to take in the older man standing quietly off to the side. He'd been there for a while, likely watching her. Grey hair peppered his black locks but extended past his shoulders, making it obvious he'd come from Lorvandas.

More than that, he was the man from the memories. The man they'd called Rildan. She knew him, and yet she shouldn't.

"Father?"

His face broke into a grin, all hesitation gone, and he rushed forward, crushing her in his arms. A laugh rumbled through his chest and enveloped her along with his hold, the sensation nearly bringing her to tears with her confusion.

"I can't believe they found you." She pulled back and soaked in his weathered skin and hunched form, a frailness masked by a tough outer shell formed by unwelcome life experiences.

He glanced at the forest behind her. "Did anyone else come?"

The hope in his eyes made her know what he was really asking.

"Mother is back at the fortress. She's doing better, but it's faster for you to go to her than it would have been for her to come with me. Besides, I wasn't sure you'd actually be here. I didn't want to get her hopes up."

His form hunched even more, but this time with relief. "Can you take me to her?"

"Of course." She stared at him a moment longer, unable to fully comprehend that he was there. After so many years of assuming her parents were dead, it felt too good to be true to have both of them alive and here with her.

She'd envisioned riding back to the fortress with Gaeren by her side, filling her in on news from Lorvandas, but now that her father was here, she couldn't leave him to walk. He'd waited long enough to see his wife.

Aeliana turned to Gaeren in apology. "I only have two horses in the woods."

Gaeren grinned. "We all need to get our land legs back anyway."

"I look forward to catching up later." Her words came out shy, her hands suddenly feeling awkward no matter where she placed them. She scanned the shore for Cyrus and Riveran and quickly added, "With all three of you."

"I don't mind if it's just us." He bent to pick the daisies growing at her feet, and his grin widened. "I've had enough of Cyrus and Riveran these last two moons."

He handed her the cluster of daisies, and her cheeks heated. Her bond mark twinged as his nearness left her flustered. Was he teasing her? Or reminding her they were childhood friends and nothing more?

"Felk is in the woods, too," she blurted out.

He raised his eyebrows. "Just Felk?"

"Lilik and the others are back at the fortress. I didn't want to overwhelm the sailors. I wanted to make sure they knew the only winex still in the area are friendly."

"Where did the others go?" Gaeren asked.

Aeliana shrugged. "I suppose there could still be some roaming free in the forest, but they've kept themselves hidden these last two cycles. Their numbers have likely dwindled now that Mayvus isn't breeding them." She pursed her lips at the memory.

"I'll warn the others to keep their weapons to themselves," he said.

"I was hoping you could share your memories with Felk." The words came out far less confident, her plan for restoring Felk's memories now tainted by her own strange experience.

"Of course. I'll be sure to highlight all the ways he owes me."

She smiled, but her heart wasn't quite in it. She'd finally come to terms with using magic because she'd learned to control it. Having something happen without her understanding, without her having control, put her right back in a state of distrust.

She shook the thought away. Gaeren's memories would help Felk.

But as she led her father to the horses and they made the trip back to the fortress, she couldn't shake the strange realization that most of the memories she'd seen had been from Cyrus' perspective.

CHAPTER 17

Gaeren watched Aeliana leave with a tightness in his chest. He'd spent the last eight weeks looking forward to returning, but the reunion had been so brief. It shouldn't matter; they were barely even friends. He remembered her as a child, but she had no memories of him. She'd even spent much of their time together unwilling to trust him because of his royal status. But when they'd finally set aside their differences and worked together against Mayvus, it had thrown them together in ways that felt far more intimate than any of his time with Lenda.

He frowned as he gathered supplies and joined the other men heading inland. He should have gone to see Lenda like Fernandus suggested, but he'd been too eager to get away from his family before they decided to imprison him for his treasonous words. He turned his palm over, examining the dark mark of raised skin. It seemed smaller, like Enla had said, less present. It hadn't itched or twinged as much either, not since he'd first left Elanesse.

But after his sister's painful experience with a broken bond, he couldn't bear to cut it out and put someone through the same, even if their bond wasn't taking. Not without asking. He'd rather Lenda made that choice for herself. Maybe it wouldn't even be considered treasonous since he'd abandoned his role as throne warden.

He wanted the freedom that would come from the release of his bond, but he didn't want the responsibility of taking it away from someone else. Did it make him a coward to hope Lenda might be willing to do that to him?

"I'm told you have memories to show me." Felk's voice rose above the murmurs of the men around them, his large blue eyes a welcome sight even if they were clouded with age. He had to be near his rebirth—was the new moon tonight or tomorrow?

Gaeren grinned and opened his arms to hug the creature, but Felk shrank away.

"I can only give you the memories if we touch." Gaeren held out his hand instead. "My spoke as a noetic progeny allows me to pull memories from people nearby, but we have to be touching for me to give them to you."

Felk stared at his hand. "Only because Mama said," he grumbled.

When Felk gripped Gaeren's hand, Gaeren sent a barrage of memories toward the winex, doing his best to keep them positive. In the past, he'd shown Felk ways that the winex had failed their party, ways he'd reverted to his more predatory instincts. But this time he saw no purpose in it. It was clear Felk and Lilik had made their home in the fortress, and there was no need to warn the creature about how tenuous his relationship with the people could be.

It didn't take long, but the energy that drained from Gaeren left him as exhausted as if he'd climbed to the northern keep of the fortress and back. The starlock around his neck burned with its effort to feed his blood's power, and he sagged under the weight of its use.

Felk's eyes filled with tears that he self-consciously batted away before dropping his hand.

"We've been through far more together than I realized." Felk frowned, staring out over the water.

"We are friends, though," Gaeren said. "That will never change."

Felk nodded. "I hope you're right."

The memories seemed to age Felk even faster than before, his shoulders hunching with the weight of all he'd seen. In some ways, Gaeren wished he'd been able to let the winex stay innocent and unaware of all their trials.

"Would you rather not know these things in your next life?" Gaeren asked.

Felk hesitated. "I'm not sure. I suspect I'll want more time to decide than I have in this cycle."

Gaeren nodded.

"It might not matter. Mama will want me to get them either way."

Gaeren's eyebrows rose. "They're your memories. It's your choice." He felt the weight of Felk's stare as if he was being judged for his words, but he wasn't sure if Felk was pleased or bothered by Gaeren's willingness to go against Aeliana.

Felk made his way through the crowd of sailors, greeting each of them and learning their names. He seemed determined to show his tame side before they all reached his clan. A wise move on his part. Erech greeted him the most exuberantly, then the two ran back and forth through the forest as they urged the other sailors to catch up.

By the time they reached the fortress, the sailors were beyond hungry. Iris welcomed them all to the kitchen and dining hall as if she'd been running it all her life. The meal was meager, making Gaeren wonder about their supplies. Mayvus had probably had stores of food for her soldiers, but they would need to bring in more from the cities further south if they all remained here for any length of time. Bartholem's offer to sell starlocks suddenly seemed slightly less blasphemous and a bit more practical.

Gaeren ate quickly, his gaze wandering the room for the faces of those he'd left behind eight weeks ago. Velden and Sylmar greeted him, but Lukai and Kendalyhn were nowhere to be found. When Iris and Holm joined him at his table, he learned that Aeliana was dining privately with her parents.

"Where's Orra?" Gaeren asked.

"She keeps to herself," Holm said, reaching over Iris for a second slice of bread.

"She hunts for the stone starbridge like the rest of us." Iris slapped Holm's hand away, then passed him the platter.

"Not just the stone," Holm muttered.

Iris shot him a look. "Not here."

Gaeren tensed. "What are you talking about?"

Iris' glare shifted to a sweet smile for Gaeren. "You'll have to ask Sylmar, dear."

"But he won't tell you until he's dragged you at least a mile from the fortress." Holm used his finger to clean out the last bits of squash from his bowl.

Iris pulled the bowl from his grasp, her lips curled in disgust. "He's being cautious."

Holm pulled the bowl back, and despite Iris' glare, he resumed scraping the bowl clean. "It's a compliment to your cooking."

Iris huffed and turned back to Gaeren. "If you're looking for Orra, she often ends her day on the balcony of the northern keep."

Gaeren shuddered. "That thing's still standing?"

"I wonder if she's strengthening it," Iris admitted. "It almost seems more stable than before."

"No," Holm said. "I don't think she's willing to use her magic on something so trivial."

"You're one to talk," Iris said, pulling the bowl away from him once more.

The two continued their banter, reminding Gaeren of Larkos and Calia in a way that made him homesick. Would he never be content where he was?

He excused himself, making his way through the maze of halls until he reached the battlements surrounding the northern keep. The sight brought back painful memories, vivid images playing through Gaeren's mind whether he wanted them to or not. Sometimes it was a gift to be a noetic progeny, to hold on to those memories so clearly, but other times it was a curse. His mentors had taught him to tamp down the memories he didn't want, but the stronger the emotions surrounding the memory, the harder it was to ignore.

He closed his eyes, remembering the sight of Aeliana, branded by Mayvus, walking toward the evil woman against her will. The need to save her, even if it required performing his own branding ceremony. He opened his eyes and ran his hand over the scar on his palm.

At one time he would have scorned someone's use of blood magic. He probably would have fought to have them detained. But now he understood that blood magic in and of itself wasn't wrong. It had far more to do with the intention behind it.

He would do it all over again if it meant he could save Aeliana.

"You've returned."

Gaeren swiveled at the sound of Orra's voice. Her skin seemed paler than he remembered, more cream than brown. The waning moon still managed to reveal her frailty, leaving him shocked, not because she looked worse than before, but because she didn't look much better. He'd thought she would have been back to her full strength, especially knowing what she was—who she was—but she seemed nearly as exhausted as when he'd last seen her.

"You look tired," he said. "You're using too much energy."

Her eyebrows rose. "Telling a woman she looks tired is the same as telling her she looks awful. It's never a wise move."

Gaeren barked out an awkward laugh. "I just mean you need to rest."

"I've spent far too long resting. There are things that need to be done, and now is the time to do them. I'll have time to rest later."

He shook his head, irritated that he'd already forgotten how cryptic her words could be. Then he reached in his pocket and pulled out the golden arrow.

She shivered as he held it out, then reached out to take it, her fingers trembling as they hovered over the starbridge. Her gaze traveled to the dancing Stars.

"Maybe I should let you keep it for me," she whispered.

"Why?"

"It seems that every time I find one of these, a different one slips through my fingers."

Gaeren considered her words, the way they'd come full circle in their hunt. At one time he'd wanted the starbridges for himself, first to find Aeliana, then as a means of leverage—whether to protect Enla or Aeliana. But Orra's need for them seemed far greater, her purpose far more important. But as always, she held her reasons close, closer than he'd been allowed.

"What exactly do you hope to gain from gathering them?"

Her eyes closed, her hand still a finger's breadth away from the arrow. "Everything. And nothing."

He sighed, tucking the arrow back into his pocket. "I think I've figured out who you are." He'd come to terms with her being a Star, with her being Sheen even, but now that he stood before her, he felt ridiculous suggesting it. "Is that why my magic doesn't work on you? Because you're a Star?"

She somehow managed to look even more tired than before. Her hands dropped to her side and balled up the fabric of her skirt. "Stars are already infused with the light of the Sun. Anything they need can be granted by taking to the skies and being enveloped in the Sun's presence. A half-light's magic is too weak to work on a Star, even one who's been grounded."

"So you're not just any Star. You're Sheen."

Orra raised her chin. "I might not announce it, but I won't deny it. Aeliana's already figured out almost as much as you."

Gaeren grinned at her regal way of refusing to admit she'd lied. It reminded him of Enla. "I might have trusted you sooner if you'd given me that name."

A shudder passed through her at the use of the name. "You shouldn't trust me. Not if you read my role in *The Sins of the Stars*."

"I read about a Star who wanted to save the people from themselves," he said softly. "I'm not sure what you read."

"I read between the lines because I lived it. I wrote that book as a warning, but even then, I left out the worst of it." She clamped her jaw down and looked away.

All this time, he'd thought she'd just been responsible for the handwritten notes in it. He wanted to laugh at the ridiculous revelation that she'd written the entire thing, but her eyes still crinkled with pain, and her shoulders were still weighed down by her shame.

"Father Fernandus told me it's best to confess our sins. Bearing that burden alone is too much for anyone."

"It's true. I can't keep the worst of my sins a secret forever." Still, she didn't offer him anything more, and when her shoulders relaxed a fraction, he decided to let it lie.

"Iris mentioned you're all still looking for the stone. I'm sorry you haven't found it yet."

Instead of responding, she took a few steps closer to the edge of the battlement so she could lean out and look at the grounds below.

Gaeren followed, taking in the sight of dozens of fire pits and tents, camps formed by the men and women who couldn't fit in the fortress. "She also mentioned you're looking for something else. Did you catch wind of another starbridge?"

Orra shook her head. "You'll have to ask Sylmar about that. His goals might align with mine, but they're not the same. Not really. All of us have our own goals. Even you." She gave him a pointed look, then let her gaze trail down to where his starlock rested under his shirt.

After years of keeping it hidden, he automatically placed a protective hand over it, but she probably already knew what it was. She probably even knew what it represented.

On a whim, he pulled it out, frowning at its teardrop shape. When he'd first begun training, he'd hoped it was a sign that he'd receive water for his rim magic, but now that his magic traveled down the destructive noetic spoke, fire was the only possible element in his future. If anything, it could represent the way water magic would someday overpower him. And that was best-case scenario. Worst case was that it represented a tear and his future held deep sorrow. Sometimes it was what fueled him to celebrate each day for what it was and to not take life too seriously.

"You still haven't figured it out?" Orra murmured.

"I have theories." His words came out defensive.

She closed her eyes, tilting her face toward the setting Sun. "Sometimes the most obvious answers elude us because we try to overcomplicate the solution."

He scowled at her evasive answer. "It's water or tears. I assume it's because I spend time at sea. Perhaps that's how I'll die. Or maybe it represents all the sorrows I'll have in life. It can't get more obvious or simple than that."

"You're still thinking of it in symbolic terms. Where else have you seen that exact mark every day of your life? Or at least that you can remember?"

He let the starlock fall against his chest, then held up his hand, lining the starlock up with his bond mark. "I considered it early on, but Lenda and I were never close. And after Enla... well, I think I sort of hated the idea of my bond being that important."

"Maybe it doesn't represent the importance of the bond so much as what you decide to do with it," Orra mused.

He blinked in surprise, then held up his starlock once more. The tear shape of his bond mark took on a whole new meaning as he held them together. Now the starlock mocked his bond, as if telling him it would define who he was whether he wanted it to or not. Did it imply he should be a man of honor and hold to his bond and role as throne warden? Could he even after the things he'd said and done? Or did it suggest his need to sever this last thing tying him to his family's throne?

His starlock could represent the defining decision either way he went.

"What am I supposed to do?" he whispered.

"Sometimes the hardest questions are when both answers are right for different reasons."

Gaeren tried to tamp down his frustration. He'd seen Orra sift the future of souls just like Enla, except she hadn't even needed to hold anything that belonged to them. Sometimes Orra's power seemed limitless, greater than anything Gaeren had seen before, and sometimes it felt like she couldn't access it at all. If she wanted to, she could sift his future and tell him which answer was more right. It felt selfish when she held back, but as he took in the dark circles under her eyes and the way she leaned against the wall, he knew she wasn't holding back. She was fading.

"Or it could just be that you're a sailor." Orra shrugged. "Maybe I'm trying to make it out to be something it's not."

Gaeren snorted and tucked the starlock back under his tunic. It had been a mystery ever since he'd received it. He couldn't expect to solve it right at this moment. "I guess I'd better find Sylmar since no one else wants to tell me what I've missed. Even though I risked my life to bring back Rildan and the arrow."

A faint smile crossed Orra's face as she pushed off the battlement's edge. "You're the arrow's protector now. Hold it close until we have the others." Her unhurried gait as she turned to the northern keep's door was almost painfully slow.

He was tempted to escort her up the stairs but felt certain her pride wouldn't appreciate it. Instead, he turned back and headed for the main hall. Sylmar had some explaining to do.

CHAPTER 18

ORRA CLIMBED THE STEPS, letting her hands run over the vines that still grew from the night she'd used her power to kill so many and save so few. She'd felt peace in that moment that she was doing what the Sun wanted, but now she let the events replay through her mind, second-guessing all she'd done. Helping Aeliana and these people had been the right thing to do, and yet she'd interfered. It went against all she knew, and it delayed all her goals. And yet it had been the Sun's will. Hadn't it?

She might have been able to get the stone's location from Mayvus, but now that Mayvus was gone, Orra had no more leads to follow. She made her way through Mayvus' rooms, ignoring the mess left behind from battle and the care for the wounded. No one else dared spend time in the northern keep because of its instability, but Orra longed for its precarious balcony. Not only could she guarantee solitude under the Stars and Sun, but she almost welcomed the keep's demise. After a thousand years of being grounded on the earth, she was ready to return to the Sun, if it would even welcome her.

She stepped out on the balcony, tracing the faint lines of ash left from the Stars who had retrieved starlocks the night of the battle. Eventually, she settled in the dark outline of where Jasperus' body had been burned up. Where Reyna had rejected her as a peer once more. She could still smell the heat and smoke coming from her former friend, could still sense her ethereal presence as if her stardust lingered.

But Reyna and the others had abandoned her. They had given up on her ability to redeem herself, and they wanted nothing to do with her.

She lay there, studying the static stars and their constellations, waiting for her old friends to begin their dance. Andreas made his entrance, a slow buzzing loop, like a bee circling a flower for its honey. Lumina had a more abrupt approach, jolting through the sky in sporadic patterns. Reyna was as graceful as always, the smooth lines of her dance a pure form of art.

Several others joined in, making Orra feel the loss of companionship with a heaviness that only highlighted how much she was bound by gravity in this form. She had once treasured the ability to take on this body and fellowship with the people, but she'd never thought she would have to give up her space in the sky. She'd never thought she would lose her relationship with the Sun.

A tightness squeezed in her gut, then spread out to her limbs until her entire body grew tense. She sat up, evaluating the way the tension felt like a string wound in an instrument, taut and plucked. Humming with its vibration.

This was far more than grief.

She placed a hand over the braid tied around her wrist like a bracelet, letting its hum reverberate through her fingers.

Someone was touching the stone.

CHAPTER 19

Watching her parents' reunion should have been inspiring, but it tickled at a sense of loss in the depths of Aeliana's heart. She tried to be grateful that they were all back together instead of counting all the years that had been stolen by Mayvus.

They sat at the table in her mother's room, her parents hardly noticing the food they ate as they stared into each other's eyes and talked over each other with all their questions. As much as Aeliana wanted the reunion to include her, she sensed they needed some time alone after so many years apart.

"I'm going to check in with Sylmar." She stood from her place at the table, setting down her napkin. She dreaded giving him an update, but the memories she'd received still ran through her mind, unwilling to be ignored. Was it possible for Cyrus to have magic? Or had Gaeren's noetic skills somehow traveled through Cyrus? Or was this just further evidence that she didn't understand her own magic?

It was the last thought that brought her right back to feeling uneasy with the power flowing through her blood. It left her wondering if she could ever feel at home with the Vendarans and their magic—if she could ever feel at peace in her own body.

Her father stood as well and wrapped his arms around her, the sensation welcome but odd enough that Aeliana didn't quite squeeze him back. There was a frailness to him that didn't match the strength in the memories both Gaeren and her mother had given her from when she was a toddler.

"In many ways you feel like a stranger, but I aim to change that." He pulled back and lowered himself to look her in the eyes. "I know you're beyond the age of needing a father, but I still want to be that for you."

Aeliana smiled tentatively. "I don't think the title goes away when a child becomes an adult. And I've had no father figure in my life. I still need one."

He hugged her again, and this time Aeliana returned his tight grip, squashing down the confusion festering within her. Everything should feel right, but nothing did. Mayvus was still alive, they hadn't found the stone starbridge, and the magic she thought she'd learned to control was changing on her.

"Maybe tomorrow the three of us can spend the day together, catching up on all we've missed." Her mother's words were met with agreement from her father, so Aeliana nodded as well.

She made her way down the hall until she came to Sylmar's quarters. He tended to turn in after the evening meal, rarely interested in socializing and often needing to soak his aching leg. Aeliana couldn't help wondering if their travels and battles were finally catching up to him and his body was resisting all he'd been put through.

She knew his scars came from the brands Mayvus had given him over the years, the brands he'd cut out when he'd left her side. But his limp remained unexplained. He was close in age to her parents, but his experience and injuries made him seem far older.

A rap on his door revealed stirrings from within, confirmation that he'd turned in for the night. When the door opened, he squinted into the torchlight of the hall, only giving a grunt of acknowledgment.

"Something happened today." Aeliana didn't bother with pleasantries. Sylmar never did. "Something I thought you should know."

His eyes opened wider, as if he was coming fully awake. He scanned her from head to toe. "You found something in Mayvus' notes?"

Aeliana shook her head. "It has to do with my magic. Or maybe just Gaeren's. But if it's not his, then I don't think I'm fully weaned."

Sylmar opened the door wide. Even right out of bed, he was fully dressed, just like he'd been during their days traveling. He always expected to leave at any moment. "Let me grab my staff, and we'll meet in the training room."

As Aeliana stepped back to wait, a shadow flickered at the end of the hall, then Orra glided toward her. The older woman's steps were far more hurried than Aeliana had seen from her since they'd come to the fortress.

"Did you sense it too?" Orra asked, breathless.

"Sense what?"

Orra placed her hands to her temples with a wince. "No, of course not."

Sylmar backed out from the room and shut the door, then hesitated when he turned and saw Orra. "You invited her?"

"No," Aeliana said. "I don't know why she's here."

"I'm here because the stone has been used." Her face pinched with worry. "It's possible Mayvus crossed the barrier."

Aeliana bunched her skirt in her fists, her mind racing. "Did you cross it to confirm? Like you did with me when you sensed I used the golden arrow?"

Orra shook her head. "My strength hasn't returned. I don't think I could do that again." The vulnerability on her face made Aeliana wish she hadn't asked.

"What do you know for certain?" Sylmar asked.

"The stone was held by a half-light, one with great power. Similar to the power that runs in her blood." She nodded at Aeliana as if she were somehow to blame. "The hum was strong, close. But then it abruptly faded, like its source was suddenly hundreds of miles away." She turned toward the window even though it was too dark to see out into the night. But beyond their view lay the northern cliffs, the Northern Sea, and Ahmranas, the icy land of the half-lights who had been on the other side of the Myndren Mountains when the land was split and the barriers put in place by the Stars. Or the Sun, if the Vendarans were right.

If Mayvus had traveled across the barrier with the stone starbridge, she was as far out of their reach as possible.

Sylmar pursed his lips. "Seems we should call a meeting, then."

It was late in the evening by the time they gathered everyone in the training room, only allowing a few generals beyond Sylmar's original group of loyal Recreants. They were carefully searched for brand marks, but Aeliana still felt wary after talk of illusions masking the marks. Gaeren, Riveran, Cyrus, and Aeliana's parents had joined them as well, their presence bringing new energy and hope. The others likely thought they were going to hear an update about the men's journey from Lorvandas, but Sylmar quickly snuffed out that expectation as he stood at the front of the room.

"Orra believes that Mayvus has crossed the barrier using the stone starbridge."

Gasps and whispers spread through the few occupied tables, and Orra shot Sylmar an irritated glance as she made her way to his side.

"I sensed that someone used the stone," she clarified. "I suspect it could have been Mayvus, but there is no way for me to know."

Holm and Iris held hands where they sat on a bench, leaning in to each other for support. Lukai sat within arm's reach of Aeliana, but the distance between them made her more aware of the closeness they lacked.

"Now what do we do?" Kendalyhn asked.

The others hushed, waiting to hear Sylmar's response.

"We can't go after her or the stone. Until she chooses to return, she's out of our reach."

"Can't we find another starbridge?" Holm asked.

Orra shook her head. "Each starbridge is designed to travel to a single land. The golden arrow takes people to Lorvandas and returns them here. The onyx stone takes people to Ahmranas and returns them here. There's no other way."

"Maybe this is a good thing," General Nels said from where he sat off to the side with the other generals. They all studied the room with their stiff postures and scowls, but their vigilance was probably what had kept them alive during the fight against Mayvus. "If we stop wasting our time hunting for one woman and her rock, we can work harder to rebuild. If she's not here, she's not a threat, for now."

Velden let out a short laugh. "Assuming that Mayvus isn't a threat would make fools of us all."

The general shifted in his chair, his face turning red. "I just meant that fortifying the grounds and rebuilding the community following the Wyndren family is the best way to prepare for her inevitable return."

Aeliana winced. It was one thing for them to respect her mother, but the Wyndren family was a mess. "What if we send dignitaries to Elanesse and request aid?" she asked. "Shouldn't part of the rebuilding process include making amends with the legitimate royal family? I thought we received some sort of invitation or apology from them."

At the other table, Gaeren sat up a little straighter. Perhaps he hadn't heard about his parents' change of heart.

"That was just an attempt to save face after their initial alliance didn't work out." Brogdon stood, his booming voice so reminiscent of Jasperus' that Aeliana felt tears tickle the back of her throat. "I'm not sure we should even acknowledge them as royals."

"Sitting right here." Gaeren lifted his hand in an awkward wave. "But I understand your hesitation."

Aeliana squirmed. All Recreants agreed that they didn't want the Elanesses on the throne, but half of them wanted the Wyndrens to replace the Elanesses while the other half wanted democracy, relegating the Wyndren authority to priesthood in the Sungazers. She couldn't help liking the idea of a democracy, and not just because she was terrified of being expected to lead. Even if the throne should have gone to the Wyndren family a thousand years ago, what did it matter now? They were generations away from that feud, and dividing the kingdom would only make things worse. If they couldn't figure out how to work together, they'd end up cannibalizing themselves before Mayvus even returned.

"We're cleaning up Mayvus' mess," Sylmar said. "And now we're weeding through her soldiers for Zealots masquerading as Recreants. We don't need to add Loyalists in the mix."

"One kingdom's loyalist is another kingdom's recreant," Gaeren muttered.

Aeliana couldn't help humming her agreement. Gaeren had been taught that Loyalists were loyal to his family's crown and Recreants were opposed to all monarchies. She'd been taught that Recreants supported her mother while Zealots supported Mayvus. Except the Zealots had also called themselves Loyalists to keep Gaeren's family from becoming suspicious of Mayvus' growing power. The range of definitions started making the terms meaningless.

"We can't just sit around," Emeris said. "If we wait for her to return, she'll win. She's too cunning to return before she has the upper hand."

Sylmar grunted. "I agree. We can build up our armies, and yes, we can play nice with the Elanesse family." He glanced at Gaeren, who gave a mock bow in Sylmar's direction. "But we need to have a weapon to defeat her." His gaze flicked over to Emeris.

Aeliana's chest grew cold. "If you're suggesting my mother sacrifices herself to test a theory that her life is connected to Mayvus', that's not a weapon—that's murder."

The room went silent as everyone avoided her gaze, even her mother.

Rildan wrapped his arms around Emeris. "I could understand her willingness to test it in the heat of a battle. She was desperate." His gaze softened as he studied her. "But now we have time to find a different solution."

"How do we find a solution if we don't even know what she's really after?" Iris asked. "Clearly she wanted the throne, but to what end?"

"Power," Brogdon muttered. "She's always looking for more power."

Sylmar shook his head. "Mayvus' goals went beyond power. What was the use in having ultimate power if that power could come to an end? Aeliana's on the right track with the winex research. Mayvus is after something much bigger. Maybe immortality, or invincibility, or maybe ascension as a Star."

"That's blasphemous," Cyrus interjected.

Gaeren leaned around the others to grin at Cyrus, remembering their religious debates, but then his smile shifted to a jaw drop and his eyes grew wide. "The starbridges." His gaze swiveled back to Orra. "What did it say about them in *The Sins of the Stars?*"

Orra fiddled with the braid at her wrist and closed her eyes.

"It said something about the starbridges having the power of a Star. I don't"—he patted his pockets in frustration—"I wish I had it on me."

"'The starbridges hum with unbridled power,'" Cyrus quoted, his gaze focused on the stone ceiling. "'Power that's both given and taken by the Sun. Some say that when combined, their power will bring down the barriers. Some say it will give that power to the one who wields them. But the truth is…'" He hesitated, either forgetting the last line or unwilling to voice it.

"The truth is," Orra said softly, "no one knows." She held the braid to her lips. "Not even the broken Star who documented their creation. But I suspect combining them will reverse all those wrongs."

"What do the starbridges have to do with my mother being cursed?" Aeliana asked. "I feel like we're losing focus. Even if Mayvus was going after the starbridges in her pursuit of immortality, which we have no evidence of, we need to find out the source of this curse and how to break it."

"Wouldn't Mayvus be wanting to break it too?" Gaeren asked. "Seems she'd be just as eager to be done with it. She's more vulnerable if killing Emeris kills Mayvus too."

"Unless…" Sylmar said softly. "Unless Mayvus thinks keeping Emeris alive keeps *her* alive too."

It was a subtle twist on Gaeren's words, but it gave a new ugly meaning to them.

"My mother can die just like anyone else," Aeliana said. Why did something she'd been so certain of moments ago sound so uncertain coming from her lips?

Sylmar's gaze drifted to Rildan. "Do you remember that winter before Mayvus came for Emeris?"

Rildan frowned. "Emeris had been sick. She was able to hide it well since Iris and Hen—I mean, Gaeren—spent so much time caring for Aeliana. Was Mayvus sick with something too?"

Sylmar nodded, his eyes focused far beyond them. "She grew deathly ill. She'd been experimenting with potions and blood, spells she'd learned from the witches that she wouldn't even share with me. It's why I first considered leaving her. The secrecy made it impossible to trust her. There was a night that she nearly died. I swear her heart stopped. But then she gasped and said Emeris' name."

Everyone turned to Rildan, his face now a stony mask.

"I can guess which night it was." He shook his head, as if unwilling to bring up the memory. "Emeris grew so cold in her sleep, muttering Mayvus' name over and over. Are you suggesting that their connection kept Mayvus alive?"

Sylmar's head cocked in thought. "I'm suggesting that the experience made Mayvus believe it would. It explains why she was determined to go after Emeris as soon as she recovered. She believes that their injuries can be shared, but so can their health."

Aeliana's stomach turned. "So she kept my mother imprisoned like some sort of emergency boost to her health?"

"Exactly," Sylmar said.

"And depending on what she discovered with the winex," Velden added, "her plan might not be as far-fetched as it sounds."

Lukai turned Aeliana's way. "The regenerative properties in their eggs. They brought people back from the brink of death."

Aeliana closed her eyes, terrified by the conclusion she knew was coming.

"If their health is connected," Lukai said, "if they can keep each other alive even moments longer, it could be enough for her to regenerate herself and avoid death every single time."

CHAPTER 20

GAEREN WATCHED Aeliana's face pale. He wanted to kick Lukai and remind the fool that his role was to comfort his bondmate. Instead, he laughed nervously and tried to minimize it all.

"I think we're all jumping to conclusions here. Even if you're right —and that's a big if—we're not powerless. We start by keeping Mayvus from the winex. I doubt there are any in the cold Ahmranan climate, so she already helped us out there." Gaeren ticked the solutions off on his fingers. "Then we figure out if there really is a curse or spell or whatever. And then we break it." He wiggled the three fingers as if a child should be able to follow the plan.

The others stared at him incredulously, making him aware of how impossible that all sounded. But that wasn't something that had ever stopped him in the past.

"How are we supposed to find answers about a curse we're not sure exists?" Kendalyhn asked.

"Maybe we can attack two problems with one solution," Velden said slowly. "If Mayvus is hunting down the starbridges in order to unite them for power, there's value in finding them before her. We have the golden arrow, and Mayvus has the onyx stone. There are only two left: an iron cutlass and a silver fish."

Gaeren tucked his hand in his pocket, letting his fingers wrap around the arrow's shaft. Orra's gaze shot to his, her brows pinching in pain. He quickly let it go. Perhaps he should wrap it with something in the future.

"But the starbridges aren't our primary problem," Aeliana said. "As long as we keep the arrow from her, she can't gain power from them."

"There's power to be had from each one," Orra pointed out. "Maybe not the ultimate power she's looking for, but think about how she's using the stone to win Ahmranans over to her side. Could she do the same with the cutlass with the Dehvlonians or the silver fish with the Sayhleens?"

The silence in the room grew thick with fear.

"That's why I suggested we attack two problems with one solution." Velden let water burble between his hands, then tossed it from palm to palm like a ball. "If we go after the silver fish that would take us to Sayhla Island, we could visit Lady Merinnia and ask about the curse."

"Lady Merinnia?" Aeliana asked. "The Seer from your story?"

"I don't remember that one," Gaeren admitted.

Aeliana turned to Gaeren. "You were back at the palace when he told it. The Sayhleens have a pneumatic progeny who's so powerful she can see just one or two paths in the future. Velden's mother went to her to ask about whether or not she should use the silver fish to cross the barrier. Whatever she saw convinced her to come even though she probably also saw her death."

Velden nodded, his shoulders tighter than normal.

"That was years ago," Holm said. "For all we know, she's no longer alive."

"Then they would have appointed a new Seer," Velden said. "Maybe not as powerful as Lady Merinnia, but they train them for that purpose."

"They've been doing it since their existence," Orra added. "The first Seer was also the first Sayhleen—the man who sought out the sprites asking to take refuge in the water. The sprites thought they were tricking him, but he saw the way their people would thrive. He chose that path."

"But if a curse exists, it's already happened," Sylmar said. "She sees paths in the future, not the past. I propose we visit Pacran's library. If anyone has information about a curse that could connect people's life sources, it would be him."

"The collector?" Kendalyhn asked. "Technically he would also be our best option for finding the starbridges."

Gaeren suspected Kendalyhn was right. In fact, Gaeren had gone looking for Pacran when he hunted down the starbridges on his own, but the swindler had been tight-lipped. Probably because of Gaeren's status as a prince. Would they have more luck with someone like Sylmar or Velden asking instead?

"What about the witches?" Holm asked. "Didn't Emeris say Mayvus often asked her about a connection between them? Maybe she was in league with the witches."

"We already have someone looking into the connection with the witches." Emeris' cheeks turned pink as the room went quiet.

"Who?" Sylmar asked.

"You call him Marnok." Emeris glanced at Rildan, and a look passed between them that made Gaeren certain Rildan knew just as much about Marnok's identity as Emeris.

"I thought he went in search of his past," Aeliana said slowly. "Because of things you showed him in your memories."

"It's complicated," Emeris said, "but his past isn't mine to share. He's looking into elements of his past, but he's also attempting to learn if the witches know anything of a curse."

Sylmar's eyes narrowed, and Gaeren sensed the old man was about to wrestle a truth from Emeris that he had no right to hear, let alone the rest of the people in the room.

"Actually," Gaeren blurted out, "I might have a lead for the silver fish." The words came out with a wince.

Riveran glanced his way, eyes wide. He was the only one who'd been there when Gaeren had made a deal with the sprite.

"I agree that Pacran might have the iron cutlass." He glanced at Orra, remembering her story of Pirate Redwood handing it over to her husband and letting it pass down the generations. It was just the type of thing a collector would hold on to. "But I also heard rumors of the silver fish being down in Andel. Supposedly it's aboard some fisherman's boat, mounted on the wall of his cabin."

Velden raised his eyebrows. "I was raised near Andel and spent my naval days there. There are hundreds, if not thousands, of fishermen's boats. That's not exactly a prime lead."

Orra's hands went to her cheeks, her voice breathy. "Maybe not, but it's the first clue I've had for the silver fish since my search began."

Gaeren couldn't help wondering when that search had begun. Was it a thousand years ago when she'd first been grounded?

"You never considered this a clue?" Velden held up his webbed fingers, wiggling them for all to see.

Orra's eyes grew troubled. "I recognized your heritage from the first time I met you, but your mother forbade you from seeking out Sayhla Island. Any hint at where the silver fish ended up died with her."

Velden's face paled. "I've never told that to anyone," he murmured. "I wasn't sure I wanted to find Sayhla Island after she died, but I did search her cove. The starbridge never turned up. I assumed it was lost in the water with her."

"Then how does Gaeren know where it is?" Cyrus asked.

Gaeren's face heated as one by one everyone's gazes rested on him. He opened his mouth, then closed it.

"If he can't even say where the information came from, I don't trust it," Holm said.

Iris smacked his shoulder. "You've been speaking your thoughts far more than usual these days."

"Still, Holm has a fair point," Sylmar said. "Is it a reliable resource?"

Gaeren's mouth went dry. Could he honestly answer that? Who trusted the sprites? They were slippery creatures, bent on tricking everyone who sought them out, but they weren't known for lying. Their deals had a prophetic nature to them, and he'd never heard of anyone avoiding the fate presented by the sprites. Which was what terrified him.

He forced a smile. "Even though I got the information when hunting down the starbridges to find Aeliana, it wasn't a typical treasure-hunting source. The instructions given to me were as trustworthy as my sister's visions." Several people's eyebrows rose since Enla's skills as a pneumatic progeny were widely known. Good thing they didn't know about her recent decline in being able to control those skills. "But my source also said I'd be better off finding the fish before the cutlass."

Sylmar let out a huff. "And you just… believe everything someone tells you when you're hunting for treasure?"

Gaeren and Riveran exchanged a glance. "Not always," Gaeren conceded. "But this time I did."

"As much as I like the idea of helping Orra find the starbridges and keeping them from Mayvus"—Aeliana shot an apologetic look toward the other woman—"I think we're getting distracted. We need to find out what connects my mother and Mayvus so we can get rid of it. We can watch for starbridges along the way, but we need to choose what's best for the danger at hand."

"Which is why Pacran and the cutlass are the better bet," Sylmar said, his tone turning dry, "despite Gaeren's mysterious insistence that it would be better to find the fish first."

"The Seer's connection with a soul's destiny is far more valuable than a collector's horde," Velden argued. "She can show us where and when we'll discover the strange connection between Emeris and Mayvus. She can show us where the iron cutlass is. She can show us how to defeat Mayvus."

"And we can also come away completely destroyed by what she tells us." Aeliana had grown quiet, her face almost green with trepidation, but now a tinge of pink came into her cheeks. "Don't leave that part out of the story. You said some people come away unhinged because of what she shows them. You said people had to be desperate to go to her."

Velden shrugged. "What do you call our circumstances if not desperate?"

Normally Gaeren would agree with anything Aeliana said. They shouldn't go to a woman whose magic seemed to spread her madness. That was reasonable. And yet the sprite had said he'd have better luck seeking the fish first, which meant he'd have more of a chance at crossing the barriers and protecting Aeliana.

He tried to push the thought away. She didn't need his protection anymore. But did that mean he couldn't even offer it? And did he even want to? The sprite had also said if he took the deal and got Aeliana across a barrier to protect her, Enla would pay the price. For all he knew, if he made an effort to cross the barriers with Aeliana, he could be sealing whatever fate the sprites had in store for Enla. Maybe he should be thinking about how to protect Enla, especially after he'd left under less than ideal circumstances.

"That seems far riskier than any of the other plans we have," Holm said.

"High risk, but high payoff," Velden mused.

"Pacran seems like the safer bet." Holm's quiet voice rang through the room more than usual. "What would a Seer across the barrier know of a curse between two sisters on this side? We can still look for the starbridges, but it doesn't seem wise to use them."

Aeliana bit her lip with an intensity that made Gaeren flinch.

"Lady Merinnia could answer questions about the curse with far more accuracy than a dusty library," Velden said. "Her magic is living and active."

"We could split up," Brogdon said, his stony gaze fixed on the table.

Gaeren hadn't even been sure the man had been listening since his last outburst negating the royal family.

"Send a team after Pacran and send another after the silver fish," Brogdon continued.

"Splitting up seems dangerous," Holm said.

"More dangerous than having Mayvus return before we're ready?" Brogdon spit the words out, startling others at his table. He crossed his arms over his chest, his jaw clenched.

Gaeren couldn't blame the other man's slip in control. He blinked away the memory of Jasperus dying in his arms, his final words of forgiveness for his son. Those were the kind of memories he wished his noetic skills could repress. It was far harder to move on from the painful things he'd experienced when they came back with the same clarity and emotional upheaval as the first time he'd gone through them.

"It just seems like we're setting ourselves up for failure if we try to do too many things at once," Holm said.

"Splitting up might slow both parties down," Aeliana added. "If Andel is as large as you say, we need everyone's help searching the harbor. And who knows what we could run into across the barrier looking for Lady Merinnia? It could take just as long hunting through Pacran's library, assuming he lets us, which means that option would also be faster with everyone present. What if Mayvus returns before we do? My mother isn't ready to travel. She'd be vulnerable here."

"The entire army will be here to defend the fortress," Sylmar said. "Including the generals."

General Nels and his three friends all nodded.

"And I'll stay with Emeris," Rildan added. "We can continue going through Mayvus' work in case we find something helpful."

"As will I." Orra's quiet offer surprised Gaeren. She was the one who wanted the starbridges. "My power will return faster if I don't push myself. Whenever Mayvus comes back, I'll be getting the stone back from her." The last bit came out with a cold ferocity he hadn't heard from her before.

"So we head for Andel or Pacran or both," Sylmar said. "I say we take a vote from the people planning to travel since they're the ones taking on the potential risks that come with visiting the Seer. All those in favor of splitting up and sending out two parties, hands up."

Gaeren raised his eyebrows. This was democracy in action, something he'd never witnessed at the council meetings run by Enla. Everyone had been given the opportunity to voice their opinions, but the decision had been Enla's or their father's alone. As a few hands raised around him, he felt paralyzed, unsure what to do with the sense of power that came with placing a vote. Did he think they should split up? Holm and Aeliana had made good points, but so had Brogdon. Even if it took a little longer, maybe they could come back with both starbridges and twice as much information.

Before he could even decide about raising his hand, Brogdon,

Lukai, and Kendalyhn dropped theirs, conceding that their minority votes had been overruled.

"All right," Sylmar said. "All those in favor of seeking out the silver fish in Andel, hands up."

Once again, Gaeren hesitated. He wanted to cross the barrier and go to Sayhla Island, but he knew that wasn't what Aeliana wanted.

Sure enough, she crossed her arms over her chest, the crease between her eyebrows deepening as more hands raised. Would there be enough for them to go to Sayhla even if Gaeren didn't vote? He quickly scanned, counting raised hands from Velden, Lukai, Kendalyhn, Riveran, and Brogdon. With eleven in the room, one more vote would make the decision.

Gaeren's hand twitched with his desire to raise it, and sweat beaded on his temple. Just as he was about to give in, Iris lifted her hand instead.

Aeliana's eyes filled with tears, and she turned away.

"Iris." Holm's voice held a contempt Gaeren had never heard from the other man.

"I'm sorry, love. I just think it's our best bet to help Emeris," she whispered, unable to hold his gaze.

"Well, then, that settles it," Sylmar conceded. "Tomorrow we set sail for Andel."

Gaeren started. "Set sail?"

Beneath his beard and scars, Sylmar's lips tilted in a suspiciously smug smirk. "It's time you made good on your offer to lend us your ship."

CHAPTER 21

As the meeting broke up, Aeliana slipped out of the room, and Gaeren followed her. Her speed through the halls made him hesitate. It seemed like she wanted to be alone. But he also felt like she maybe shouldn't be right now.

He kept his distance as she made her way to the bailey, noting with curiosity that the soldiers gave her the same customary bow many of the men on his ship would give him, two fingers to the forehead followed by a slight nod. And while Aeliana didn't snub them, her pace sped up with each encounter, as if she grew more desperate to escape the attention.

To his irritation, the soldiers didn't stop her from leaving the fortress walls even though it was nearly the moon's reign, but they questioned him. The delay nearly made him lose track of her, but eventually he caught up to where she sat at the edge of the woods on a stump. She placed her face in her palms, then bent over her lap, her hair forming a curtain on either side, blocking her out from the world. He paused, wondering if he'd made a mistake, if this moment was too vulnerable for her to want him here.

He was about to leave when she let out something between a cry and a yell, then bent forward and grabbed a pinecone before chucking it just past his right ear. He ducked to avoid it, and she gasped.

"I didn't know you were there." She stood, wringing her hands. "Are you all right?"

He chuckled. "I think I'll live."

Even in the waning moonlight he could see her concern shift to a frown. "Serves you right for sneaking up on me out here."

He glanced over his shoulder at the open space between the woods and the fortress. "Even in this darkness you could have seen me coming if you'd been looking."

Her frown deepened, and he tried to backtrack.

"I just came to make sure you're all right. You seemed upset." He stepped closer and she looked away, wrapping her arms around herself.

"I'm just frustrated. For all Sylmar's talk about wanting me to step into some sort of leadership role, he let the group override the decision. It makes no sense. He wanted to go to Pacran as well. That's what we should have done."

"Maybe he was waiting to see if you pushed back."

The glare she'd reserved for the stump shifted to him. "So you're saying I failed his test?"

"I don't know if anyone passes any of Sylmar's tests." He grinned, and when her frown smoothed out and the edges of her lips curved upward, he felt a strange rush of satisfaction.

"We should be going to Pacran's library," she said again, as if wanting reassurance she'd been right. "How can we trust anything that crazy sea witch tells us? Even if it's right, what's the benefit if knowledge of the future drives us all to insanity?"

The sprite's instructions for finding the silver fish were on the tip of his tongue, but somehow he didn't think that detail would change her mind. If anything, it would get him in trouble for siding with those wanting to go to Andel. So he kept his silence, letting her assume he agreed. It wasn't exactly a lie, was it?

Guilt wormed through him, a response usually only triggered by Enla. The thought made his guilt double, considering this journey could potentially set the sprite's prediction in motion, resulting in Enla paying a heavy price. Or maybe it would result in Gaeren paying that heavy price since he'd tried to trade his own life for hers. Riveran may have saved his life by killing the sprite, but he also might have solidified Enla's danger. Or maybe the sprite's death had canceled out all the deals he'd tried making.

Aeliana sat back on the stump. "I suppose I don't understand Vendarans enough to think the way they do. I hate that my mother's so confused. I hate that the Recreants expect me to follow in her footsteps."

"Ah." He squatted next to her, dragging a stick through the pine needles scattered on the forest floor. "So that's why they bow to you." He should have figured it out, but his politics were far more focused on how to help the Recreants get out from under his father's thumb to consider the Recreants' divided interest in placing Emeris on the throne instead.

"The ones who don't know me bow," she spat out. "Those who do are well aware that I'm more Lorvandan than Vendaran. I'm not fit to be a part of their cause, let alone lead it."

"Then don't."

She huffed in disbelief.

He tapped her knee until she looked at him. "I mean it. You don't have to be Lorvandan or Vendaran. You're just Daisy."

Her eyes grew troubled. "I'm only Daisy to you."

His face warmed when he realized what he'd said. "Sorry, you're just Aeliana." He sat back on the grass and pine needles. "Just... don't try to be something you're not."

She sighed. "Orra said something similar. It's a nice sentiment, but Sylmar, Iris, and Kendalyhn—even my mother—they're all pushing me to accept the culture. To be one of them." She toyed with the hem of her skirt. "They want me to wear leathers instead of dresses."

A laugh burst out of him before he could hold it back, and she turned hurt-filled eyes his way.

"Sorry, it just seems ridiculous. But if it makes them happy, why not try it? Then maybe they'll realize you can't throw pants on a woman and make her something else, and you can go back to wearing these." He gestured toward her dress.

She grimaced. "They also want me to cut my hair." She pulled her hair around to one side, combing her fingers through it and twisting it up as if testing how it might feel to be short.

"It would make you *look* more Vendaran." Gaeren studied her with a critical eye, trying to see why Sylmar and Iris might think that was so important. "But you can't exactly throw it back on if you change your mind later."

He'd grown used to the look of her long hair, even come to prefer it. But if it gave her a sense of ownership for this place and these people, he wouldn't stop her cutting it. And it wouldn't hurt to have it out of her way in battle—especially now that another confrontation with Mayvus was likely imminent.

"I feel like I should try to be more Vendaran." She pulled out her dagger—the one he'd given her—and ran a finger along the daisy pattern, just like he'd done a million times while searching for her. "Not just because they want me to, but because it's my heritage, whether I understand it or not. It's just hard to make the switch, to go against what the priests and priestesses taught me in Lorvandas. Dresses were more modest and cutting hair was like defying the Stars."

"Because they all have long hair?" Gaeren asked. He frowned, something about that niggling at the back of his mind. "I'm pretty sure we keep our hair short for the same reason, but from a different angle. It's disrespectful to grow our hair as long as the Stars, who are far greater than us. Although I know it has something to do with Queen Amaya as well. It could be as simple as her setting a trend with her short hair."

Aeliana breathed out a light laugh. "Maybe we're both wrong. The only Star I've seen is Orra, and her hair isn't long."

That niggling feeling came back. "You're right. Unless she cut it all off for starlocks. Maybe that's the real reason why she was grounded." Now that he thought about it, maybe that was the reason fewer starlocks were being handed out. Maybe they'd all come from Orra and the Stars were running out of her hair.

Aeliana smiled. "That seems like something she would do." Her smile faded. "She also might have cut it off to fit in with the Vendaran people since she was grounded with them. Maybe that's an example I should follow."

Gaeren shrugged. "Sometimes the effort alone can help. As you try blending in with our culture, you'll figure out what works for you and what doesn't, and when you slip back into some of your Lorvandan ways, the fact that you tried will go a long way. Maybe you'll even like some of the changes. You'll become your own blend of cultures that people can appreciate."

Her gaze turned thoughtful, then she gave a decisive nod. "You're right. And hair can always grow back." She held the dagger out to him. "Will you cut it before I change my mind?"

He leaned away as if she offered him poison. "I don't think you want me anywhere near your hair."

"I'm sure Iris can make it look prettier when you're done."

He still didn't grab the dagger. "Then why not ask her to do it?"

"I might change my mind before I get to her." Her eyes pleaded with him. "Please, Gaeren. I'm already about to lose my resolve."

Against his better judgment, he took the dagger and stood. She spun on the stump until her back faced him, then bent forward to reveal the smooth skin at her neck. He shook his head at the irony of the dagger in his hand and her exposed neck. His father would see this as an opportune time to take out a perceived enemy.

But Gaeren was not his father.

He placed his free hand at her back, letting it linger over her neck as he gathered her hair in his hand. Her warm skin left his fingers on fire, even as he watched a shiver run through her, making him wonder if she was afraid or if she felt the same pull as him. Before he could examine the sensation too closely, he began hacking her hair off at the nape of her neck.

She sucked in a breath when shorter strands hit her cheek, making him pause. A wave of daisies bloomed at her feet, spreading out in a circle around them.

"Keep going." Her voice came out raw, and her hands balled into fists in her lap.

Why had he agreed to do this?

Within moments, a fist full of her hair was in his hand, and what remained on Aeliana's head barely brushed her neck. It was a sorry excuse for current styles. Aeliana turned and glanced up at him, placing a hand at the back of her head. Hair fell across her cheeks and into her eyes, which grew as wide as a winex's. The clearing around the stump was now filled with daisies, reminiscent of the ways she'd filled entire fields when they were children. A lump lodged in his throat, and he fought to swallow around it.

She glanced over at the hair in his hand, then closed her eyes. "It's done," she whispered.

A war of emotions crossed her face, making the temptation to brush the hair out of her eyes too strong. His gaze dropped to her lips, and the bond mark on his palm burned.

He took a step back, and the skin surrounding his mark cooled. He tightened his grip on her hair, then held out the dagger, hilt first, searching for something to say, anything to make the moment feel less intimate.

"Do you need me to help you with the trousers, too?" he teased.

Her eyes flew open and her face turned red. She yanked the dagger from his hand and stood. "Very funny." She shoved the dagger back in its sheath before pushing past him with an eyeroll. "I'll go find Iris for that."

A twinge of regret wove through him as she left. He'd embarrassed her and ruined the moment, but at least her pain had been replaced by irritation. That was good, right?

He could practically hear Enla raving at him for his stupidity. Of course it wasn't good. But if he hadn't teased Aeliana, he might have done something stupid, like kiss her, and that would have been far worse.

His bond mark itched again, a reminder of how much he loathed the idea of breaking it and how desperate he was to be free of it.

Instead of chasing after Aeliana, he sat down on the stump, separating out a chunk of her hair and tying it off at one end. He double braided it like the mainsheet on his ship, the familiar motion calming after the chaos of the night. Once it was the length of his hand, he wrapped it around his left wrist, testing the feel of it. An old memory of Orra toying with her braid came to him, along with her words telling him it belonged to someone who had been much more than a bondmate.

He wasn't sure what Aeliana was to him, but "more than a bondmate" felt right.

He let his starlock warm at his chest before sending its energy out to his wrist, singeing the ends together. The bond mark on his palm burned with it, the searing pain forcing him to close his eyes until he sensed the braid made a full circle.

The pain receded, but the bond mark had faded with it. The edges had grown thinner, the shape disfigured. He ran a finger over it, wondering if Lenda had felt it, wondering what exactly it meant. But then he ran his finger along the braid, grateful he once again had a token, like the dagger, to remind him of his purpose. It had grown much bigger than protecting just Aeliana. He needed to protect Enla from whatever the sprite had seen in her future. He needed to protect the Recreants from his father's rule. He needed to protect all of Vendaras from Mayvus' impending threats.

And yes, whether she wanted it or not, he still felt the need to protect Aeliana.

He pressed his nose to the soft hair, inhaling the earthy smell of daisies and a hint of salt, his mind rushing back through the memories of her as a toddler, the scent of the sea forever in her hair. Except this time the memories were faded, the current impression of her as a woman far more pressing in his mind.

He slipped his sleeve down over the braid before he was forced to acknowledge what that change might mean.

CHAPTER 22

AELIANA WOVE her way through the troops at the gate, unable to keep her hands from the strands of hair tickling her neck and cheeks. After talking to Gaeren, she'd thought it would be freeing, that it would make her feel ready to step into her identity as a Vendaran. Instead she felt naked and vulnerable, especially after Gaeren had turned it all into a joke.

Tears burned behind her eyes, and whatever sense of loss she'd felt shifted to frustration. It was only hair. It shouldn't matter.

She made her way toward Iris and Holm's room, avoiding eye contact with everyone she passed, unwilling to accept any more bows. When she reached their door, shouts came from within, and Aeliana's hand froze where it hung, poised to knock. She couldn't make out what they fought about, but she suspected it was the vote.

"What did you do?" Kendalyhn's horrified whisper came from behind.

Aeliana whipped around, causing uneven strands to fling into her eyes and make her flinch.

Kendalyhn reached out to touch the edges of Aeliana's hair where it brushed against her cheek. Down the hall, half a dozen soldiers stood in silence, their eyes holding a strange hope as they gave the bow Aeliana had been so desperate to avoid.

"Come here," Kendalyhn hissed, dragging Aeliana by the elbow toward her own room, beyond the prying eyes of the soldiers. Inside, she gestured for Aeliana to sit on a stool and folded her arms over her chest. "What made you finally do it?"

Aeliana swallowed hard, not wanting to explain Gaeren's role in it. "You and Iris were right. I should have done it a long time ago."

Kendalyhn's eyes narrowed, her gaze flicking back to the door.

Aeliana twisted her hands together. The other half-light probably sensed Gaeren's involvement with her pneumatic abilities.

"I'll never understand you." Kendalyhn huffed the words out before digging out a pair of shears from a drawer. She roughly spun Aeliana around and began snipping at the choppy ends. "Sylmar and Iris speak as if you're here to change the world even though you know nothing about it. You're like a child, too caught up in your own woes to recognize how much the people around you are hurting. And now, just before we leave the troops, you manage to do the one thing that might rally them to follow you to the ends of the earth. But you have no idea that you've done it. And now you're leaving before you can follow through on it." The longer Kendalyhn spoke, the more her words lost their hard edges. She kept snipping, making Aeliana wonder if she'd have any hair left by the time this was over.

"I didn't come here to change the world. And I know the people around me are hurting. I know I caused a lot of it." Aeliana's words came out like a whine, further proving Kendalyhn's assessment. "And I wasn't trying to rally the troops. I'm stuck between two worlds, not fully Vendaran and not fully Lorvandan. I just wanted to show I'm here to stay. I'm willing to learn. If different clothes and hair are the way to communicate that, then fine. I give in." Her conviction drained as she went on.

She'd been a fool.

Kendalyhn sighed but didn't respond, continuing to clip the ends of Aeliana's hair. As the silence grew between them, the sounds of the soldiers out in the bailey drifted up through the window, mixing with the crackle of the fire in Kendalyhn's room. Aeliana closed her eyes, imagining they weren't about to embark on a dangerous journey and there wasn't hatred constantly brewing between her and Kendalyhn.

The shears went still, and Kendalyhn hummed. "That should do for now." She spun Aeliana back, turning a critical eye on the hair falling in her face. She snipped a few more pieces.

"I feel like short hair is going to get in my way just as much as long hair," Aeliana mumbled. "At least I could tie my hair back before."

"You get used to it. Sun's fire, your head has to at least feel lighter."

"True." Aeliana gave the other woman a tentative smile. "Thank you."

Kendalyhn looked down at the shears, her face a mask.

"Why does it matter so much that I cut my hair? Iris always pushed me to do it, but I thought it was more symbolic. You seem… angry. And the soldiers…" Aeliana glanced back toward the door even though it was closed to whatever soldiers remained in the hall. "They stared at me like they'd seen a ghost."

"I'm not sure even Iris realized what it would do." Kendalyhn reached out and tapped Aeliana's chin right and left, studying her face. "But you look exactly like your mother. You've basically laid claim to your heritage. You haven't just proven that you're Vendaran and here to fight with the people. You've proven you're a Wyndren." Something close to admiration came through in Kendalyhn's voice, but her words only made Aeliana anxious.

"I can't ever live up to their expectations."

Kendalyhn snorted. "I know. And I'm glad you know it." Her gaze softened. "But those people don't need to know it." She gestured toward the door. "Let their ignorance build their confidence. When we leave in two days' time, you're going to wave goodbye with your head high, reassuring them that they're staying behind to fight for a future out from under the rule of the Elanesses. A future filled with freedom."

"Eventually they'll discover I'm a failure." Aeliana bit her lip.

"Maybe." Kendalyhn squinted at Aeliana, but for once she didn't seem angry. "Or maybe you'll grow into their expectations."

A wave of shock rippled through Aeliana. "Are you—did you just give me a compliment?"

Kendalyhn rolled her eyes. "Don't read into it. I can still despise you. But for now you're the ally of my allies, and I have to make it work." Despite her words, a small smile graced her face.

"Well, ally of my allies," Aeliana said, hiding her own grin, "any chance you have a pair of trousers I could wear?"

That night Aeliana said her goodbyes to the ailing Felk, and in the morning she fussed over the baby winex she was being forced to abandon. Emeris promised to give him memories of Aeliana, and Orra swore she'd watch out for all the winex in Iris' absence. But it still hurt to pry the toddler from her legs the following morning when those traveling headed to the shore.

Saying goodbye to her parents was equally difficult after having just gotten them both back, so by the time Orra found her in the bailey, her emotions were raw.

"Are you ready to go?" Orra's question seemed too simple considering who it came from. If anyone else had asked it, Aeliana would have said yes, because physically she was packed and ready. But Orra always got to the heart of the matter, and Aeliana couldn't honestly tell the other woman she was ready.

"I want to be," she said instead.

Orra smiled, and they stood in silence for a while, watching as dozens of horses lined up for the short ride to Gaeren's ship. Three wagons filled with supplies were already being driven out through the gate, and four more had been sent out during the night. Aeliana marveled at the amount of work people were putting in to ensure the success of their trip. It should have made her grateful, but instead it made her nervous. Everyone was counting on them to succeed. What if they didn't?

Her parents stood with Holm and Iris, the faithful maidservant giving final instructions to Rildan on how to care for Emeris, which he humbly took, either because he really needed them or just to humor her. Holm tugged on Iris' elbow, likely trying to save Rildan from the barrage.

Sylmar and Velden were having a meeting with General Nels and a few of his men. All their faces seemed even more serious than they'd been during the meeting two nights ago, which brought a new round of nerves to Aeliana.

Brogdon seemed to have found his place among the sailors, working alongside Riveran and Thallahan to secure the cargo in the wagons. She suspected Larkos and the other sailors were already at the ship, organizing the wares delivered the night before and doing final preparations, but she had no idea all of what went into sailing a vessel.

For the first time, she felt a twinge of excitement. Being out on the open water sounded thrilling, even if their final destination didn't.

"I'm glad you held your ground the other night," Orra said.

"What?" Aeliana pulled her gaze from the chaos to try to process Orra's words.

"When others wanted to go to Andel, you didn't change your mind."

"Did you sift the future? Is this the right choice?"

Orra's eyes grew troubled. "My powers have grown too weak for me to know that for certain. Both paths have options for success and both have options for failures. It's the decisions along the way that will make the journey's end a success or failure."

"Isn't that always the way of life?" Aeliana tried to hold back her frustration. What was the use in being able to sift the future if that was the only answer Orra had?

Orra hummed. "A very wise assessment. Just like it was wise of you to step back and let the vote run its course. If you were certain there was no chance of success on this mission, it would be one thing. But knowing each has potential makes it a fight not worth having. It might feel backward, but letting them make that decision shows leadership skills that will pay off in your future."

"It wasn't exactly intentional," Aeliana muttered.

"You could have refused to go," Orra said. "You could have set off for Pacran on your own. You're still showing faith and trust in them, and that will pay back tenfold in the future."

Aeliana sighed. "Asking Lady Merinnia about the future seems like a gamble that risks insanity. And before we can even do that, we have to locate a starbridge that you've been trying to find for a thousand years." She tried to focus on the fact that Velden's mother had been to see Lady Merinnia and that she'd come away with purpose and resolve—that she'd known the future and faced it with joy despite how much sorrow it held. But what about all the others who'd come away destroyed by what they'd seen?

Orra patted her arm. "When you reach her, you can choose not to ask her a question. You can choose to remain ignorant if you feel that's best."

The suggestion loosened a lingering tightness in Aeliana's chest, but her thoughts still felt tangled as Lukai and Kendalyhn mounted their horses. "It might take the entire journey for me to decide which is more brave: to deny myself the knowledge or to face it head-on." The admission burned. Neither option seemed good.

"There's no need for you to prove your bravery," Orra said. "When the time comes, you'll know. Let the Sun's warmth fill you, and you'll sense what's right." She gave Aeliana an uncharacteristic hug, and Aeliana squeezed her back, her throat tight. Who knew what would have transpired by the time they saw each other again?

Her parents finally escaped Iris, and they wrapped Aeliana in one last hug as well. She was grateful her father was staying behind with her mother and even more grateful that Orra would be there to aid them. Even if the older woman remained aloof, she would be an asset if Mayvus returned. Aeliana knew she could count on Orra for that. Perhaps her mother would even find something in Mayvus' journals that Aeliana and Sylmar had missed.

As Aeliana mounted her horse, another pranced in front of her, carrying Cyrus in backward circles toward the general direction of the wagons. He fought with his mare's reins, clucking and tugging in his attempt to turn her around. But the mare seemed determined to do the opposite, making Aeliana laugh, and her friend looked up.

A grin split his freckled face. "Want to trade?"

She shook her head. "You should ask Riveran for help. I hear he's excellent with animals."

Cyrus tried guiding his horse to the quiet half-light's place in the line, his failed efforts making Aeliana laugh harder. She suspected he'd gladly ride backward the entire way to the ship if it meant he could go on this adventure. She'd wanted him to stay back in Lorvandas for his safety, but it would have been selfish to make him. He deserved to be here as much as anyone else.

"Orra!" The sound of Gaeren calling out the Star's name spread a warmth through Aeliana that finally gave her a small sense of peace. Despite his teasing the other night, he'd come through for her in her moment of need. Having him on this journey made it feel slightly more possible.

She craned her neck to find him at the head of the line, standing in his stirrups and hailing Orra with an obnoxious wave. "How many Stars are there?"

Several onlookers turned toward Orra to see if she would bother responding. Her chin rose, and for a moment it looked like she would rebuke him for even asking. "There were one hundred." Her voice rang out clear and loud. "After Lucian's death, there were ninety-nine, and only ninety-seven can currently take to the skies."

Gaeren grinned. "Thank you!" He blew her a kiss that made something in Aeliana's stomach twist, then sat back in his saddle and led the way out the gates. Riveran and Thallahan followed, along with Brogdon. Riveran's shoulder was unusually bare, as Gullet remained behind in case the others needed to quickly send a message.

"What was that all about?" Aeliana asked.

Orra shrugged. "I believe it's something he needs to prove to his sister, but you'll have to ask him." She gave a regal nod, and Aeliana took that as her cue to lead her horse to join the pack. She gave one last wave to her parents, then held her breath as a handful of soldiers placed their fingers to their foreheads before bowing their heads, not to her mother, but to her. The motion was picked up by others and became a wave that rode through the crowd.

Aeliana's face heated as her mother and father made the same motion.

"When used in a procession or send-off," Sylmar said from beside her, "it's appropriate to return the signal, as though accepting the respect they offer."

Aeliana's fingers shook as she copied the gesture, but it was better than her awkward nods in the hall where she was unsure how to respond.

His horse whinnied its approval, but Sylmar gave her a strange look. "Did Kendalyhn not teach you anything in your lessons?" He and Velden fell in line with Aeliana for the ride to the ship.

"She taught me to do a crown braid," she mumbled. Which was pointless now that her hair tickled her neck and cheeks, driving her mad with its constant movement. "And she yelled at me for pulling at my pants too much." Aeliana pulled at them now, hating the way her position on the horse made them tighten around her legs and waist. She felt both claustrophobic and naked.

"Pants are easier for riding," Velden pointed out.

Eager to change the topic, Aeliana turned the tables on Sylmar. "You looked concerned when talking with General Nels. Is everything all right?"

Sylmar frowned. "It seems some men have gone missing in the last two nights. We suspect they might have been among the branded, but we don't know if they're headed for the starbridge's drop-off point to join her or if they're out sabotaging our efforts to secure the fortress. Either way, it seems to confirm that it was Mayvus who used the stone. Not that any of us had any real doubt."

Aeliana wrapped her cloak tighter around her, wondering if they would ever know who was loyal to Mayvus or whom they could trust. At least when it came to people outside those she'd traveled with from her initial arrival on Bamboo Island.

"Have you checked in with Durriken?" Sylmar asked. "Maybe he could help watch over the fortress."

Aeliana cringed. "Just because I have a brand on him doesn't mean he's mine to control."

"I never said you had to command him." For once Sylmar seemed more offended than irritated. "Now that you know he can understand you across the brand, you can use the connection to communicate what we've learned. Tell him our vulnerabilities, and then ask if he's willing to help. I never said command."

Aeliana bit her lip. It still felt like it was asking too much of the dragon who'd been enslaved by Mayvus, but she supposed she needed to at least tell him what they knew of Mayvus. "I'll try reaching out to him soon."

Sylmar grunted his approval. "I haven't forgotten that you had something to tell me the other night. Orra's news took precedence, but it's important that we address any issues with your magic—especially if you feel like you haven't been properly weaned."

Her questions felt silly in light of everything else going on. "I think it was just Gaeren giving me memories. It seemed… different from when he had in the past. I thought maybe my magic was somehow changing his. I don't know."

"The Wheel of Magic is as unchanging as the Sun." Sylmar's words came out stern, like he'd told Aeliana that a dozen times in lessons before. He probably had.

"It's meant to be a reassuring thing," Velden added, "even if Sylmar makes it sound ominous."

"But an individual's magic can change," she pressed. "You said I could grow to develop rim magic."

"Grow, yes," Sylmar admitted. "But never change. Gaeren will always have noetic magic. You will always have somatic magic. But magic can also wither if it's not cared for."

"Here we go," Velden muttered.

"I've noticed your light shields have been dimming," Sylmar said.

Aeliana winced. His words felt like a rebuke, even though he was merely voicing some of her own concerns.

"It's expected now that you're fully weaned," Velden said. "Your magic was never going to stay that strong."

Sylmar grunted. "It's also a sign that you could be training more to bring it back to the strength you'd reached."

"He would have said the same thing if your light shields were stronger," Velden whispered. "Would have made it into a challenge to reach your rim magic younger than any other progeny."

"I'm sure you're both right," Aeliana said slowly. "I haven't put as much time into my training because we all had a false sense of security. But there's more to it than that."

Sylmar's brows rose, and as his interest piqued, she felt that same hesitation from her early days in Vendaras rise.

"The memories I saw weren't Gaeren's. They were from Cyrus'

perspective. I'm wondering if my somatic skills somehow temporarily transferred his magic to Cyrus."

Sylmar and Velden exchanged a look that made Aeliana regret asking her question.

"If the memories were Cyrus', that wasn't Gaeren's magic," Velden said softly. "It was yours."

"My magic?" Aeliana frowned as their horses fell a bit behind the others. "But I'm a somatic progeny. Are you saying I'm developing a second spoke?"

"Maybe." The way Sylmar studied her left her uneasy.

"Maybe she's still not fully weaned," Velden suggested, "and she's tapping into some of that extra magic? Could it be temporary as it works itself out of her system?"

"Or maybe we never got her spoke right in the first place," Sylmar murmured.

The thought left Aeliana exhausted. Would that mean starting over with testing and training? Their horses caught up to the wagons and the mix of sailors and soldiers, and Aeliana sensed Sylmar's wariness grow alongside her own.

"We'll continue this conversation after we've gotten settled on Gaeren's ship," he said. "In the privacy of the captain's quarters."

Sylmar nudged his horse ahead, and Velden grinned while leaning toward Aeliana. "I can't wait to see how Gaeren reacts to Sylmar commandeering his quarters."

CHAPTER 23

As *To the Deep and Back* came into view, Aeliana couldn't help the thrill that ran through her. Something about the salty scent of the sea and the wind in her hair felt like home. She supposed it was because she'd grown up in the Sungazer by the sea with her parents, but she'd been taken from them at too young of an age to hold on to any of those memories.

She would just have to make new ones.

Thallahan and Riveran helped get Aeliana and the other newcomers settled aboard the ship. Gaeren directed his sailors in their final preparations, and Aeliana couldn't help admiring this new glimpse of him. She'd sensed his strong leadership skills in their time together, but because he'd always been under Sylmar's watchful eye, he'd never had a need or opportunity to display it.

A few of the men grumbled and made comments about the women on board as Aeliana, Iris, and Kendalyhn were given Gaeren's cabin. But Thallahan was quick to remind them that Orra had brought them luck. And then they kept their mouths shut.

"What luck did Orra bring?" Aeliana asked.

Thallahan chuckled. "I don't know if it's actually luck, but everyone loved her all the same. It doesn't hurt that Gaeren landed squarely on the side of the Recreants after her influence."

"I heard he was back in his parents' favor," she said, unsure if she should mention his parents had been branded.

Thallahan bobbed his head back and forth with a roguish grin that fit perfectly with his eye patch. "Yes, but then he had the nerve to tell them they were horrible rulers and they should step down. So it's anyone's guess if he can return without fear for his life. You'll have to ask him for more details. That's all I've got."

A young boy on the crest of adolescence ran up to Thallahan. "Master Gaeren needs you at the helm. He's asked me to see to the ladies' needs." His face took on a pink hue, whether because the idea gave him pride or embarrassment, Aeliana wasn't sure.

"Aeliana, meet Erech," Thallahan said. "Erech, this is Aeliana."

She held out a hand. "It would be an honor to have your help. I've never sailed on a ship before, and I need someone with your experience to make sure I don't make a fool of myself."

Erech took her hand and ducked his head. "This is only my third voyage, but I might have some tips, especially if you get seasick or homesick." When he finally looked up at her, his eager grin made her think of Felk, even though this boy had half as many teeth and no feral instincts.

It wasn't long before the motion of the ship shifted and they headed out to open waters. Aeliana left the cabin to take in the coastline, marveling at the speed with which they would be able to make it to Andel.

"We should have sailed here from Bamboo Island in the first place," she muttered as she leaned over to let the sea spray her face.

Sylmar's unexpected response startled her more than the water. "Even if we'd had a ship, it would have been much harder to arrive undetected, and we would have beaten the army by moons."

She turned to face him, then sighed at the determined tilt of his chin. "I don't suppose we can put this off until tomorrow and simply enjoy being on the water?"

His beard shifted into one of his rare smiles. "No, we can't."

Gaeren approached, his face more relaxed than Aeliana had ever seen it, his eyes practically sparkling with the joy of being back on his ship. "Did Erech and Thallahan get you settled?"

"Yes." Aeliana glanced at the overeager boy climbing the rigging. "Erech even promised he'd share his secret stash of sweets if I kept it between him and me. I'm not sure if you suggested he show me the ropes for his sake or mine."

Gaeren shrugged. "Can't it be both?"

"I'll take one of those sweets," Velden said with a grin as he joined them.

"Sorry," Aeliana said. "He said he'd only share them with me."

Velden's overdramatic pout didn't concern her.

"I've asked Kendalyhn to make sure no one disturbs us." As always, Sylmar got straight to the point. He led them toward the captain's cabin, where Kendalyhn leaned against the door, looking beyond bored.

"Wait." Gaeren rushed to catch up. "What are you doing?"

Aeliana glanced around, but those who were above deck were too far away and too busy to pay attention to her words. "It's possible we got my spoke wrong when we first tested it."

Gaeren's eyebrows rose. "I saw your light shield. There's no mistaking that."

She tamped down the warmth rising at his admiration. "Maybe, but it's been dimming. And when you arrived, I saw memories of your time in Lorvandas. The memories were from Cyrus."

Gaeren's brow pinched in confusion.

"We need to test it again," Sylmar said, confirming Aeliana's fear.

"In your cabin," Velden added, then raised his brows.

"Absolutely not." Gaeren crossed his arms over his chest.

Velden steepled his hands under his chin and glanced back and forth between Sylmar and Gaeren, thoroughly enjoying the moment.

"It's where the women are staying anyway. Where else can we do it without prying eyes?" Sylmar asked as Kendalyhn opened the door and shooed them all in.

"Which test will you be using?" Gaeren asked. "At the academy, they almost always ended in fire or with something broken. I'm not exactly eager for you to destroy my ship or endanger my crew."

Lukai hurried across the deck, stepping in just before Sylmar shut the door behind him.

Aeliana twisted her hands. Velden was still amused, but now she had only fear. "I agree. We should wait until we're on land where it's safer."

Her first test had been terrible. It had come on the heels of her years with Arvid and Vera, who had taken her blood to do terrible things. Sylmar hadn't meant to prod at that painful past, but the test he'd given her had been an illusion, showing Sylmar taking blood from Cyrus. It had been meant to push her to heal his wound, recall the memory, or identify it as a falsehood, depending on which spoke was her strength. If she was a somatic progeny, she would have tried healing him, which is what she had done and why they'd suspected that was her primary spoke. But she'd also seen the vision of Cyrus being cut, and she'd recognized it as a lie. At the time, her body had been so bloated with magic, it had been impossible for them to obtain a definitive result.

"It can't wait." Sylmar began clearing Gaeren's desk, placing instruments and papers on shelves.

Gaeren came behind him, rearranging them all with a scowl.

"We've already put it off for too long," Sylmar continued. "Your magic was muddled by its sheer capacity. We meant to test it again, but then your affinity for healing seemed to make it pointless. Especially once you were able to make light shields. But perhaps that's your secondary spoke, and we've been developing the wrong one. Now that you're fully weaned, your magic is settling. You may not be able to develop that constructive somatic spoke any further, which means we need to identify your primary spoke and develop that."

He patted the chair at the desk, and Aeliana reluctantly sat. "Wouldn't this skill have shown earlier if it were my primary spoke?"

A strange cross between a grunt and a laugh escaped Sylmar's lips. "I'm beginning to wonder if it did show earlier and we simply missed it. I always thought it was odd that you saw Cyrus wounded in your initial test. Even if constructive somatic is your secondary spoke, that leaves constructive noetic or destructive pneumatic as your primary spoke, because they have to be adjacent. Receiving memories is found on the destructive noetic spoke. So it still doesn't quite fit."

"Unless she's a constructive noetic and she was tapping into her opposite spoke," Gaeren mused. "It's far easier for me to take memories, but I can still give them if I'm touching someone. They're just not as clear."

Aeliana's head swam, and she wished she had a copy of the Wheel of Magic in front of her so she could line up their words with a picture of the spokes on the Wheel. "Your memories were clearer than my own when you shared them with me."

The whole room went still, her words confirming their suspicions.

Sylmar stroked his beard thoughtfully. "It's possible the combination of you each giving and receiving the memories made them stronger."

"So I helped draw Gaeren's memories out?" she asked, "and then I took the memories from Cyrus? How is that possible when I'm not a noetic?"

Even Sylmar seemed stumped.

"So much for magic not changing," Aeliana mumbled.

"Just because our understanding shifts doesn't mean the magic has changed." Sylmar continued studying her, like she was a bug he needed to identify. "Have you received memories any other time?"

She shook her head. "Even the images from Durriken have been more like what's happening in the moment rather than a memory."

Velden and Sylmar exchanged a glance. "You see what Durriken sees through your brand?"

"Of course. Isn't that just because of the brand?" Even as she asked the question, she knew it was more than the brand. She hadn't seen things when she'd been branded to Mayvus and Gaeren. Unless—had they seen things from her? A new thought occurred to her that left her insides cold. "I think I actually saw Durriken's memories when we trapped him in Islara."

Sylmar straightened. "You never said anything."

"There was a lot going on. I thought it was Durriken's magic, not mine."

Sylmar rubbed his hands over his face.

"I'm sorry," she mumbled.

He waved away her apology. "If it is his magic, I suppose you could be tapping into that through the brand. Anything else we should know?"

"I also saw visions in my Awakening." Aeliana let the words tumble out. Now that she was confessing one thing, it seemed she would confess it all.

"What sorts of visions?" Velden asked.

"Little snippets of memories, or maybe future memories. I can't remember them all, and they faded soon after I saw them. But I remember seeing Durriken with his collar removed. When we took it off, that vision came back to me as if confirming it had been prophetic. It gave me peace that I was always meant to free him."

Sylmar's face grew more somber. "What else did you see?" he asked.

She shook her head. "I remember so little. I saw Cyrus dead in the water, just like he was that night by Lovers' Falls. I saw a girl Arvid and Vera had killed back in Lorvandas. I saw the sprites and the winex. I saw people I don't know. The visions have all become too blurry for me to recall unless they're things that have already happened."

Sylmar's eyes closed. "That could still be a symptom of your bloated magic at that time. It doesn't necessarily mean anything."

"Same for the things Durriken showed me?" she asked.

His brow furrowed, and his scars puckered. "That could be his magic, like you suggested. Even if we retest you and you show an affinity for noetic skills, it could just be a result of your brand on him. Although the distance should be impacting it. The closer he is, the easier it would be to use his magic."

She shivered. "Then I'll remove it. Free him. If nothing else, it will help us know for sure if that was the cause for the change."

Sylmar opened his eyes and studied her. "You could. But he may want the brand for his own protection now that Mayvus is back."

Aeliana winced. She'd put off updating Durriken, but she couldn't wait any longer.

"At this point," Sylmar said, "I'm not sure we can test you again. Not if your brand is interfering with your magic. The tests were already going to be skewed toward constructive somatic skills because that's what you've learned. But if your true primary spoke lies on either side, we should be able to get a sense of that. We may never know whether this new spoke or the constructive somatic spoke is your primary until you've trained more. One will eventually outpace the other, and you may show affinity for skills on the opposite side of your primary spoke. But until then, we're likely going to be stuck training and developing both spokes equally."

Velden rolled his eyes. "I'm sure you're terribly disappointed to have to do that." Then he leaned toward Aeliana. "It's like Winter Solstice for him, being told he can train someone along two spokes simultaneously. You've made his entire year."

Aeliana tried to smile, knowing Velden was lightening the mood for her sake. It was something she always appreciated about him, but this time it wasn't working. "So, now what?"

"Like Gaeren suggested," Sylmar said, "if it's not coming from Durriken, I'm inclined to believe you rest on the constructive noetic spoke. It's adjacent to the constructive somatic spoke, and it's clear you're showing an affinity to tune in to memories. We've likely switched your primary and secondary spokes."

Aeliana frowned at his choice of words. Noetic progenies usually spoke of tuning in to the mind, whether it was memories, emotions, or thoughts. But she'd been training as a somatic progeny up until now, and she'd learned to adjust the body, whether it was healing or creating protective barriers. It would be hard to change her thought process.

"What if I'm..." She trailed off, picturing the Wheel inside her mind and tracing the other spoke adjacent to the constructive somatic spoke. "What if I'm a destructive pneumatic and it's all still muddled from how much magic I had in the beginning?"

"That's why instead of testing all the spokes, we're going to do a single test to rule out pneumatic skills." Sylmar gestured for Lukai to sit on the desk. "I'd offer you the bed, but everything's nailed down and this is the easiest way for you two to sit close—unless you'd both rather sit on the floor."

Lukai eyed Sylmar warily. "It's not the desk I object to. What exactly are we doing?"

"I want Aeliana to try sifting your soul."

Lukai laughed uncomfortably, then shrugged, settling on the desk so his knees brushed Aeliana's hands. She pulled them back nervously, glancing at Velden and Gaeren, who both seemed far more interested in the results than Aeliana.

"The bond should help." Sylmar gestured for them to hold hands. "It could give us a false positive result because in general you can sense each other's well-being, but if you can't even sift the soul of your bond, it's clear you're not pneumatic."

Their awkward positioning left their clasped hands resting on the tops of Lukai's thighs, and Aeliana willed her hands not to grow even more clammy. She closed her eyes, more to block out Lukai's proximity than anything else.

"I'll let Velden take over." A thump against the wood floor gave Aeliana the sense that Sylmar had backed up with his staff, leaving room for Velden to step in. Sure enough, the half-Sayhleen's low voice came close to her ear, as if he kneeled beside her.

"Sifting the soul has a bit more art to it than the crude simplicity of adjusting the body."

"Velden." Sylmar's expected warning tone made Aeliana smile, and her entire body relaxed a fraction.

"What? You teach your way, and I'll teach mine."

Aeliana peeked between her lashes to catch Velden's grin.

"Where was I? Ah, the artistic quality of sifting souls. It's about separating truth from lies, confidence from guilt, humility from pride. It's easiest to sift the things that weigh heaviest on our souls, which is why novices often find lies and guilt more quickly, even if their eventual strengths lie more on the constructive side that sifts truth or possible paths in the future."

She closed her eyes again and tightened her grip on Lukai's hands. "But I would have destructive pneumatic skills anyway, wouldn't I? I'd sift to find the lies and guilt in a soul."

"Exactly," Velden said. "And the lies of the past."

Aeliana frowned. "How is seeing the past different from seeing memories?"

"How is sifting the past different from tuning in to memories," Velden corrected.

They still sounded the same to Aeliana.

"Sifting someone's past is far more about sensing the state of their soul during their past experiences. So while tuning in to a memory might give you a sense of that person's emotion or senses during the memory, you're not catching the way it affected their soul. A destructive noetic might tune in to someone's sadness during the memory of attending their mother's funeral, but a destructive pneumatic would sift through the soul's past to know if the sadness was fueled by guilt or if losing their mother shifted how they viewed their father. The destructive pneumatic will never even see the memories the way a destructive noetic would. They'd simply feel the status of the soul."

Aeliana bit her lip. Velden's claim that this was a far more artistic spoke wasn't as far off as it had originally seemed.

"So I reach in to get a sense of his past, not the memories, but the heart behind them."

"Exactly." Velden's voice brightened, making Aeliana wonder if even he'd thought his own words were too abstract to be understood. "Lukai, make it a bit easier for her by sitting in something you feel guilty about in the past."

The memory of Lukai handing over her blood to Sylmar, his willingness to go against her wishes so he could protect her, flashed through her mind, but that was her memory, not his. Lukai shifted on the desk. Was he thinking of the same thing—and feeling just as uncomfortable? It still sat between them, this ugly history that made it impossible for them to work at growing their bond. Or at least, it made it impossible for her.

The tension in the room thickened as the silence went on, but Aeliana was hesitant to truly try. She didn't want to sense his guilt and shame. It might make it too easy to forgive him.

"If she's getting nothing, is it safe to assume she's not a destructive pneumatic?" Lukai's hands twitched in hers as he spoke.

She opened her eyes and frowned, taking in the sheen of sweat on his forehead. He wouldn't be this stressed about her seeing his guilt and shame over the blood. It wasn't like it was a secret she was about to discover. Unless… was there something else he'd kept secret?

Velden still kneeled beside her, and he cocked his head with a knowing glance. Hadn't Orra said everyone had secrets?

A desire to know filled her, and this time when she shut her eyes, she felt her starlock warm against her chest. She let that warmth travel across the thread of magic, but instead of letting it look for things physically broken and in need of fixing, she urged it to look for other forms of dissonance. It felt unfocused, like fingers blindly reaching for what might be within their grasp. But when she finally latched on to something, the focus became far too clear.

Kendalyhn sat before her, slightly younger, her face holding none of the contempt Aeliana was used to seeing. It was amazing how beautiful the other woman was when her lips weren't tugged down in a frown. Smooth light brown skin, dark braids holding the hair from her eyes, but the rest curling around to frame her face.

Without warning, Kendalyhn bent forward, as if she might kiss Aeliana. Except this was a memory, which meant she was leaning in to kiss…

"I love you, Lukai," Kendalyhn whispered, but before their lips could brush, Aeliana felt Lukai's body jerk away.

"I'm sorry, Kendalyhn. It's not right."

Aeliana caught a brief glimpse of Kendalyhn's frustration before Lukai rubbed his palms over his face and blocked her view.

"What if she's dead?" Kendalyhn asked.

"I'd know if she were dead." He rubbed the mark on his palm, the motion all too familiar to Aeliana since she'd rubbed the same mark on her own hand hundreds of times.

"What if she never returns? What if Rildan lost the starbridge?" Kendalyhn's face held a strange mix of hope and fear. "When will you decide you've waited long enough and live your life?"

The memory cut off abruptly, and the sway of the ship left Aeliana disoriented. She pulled her hands from Lukai's, her gaze resting on his chest. She didn't dare meet his eyes for fear of the truth being written in hers.

The thump of Sylmar's staff sounded beside her, and Sylmar nearly shoved Velden aside. "Did you sift his soul? Did you sense his shame?"

She was more confused than she'd been before. Sylmar said it wouldn't come in the form of a memory, but this was clearly the thing Lukai felt guilt over. Was her history of blood magic still affecting the way her magic worked?

"I sensed no shame or lies," she said slowly. "I don't think I'm able to sift his soul."

Lukai's shoulders dropped, his relief palpable. Sylmar stepped back and grumbled about how they'd have to start training her constructive noetic spoke simultaneously with her somatic skills even though, like Velden had said, Sylmar was likely thrilled at the prospect.

She continued to carefully avoid Lukai's gaze, which meant she soon found herself looking at Gaeren. He studied her, then raised his eyebrows as if challenging her words.

But they hadn't been a lie. It was clear she hadn't sifted Lukai's soul. She'd gotten a memory. And she hadn't sensed guilt or shame in the memory.

She'd only sensed frustration and longing.

CHAPTER 24

After a restless night debating searching the future of those aboard the ship, Orra wandered the fortress halls, her magic levels unaltered, but her worry at an all-time high. Perhaps she should have gone with them. If they didn't return, eventually Orra would have to hunt for the starbridges by herself, something that had once been a given but now felt like too much to bear on her own.

Everyone around her had a task, whether self-imposed or assigned by General Nels. Even Emeris had returned to the makeshift Sungazer, praying with soldiers on break until Rildan forced her to rest.

Orra wanted to do her part to aid the Recreants' efforts, but only the Sun knew what that might include. The onyx stone was beyond her reach, and she felt its absence like a lost limb. If she wasn't searching for a starbridge, what purpose did she have?

A blur of silver sped passed her, followed by almost three dozen more. At three days old, the winex were like small school children, always in trouble but learning quickly. She smiled as Felk led the others to the kitchen, then winced as she heard howls mixed with clattering pans. She rounded the corner to find one of the soldiers' cooks chasing them out of their favorite room.

Yesterday Iris had set aside meals for them before she left, but now they were on their own.

"Are you hungry?" Orra called.

Several stood tall, peering over their clan members to see who spoke. Felk rushed forward, tilting his head as he studied her. "You have food?"

She bent down at his eye level and patted his head. "If you can be patient enough for me to saddle a horse, I'll show you where you can get an endless supply."

Felk's grin revealed dozens of new teeth that had cropped up during the night. The others all clambered to join them, practically pushing Orra down the hall.

By the time she led them to the beach, they'd begun whining about the wait, but the moment she pointed out a school of tilapia, they went wild with anticipation, scrambling over each other to get first pick. Orra kept her distance, settling on the sand to watch them struggle, then adapt, until all were well fed and there was more splashing than hunting.

Felk returned first, settling on his haunches beside her, his knobby knees near his ears and his full belly protruding. "Thank you."

"You're welcome." She smiled and patted his back. "I suggest you all gather more to take back for your evening meal. You can return each morning and do the same so you don't have to rely on the soldiers to feed you. They won't be as accommodating as Iris was."

He nodded, then hesitated. "Emeris showed me memories. Iris and Mama helped us, but I don't remember you."

"I'm Orra, a friend of Aeliana's. I've been with you for much of your journey with her, but I usually keep to myself." She glanced back in the direction of the fortress even though she couldn't see its turrets. "It seems we both have to make adjustments if we want to fit in here."

"The soldiers don't like us," Felk said, trailing a finger in the sand.

"They're afraid of you," Orra corrected. "And I supposed they're afraid of me too."

He threw back his head, the tinkling laughter having no effect on Orra. She smiled, once again amazed at how little attention she'd given the winex before meeting Aeliana. What if she'd befriended one hundreds of years ago? Perhaps she could have had a companion who didn't wither away like all the people she'd known.

"I think if we work hard to help them, we can gain their trust," Orra said. "Can you do that?"

His backside wriggled like a dog's as he shoved to all fours. "We can work hard."

She stood. "Gather more fish, and I'll race you all back to the fortress."

He rushed off to tell the others while she mounted her horse. She patted the mare's withers and leaned in, brushing its hair softly. "Let's go. They'll still beat us back."

Orra settled into a routine with the winex, showing them how to help the soldiers with menial tasks. By the sixth day of their cycle, when their bodies were the size of a twelve-year-old but their strength matched that of the soldiers, they graduated to more difficult labor.

Despite how much time and effort the winex saved the soldiers, General Nels' men showed little thankfulness. If they'd been men aboard her ship during her time as Pirate Redwood, she would have shown them the plank. Instead, she took her complaint to their superior.

She found General Nels working alongside the soldiers, building supports for the outer wall so they could double its width with an additional layer of stone.

"I don't know what you want me to do." He didn't even look at her as he nailed the wooden planks together. "Most of these men watched friends or family members torn apart by the winex. Maybe not these winex, but ones just like them. I can't force them to be friendly."

"But they're proving themselves with their hard work," Orra insisted. "We can at least show gratitude for the help. They have no obligation to work alongside your men."

"I think you need to give it more time." He took out a cloth and wiped the sweat from his brow, his gaze finally meeting hers. "If they continue to work hard, the men will see that. Give it a few moons."

Orra huffed, ready to tell him that was lifetimes to the winex, but a tickle started at her wrist that grew to a familiar hum. She reached out a hand to steady herself on the temporary stakes, closing her eyes as she perceived the change. She could sense the onyx stone again, but it was too faint for it to tell her much.

"She's back," she murmured.

General Nels shook her elbow, and she opened her eyes to find him standing in front of her. "Mayvus has returned?"

Orra pursed her lips and did the math. "If she's done building her army, she'll reach us in ten to twelve days."

CHAPTER 25

It had taken a few days to find the right moment, but with the women's cabin finally free, Aeliana wasted no time lying down on the bed and closing her eyes. She set aside all of Sylmar's attempts to train her in noetic magic, instead focusing on the thread of connection formed by her brand on Durriken. If this worked, and if their theories about her noetic magic being stolen from Durriken were right, she wouldn't need to work on her noetic skills anymore, because they wouldn't exist.

As always, it felt invasive and wrong, but this time the thread connecting them seemed thicker than before, and once she recognized the path toward Durriken's presence, it was like he was there with her —or really, she was with him. He sat in the same clearing where she'd last left him, only now the little boy held a squirming baby girl. Her smiles lit up her face as her pudgy hands reached for Durriken's snout. It was a strange sensation for Aeliana to feel the girl rubbing his nose as if it were her own, like a tickle that made her want to sneeze. The dragon held unnaturally still as if knowing sudden movements might frighten the baby, and he barely breathed, likely concerned the warmth of his breath might be too hot for her tender skin.

"Adella? Ahndru?" The older male's voice carrying through the trees caused Durriken to stiffen. His body drew inward as if he could slink away and hide from whoever approached, but Aeliana couldn't sense if it was fear or something else making him cower.

When the stranger reached the clearing, his jaw dropped and his face paled. He crouched and waved the children toward him, his eyes never leaving Durriken's. "Quickly, come to me."

Even though it was clear the man had far more fear than Durriken, the dragon took slow steps backward, his tail bumping into the trunks behind him. Aeliana sensed his desire to leap into the air, but something held him back.

I might kill them. The thought rumbled through her as if in answer to her question. *The brush of the air from my flight could knock the wee ones to their deaths.*

"Grandpa, you have to meet him," the little boy said.

"Come to me now," the old man demanded, his voice shifting to a panicked plead.

"But he's our friend. He's nice," Ahndru insisted. "He won't hurt you."

"Are you so sure?" The old man's voice shook, but this time from rage. "This dragon killed your mother and father."

The words were like an arrow to Durriken's heart, and Aeliana felt the pierce of their point along with him.

The boy's face crumpled. "No. He wouldn't do that." He turned back to Durriken.

The dragon merely lowered his snout to the ground like a dog who'd been shamed by his disobedience.

"Did you?" the boy whispered. He was too old not to catch the meaning behind Durriken's actions, but too young to fully understand. Tears filled his eyes, and he pulled the baby away, back toward their grandfather.

I'm sorry. The words reverberated in Aeliana's mind again, the boy unaware of the dragon's apology.

Aeliana stayed silent with Durriken long after the people left the clearing, unsure how to help him. But a strange warmth invaded the brand binding them, as if this time he was grateful for her presence as he curled up in a ball.

I've come to set you free. Letting the words cross their connection felt easier this time, and she felt confident they reached him even before she sensed his curiosity. *I knew the brand connected our thoughts in some way, but I thought you were giving me memories with your magic. I didn't know I was taking both your memories and your magic.*

A grumble passed through their shared space. *I never let you see anything I don't want you to. And any magic stolen from me has been too little to be missed. Unlike Mayvus, you've never forced me. Was he...* grateful?

Either way, I want to set you free. There are some things you should know first, but I promise I will remove your brand today. I don't want to risk using you in ways I shouldn't, in using the brand in ways I shouldn't.

Durriken uncurled to lift his paw, holding it before his face to give her a view of the brand mark on it. Without his other paw available to balance, he was forced to sit back on his haunches. Even so, he managed to lift a hind leg and bring a claw to the edge of the bond mark. *I could have cut it out at any time. Mayvus would have stopped me from cutting out hers, but not you.*

Aeliana hesitated, her update on Mayvus on the tip of her tongue and at the edge of her mind. But his admission left her curious. Why *hadn't* he removed it? She shook away the distraction.

Mayvus is alive. The thought came out in a rush as she tried to move on from what his words implied. The tension in Durriken's muscles left Aeliana's own body trembling in a way that made her too aware of the fact that her body was back on a ship. It made it difficult to maintain a constant connection through the thread of the brand.

How?

We're not entirely sure. The admission burned. *We're trying to figure it out, but... either way, we suspect that she's crossed the barrier to Ahmranas using a starbridge. She's out of our reach. Sylmar wants me to ask you to watch the fortress, maybe intervene on our behalf. I'm not willing to force you to do anything. This is our battle, not yours. So I want to release you.*

The quiet that settled between them was comfortable, punctuated only by the twitter of birds in the forest, who somehow seemed unconcerned about Durriken's presence.

And what if I wish to make it my cause? She is my enemy as much as she is yours.

His answer left Aeliana stunned into silence. At most she'd expected him to want the brand as a protection like Sylmar had suggested. But it almost sounded like he wanted to be allies.

His words slowed as he sent his thoughts her way. *A connection like this isn't all bad. My ancestors tethered themselves to half-lights. Maybe not with a brand, but it was still a voluntary submission of vulnerability. A willingness to work together that was blessed and sealed by the Stars. I'm willing to accept this form of connection for now if it allows us to communicate.*

Her presence in Durriken's mind flickered as her gratitude swelled. She wanted to shout with joy or throw her arms around him, and the inability to do so reminded her that this wasn't her body, that this was unnatural. Daisies unfurled in the grass near his paws, and while he nosed at them, this time he let them grow and blossom.

She dared to voice her suspicions. *It almost sounds like you trust me.*

A growl emanated from his lips. *I have no reason to trust people. But perhaps I trust you above the others. Enough to sacrifice some of my freedom and preferred solitude for an advantage over an enemy.*

His attempt to salvage his pride wasn't lost on her, but rather than call him out, she gave him an even better reason for his offer. *There's also the possibility she has more of your blood somewhere. Since I branded you on Summer Solstice, her brand wouldn't be as strong as mine. If she tries again, I could help you fight it.*

A shudder ran through him. *Another excellent point.*

So you'll watch for her return?

He yawned and smacked his lips. *I won't go back to the fortress again unless I can destroy it.*

No. Aeliana said the word perhaps too quickly, and she sensed his interest pique. *My parents are still there, along with Orra and many of the soldiers who aim to protect them. You would do more harm than good to destroy it.*

His sigh was almost comical, but it gave Aeliana confidence he wouldn't attack them. *I will let you know if I hear anything from afar, then. And for now, we remain tethered, little one.*

There was that word again. *Tethered?*

It's what they called the connection with your kind. Not through something as barbaric as a brand. But this will do for now. He curled up in a ball on the forest floor, tucking his snout under his tail. She sensed his grief over the boy's sorrow returning. *Now I wish to be alone.*

Even though it was a clear dismissal, something warm rushed through her with his acceptance of their connection, something that made the string connecting them feel thicker, sturdier. It also made her concern for him grow.

Will they come after you for revenge?

He didn't answer right away, and she wondered if he would. But then he sighed in disappointment. *They can't hurt me.*

As she released the string binding them, she sensed that he almost wished they could.

The sway of the ship left her dizzy after having briefly returned to solid ground. She stood, holding on to the furniture to make her way out of the cabin and back on deck.

"Are you all right?" Velden asked. He lazily sprayed the deck with water so one of the sailors could swab it.

"I'm not sure," she said.

He eyed her more closely. "What happened? Should I get Sylmar or Lukai?"

"Durriken just—he requested to remain branded to me. He said it's as if we're tethered."

Velden's jaw went slack. "Tethered? Dragons haven't been tethered to people since before the Great Divide."

She shrugged. "That's what he said."

"If he used that term, he meant it. And it's an honor you should not take lightly."

"I won't." She stood a little straighter, almost offended. "I just—I don't really understand it. I never expected him to see us as allies."

She held up her hands, studying the scars on her palms, tracing the dark, bubbled brand mark on her right palm before placing her thumb over the small, tear-shaped mark on her left, hiding it from her view.

"It's funny how his acceptance of it seems to change it," she mused. "Perhaps when a brand is wanted, it gives that connection more power."

Her gaze drifted toward Kendalyhn and Lukai. He had a shell on his knuckles that he kept flipping around to his palm, entertaining her with his sleight of hand. She smiled and shoved his shoulder, a light-heartedness in her actions that Aeliana rarely saw. Lukai glanced up, his brow furrowed, and he rubbed his palm when he caught Aeliana's gaze, then stepped nervously away from Kendalyhn.

"Ah," Velden said. "Something tells me you're no longer talking about brands."

"Or maybe I'm realizing bonds and brands are more similar than everyone makes them out to be."

"Maybe. But don't ever forget that a bond goes both ways." He raised his eyebrows, but she still didn't see much difference.

"Is my bond with Lukai not taking because he and Kendalyhn are in love?"

Velden gave a nervous laugh and shot a glance in the couple's direction. For that was how Aeliana thought of them now. Now that she was looking, they were always together—always talking, training, assisting each other.

Before, when they'd traveled to the Myndren mountains, she'd thought it was more out of habit from their growing up years, especially after Aeliana had accidentally injured Kendalyhn while training. She thought Lukai had been such a gentleman to offer to be friends with Aeliana instead of more despite their bond, but now she suspected it was because he didn't want the bond. He never had.

"There's always been a mutual attraction," Velden said, "but it was understood that he was bonded to you."

"Well, that makes me feel worse."

"Why?" Velden asked

"If he'd never been bonded to me, maybe they would've bonded and sealed it with marriage ages ago."

This time Velden's laugh was more genuine. "They're only a few years older than you. I doubt they would have done that ages ago."

"You know what I mean."

His smile fell. "I do. Their feelings for each other certainly don't help your bond."

His admission and acceptance of her accusation made the revelation raw and fresh once more. Heat bloomed in her chest, a strange sensation that left her unsettled. She didn't like the idea of a magic mark on her palm stirring up jealousy, and she didn't need any more reason to feel a growing dislike for Kendalyhn. "It would explain a lot about why Kendalyhn hates me."

"Bonds are complicated enough when they're done by two adults who are in love and fully aware of the decision they're making." He turned over his palm, revealing a scar running along its edge, nearly hidden by his webs. "I can only imagine the added complication of a loveless childhood bond."

"You were bonded?"

A wistful smile flitted across his face. "The point is, instead of asking why it's not taking, maybe you should be asking what would help it take? Or maybe why it was done in the first place? Or maybe whether or not it's even needed now?"

Her surprise must have shown on her face because he gestured to her hand.

"You've found a purpose for your brand, so you're keeping it around. Seems the same logic should be used on your bond."

She ran a finger over the bond mark once more. "I thought my parents bonded us for my protection."

Velden nodded. "And maybe that will come in handy someday. Maybe Lukai will save your life. I don't know. But if you decide it's worth keeping for that, then you need to ask how to make it take. And remember my initial point: a bond goes both ways. You'll have to be ready to give him your heart just as much as he's ready to give you his."

She frowned, well aware that he'd neatly avoided her question about his own scar. "What about Kendalyhn?"

"Kendalyhn isn't bonded to anyone." Velden's words were soft with a gentle warning. "Her heart is free to choose, but even then, the choice isn't always an easy path. Sometimes it requires stepping back to let someone else take the journey you want."

"Everyone's heart should be free to choose." Her words lacked conviction, her thoughts muddled by their conversation.

Iris and Holm had chosen to be bonded, and it seemed to have made all the difference in the health of their bond and marriage, even if lately she'd caught them fighting more. Perhaps that was expected in any relationship. But had her parents really believed the protection of a bond was worth losing that right to choose? For the first time, she felt a pang of frustration with her parents, a sense that maybe they'd made mistakes just like she had.

"Bonds used to be used between parents and children, not just couples," Aeliana said, recalling her lessons from Sylmar. "If it can be used solely for protection, can't Lukai and I be bonded for protection, but each choose someone else to marry? Can't he choose Kendalyhn?"

Velden winced. "I can't imagine that would work, but feel free to give them permission to try." He chuckled and went back to squirting the deck with water. "Then let me know how that goes."

Aeliana lifted her chin, ignoring Velden's laughter as she made her way to Lukai. Kendalyhn's eyes narrowed with Aeliana's approach, but she didn't budge from her spot beside Lukai.

"Could I speak with you…alone?" Aeliana asked Lukai.

He glanced nervously between the women, and when he didn't respond, Kendalyhn let out a huff before mumbling something about Sylmar needing her. As she disappeared below deck, it should have gotten easier to confront Lukai, but instead Aeliana's tongue felt too dry to form words.

"Are you wanting to train?" he asked.

She shook her head. "I wanted to ask you about the memory I saw. The one with Kendalyhn."

His face heated, and he dropped his gaze. "I've never acted on it, and I never will. I swear on the Sun and Stars." He flexed his palm, studying his bond mark. "It's changing things anyway. I don't—I'm not sure how I feel anymore."

"If you love her," Aeliana said softly, "you can't let me get in the way."

His gaze shot to hers, surprise flickering across his face before being replaced by confusion. "But you're my bondmate."

"Cut it out." Aeliana pulled her dagger out from her belt and offered it up.

Lukai shuddered and backed away. "I know stealing your blood was wrong. I don't expect you to forgive that anytime soon. But even if neither of us is ready to let our bond grow, I'm not going to remove something your parents put in place for your protection. Our parents made a promise to each other when we were young. I made a promise to your parents to uphold the bond to keep you safe. I won't go back on that."

Aeliana shoved the dagger back in her belt and pursed her lips. "So we keep this awkward friendship that's supposed to be more, and I just let Kendalyhn hate me for it?"

He winced. "I guess so."

She studied the mark on her palm, contemplating cutting it out on her own. It wasn't like Lukai could single-handedly protect her from Mayvus. How necessary could their bond be?

They stood in an uncomfortable silence for a few more moments until Lukai tugged on the collar of his shirt and made some excuse about helping Thallahan with the sails. A cheerful whistle carried across the ship, and Aeliana turned to find Velden dancing her way with his mop. He winked at her before dipping his imaginary partner.

"How'd all that work out for you?"

CHAPTER 26

GAEREN HAD NEVER FELT SO out of place in his own cabin. It had been five days since they'd set sail and experimented with Aeliana's magic. Apparently Sylmar's attempts to train her in noetic magic weren't going well, so he was enlisting Gaeren's help.

Aeliana sat in his desk chair with Riveran and Cyrus on stools beside her. That left standing room only for Sylmar and Gaeren. When the older man crossed his arms and frowned down at Aeliana, Gaeren uncrossed his own arms and smiled, not wanting association with Sylmar's anxiety-inducing instructor stance. Then he felt like a child, back with his parents and Enla, doing the opposite of what they wanted and expected just to prove some point.

"Are you sure you have time for this?" Aeliana asked.

Gaeren shrugged. "I may be the captain, but it's often Larkos who runs this ship."

Riveran snorted but made no other comment. A wise choice.

Aeliana's hands twisted in her lap, and the motion made Gaeren feel oddly more at ease. Her nervousness allowed him to focus on making her more comfortable rather than examine his own discomfort.

"Gaeren is the best person to help you with this because his noetic skills are the most advanced in our group," Sylmar grudgingly admitted.

"Why, thank you," Gaeren said, placing a hand over his heart in mock surprise. "I think that might have been a compliment."

Sylmar rolled his eyes and sat heavily on the bed, leaving Gaeren still hovering awkwardly over the other three. "Let's start with Cyrus."

"I thought we should start with me." Gaeren might have been a little too eager to contradict Sylmar's plans, but he rushed on anyway. "It will be hard to tell whether she's using her magic or I'm using mine, but it will give her a sense of what she's aiming for since the other instances were more accidental."

Cyrus stood, gesturing toward his stool for Gaeren to take his place.

"Very well," Sylmar muttered.

Gaeren sat beside Aeliana and Riveran, holding out his hand, palm up.

Still, Aeliana hesitated. "How do you keep yourself from getting memories people don't want to give you? How do you stop yourself from invading their privacy?"

Gaeren winced, remembering his own fears when he'd first learned. He'd hardly wanted to touch anyone for fear of seeing something he couldn't unsee. "It's difficult to get someone to show you a memory they don't want you to see, especially when you're first learning. And in your case, you're going to focus on giving me memories since that should come easier to you if it's your primary spoke."

"I don't think it is," Aeliana said. "I meant to test it yesterday by cutting out my brand on Durriken. If the magic had stayed, we'd know it was my magic, and if it didn't, we'd know it was Durriken's. But... Durriken wanted to maintain the connection. He called it a tether. He's fine with me using his magic."

Gaeren whistled low and long. "A tether? I didn't think those were possible anymore."

"They aren't," Sylmar said.

"It's not a real one," she rushed to add. "He just seemed to think we could treat the brand like one. For now. It's the only reason I'm willing to train in magic I'm basically stealing from him. Because he's offered it." A pink tinge came to her cheeks, one that made Gaeren want to tease her, but something about the topic felt off limits to him, at least if he wanted to maintain the growth in their friendship.

Besides, the idea that this skill came from Durriken made sense. With her ability to receive so many memories, it would make more sense for her to be a destructive noetic, but he understood why the old man assumed she'd be a constructive noetic after seeing her light shields. If Durriken gave her noetic magic, it didn't have to follow the rules of the Wheel of Magic.

He tapped her knee, then held his palm up once more. "Then let's get started."

"What if—what if there are memories I don't want to give?"

"Then you let go of my hand," Gaeren said. "Any memory you're giving me will cut off if you let go. At least for now, while you're still learning. If it's your primary spoke, you'll eventually be able to use it without touching. Technically I could continue to take the memory from you with my own magic, but I've trained not to do that. Losing people's trust is not worth gaining whatever knowledge they want to keep secret."

She nodded but still seemed uneasy.

"Instead of thinking about the things you don't want me to see, it's important that you think of something you *do* want me to see. Shove those other memories to the background and bring the memory you want to share to the front."

She nodded again and tentatively placed her hand in his.

Gaeren didn't need to close his eyes, but he did so anyway. She was already nervous enough without being watched. "I'm going to reach out for your memory now. For me, it's like tuning in to a specific note on an instrument." His starlock warmed as he said the words, and he felt the thrum through his arm and into his palm. "At first the images will be blurry, but just like an instrument can be tuned to the perfect pitch, I can find the right note to make the memory clearer."

Even as he spoke, the image came to his mind.

It was a fleeting moment with all of them on horseback, long before they'd reached the Myndren Mountains. Maybe even before Aeliana and the others had found Gaeren in Islara. Sylmar was instructing Aeliana on the Wheel of Magic, and Velden was behind him, mimicking the way the older man spoke by overexaggerating his gestures and pompous expression. Then the half-Sayhleen shifted into a bored listener, falling asleep and nearly tumbling from his horse. Cyrus snorted from beside Aeliana, and he felt her turn to hide her own smile.

Gaeren pulled his hand back and let the memory snap closed. He and Aeliana grinned at each other.

"What did you see?" Sylmar asked.

"She just showed me a memory of Velden being Velden."

Aeliana's eyebrows rose, as if challenging him to admit the full scene.

Sylmar grunted. "That man needs a leash."

Aeliana burst out laughing, the sound stunning Gaeren with the same mesmerizing power of a winex's chime. He tore his gaze away from the dimple in her cheek to find Sylmar grumbling.

"It wasn't a joke."

Gaeren turned back to Aeliana. "Did you sense how the memory could be tuned in to? Sort of singled out from the others in your mind?"

Aeliana's smile faded. "Maybe?"

"This time I'm going to give you a memory. Instead of just taking it in as your own, I want you to focus on where you sense it. Use your starlock to feel where it's coming from and how to grasp it so you can then pass it to someone else."

Her face clouded over as if his words held no meaning. He remembered the sensation all too well from his time with his earliest mentors.

"Think of it like a game. In fact, it's one we played often in school. All the noetics would train together and we would transfer one memory through the entire group. It was meant to test our accuracy to see how much the last person's interpretation of the memory matched the first person's original memory." He grinned. "It usually ended up being more of a game for who could throw in the funniest alterations to irritate our instructors."

Sylmar's hum from behind Gaeren showed the older man's lack of surprise, but Aeliana's shoulders relaxed, and she smiled as she closed her eyes.

"Secretly, I don't think the instructors cared," Gaeren added. "It's much harder to falsify a memory than it is to keep it accurate, so we ended up pushing our magic harder than we would have otherwise."

He studied her a moment longer than necessary, watching the way a little V formed between her brows as she focused. Her hair swung across her cheeks and neck, practically inviting him to brush it back and feel its silkiness once more. For the hundredth time he worried she might catch a glimpse of the braid on his wrist, then berated himself for caring. It was a reminder of promises he'd made, nothing more.

Despite the becoming way Kendalyhn had fixed his poor cut to frame Aeliana's face, he missed the way it used to brush her elbows. Why were Vendarans so eager to cut their locks anyway? Was it really such a shameful thing to have long hair like the Stars when it was a reflection of their beauty?

Sylmar cleared his throat, and Gaeren squeezed his eyes shut but not before catching Riveran's smirk.

He tried to push the image of Aeliana's hair out of his mind, but instead it brought him back to the idea that Orra's short hair didn't match her history as a Star. Instead of completely shoving the thought aside, he pulled up his memory of Orra and her admission at being Sheen. Did the details Orra had given him match the ones she'd given Aeliana? This was an opportunity to test it.

When Aeliana gasped, he opened his eyes, curious at which part had shocked her. Her grip on his hands tightened. "She's—

"No!" he cut her off. "I don't want you saying anything out loud about the memory. Not yet."

She frowned, glancing at Sylmar.

It wasn't that Gaeren wanted the information kept secret. It was that he wanted to test her ability to transfer the memory to Cyrus. He pulled his hands away from hers and stood, the absence of her soft skin leaving his hands feeling awkwardly empty until the mark of his bond twinged its irritation. He scratched at it, then gestured for Cyrus to take his seat.

"Can you still feel the presence of the memory?" he asked Aeliana. "Not just the knowledge of it but the thread it hangs on?"

"I think so," she murmured, closing her eyes once more.

"Try sending that thread through to Cyrus."

The almost-priest held out his hands, eager, as always, to participate in anything with magic. At least Sylmar had chosen Cyrus instead of Lukai for this task. The thought surprised Gaeren and made his bond mark itch once more.

"It sounds like it was an interesting memory," Cyrus said. "I'll take it."

Aeliana grimaced. "You might be waiting a while."

The silence stretched, and Riveran yawned, gaining a glare from Sylmar.

"I feel like it's fading," Aeliana said. "The thread and the memory. It seems stuck where you left it."

Sylmar stood. "Think of how you push out your light shield, how you send your energy through to others to heal them. Think of the ways you've already used your magic and do it again, but with the memory."

Her brow furrowed once more, and this time Gaeren allowed himself to study her even longer. The way her lashes brushed her cheeks and how her lips pursed in concentration. He could still see faint traces of the toddler he'd known as a child, of the Daisy he longed to protect, but he could no longer think of her that way. He wanted to protect her, but not because she was a small child unable to protect herself. He simply cared what happened to her.

He cared about Aeliana.

He squirmed at an admission that felt forbidden. She had all the grace and beauty of the women in the noble courts back at the palace. But she also held a humbleness that set her apart from the women he was used to dealing with. Even Lenda had held him at arm's length, as if she knew he could never truly love her. As if she saw their future as political and transactional just like he had.

But could he break his bond because he cared for someone else? Was there dishonor in doing it if it was for the right reasons? To free Lenda and to free himself from something neither of them wanted— maybe something neither of them had ever wanted? To free them up for something more? Something better?

Cyrus' confused voice startled Gaeren out of his unexpected spiraling thoughts.

"I'm not really getting memories, but I feel like you have some sort of story about Orra and Sheen in there." Cyrus' face only held more questions when Gaeren started clapping.

Aeliana's face grew pink. "That's hardly worth applause."

"Did you show her our conversation about Orra?" Cyrus asked.

"No. I showed her my conversation with Orra, who confirmed she's Sheen."

Riveran gasped, but Sylmar seemed unsurprised. How long had he known?

Cyrus let out an exasperated groan. "I should have talked to her before we left. What else did she say?" He pulled his hands away from Aeliana, drawing Gaeren's attention to the red stains on both of their skin.

"You're bleeding," he said, bending forward to see which one of them was actually injured.

"Oh, no," Aeliana said, pinching the cut on her palm. "How did that happen? Did I push too hard?"

"I'll get Lukai," Riveran was quick to offer, reminding Gaeren his old friend had always been a bit squeamish.

"I can heal—" Aeliana started, but Riveran was already out the door.

"It's a good thing his X is on his forehead," Gaeren said. "He might have fainted every time he saw it otherwise." He grabbed a rag from his desk drawer, then poured water on it from his waterskin before passing it to Cyrus. "And you can't cut yourself from pushing too hard. Not unless you had an old wound that reopened."

She frowned at her hand. "I feel like I'm always getting cuts and bruises, but I don't know where they come from."

"You're almost as klutzy as me," Cyrus said. "You probably just didn't notice it before because Arvid and Vera kept bleeding and healing you."

Aeliana shuddered.

"It will be hard to switch skills after training so much." Sylmar studied Aeliana a little too closely while she attempted to heal the cuts on her palm. "It will be a bit like reversing the Wheel's spin or pivoting to roll down another path."

"It feels wrong again." She took the rag Cyrus offered now that his hands were clean. "I don't like it."

"We'll take a break." Sylmar shuffled toward the door. "Try again tomorrow. We need to go back to your somatic skills and get your healing and light shields back up to speed as well. Perhaps the brand is interfering by presenting new options to you, but that should never override your primary spoke."

"Is there any chance Mayvus branded me again?" Aeliana's eyes flashed with fear. "Why does it feel this way?"

Sylmar turned, his face a storm of fury that didn't seem directed at her. "Branded progenies give up their magic; they don't receive it. Mayvus wouldn't want you gaining any extra skills or advantages. Plus, you'd have another mark on your hand unless you've learned illusionary magic without my knowledge. I think we can all agree that this must be from Durriken."

"Mayvus had marks all over her body." Aeliana looked like she wanted to say more, maybe reference the marks he'd had all over his body at one time. Her eyes grew wider with her rising panic. "What makes you so certain it would be on my hand? Should we search the rest of my body for marks?"

"The person performing the branding can place the mark wherever they want on their own body, but the recipient's mark will always be on their hand." Sylmar's rage simmered until his words held sadness. "You're fine. You're safe. You don't need to be afraid."

Aeliana's face still held a mix of emotions as Sylmar left. Cyrus patted her back awkwardly before following the old man, leaving Aeliana and Gaeren alone.

The room suddenly felt smaller, and yet Gaeren was too far away to comfort her. When she wrapped her arms around herself, he knew he should go to her, but the two steps it would have taken felt too forward. What if she didn't want his comfort? He wasn't her bondmate.

When a visible shudder passed through her, instinct won over his internal debate. He took one step, and her gaze snapped to his. With his second step, her muscles loosened and she leaned in. Just as his palm brushed the smooth skin of her arm to pull her close, the door opened, and Lukai rushed in.

"Are you all right?" He pushed past Gaeren, scanning Aeliana from head to toe as he gripped her upper arms. "Riveran said you were hurt, but I hadn't felt anything, so I didn't think it could be much, but—"

"I'm fine." Aeliana's smile was tight. "I'll be fine."

Lukai steered her from the room without even acknowledging Gaeren's presence, and suddenly Gaeren was alone, his bond mark flaring and the braid on his wrist too constricting.

He yanked his knife from his belt, his thumb automatically feeling for the flower that wouldn't be on the pommel, because he'd given that knife to Aeliana. He held the point to his wrist, debating cutting off the braid but instead letting the tip rest against the innocuous bond mark that suddenly felt like poison he needed to cut out.

His heart pounded, his spirit eager to be rid of the thing once and for all. What did it matter if he cut it out? He let the point break his skin, the sharp cut hardly noticeable, but it brought forth a rush of memories: Enla bent double, tears streaming down her cheeks. Painful moans escaping her lips as Gaeren carried her to her room. Screams of hatred for their friend that Gaeren had echoed in his own mind. Then the stillness. The numbness. When he thought he'd lost her completely.

How had he left his sister back in Elanesse after swearing to protect her? How was he any better than Riveran, who hadn't protected her from their parents' decision to break the bond? What kind of brother was he to turn his back on her and leave her to the fate predicted by the sprites?

His knife clattered to the floor, pulling him from the memories that had swallowed him. A knock sounded on the door, and rage swelled in Gaeren. He pulled the door open, almost wanting Riveran to be on the other side, desperate to give the other man a solid punch. Maybe wanting Riveran to return the punch even more.

Erech stared up eagerly at Gaeren for just a moment before shrinking away. "Um, sorry, Captain, but Larkos needs you at the helm. Says his leg is bothering him. Sorry."

All the anger drained from Gaeren, leaving him as exhausted as if he'd sailed through a summer storm. "It's all right, Erech."

He bent to retrieve his knife, noting his bond mark no longer throbbed. His desire to cut it out now felt like an act of insanity that left him unsettled by his own behavior. Like always, he shrugged it off with humor.

"Tell Larkos that next time he shouldn't get new tattoos right before we sail out."

"I don't think he'll laugh if I say it, sir. He might actually growl at me."

Gaeren chuckled and tousled the boy's hair before following him out on deck. "He'll growl at me too. That's what makes it so fun."

CHAPTER 27

Aeliana stood in a field of daisies. At her feet, a little girl hunched over, her back blocking Aeliana's view of her hands and face.

"What are you doing, Daisy?" The voice that came from Aeliana's lips was young and male, reminding her that this was Gaeren's memory and not hers.

The little girl didn't turn. "Nothing."

"Your mother told me that always means you're up to something." Gaeren leaned forward and tugged on the little girl's elbow, forcing her to turn and allowing Aeliana to see black and purple marks running across the girl's face and arms. Gaeren gasped. "What did you do?"

Aeliana recognized her own face from the memories Gaeren had shown her before. Her toddler self lifted her chin, exposing more marks down her throat. "I want to be pretty like the sailors who come in town."

Gaeren's high laughter floated across the field until it cut off as Aeliana pulled her hands from his. His captain's quarters came back into view along with Iris sitting on the bed, mending one of Holm's oversized shirts.

"I did not draw tattoos all over myself." Aeliana's horror warred with the humor of the memory, and her face heated as the adult form of Gaeren echoed his childhood laughter from his place on the desk. The nailed-down furniture left him far closer than she wanted, and she shoved his knees away until he slid off the desk and gave her the space she needed.

"You did."

Were those tears forming in his eyes?

"And you used the dyes your mother had for ceremony fabrics. They were the brightest colors you could find, and they lasted for weeks." Fresh chuckles bubbled up, making his sentences break up. "The high priestess was especially embarrassed by a voluptuous Sayhleen tattoo you'd copied from a regular worshiper whose trade route crossed Celanoft every moon."

Aeliana shoved his arm, making him nearly fall into Iris.

She glanced up from her mending, but her fingers kept moving. Her eyebrows rose and the corner of her lip lifted, which made Aeliana's face heat even more.

"I think you're making it up." She crossed her arms and narrowed her eyes.

"Memories don't lie." Gaeren's laughter settled into a smile. No, it was definitely a smirk this time. His ability to get under her skin gave him power over her, and he knew it. He seemed to enjoy driving her crazy when they trained, and instead of hating him for it or even ignoring him, she found herself rising to his challenges. She looked forward to their banter more than she'd ever looked forward to Lukai's interest, which had all but disappeared after his betrayal.

"The tattoos were real, love," Iris confessed, her eyes shining with mirth. "Your mother threatened to keep you indoors for two moons if you ever did such a thing again. Especially after you tried showing a visiting priestess how the Sayhleen could swim if you moved your arm just so."

This time, Iris and Gaeren both burst out laughing, and Aeliana gave in to the ridiculousness of the image, shaking her head and smiling. It felt good to let down her guard, even if that meant inviting more of Gaeren's teasing. At least she could trust these feelings to be real. When she'd regretted her anger over Lukai's betrayal, she'd wondered if the bond was forcing her to be too forgiving. When she'd felt sorry for the way the bond had driven a wedge between him and Kendalyhn, she'd felt a flare of jealousy that she hadn't wanted.

Could that kind of confusion ever grow into a bond truly centered on love? Was it even worth trying when underneath the bond, Lukai loved someone else?

It was one more thing she didn't have time to examine while chasing after starbridges and beating Mayvus back home. Her focus needed to remain on identifying and breaking whatever curse bound her mother to Mayvus.

"I thought you said you could alter the memories shared with your classmates," Aeliana pointed out. "Couldn't you have altered yours just to trick me?"

Gaeren's smirk fell. "Both are difficult, but altering someone else's memory is far easier, because it's been passed on to you rather than being an intrinsic part of your own past. Altering my own memory would require illusion on top of a memory, which is more of a theory and a skill I don't have." He leaned against the desk and pulled out a small knife, balancing it on his knuckles before letting it spin back to his hand. "Besides, then I would have given you a memory of Iris with the tattoos."

"Oh, stop." Iris tossed a pair of Holm's pants at Gaeren, then shook her head, her smile as big as Aeliana's.

"I wish I remembered it myself," Aeliana admitted.

"I wonder if you could," Gaeren said. "Over time, as your skills grow, you might be able to tap into memories you've forgotten. You were young enough that it's possible the memories are truly gone, but I suspect some of your time with Arvid and Vera caused you to lock them away. Almost in self-defense out of fear that you would lose them."

"Is that even possible? To lock memories away?" she asked.

His face grew serious, and he studied her too closely. "It is. I've done it. I kept my memories of you locked away for many years. Not necessarily to protect the memories, but to protect you."

Her previous irritation with him was replaced with a warmth she couldn't define. At one time it had felt unwarranted, but the more she saw of their past, the more she appreciated it.

"I knew there was something important about you even when I was a child. Toddlers don't make daisies grow, not even the royal family's toddlers who all have ridiculously high levels of starblood." He tilted his head in thought, making Aeliana aware of the fact that they still had no explanation for that, especially if they'd gotten her spoke wrong. "I was afraid one of my instructors or fellow students would find my memories of you, even accidentally, while training."

She glanced down at her hands, grateful for all the ways he'd protected her, but she didn't like when he looked at her like she was a sister or a child. She told herself it was because they'd barely agreed on friendship after their families' history as enemies. But her bond mark twinged as if it was because she wanted something else entirely.

"I was going to have you try giving that memory to Iris," he said, "but since you blurted it out, I'll have to pick something else. Otherwise, I'll have no way of knowing if you succeeded."

She snorted. "Not to spoil the surprise, but I wouldn't have succeeded." They'd been sailing for over a week, and her noetic skills had hardly grown. The progress was even slower than it had been before, probably because her magic had weaned to a more normal amount. Her light shields were barely more than a flicker, and her ability to heal had been reduced to surface cuts and minor ailments. "At this rate, I'm not sure I see the point in practicing. I seem to do better when I use it by accident."

He waved away her concerns. "That's how it is for everyone when they're first learning. Don't let Sylmar tell you otherwise." He held out his hands, and she took them, fully aware of the irony that she'd grown so used to touching him. She was more used to holding his hands than Lukai's, and with that thought, her bond mark flared.

A knock on the door prevented them from returning to their training, and Aeliana snatched her hands back to her lap. The door opened, and Erech's head popped in, his youthful zeal always a welcome sight.

"Is it that time?" Gaeren stood, his eagerness matching Erech's.

Erech nodded. "Yes, Captain Elanesse." He glanced at Aeliana before ducking back out from the cabin, face pink.

"Time for what?" Aeliana's voice betrayed her disappointment, and Gaeren's grin widened.

"There's something I want to show you." He led her out on the deck and steered her to the starboard side.

Her breath caught as she took in the view of the coast. They'd mostly stayed farther out to sea, where she could catch glimpses of the shimmering barrier now and then. But for some reason, they'd traveled closer to the mainland today, allowing her to see small towns and ports.

Gaeren stood behind her, bending down so his cheek was nearly lined up with hers, and he wrapped his arm around her so he could point and direct her line of sight toward a barren ridge. "Do you see where the bluff hits its peak?"

She nodded, the warmth of his breath on her cheek making it difficult to pay attention.

"You can barely make out ruins before it slopes back down into the valley beyond, but that is Celanoft. That's where your parents meant to raise you, and that's where you and I first met."

Her shock chased away any confusion over his nearness, and she leaned forward over the ship's edge, ignoring the spray that caught her blouse. "That was my home?"

Instead of answering, he passed her a spyglass. She fumbled with it, mixing up the front from back until he gently guided it to her eye, showing her how to bring the distant coast into focus. "That's where the Sungazer was, isn't it?"

He hummed his confirmation, and her chest tightened. It had been completely razed, maybe not by Mayvus herself, but on Mayvus' orders. The remains were little more than a foundation of stone, but they seemed well cared for, like the people in the surrounding area still honored the site.

The area was too barren to match glimpses from the memories Gaeren had shared, but the lines of the various paths—down to the beach and out to the forest—were a perfect fit. Most of their time had been spent on the other side of the ridge where she knew a creek flowed through the valley and out to the sea. She relished the way seeing it now made the memories feel more certain. Even the salty breeze dancing through her short hair made the memories feel more alive.

"I wish we could stop and see it." She passed him the spyglass, and he took a turn studying the land that had once connected them.

"We'll come back sometime." He said the words almost too casually, like he was testing out her response, or maybe testing out the promise for himself.

"I'd like that," she said. They stood side by side at the ship's edge, ignoring the bustle of the sailors around them as they sailed farther south and Celanoft grew smaller.

"I don't mean to keep you from your duties," she murmured when she realized how much time had passed.

"There are times I take full advantage of being a prince." Gaeren's words held mischievousness, and his sly grin returned. "Larkos is the only one on this ship who'll ever tell me I'm being lazy, and even he picks and chooses when—"

"Gaeren!" Larkos' voice carried across the deck.

The smile on Gaeren's face disappeared, and his eyes widened like a schoolboy caught cheating on a test.

"I shouldn't have to send Erech to hunt you down every time it's your turn to be at the helm," Larkos continued, his voice growing louder. "What kind of captain shirks his own duties? You owe me at least three shifts for all the times I've covered for you on this voyage."

The clomp of the older man's boots grew closer, and Gaeren scanned the extra sails and food tied down, crouching as if he might crawl between them and hide.

Aeliana's laugh gave them away, and Larkos rounded the mast, glaring at them and making Aeliana grateful it was Gaeren he was after, not her.

"I should probably get back to training." Aeliana bit her lip to hold back a second laugh when Gaeren shook his head, his eyes pleading with her to stay.

He caught the sleeve of her shirt in his fist. "At least be my alibi. Make sure he knows Sylmar wanted us training together."

"Somehow I don't think that excuse will change anything. After all, aren't you captain of the ship, not Sylmar?"

His eyes narrowed, giving her the impression that she'd managed to get under his skin this time, and she found that knowledge rewarding. As Larkos began railing at Gaeren, she gave him a mock salute and yanked her sleeve from his grasp, turning to head back to his quarters that she'd stolen.

The satisfaction stayed with her as she returned to the room, and when Iris was nowhere to be found, she decided to take advantage of her stolen time. She lay down on the bed and closed her eyes. As she reached for the tether tying her to Durriken, she wasn't sure if the smile lingering on her lips was because of her remembered time with Gaeren or the time she anticipated having with Durriken.

CHAPTER 28

After a verbal beating from Larkos, Gaeren fulfilled his shift at the wheel, his mind still on his training session with Aeliana. It was the start of a predictive pattern over the next five days: training with Aeliana in the mornings, getting berated by Larkos in the afternoons, then taking a turn at the helm until the evening.

There was no shortage of work to do on the ship, but even while working, his mind remained preoccupied with Aeliana. It shouldn't have been any different from the years before when he constantly thought about rescuing her, but now his thoughts dwelt on how much easier she laughed with him or how glimpses of the memories she shared gave him new insight to the woman she'd become instead of the toddler he'd lost.

"The men are getting restless." Larkos' gaze never left the water, and his hands remained tight on the ship's wheel.

"They usually do after fourteen days at sea," Gaeren said. "It can't help having so many extra hands on board who need even more training than Erech."

Larkos grunted his agreement.

"You haven't exactly been pleasant either," Gaeren pointed out, even though he risked receiving another dressing down. "Not since we left Elanesse. I should have let you stay home with Calia."

"You've kept me from my wife far too long. I won't deny that. But that's not what's left me irritated." He scowled at the horizon.

"Then what has?" Gaeren crossed his arms. "Get it off your chest."

Larkos glared at him. "You finally understand the Recreants, even fight alongside them. Then your sister hands you the opportunity to stay in a position of power—one you can use to aid the Recreants—and you throw it away."

Gaeren's jaw fell open. "You wanted me to stay in Elanesse?"

Larkos grumbled something unintelligible.

"What was that?"

"I don't know," the older man admitted. "I did. Thought it was the perfect setup. Maybe it still is. But something about this journey feels right. I'm trying to keep an open mind."

Gaeren grinned and shook his head, trying to imagine his first mate being so agreeable.

Larkos grunted again. "Maybe you should have Thallahan pull out his fiddle tonight."

Gaeren scanned the ship for his friend, who happened to be letting another sailor paint his eye patch. "I'm sure he'd be eager for an excuse to work even less," he said dryly.

They'd reached the Darkwater currents near Vendaras' southern tip, and Larkos adjusted the wheel more than usual to account for the unpredictable shifting currents. The flex of his forearm brought Gaeren's attention back to his Wheel of Magic tattoo. Something about it still seemed off to Gaeren. It was probably just the way the rim remained unfinished. But he studied it all the same, looking for how Larkos might have twisted the image to fit his Recreant ideals.

"You still don't like it?" Larkos asked.

"I don't like it any more or less than the rest of your tattoos."

Larkos' brow furrowed. "What's wrong with my tattoos?"

"Nothing. They're just so permanent. I can't think of anything I'd want to make that permanent on my body."

Larkos' grin turned sly beneath his beard. "Like a bond mark? How's that been feeling these days? Twitching and tingling quite a bit?"

Gaeren flinched, his hand automatically brushing what was further proof that permanently placing things on his skin was a bad idea. "You know, Fernandus basically gave me permission to cut it out."

"Is that so?" Larkos said. "Then why haven't you?"

"I've tried more than once. It'll happen when the time is right." He let his hand drift to his starlock, the renewed idea that its meaning might be connected to his bond almost more daunting than helpful. Was it significant because he should keep it? Or because he was meant to break it?

Larkos snorted. "Sometimes your vision is awfully narrow for someone trained to rule an entire nation."

Gaeren leaned back against the bulkhead. "How so? You think I should keep the bond?"

Larkos glanced back at Gaeren's palm. "Calia might think so, romantic that she is, but I suspect that bond will never fully take. Maybe it never had a chance, but it certainly doesn't now."

Gaeren frowned, trying to parse out what the older man left unsaid.

"That's not what I'm talking about anyway." Larkos held out his arm. "You keep staring at my tattoo, distracted by the faded rim and trying to figure out what that might mean, but you've never paid attention to the rest of the tattoo around it."

Gaeren leaned forward, taking in the strange scene surrounding the Wheel. He hadn't noticed it before because it connected to the rest of Larkos' tattoos, forming a sleeve on the man's arm with images all blending together. He couldn't keep track of which ones were new all the time. But now as he studied it, different elements began to stand out. Crowns and swords. A mix of winex and soldiers. It almost resembled the scene at the Myndren Mountains when they'd worked together to fight against Mayvus, but he'd gotten this tattoo long before that battle. Besides, the longer he studied it, the more he realized they were taking down a dragon.

"You have a problem with Durriken?" Gaeren asked.

Larkos huffed his irritation. "No more than the rest of the Vendarans."

Even as Larkos spoke, Gaeren finally caught the hidden meaning.

The dragon bore the Elanesse coat of arms. "Is this some sort of Recreant symbol?"

Larkos shrugged. "It's more of a reminder that as individuals we can't do much to stop the throne, but together we can take it down. One piece at a time."

His words were strangely reminiscent of something Orra had said to Gaeren a while back about needing to devour the moon one bite at a time. The image should have disturbed him. It might have a year ago, but he'd seen the way his parents abused their power and he'd also seen alternatives. Now that he saw the Wheel of Magic tattoo as part of the larger picture, it made more sense.

"Are you suggesting that by bringing down the throne, you're also going to be weakening the Wheel of Magic?" Gaeren asked.

"Your family has controlled most of the progenies over the years. Clearly not all since we saw how Mayvus stole them from the schools. But if we're not careful with how we handle the transition of power, a lot more could be at stake than our freedom. Most Recreants want an immediate power shift, but without a plan in place, the results could be detrimental—and not just for your family."

Gaeren's gut tightened as his age-old fears rose to the surface. How could they remove the monarchy without hurting his family? Would the Recreants even want to? Or were they bent on revenge?

"I think the ramifications will be bigger than even the Recreants realize," Larkos went on, shifting the ship's wheel once more as the current threatened to send them farther east. "But I'm honestly not sure if the crumbling magic system will help us take down the throne or if taking down the throne will weaken the Wheel of Magic even more."

Gaeren nodded slowly, thinking of his question for Orra about her hair, the way starlocks were no longer being handed out as frequently. But if Orra had been grounded for the last thousand years, would she even know?

The last bit of the Sun's glory sank beneath the Vendaran coast as it went to sleep. They were close to rounding the Southern Horn, and by the next Sun's sleep, they'd be aiming west instead of south, watching it sink beneath the waves instead of land.

"I wish I had an answer for you," Gaeren said, "but everything I've learned about politics has come from you. It's almost like the Recreants tasked you with training me." He laughed a bit, but the older man shot him a nervous glance.

"Just because I was tasked with it doesn't mean I was manipulating you."

Gaeren tensed before pushing off the bulkhead. "Are you saying—was I an assignment for you?"

Larkos sighed. "When a priest or a priestess is tasked by the Sun to teach the people about the Sun's glory, does that mean the servants of the Sun don't care about the worshipers? They believe in their cause and want to share it with those they care about. It doesn't matter that they were also instructed to do it. It was still done from love."

Gaeren clenched his jaw, wanting anger to brew from his frustration. "I still feel a fool for only recognizing it now."

"If it makes you feel any better, I think you would have gotten there on your own. Your parents saw to that by sending you out to sea so much. And then Enla kept sending you too."

"At her own expense," Gaeren muttered, thinking of the ways she'd suffered staying behind to take the brunt of her parents' training and focus. Not only had she become entrenched in their ways, but she was slowly going mad because of it.

"Also an act of love," Larkos pointed out. His face still held guilt.

Maybe Gaeren could have said something to alleviate the other man's discomfort. But he wasn't ready with the bruise to his pride being so fresh. "I'll go get Thallahan. Since you suggested we turn the night into a party, I assume that means you're willing to put in an extra shift at the helm."

Larkos chuckled. "It's not like I'm much of a dancer anyway."

As word spread through the ship that the reserves of ale were being brought above deck and Thallahan was pulling out his fiddle, the men rushed through the remainder of their chores, the mood on the ship already perking up thanks to Larkos' sage advice.

"I've never seen them so focused." Aeliana's eyes glinted in the moonlight. "You should motivate them with a party every night."

"You'll see why I don't in the morning when they're all crankier than ever."

She smiled, then got lost in the crowd as Thallahan began playing. The three women showed great patience in being led across the deck by the clumsy sailors, though Gaeren noticed Aeliana was just as bad. He supposed she hadn't had much training in the finer arts of dancing while being carted around Lorvandas by two Zealots and their blood magic.

Even so, the flush in her cheeks made it clear she enjoyed it, and he was quick to agree when she tugged him out on the deck for a dance. He chuckled as she stepped on his toes, then tightened his grip, forcing her to let him lead. It took her a while to relinquish the control, but when she realized their steps were smoother from his training, she gave in to following him.

He grinned down at her, appreciating the way her lips pursed in concentration as she studied their feet. Her right hand felt rough against his, the scars of her past a painful barrier between them. It didn't matter that he'd been a child. He would always feel responsible for all she'd gone through, and he still felt burdened to protect her. He tightened his hold on the small of her back, drawing her slightly closer, and his bond mark twinged.

As they spun, he caught sight of Larkos on the other side of the main mast where he watched their revelry from the helm, a knowing look in his eye. Their earlier talk of bonds came back to Gaeren's mind, making him miss a step as he grew flustered.

Aeliana laughed, and his skin's tingling response made Gaeren further aware of the way he felt more alive in her presence. His heart beat faster and his starlock warmed against his chest. In this moment, the idea of cutting out his bond mark was clearly not an act to free Lenda but rather an act to free himself.

Except he still didn't know if that made it any more right or any more wrong.

"Whale on starboard!" a sailor in the crow's nest called down just as a gentle nudge against the ship knocked Aeliana closer into

Gaeren's embrace. He tightened his grip to steady her, and her eyes grew wide.

"A whale?"

"They're harmless," he said.

She scanned the deck as if it might suddenly appear on board, but her gaze landed on Velden. "Is there such a thing as a giant squid?"

The sudden change of topic made Gaeren pause. "You mean the kraken? They exist, but they stay in the deepest parts of the water. Sometimes I wonder if they're a bit like Durriken and maybe only one or two still exist. I'd love to see if Riveran could tame one. All creatures seem to take to him."

The music stopped, and several of the Recreants stepped to the side of the boat to glimpse the whale. Aeliana and Gaeren joined them, and she exclaimed in delight as the whale shot water from its blowhole.

"Have you heard Velden's story about his Awakening?" she asked.

"He told you about his Awakening?" Awakenings were private affairs by tradition, but maybe Velden's Sayhleen background left him more open about it. For all Gaeren knew, Sayhleens might share their story with everyone they met. Still… "I think any story told by Velden is likely exaggerated."

Her carefree smile widened, drawing his gaze. "That's a good point."

As the whale moved on, the others returned to gather around the main mast, but Thallahan had a glass of ale in his hands and seemed to be taking a break from his fiddle.

"Any chance you're as good a storyteller as your father?" Cyrus asked Brogdon.

Gaeren tensed, wondering if the question would offend Brogdon. But the petite man just smiled and shook his head. "No one could tell stories like my father."

A few people raised their glasses, and the gazes around the circle of sailors and Recreants grew more solemn.

"And no one could burn food like Breeve," Thallahan added, bringing about a round of chuckles and more raised glasses.

"They're in a better place now," Cyrus said. While Gaeren believed that to be true, it didn't remove his sorrow that they'd been taken from the world too soon.

"Maybe Velden could tell us a bit about Sayhla Island," Gaeren suggested.

"He's never been there," Aeliana said.

"True," Velden admitted, swirling his glass of rum as if it were fine wine at a dinner party. "But my mother spoke of her homeland often. It was clear she missed Paelen's Waters and Sayhla Island whenever she was here. Always made me wonder why she didn't just stay there."

"Probably because she loved you more," Iris said.

Velden smiled wistfully. "My mother was beautiful, I'm guessing even for a Sayhleen. She had red scales from the waist down with a single tail and fin, which spread out like a rainbow of shimmery skin. She told me they all have different colors and shades, and some have two fins while others have none."

"Is it true that some are like sirens and others more like people?" a sailor asked.

"Sirens haven't been seen since the Great Divide." Velden set down his glass. "They're predators, like lions of the sea. They reel men in with their wordless songs to devour them. My mother was nothing like that, and she never gave me the impression that the other Sayhleens were either."

He held up his webbed hands before his own eyes, as if seeing them for the first time. "But you're right that physically they're probably a cross between the two. On land, they look and function like half-lights, but in water, they all form gills and scales, allowing them to dive deeper than any warm-blooded half-light should be able to. Some only gain webbed hands and feet like me, while others form full tails and fins below their waist." His tone turned forlorn.

What would they find on Sayhla Island? *If* they ever managed to find the starbridge in Andel…

"It's said they were cursed or blessed by the sprites," Velden said, "depending on how you look at it. A man came to them asking for the ability to dive deep and swim leagues. They twisted his request into forming a new race, subjecting him and his family to a life so tied to the water they could never leave."

"That definitely sounds like the sprites," Gaeren muttered.

Velden's eyebrows rose in satisfaction. "And yet...they worship the sprites."

"What?" Cyrus asked, his face holding the same shock that Gaeren felt.

"Think about it." Velden leaned forward, elbows on his knees. "Vendarans worship the Sun because they believe it created them. Lorvandans worship the Stars because they believe they created them. If Sayhleens believe sprites created them, why would they not worship them?"

"Because they're terribly cruel?" Gaeren suggested, and Riveran snorted from beside him.

"Well, where do the sprites come from?" Cyrus asked.

"Where do the winex come from?" Sylmar countered. "Or the dragons? They're created the same as any other creature."

Gaeren frowned. He supposed that made sense. But unlike the winex and dragon, who seemed to have the choice to seek good or evil, all the sprites seemed bent on twisting truth and causing havoc.

"That might be a better question for Orra," Gaeren said. "There's something evil about the sprites. I'm not sure how they could have been created by the Sun just like anything else."

Cyrus nodded, his show of support surprising when he still likely believed the Stars to be the creators.

Riveran leaned over, his words for Gaeren's ears only. "I've thought the same ever since that blackness came out of the one I killed."

Gaeren stilled as his mind went back to the moment they'd escaped the sprites. It had been chaos, and they still didn't know which deal the sprites had taken, if any. But Riveran had killed the sprite they'd bartered with, and in that moment, a darkness had fluttered out of the sprite and escaped from the cave.

Gaeren had wondered if they'd released something far worse into the world with that action, but then he'd forgotten about it. Now, Riveran's reminder combined with more recent events brought a truth that made him go cold all over, despite the warmer breezes in the southern currents.

"It was a dark spirit," Gaeren whispered.

"What?" Riveran asked.

"I saw them enter Arvid and Mayvus. The dark spirits that feed on blood magic. I thought the ones in Myndren were the first I'd seen, but you're right. A dark spirit came from the sprite."

"What are you saying?" Riveran asked. "That the sprites fuse with dark spirits? That they're doing blood magic?"

Gaeren shook his head slowly, remembering the way the dark spirit had been evident in Arvid and Mayvus, how their eyes had turned black and smoke had come from their ears and nose. The cold darkness he'd sensed from the spirits hadn't been present in the cave. Not until Riveran had killed the sprite.

"I'm saying we may not know where sprites come from, but now we know where dark spirits come from. They're dead sprites."

CHAPTER 29

ORRA FOLLOWED the path around the lower bailey until she reached the weakest part of the wall, where the winex worked alongside the soldiers. Sixteen days into their cycle, they were at their prime—able to lift twice as much as the soldiers. But several of them grumbled and dragged their feet as they laid stones and mortar to strengthen the ramparts. They took their cue from Felk, who hadn't quite settled in with the people this time around. Perhaps it was because he'd only had one day with Aeliana before she'd set sail.

"Day eleven and no sign of Mayvus," General Nels said as he came up behind her.

She kept her tone even as she turned. "I already told you she went back to Ahmranas five days ago."

"And yet our soldiers lost sleep pulling extra guard duty the last few days on the off chance you were wrong and she still came, arriving early by boat."

She turned back to the winex. "That decision was not suggested by me."

"It's awfully convenient that she went back so fast."

"You don't have to be coy about it. You think I'm covering my tracks because I was wrong. But I'm telling you the truth."

"And you know this because the braid on your wrist hums." His words held a disbelief so thick it bordered on disrespect.

"I won't pretend to understand the way you direct your men, so I don't expect you to understand the way my magic works." She stepped forward and called out to the winex. "I have your fish laid out in the kitchen."

Several of the soldiers turned and made faces, but the winex all loped toward her, weaving around her with tongues lolling in their eagerness, nearly knocking General Nels over in their zeal. Orra hid a smile as he cursed and dodged out of their way.

She'd started feeding the winex separately from the soldiers because the men couldn't stomach watching the winex eat, especially now that there were so many of them. As she followed them in and served up their plates, some of the creatures thanked her, but most merely grunted.

She wasn't sure if it was the particular labor the soldiers had asked them to do this cycle, or if Emeris hadn't shown them enough memories of their past cycles, but she suspected some of the winex were unhappy enough to leave before Aeliana and the others returned. She settled in a chair next to Felk, folding her hands under her chin as she studied him.

"What?" Fish and spittle flew from his mouth with the question.

Orra ignored his poor manners. "Immortality is a difficult thing. It sounds enviable. But it comes with burdens others don't feel."

His brow furrowed, and juice from the fish dripped down his chin back into the bowl. The tear mark on his cheek that made him stand out from all the others felt poignantly symbolic of the weight he carried with his constant rebirth.

"Why are you telling me that?" Felk asked.

"I imagine having infinite lives and no memories would come with similar burdens that others couldn't understand."

He slowly spooned a fish head into his mouth while holding her gaze, and Orra tried not to grimace at the way his dozens of teeth mutilated the flesh. "Maybe," he said around the mouthful.

Even though they were full-grown and past their middle age, he still had a sullenness that normally only appeared in the first third of his cycle, when his attitude was that of an adolescent. "Maybe forgetting my past lives is a gift that keeps getting taken when you people give me memories." A flicker of hatred that shocked Orra crossed his face.

Perhaps they'd pushed their luck in having the winex stay with them for so long. Or perhaps the Sun had never intended for them to relate in this way.

She knew he'd questioned the need for sharing memories, but she hadn't realized it might have felt intrusive to a fresh start. "I suppose when Emeris and Gaeren gave you memories, it gave you the burdens of immortality instead of infinite lives," she mused.

"We know how to start over each month. How to nest and prepare. When you make us do something else, it feels wrong, even if you say you'll help us transition."

She nodded, understanding far more than he probably realized. "And yet we haven't helped you as much this cycle. You feel like slaves."

His gaze darted around the room as if afraid they might be overheard. Perhaps it was something the winex had discussed. Or perhaps he feared there would be some sort of retaliation for his rebellious words.

"The gates are currently open," she said. "No one will prevent you from leaving if you so choose. But know that in a future cycle, you will be prevented from returning. We have survival instincts as well."

He nodded slowly, and it looked like he might say more, but a hum started in Orra's braid, and she lost all awareness of her surroundings. She closed her eyes, wrapping her fingers around the braid to absorb the life flowing through it. She longed to reach out the way she had with the arrow, to let her soul leave her body and follow the thread connecting the braid to the stone. But her power remained limited. Following the stone could drain her completely.

"Miss Orra?" Felk mumbled. "You all right?"

Her eyes fluttered open, the sounds of a dozen winex smacking and slurping their fish soup bringing her back to her present reality. "She's come back again," she whispered.

Emeris glared at General Nels, whose face remained stubbornly skeptical.

"You said this almost two weeks ago." General Nels and two other generals sat across from Orra and Emeris in the quarters they'd deemed the war room. Outside of chairs, desks, and maps, the room was bare and scrubbed thoroughly clean since it had been one of the rooms overtaken by winex in the fight against Mayvus' Zealots.

"As I said," Orra repeated, barely holding on to her patience, "she left seventeen days ago, then returned eleven days ago, then left five days ago, and now she's returned again."

"We would be fools not to listen to her," Emeris said. "If Mayvus is going back and forth, she's rebuilding her army."

General Nels sighed and glanced at the other generals. One shifted in his chair, glancing out the window as if Mayvus might somehow fly through the glass at any moment, but the other remained stoic and unreadable.

"I will continue to keep our normal guard up, but I will also inform the men of your… update," he conceded. "But I can't put out any extras. I can't make the men labor all day and stay on guard all night."

"Perhaps instead of waiting for her to come," Orra suggested, "we should go look for her. I told you the stone drops her off at Ahmranan's Viewpoint."

"It would take a week or more for me to send scouts," General Nels pointed out. "Isn't it likely she'll leave again before they get there?"

She shrugged off his irritation. "She might be gone, but whatever army she's building will have to wait for her return."

General Nels' lips thinned into a grim line. "We can see how big of an army she's bringing back."

Orra nodded, a headache forming between her eyes. "I have no idea how many she can bring at a time. But at some point, she'll stop finding recruits to bring back, and she'll start marching south. If we can see where her numbers are at now, it will give us an idea of how likely we are to maintain a defense with our soldiers."

The three men exchanged glances, and General Nels stood. "Thank you for the update."

Orra adopted a serene smile, ignoring the way he struggled to acknowledge the full value of the information she'd brought.

"We'll keep you posted on what our scouts find."

"Should we send Gullet after Riveran with a note?" Emeris asked, brow pinched.

The men all frowned in hesitation, but General Nels eventually shook his head. "Let's see what the scouts have to say first."

"I wish there were a way to let my husband know," Emeris said.

General Nels and Orra exchanged a glance, only this time it was a shared concern.

"Rildan is in the fortress," Orra said gently. "We can go see him now and let him know."

Emeris' gaze clouded over. "That's right. So much has changed…"

As her words faded, the generals left with respectful bows and purposeful steps, but the uneasy sensation lingered in the room.

"I found more of Mayvus' research," Emeris added, and Orra couldn't help noting the other woman waited to share this after the generals had left. For all their loyalty as Recreant soldiers, she seemed to trust them even less than Orra did.

"What else was she up to?"

Emeris sighed. "It seems she wasn't content with just the stone either."

Orra went still, her hands itching to hold the arrow once more, her heart regretting her decision to let Gaeren leave with it in his possession. "Did she have any of the others?"

"I'm not sure, but she seemed to know the silver fish was in Andel. She may have already gotten it."

"Making our mission failed before it had even begun," Orra mused. "She always seems to be five steps ahead."

Emeris nodded. "She also believed combining the starbridges would give her immortality."

Orra flinched. "How so?"

"She didn't say. But it not only confirms Aeliana and Sylmar's theory that immortality has been her ultimate goal—it proves she had multiple methods in the works."

An uneasiness settled over Orra. Did Mayvus know what would happen when the starbridges were united? The Sun's prophecy had told Orra she'd receive help combining them, but it hadn't said anything about the half-light's motivation. What if it wasn't Aeliana or Gaeren who was meant to help her? What if it was Mayvus, except she had far darker purposes in mind?

"I'm grateful Aeliana won't be here when she comes," Emeris said.

Orra pulled herself from her thoughts, from the temptation to reach for Mayvus' future. It wouldn't show her what she wanted. Magic didn't work on Stars, not even their own magic, which meant Orra could never see anything perfectly if she was involved. It would be a waste.

Instead, she tried focusing on the half-light here with her, in the present. "What did you say?"

"I think we got a bit lucky last time," Emeris said. "I don't want Aeliana to be here when Mayvus returns." She studied her hands, letting them twist together in her lap.

"Hmm." Orra sensed something deeper behind the other woman's words. "But aren't there things you didn't have a chance to tell her?"

The high priestess' gaze shot to Orra's. "The timing wasn't right. The Sun hadn't sanctioned it."

Orra nodded slowly. "And now you're worried you won't have any time at all."

Emeris bit her lip and looked away.

"If your fears should come to pass, do you wish for me to tell her your secret?" Orra understood the weight of such a layered secret. How the knowledge could both free and completely undo someone.

"If the timing is right." Emeris' brow still furrowed.

"Only if the Sun wills it," Orra promised. "Or not at all."

The other woman's features finally relaxed, and she reached over to squeeze Orra's hand. "Thank you."

A faint glow hovered in the room, likely not noticeable to Emeris' half-light eyes, but Orra held her breath, basking in its presence. It reminded her of her days communing with worshipers in the Sungazers, guiding them to follow the Sun, helping them through problems large and small in a simple conversation, just like she'd done with Emeris now.

She blinked back tears, longing for what had once been but knowing it was beyond her reach. She squeezed Emeris' hand back. "Thank *you*," she whispered.

CHAPTER 30

As they pulled into Andel's harbor, Aeliana's jaw dropped. The city seemed to stretch on as far as she could see along the coast as well as inland. They passed ships at least three times the size of *To the Deep and Back*, with masts towering high above. Brightly colored homes dotted the cliffs, the structure surprisingly similar to the fortress in the Myndren Mountains. The cheerful view made her want to repaint the fortress, perhaps bring back its former glory as a Sungazer, if Orra's stories of its origin could be believed.

She joined Gaeren at the helm, eager for a better view and curious how he'd maneuver the boat through such congested waters.

"You're a natural sailor," Gaeren said.

Aeliana laughed to hide how much that compliment pleased her. "What does it look like to be a natural?"

"Haven't you noticed Holm has been stuck down in his room, sick as a dog?"

She grimaced. "Fair enough. I wonder if that doesn't bode well for him when we find the starbridge and travel to Paelen's waters."

Gaeren shifted the wheel and called out instructions to the sailors, the change in direction making the wind ruffle his hair. He turned back to her, eyebrows raised. "Do you think it's likely we'll find it? The starbridge?"

Doubt niggled at the back of Aeliana's mind, but she refused to give in to it. "We have to in order to save my mother, so we will." She ran her hand over the smooth wooden rail separating her from the water. "It will be hard to leave the water for land again."

"It always is," Gaeren murmured.

Aeliana hadn't expected to enjoy sailing as much as she did. At first, she'd been like a passenger, wandering aimlessly along the deck to enjoy the occasional spray of water from the ship's edge. But as they'd progressed down the eastern coast of Vendaras, she'd found herself learning from the sailors. More than once, Iris had pointed out she was only able to climb the rigging because she'd finally given in to wearing trousers. It was true, but Aeliana wasn't going to admit that to Iris.

"Despite being the capital, Elanesse is probably half the size of this city. This is a good place for you to practice pulling back on your access to memories. In crowds you'll get flooded with glimpses that you have to push away, or they'll overwhelm you."

She grimaced, wishing her connection to Durriken hadn't altered her magic. She still couldn't heal as much and she hadn't gotten the strength of her light shields back, and she found that she missed that part of her magic.

"It's not all bad," Gaeren said with a smile, misinterpreting her disappointment. "I always wanted to travel through Andel and lose myself in it, but I usually had an entourage that made it impossible not to be recognized. Probably kept me safer, but I would have preferred the anonymity."

"Are you in danger coming here now?" Aeliana asked.

"Probably not? Larkos claims the southern Recreants aren't concerned about me after hearing how I left, but I can't help wondering if there could be a few rogue people who still don't care for my bloodline."

Aeliana shuddered. "It would be nice if we found the starbridge quickly, but with a city this size and an artifact being lost for so long, I doubt we can expect it."

"I don't have my hopes up either." He scratched at his bond mark, drawing Aeliana's attention.

"Is your bondmate bothered by the fact that you haven't returned?"

Gaeren hesitated, making Aeliana wonder if her question was too personal, but then he shrugged. "Lenda and I have never been as close as we should be for bondmates. My sister actually wanted me to break our bond."

Aeliana's eyebrows rose. "Whatever for?"

"I'm starting to wonder if she wanted me to be free to leave again. It's hard to tell when her advice changes on a whim depending on what visions she sees."

"I suppose you'll go back after all this. Continue on as throne warden." She let her real question hang there, unspoken between them. Was there any chance he'd remain with the Recreants? She didn't feel like she had a right to the answer, but she wanted it anyway.

"I'm not sure I'll be welcomed back after the way I left, but I'm determined to go back for Winter Solstice. Thallahan is getting married, so it's as good a reason to return as any." He stared down at his bond mark, and the sadness and confusion on his face reflected everything Aeliana felt about her own bond.

"If she gave you permission to break it, why haven't you?"

A rueful smile crossed Gaeren's face. "Because I'm a coward?"

Aeliana scoffed. "I don't think anyone could say that about you."

"I thought Riveran broke his bond with my sister. I found out later, very recently, that it was my parents who forced them to break their bond. Riveran wasn't good enough for them because he hadn't earned a starlock."

Aeliana glanced at Riveran, who sat repairing a net on the other side of the ship. He'd begun growing out his hair, and while it still had a long way to go to hide the X on his forehead, the thick darkness across his scalp made it stand out a bit less, drawing more attention to his gentle smile. "Riveran would make an excellent queen's consort. What would it matter if he had a starlock or not?"

"In some ways the royal family is as power-hungry as Mayvus. They might not seek it out with blood magic, but they are determined to keep high concentrations of starblood in the royal line. Enla's descendants wouldn't be guaranteed to be progenies if their father wasn't one. At least, that was the thinking. No one's guaranteed to be a progeny regardless of their starblood concentration. Not anymore."

Aeliana's hand drifted to her starlock, which she kept tucked under her shirt and out of sight. It warmed against her skin in a reassuring way. "I take it you didn't enjoy seeing their bond get broken?"

Gaeren's frown deepened, and Aeliana regretted her question. "My sister's pain was excruciating. There was physical pain, but it was more that she was emotionally broken. Riveran had been the center of her life. They'd grown up loving each other in a way that Lenda and I never experienced. I don't know if it was the bond or if they would have loved each other anyway.

"I tried taking the pain from her by removing the memories and almost broke both of our minds. My mentor at the time was able to rein in my magic. But I've been cautious ever since about how much I use my ability to take memories. It's one thing to receive them willingly, and it's another to take them by force. And removing them completely? Even if I had been ready at that point in my life, that level of magic would have done permanent damage."

Aeliana couldn't help thinking of Marnok. Had someone done the same to him? And yet he'd gotten some of his memories back from her mother. What secrets did he still hold? If he wasn't an enemy, why hadn't he shared who he was?

"Your bond doesn't seem to be taking any better than mine." Gaeren grinned, enjoying pointing that out far too much.

Before she could respond, Velden leaped onto the helm and dragged Aeliana across the deck. "There's the Naval Yard where I trained." He pointed out a shipyard that kept its cargo sealed off by stone walls. "Ludo and Barny still work there, and I have three good guesses of where to find them tonight."

Aeliana welcomed the distraction. "Barny?"

He grinned. "Short for barnacle. When you see him, you'll understand why."

"Who are they?"

"My old naval buddies." His excitement was contagious.

"I never understood why the navy trained down here to protect the king and queen up north."

Velden nodded. "It's become a bit of a farce. Several Loyalists come down here, expecting to hold on to their ways, but out here the hatred for the royal family runs deep enough that most are converted to Recreants. It wasn't as bad when I was a recruit thirty years ago, but Ludo says it's pretty impossible to support the crown in Andel. Fewer people are getting starlocks, and the ones who do stay north with the nobility. It's widening the economic disparity between the regions and the people enough that it's a hard split."

Aeliana glanced back at Gaeren, her concern for his safety heightening. Larkos had joined him, and they pointed at various docks, arguing over where to berth. "Do we need to encourage him to wear a disguise?"

"In some ways it might be better for him to get his identity out in the open and deal with it as it comes." Velden leaned over the edge, letting his webbed hands pull in the water's spray. "It could be a rough transition, but in the end word will spread faster that he's a Recreant supporter if he doesn't hide himself."

They continued passing ships at docks, drawing closer to the large buildings that likely made up the center of the city. The ships they passed in the bay area all held fisherman and lay workers, their tanned skin making even Gaeren look pale. Most of them stared with narrowed eyes at Cyrus, probably equally confused by his long red hair as they were by his pale and freckled flesh.

The Sun sank lower in the sky, partially blocked by the other half of the city they hadn't even sailed by yet.

"When did you last visit?" Aeliana asked.

Velden's gaze hardened. "I don't visit. I haven't been here since my mother was killed twenty-five years ago."

"I'm so sorry, Velden."

"I stuck around for a few moons to take care of my father, but a lot of him died with her." He hesitated. "He never really knew what to make of me. He always wanted a son, but he didn't know how to share me with the people around him when I was so different. I think without my mother, there was very little we had in common."

"Are you going to see him now?"

"He died a long time ago. But I'll visit my old naval friends. I've kept in touch with them over the years, and they'll share anything with me that they think can help our search."

"Twenty-five years is a long time to go without seeing people you call friends," Aeliana mused. "You and Sylmar met up fourteen years ago when he left Mayvus, right? So what did you do all those years before that?"

A ghost of a smile crossed Velden's face. "Every man should have a secret or two, shouldn't he?"

A hand settled on Aeliana's shoulder, and she turned to find Lukai's eager grin.

"I can't wait to get off this ship."

She stiffened, unsure if she wanted to defend Gaeren's brig for his sake or out of spite. She'd avoided Lukai for much of the rest of the voyage, partly because she'd spent so much time training and partly because she didn't know what more to say to him.

Maybe the more she let Lukai flirt with Kendalyhn, the sooner he'd come around to wanting to break his bond with Aeliana. Besides, she still found Lukai's direct betrayal of handing her blood over to Sylmar far less forgivable than Gaeren's status and connection to old family feuds.

"I'm going to miss the rhythm of sailing." She surreptitiously stepped to the side to peek over the rail, forcing Lukai to drop his hand. Velden stalked off toward Iris, likely pointing out all the same haunts he'd shown Aeliana, but Kendalyhn filled his empty spot, which was no surprise now that Aeliana was watching for the way she dogged Lukai.

"Seems like we have a lot of ground to cover." For once the pessimistic woman's irritation seemed warranted.

The silence between the three of them grew uncomfortable.

"I suppose I should gather my things," Aeliana said.

Lukai placed a staying hand on her arm. "We're staying on the ship at night. There's no need."

"Well, at least my satchel. Velden plans to take us into town right away."

"I'll get it for you," he offered, stepping away before she could even protest.

Kendalyhn snorted, tucking stray strands of short dark hair behind her ears—a losing battle with the sea breeze. She had a fierce beauty that didn't line up with her small frame. Aeliana pictured that fascinating incongruity being part of what had made Lukai fall in love with her in the first place.

Kendalyhn turned her glare on Aeliana. "What are you staring at?"

There wasn't any answer that would make her happy, so Aeliana didn't bother trying. "I know you and Lukai had a thing before I came. I'm sorry."

Kendalyhn huffed. "You're sorry," she muttered.

The silence stretched, but for once it wasn't uncomfortable. It was almost as if having that truth out in the open loosened the taut strings between them. Gaeren and Larkos eased the ship against the dock, and the sailors went into a frenzy, dropping the anchor and tying up sails.

"Will you always hate me?" Aeliana asked.

Kendalyhn gave a short laugh. "It's an interesting question. My answer might have been yes if I hadn't sifted Gaeren's soul."

Aeliana frowned. "Gaeren? What does he have to do with anything?"

"When we first found him, he was one big bundle of confusion." She leaned forward, a sly tilt to her head. "Loving the memory of you as a child, hating the family you represented. Hating who you should have been, but not quite sure what to think of who you actually were. Usually when I sense hatred, there's a wall. A desire for indifference at best in those who have integrity, an ugly desire for their enemies' death, even pain, in those who don't. But he was far too curious for pure hatred. He was anything but indifferent."

Her carefully chosen words stirred something in Aeliana's gut. She tried to keep the reaction hidden, but Kendalyhn was likely sifting the edges of her soul whether Aeliana wanted her in there or not, sensing her response even if she couldn't experience it in full like she did when she had physical contact and sifted someone's past. She was likely seeing the hope Aeliana felt, maybe misinterpreting it for something more. Unless it was Aeliana who was misinterpreting her own confused heart.

"And now?" she asked, hating herself for succumbing to Kendaly-hn's bait.

"Now is always fuzzy. My spoke's strength is sifting the past. But in the most recent past, he's still confused, for different reasons." The right side of her mouth curved in a frustrating smirk. She wasn't going to give Aeliana any straight answers.

"I don't understand why that changes anything," Aeliana said. "If Gaeren doesn't hate me, why would that make you hate me any less?"

Kendalyhn gave her a scathing look. "I don't know if it does. We'll have to see how it plays out." Her piercing gaze made Aeliana feel even more exposed than when Kendalyhn had held her palms and sifted her soul. "The problem is, I can't decide if I should hate you for taking away Lukai's love for me or because you're not loving him back."

Aeliana stilled, the familiar tightening in her gut almost making her nauseous.

Kendalyhn glared up at Aeliana. "If he and I can't be happy together, at least make him happy. That would help me hate you a little less." She stalked away, leaving Aeliana alone to wrestle with her guilt.

"Ready?" Velden called out to no one in particular, rubbing his slimy hands together. "The day is just beginning for my old friends. I hope you all know how to hold your liquor."

CHAPTER 31

"Ah, there he is." Velden's face lit up with a grin as he led Gaeren and a handful of others from their group to the back corner of the fourth pub they'd tried that evening. He stopped at a table where an eerily still lump of clothing and shaggy hair remained affixed to its chair, the half-full mug in front of it the only evidence that it might truly be a man.

"You're alive." The gruff words escaping the man managed to sound pleased, and Gaeren caught a glimpse of shiny brown eyes between strands of hair. If he stood, he'd likely rival Holm in height and girth, but it was hard to tell if his size was due to an abnormally large number of layers of clothes or actual muscle and fat. It made Gaeren sweat a little more, uncertain why anyone would voluntarily suffocate themselves in the heat of southern Vendaras.

Velden slapped the other man on the back. "You sound surprised. Everyone, this is Barny." He gestured toward the lump of clothes. "Barny, meet everyone."

Aeliana and Cyrus each gave a small wave, but Sylmar and Riveran simply pulled out chairs and sat. Lukai brought a chair from an extra table, passing it off to Kendalyhn, so Gaeren did the same for Aeliana before claiming one for himself.

Velden flipped one around and straddled it, leaning in close to his friend. "Where's old Ludo? I figured he'd beat you here."

Barny grunted and lifted his mug to his lips.

"It's that wife of his, isn't it?" Velden asked. "Ludo always swore he'd never become like our stuffy professors. And look at him now—married, staying home, and teaching all the young bucks down at the naval academy."

This time Barny's grunt sounded more like a laugh, and his layers of fabric shook. "He'll come," was all he said.

Velden grinned and raised a hand to hail a waitress. "Barny's a man of few words, if you couldn't tell."

As the waitress came and took their orders, Barny slowly scanned the newcomers. His eyes narrowed when he took in Gaeren, but he didn't say anything. Gaeren could have kicked his father's advisors for insisting portraits of the royal family be placed all over the continent. Would he have to start wearing a hooded cloak or shear his hair? On the flip side, Barny's lips lifted as he took in Riveran's X. Maybe that would be a sign of honor down in these parts.

Just as the waitress took their final order and gave Velden a wink, the door to the pub creaked open. Several shouted out greetings to a man with greying hair and a grin that rivaled Velden's.

The half-Sayhleen jumped to his feet. "Ludo," he called out.

The other man's grin grew impossibly larger and the two ran at each other, their reunion looking more like two schoolboys rough-housing than old friends meeting up. Gaeren glanced at Riveran, feeling a strange sense of gratefulness that they were back in each other's good graces.

"As slimy as always. And I see you brought friends." Ludo wiped his hands on his trousers and scanned the group in surprise. "Lots of friends. I didn't think you were capable of having so many."

"And I didn't think you were capable of snagging a wife." Velden jabbed the other man's shoulder.

Despite the low lighting of the pub, Gaeren caught a blush rising in the other man's cheeks. "I was just waiting for the right woman. One who cooks me dinner, turns in early, and still lets me come to the pub at night."

Barny's clothes jiggled again, and Velden shook his head. "You still became everything we despised when we were young. No matter how you paint the picture."

"I seem to remember you giving it a try once," Ludo said. "Besides, it could be a worse life."

He took Velden's chair for his own, studying everyone a little closer while Velden grabbed a new one. Just like Barny, his gaze settled on Gaeren a moment longer than the others, his silence speaking more of an enhanced alertness than a dismissal of Gaeren's heritage.

"Now," Ludo drawled. "Tell me why we're having a party tonight."

Velden introduced everyone around the table, making no effort to hide Gaeren's identity, but instead heralding the way he'd defied his parents to protect Emeris' daughter. Sylmar's staff jabbed Velden a few times when his lengthy introductions spilled more information than they should, but the longer Velden talked, the more Ludo and Barny relaxed.

He left Cyrus for last, because most of their plan centered on a half-lie they'd concocted about his quest for truth.

"Cyrus here is a priest-in-training, but he has little to no starblood." Velden stretched his webbed hands out toward the fidgeting younger man.

"That explains why I can practically see through him," Ludo squinted at Cyrus. "His freckles are unusual though. Where're you from, lad?"

Cyrus' smile faltered, and Gaeren inwardly groaned. His priestly nature was going to ruin their story. Cyrus had tied his hair in a knot and hidden it under a cap, but the moment he opened his mouth, it would all be over.

Gaeren leaned forward, drawing Ludo's and Barny's attention. "Would you believe me if I said the royal family has a strange obsession with collecting those with little starblood? I suspect my ancestors watched for them each time they tested the people's blood for their children's bonding ceremonies."

It wasn't a direct lie, and he said it with such earnestness that even Aeliana looked a bit rankled.

"Wouldn't surprise me one bit," Ludo admitted. "They probably take satisfaction in surrounding themselves with people they think are far lower than themselves."

Gaeren did his best to hide his wince by gripping his knees a little tighter. The man was only saying things Gaeren had said about his own family. It shouldn't bother him to hear others say it too. Aeliana's hand twitched as if she might place a steadying hand on his arm, and his bond mark twinged its disapproval that he wished she would.

"Because of Cyrus' lack of starblood," Velden went on, "he's become a bit of a historian and collector. He's out to prove history's veracity. Which brought us here."

"Velden says you two know where to find everything on the market," Cyrus said. "Every *kind* of market."

Gaeren wanted to smack his hand over Cyrus' mouth at his lack of subtlety.

Barny took a long swig of his ale, and Ludo let out a guffaw. "He's not one to beat around the bush, is he?"

Velden rolled his eyes. "It's more a lack of social grace than efficiency."

"So you're actually a group of treasure hunters," Ludo said. "That's what you've become now, Velden?"

Velden shrugged, his lazy grin returning. Ludo and Barny didn't seem at all put out by the idea.

"What treasures do you seek? The Fearsome Pirate Redwood's lost ship? Queen Amaya's crown jewels?" Ludo's gaze strayed to Gaeren again. "I suppose if he doesn't know where they are, no one does."

"Anything, really," Cyrus said. "Send us to the best contacts with information on the oldest of artifacts—even the starbridges themselves."

Gaeren tensed. They'd agreed not to bring up the starbridges, but in Cyrus' nervousness, of course he'd gone and done exactly that.

This time it wasn't just Barny's clothes that jiggled. His entire body shifted, his laughter finally audible. He shook his head and took a long draw of his ale.

"Well, that would keep you busy for the rest of your lives." Ludo slapped the table in his glee. "Assuming you didn't give up when you realized they didn't exist."

Gaeren was tempted to pull the golden arrow from his pocket. These men may have been Velden's friends, but their banter was currently more irritating than fun.

"I guess there are worse things you could have come back for." Ludo's eyes held regret the moment the words left his lips.

A dark look passed over Velden's face, something so foreign he almost looked like a stranger. "Be grateful they convinced me to come back at all."

Ludo pursed his lips, eyeing each member of the group as if weighing their worth. Perhaps he assumed they were all swindling Velden, or maybe he thought they were blackmailing him, but when his gaze finally settled on Cyrus, who nonchalantly leaned back on two legs of the chair before managing to spill not only his ale, but himself, all over the floor, the old naval officer grinned. "I might have a few leads for you."

They spoke well into the night, gathering a list of museums, collectors, and black market traders in the area who might have heard rumors about ancient artifacts. The starbridges weren't brought up again, and Lukai and Kendalyhn even spent a fair amount of time referencing dragon bones to misdirect their focus.

Barny's contributions came in one-word grunts that Ludo translated, which was the only evidence that the quiet man was equally invested in helping Velden. The list was overwhelming as it was, but as they said their goodbyes, Ludo added, "Stubs might have some more ideas if we can find him."

Velden's smile fell. "It was a shame to hear about Dirk."

Ludo's eyes held a new heaviness. "We can't all live to be ancient."

"How did it happen?"

Ludo and Barny exchanged a glance. "Just a freak accident at sea," Ludo mumbled.

"It's even worse that Stubs took it so hard," Velden added. "It's like you lost two friends instead of one."

Ludo's grin returned. "Which is why it feels so good to get one back. Even if it's temporary."

As Gaeren and the others rose to leave, Ludo sat back down, calling the waitress over for another drink. "You know where to find us if those leads are dead ends. We'll keep cheering you on from our place here." He lifted his nearly empty cup, and Velden responded by squirting him in the face with water from his hand.

"Your tune might be different if we'd promised you part of the spoils."

"Rightly so." Ludo passed that same cautious gaze over their group and settled it warily on Gaeren. "But something tells me I don't want any part of what you all are up to."

Velden spun his chair on one leg until it faced forward once more and tucked it under the table. "I knew getting married made you less fun."

Ludo raised his cup higher. "You all take care of my old friend. I don't want to wait another twenty-five years before I see him again."

CHAPTER 32

BY THE TIME they returned to the ship, most everyone was ready to sleep, determined to start fresh and early in the morning by divvying up Ludo's list. Gaeren waffled over whether this was the right direction to take. The sprites had told him the starbridge was nailed on a boat in Andel's harbor. He suspected they'd have more luck searching the boats than looking for black market traders or museums, but how could he explain that without giving up his source of information?

His gaze swept over the hundreds of boats in the harbor before he slipped below deck, and the deeper he went into the belly of his ship, the more his hope sank with him. Even if he told them what the sprites had said, searching that many boats would be impossible.

He stepped around several sailors already passed out for the night in their overstuffed quarters. Just as Gaeren reached to remove his trousers, Larkos elbowed his side.

"Ready to head out?"

Gaeren started. "Now? Where would you want to go at this time of night?"

Thallahan rose from his bed, fully dressed, and gave Gaeren a wink while adjusting his eye patch. Erech joined them, practically bouncing from foot to foot in his excitement.

"There's something we want to show you." Without any more

explanation, Larkos headed back toward the stairs to the upper deck, Thallahan and Erech in tow.

Gaeren swore under his breath. Those cryptic words might have been the only thing that could convince him to keep his pants on and head back to land.

Instead of answering Gaeren's questions, Larkos gave him mundane updates about the ship and sailors while they wove their way through the docks, and Erech peppered them with questions about the various ships. Gaeren sensed his first mate growing more tense and wary, but Thallahan seemed to loosen up the farther they got from the ship. Before they made it very far into town, Larkos pulled out a strip of cloth, regret on his face.

"It's not that *I* don't trust you…" He let the words hang until Gaeren grasped their meaning.

"You're taking me to meet with southern Recreants."

Larkos winced and nodded. "They gave me permission for a meeting only if you were willing to be blindfolded. Their regular meetings are constantly changing locations, but they want to be extra cautious because of who you are."

Gaeren sighed and glanced at Erech. "And what if things go badly? You're willing to put Erech in harm's way?"

"He brought me because he thinks I'll keep the others from taking things too far." Erech's grin was positively cheeky. "No one wants an innocent to accidentally get hurt because of a misunderstanding." His grin dropped and his face melted into the expression of a forlorn puppy.

Bringing the boy was probably a brilliant idea.

"I could say the same thing about you." Gaeren turned to Larkos. "It's not that I don't trust *you*…" He left the sentence unfinished like Larkos had, and the other man chuckled.

"It could go a long way for them to hear from you directly instead of through an old man like me, who they think cares a little too much for the prince he was told to convert."

"They suspect you of being loyal to the crown because of me?"

Larkos shrugged. "Some of them are stupid, right?"

Gaeren shook his head and turned his back to Larkos, waiting for his first mate to conceal his vision. In many ways, it was a wasted effort. He could take the memory of approaching the meeting from Larkos or any other of the people there. But hopefully they all knew of his respect for privacy with his magic just like they knew of his evolving politics.

"Not as roguishly handsome as my eye patch," Thallahan said from his left, "but it'll do."

Gaeren reached out to punch him, but the other man must have moved, because his fist met air.

An awkward half a bell later, Gaeren was led up steps and through a door, where the blindfold was removed. It took his eyes a frustrating amount of time to adjust considering it was almost as dark in the room as it had been under the blindfold. Nearly a dozen men and women eyed him nervously, and Gaeren realized he was probably looking at the core members of the Recreant rebellion.

Unlike Sylmar and Velden's group, these people wanted a full democracy instead of even a spiritual leader. They would kill his parents and sister without question. They might still kill him if he didn't give them the right answers.

He glanced at Larkos, wondering if he'd made the right decision to come.

"He's just as pretty in person as he is on his posters," an old woman from the back yelled.

The tension dissolved with chuckles around the room. When Thallahan shoved Gaeren into a chair, a drink was passed his way, and Gaeren couldn't help wondering if it was laced with poison. As if reading his mind, Larkos traded mugs with him.

"I'm not sure I trust them any more than you do," he muttered.

The tension in his first mate's shoulders had only increased since they'd left the ship, and his hand strayed awfully close to his sword's pommel. Erech had already taken to his role of deflecting tension by asking a few of the attendees to watch the magic tricks Thallahan and Riveran had taught him. Even Thallahan greeted several people by name, leaving Gaeren feeling strangely out of place. Despite the relaxed chatter, Gaeren knew he needed to maintain vigilance just like Larkos had.

He barely had time to let the thought register before the interrogation began.

"Larkos tells us you left your family because you don't want to rule with them." A middle-aged man with squinty eyes said the words like an accusation.

Gaeren nodded, but a second question was fired his way before he could expand his answer. As the questions grew more specific, Gaeren set his drink aside. He wouldn't have time for swigs, but he also couldn't risk his mind being addled when they watched for him to make a mistake. Instead, he toyed with the braid hidden beneath the cuff of his sleeve, reminding himself that far more was at stake than how these people perceived him.

The youngest man sitting in the front was still at least ten years Gaeren's senior, with stringy black hair and a shave well overdue. He didn't ask any questions, but Gaeren noticed his knuckles grow white on the handle of his mug every time Enla's name came up. The man's anger wasn't just for Gaeren's parents, whose rule had much to question even in Gaeren's eyes. The man and his animosity toward Enla made Gaeren more nervous than any of the other patrons, who seemed to be warming up to Gaeren based on his answers.

When the questions subsided, Gaeren decided to ask one of his own. "How do you expect to overthrow a time-tested monarchy without a unified front?"

Several people blinked back at him, brows furrowed.

"I just spent the last several moons with a group of Recreants determined to undermine a high priestess' power, not the royal family's. They want Emeris Wyndren to rule instead of my family, but down here in the south, you all want to rule yourselves."

Understanding flashed, and a few of the attendees exchanged nervous glances. This wasn't a new topic, but maybe one they weren't ready to discuss in front of him.

"We respect the priests and priestesses in the Sungazers," one woman said, "but we don't want them making decisions for us."

"Are you able to set aside those differences and work together? Or will you take my family off the throne just to have another battle to fight with people who were supposed to be on your side?"

"Most of those Recreants are in the eastern provinces," another man said, waving his hand in dismissal. "Let them live the way they want out there and we can live the way we want down here."

"So now we're talking about dividing the nation with a theocracy in the eastern provinces and a democracy in the southern provinces. Why not allow a monarchy in the northwestern provinces to keep all the nobility there happy? After all, if it's what they want, let them live the way they want out there and you can live the way you want down here, right?" He tried to keep his tone light even though he clearly threw the man's words right back in his face.

Some seemed to consider the idea, but others pursed their lips. One woman in particular laughed. "Because the royal family won't settle for less than everything."

Gaeren laughed with her, easing some of the tension. "Maybe you're right. But they did give the eastern provinces to Mayvus before Mayvus died. We were already partway there."

This gave the group pause. Maybe Gaeren should have mentioned it was done under the duress of a brand or that Mayvus was still alive. But those things didn't change the fact that Emeris fully expected to maintain authority in the Myndren Mountains. He even suspected his parents would allow it in order to keep the peace.

"I understand the complaints you have with my parents. But do you assume Enla would make the same mistakes, or do you all have some other reason to despise her being on the throne?"

The man before him took the bait, answering the question before any of the others could. "It wasn't your parents who last raised taxes. It wasn't your parents who decreed that those who couldn't pay would become vassals." His voice rose until it finally broke. "It wasn't your parents who sent the order for my boy to be taken away to the schools."

Gaeren sucked in a breath, the man's words hitting him hard. Enla had almost said as much when he'd last met with her. She'd questioned if the mistakes made were her fault, since she'd made so many decisions while their parents were branded.

But these weren't the kinds of mistakes she was talking about. These were probably papers she'd signed off from the advisors without a second thought. Because in her mind, what Vendaran family wouldn't be grateful enough to pay back the royal family's protection in the form of taxes? What man should be governing his own land if he couldn't produce enough to pay those same taxes? And what progeny wouldn't want to train among the nobility?

He'd thought his sister was still moldable, but maybe he'd been even more blind than he'd realized. *He* was the one who had been open to change. It wasn't just that Larkos had infected him with Recreant ideals. Gaeren had been open to them.

And Enla never had.

As much as he hated the idea of his sister's philosophies being so different from his, he still longed for a way to make things right, not just with her and not just with these people, but between her and the people.

"I'm so sorry." He held the man's gaze even though it physically pained him to sit under the harsh judgment his family rightly deserved. "I can't promise I can reverse any of that. I can't even promise I can change their minds for the future."

Whispers started in the back of the room, the faces that had begun showing warmth and acceptance now closed off with furrowed brows.

"When my ideas differ from theirs," he admitted, "they remind me I'm trained as a throne warden, not as a king. My parents are too far gone to reconsider the way their actions are harming Vendaras instead of healing it. There might not even be hope for my sister. But that doesn't mean there isn't hope for all of you. I don't deny that I would be eager to see my parents step down from the throne, but that would only lead to my sister taking their place, with me as her throne warden. Something I have no interest in."

He watched that same man's reaction, and his knuckles grew predictably white.

"And what if that's the exact place you should be in?" It was the first time Larkos had spoken since they'd arrived, his words quiet, as if he feared they were disrespectful even though he'd spoken them before.

This time the question stirred up Gaeren's own fear and regrets. Had he made the wrong decision in leaving Enla? Not just for the sake of the Recreants like Larkos had suggested, but also to protect his sister? By widening the divide between them, he might have sentenced her to the fate he'd sworn to protect her from. He'd much rather work alongside Aeliana and the others to find peace in Vendaras. To help Orra find the starbridges. To maybe even be rid of his useless bond and sever the last of the ties to his family.

But after hearing these people question his views on taxes and feudal servitude and knowing the trials they experienced that led to their frustrations, he understood Larkos' suggestion on a deep and painful level. What if he could do more good for these people by staying in his role of power? By placing himself in the right place at the right time so he could defend and support them when they made their final move to take Enla off the throne? And what if that was the move that would put him in place to protect Enla when she needed him most?

He almost laughed, thinking of Orra and all her talk about throwing stones and moving things in the paths of ripples.

Perhaps when they found the starbridge, he should return home and make amends, both for the sake of the people and for Enla. The image warred with his desire to defend the people and help them find freedom on his own terms, as a treasonous vagrant. The longer Larkos waited for an answer, the less Gaeren felt prepared to give one.

"I hope I'm not meant to remain on as throne warden, but…maybe. It's something I'll have to consider. Either way, I will do everything in my power to sway her. I want you all to have the opportunity to build the democracy you crave, whether it only takes in the south or whether it spreads to all of Vendaras."

"And what if you can't sway her?" the bitter man sitting before him asked. "Will you join us in fighting against her?"

The entire room held their breath as Gaeren weighed the question that had plagued him for moons. He couldn't fight against his family. He didn't even think it was fair for the other man to ask him that when that same man wanted his son returned.

"Just like you would never take up arms against the son she sent to the schools, I won't help you harm her."

Grumbles started throughout the room, and Larkos' hand went straight to his sword.

Gaeren raised his hands in defense, his voice as well. "I won't help you harm her, but I will help you remove her from the throne."

A few guffaws replaced the disgruntled murmurs. "She'll find her way back," one man called out. "The royal family always will."

Gaeren patted his pocket, reassured by the presence of the golden arrow but uncertain if it was his secret to reveal. In some ways it felt like it belonged to Aeliana. In others it was clearly Orra's. But for now, it was his pocket the arrow rested in. He wouldn't be telling the Recreants Aeliana still sought the other starbridges. He would just be making sure they knew he could follow through on his promise.

Decision made, he pulled out the arrow, unwrapping it from its protective cloth and holding it up for everyone to see.

"If my parents and Enla won't see reason, I promise to take them all across the barrier and leave them in Lorvandas."

CHAPTER 33

AELIANA TOSSED AND TURNED, watching the moon through the porthole of the ship. After a week of dead ends, she tried contacting Durriken, wondering if he might have leads on the starbridge. As much as she wanted to reach out to the dragon, she was distracted by the new moon and what it meant, making it impossible to follow the threads tethering them.

When the sliver of light moved beyond her sight, she finally gave up, throwing off her covers. She changed into her blouse and trousers, which she'd finally grown used to. She pinned back her hair with a small braid the way Kendalyhn had taught her, but then tugged on the ends, wishing it would grow back faster.

By the time she made her way to the deck, she'd worked up a sweat from the muggy air and relished the slight breeze coming off the waves to cool her skin. The Sun's morn would come soon, but she could still see that sliver of moon in the distance.

"You're up early." Gaeren's voice startled Aeliana into turning around. She took in his disheveled hair and sleepy eyes and held back a grin.

"That makes two of us."

His smile held less bite than usual, softened by the early morning. "Larkos snores like a bear. Every morning is early when I bunk with him."

She smiled, but his words only made her think of Felk's nocturnal habits and the way he'd made her rise far earlier than she wanted on more than one occasion. She turned back to the water. "It's a new moon this morning."

Her back grew warm as he stepped closer. "You're thinking of Felk."

Tears pricked her eyes at his understanding. "It will be the first time he has a cycle where he hasn't met me. He won't even know me."

They stood in silence, and Aeliana let herself run through all the times she'd taken care of the winex, all the ways he'd taken care of her.

"He may have had hundreds of cycles before he knew you."

Gaeren's words struck her as insensitive with her lack of sleep, and she turned to frown at him.

"And hopefully he'll have hundreds more," he added. "You've changed the nature of the winex whether you meant to or not. I'm guessing they'll no longer be content forgetting their past lives."

Her heated words froze on her lips, and she stared at his collar, unsure what to say.

"In sixty years, when you lay on your deathbed, maybe Felk will take care of you."

She shifted her weight so she could bump her shoulder against his. He wrapped an arm around her to regain his balance but kept it there far longer than necessary.

"You have me dying far younger than I plan to live."

He snorted. "At the rate you seek out trouble, I thought I was being generous."

"I wish we'd had a little more excitement this last week." Aeliana couldn't keep the bitterness out of her voice. The night before, they'd reached the end of Ludo's and Barny's leads with no luck.

"I'm not sure we're looking in the right places," Gaeren said.

"Clearly."

He laughed, and despite her exhaustion, grief, and frustration, she laughed with him, grateful for the ways he helped her see the lighter side of life.

He looked like he might say more, but the Sun rose to the east, cutting off their conversation as they watched it rise in all its glory.

Now that Orra had all but confirmed the Vendarans were right, that the Sun was their creator and deserving of worship, Aeliana still wasn't sure how to worship such a distant creator. The Stars had always seemed approachable and loving—as eager to please their creation as their creation was to please them.

She nearly asked Gaeren about his own faith, but Cyrus joined them, arms stretched overhead and his jaw popping with a yawn. When he finally settled back into a sleepy smile, he pulled his hair into a knot. "Ready for another day of fruitless searching?"

Gaeren snorted. "Sylmar's starting to rub off on you. And no, we're busy enjoying the Sun's rise."

Aeliana's face heated at the way his words sounded more like they'd had a clandestine meeting.

Cyrus rolled back and forth on the balls of his feet. "Good. Me neither. Because today's the day. I can feel it. We're going to find the starbridge."

"I can't believe we didn't find it." Cyrus' words carried across the tavern they entered, drawing heads in his direction.

Aeliana grimaced as several eyes narrowed at his pale freckled skin.

"Failure makes me hungry," he went on, rubbing his belly. "I could use a big bowl of beef stew."

"You're always hungry," Aeliana pointed out.

"But tonight it's justified, right?" He sat down heavily next to Barny, whose only acknowledgment of their arrival was a twitch in his hand as he tightened his grip on his mug.

"Have any more leads for us, Barny?" Cyrus asked, elbowing the other man in his oversized gut.

The grunt he received in response could have been a confirmation or denial—or maybe just the expected result of an elbow to the gut.

Gaeren and Riveran soon arrived, followed by Velden and Ludo, and Aeliana and Cyrus scooted aside to let them in at the table.

"I know we haven't been here long," Gaeren said, "but this feels impossible."

He leaned back with a look of defeat that echoed Aeliana's feelings, and Riveran hummed his agreement. Today they'd scoured the darkest parts of the harbors, meeting a wide range of seedy individuals. Some had even produced items that could be labeled as a silver fish, but none of them hummed at Aeliana's touch.

"You're not going to let the rougher residents of Andel scare you away, are you?" Ludo sent a sneer in Gaeren's direction. He would likely always be the enemy in the old navy man's eyes.

"Oh, I've been scared of them since we arrived," Gaeren said. "But now I'm frustrated."

Ludo grinned, and a waitress brought another round of drinks, taking the empty glasses as well as the newcomers' orders. Her eyes lit up as Cyrus selected half the menu. Aeliana raised her brows as the woman walked away.

"What?" His ears turned pink. "Sylmar and the rest should be here soon. Now they won't have to wait as long to eat."

"Unless they take too long to get here and you finish it all for them," Velden said.

"How far have they made it down the coast?" Gaeren asked.

Sylmar, Kendalyhn, Lukai, Iris, Holm, and Brogdon had started approaching ships at harbor. They'd developed a story about a lost heirloom that they were offering a reward for, but so far they'd only had swindlers trying to convince them the metal trash they'd drudged up in their lobster traps had a fish shape to it.

They'd even brought Ludo and Barny in on parts of the truth in the hopes that they might have better leads, but the navy men still consider the starbridges to be tall tales, despite having a friend who clearly held Sayhleen ancestry.

"They might have made it halfway down the coast," Velden suggested. "But approaching docks is tricky. If a sailor has it, they might have already gone past his berth, only he was out at sea when they did."

"It feels like there has to be a clue we're missing," Gaeren muttered. "Something."

"You're the one who was so certain this was the plan of action to take." Aeliana still wished they'd gone after Pacran instead. Especially when they hadn't made any progress in so long. "Where did you get your information anyway?"

Gaeren hesitated. "I'm not proud of the source, but I feel like it's reliable enough."

"Gaeren." Riveran stretched out his name in a warning that only served to make Aeliana more curious.

"I think we've all done our fair share of questionable acts to get information." Aeliana scoffed. "I can't judge anyone. I went to the sprites for help."

This time the look Gaeren and Riveran exchanged was thick with guilt.

Aeliana's chest tightened, and she leaned forward. "Please tell me it wasn't the sprites."

Gaeren grimaced. "All right. It wasn't the sprites."

Riveran groaned, and then Ludo and Velden guffawed, clearly pleased that Gaeren was about to be in trouble. Even Barny shook with silent laughter as he raised his glass to his lips.

"You're almost as bad a liar as Cyrus," Aeliana said.

"Hey!" Cyrus feigned offense. "I've come a long way in my deception skills."

Aeliana rolled her eyes. "Are you telling me we've been following the directions of the sprites? What condition did you have to make to get their advice? Does it feel worth it now that they've sent us on a wild chase?"

Gaeren winced. "I thought you weren't going to judge."

"She's not judging," Velden said. "She's just asking questions. But the rest of us have all found you very guilty." He gestured at his friends, who laughed again and clinked their glasses together.

Aeliana leaned an elbow across the table to block the idiots from Gaeren's view. "Just tell me what they said."

"Technically we didn't hear all their advice."

Riveran shuddered. "Their price was too high."

"You didn't take their deal?" Aeliana sat up straighter. "They didn't let me go back on my deal. Said the deal was made the moment I asked."

"Which ended up saving my life," Cyrus added. "So not an altogether bad thing."

Riveran stared at the table, as if the grooves had suddenly sprouted letters worth reading.

"Come on." Ludo nudged Riveran. "You can't tell us half the story. This is one that might rival some of Velden's tall tales."

"I never embellish any of my stories," Velden lied, his grin as cheeky as ever.

"What happened to you in the cave?" Aeliana asked.

"I tried making a deal," Gaeren admitted. "Riveran didn't trust them, and he didn't want me to take the deal. He did the best thing he could under the circumstances."

Riveran looked up, his eyes holding a mix of confusion and appreciation.

"But he did kill the sprite before it finished giving us the information."

Aeliana gasped, then placed a hand over her mouth as if she could take it back. "How in Rhystahn did he manage to do that?"

Riveran shrugged. "Their blood might be cold, but it's their source of life like any other creature in this world. If you stop its flow, they'll die."

She winced. "I was wondering more how you managed to do that and survive."

"We almost didn't." Gaeren shuddered.

Both men looked chagrined, and Aeliana decided to put them out of their misery. "Fine. So you maybe took the deal and killed a sprite in the process. What words *did* you hear?"

Gaeren's eyes closed briefly, and he went still, likely calling up the memory for the exact lines. Part of her wanted to ask to see it for herself, but when Riveran continued looking haunted, she supposed she was better off without it.

"They said 'a fisherman in Andel has the fish. He doesn't know what he holds. He mounted it on the wall of his ship's cabin, along with the hide of—'" Gaeren cut off abruptly. "And that's when Riveran —you know."

This time Ludo and Barny exchanged nervous glances. It was the strongest reaction they'd ever seen from Barny, and Velden perked up. "Does that sound familiar to you, old Barnacle?"

Ludo and Barny busied themselves taking long swigs of their drinks.

"You all know that Gaeren could take your memories if he wanted-ed," Aeliana said. "He respects you enough not to do that, which is why we hope you'll tell us what we need to know on your own."

"We've cooperated with all of you ever since you arrived," Ludo said. "We owed it to Velden, not to you." He directed his words at Gaeren. "But we won't talk about that sailor or the hide that he shows off like it's a carnival booth."

Aeliana sat up straighter. "Then you know who it is."

Barny shot a dark look at Ludo.

"Aye," Ludo agreed.

Velden clapped a hand on Ludo's shoulder. "Come now, what would be the harm in giving us his name? You don't have to approve of what he does. But we can go settle with him."

Ludo and Barny refused to meet Velden's gaze.

"You'll kill him," Ludo finally said.

Velden rolled his eyes. "You think I've become a murderer since I left the navy?"

Ludo remained quiet long enough that Aeliana grew uneasy. What was it about the sailor? What hide did he have that would—

Understanding hit Aeliana a moment before Velden. He stood, his knee bumping the table and sloshing the drinks. "Give me his name." His words dripped with vengeance, a hateful tone Aeliana had never heard on his tongue.

Aeliana stood as well, laying a hand on Velden's arm. "Maybe we should have them give the information to Sylmar."

Velden shook her off, then slowed his words as if the sailors had been unable to hear. "Give me his name."

"What's happening?" Gaeren asked.

The waitress chose that moment to bring several dishes, oblivious to the showdown occurring at her table. While most were placed in front of Cyrus, Aeliana sat back down to whisper, "Velden's mother was murdered by a sailor. He harpooned her. I assume that's the hide this man shows off alongside the silver fish. He stole two prizes that day."

Gaeren's face paled. "That's sick."

The waitress grinned at the group, then finally seemed to sense the tension before scooting away and mumbling something about "too much to drink."

"Give me his name." Velden's hands shook, water dripping from the webs as if he couldn't contain the power inside him. Perhaps that was what made Ludo finally give in.

"Dreyfus. His berth is on the west side of Andel near the tallest Sungazer."

Velden stepped back, then kicked his chair in.

"But you can't go now," Ludo rushed on, standing and raising a calming hand. "Dreyfus is on a run and won't be back until end of next week or middle of the next. At least ten days."

Aeliana stood and tugged on Velden's sleeve. "It's all right. That gives us time to prepare." She didn't bother adding, "And to calm down."

"Seems like you're well acquainted with the beast." Velden's words came out through gritted teeth.

Ludo sighed and lowered his head. "We've been after him for years to give her a proper burial. Even tried stealing her tail one night before he warned us he would turn us in."

"Why didn't you tell me?" Velden's hands remained fists, dripping water all over the tavern floor.

Ludo looked to Barny for help, but his gaze remained fixed on his glass. When Ludo glanced back at Velden, he winced.

"Because the story he tells mentions you as his next prize."

CHAPTER 34

FEAR FLASHED on Aeliana's face, stirring up Gaeren's own concern for Velden.

But the half-Sayhleen only laughed bitterly. "That sounds like a challenge. One I will gladly accept."

"No." The forceful word came from Barny's lips, surprising everyone.

Even Velden sat down, his anger deflating to irritation. "Why not?"

This time, when Ludo and Barny exchanged nervous glances, Ludo sat back, bringing his glass to his lips.

A deep sigh emanated from Barny. "Dirk went after him."

Gaeren frowned, not remembering who Dirk was.

"Your friend who died?" Cyrus asked.

Aeliana shot him a glare, likely irritated by his lack of tact. But it helped Gaeren remember their initial meeting of these two men and the shared grief over another friend of Velden's.

Velden leaned forward, his voice low with fury. "You said it was an accident at sea."

If Barny and Ludo thought to deter him from going after Dreyfus with this information, they didn't know their friend as well as they used to. This was only going to fuel Velden's motivation.

"It was meant to be an accident that sank the man's carnival ship,"

Ludo said. "If the murderer went down with it, so be it. None of us understand how Dreyfus' ship came back and Dirk didn't."

"And you just…let him get away with it?" Velden's hands balled into fists on the table, water leaking out to pool across the surface. Cyrus rescued a couple of plates by bringing them closer to his corner.

Ludo sighed. "It's not that simple, Velden. We've been chasing after revenge in your honor, waiting for the day that we could tell you your mother was finally at peace. It suddenly seemed like a waste if it made us lose one of our own as well. And that's why we don't want to lose you either." He jabbed a finger into the table, his face bunched up with passion—or maybe pain. "This man has evaded us for twenty-five years. Every time we've gone after him, he's known. Sometimes I think he's laid traps to play with us. It feels like he controls the wind itself, finding ways to escape us at every turn."

"Sometimes vengeance is best left to the Stars," Cyrus murmured. "Or the Sun." He cast a sheepish look around the table.

Velden pursed his lips and looked away.

"So he's a destructive noetic?" Riveran asked.

"I don't think he has a starlock." Ludo shook his head. "He's just lucky."

"Well, his luck's run out," Aeliana announced. "Regardless of whether the man deserves Velden's revenge or whether it's even possible, we're still going after him."

For a moment their companions seemed confused, but then understanding dawned. "He has the silver fish." Ludo shook his head. "All this time I thought Velden's mother came from some underground community of Sayhleens hiding from the half-lights. But she really came from across the barrier?"

Aeliana nodded. "Perhaps instead of trying to kill the man or sink his treasures, we should be figuring out how to perform a heist."

A slow grin spread across Velden's face, making Ludo groan. "I'm in," the half-Sayhleen said.

"This means we can start eating now, right?" Cyrus asked, a forkful of meat pie already halfway to his lips.

Sylmar and the others arrived soon after, requiring the information to be repeated. Their discussion went well into the night, the plan growing more involved than Gaeren wanted.

He may have been a prince, but he was also a sailor. And he would be lying if he said he'd never stolen a thing or two in honor of the pirates he looked up to. But Velden's plans were overcomplicated and involved far too many people. Supposedly Dreyfus had wonders of the world aboard his ship that couldn't be found anywhere else, so Velden intended to turn *To the Deep and Back* into Dreyfus' competition. They'd lure the man aboard their boat while Velden and Ludo boarded his.

It was a good thing Dreyfus wasn't expected to return until the following week, because they had dozens of people to contact and supplies to procure. It left Gaeren uneasy. There were too many ways for Dreyfus to hear of their plans. There was too much room for error.

"It's not going to work," Riveran whispered as they settled into their bedrolls that night. Most of the sailors around them snored, and all seemed asleep. "If two years in the seedier parts of Elanesse taught me anything, then I guarantee our plans will already be in that man's ears before he's even docked his ship."

Gaeren grunted his agreement, too tired to say much more.

Cyrus had stayed above deck worshiping the Stars, and Lukai had tagged along to say good night to the women. Sylmar and Velden had remained back at the pub, finalizing plans, which left only Holm and Brogdon still getting settled in the bunk room for the night. Thankfully they were across the room, oblivious to Riveran's assessment of their situation.

"If he's docking in all the major ports between Valorian and Andel to sell his wares, he'll hit up Melford just before heading here." River-an's voice grew even lower as he lay down, hands behind his head. "You could hire a ferryman to get you across the inlet and beat him there by a day, maybe two. If no one else knows about it, he won't be expecting it."

Gaeren lay back, studying the rivets holding the mast in place in the ceiling where it cut through the ship's core. It was a decent plan. Far better than Velden's overdramatic flair and overcomplicated steps. "We might even talk a little louder about Velden's plans to keep Drey-fus' focus on his arrival here."

"Exactly," Riveran agreed.

Gaeren mulled it over in his mind. It would take five or six days to reach Melford without *To the Deep and Back*. Dreyfus would probably reach it in six or seven, maybe stay a day or three for his "show." They could go on board, show interest in the Sayhleen tail. Gaeren grimaced at the thought, but it would also allow them to see the starbridge, Dreyfus' methods for protecting it, and all the entrances and exits to the place they'd need to perform their heist.

Worst-case scenario they could stow away in the hull of the ship and steal it while Dreyfus was sailing back.

"It might work," he said.

"Only if it's kept quiet. And only if you take just one or two others."

"Are you volunteering?"

Riveran's laugh was short, and he rubbed the X on his forehead. "Not with this."

Gaeren frowned, his thoughts taking a new direction. Once again this was an instance in which he could do more good back with Enla. "My parents were willing to remove it for you. If I got back in their good graces—"

"Nah. I'd rather have this brand for everyone to see than owe your parents something in secret."

Gaeren flinched even though Riveran had said the words without malice. It almost made it worse that his response didn't come as an emotional deflection but more of a statement of fact. That was just how terrible Gaeren's parents were, and everyone knew it.

"What about Enla?" Gaeren asked.

"What about her?" Riveran frowned, turning to take in what little he could see of Gaeren's face in the moonlight through the porthole.

Gaeren tried to keep his face passive. "Would you be all right if you owed Enla something in secret?" It was a poor way to ask what he really wondered, and Riveran's confused face proved it. "Do you still love her?"

A mix of emotions crossed Riveran's face before he schooled his features too.

"She's bonded." The words came out flat as he lay back on his bedroll.

"Bonds can be broken," Gaeren whispered, surprised at his own words.

"Well, she also got married." The pain in Riveran's voice confirmed what Gaeren already knew. "She should have at least told me in her letter," he muttered.

"I'm sorry." Gaeren was still sorry for all the ways their friendship had soured over misunderstandings. But he also felt sorry for Enla and Riveran. They'd lost even more.

"Whoever you choose to take," Riveran said, forcing Gaeren back to the plan, "it should be someone you trust with your life."

Gaeren nodded, and several of the sailors' faces passed through Gaeren's mind.

But they were all overshadowed by a woman with green eyes and daisies at her fingertips.

Convincing Aeliana wasn't the difficult part. It was getting her alone to ask. Sylmar and Velden kept everyone busy with redecorating Gaeren's ship, the tasks more suited to Enla's event planning than a group on a mission to find a starbridge.

Eventually he grew impatient, and as Aeliana organized jars of random sea creatures on a table, he placed a hand on her shoulder, drawing energy from his starlock and doing his best to pass her the memory of his conversation with Riveran.

She stilled, her hand going to her own starlock, which lay hidden under her shirt, then glanced up at him, a slow smile spreading on her face. "Absolutely."

He smiled back, then glanced around, knowing the look on his face would make anyone suspicious, but everyone seemed too preoccupied with Sylmar's and Velden's orders.

"Will you be ready at the moon's reign?" he asked.

Her brow furrowed. "Is that midnight for Vendarans?"

He grinned, remembering she'd been raised in a different culture. "You got it."

"But you don't even worship the moon."

"It's more of an expression. At its peak, the moon is reigning over all of Rhystahn."

"I'll be ready." She glanced at Iris, who fought with Holm over a sign he was painting.

Gaeren winced at the permanent damage being done to his best spare sail. If nothing else, this side adventure would allow him to miss seeing all the ways they were ruining his beautiful ship.

He snuck into his cabin to remove some of the money he'd hidden under a board, and Riveran helped him pack a bag, which they hid in a storage room.

"I won't tell Larkos or Thallahan that you picked her over them." Riveran didn't even try to hide his smile.

Gaeren's face heated, but he grinned back at his old friend. "I need them to take care of my ship. Sylmar and Velden are close to ruining it beyond repair."

***

Hours later, Gaeren waited in the shadows of the dock while watching for Aeliana to disembark the ship. Despite his confidence in her word, nervous energy kept him pacing. What if Iris caught her? Or what if she changed her mind? What if she told Lukai and he refused to let her go?

His bond mark itched and he frowned, still caught in his confusion over whether or not to cut it out. It felt like it represented so much more than his bond with Lenda. Now it represented all his ties to his family and Elanesse.

But then Aeliana was running across the plank, the wind tangling the short bits of hair in front of her eyes. He smiled but couldn't help missing the way it had wrapped around her when it was long, like a cocoon protecting her. When he stepped from the shadows, she sucked in a breath, and a spark of light grew between them that temporarily blinded him before it sputtered out.

"You can't do things like that," she gasped out. "I might have hurt you."

He chuckled. "With your half-formed light shield?"

She stuck her tongue out at him. "Hopefully that's all it would have been, but I still don't have great control of my magic." She stepped away as if he were to blame for that. "With the change of tactic in training me, I feel like my control has gone backward."

"So…you might have given me a memory when I startled you?" He gasped in mock fear. "I don't know what I would have done."

She slapped his shoulder, then glanced around nervously as she adjusted her pack. "Now what?"

For some reason, it hadn't dawned on Gaeren until now that they would be traveling alone for five days. He suddenly felt out of sorts, like he should have considered how intimate that might be.

"Um, we head for the ferry on the south side of town. Riveran arranged a ride for us."

Her eyebrows rose. "What's he going to tell Sylmar and Velden in the morning?"

Gaeren shrugged. "That he has no idea where we are. Because by then we'll be across the inlet and we could be anywhere."

She snorted out a laugh and started toward the southern half of the city, all awkwardness dissolving.

Conversation lulled as they both grew tired, their bodies clearly feeling that it was the middle of the night even if their minds weren't. By the time they reached the ferry, Aeliana's eyes were barely open.

Gaeren put an arm around her and let her lean against his shoulder while they stood in line to board. "We'll be able to sleep on the boat until the Sun's rise. It will be enough to get us through the day."

She nodded against him but didn't pull away.

Out of habit, Gaeren scanned the others lined up to board the ferry. A midnight run wasn't unusual, but it was more likely to hold seedy individuals. He kept his hood covering most of his face, unwilling to let his identity be the thing that foiled their plans. His eyes narrowed as he caught sight of a familiar nearly shaved head from behind, with fish hook earrings dangling.

"Velden?" Gaeren called out.

Aeliana's head shot up from his shoulder, and her entire body stiffened.

Velden turned, eyebrows raised, and he stepped out of his place ahead of them in line to join them. "Well, this I did not expect." Even so, he rubbed his webbed hands together as if it was exactly what he'd hoped for.

"What are you doing here?" Aeliana asked.

"Probably the same thing as you. Although I'm curious—did you know my plans were a ruse? Or did you think you were the only one fooling Sylmar?"

Aeliana blushed. "We weren't trying to fool Sylmar. We're just trying to get the starbridge."

"As am I." Velden held out his hands in mock surrender.

Gaeren frowned. "I call your bluff."

Velden's eyebrows rose. "You think I'm bent on revenge?" He looked away, his gaze going out over the water. "Maybe. But I want that starbridge just as much as you. Maybe more." He tightened his grip on his pack, readjusting it on his shoulder. "Maybe I can avenge my mother this way, maybe not. But I can at least find her people—my people. I can gain closure on a different part of my past."

Gaeren and Aeliana exchanged a glance.

"What if you let us do this for you, Velden?" she offered, placing a hand on his arm. "It's not that I don't think you can do it, but what Ludo and Barny said…" She trailed off, biting her lip.

"I'll be fine." Tight lines formed around Velden's mouth even though his tone remained light. "That old fool can't hurt me."

She shook her head. "You don't know that."

"Well, I'm willing to find out." His lazy grin returned, then, as his gaze flicked between them, it turned wicked. "Besides, it seems like you two are in need of a chaperone."

The heat in Gaeren's cheeks rivaled the red in Aeliana's.

"You should be thanking us instead of teasing," Aeliana mumbled.

"Is it teasing if it's true?" Velden turned as the line started moving, leading the way on the ferry and talking over his shoulder. "Three is a good number for this mission anyway."

"Why three?" Gaeren asked.

Velden glanced back to wink at them. "Oh, let's be honest, shall we? Any number is a good number if it doesn't include old Sylmar."

CHAPTER 35

After a week of listening to Velden rant about everything he planned to do to Dreyfus, Aeliana was relieved to reach Melford. But the moment they found the docks, Aeliana regretted it. The carnival ship could be spotted a half mile away, its sail boasting a large painted sign reading "Boat of Wonders." As they drew closer, a young girl called out to onlookers, offering tickets to people wanting entry.

After a heated debate amongst the three of them and listening to far too many renditions of the young girl's "money-back guarantee" speech, Velden finally handed over coin in exchange for tickets, which he promptly soaked in his anger.

Aeliana and Gaeren exchanged nervous glances. How much of their energy would be spent on keeping Velden in check?

With Velden rumored to be Dreyfus' next prize, Aeliana had forced him to wear a ridiculous floppy hat and continually reminded him to keep his webbed hands hidden. More than a dozen people milled across the deck, studying the conman's outrageous wares. Pickled octopus to cure one's warts, pearl-infused oils to slender one's waist, kelp perfume to attract a bondmate. Not a single woman besides Aeliana graced the dirty vessel, and a second young street rat had already served far more ale than Aeliana had seen in the taverns the week before. She suspected most of Dreyfus' displays only looked legitimate if someone had blurry vision.

As the three of them weaved through the makeshift tables, several men leered in her direction, making her starlock heat with the urge to put them in their place. Gaeren seemed to notice too, and he wrapped a possessive arm around her that she didn't shove away.

"I don't see it," Velden grumbled.

"I'm guessing it's hidden away as some sort of grand finale," Aeliana said.

The crowd had grown to hold at least thirty men, and the young girl selling tickets slid the plank away from the dock.

"Full capacity! We've reached full capacity!" she yelled out to those still on the dock.

Her shouts also served to draw a short man with curly blond hair and tattoos peeking from his collar out from the captain's quarters. Muscles bulged beneath his thin white shirt and black suspenders, and hatchets and knives lined his belt. The number of weapons was so ridiculous Aeliana almost snorted. Clearly the man had something to prove.

Velden stiffened, and Aeliana leaned over. "Tuck your hands in your pockets."

He did as she asked, his jaw tightening.

Dreyfus made his way through the crowd with slow, measured steps, his beady eyes taking in the people more than the objects they perused. His barrel chest seemed to swell even larger as he passed people exclaiming over the oddities he'd assorted. When someone stopped him to ask a question, he adopted a salesman smile that didn't reach his eyes but was full of teeth. He hooked his thumbs in his suspenders and raised his voice for everyone to hear.

"Why, those coins were found in the belly of a fish my fifth year of sailing. You'll notice the dates go back to before the Great Divide."

The man questioning him squinted and held the coin closer, then his eyes widened, and he pointed excitedly at the sorry excuse for metal before shoving it under his friend's nose.

Dreyfus continued down the aisle, doing his best to verify the authenticity of each item on display.

Aeliana watched him pass, checking his hands for signs of a brand or bond. There was neither, but the tattoos on his neck were similar to some of the secret anti-royalty tattoos Larkos had shown her—enough to make her suspect Dreyfus was a Recreant. She supposed there could be terrible Recreants just like there were some good Zealots.

"What about the Sayhleen hide?" one man shouted.

"Yeah, that's what I came to see!" Similar shouts rang out through the crowd, but Dreyfus showed no concern. If anything, the smile on his face grew bigger, and he ran a hand through his golden curls, relishing the attention.

"My museum of wonders boasts many artifacts, but if you're finished looking at the items on deck, I can take you below for my prized possession. The stairs are steep and the room is small, so I can only take two at a time."

Men stumbled over themselves to get in line first, but Aeliana, Gaeren, and Velden held back. At least Velden's anger wasn't making him do anything rash… yet. It would be far better to deal with Dreyfus without a crowd.

As the Sun rose higher and the line grew shorter, Aeliana began to wonder if it would have been better to go first. With each pair that left, Aeliana and Velden were forced to listen to people's comments on what they thought of the tail nailed to the wall. Occasionally men would come out, describing it in detail in a way that made Velden flinch. Others made fun of it, which swung Velden to a state of agitation. One man immediately kneeled to worship the Sun, as if the sight had restored his faith.

Velden pulled his webbed hands out of his pockets to wipe his face, but she wasn't sure if the water came from his hands or his eyes.

Eventually, the crowd dwindled, and Aeliana, Gaeren, and Velden took their place in line.

"Velden and I can go first," Aeliana said. "Be prepared to back us up if we have any trouble."

Gaeren nodded, but his eyes narrowed. She expected him to argue, maybe suggest that Aeliana stay behind instead, but the young girl who had sold them tickets stood back on the dock, shouting that the next view time would start soon. Eager onlookers formed a line on the dock, and Velden frowned. So much for waiting to avoid an audience.

"We're just scoping it out to steal later anyway," Gaeren said, his gaze shifting to Velden. "Right?"

Velden nodded, but the tightness in his jaw made it hard to believe him.

When their turn came, Dreyfus held out of hand for Velden.

"Name's Dreyfus."

The conman peered under the hat's rim, but Velden kept his face hidden in its shadow. He didn't introduce himself or take his hands from his pockets, leaving Dreyfus awkwardly holding out his arm.

"It's not often I get a pretty lady aboard my boat," he continued, adjusting his hand for Aeliana to offer hers for a kiss.

The thought of his puffy lips against the skin of her hand made her nauseous.

"It looks like you're ready to start a new show, and we want to get our money's worth," she said shortly.

Dreyfus' smile faltered. "Of course." He recovered quickly, gesturing for them to follow him below deck. As he walked, he began his story, sharing how he had gone out early one morning to empty the crab traps when he saw the flicker of an orange and mauve tail.

Aeliana glanced back at Velden, whose eyes slid shut.

"I didn't expect it to be a Sayhleen. Who would?" Dreyfus' deep chuckle sounded sinister in the dark hull of his ship. "But I thought it might have some pretty scales to sell at the market, and it seemed large enough to be worth the pursuit. So I unfurled my nets and cast them wide."

"But you didn't catch her within the net, did you?" Velden asked.

Dreyfus turned back, his eyes narrowed. "Yes, I did. Unfortunately, she was injured, and by the time I pulled in the net, she was already dead."

Velden's jaw clenched, and Aeliana placed a hand on his back in warning. They needed to find the starbridge before he addressed what this man had done. Her mind flashed back to Cyrus' insistence that vengeance be left to the Stars or Sun, and she did her best to push that memory on Velden.

If he received it, he didn't acknowledge it.

Dreyfus made a show of unlocking the door and ushering them in to a small room, its portholes shining light directly on a glittering object.

Gorgeous ombre scales bled from a bright sunset orange to a deep blood-tinged mauve, like the depths of a fire in solid form. The tail's length rivaled the height of a man, and the span of its shell-pink translucent fin stretched out just as wide. Despite its elegance, the thickness of the tail gave evidence to muscle that had once propelled the Sayhleen through the waters with ease.

She reached for Velden's arm, needing to steady herself as much as him.

"How did you preserve it?" Velden asked.

"My skills are no different from the taxidermist who stuffs birds and beasts."

A cold chill ran down Aeliana's spine.

"And what of the top half of the body?" Velden's voice shook, signaling that Aeliana's time to find the starbridge was running out.

For the first time, Dreyfus looked uncomfortable. "I couldn't very well stuff a woman's body. People would be horrified to come look at that." He shrugged. "Even though she had been beautiful."

Aeliana stepped between the two men, and the shift in proximity brought her gaze to a second object on the wall, placed almost as an afterthought. She held her breath as she took in the silver fish that would fit in the palm of her hand, ancient symbols inscribed on its surface instead of eyes or scales. The smooth symmetry of its shape was otherworldly, like something no human, half-light, or other being could create.

"Oh, I see you found the Sayhleen's treasure." Dreyfus joined her by the fish. "Even in death she gripped that tight. I suspect it's worth a lot to her people."

"You didn't once think"—Velden's voice was gruff as it rose in volume behind them—"that stuffing the bottom half of a woman's body was just as horrific as stuffing the top?"

The sailor's eyes widened, and Aeliana turned to find Velden's hat thrown off, his webbed hands splayed and filling the room with a hot steam reminiscent of his anger. Their time was up.

"You!" Dreyfus backed away until he hit the wall between the tail and silver fish, his gaze fixated on Velden's webs.

"So you remember me? I'm her son. We went out to the deeper waters that day because there were things I wanted her to show me. Things she needed to tell me in case something happened to her. Except you got to her first." Velden's eyes narrowed, and the steam shifted to a spray.

Aeliana sucked in a breath. For some reason she'd always thought, or maybe hoped, that Velden's knowledge of his mother's death was something he'd received secondhand.

Dreyfus nervously batted the water away from his eyes. "I told you she was already injured. Some beast or other got to her before me."

"I could've healed her," Velden ground out. "It wasn't a serious injury. We were far from land and supplies, but Sayhleens heal well in the water. She might have been fine without your harpoon going through her chest."

Dreyfus went still, guilt flashing in his eyes, but then he schooled his features. "I caught her in my net and she was already dead."

Had he told the lie for so long he believed it? Or did he think he could fool Velden into suspecting his own memory was flawed?

Aeliana bit her lip, tempted to reach out and grip the man's arm, to try receiving his memory, but if he didn't want to share it, it likely wouldn't work. Not with how poorly her training had been going.

"Liar." Velden cut off his spray and pulled out knives instead. "She could have at least finished telling me all the secrets she'd kept if you'd let her live. She could have said goodbye. She could have died in my arms instead of while being dragged aboard your ship."

Footsteps rang above them.

"Velden," Aeliana said. "I think it's time we go."

"I would listen to the little lady if I were you," Dreyfus said. "There's nothing more for you here. Your mother is still inspiring generations and will continue to do so. I've kept her alive in that way for you."

Aeliana groaned inwardly. She wasn't sure she'd be able to hold Velden back if it came to it, and not just because he was too strong for her. Dreyfus wasn't doing or saying anything to make himself seem redeemable.

"I will be taking both my mother and the silver fish."

Dreyfus frowned, pulling the hatchets from his belt. "I don't think so. This is my livelihood. More than half my income comes from people wanting to see the treasures of the Sayhleen."

"Then you'd better learn to live on half as much." Velden shrugged. "Or if you'd rather, I can remove half your body like you did for my mother. Remove your need for any income at all."

"Velden," Aeliana hissed. "Murdering a man, even if it's warranted, won't make it easy for us to leave this ship."

"Maybe I don't need to leave." His gaze hardened with resolve, the lines on his face showing his age for the first time. "It's enough if you do."

Dreyfus' eyes darted around the room, leaving Aeliana unnerved.

"I'd much rather add your webbed hands to my collection." Dreyfus spun the hatchets in his hand with a dexterity that gave her pause. Maybe the weapons hadn't just been for show.

"Then you should know I also have webbed feet." A wicked grin crossed Velden's face, as if he relished the thought of tempting this man into attacking first.

Aeliana sighed. There was no way they were getting out of there alive unless they were willing to incapacitate Dreyfus in some way.

The sailor's eyes gleamed.

Aeliana didn't wait to find out why. Pulling energy from her starlock and into her hands, she let the energy out in a burst of light that formed a wall between them and Dreyfus. It flickered and faded, like starlight winking out behind clouds, inciting her panic. Why were her light shields so weak? Why hadn't she demanded Sylmar focus on that instead of the new noetic skills?

The momentary fear on the sailor's face gave way to dark humor. As he threw his first hatchet with practiced precision, Aeliana pulled on her starlock's power, feeding it into the light shield until it shone bright once more. When the hatchet clinked off the shield, Dreyfus' confidence waned. "Is this why you brought the girl? To fight your battle for you?"

"I hunted you for three moons while watching my father fade away. I only stopped because my mother wouldn't have wanted me chasing vengeance. Not when I could chase love instead. But if I'd known what you did with my mother's body, if I'd found this sorry excuse for a show, I'm not sure it would have mattered. I would have come the same day and killed you myself."

Dreyfus' eyes flicked between the stairs and the tail, but he pulled another hatchet from his belt. "Maybe we can work out a deal."

"I don't make deals with liars and swindlers. And definitely not with murderers."

"Swindlers?" Dreyfus scanned their necks and hands, likely assessing the source or strength of their power.

He was using conversation to stall, and it made Aeliana uneasy. Just because he didn't have magic didn't mean he didn't have ways to trick them. And just because she couldn't see a starlock didn't mean he didn't have magic.

"I give people exactly what they came for. A glimpse of the beauty of the Sayhleen."

"Let's go, Velden." Aeliana stepped forward with her shield, forcing Dreyfus away from his prized possessions on the wall. He stepped to the side, reluctantly, hissing as the edges of her shield touched his skin.

She reached for the silver fish first, mostly because she wasn't sure how easily they could get either off the wall. Sure enough, nails were bent to hold the fish in place. As her fingers brushed the metal, a warmth surged through her, followed by a humming vibration.

Her shield flickered with the distraction, and Dreyfus lunged for her.

He knocked her to the floor, and his axe came within a handsbreadth of her face before she regained control. As her energy shifted to strengthen her arms and hold him at bay, Velden stepped in, pulling Dreyfus away by the collar and placing a dagger at his neck.

Aeliana stood, brushing off her pants and giving Velden a warning glance. "We'll get out of here faster if you don't kill him."

"You're right. Maybe I won't kill him. Just take what he took from my mother." He let his dagger slide down near the man's thighs. "Only seems fair."

Dreyfus elbowed Velden and knocked the dagger from his hand, then each man drew another weapon.

Aeliana turned her back on their match to face the silver fish. Velden could use his magic on Dreyfus at any moment and tip the scales. Both men had to know that. So what game were they playing?

She pried the nails apart until she could loosen the fish and tuck it into her pocket. Next, she moved to the tail, but she hesitated over the way to get it down most respectfully.

"My mother once told me that each Sayhleen takes their form in the water in different ways." Velden's voice held an unfamiliar edge that added urgency to Aeliana's choice.

She worked at the nails holding up the tail, bending them like she'd done for the silver fish.

"Some form a single tail like she did." His words were punctuated by grunts and thuds as they continued attacking and blocking. "Others retain most of their lower legs but gain dual fins and scales. Still others transform with scales and fins covering their entire body, a shift so intense they rival the skills of the most powerful somatic progeny. No magic required."

Aeliana glanced back. Dreyfus' eyes gleamed with this information, and Velden used his distraction to finally draw blood on the sailor's cheek. She went back to her work.

"Aeliana," Velden called lazily. "I think we should take him with us. See if the Sayhleens want to put him up in one of their museums."

"That's enough, Velden," Aeliana muttered, more frustrated with the nails holding the tail in place than her friend.

"As if you can reach Sayhla Island." Dreyfus guffawed, but he couldn't hide the curiosity in his voice.

Aeliana finally bent enough nails away to loosen the tail and slide it free. Its weight nearly toppled her until she infused her arms with strength from her starlock. Even then, it was awkward to carry. She didn't see how they could get above deck and off the ship without being swarmed.

"We can now, thanks to you."

Aeliana turned to catch Velden's mock bow. Dreyfus made one last lunge with his hatchet, but Velden easily dodged it, water snaking out from his hands to wrap around Dreyfus' wrists. It was unusually effective considering it was water, but Aeliana had seen him do it once before to Felk and remained confident it would hold.

"Did you really not know you had a starbridge all this time?" Velden's sneer lent more contempt than curiosity to his question, and Dreyfus' eyes widened in shock. Velden pulled his dagger back out. "Come on. Let's take this liar above deck and let him put on his final show."

CHAPTER 36

ORRA SHUT the door on the eastern garden where Felk and Lilik settled with the other winex. She leaned her forehead against the door, wondering if it was worth keeping them here when they grew more discontented.

The braid on her wrist hummed ever so slightly, and she stilled. Had Mayvus crossed the barrier again? But it felt different, more distant. She smiled softly.

No. This was a different starbridge. She supposed Gaeren could be holding the arrow, but something about this felt different.

New.

A year ago she would have known exactly which starbridge and where it was held. While the weakness concerned her, it also gave her hope that her search was coming to an end. That with the end of her magic, she would finally fulfill the Sun's prophetic words.

A growl pulled her from her satisfaction, and she opened her eyes to find a straggler from the winex clan crouched by the door, waiting for her to move. At least he hadn't snapped at her. She sighed and opened the door, stepping aside so he could go through to the garden.

A dozen or so had left with this last cycle. The memories Emeris had given Felk apparently weren't strong enough for him to be confident in their ties to the people. It would break Aeliana's heart if she came back and Felk was gone, but he wasn't a pet for them to keep on a leash.

Twelve days into this new cycle and they'd finally made it through their most rebellious stage. Still, Orra fully expected another dozen or more to leave.

Shouts echoed down the hall as she shut the door once more. If she hadn't just watched the winex all settle in to sleep for the day, she would have assumed they were causing trouble again. She followed the sound, wondering if it was possible that General Nels' scouts had returned early. But this would be far too early.

She quickened her pace, tempted to unfurl the tendrils of her magic that had been growing in the last moon. The quiet and rest had been good for her, even if feeling blind without using her magic had left her on edge. She wasn't sure it could ever be what it had been, but it was returning. Even so, it wasn't enough for her to waste on something as trivial as seeking the future she was about to experience.

When she rounded the corner to enter the main hall, a fire blazed in the hearth, giving light to the pockets of soldiers gathered around on their day off. The rest were out guarding the fortress or rebuilding the ramparts, but these soldiers weren't all relaxing. Several of them stood on tiptoe, trying to catch sight of who was coming through the main entrance. Gullet flew past and up into the rafters, where he anxiously hopped side to side.

When the crowd parted, Orra glimpsed Emeris, her face unusually bright. She had been growing stronger too, but this lightness had nothing to do with her magic. Behind her, a man with shorn hair and tattoos on his hands followed, his face far wearier. His years rested somewhere between Aeliana and Emeris, too old or young to be either's contemporary.

"Marnok's back," Orra breathed out.

Rildan brought up the rear, ushering them both through the crowd and instructing people to give them space.

"Orra," Emeris called. "Come to my sitting room so we can hear about Marnok's travels."

Without her meaning it to, Orra's magic stretched out toward

Marnok, snatching up snippets of furious witches and calculating sprites. Her eyebrows rose. "I wouldn't miss it."

Despite the lack of trust Emeris had shown for General Nels, he'd been invited too. But this time he came alone. Rildan and Emeris took a seat on her settee, hands clasped as Emeris beamed at Marnok, who looked unsettled on the chair across from them. General Nels opted to remain standing by the door, arms crossed. Perhaps he viewed himself as some sort of guard. Or perhaps that was just his preferred stance.

Orra pulled up a chair next to Marnok, giving him a smile. "It's good to see you. I hope you've come to terms with who you are."

A flicker of surprise crossed his face. "Did you know all along?"

Orra lifted her shoulder noncommittally. "Only bits and pieces. Enough. If I haven't shared it with anyone yet, I have no reason to start now."

He nodded but still shot Emeris a nervous glance.

"Tell us about the witches," Emeris prodded.

"Yes, the witches." Marnok took a deep breath, wiping his palms on his trousers. "It turns out they have about as much love for the Wyndrens as the Elanesses do." He smiled wryly. "And now they hate me just as much."

Emeris' eyes held compassion. "I'm so sorry."

General Nels shifted from his place at the door. "Why would you be sorry?"

She and Marnok exchanged guilty looks.

"Because my mother is a witch." Marnok's words held no pride, but there was a hint of defensive disdain.

"We can't choose whom we're born to," Emeris said.

"I take it you told them you're a friend of the Wyndrens?" Orra asked.

Marnok sighed. "Not at first. When Emeris showed me what she could of my past"—he glanced at the high priestess, uncertainty in his eyes—"I knew I not only needed to face my origins, but I had to do it in secret. On top of being born to one of the highest witches, I was raised with purpose. I was sent to infiltrate the Wyndren household. My mother wanted me to end their line."

Rildan's grip tightened on Emeris' hand, but he didn't seem surprised.

"And yet...you didn't." Orra smiled. He'd left out half the story. She suspected everyone in the room knew what he'd left out, except for General Nels. There was no need to make him spill everything. The full truth would come with time.

"I didn't. Perhaps I left the witches with the intention of doing just that. Or maybe I never fully believed in my mother's obsession. Emeris' memories can't tell me those parts of my story. But in the end, I trusted Emeris over my mother." He glanced at Emeris. "Or at least her memories of me suggest that."

"Then why bother going back?" General Nels asked.

"When I was healing Emeris, her wounds would grow worse, like she was gaining new ones. She told me it was because Mayvus was gaining new ones from Durriken."

"You believed me about the curse because you could see it happening." Emeris' eyes clouded over. "I thought I would die from those wounds. It probably wasn't fair for me to give you so many memories at once. It was too much. But I was afraid I wouldn't have another chance. I knew you were the only one who would take my suspicions seriously. That you were the only one who could find out if Mayvus and I had been cursed by the witches."

"So you went to the witches," Orra mused, "pretending you still intended to end the Wyndren line?"

Marnok nodded. "I was only able to stay with them for a couple of weeks, and it was difficult to learn much. They spent so much time with their rituals, and while I wasn't forced to participate, even watching for the sake of maintaining my supposed allegiance was hard to stomach." He shuddered, and Orra's own past experiences with the witches rose to the surface, leaving her uneasy.

They may worship the Stars, but that hadn't stopped them from poisoning her, bleeding her, and abusing her for their own nefarious purposes. The dark spirits had hovered, constantly waiting for their feeding frenzy, leaving a persistent blackness that had drained her of hope. It had been one of the darkest seasons of her existence.

"Did they question your story?" Emeris asked, her careful words leaving much unsaid.

Marnok shrugged. "They've seen Mayvus' rise to power. They knew I had my work cut out for me. But they seemed satisfied with the fact that Mayvus had been dragged off by Durriken and you were near death when I left. I told them I felt like my mission had been accomplished. Even so, I wasn't able to gain any understanding of why I was given the mission in the first place."

"So you think the witches cursed the Wyndren family?" General Nels asked, eager, as always, to get to the main point.

"I doubt it." Marnok's brow furrowed. "Why would they have sent me after Emeris and Mayvus if they'd already successfully cursed them?"

"Maybe they cursed them after you left," Rildan suggested.

Marnok frowned. "Maybe. Whether they did the cursing or not, I feel like they know something about it. When I didn't have bodies to show them as proof, they seemed strangely certain the Wyndrens were already doomed in some way. I just couldn't tell if that was their over-confidence in some measure they've taken or if it was because they knew of some other endgame that was already in place."

General Nels made a frustrated sound in the back of his throat. "That's all you discovered in two weeks with them?"

Emeris shot him a disapproving glare. "He risked his life to go back to people who would kill him if they knew where his true loyalties lie. I'm grateful he was cautious enough to get out safely."

"They grew suspicious after a while," Marnok admitted. "My mother asked me things about my childhood that I couldn't remember. Even though I told her I'd had memory loss, I think it scared her. I assume she'd rather eliminate a possible asset than set loose a suspected traitor." He shuddered. "I barely escaped. It's likely I would have been their next sacrifice to the Stars if I hadn't sensed the change in my mother."

"What change?" Rildan asked.

"She almost grew...sentimental. She may be a witch, and I may have been her pawn, but she loved me at one time. In her own twisted way." His jaw tightened.

Emeris reached across the space between them, patting his hand. "The others have gone hunting for the starbridges. They're going to see Pacran."

"No," Rildan corrected gently. "They're headed for Paelen's waters to seek out the Sayhleens and find Lady Merinnia. If anyone knows about a curse or a prophecy or something that binds you to Mayvus, she will."

Emeris frowned, her eyes clouding over. "I could have sworn…"

Rildan and Marnok exchanged a curt glance.

"Either way," Emeris continued. "We won't make you go back to the witches."

His shoulders slumped, making Orra aware of just how tense he'd been. There was far more to his story. And perhaps he would share it all at some point. But it was clear he still wasn't ready to reveal his secrets.

"You've been gone far more than two weeks," General Nels pointed out. "Even with travel time. That can't be all you did."

"This isn't an interrogation, General," Emeris said. "I invited you here as a courtesy and out of respect for the ways you've protected us. But there's no need to put him on trial."

Marnok held up a hand. "It's all right. He's being thorough. I would ask the same questions if I were him."

Orra licked her lips, already knowing part of his answer. "You went to see the sprites," she said.

"No," Emeris said. "He wouldn't—" She cut off as they all took in the guilt on Marnok's face.

"I went there—not to seek a deal, but to verify why I went there in the first place."

"In the first place?" General Nels asked.

"The first memory I have is from that cave. It only makes sense that I made some sort of deal with them, and the price was my memory." He glanced at Emeris, his need for her approval or forgiveness written in the raw emotion on his face.

"You were desperate," Emeris whispered.

He nodded. "And as much as I don't care to admit it, the sprites gave me what I wanted." He squeezed his eyes shut. "I'm not sure I regret it."

Emeris sighed and sat back in her chair, her face uncertain for the first time since Marnok had started his story.

This time, Marnok reached across the space between them and squeezed Emeris' hand. Her gaze went blank, and Orra sensed she was receiving memories from Marnok, secrets he wasn't willing to share out loud, whether it was because of General Nels' presence or Orra's and Rildan's.

She itched to seek out the information on her own. Her magic flowed not just in her blood, but in her very skin and hair. Every bit of her tingled with the opportunity to stretch out her power and draw in the information she sought. But even if she was willing to waste the magic she'd slowly regained, Marnok wanted to keep those memories private for a reason, and she would not interfere.

Emeris blinked back tears and nodded. "You've sacrificed so much. I can't judge you for your choices. It's between you and the Sun."

He smiled, his lips wavering, and dropped her hand. "Thank you."

Emeris' gaze remained distant, and Orra feared she was falling back in the past once more, giving in to the safety of her memories instead of the unknowns of the present. Rildan nudged her, likely having the same suspicions. Emeris blinked and sat straighter, clearing her throat.

"And what about the witches?" General Nels asked. "How big of a threat are they to the Wyndrens?"

Marnok gave a short laugh. "If Mayvus survived a dragon attack, then I'd say we have far bigger things to worry about. Maybe we can let the witches and Mayvus go at each other while we quietly find the starbridges."

A small smile crossed Emeris' face, one that Orra tried to mirror for Marnok's sake, but she felt the fear behind his words. They weren't through with the witches yet.

CHAPTER 37

GAEREN WAS ABOUT to force his way into the ship's hull to go after Aeliana when the door leading below deck opened with a crash, slamming into a table before flinging back to catch on Velden's boot. Gaeren froze as Velden's dagger came into view, followed by the water shackles around Dreyfus. Gasps from the crowd made it clear he wasn't the only one who noticed.

Guess it was time for a new plan.

Velden swung his dagger around wildly, ensuring a wide berth from the next set of ticket holders who had just crossed the plank.

"You all came for a show, so today you get one." His voice rose even louder. "And I won't even distinguish between buyers and onlookers. It's a free show, and it will be a grand one, because it will be this man's last."

Behind Dreyfus, Aeliana emerged carrying a magnificent Sayhleen tail that almost looked fake with its brilliant colors. She caught Gaeren's eye over her hefty cargo, but he couldn't get close enough to tell if she'd already come up with a new plan. He could try pulling it from her memories, but it seemed more prudent to focus on Velden's current chaos.

"This man shows off a beautiful Sayhleen tail." Velden turned back to Aeliana, gesturing for her to hold it out as evidence.

She did as he wanted, but Gaeren could see she didn't like it.

Velden's grief was driving him mad. How were they going to rein him in?

"But he hasn't been honest about how he came by the tail. Tell us, Dreyfus, how did you find such a prize?"

Dreyfus licked his lips, his eyes scanning the crowd, looking for an escape. "I caught her in my nets. I tried to save her, but by the time I got to her, she was already dead from another injury."

Velden clucked his tongue. "So, shall it be your word against mine?"

"No." Dreyfus' voice rose a little higher. "She was injured or something. She left a trail of blood in the water. If I hadn't gotten to her first, the sharks would have."

"It's funny," Velden said. "I'd think if you saw a woman bleeding in the water, you would attempt to help her instead of harpooning her."

"Maybe," the man said, narrowing his eyes at Velden. "But she bared her teeth at me, and I got the sense she wasn't quite tame."

Velden flinched, his dagger drawing nearer to Dreyfus' neck. The other man leaned back, exposing his neck more as he avoided the glint of steel.

Aeliana tugged on Velden's sleeve, and he glanced her way, his gaze softening a bit.

"I need you, Velden," she said. "If I don't have you, who will keep Sylmar in check?" Her smile wavered, but Velden shook his head.

"I've waited twenty-five years for this moment."

Gaeren's mind raced through their options. All Velden's antics had done was bring on more witnesses and more obstacles. Several men and women covered their children's eyes, backing away. It wouldn't be long before local soldiers were sent to intervene.

He stepped forward, and for a moment, Velden's wild eyes seemed to forget that he was a friend. The watery shackles tightened, making Dreyfus cry out, and the dagger shifted toward Gaeren. But then Velden pivoted the dagger back to Dreyfus once more.

"How shall we do it, oh mighty prince? Drown him at sea? String him up from his own mast? I still favor gutting him like he did my mother." The last option was said on a growl.

Gaeren stepped around Velden, placing his hands on Dreyfus'

shoulders and pulling the two men apart a half step. The shackles loosened a hair but remained in place.

"I'm not sure we should do any of those things with this number of witnesses."

Dreyfus nodded quickly. "I knew you had the most common sense out of all the royals."

Gaeren grimaced, finding it hard to maintain objectivity when the man was proving to be as obnoxious as his reputation. "Do you have the fish?" he whispered to Aeliana.

She nodded.

Despite their impossible situation, Gaeren felt light. It didn't matter that they were attempting to steal something from a murderer in broad daylight. They'd found the starbridge. If they could cross that hurdle, escaping this was nothing.

"Tell them what you did when you saw the wounded Sayhleen in your nets," Velden continued, drawing more eyes. He was an even better performer than Dreyfus, since he used his free webbed hand to spray waves of water to draw attention.

"He's like the green-eyed goddess," one of the closest observers told his friend, distracting Gaeren with the memory of an old lead he'd chased when looking for Aeliana—a green-eyed goddess rumored to control the seas.

"She was dying." Dreyfus interrupted Gaeren's thoughts, his voice turning into a whine as Velden lost more control. "When animals are dying, you put them out of their misery."

His final word ended on a screech as Velden's shackles rose him half a foot off the deck, tugging his shoulders at an awkward angle and pulling him out from Gaeren's grip. Gaeren placed his hands on the man's back, unsure if supporting him would prolong his misery or save his life. Surely Velden knew they couldn't kill him with this many witnesses.

"And what about the young naval student you saw swimming with her?" Velden asked.

"She was alone," the man said. Gaeren sensed the lie through the man's back with his underused pneumatic spoke. He frowned, but instead of testing it further, he dove into the man's memories, feeling no remorse over the invasion of privacy.

The memory was already at the tip of Dreyfus' mind, giving Gaeren quick and easy access. From within Dreyfus' memory, Gaeren drew the net closer, heaving it out of the water and into his boat. The body dropped with a heavy smack, blood splashing across his thigh.

The beautiful woman's eyes stared back at him, glassy and sorrowful.

"If you hadn't fought back," Dreyfus muttered, shaking his head. "I might have been able to let you live. Imagine how much people would pay to see a live Sayhleen."

Gaeren wanted to retch, but Dreyfus kept cutting the net from around the Sayhleen.

"Except you would have talked. Maybe even escaped. This is the safest way to cash in on a prize." Gaeren felt a grin stretch across his lips—until a man's cries reached his ears.

Dreyfus squinted out over the water, giving Gaeren a glimpse of a much younger Velden swimming through the water unreasonably fast. Dreyfus grabbed his harpoon once more but seemed aware that the man coming his way was in fact just a man. Hardly something he could harpoon.

"Did the siren reel you in?" he called out good-naturedly. "Don't worry; I've taken care of her. She won't bother you anymore." Velden's approach didn't slow, making Dreyfus hesitate. Gaeren sensed the calculated decision over the risk Velden brought to Dreyfus' prize. Decision made, he swapped out the harpoon for a dart. The poison wouldn't kill the man, but he'd likely drown before he regained consciousness.

"Can't have any witnesses," Dreyfus muttered.

His aim was true, but at first Velden's stride hardly slowed. As he neared the boat, his face grew slack with understanding. "I'll kill you," he said slowly before his head sank below the waves.

"Not if I kill you first." Dreyfus turned back to the Sayhleen, pulling a hatchet from his belt.

Gaeren cut the memory off in a panic, horrified at what likely came next, disgusted by what he'd already seen. He pulled his hands off the man's back as if touching him made his evil methods contractable.

"I won't blame you if you end him in whatever way you wish," Gaeren ground out.

"Gaeren," Aeliana hissed. "That's not helping."

"I saw what he did." Gaeren's voice rose. Now the eyes of the bystanders turned his way. "He harpooned her so he could make money. Dead slaves can't complain or escape. Then he shot the only witness with a poison dart, assuming he would drown, not knowing the man was her son and fully able to breathe underwater."

The crowd gasped, but Gaeren wasn't sure if their reaction was over Dreyfus' depravity or the shock of Velden's ancestry.

"He's a murderer two times over."

Instead of the words rallying Velden further, the older man's arms dropped, the shackles and Dreyfus along with them. "He killed her." His webbed hands covered his eyes. "She shouldn't have even been out in the water that day. But I insisted she take me. I wanted her to take me home. To her home."

Velden's vulnerability was all Dreyfus needed to rise and backhand the broken man. Velden fell back, his dagger clattering to the deck.

Gaeren's sword was out to block the man before he could turn, except Aeliana had the same idea. She used Velden's mother's poor tail to knock the conman to the deck, and Gaeren had to stay his sword before he accidentally ran her through in his haste to disarm Dreyfus.

Her face held shock and guilt at her own actions, and she picked up the Sayhleen tail, practically cradling it. "I'm so sorry," she whispered, her words more for the tail than anyone else.

"If you think this man's lies ended with his murders, you're all fools," Gaeren shouted, pulling Dreyfus up to face the crowd. The tail must have hit his head just right because his eyes fluttered as he fought for consciousness.

Velden recovered enough to grab his dagger and sheathe it, but his body still shook with sobs, his hands back to covering his face. He was no longer in danger of publicly murdering his enemy, but that still didn't mean they had a way out.

"How well can you swim?" Gaeren whispered.

Aeliana's laugh came out on a choke. "Decent, but not when I'm holding this." She angled her head toward the Sayhleen tail in her arms.

Gaeren grimaced, guessing it weighed more than half of what she did. "We'll have to leave it," he said.

"No." Velden stood, surprising Gaeren. He took the tail from Aeliana's hands and leaned his forehead against its scales, murmuring some sort of prayer or homage.

Gaeren put his sword away and let Dreyfus slump to the side, but the bystanders were getting braver. The young girl who'd helped swindle attendees stood with her jaw hanging open as people crossed the plank without buying tickets.

"We need to get out of here." Gaeren said the words in a singsong to hide the fear crawling up his throat. Until an idea struck. "Can we use the fish?"

"Only as a last resort," Aeliana said.

"I think we're on last resorts." Gaeren held out his hand, beckoning for her to hand the starbridge over.

"If we use it now, it could be a week or more before we can return for the others, and who knows where it would drop us? We need to get back to your ship first."

He debated pulling out the golden arrow. At least they knew where that would take them. But it would also set them back by weeks they didn't have.

"I'll hold them off while you leave," Velden said, tightening his grip on his mother's tail. "I got what I came for."

"We're not leaving you." Aeliana's tone was firm, but she backed up against the ship's railing as the people grew closer, their cries holding demands for the imprisonment of not just Dreyfus but also Aeliana, Velden, and Gaeren. "Can you swim with her body?"

"It will slow me down, but I'm faster than you."

"Good enough for me," Gaeren said. He hopped up on the railing, awkwardly pulling and forcing both of them up with him before unceremoniously pushing them into the water. A hand grasped at his ankle as he jumped after them, but he slipped from the stranger's grip and plunged beneath the sea.

CHAPTER 38

It was probably one of the worst plans Gaeren had ever had, but he was counting on the fact that they had two starbridges in their possession for an emergency escape. The longer they swam through the harbor, the more likely it seemed they'd need to use one.

"Where exactly are we going?" Aeliana switched to her back, her quick breaths signaling Gaeren that he should probably slow even more than their already agonizingly slow pace. With Velden's unwillingness to let go of his mother's tail, it was a wonder they'd even made it away from Dreyfus' ship. For now, they weaved between boats, utilizing stealth more than speed.

"If we can make it past the main harbor to a beach with fewer observers, we can pause and reassess," Gaeren said. He felt the skeptical look crossing Velden's face down to his core. That was still a few miles of swimming. "We'll need to tap into our starlocks to make it."

It felt dangerous to use up magic they might need if they were being pursued, but as far as Gaeren had been able to tell, the mob had turned their attention to the conman, letting the lesser threats make their escape. They'd have to decide if they should risk going back to the tavern for the few things they'd left behind or forge ahead.

He glanced at Velden between strokes, noticing that even his webbed hands weren't enough to keep him from being dragged down by his mother's tail. How in Rhystahn were they going to transport that all the way back to their ship?

As they reached the harbor's edge, all three of them were out of breath and weary despite pulling energy from their starlocks. Even so, they swam a bit farther until they reached an empty beach, where Gaeren helped Velden drag the tail far enough up the shore that it wasn't at risk of being pulled back out to sea. But then the three of them collapsed in the sand. They stared up at the clouds in the sky, the only sound the waves crashing on the beach and their own deep breaths.

"I'll admit I've been eager for a swim," Aeliana said, "but that was not the kind I had in mind."

For some reason, a giddiness bubbled up inside Gaeren, eventually breaking into uncontrollable laughter over the ridiculousness of their situation. Aeliana chuckled too, and even Velden cracked a smile, though the sadness in his eyes still lingered. It sobered Gaeren enough for his laughter to fade, but still left a grin that hurt his cheeks.

Now that they were out of immediate danger, Gaeren vowed to do whatever it took to help Velden get his mother's tail wherever it was Velden felt she deserved it to be.

"I'd give anything to see Gullet swoop in right now," Gaeren admitted. He hated the bird, but sending Riveran directions would have been ideal.

"What about your ship? Wouldn't that be better?" Velden sat up, his gaze on the water and one hand resting on his mother's scales.

Gaeren snorted. "Now you're asking for a miracle." He found a cloud shaped almost exactly like a tear, reminding him of the mystery still surrounding his starlock.

"Is it still a miracle if I told Larkos to come?" Velden asked, his voice regaining some of its dry humor. "Because I kind of like the sound of it being a miracle."

Gaeren sat up, sand sticking to all surfaces of his skin. "You did what?"

"Maybe the real miracle is that he did as I asked." Velden shielded his eyes from the Sun, and Gaeren followed suit. In the distance, a black ship angled its way toward Melford's harbor. Its profile was both unfamiliar with its pathetic sail and black wood and achingly familiar with its perfect way of cutting through the water. The reckless angle was Larkos' tell, and Gaeren felt a fresh surge of energy unrelated to his starlock's warmth. He stood with a whoop and waved, even though the sailors were unlikely to see them this far out, not unless one had a spyglass and was randomly searching the beaches.

"I may have also left a note with Cyrus," Aeliana admitted. "I told him to open it in five days' time." She stood beside Gaeren with a sheepish grin.

He swept her up in his arms and spun her around, making her yelp.

"That was brilliant," he said, setting her down and placing his palms on her shoulders, almost shaking her in his relief. "Why didn't I think of that?"

"Where's my celebratory spin?" Velden's eyebrows rose, but he remained on the sand, guarding the Sayhleen tail. "Why aren't you calling me brilliant?"

Gaeren grinned, mostly relieved that a ghost of Velden's confident smile crossed the older man's lips. "I'm still in shock. Why Larkos? I've never even seen the two of you talk."

Velden groaned and made a show of rising to his knees and standing. "I knew he wouldn't tell Sylmar, and that was my only real qualification when looking for someone to confide in. Besides, he's the only one who could give the command to bring the ship here. That seemed a bit important."

Gaeren shook his head. "Whether it was your confession to Larkos or Aeliana's letter to Cyrus, someone had impeccable timing."

"Or a lot of luck," Aeliana mumbled.

"If I can't have it labeled a miracle," Velden said. "I want it to be called impeccable timing. After as many years of experience at getting into trouble as I have, very little is left to luck."

By now, the ship was close enough for them to make out individuals on board. The three of them used their last dregs of energy to jump and wave like children until it was clear they'd been spotted and Larkos had corrected his course. It didn't take long for the boat to near the beach and anchor. By the time Velden, Gaeren, and Aeliana had been collected by rowboats, they were mostly dry but still sandy and exhausted.

Sylmar's rage kept him mercifully quiet, but Iris had plenty of heated words to fill the silence, her anger directed at Gaeren as she wrapped Aeliana in unnecessary blankets and dragged her to their quarters. The sailors all eyed the Sayhleen tail warily, though Gaeren noticed a few had guilty expressions, as if this wasn't the first time they'd seen the beautiful scales.

Gaeren instructed Larkos to sail farther west around the southern coast, aiming for Valorian even though that wasn't their final destination. If all went well, half of their party would be headed for Sayhla Island, but gaining distance from Melford's harbor seemed wise considering how they'd left it.

"I take it your mission was successful?" Riveran asked, following Gaeren below deck.

"Aye," Gaeren said, "though I think Aeliana and I would have failed without Velden, and he most certainly would have gotten himself killed without us." Gaeren found his spare set of clothes and changed, shaking off grains of sand from his hair and skin, eager to wash off the remains of his time with Dreyfus.

He would have liked to have seen justice come to a man like that, but in this instance, he had to count on the people to make sure that happened. He only hoped they had enough power to protect themselves from someone so corrupt. A nagging fear made him wonder if his family's soldiers could be bought off by a conman like Dreyfus.

"So now what?" Riveran asked as Gaeren switched the carefully wrapped golden arrow from his damp clothes to his fresh ones. "Are Aeliana and Velden crossing to Paelen's waters?"

"I think most of us are." Gaeren paused, taking in Riveran's nervous expression for the first time. It brought out Gaeren's own twinge of apprehension. "You don't think I should go."

"Do *you* think you should?" Riveran asked. "I'm still not sure which deal you took from the sprites."

"Maybe I didn't take any," Gaeren said. "They told me I would cross the barrier with Aeliana regardless of any deals. This shouldn't make a difference." The words felt like a lie since he'd been asking himself the same question ever since Larkos had taken him to see the Recreants. Maybe he should go back to Enla and protect her as throne warden. Set himself up as a secret ally to Aeliana and the Recreants from afar, waiting for the moment when he could help them while still protecting Enla.

But leaving Aeliana now, in the middle of all this, felt just as wrong.

"What if this is what starts it all?" Riveran asked. "What if by crossing the barrier, you set things in motion that put Enla in danger? What if it puts you on a path to where you need to sacrifice yourself to keep her out of danger?"

Gaeren had no answers for Riveran. If he was honest, he was terrified that his entire family had already gone down a path they couldn't return from, that Enla was already lost to him even if he still had access to her a bit longer.

His lack of knowledge and control over the situation left him agitated. "If you didn't want me crossing, why were you so eager for Aeliana and me to go find the starbridge in the first place? You could have let Sylmar and Velden continue with their pointless plan and never said anything at all."

Riveran scoffed. "Their plan would have caught us all in Dreyfus' trap. I was pulling us out of one fire, knowing we were likely jumping into another."

They stared at each other, the tension between them familiar but unwanted. "I may not want the role of throne warden," Gaeren said, "but I will still protect Enla to my death."

Riveran sighed. "Maybe that's what I'm afraid of." His soft words knocked all the fight out of Gaeren.

"You know I have to go," Gaeren said. "I will protect Enla, but I have to do this first."

Riveran gave a short nod. "Which is why I'll go with you."

The undeserved loyalty left a lump in Gaeren's throat, and all he could do was clap a hand on Riveran's shoulder in thanks.

When they headed back to the main deck, Iris and Aeliana still hadn't emerged from their quarters, but Sylmar and the others had gathered around Velden, demanding answers. Even some of the sailors listened in, their knowledge of the hunt for starbridges always dependent on what they could glean from eavesdropping and gossip.

The poor half-Sayhleen still hugged his mother's tail to his chest, his lips pressed together in a grim line and his eyes haunted by memories Gaeren didn't want to access.

"We can share the details of what happened later," Gaeren called out, drawing everyone's attention away from Velden and onto him. "The important thing is that we have the starbridge. Right now we need to figure out a plan moving forward."

"You all deliberately went behind our backs," Sylmar said. "The events that transpired over the last few days might very well inform us on how to move forward."

"Fine," Gaeren said flatly, and he began rushing through the events like he was reciting the contents of his desk drawer. "The plan to fool Dreyfus was terrible. He's a black market trader, a conman, a swindler, and a murderer. Our efforts to fool him would have been seen through before we were able to act on them. Aeliana and I saw that, but we didn't realize Velden concocted the plan in the first place as a distraction, both for you and Dreyfus."

Sylmar stiffened a bit but let Gaeren continue.

"We figured if word got back to Dreyfus that a trap lay in wait in Andel, he wouldn't be looking for one in Melford. So we caught him unaware, and we took the starbridge from him. Now we can use it to get answers, and…" He paused, abandoning his emotionless tirade so he could give proper respect to his final words. "And we'll use it to take Velden's mother home for a proper burial."

Cyrus and Holm dropped their eyes, as if finally aware of how their curiosity might have been painful for Velden, but several sailors grew more excited, making Gaeren want to string them all up with the sails.

"That should sum it up," he said even louder, "and now we can move forward."

Thallahan took the hint and elbowed a few men before sending Erech off on an errand.

Velden shot Gaeren a grateful glance, but Sylmar's frown didn't fade. He leaned on his staff, glancing back and forth between Velden and Gaeren. "Do we know where the starbridge will take us, or where it will return us?"

Gaeren shrugged. "I suppose we're about to find out."

Lukai and Kendalyhn bent their heads together, whispering, while Holm glanced back toward the women's quarters, still waiting for Iris and Aeliana to come out. Thallahan frowned, rubbing at his eye patch.

Velden finally cleared his throat, his voice once again subdued, making Gaeren mourn the little progress they'd made with him during their escape. "I suspect it will bring us back somewhere in the southern waters, most likely on the western coast. My mother would return home sometimes, and when she would come back to Andel, she always came from the west."

Sylmar nodded, then turned back to Gaeren. "Didn't you say you left friends in Rykarn?"

Gaeren and Riveran exchanged glances. "Breeve's mother and Riveran's..." Gaeren hesitated, no longer sure if he should refer to her as Riveran's wife.

"My sister and her son," Riveran finished.

Gaeren couldn't keep his eyebrows from shooting up.

Riveran leaned in to mumble, "We agreed there was no reason for the marriage charade. When we last spoke, I still wanted Rox to be family, and this seemed the easiest way."

"Was that before or after you knew my sister got married?" Gaeren hissed.

Pain flashed across Riveran's face, and Gaeren regretted the question, even though he still wanted to know the answer. Had Riveran made that decision because he thought there was hope for him and Enla?

Sylmar's staff thumped on the deck, breaking up their awkward impasse. "I say those of us who came from the Myndren Mountains cross the barrier and meet with Gaeren and his men in Rykarn."

"I'm crossing the barrier," Gaeren corrected. "Riveran too."

Sylmar's lips pursed, making them disappear beneath his mustache and beard. But he didn't argue.

"I wouldn't mind staying on the ship," Brogdon admitted. "Maybe even after we return to the fortress. I'm not sure I can return to a soldier's life." The raw statement was directed at Gaeren as if asking permission.

"You'll always be welcome aboard my boat," Gaeren said, and he meant it even if he now saw the boat as a Recreants' tool more than his toy. Jasperus' son had turned out to be a fine sailor, and he couldn't blame the man for wanting a fresh start away from the reminders of his past. "Even if Larkos paints her and changes her name without my permission… again." He waved to Larkos, who stood across the ship at the helm.

Larkos waved back, blissfully unaware of the slight directed his way.

Iris and Aeliana chose that moment to step out from their quarters, drawing everyone's attention as they crossed the deck. Aeliana's hair had been freshly braided at her crown—so tight it looked painful. It seemed like Iris had taken her fears from the last week out on the plaits, and he winced in empathy for Aeliana.

She stood next to Cyrus, practically leaning on the almost priest for support.

"Does anyone else want to stay behind?" Sylmar asked, his gaze lingering on Cyrus, who only seemed to raise his chin and stand a little taller in response.

"I know you already said I'd stay behind," Thallahan said before turning to Gaeren, "but I'm just making it clear I'm not delaying my wedding again. And if you want to be welcomed in my home by my wife, you'll make sure you're back in time for it too—with that princely gift you promised."

"I'm pretty sure you promised it on my behalf." Gaeren chuckled.

Thallahan shrugged. "It's still expected by the bride."

"We still have a few moons. It shouldn't be a problem."

Thallahan squinted his good eye. "Do I have to remind you what happened last time?"

"We'll take a few days to let the three of you recover," Sylmar said, ignoring their side conversation. "Maybe stop for supplies we might need on Sayhla Island."

Gaeren didn't bother hiding his relief, and neither did Velden nor Aeliana.

Sylmar's scars bunched together with his favorite overly dramatic grim face. "Who knows what we'll find across that barrier?"

Over the next four days, they let their starlocks and blood recharge in the Sun's light while Sylmar attempted to make plans for every possible circumstance. Larkos continued heading toward Valorian, taking a slow and aimless pace, suspecting they'd get to Rykarn days, if not weeks, before those using the starbridge.

After Bartholem's reverence for their use of the starbridge, it almost felt sacrilegious for the ten of them to stand on the deck and crowd around the silver fish under the moonlight. Velden's grip tightened on his mother's tail as if fearing it might not cross the barrier with him.

"I wish we were leaving during the day," Cyrus said. "I want to see everything."

"But we don't want the Sayhleens to see us," Sylmar pointed out. "At least not right away. Not until we know we'll be welcome."

"Is there a limit to how many can cross at one time?" Aeliana asked, her gaze on their linked hands.

"I guess we're about to find out," Gaeren said.

"Can I say it?" Cyrus eagerly held out his hand for the fish. His face reddened. "It's the only thing I can really do."

Aeliana gave Cyrus an encouraging grin as Sylmar grunted his reluctant assent and set the fish in the Lorvandan's palm. As they all linked arms, Cyrus reverently recited the foreign words that matched the script on both the arrow and the fish, and Gaeren let them sink into his memory, determined to be able to repeat them if he ever needed to follow through on his promise to the Recreants to take his family across the barrier.

Then Gaeren felt the deck of his ship disappear from beneath him.

CHAPTER 39

Aeliana's stomach dropped, the experience uncomfortably familiar. But this time she waited for the grounding sensation she knew would follow once they crossed the barrier and reached Sayhla Island.

Except this time the sensation didn't come.

Her stomach continued dropping as her body fell with it. Bright light was replaced by dark skies and flashes of lightning. Rain lashed against her skin, and screams carried on the wind around her. They were quickly swallowed up by the thunder of waves and the slap of bodies hitting water before Aeliana was swallowed up by the sea. Panic engulfed her as she was swept back to the memory of being pushed off Lovers' Falls by the sprites. That same loss of direction left her fighting the waves around her for what was up and what was down.

Her hands brushed fabric and hair, arms and legs, making her desperate to drag all her companions to the surface with her, unwilling to repeat her failure with Cyrus. But she couldn't maintain a grasp on anyone, let alone find her way to the surface.

The thunderous roar of the storm above was muted beneath the water, the quiet foreboding. Her lungs burned and her mind fought the intense need to inhale as she stretched her fingertips, reaching for relief.

When she finally broke the surface and gasped in air, she was quickly overcome by a monstrous wave that rolled her again, leaving her sputtering and coughing as she surfaced a second time. Rain pummeled her face, making it impossible to catch a full deep breath, and the waves tossed her around until she no longer knew if her companions were still with her or if she'd been lost farther out at sea.

Then again, she had no idea how far out to sea they'd even been to begin with. Sylmar certainly hadn't considered this possibility with all of his preparations. Did any of them even have the bags they'd packed? Hers had quickly been lost in the storm's rage.

Lightning flashed, giving her a glimpse of at least six others struggling at the surface. She begged the lightning to return once more so she could find the rest, so she could know they were safe. Shouts rang out but were lost on the whistling wind. Her own cries came back to her, likely unheard by her companions, especially when the thunder returned the lightning's call.

Velden would be fine, but what about the others?

Her body felt weighted, making her grateful she'd given up the skirts that would have instantly made her sink. Her short hair still whipped in her face, ripped from her braids, but she felt certain half of what she wiped off her face was seaweed. The waves dragged her down again, and exhaustion swept through her. They'd been doomed before they'd ever even found the starbridge.

Her arm latched on to someone else's, maybe Kendalyhn's or Iris', but their slippery grips didn't hold, and Aeliana felt herself sinking, her energy spent. She reached for the magic deep within her blood, and her starlock glowed green in the water around her from where it floated out in front of her. But her magic wasn't equipped for this environment. It boosted her energy, but it couldn't give her air, and eventually her energy would run out.

It would be the same for the other progenies, and if their magic couldn't outlast the storm, it would be their end. And for those who weren't progenies? Cyrus', Holm's, Riveran's, and Iris' faces came to mind, pushing her to fight harder, to survive so she could help them.

As she pushed again for the surface, another hand gripped her wrist. In the dark water she couldn't see who latched on to her, but this grip was steadier, its webbed surface almost suctioning to her skin.

Velden.

As he pulled her to the surface, she felt a sense of relief, but he couldn't save all of them. He should be helping those who didn't have starlocks.

"What are you doing out here?" a voice screeched at her—a female voice that was clearly not Velden's. "Why didn't you transform? Do you have some sort of death wish?"

As the lightning flashed, it lit up a face patterned by scales and a neck boasting gills. The Sayhleen's hair floated wildly around her, more reminiscent of kelp. The moment Aeliana recognized the Sayhleen for what she was, the Sayhleen seemed to recognize what Aeliana was not.

Her eyes widened, and she kicked and swept out her hands, pushing more of the sea between them as she sought space from Aeliana.

"Who are you?" She scanned the water's surface, which was only slightly calmer than it had been. "Are all of you…human?"

"Half-lights," Aeliana corrected, still fighting to stay above the waves while also straining to be heard. "Well, and one human."

The Sayhleen's eyes narrowed, but she didn't seem to be having the same trouble as Aeliana. Her body buoyed in the waves in an almost gentle, relaxing manner as Aeliana coughed and sputtered.

"Please," she begged. "We can explain everything, but we can't swim in a storm like this. Not like you can."

The Sayhleen's head whipped around, taking in the struggle of those nearby before nodding. Then she dove below the surface.

And stayed below the surface.

Aeliana's breaths turned to gasps and near cries as she waited for the woman's return. Where had she gone? Did she see their vulnerability as a sign to abandon them? Was she looking for those who struggled more than Aeliana?

As she slipped beneath the surface once more, she wasn't sure anyone else *could* be struggling as much as her. It was humbling, knowing her starlock could do her no good in this place, and it made her realize how much she'd come to depend on the thing she'd once despised.

The kelp-like hair rose from the water along with two other Sayhleens, the skin around their scales rougher with age lines and their mouths twisted in frowns. Still, they split up, practically flying through the water to gather up her friends.

A smooth hardness brushed against Aeliana, making her yelp, then a dolphin rose beside her, cocking its head as if assessing her intelligence.

"You can ride Eyelee to the shore. Grasp her fin like this." The Sayhleen demonstrated, then pulled Aeliana's hand to do the same. "And swing your body over hers."

Aeliana fumbled to do as the Sayhleen instructed, but the waves pulled her back down. When she was finally settled, the Sayhleen patted the dolphin, and the dolphin took off in the water, nearly making Aeliana lose her grip. She tried to look back, to see if the Sayhleen was helping her friends, but the dolphin dove deep, forcing her to hang on tighter and face forward, grabbing air when the dolphin surfaced and leaning her head close against the sea animal each time it dove.

Within moments the darkness beneath her shifted, slowly lightening as the sandy surface of the ocean floor sloped upward toward the beach Aeliana had been desperate to find. The dolphin came to a sudden stop, and Aeliana slid off.

"Um, thank you?" She patted the dolphin the way she'd seen the Sayhleen do, then flinched as the dolphin took off, hopefully to help someone else.

The waves still lapped at her waist, so Aeliana walked farther up the beach, hugging herself as the wind whipped her wet clothes. From her new vantage point, the storm didn't look as severe, but she suspected it was still terrifying to those out in the water. She prayed to the Stars and then, for extra measure, to the Sun, begging for all her friends to be spared, thanking them for the Sayhleen's willingness to help.

The moonlight revealed little on the wild surface of the waves, but the next flash of lightning showed her five more people being swum to shore, whether by dolphins or Sayhleens she couldn't tell at first. As Cyrus, Holm, Iris, Riveran, and Kendalyhn were deposited beside her by chittering dolphins, she gave them all wet and exuberant hugs, even Kendalyhn. Riveran looked the most at ease, bending forward to rub his dolphin's nose affectionately before sending them off to rescue the rest.

It seemed the Sayhleen had recognized who could withstand the waves a little longer after all.

Kendalyhn pushed Aeliana aside with a glare. "I'm going to kill that idiot for bringing us all over here."

Aeliana smiled in her relief. "Velden or Sylmar?"

"Maybe both," Kendalyhn muttered. As she headed up the shore, squeezing water from her blouse, Iris, Holm, and Riveran followed, but Cyrus seemed frozen in shock, his face pale and his body still being buoyed by the waves. Aeliana tugged on his hands, bringing him farther up the shore to ensure he wouldn't be pulled out again by a rogue wave.

"It's all right, Cyrus. You're fine."

He nodded, not really looking at her, and she suspected he was back in Lovers' Falls, drowning all over again. She put her hands on his cheeks and forced him to look at her.

"Take a deep breath. You are surrounded by air. You will not drown." She emphasized each word like she was speaking to a child, and this time his nod was a bit more sure, his freckles no longer standing out so intensely against his pale skin.

"I won't drown," he repeated. Then he seemed to truly see her for the first time. "Did you see me riding the dolphin? I rode a dolphin."

A laugh burst from her throat, and she hugged him even tighter than she had when he'd first ridden in. "You were an amazing dolphin rider."

Another flash of lightning revealed the others arriving, this time led by the Sayhleens themselves. As the dolphins dropped off Sylmar, Lukai, and Gaeren, Aeliana finally breathed easier. She saw her relief reflected on Gaeren's face as he came to check her over, but Lukai beat him to her, sweeping Aeliana up in a hug that felt more smothering than comforting.

Velden was suspiciously absent, and while Aeliana wasn't concerned for his safety, she wondered why he held back. Was his mother's tail dragging him to the sea's floor? Or was he using it as an opportunity to put her in her final resting place?

The Sayhleens who had escorted them to safety rose from the water, their fins and tails morphing into legs and feet. Aqua and amethyst scales remained on their skin, and gills still flapped at their necks, as if they had no intention of staying on land for long.

"Why, Nori?" Deep disappointment laced the older male Sayhleen's voice as he frowned down at the younger one who'd found Aeliana. He made harsh hand motions that brought the woman's head low in shame.

"I'm so sorry, Father," she whispered, her own hand motions much more subdued, but clearly communicating far more than they were saying. Her hands paused in hesitation, her gaze taking in all the Vendarans in confusion.

"It's rude for us to use Water Words in front of guests." The other female Sayhleen's voice held a bit more softness. "What did you think you saw?"

"I thought I saw..." Nori tucked her hands behind her back, then stood a little straighter. "I thought I saw Rhoda's scales."

The older woman sighed. "You've never even met her."

"But I've heard you describe her," Nori rushed on. "Scales that bright are unusual. But... perhaps it was the storm's light that confused me. I'm sorry, Mother." Her head bowed once more.

The woman frowned. "I barely remember her scales. It was more fanciful daydreaming, and one of these days it's going to get you killed."

Nori's chin rose a fraction. "Perhaps it was the sprites calling me up to save these people."

Before her parents could respond, a final figure rose from the sea, weighed down by the heavy burden he carried in both his arms and heart. A flash of lightning revealed a glimmer of orange and mauve, brilliant scales and full fins.

Both of the older Sayhleens gasped.

"I knew it," Nori breathed out.

But as Velden drew closer and it became apparent he carried only half the body, all three of the Sayhleens stiffened, and the man snarled.

Chaos ensued as a net shot out from the belt at the man's waist, encompassing half of the Vendarans, who immediately drew weapons to defend themselves. Another came from the woman's, effectively trapping the rest of them with a substance that seemed impervious to their daggers. When Sylmar's staff turned molten, singeing the net even as the rain sizzled against it, the older Sayhleen pulled a three-pronged dagger out from his belt, snarling once more.

He held the dagger against Sylmar's neck. "What have you done to my sister?"

CHAPTER 40

GAEREN STEPPED in front of Aeliana, attempting to shield her even though the Sayhleen man threatened Sylmar under the opposite net. As Velden drew closer, Nori released her own net, easily ensnaring him because he made no move to run. Instead, he lay his mother's tail down and kneeled as though presenting an offering.

"Your sister?" Gaeren asked. "Then you would be Velden's uncle?"

Velden's head snapped up at this, his eyes holding a mix of hope and confusion.

But the Sayhleen kept his trident and focus on Sylmar, waiting for an answer.

"We brought your sister here for a proper burial," Sylmar said, his tone more even and placating than Gaeren had ever heard it. "We mean her no disrespect."

The Sayhleen still didn't move, but his gills flapped as though searching for water that might calm him. "Why should I believe you?"

"Because I can show you," Gaeren said.

This time the older woman stepped forward, her eyes rimmed red and the wetness on her cheeks likely more than rain. "Show us what?"

"I'm a noetic progeny. Velden, Aeliana, and I rescued his mother's tail from a poacher. We brought her body here so Velden could say his goodbyes. And now it seems she has family who could benefit from that closure as well." He held out his hand. "Let me show you."

"Don't," the man growled, and the woman stepped back, distrust written on her features. But to Gaeren's surprise, Nori stepped forward, placing her hand in his.

He was already spent from his fight with the sea, his starlock nearly drained. But he pulled up the memory of their fight with Dreyfus and their escape to the water. He made sure to remember Velden's grief for good measure.

The memories broke off with a painful snap as Nori's father tore her hand from Gaeren's.

"He could have killed you," he said.

Nori's eyes shone with awe. "They saved her," she whispered. "They're telling the truth."

"You'll let the elders decide that," her father said. "And we won't hear any more of their lies until then."

The man dislodged Nori's net just to lift the Sayhleen tail, then tightened it around Velden once more. To Gaeren's dismay, they were dragged back into the water with far less care over how they fared. Even though they could still touch the sea's floor, the Sayhleens swam them along the coast, dragging them along like the day's catch. The nets made it difficult to stay above water, much less plan any sort of escape. But the Sayhleens were able to transport them faster than they would have made it on land.

By the time they'd reached a different beach, one that held a small town's harbor, the storm had mostly abated and other Sayhleens were rising from the water. Gaeren's mouth hung open as wide as Cyrus' as they watched the people transform their scales, sliding them away for leathery skin and shifting the kelp-like hair to a range of colors silkier and smoother. Tails and fins transformed to arms and legs. Minimal scales remained on torsos to maintain modesty. Was that how they clothed themselves, or would they eventually don trousers and tunics? Even the Sayhleens who had captured them shifted more than they had before, their gills folding in against their neck and the webs of their hands smoothing out to fingers.

Velden held up his own webbed hands in curious comparison, drawing Nori's gaze.

"Oh." She leaned over to inspect him through the net. "Are you really Rhoda's son?" she whispered.

"No more talking," her father chided.

She stepped back, biting her lip and bowing her head in deference.

A crowd gathered around them, making Gaeren more anxious as possible escape routes diminished. Cries rose as people recognized the Sayhleen tail, and within moments there was a sea of people kneeling down and wailing in their grief. Their mournful sounds rose almost like a song that was both horrifying and awe-inspiring, leaving Gaeren uncertain if he wanted to cover his ears or hold on to the memory to revisit later.

Velden kneeled as well, his face in his hands as he wept.

Several young men approached, their scales remaining in place like armor, weapons at their sides. Gaeren couldn't hear the words exchanged because of the wailing mourners, but it was clear they were about to be carted off to some sort of waiting place or prison.

Holm and Lukai exchanged grim looks, determination on their faces as they reached for their weapons.

"Wait," Gaeren hissed, trying to be heard over the wails but not by the soldiers. "What if they're willing to listen? If we fight back now, we immediately make ourselves enemies. But if they listen, we have a chance."

"And if they don't listen?" Sylmar asked.

Gaeren frowned, glancing back at Aeliana.

"I agree with Gaeren," she said. "I don't want to fight these people, not when they're mourning the same woman we are." Her gaze rested on Velden, her eyes filled with compassion. "Besides, we came for a purpose. We need them to take us to Lady Merinnia. We need to get our questions answered."

Sylmar sighed, but his tense posture relaxed. "I doubt our weapons can do much against these nets anyway. The Sayhleens would have removed them from us otherwise."

As the soldiers began leading them away, Velden finally put up resistance. "Please, no," he cried as they pulled him to his feet. "I know you'll take her out to the sea. I know you'll release her to the water, to the sprites."

Gaeren tensed at the absurdity of that part of the ritual. How could he respect anyone who worshiped such vile creatures?

"I wasn't able to hold her in her death." Velden went on. "Please don't deny me the chance to release her to the sea." He made similar hand motions to the Sayhleens, far slower, but with purpose.

The soldiers hesitated, glancing at the man who'd brought them in. Even he looked momentarily uncertain as he followed Velden's hand motions. "How do you know Water Words? And of our rituals?"

"My mother taught me." Velden's shoulders slumped and he squeezed his eyes shut. "She came every year when the water was warmest, even after I was grown. She told me of her people, my people. She told me of the Seer and your Awakening celebrations. She told me she would never regret coming to Vendaras, that she would never regret me.

"But then she died," he said flatly. "She left me without a true place in this world, straddled between two people groups. She told me so much, but it turns out she told me very little."

The wails had died down by now as people listened to his tirade, which was more of a tribute.

Nori stepped forward, tugging on her father's sleeve. "Look at his hands," she said. "He tells the truth."

Everyone's eyes strayed to Velden's webbed fingers. Even he held them out and studied them as if he hadn't seen them before. Then he looked up at the man, his chin raised with pride.

"Look at my eyes. My father always said I had her eyes. It made it difficult for him to see me after she died." His lips pressed together in a thin grim line, hinting at a different sort of grief he'd yet to share with his companions.

This time, the Sayhleen man's eyes grew misty. "Let him come," he said gruffly. "But take the others to the hut."

***

The hut turned out to be exactly what it sounded like: walls made from bamboo shoots and other sticks, a dirt floor, and a thatched roof. But the entire thing was lined on the outside with the same net that had been used to catch them, some sort of seaweed-like substance that felt more alive than the ropes they'd used in Vendaras.

As the nine of them were shuffled into the fifteen-foot round room, they were relieved of their weapons, except for Sylmar's staff, since he needed it for walking. The soldiers stared extra long at Riveran's forehead, a stark reminder that even without context it was a clear sign of distrust across cultures. Even the silver fish and golden arrow, their guaranteed chances at escape, were taken into the Sayhleens' custody. They didn't disrespect the travelers so much as to remove starlocks, but they gave several warnings that no second chances would be given if magic were used.

Sylmar and Lukai immediately began scouring the walls of the hut for any weaknesses, but Gaeren simply sat, leaning back against the sticks. Their fate rested in the hands of the Sayhleens and in Velden's ability to convince them of the truth. After seeing Velden grieve his mother, he held a fair amount of confidence in the Sayhleens. He just wasn't sure how long it would take.

The warm, humid air made it impossible for their clothes to completely dry, but the longer they sat there, the stiffer their tunics and trousers grew with the salt. Aeliana's blouse crunched with her every movement, and sand stuck to every bit of skin on Gaeren's body, exposed or not. The inability to wash it off left him agitated.

"What happened?" Gaeren asked Aeliana, gesturing to the blood on her blouse and trousers.

She frowned at it, then tugged on her sleeves and flipped her hands around until she found cuts on her palm. "Maybe shells in the water?"

Her uncertainty left him anxious even though it wasn't the first time she'd had unexplained cuts on her skin—maybe because it wasn't the first time. Lukai joined them, smoothing out her wounds even though Aeliana could have done it herself.

Gaeren rubbed the braid under his cuff while debating if he should get up and give them some space. One glance at Kendalyhn, who glared daggers at Aeliana, made him decide that space would only get filled by someone else with far more animosity.

Eventually, even Sylmar joined the others on the floor, and Holm's snores filled the room, lulling several others into an uneasy sleep.

Gaeren couldn't find rest. As the Sun's light finally peeked through cracks in the hut walls, footsteps sounded, followed by low voices. The hut door opened, and Velden was escorted in.

His eyes were puffy and his smile absent, but there was a peace on his face that Gaeren hadn't seen since they'd discovered what Dreyfus harbored. Without a word, Velden walked to the back of the hut and lay down, curling on his side away from the others.

"Sylmar?" one of the soldiers asked, scanning the group.

Sylmar stood, leaning heavily on his staff. The soldier beckoned for him to come out. "Velden says you're the one we should talk to."

Gaeren grimaced, then murmured, "If we want to start a war."

Cyrus was the only one close enough to hear, and he snorted out a laugh.

The soldiers glanced their way warily, but when no one else spoke or moved, they shut the hut door behind Sylmar.

A second round of waiting began, punctuated by intermittent naps. Food and water were delivered by Nori, who lingered within the hut as she handed them each a cup and plate filled with fish broth. Even Velden rose to eat, and Nori gave him a tentative smile.

"Rhoda never told my parents she had a son. I think that's the only reason they're hesitant to believe you. Why would she keep you a secret?"

Velden smiled, but it was a fraction of the carefree manner he usually exuded. "She kept many secrets, most of which she learned from Lady Merinnia."

Nori's eyes widened. "She went to see the Seer?"

He nodded. "I suspect that's why she told me she had no regrets. She knew the outcome before she made her choices. I only wish she'd explained things a little more. Maybe given me some warning."

Nori's face grew troubled, and a soldier cleared his throat. She stood, backing away, the indecision on her face giving Gaeren hope. The elders didn't seem to believe Nori, but as long as she kept asking questions and listening to their answers, they might end up with an ally.

"Thank you for the food," he said.

She turned his way, and he gave her an encouraging smile.

This time, the soldier pulled on her arm, and she disappeared outside the hut.

When Sylmar finally returned that evening, he had little to tell them. "They asked all the questions." He used the wall to ease down into a sitting position, wincing the whole way. "Nori's father, Elder Algaen, wanted me to identify everyone in our party and why they'd come. I'm not sure they believed me much, but at least they let me talk. I suspect they mostly wanted to see if my story matched Velden's."

Velden chuckled, the corner of his lip regaining its teasing lift. "Considering we never see eye to eye, I doubt that worked in our favor. You may have just gotten us all killed."

Sylmar grunted but didn't say anything, and Gaeren suspected the old man was secretly pleased that Velden's humor had returned.

"What did they say about the Seer?" Aeliana asked.

Sylmar frowned. "She's not available to outsiders. That was the most I could get from them."

"But Velden's not an outsider," Kendalyhn pointed out.

"Just because I'm not fully Vendaran doesn't mean they don't see me as an outsider." Velden gave a wry smile, and Aeliana squeezed his arm. Her face held an understanding that surprised Gaeren, reminding him that she was only half-Vendaran.

For an ironic moment he considered how Enla would never approve of him choosing anyone with so little starblood as a bond-mate, no matter how much power she clearly had. And the knowledge that it would irk his sister made it all the more appealing. Then his bond mark burned with a fire he'd never felt before, and he winced away the thought.

"So now what?" he asked.

Before Sylmar could respond, the hut door opened again. The Sun's glory was fading as it headed for sleep, and Nori's silhouette broke up their view of the outside world. As Gaeren's eyes adjusted, he took in her beaming face.

"I've come to escort Velden, Gaeren, and Aeliana on a tour."

Everyone exchanged confused glances at the strange offer. Velden stood, but Gaeren and Aeliana remained seated.

"Why them?" Riveran asked.

"Some are convinced that Velden is Rhodasepha's son—and my cousin." Her smile grew impossibly bigger as she looked up at him.

He smiled back, as charming as ever.

"I don't have any other cousins. Or siblings." Her smile faded. "Or friends really..." She frowned at the dirt floor, then finally seemed to remember the initial question. "They wish to welcome Velden into the community. I think many of the people want to see him for themselves. Rhoda was well-loved among the Sayhleens. Even those of us who were too young to have met her know so much about her. She was slated to be the next Seer. Her disappearance was felt deeply across the island. The confirmation of her death even more so."

"What about Aeliana and Gaeren?" Iris questioned further, her crossed arms and furrowed brow almost as foreboding as Lukai's protective glare.

"Oh," Nori said, as if she hadn't realized their inclusion was odd. "Velden made it sound like Sylmar was your leader, but when the elders questioned Sylmar, it was clear that Gaeren and Aeliana hold higher rank as the son of a king and the daughter of a high priestess. They would like to show them our refuge as a peace offering. We consider them ambassadors of Vendaras and would like to treat them as such."

"While keeping the rest of us locked up in the hut?" Holm asked.

Nori gave an embarrassed shrug. "It's a start in the right direction. Think of it as a test of diplomacy. If things go well with Velden, Gaeren, and Aeliana, I foresee them going well for all of you."

Kendalyhn groaned, placing her hands over her face. "We're doomed."

CHAPTER 41

INSTEAD OF WALKING through the village, Nori and the soldiers led Velden, Gaeren, and Aeliana around its perimeter until they reached the beach. Aeliana's stomach clenched when she saw half a dozen dolphins and Sayhleens waiting several lengths into the water.

"Where are you taking us?" Gaeren asked, wariness bleeding from his voice.

"It would be an honor for us to show you our Coral Coves," Nori said. "It's our sanctuary from the storms and where many of us seek solitude for worship. Many women even come here to nest before birthing, because the weight of their child is less burdensome in the water."

Aeliana scanned the horizon. While the waves had calmed, there was nothing else to see for miles. "Is it underwater?"

Nori laughed. "Of course. That's where coral lives."

Gaeren backed away, but the soldiers blocked him. "Maybe you're not aware, but we can't breathe underwater like you."

"Even I can only last an hour at most," Velden admitted.

Nori gestured up the beach where several more soldiers carried heavy clothing and strange glass helmets. "That's why we've brought our training suits."

"Training suits," Gaeren echoed uncertainly.

"They might be a bit snug on you," Nori continued. "Most of our children learn to control their transformations in their adolescence, so our suits are small. But we have a few larger ones that we think will do the trick. Some of our eldest have to use them again in their final days."

"I don't understand." Aeliana said, even as she took the clothing passed her way.

"Transforming into our water forms might seem as simple as breathing," Nori said, "but it's more like walking. It's something we learn to do when we are young, and we often stumble and fall. But when we're older, it becomes natural. The suits are used for those who have not yet learned to control their transformation to ensure that they don't transform underwater and drown themselves."

Aeliana shuddered.

"It's perfectly safe," Nori reassured her. "We wouldn't use it for our own children if there were any danger."

Velden pulled on the suit without hesitation, but Gaeren and Aeliana glanced between the suits and the water.

"No offense," Gaeren said, "but this would be an easy way for you to accidentally get rid of us all."

Nori gnawed on her lip before responding. "I know we've not had a great start. Our hope is that showing you our prized cove will give you confidence that we truly wish to get along."

"Releasing our friends from prison would probably be more convincing," Gaeren said.

Nori winced. "You have to understand that we're also waiting to gain the same assurance from you."

"Maybe only one of us should go," Aeliana said.

At this, Gaeren tensed. "Absolutely not. I stay with you."

She held his gaze for another indecisive moment, then nodded and pulled on the suit's trousers. Their weight alone was surprising, and she suspected it might weigh her down to allow her to walk along the sea's floor. The glass that went over her head felt suffocating until Nori took Aeliana's hand in hers, her webbed hand suctioning to the only exposed part of Aeliana's skin.

"I can share my air with you in this way. If it ever feels like too little, ask for more." She demonstrated a gesture of pinching her thumb and fingers together and drawing them toward her body. "If we get separated, you have permission to remove your suit and swim to the surface. It's deep, but not so deep that you couldn't make it."

Her voice sounded muffled through the glass, but Aeliana nodded her understanding.

"It will be difficult for us to communicate through speech," Nori admitted. "It's why we use Water Words. But if you truly must tell us something, signal to Gellen, and he can tune in to your current thoughts to translate to us." She pointed out a soldier with dark green scales and deep purple seaweed-like hair, but the words felt more like a warning than an offer for assistance.

This man could tune in to their thoughts at any time. That might have caused her fear in the Myndren Mountains, when they approached Mayvus, but here it almost felt like an asset.

"We have nothing to hide," she said. And it was true. Sylmar had told them they wanted to see Lady Merinnia, and that was all they'd come for. That and giving Velden the closure of returning his mother's tail. She almost wanted Gellen to sift her mind if it would get them past their mistrust.

But she supposed they'd already done that with Sylmar. That was probably why they were even being offered this tour of the coves. The trust process was slower than Aeliana would have liked, but she had to have faith that it would eventually bear fruit. She needed answers to save her mother.

Even though the suits prevented them from floating, they were still able to swim through the water, partially pulled by their much faster, and somewhat impatient, Sayhleen guides. The journey was lengthy, but after a time Aeliana grew comfortable with the strangeness of remaining under water, obtaining air from Nori's hand. Velden and Gaeren each had a soldier doing the same, and they made a strange procession among the school of fish and bottom dwellers. The dolphins swam ahead and returned, like dogs on a hunt leading the way. One looked familiar enough that she thought it might be Eyelee, but there was no way for her to confirm the suspicion.

Their surroundings grew darker as the sea floor sloped, but then light shone ahead, a mix of fluorescent seaweeds and unnatural light that had been produced by progenies. It helped highlight the full spectrum of colorful plants and sea life, an entire jungle of foreign creatures inhabiting a space Aeliana had never thought she'd be able to explore.

A coral reef spread out before them, a maze of amethyst, aqua, and turquoise fingers beckoning them to enter. Unlike the few Aeliana had seen in Lorvandas and Vendaras, this was not only an intricate pattern of plants but one that created a structure suitable for living.

Gellen turned back, his smirk directed at Aeliana.

Nori frowned and signed something to him. When he signed back, she grew angrier, her hand motions faster. Finally, Gellen rolled his eyes and swam back to Aeliana, taking her free hand.

They're not plants. They're animals. Gellen's voice spoke into her mind almost the same way the sprite's had, leaving Aeliana feeling invaded even though she found the information helpful. *They created this haven for us because we also provide for them. But they're fragile. Don't touch them.*

Gellen's hand left hers the instant the words reached her mind, as if he couldn't stand touching her a moment longer. Guilt flashed across his face, and she knew he'd received her own thoughts identifying the snub. Even if that hadn't been enough proof, the fact that he'd known she'd thought of them as plants made it clear that he was constantly evaluating her thoughts, whether it was his assignment as a soldier or his preference as a progeny.

She couldn't help appreciating Gaeren's careful use of his noetic skills a little more.

Even so, she had nothing to hide. Might as well let Gellen keep digging.

As they made their way under an arch of chartreuse skeletal coral, the ocean floor gave way to a bed of seagrass, the blades swaying in the current like they all danced to the same song. Inside the reef's center, a calmness pervaded the space. The sea life they'd walked among was now replaced by only a few schools of fish among dozens of Sayhleens, all watching the newcomers with wide eyes. Small Sayhleens inside their own training suits were tucked behind fins, left to peek between their parents' tails.

Even Nori hesitated at the way everyone held back before she swam forward to sign at the Sayhleens, making a full circle and repeating her gestures a few times for everyone to see. Several smiles and nods came in response, followed by a few of the men coming forward to sign to Velden. He attempted to sign back, but the clumsy suit made it impossible, and he glanced up at the water's surface in frustration. Finally he held up one finger in some sort of warning, then he pulled off his helmet.

"What are you doing?" Aeliana cried, but her words likely didn't carry beyond her own glass. She trusted he really could last an hour, but what if they didn't surface that soon?

Velden pulled down his suit and gestured at the tiny flaps on his neck, lines Aeliana had never noticed before. Maybe they weren't even visible outside of the water. Their size and sporadic movement proved they weren't as functional as the Sayhleens', but they'd give him that hour he'd promised.

Several Sayhleens crowded closer, and some even reached out to touch him. They signed so quickly that laughter made bubbles come from his lips, and his fumbled attempts to sign back were met with understanding as they took turns and slowed their own gestures.

Aeliana felt both privileged and out of place to watch this strange welcoming of Velden. The silence stretched around her, her own breathing the only noise reaching her ears. But it was a misleading calm when the excitement of the Sayhleens, and even Velden, was palpable through the water.

Nori grinned and winked at Aeliana, clearly pleased with the way he was being received.

His gestures shifted to more common ones Aeliana recognized as he pointed the others toward her and Gaeren. She smiled and gave a hesitant wave as the Sayhleens' attention turned her way. The Sayhleens came closer, almost too close, as they reached out to touch her glass and suit and gain a better view of the strangers in their midst.

Eventually a woman with a tail almost as brilliant a mauve as Rhoda's had been swam forward, two open clamshells in her hands. She placed them before Aeliana, weighing them out as if Aeliana was to choose.

She glanced at Nori, who nodded, and Aeliana studied the shells more closely. The one on the left held a rose pink pearl the size of Aeliana's smallest nail and the one on the right held a similarly shaped gem, but it was more transparent, its multi-faceted surface taking on the various shades of the bright coral around it like it reflected an entire rainbow.

Aeliana bit her lip, wishing she understood, wishing she could ask questions. Gellen swam beside her and placed a hand on her arm.

You can *ask questions. And no, your questions aren't rude.*

She grinned uncomfortably. "Is this a gift? Am I meant to choose one? I have nothing to offer in return." The words echoed back at her within her helmet, but she knew Gellen would likely hear them in his mind.

She glanced at Gaeren, but he shrugged, unable to hear her question or offer advice. He was probably used to these sorts of diplomatic affairs, but the choice had been offered to her.

Gifts are given without expecting anything in return. And while asking questions isn't rude, refusing a gift would be.

She studied the two offerings again, unsure of their value or meaning. Why hadn't she asked Velden more about Sayhleen culture?

She turned to Nori. "Which would you choose?"

Nori looked to Gellen, who narrowed his eyes but signed the question to Nori.

Her scales flashed in the light as a smile bloomed on her lips. She pointed at the one on the right, with its prism-like surface reflecting the azure of her fins.

Aeliana copied her motion, then bowed in what she hoped was an appreciative gesture to both Nori and the woman before her. The woman bowed back, then swam away with both shells, leaving Aeliana to wonder if it really had been a gift or some sort of test.

Then a small hand gripped her glove, and she kneeled down in the seagrass until she was eye level with someone in a tiny suit. The child couldn't have been much more than five or six, and when he grinned at her from behind his glass helmet, sharp teeth made her think of Felk. Scales fluttered across his face, as if he had little to no control over which form he took in the water.

"Hello," she said softly, even though she knew he wouldn't be able to hear her.

His mouth moved and then his hands. It was a question she couldn't catch, but she glanced at Nori, who nodded her approval.

Then Aeliana was being pulled through the water toward another archway, where her fear of accidentally harming the coral within its maze made her lose her sense of direction. The boy brought her to a small section that clearly belonged to him, with various toys tied down to a table and a sea turtle in their midst. He reached for the sea turtle and brought its nose against his glass, making kissing faces at it until it licked his glass.

Aeliana laughed, then did the same as he brought the turtle up against her helmet.

For the next hour, she was led from room to room where the people showed off their families and homes, the unique experience giving Aeliana hundreds more questions. Nori stayed with her, but she lost track of Gaeren and Velden until they all wound up back in the reef's entrance, where Velden signaled that he needed to leave. He and his guard swam to the surface, while Aeliana and Gaeren waved farewell to the submerged Sayhleens.

Before they left, the Sayhleen with the bright mauve tail tugged on Aeliana's arm, placing a closed clamshell in her free hand. Was this the gift Nori had suggested she pick? She moved to open it, but the Sayhleen shook her head, then pointed to the surface.

"I understand," Aeliana said, nodding at the woman. "Thank you."

The woman smiled and swam away, leaving Aeliana and Gaeren to make the trek back to the beach with Nori, Gellen, and Gaeren's guard. It felt even longer than the first time as Aeliana's questions swirled inside her. Did those people all live there all the time? Or did they rotate with the villagers? Did they work down there, or did its status as a refuge make it a place for only rest? Was that where they would find Lady Merinnia?

When they rose from the water, Aeliana and Gaeren pulled off their helmets and the clothing that was even heavier now that it was wet. Aeliana wanted nothing more than to flop on the beach and stare up at the sky while begging Nori for information, but she suspected that wasn't on the agenda.

Nori, Gellen, and Gaeren's guard all made their shift from scales to skin, retaining minimal modesty. Aeliana's face heated, and she looked away, wishing they'd kept more scales in place until they'd pulled on the clothes they'd left on shore.

Gellen chuckled, making Aeliana's cheeks grow even warmer.

She turned the shell over in her hand, wondering if it was finally safe to open. Gellen snatched it from her grip and tucked it into his belt pouch.

"That was a gift," Nori protested.

"She can have it back if she's released."

The two Sayhleens glared at each other, making Aeliana wonder what other disagreements lay between them. She had no use for a gemstone anyway. She'd trade it for the chance to talk to Lady Merinnia.

Gellen's glare was replaced by confusion as he turned to study Aeliana. She ignored his perusal, not wanting to care what he might be pulling from her mind.

"Thank you for showing us Coral Cove." Aeliana's words for Nori were true, even though she now knew the real reason they'd been brought on this tour in the first place was for Gellen to access their minds. Had they passed whatever test they'd been given? She supposed he would report back to the elders tonight.

"You did well enough," Gellen grudgingly admitted.

Nori's eyes narrowed, and her hands went to her hips. "Got enough information? Maybe now you can stop telling my father to—"

"Nori!" the other guard hissed.

She crossed her arms over her chest and looked away. "Let's take them back," she muttered.

No more words were exchanged before they reached the hut, where Velden greeted them like a hospitable host instead of a co-prisoner.

"Come in, come in! What took you so long?" He grinned and winked at them, gesturing for them to enter. "I was beginning to think we'd never see your sorry hides again."

"We couldn't have beaten you even if we'd sprouted wings," Gaeren said.

His words made Aeliana think of Durriken and how long it had been since she'd been able to reach the dragon. She hadn't thought to tell him goodbye before leaving Vendaras, hadn't considered she might not be able to access him after crossing the barrier. But ever since arriving on Sayhla Island, she'd felt like the brand connecting them had been temporarily severed even though it still looked solid on her palm.

The inability to sense his presence was uncomfortable, like when her bond mark would twinge if she sensed Lukai in danger. But this was more like the phantom pain of a lost limb, and her efforts to reach him had become more of a desperate habit than true attempts. She supposed that meant her noetic magic would be dulled. Would her somatic skills automatically be strengthened? Or was it a muscle she had to retrain first? There was no way for her to test it with the Sayhleens guarding them anyway.

Before Aeliana could follow Gaeren into the hut, Gellen's hand shot out to grab her wrist.

She stiffened, but then his question reverberated in her mind.

Who's Durriken?

Her brows rose in surprise, but instead of answering, she let the image of Durriken fill her mind—not the docile creature in the woods playing hide-and-seek with a little boy, but the terrifying beast who'd annihilated thousands of soldiers in the Valley of Krahn.

Gellen stepped back and dropped her wrist, his face pale. "You're trying to frighten me."

She'd simply wanted to shock him, but frightening him felt equally rewarding. "Is it working?"

His brow furrowed and his color returned, along with a few sapphire scales. "Or you're trying to make a fool of me."

She sighed. "What would I gain from that? What is it you think we've come for? If not for the reason we've stated—to gain an audience with Lady Merinnia—then why?"

He pressed his lips together in a thin line, then stepped back just enough to slam the hut door in her face.

CHAPTER 42

VELDEN, Gaeren, and Aeliana spent the evening rehashing their excursion, but Sylmar and the others couldn't make sense of it either. Which made Aeliana even more confused when Nori showed up again the next afternoon, informing them that Velden, Gaeren, and Aeliana were all invited to her friend Ailah's Awakening celebration.

This time they were led away from the hut, which sat on the far eastern edge of the village, toward the center of town. Their procession drew attention from children and even adults who stopped to stare, making Aeliana relieved when Nori led them to a large gated home, away from onlookers.

They were offered the chance to freshen up, and two of the soldiers followed Gaeren and Velden into private rooms, but to Aeliana's relief, it was Nori who led her to an already steaming bath. After pointing out soap and towels, the young woman turned her back but kept up a steady stream of chatter, telling Aeliana about the people she'd meet and the meal they'd be serving, all while giving little tips to ensure she didn't offend anyone.

"This is the most exciting thing to happen to our village in years, maybe decades. Obviously it's not exciting that Aunt Rhoda is gone, but visitors from across the barrier…"

Aeliana couldn't see Nori's face as she stepped from the bath to dry off, but the awe was evident in her words. "Velden made it sound like everything over here was exciting."

Nori snorted. "He'd never even been here before, so maybe it's that Aunt Rhoda made it sound exciting. And it probably was for her. Crossing the barrier, having a secret romance, slated to be Seer." Her voice came out wistful.

"I'm sorry you were never able to meet her," Aeliana said as she pulled on a fresh set of clothes.

Nori sighed. "I think I'm probably more like her than I'm like my parents."

When Aeliana tapped Nori's shoulder, the other woman turned and grabbed a brush from the table, pushing Aeliana to sit in the chair and face the mirror. When she came around Aeliana to comb through her hair, Aeliana stiffened, Nori's familiarity feeling out of place. But in many ways, it was no worse than when she'd been forced to do the same with Kendalyhn. Besides, it kept Nori talking, and she was a wealth of information.

"Sometimes my father tells me I'm like her when I get in trouble, almost like it's an insult. My parents take everything so seriously. I know it's because they bear the weight of our entire people group, but that almost makes it worse. I can't live under that kind of pressure." Her strokes turned rough, making Aeliana wince.

This was all news to Aeliana, but she held back her surprise, worried it might clue Nori in to the fact that she was likely giving out more details than she was supposed to. "My mother bears a heavy load as the high priestess. Many Vendarans want her to rule instead of the royal family."

"Yes." Nori paused in her strokes, studying Aeliana in the mirror. "That was how Sylmar made it sound when the elders questioned him. It's good that your stories match. It will matter to the elders you meet."

Aeliana nodded, and they fell silent as Nori switched to plaiting Aeliana's hair.

"It can be hard to follow in footsteps like that," Aeliana added, hoping to get Nori talking about her own family again. But the words were also true, giving her a sudden shared kinship with this Sayhleen woman.

Nori hummed her agreement. "I don't really want to follow in my parents' footsteps, but I don't have much choice. I haven't received a starlock, so I can't go to the Seer's Sanctuary school. I always dreamed of being the next Seer. I'm sure every child does at some point, but a part of me still wants it. To see the future with such certainty, to do so much good with that knowledge. To pick up the mantle Aunt Rhoda couldn't take." Her hands stilled once more with her wistful tone.

"Why is the Seer not available to outsiders?" Aeliana asked.

"Is that what my father said?" Nori picked up plaiting Aeliana's hair once more. "I don't know that we have a true rule about it. There haven't been outsiders before now. Why do you want to see her anyway?"

Aeliana hesitated, but the curse wasn't exactly a secret. If Gellen hadn't already gotten it from her mind, Sylmar or Velden had probably told the elders. "My mother's been cursed. Her life is tied to another's, and we need to know how to break the curse."

Nori frowned. "Her pneumatic skills are highly focused on the future, not the past."

"But if we have a chance of breaking the curse in the future, won't she see that?" Desperation leaked into Aeliana's words. They couldn't have come for nothing.

"Probably. It's just an unusual use of the Seer. But far worthier than most," Nori added dryly. "I suspect the elders are afraid of what she might show you. What you might think of her. People go to her under the rarest of circumstances. Predictions for a loved one's future, resolution for crimes, decisions they can't possibly make on their own. We're each given one chance in our life to consult the Seer, and we must save it and use it wisely."

"Just one?" Aeliana asked.

Nori nodded. "We have to invoke our right by making an official request to the elders. Some wait so long to use it they never end up getting the chance. Others use it too early and regret that they wasted it. Others choose to never go, afraid of how often people return... changed. Sometimes mad."

"Velden said as much," Aeliana admitted. "Which shows how desperate we are."

"It's not always bad. She's proven people's innocence and saved lives. She's not just a Seer but a judge. Her words are the final answer on everything, even if we don't like the answer. That kind of authority is the only thing that made me nervous about accepting such a role."

Her gaze took on a faraway look, but instead of prying further, Aeliana let the other woman sit in her sorrow.

"Well"—Nori's voice turned flat—"without a starlock, I'll most likely be married off to someone who cares more for the proximity to my father's power than my lack of it."

"Aren't you young? I just received my starlock this year. There's still time."

"Now you sound like my mother." Nori's voice held a smile. "And while that may be true, fewer people are getting starlocks. Ailah's Awakening is the first we've had in two years. The next likely won't be for another two years or more, and by then I'll be far too old. I'm happy for her though," Nori was quick to add as she tied off Aeliana's braid.

Aeliana turned to face her. "You can be sad over your own loss and still be happy for someone else."

Nori snorted. "You will do far better at following your mother's high priestess footsteps than I'll do at being an elder's wife." Her laugh shifted to a disgusted face that left Aeliana grinning.

"Maybe you'll become an explorer now that there's a way across the barrier. You could always come back with us."

Nori leaned forward, her face a handsbreadth from Aeliana's. "Do you think that's possible? I've always felt like my future had to hold something more, something bigger. Something beyond this small island and our coral."

Aeliana smiled. "Of course. Why couldn't it?"

Nori bit her lip and looked away, indecision making her hesitate. But then her face hardened with a serious resolve. "It's important that you make a good impression tonight. This is a test as much as it is an invitation, just like yesterday. They won't give you back the starbridges unless you pass."

Aeliana felt the warning in Nori's words deep within her soul. Still, Nori wanted her to succeed. She was on their side.

"I will do my best, not just for my own future, but for yours as well," she promised.

Nori smiled and stood, holding out a hand to pull Aeliana up. "Compliment Elder Mishkel on his fin." She rolled her eyes. "He keeps it visible even outside the waves because the rainbow scales are coveted by everyone. He's an obnoxious show-off, but he'll be the easiest to win over because of it."

"Elder Mishkel, beautiful rainbow scales. Got it," Aeliana recited.

"Elder Perla's wife just had a baby even though Gellen, their oldest son, is in line to take his place once he marries."

Aeliana couldn't help her eyebrows rising. "Is he the one interested in being close to your father's power?"

A few of Nori's scales surfaced on her face, as if her embarrassment made her lose control of her transitions. "He's offered more than once. I'm not sure how much longer I can convince Father to say no."

"All the more reason to bring you to Vendaras as an explorer?"

Nori bit her lip and nodded. "We would be miserable together. Always fighting."

This time Aeliana hesitated, catching uncertainty in Nori's tone. "Sometimes we fight the most with the people we love the most. Usually it's because we're afraid for them."

Nori sighed, then shook away whatever else she might have said. "When his mother brings her baby over, don't ask to hold him until she offers, but then immediately say yes. He loves being rubbed under his chin, and then you'll win over their whole family, including Elder Gerot, whose wife is sister to Elder Perla's wife."

"Elder Perla, baby's chin. All right." Aeliana's words were less certain this time as the extra names fought for a place in her memory.

"Elder Kraken already likes you. He likes anything that stirs up drama. But don't make fun of his name, or you'll lose his support. Elder Corantun may never be swayed. He's very set in his ways. But if you can win the other four, you'll have the majority." She turned to leave, clearly expecting Aeliana to follow.

"What about your father?"

"Oh, don't expect to win him over." Nori winced an apology. "My mother likes you, but he never will. That's why it's so important you win the others over."

Aeliana followed her down the hall, and the moment they stepped outside where Velden, Gaeren, and their soldiers waited, Nori became silent and submissive once more.

The crowd gathering in the village square felt overwhelming to Aeliana. She'd never be able to meet everyone, and she worried she wouldn't even be able to put Nori's advice into practice. But the hundreds gathered also felt small when she thought of Vendaras and Lorvandas. Had the Sayhleens' population been limited by their small island? Or did the majority of them live deep in the water?

Velden was the quickest to relax, settling in among the people to answer their questions and ask his own. Many of them wanted to know about his mother's life among the Vendarans. Some of the questions felt stilted, like they'd been planted by the elders for a specific purpose, but Velden answered them all with ease.

Gaeren seemed in better spirits after his own bath and clean clothes, giving Aeliana a sense of the side of him that had grown up a pampered prince. But now he was on full alert, watching everyone who approached them with the caution of a hardened soldier, his hand often straying to his hip where his hilt should have been.

"We'll get nowhere with these people if you keep glaring at them," she whispered.

His face softened a fraction. "More than half of them are remembering the sight of our arrival with a severed Sayhleen tail. It's hard not to be on edge when there's an underlying hostility in their approach."

"They don't sense you pulling out the memories, do they?"

He shook his head. "Some of the elders or those with more established magic might. They might even attempt to block it. But otherwise, no."

"You need to search their memories," she whispered. "Maybe even the elders' memories. I can try, but I suspect it won't be possible with Durriken so far away. Either way, you'll be much faster at it."

He frowned, glancing around as if worried people might have

heard her. "I'm trying *not* to search their memories. It's a defensive reaction because I feel threatened, but I don't like it."

"What if one of them remembers how to find Lady Merinnia?" She leaned closer. "What if one of the elders remembers where the star-bridges are kept? Hopefully they'll tell us these things, even help us. But if they don't…"

An elderly woman approached before Gaeren could respond. She reached out to touch Aeliana's hair. "It used to be long, like the Stars'," she murmured.

Aeliana's face heated with the realization that this woman was searching through her past. "It was the Lorvandans' way. I cut it after traveling to Vendaras." It felt silly explaining it when the Sayhleens had varying lengths of hair, but theirs held a texture unlike Aeliana's, more suited to the water.

The woman still didn't smile. "Far prettier than the others we snared. Maybe that's how we'll decide which of you to put on display like your people did with Rhoda."

Aeliana winced as Gaeren tensed beside her, but before he could respond, Gellen approached.

"Grandma. Leave them be." He tried to escort her away, but she harrumphed and stalked off on her own.

For once the Sayhleen looked chagrined. "She always says what she's thinking, and lately her mind hasn't been as clear as it once was. It's hard for me to look into it and see her confusion. Today she remembers Rhoda is dead, but not that you rescued her body. Tomorrow she'll remember it differently."

"I'm sure it was a shock to see it." Aeliana shuddered as she remembered it on the wall in Dreyfus' cabin, and Gellen grimaced as he likely saw the same. "Are you just constantly tuned in to my mind?"

He shrugged. "It's not something I normally do, but my father suggested it was prudent until we understand your true motives."

She rolled her eyes, then turned to Gaeren, except he wasn't there. Which meant he'd probably taken her advice.

"What advice was that?" Gellen asked.

"To find the elders," she lied, then looped her hand through his arm, ignoring how he tensed beside her. "I'd actually like to talk to them myself. Can you take me?"

He grimaced. "You might be better off finding Nori first. I think she was—"

"No, I think it should be you." Aeliana smiled sweetly, thinking about how his presence would guarantee the elders trusted their interactions with her.

"Oh, fine," he grumbled. "I'm not sure why you want to talk to them anyway. They won't tell you anything about Lady Merinnia."

She nudged him forward until he started walking. "Maybe not, but if they're going to condemn us, I'd rather it was because they'd actually met me."

CHAPTER 43

GAEREN DUCKED between a flirting couple and a woman reprimanding her children, hoping that Gellen wouldn't notice his absence. Aeliana's suggestion had been good, even if it was risky. At any point, Gellen could read Gaeren's mind and discover what he was doing. And that could easily put them back in the hut, even further from their goals. He'd already tried seeing if Nori knew where the starbridges were held. But her only memory was of her father acknowledging that he had hidden them.

Which meant it was time to find Nori's father.

He scanned the crowd, attempting to smile at those who recognized him as the stranger in their midst. For once, his friendly nature almost seemed to turn people away instead of draw them in.

He half-heartedly searched a few for any memories surrounding Lady Merinnia. But most centered around gossip they'd heard about others who'd gone to see her—names of people he didn't know, people who might no longer exist. All of their rumors made Lady Merinnia out to be a witch who cursed those who came. With each perspective, he gained a new understanding of Aeliana's hesitance to come to Sayhla Island.

If they had sought out Pacran's dusty tomes, would they have answers by now?

The same guard who'd escorted him to the Coral Coves the day before now followed him. He wasn't surprised, but he hoped the man didn't have the same skills as Gellen. There was no starlock around his neck, but Velden's fishhook earring was proof that empty necks didn't always mean someone didn't have magic.

When Gaeren finally caught sight of Nori's father, he weaved his way through the crowd, taking a few detours to disguise his final destination. The guard still tailed him.

Aeliana would berate him for not having a plan, but by the time Gaeren drew close enough to see the green hue of the elder's eyes, his only idea was to get the old man to tell him a long boring story that might make Gaeren's eyes glaze over even if he wasn't doing magic.

Before he could get close enough to ask about the infrastructure of the Coral Coves or the history of the sprites, Nori's mother caught his arm, holding him back in the crowd. "Where do you think you're going? Did you lose Aeliana?"

He laughed nervously. "I guess so. We got separated when talking to other people by one of the fires, and I haven't been able to find her since." He also hadn't been looking, but he didn't tell her that.

He was surprised when she grinned mischievously. "I've seen the way you two look at each other." She turned his palm over to find his bond. "I thought so."

His face heated, and this time his nervousness wasn't for show. "Oh, we're bonded to other people. We've known each other since we were children, that's all. We're just friends."

She raised her eyebrows, and he glanced down at the cord around her neck, wondering if she could sense lies, then wondering if he *had* just told a lie.

"Well, you can stay with me while we watch the official induction ceremony," she said, patting his back. The familiarity made him stiffen. Maybe she was using his exact same strategy to tune in to his mind in some way. Except, the defensive blocking strategies his mentors had ingrained in him over the years came up with nothing. Maybe she just wasn't as concerned about the Vendarans as her husband was.

Which might also mean her guard would be down for him to access her memories.

"Thank you..." He hesitated over her name. Were there titles for the elders' wives?

"Call me Aquana."

He nodded, then turned to the dais. "What's an induction ceremony?"

"It's a celebration for an Awakening. Ailah will tell us about her experience, and as her community, we accept her appointment and authority as a progeny. Next week, she'll head to the Seer's Sanctuary for school."

"The Seer's Sanctuary?" His eyebrows rose. "How far away is that?"

Aquana smiled. "It's on the other island."

"The other island?" He felt like a parrot, but this was all news to him. "How many islands are there?"

"There's only one that's very inhabitable. The Seer's Sanctuary is more like a lump of rock that's risen from the sea. The Seer prefers to remain there away from the people so she's not burdened by their futures."

"Sometimes I wouldn't mind a place like that," Gaeren said wryly, and Aquana laughed.

"Her magic is so strong that she can get overwhelmed by receiving so many people's futures at once. I actually think she likes people. They did manage to build a small school for the progenies close enough to Lady Merinnia to benefit from her assistance with education and clarification. In addition to studying all the prophecies of the previous Seers, they train in the Wheel of Magic. Most of them return, and many become elders. But a few stay and continue on as teachers and servants of Lady Merinnia."

He warily filed all that information away, worried her remote and protected location might be both hard to find and difficult to infiltrate.

"Oh, look!" Aquana pointed toward the center of the square where a raised dais revealed a young woman standing with Nori's father and beaming. Disappointment flooded Gaeren at the lost opportunity of searching the elder's memories. He'd have to make do with whatever Aquana might remember.

Before he could tune in to her memories, Elder Algaen's voice boomed across the square. "We're gathered here tonight to honor Ailah, who has been chosen by the sprites and gifted by the Stars. May her magic always be used for the sprites' glory, and may she prove the sprites' choice to be a wise one. Before we send her off, we long to hear of her Awakening."

Gaeren cringed, both at the worship of the sprites and the openness of the Awakening. Only the sailors who'd been on his boat during the time he'd earned his starlock knew what had happened—minus most of the details. He couldn't imagine standing before a crowd this size and letting them all in on such a vulnerable moment. Even Enla hadn't shared her Awakening with him.

But Velden had said it was different here. And Gaeren couldn't help being curious to hear about someone else's experience. As the girl told her tale, Gaeren warred between listening in and using the chance to tune in to Aquana's memories. Eventually practicality won out, and he tuned in to the memories of the woman beside him, pulling up his sleeve and leaning in until their arms touched so he could find things a little quicker and easier.

Most of her memories held a sense of concern for Nori, as if her motherly fears clouded all of her experiences. And that led him to several memories centering around their parental efforts to bond Nori and Gellen. He tucked that information away in case it became useful later.

Because they'd recently discussed Lady Merinnia, some of the memories surrounding her were closer to the surface, allowing him to note that the Seer's Sanctuary was not only on a different island, but an island on the other side of this island—a few days' journey and a boat ride away. He winced at that revelation, knowing it was far too long for them to sneak away and find her on their own. They would only be going to Lady Merinnia if their visit was sanctioned.

Laughter rose around him, drawing him out from his perusal of the Sayhleen's memories, reminding him that he was in a crowd of strangers listening to a woman describe her Awakening.

It sounded as if her story was coming to a close, so he needed to be quick. As he tuned in to Aquana's memories surrounding their arrival and worked his way forward, he caught sight of the starbridges being taken to Aquana's bedroom, where she and her husband looked them over, studying the inscriptions on their sides.

"Place them in the box," Elder Algaen said before standing to watch over his wife.

She pried a loose board from the floor and reached down, dragging out a box the size of her hand. When she lifted the lid, she hesitated, and her husband tensed.

"Why do you keep that?" he asked.

"So I can remember." Her words came out defensive.

He grunted his disapproval and left the room, but Aquana pulled out a pink shell, which brought up a memory within her memory. These were the worst for Gaeren, because they came through fragmented or distorted, like they were stuck behind a veil that threatened their veracity.

Two paths were given to Aquana by a woman covered in blue scales and red seaweed. Her eyes were a milky white, her haunted expression leaving Gaeren as terrified as Aquana was in both that moment and the memory recalling it. The first path flashed before Gaeren, showing Nori happily snuggled against Gellen, a baby in her arms. The other path held a bright light, followed by Nori's glassy eyes staring up at him from her still face.

Aquana's gasp pulled her from the second memory, bringing Gaeren back into the first. She shoved the shell and starbridges in the box before tucking them under the floorboard. Then Gaeren's own gasp pulled him out from the first memory.

"Are you all right?" Aquana peered up into his face. Applause rang out around him as Ailah continued beaming from the dais.

"I'm fine," he mumbled, but he couldn't unsee the sight of Nori dead. "I'm just not used to Awakenings being a public affair."

She patted his arm. "Vendarans are strange creatures." Then her gaze caught on something, and she stood on tiptoe. "Oh, look! There's Aeliana. The two of you should go near the dais. Soon the music and dancing will start." She winked and gave him a light shove. "It would be a good test for these so-called bonds that you have with other people. And make sure you watch for the light show. The Stars always show their blessing over these affairs. You'll never catch them dancing like it any other time."

He headed toward Aeliana, glancing at the sky and wondering what the Stars' blessing might mean. Did the Stars approve of their Awakening celebration? Did they approve of their worship of the sprites? His mind was still too muddled by the memories he'd taken from Nori's mother. It was difficult to find something solid to hold on to, especially when he saw Nori and Gellen standing at Aeliana's side.

"I don't know how I lost you." Gaeren stood a little closer than necessary to Aeliana, unsure how close Gellen needed to be to access his thoughts. He stared at Nori, who was very much alive, trying to fill his mind with her vitality instead of the possible death he'd seen.

Aeliana smiled up at him, a question in her eyes. "Gellen and Nori introduced me to a couple of the elders. It went well."

He glanced at Gellen, and as much as he couldn't stand the Sayhleen, he prayed to the Sun that Gellen would find a way to marry Nori and keep the second path in Aquana's vision from ever happening.

"You just have my parents left to meet." Gellen's eyes drifted over Gaeren's shoulder, and he called over a couple with a sleeping baby. Aeliana stood a little taller, receiving an almost imperceptible nod from Nori.

"Welcome to Tideholm," the man said, nodding at both Gaeren and Aeliana.

She gave a slight bow, reminiscent of the submissive stance Nori often gave the elders. "Thank you. That's very kind of you."

Gaeren mumbled something he hoped was appropriate, but his gaze was on the baby. Was this the baby in Aquana's vision? He glanced between the baby and Gellen and then the baby and Nori with a frown until Aeliana cleared her throat, shooting him a death glare.

"How old is your son?" Aeliana asked.

The woman's face lit up. "Ten moons. We're grateful the sprites blessed us with him."

Gaeren's jaw clenched, and Aeliana placed her hand on his arm. He knew it was meant to hold him back, but Aquana's visions combined with his hatred for the sprites overrode her warning. He was proud of the controlled way his question came out. "Do you have any sprites on this side of the barrier?"

Elder Perla's lips pursed, and his wife answered for him. "No. There haven't been any sprites here for ages. Almost as long ago as when the Stars stopped communing."

"So you worship them unseen?" he pressed.

She laughed lightly. "Just because they're not visible doesn't mean their presence can't be felt. During the night, your Sun goes away. Does that mean it doesn't exist in the night? It wouldn't be faith if they were always seen."

Aeliana smiled. "What an excellent way to describe it. You would enjoy talking to Cyrus. He's a Lorvandan priest-in-training, and he's eager to compare people's experiences with their faith."

The woman smiled, and her baby chose that moment to stir in her arms, his eyes opening to reveal a brilliant shade of blue that Aeliana leaned in closer to examine.

His mother noticed Aeliana's interest. "Would you like to hold him?"

Nori nodded eagerly behind Elder Perla's back, and Aeliana took the boy into her arms, tapping his nose with her finger, stroking his cheek, and then letting her finger rest under his chin, where she tickled him ever so slightly. Gaeren's lingering frustration melted away as he watched Aeliana's face light up.

The baby giggled, and blue scales popped up along his face and neck, startling both Aeliana and Gaeren. The parents merely smiled their approval.

"He's beautiful," Aeliana said.

"Perhaps the two of you will be just as blessed by the sprites," the woman said as Aeliana handed him back.

"Oh, um." Gaeren stumbled over his words. "We're not..." Really? Twice in one night? He scratched at the bond mark on his palm and noticed Aeliana doing the same.

"Gaeren's bondmate is back at his family's palace, and mine is in the hut," Aeliana clarified.

"Oh." The woman looked horrified at her blunder. "The elders made it sound like the two of you are next in line to rule."

Aeliana and Gaeren exchanged a glance. "It might be more accurate to say there are two different factions who each want one of our families to rule," Aeliana said.

The woman looked uncomfortable as she settled her baby on her hip. "Well, then, I hope the sprites bring peace to your nation and between your factions."

Gaeren gave a half snort before catching himself and turning it into a cough.

Aeliana shot him a dark look, but the damage was already done.

"Do you not think the sprites can grant such peace?" Elder Perla asked.

"It's more that we think the factions don't desire peace." Aeliana tugged on Gaeren's arm, clearly ready to make her escape. Even Nori and Gellen moved to leave, but then Gellen paused, his brow furrowed as he neared Gaeren.

"He disagrees," Gellen mused. "He can't imagine the sprites pursuing peace because the ones he's met… he thinks they're unkind."

Gaeren's starlock heated as his defenses rose. He let his mind go blank, then pictured a river running, the gentle hum of its power drowning out his background thoughts, leaving room only for the conversation at hand. "I think the one I met in Vendaras was unkind. But that's why I wondered about the sprites on Sayhla Island. Maybe they're much nicer."

Elder Perla's eyes narrowed, and his wife took a small step back, casting a nervous glance at Aeliana and Nori.

"Perhaps it has less to do with the sprite's kindness and more to do with a lack of worth they found in you." The elder's words came out flat.

Gaeren blinked in surprise, then laughed, making the others chuckle nervously too. "Maybe. They wouldn't be the first to find me unworthy of something. But they did lead me to the silver fish starbridge, which led me here. So you could say our presence here is guided and blessed by the sprites."

Aeliana held her breath as the elder considered Gaeren's words.

"We don't worship the sprites for their kindness," he finally said. "We don't expect kindness. We worship them for their power. Our existence comes from that power, and regardless of any… kindness, or lack of, we are grateful to them. The last two sprites on this side of the barrier worked closely with our Seer until they had a disagreement. The Seer foresaw their deaths but promised they would return. We await them."

Despite Gaeren's need to escape the dangerous ground of the conversation, he couldn't help being intrigued. "You await the return of those two sprites? Or any sprites?"

The elder hesitated. "We're not sure. It could even be their spirits alone, returned in some form we don't recognize."

Gaeren focused on the river running in his mind, but Gellen saw through his tactics and reached out to grab his arm. The Sayhleen frowned. "He wants to know if we'd still worship them if they returned as dark spirits. He wonders about when the sprites died—he wants to know if people saw dark spirits rise from them."

Aeliana inhaled sharply.

"How could you know that?" Elder Perla asked, his face holding more surprise than concern.

Gaeren's gut twisted, both at this revelation and the precarious position it put him in. Answering this question would be difficult. He shook off Gellen's hand and asked one of his own instead.

"Are there other dark spirits on Sayhla Island? Do your people call them with blood magic and fuse with them?"

The elder's face paled and he stepped to the side, placing his wife and son behind him. His voice rose, drawing attention from those nearby. "Blood magic? Of course not. And what do you mean by fusing with a spirit? Is that something Vendarans do?"

Gaeren shook his head. "Only our enemies do that."

The elder looked momentarily placated. "It sounds…awful. But how did you even know our sprites became dark spirits? Has the same happened to sprites in Vendaras?"

Gaeren glanced at Aeliana, longing for her to say something to get him out of this. What could he say that wouldn't push this Sayhleen over the edge?

Gellen frowned. "He's hiding something. He's blocking me."

Before Gaeren could guess what they might do, Elder Algaen

slapped a hand on Gaeren's wrist, his face going momentarily blank. All Gaeren's efforts to block the intrusion fell apart, the river in his mind draining to expose his encounter with the sprite.

Elder Algaen wrenched his hand away, nearly tripping over his wife in his haste to leave Gaeren's side.

"Murderer," he hissed. Then his voice rose over the crowd. "They killed a sprite!"

CHAPTER 44

As soon as the three of them were tossed back in the hut, Aeliana turned on Gaeren, her face a mix of exasperation and rage. "What were you thinking?"

"I tried blocking them." He shook his head, still baffled over the turn of events. "I kept Gellen out, but Elder Perla was too strong."

The conversation about the sprites had started as a way to keep thoughts of Nori and her mother's visions out of his head and, in turn, out of Gellen's mind. But he'd simply swapped that out for a far more condemning revelation.

"What happened?" Sylmar asked.

"He decided to get into a theological debate with one of the elders by insulting their worship of the sprites," Aeliana spat out.

"What?" Cyrus' face paled, making his freckles stand out. "Even I wouldn't risk that."

"I want answers about the sprites just as much as you." Aeliana started pacing in the little space not occupied by the others. "But this wasn't the time to get them. You should have saved your questions for Orra."

Gaeren held up his hands in defense. "Wait—that's not how it went. I wasn't questioning their beliefs. I was asking them to tell me about their experience with sprites. And only because they snuck into my head and asked me about mine."

Riveran placed his hands over his face. "That's even worse," he moaned.

Guilt pricked at Gaeren's conscience. If they went after anyone, it would be Riveran. And it was Gaeren's fault. "They know you killed one," he warned his friend.

Velden, who'd been strangely quiet, finally chimed in. "That probably wasn't the best thing to tell them."

"I didn't tell them," Gaeren said. "I didn't know Elder Perla could see memories."

"It's your spoke," Kendalyhn said. "You should assume anyone out there possibly could. We all should."

"Fighting amongst ourselves isn't going to help anything right now," Iris said. She cocked her head in the direction of the guards. Nori had told them the guards had no magic, but that didn't mean they weren't listening in.

Holm nodded, and they all leaned in to catch his words. "Escaping the hut won't do us any good unless we have the starbridges."

"Did you figure anything out before you set us up as their enemy?" Aeliana asked.

Gaeren huffed his irritation but latched a hand on to Aeliana's and Sylmar's arms. He showed them the box under the floorboard, making sure to cut off the memory before Nori's mother relived her time with the Seer. He dropped their arms and looked away, his mind full of Nori's lifeless eyes. He shuddered.

"What else did you see?" Aeliana asked.

When he glanced back at her, the anger had receded, and concern filled her face. "Nori might be in danger. I don't know." He rubbed his palms against his eyes. "I saw something in her mother's memory. I think they're trying to get her to marry Gellen to protect her from an alternate future in which she dies."

The room grew even quieter. Nori had only taken Velden, Aeliana, and Gaeren out of the hut, but after she'd delivered meals and given them bits of information, they'd all grown to see her as an ally.

"Even if that's true," Sylmar said, "she's not likely to believe us at this point. We may have to leave that problem to her and her people."

The thought didn't sit well with Gaeren, and when Aeliana bit her lip and stared down the hut's door, he knew he wasn't the only one.

Loud pops filled the air, and bursts of light shone through the nooks and crannies of the hut.

"A celebration like this would have been an excellent time to make an escape," Sylmar muttered.

"We don't have time to wait for another one," Aeliana said. "Nori told me they only have one of these every couple of years, and I doubt we'll last a couple more days."

"For now, we should rest up," Iris said. "We'll all think more clearly in the morning, and maybe Nori will bring us food. We'll get a better sense of our odds after talking to her."

"If she's even willing to talk to us," Kendalyhn muttered, her glare centered on Gaeren.

They all found places to lie down. No one seemed eager to be close to Gaeren or Riveran, but with their cramped quarters, Cyrus eventually ended up on Gaeren's right. His tossing and turning made it clear he was having just as much trouble sleeping as Gaeren.

"What do you think of the Sayhleens' worship of the sprites?" Gaeren whispered.

Cyrus didn't respond at first, making Gaeren wonder if what he'd assumed to be insomnia was actually nightmares.

"I think we're all genuine in our worship, and that's something to be admired. But we can't all be right." Sorrow colored Cyrus' words, making Gaeren wished he'd kept his questions to himself.

"And you think I'm just as wrong to worship the Sun as they are to worship the sprites?"

Cyrus sighed. "I wish I'd taken the time to talk to Orra before we left. Everything happened so quickly. But if she's a Star—or was a Star—I can't imagine why she would worship the Sun… unless the Sun is what you believe it to be."

Gaeren stilled, recognizing this was what made Cyrus sad. Not that they couldn't all be right, but that he'd come to the conclusion that he hadn't been.

"Go ahead," Cyrus offered. "You can say 'I told you so.' You were right, both about me being afraid and about me being wrong."

"Do you think I'm that heartless?" Gaeren cringed. "I'm sorry things didn't turn out to be what you thought."

"I'm not," Cyrus said. "I'm only sorry that I led people astray. That my family's Stargazer is a farce. I feel a burden to take this knowledge to Gamps, to help him understand and spread the truth throughout all of Lorvandas. But I can't do that until I understand it and learn it for myself. I need to get answers from Orra, and I need to make sure others know the truth, even if I don't like the answers I get." His whispers grew heated with his passion. "And if I feel burdened for the Lorvandans to know the truth, why not the Sayhleens? But how can I help them understand if they worship the sprites?" He shuddered. "Especially if the sprites turn into dark spirits like you suspect."

Gaeren hesitated, unsure if Cyrus wanted advice, especially from the likes of him. "Orra once told me that so much of what we do wrong isn't in our actions, but in our decision to act without consulting the Sun. The burden you feel, if it's from the Sun, you should act on it."

Cyrus hummed. "I guess it doesn't do me any good either way if we can't get out of this hut."

Gaeren's guilt returned, and he wasn't sure what else he could say.

"I still have faith that there's more for us to do," Cyrus said. "Whether it's by the power of the Sun or the Stars, there's a way out of here for us. I look forward to seeing how it's possible."

The next morning came quickly, but Nori didn't come with it. They continued discussing their options in hushed tones, but outside of using Sylmar's staff and magic to melt a hole through the hut, which probably wouldn't get them past the strange seaweed net, and making a mad dash for Elder Algaen's home, which would result in most of their deaths, they had very few ideas.

"At some point, they'll need to take us out," Sylmar said. "Whether to put us on trial or to execute us. That's our best chance to make a move."

"Or they could just burn us down in this hut," Kendalyhn said, making several others wince.

"What if I offer myself as a sacrifice?" Riveran said. "They know I killed the sprite. I'm the one—"

"No," Gaeren interrupted. "It was self-defense. Or at least, you were defending me. I won't let you take that fall for me."

"Not even if it saves everyone else here?" Riveran asked.

Gaeren glanced around the room, his gaze resting on Aeliana. He adjusted the cuff of his sleeve, letting his finger run across the braid on his wrist. His jaw tightened, and he didn't answer.

"It's noble of you to offer," Iris said, laying a gentle hand on Riveran's arm. "But we'll make every effort to find a way for all of us to survive this." As she spoke, the rattle of the door met their ears, and everyone straightened, anxiously awaiting who might be on the other side.

A sliver of hope bloomed in Gaeren when Nori peeked around the door's edge. She squinted at the prisoners, letting her eyes adjust, before glancing back out at the guards. "I'll just be a moment," she said and shut the door behind her.

She smiled hesitantly. "They wouldn't let me bring food. But I did bring a poultice for Velden's injury."

"My wha—?" he started.

But she held up seaweed and repeated again, a little louder, "This is for your injury, Velden."

A slow grin spread across his face. "Thank you." He shouted his words toward the hut entrance. "Oh, it hurts. This will make it *so* much better." He wrapped the seaweed around his arm, then whispered, "Actually, this does feel really nice."

Aeliana rolled her eyes, then stepped closer to Nori. "Do we have any hope?" she whispered.

Nori sighed. When her gaze landed on Gaeren, it held more curiosity than animosity, but she still shook her head. "The elders are discussing your fate, and unfortunately, Elder Perla has shared your memory with all the others."

Gaeren and Riveran exchanged a glance.

"I'm the one who murdered the sprite," Riveran said. "The others are innocent."

"I suspect they'll find you all guilty by association, but I don't know." She bit her lip and glanced back at the hut entrance. "They've said they'll give an answer tomorrow, but they're still deliberating. Everyone seems confused as to why they haven't already condemned you."

Sylmar's gaze turned thoughtful. "So you think their verdict might not be that cut and dry?"

"I think I don't want to wait to find out. If I knew where your starbridges were, I would bring them to you."

"Why are you willing to help us?" Gaeren asked.

Voices sounded outside, and Nori's whisper picked up its pace. "Look, I don't think it's right that you killed the sprite. But your culture is different from ours. I don't know that I can hold it against you either. And while tradition in itself isn't wrong, forcing people to do things isn't right. I'm ready for a change, but I don't think my people are."

The door opened, and Nori straightened.

"What's taking so long?" one of the guards asked.

"Nothing," Nori said. "I'm done." Her eyes held an apology that made Gaeren's decision.

He grabbed her arm and fed her the memory of the box under the floorboards. The guard pulled out a dagger and rushed forward, but Gaeren held up his hands.

"I was just thanking her," he said.

"You're welcome," Nori whispered, her eyes bright with hope. The guard dragged her out and slammed the hut door shut.

"What did you show her?" Aeliana asked, her voice surprisingly grim.

"The starbridges."

"Did you show her the futures her mother saw?" she demanded.

Gaeren shook his head. "I don't trust memories within a memory. I don't want to scare her into doing something stupid."

Aeliana's eyes brimmed with tears. "You just challenged her to go against her parents' authority and find the starbridges to free us. I think you've already given her something stupid to do."

He squirmed under the truth of her words and prayed to the Sun that she was wrong.

CHAPTER 45

ORRA'S SKIN practically glowed as she basked in the Sun's light from her perch on the northern keep's balcony. She'd sensed the scouts coming in from the north all morning, but she'd resisted the urge to reach out for the information they brought.

Her power was finally starting to replenish, not to the amount she'd had before Aeliana had crossed the barrier, but more than she'd had before they'd faced Mayvus. If she continued to fast from using it, she might be able to find the balance she'd once had, giving her just enough magic to continue tracking down the starbridges.

As she made her way down the tower steps, the scouts arrived at the gate, and she sensed the mood of the entire fortress shift as word spread of their arrival. She stopped at Emeris and Rildan's room to invite them to the main hall, then again at Marnok's door. By the time they all arrived there, General Nels was instructing the scouts to head for the training room to give their report.

A surge of compassion for the scouts rushed through Orra. One of the men was young—a fresh recruit who'd likely just left home for the first time. The other two had battle scars and age lines, but all of them had weary eyes and dragging feet. The older two gave suspicious glances to Marnok, but the third seemed too exhausted to notice or care.

They'd barely had a chance to sit at the table before General Nels demanded they give their update.

"The Ahmranans were gathered at Ahmranan's Viewpoint," one of the older men said, glancing at Orra. "Just like she told us. At first we thought there were only a few dozen, but there's a network of caves there, and the longer we watched, the more it seemed like there were hundreds, if not thousands, hidden in the caves."

Orra sat up a little straighter. "Thousands?"

The second scout nodded. "We didn't recognize any of them, so it took us a while to catch that it was different people coming out each day. Once we realized our mistake, we snuck into the caverns and found one that had over a thousand men and women. We suspect there are several other caverns that size, but we weren't able to assess further without putting ourselves at risk, and we felt it was more pertinent to return with the information we'd gathered."

"Of course," General Nels said, waving off the apologetic excuse. "But are you suggesting none of these men were the soldiers who deserted after the battle?"

The first man hesitated. "There might be a few. I didn't know any of them personally, to be certain, but it seems as if they're all from Ahmranas." He glanced around the room as if concerned his suggestion was outrageous, but everyone else's lips pressed into grim lines.

This was what they'd expected.

"So she's bringing back an army," General Nels said. "One that's far larger than ours."

A tear tracked down the young scout's face, and he quickly wiped it away.

Despite Orra's determination to hold back her energy, she placed a hand on his shoulder, letting her power flow through and bolster his courage. He blinked a few times, then sat a little straighter.

"We watched for several days," he said. "Longer than you told us to, because we wanted to make sure we had accurate information. We saw a group of three leave with the starbridge once more—"

"You saw the onyx stone?" Orra's eyes briefly slid shut.

"From a distance, but it couldn't have been anything else with the way they disappeared. "We couldn't wait any longer to watch for their return. But yes, we assume she's building an army of Ahmranans."

"We never were able to tell if they were aiming for a certain number or a certain date." The first scout shook his head in his frustration. "For all we know, they could have been following right behind us."

"With Summer Solstice long past," Orra said, "I doubt she's aiming for a date. Now it's going to be a matter of when she feels like her numbers can tip our scales."

General Nels hummed his agreement. "If she already has a few thousand, she could be bringing back a thousand or more each time."

Orra tried to imagine a thousand soldiers crossing the barrier at once. The power of the starbridge was astounding. And yet it was a fraction of what it had once been. She rubbed the braid at her wrist.

"She knows our numbers have dwindled," General Nels continued. "It might only take her two or three more trips to feel secure enough to come back and stake her claim."

For the first time, Emeris showed concern. "That soon? Aeliana and the others won't be back by then."

"Which means they'll be safe," Orra said softly.

Emeris nodded, but her gaze clouded over as she descended into one of her occasional states of confusion. It had grown worse with Aeliana's absence. In some moments, like now, it seemed like a self-defense mechanism, where she allowed herself to retreat into her mind so she didn't have to face the terrible reality.

"There's more," the first scout said. His gaze flicked to Orra, and he licked his lips nervously.

"Spit it out," General Nels growled.

He winced, his gaze somewhere around General Nels' chest. "They're communing with the Stars."

"The Stars?" Orra's mind raced as she took in the meaning. "The Stars are communing with Mayvus and the Ahmranans?" He might as well have said the Stars were communing with the witches.

It stung to be told something she hadn't foreseen. Her magic had grown so weak over the years that she couldn't search many paths, but her experience gave her wisdom to search the right ones. Or it had until recently.

"Are you certain?" General Nels asked. "No one has communed with the Stars for hundreds of years. Did you see light come down from the heavens? Maybe Mayvus is doing something with her magic, some sort of trick that mimics their descent."

"They've begun communing again," Orra said slowly. "Reyna told me as much. She just didn't say who..." She frowned, thinking through Reyna's words. The Star had come to collect Jasperus' body and starlock after they'd defeated the Zealots, but she'd been as aloof as ever with Orra. After making the cryptic comment that they'd found people worthy of communing with, she'd taken to the skies, leaving Orra alone with her regrets.

"We saw the lights come down," the scout continued, his tongue loosening after Orra's confirmation. "Not every night, but most nights. Two or three separate lights. At first we thought someone had died or had their Awakening, but it was happening so much we knew that couldn't be right. We snuck closer one night, and..." He trailed off, exchanging glances with the others.

"We only saw them from afar," the second said, "but they were brilliant." His face shone with the memory, and tears sprang to Orra's eyes. "And they stood among the people, talking to them."

Orra blinked the tears away, remembering the sense of completeness with communing, the joy of giving people the briefest glimpse of the Sun's glory, of leading them to reflect its power in the same way. She pinched her temples between her thumb and fingers, warding off the headache she sensed coming. "Why the Ahmranans?"

Reyna had told her they were communing with a select few. It was exactly how it had begun all those years ago. The Sun had created the humans and the Stars, allowing them to mingle together on the earth. At first, the Stars' visits were rare. They couldn't bear to leave the Sun's presence in the sky, to give up the opportunity to reflect its glory. The privilege of communion with a Star was highly sought after by the humans, and Orra supposed that history was how they'd begun to be worshiped on the other side of the barrier.

But the Stars grew to love the humans, even bonded with them and created a new people group with starblood in their veins—magic that had to be taught and tamed. Stars gave up locks of hair to enhance their children's magic, encasing them in intricate stones that the half-lights wore around their necks. But all of that had been good, blessed by the Sun.

There was nothing good about this. Even if Mayvus hadn't been involved, she questioned it. Before the Great Divide, the Ahmranans had been a bitter people group who had hidden in the north to breed the highest starblood concentrations possible. They'd sought power for themselves, not for the glory of the Sun. After the Great Divide, they'd been stuck there, forced to become as hard as their frigid surroundings. The people brought over in her days as Pirate Redwood were evidence of that. Could their descendants have changed so much that the Stars chose to commune with them?

It seemed unlikely if those same descendants were following Mayvus.

"I'm not sure the why matters," General Nels said. "What matters is that they have Stars on their side. Our numbers aren't likely to matter in that case."

Orra swallowed hard, afraid to confirm his words even though they were, without a doubt, accurate. Perhaps she'd taken too long to reunite the starbridges. Perhaps she'd failed in the mission the Sun had given her so long ago. Would the rest of the Stars make their own mistakes? Would more be grounded? How much more would Rhys-tahn feel the effects of the stone she'd thrown?

"We need to warn the others," Rildan said. "Now's the time to send Gullet."

"Gullet can't cross the barriers," Orra said. "If we send him now, he'll grow confused if he can't find them. Who knows if he'd come back here or await Gaeren in Elanesse?"

"Aeliana crossed the barrier?" Emeris asked, rising from the cloud of confusion she'd been under.

Rildan and Marnok exchanged a glance.

"About a week ago. Soon after I arrived," Marnok said.

"Where will they return?" General Nels asked.

Orra shrugged. "I suspect somewhere on the west coast. I know the least about that starbridge. I found the stone and cutlass ages ago, but the fish and arrow were only found and used in the last hundred years."

The scouts squirmed at her casual mention of her longevity, the youngest even flinching away from her despite the comfort she'd previously offered.

"We thank you for the update," Orra said. "Is there anything more? I'm assuming you'd all love to wash off the dust of the Bahlric Desert."

General Nels frowned at her but didn't disagree, so the three men took their leave.

"So now what?" Emeris asked. "Do we send a delegation to the Elanesses asking for aid?"

"I was thinking more that we send you away for your safety." General Nels raised a hand to silence her protests. "But if sending you as part of a delegation makes it seem more tasteful, I'm open to that that."

"I can't leave these people," Emeris said. "They fought to rescue me, and you want me to abandon them?"

"They rescued you to keep you safe," the general amended.

Orra was tempted to search the general's fate, to know if staying here with the soldiers would mean his death. But knowing his fate wouldn't allow her to impact it, so it was best left untouched.

"What if we travel by sea?" Rildan suggested. "We can't go north and risk running into Mayvus, but traveling around the Southern Horn is still faster than traveling across land. We could even watch for Aeliana and the others so we can be there to warn them whenever they arrive."

"Be where?" Marnok asked. "The west coast is a large expanse of land."

"I might be able to trace them when they return," Orra said, wincing at the thought of the magic that would require. "Or we can take Gullet and tell them where to find us. In the meantime, we can maybe catch wind of where Larkos is. They would have made plans to meet up with him on their return. If nothing else so Gaeren can collect his ship." A faint smile crossed her lips at his connection with the vessel, but her mind was back hundreds of years, relishing her own connection with a ship that had saved her life a hundred times over.

"Maybe you should stay with them instead of going to the Elanesses," General Nels said. "Asking them for aid reveals our weaknesses and sets us up for an attack on two fronts. It might be better to wait and only contact them if Myndren falls."

"Then you should keep Gullet," Orra said. "Send him to Gaeren if Myndren falls so we know what to do." As General Nels pursed his lips, Orra sensed he knew Myndren's fall was a matter of when, not if.

"Then we're not leaving as delegates." Emeris lifted her chin. "It sounds like we're just running."

"We can't protect Aeliana if we're under siege here," Rildan pointed out. "Aeliana is the hope for these people. Reaching her might be a more worthy destination than seeking aid anyway."

Emeris sighed. "Is it just the four of us, then?"

Orra glanced at Rildan and Marnok, who nodded, and she did the same. "How soon can we leave?"

"We'll need a day to prepare," Rildan said, "but we can leave the next."

"On one condition," General Nels said.

"Only one?" Orra said in mock surprise. "Name your price."

Instead of cracking a smile, the lines of his face grew harder. "You send away the winex."

CHAPTER 46

THE NEXT MORNING dawned without any immediate answers for the prisoners in the hut. Aeliana sensed the tension rising as the day wore on and Nori still hadn't arrived with food or news. Had she found the starbridges in her parents' room? Would she help them escape?

"If there's no sign of Nori or the starbridges by the time they come get us," Sylmar whispered, "we'll have to rush the guards. Gaeren and Riveran can get the starbridges since Gaeren's seen where they're at. We'll cover them as best we can before running to the hills in the east. Then we'll meet up there."

Velden had Gaeren tear off a strip of his clothing to help him locate Gaeren in the hills with his pneumatic skills, but Aeliana still hesitated.

"What if their verdict is to let us go back?" she asked.

Several others' faces matched Sylmar's incredulous glare. "After hearing Riveran killed a sprite?"

"I just wonder if we should give it more time," she said. "We don't understand their culture. Maybe Nori is convincing them to wash their hands of us and send us back to Vendaras right now."

"Waiting for the verdict will make it harder to escape," Kendalyhn said.

"Will it though?" Velden asked. "We may not have our weapons, but we still have magic. I know I'm biased, but I'm inclined to wait as well. No sense ruining our chances with these people if we don't have to."

Indecision warred on the faces of most everyone else. Holm reached for Iris' hand, giving it a reassuring squeeze.

"Fine," Sylmar conceded. "We can try waiting for the verdict. But if you see my staff turn molten, we're not waiting any longer."

Aeliana wasn't thrilled that he was going to be the one to decide when enough was enough, but at this point, she didn't have other options.

When the day stretched into the evening and their stomachs all growled their protests, the door to the hut finally opened, but it wasn't Nori whose head popped in.

"The elders have agreed to hold your trial publicly in the square," one of the guards announced.

Aeliana and Gaeren exchanged glances, unsure about this new turn of events. Even Sylmar seemed taken aback.

"Publicly?" he asked.

The guard nodded. "It was Nori's request."

At this, they all paused. Any thoughts Aeliana had of rushing to escape were put on hold. If this was Nori's request, maybe she had a plan. Sylmar seemed to come to the same conclusion, because he was first in line to leave the hut, his staff remaining a deceivingly plain metal.

Because all ten of them were being escorted from the hut, a few more soldiers showed up this time, dividing them in groups of two. Aeliana ended up with Velden, who still managed a grin for their parade through the village. When he started waving at onlookers, Aeliana smacked his hand down.

"Don't you think that's a bit disrespectful after all that's happened?" she asked.

He shrugged. "I'm innocent. And I'm going to maintain my innocence while on trial. Hopefully they won't kill Riveran. But I doubt they'll kill the rest of us for something he did."

"And you're fine with him dying?"

"Of course not." He frowned. "But I'm not going to walk around looking guilty because I know someone else in our party is." Then he picked up his hand and smiled and waved once more at a few curious children, who giggled as green and purple scales sprinkled across their cheeks.

"You're going to miss being here, aren't you?" Aeliana asked.

"You make it sound as if we're leaving," he said.

She snorted but didn't bother responding. They entered the square, where atop the dais, gallows had been arranged.

Aeliana swallowed hard. "Do you think this means their verdict has already been made, and we're not actually on trial?"

Even Velden's shoulders tightened. "It's possible. But I don't think Nori would lead us astray."

The guards hushed them at that point, herding them up on the stage like cattle before making them sit on the rough wooden floor.

Aeliana was forced to hope that Velden was right. She scanned the crowd, but she only saw the hard faces of the elders and their wives. Even Elder Mishkel, whom she'd managed to compliment on his fancy rainbow fin, had apprehension in his eyes.

Where was Nori?

The crowd continued to grow. Those in the back were so far away their faces blurred, and the number of attendees quickly became impossible to estimate. Some even entered nearby homes and businesses to lean out verandas for a better view, then a few climbed on rooftops. The air almost turned festive as everyone discussed the foreigners' fate.

It made Aeliana sick to her stomach, and when she glanced at Riveran's pale face, she feared he truly would retch. He'd overcome so much and had been through even more. This couldn't be his end, not after all he'd done to protect Gaeren.

A glance at the prince made her realize his mind was moving in the same direction, his eyes darting around for a possible escape. Her heart seized with the realization that if Riveran was deemed guilty, Gaeren wouldn't make it out alive either. He wouldn't let his friend die on his behalf.

Nori's father stood, joining the prisoners and their guards on the stage. He raised a hand, and the crowd hushed like a wave receding on the sea. "As many of you know, it has come to our attention that our guests have not been completely honest about their history."

Gaeren scoffed, the noise almost imperceptible, but Aeliana frowned, both at his risk of angering the Sayhleens and at Elder Algaen's inaccurate representation of them.

"We have spent the last two days deliberating their actions. Because their murder of a sprite was seen through Elder Perla's noetic skills, there was no need to question them for more information. Their guilt is clear."

Aeliana tensed, but the crowd seemed to expect this. She supposed the elders' deliberations had been kept from the prisoners, but they'd likely spread through the Sayhleen people like blood in water, attracting more sharks with each tiny spurt. They'd never even had a chance.

So what had made Nori request this public trial? Aeliana scanned the crowd wildly once more, and this time she caught sight of the younger woman at the dais' edge, mostly hidden beneath a cloak. Despite her tense posture, she gave Aeliana an encouraging smile, a promise in her eyes.

"Instead," Elder Algaen continued, "we deliberated how to address their guilt. It was clear the murder was committed by only one member of their group, with a second possibly complicit observer. Some among us felt only they should be held guilty for the crime. Others felt their group was guilty by association."

His lips pursed, but Aeliana wasn't sure which side of the argument he stood on.

"As much as we would like to collaborate with people across the barriers, we do not want to put our own people at risk. If these Vendarans are willing to kill a sprite, one of the creators we serve, how much less respect do they have for our people?"

Murmurs started up in the crowd, but they weren't all in agreement. A tiny sliver of hope threaded its way through Aeliana, and she worked at it, trying to draw it out into something larger to latch on to.

"We also debated what punishment would fit the crime. An obvious option would be death." He gestured toward the gallows.

Gaeren straightened, the defiance written all over his face in a way that made Aeliana even more nervous for him.

"But is it better to show justice for the crime or to lead by example and show the mercy we wish they would have given the sprite?" At this, the elders all stood, joining him on the stage. "We give you the results of our deliberation."

"Are we not given a chance to speak in our defense?" Gaeren called out, earning him a boxed ear from his guard.

This time the murmurs grew louder, and Aeliana couldn't get a sense of whether the people were affronted at his outburst or if they agreed with his question.

Elder Algaen raised his hand once more, and while the people closest quieted down, those farther away continued talking. Aeliana imagined his announcements being spread to the people in the back who likely couldn't hear him, wondering how accurate the news traveled given its speed.

"As I said," Elder Algaen repeated, "Elder Perla saw your memory. The guilt is uncontested."

"And will he not let me show him the memory of what the sprites did to us first?" Gaeren asked.

A smile twitched on Nori's face, and Aeliana sensed they were reaching the reason she'd asked for a public trial. Would receiving this evidence before the crowds work in their favor? Or had Nori found the starbridges and a public trial was the only way she could get it to them?

The elders exchanged glances, curiosity evident on Elder Kraken and Elder Mishkel's faces.

"I can't imagine how that would change our view," Nori's father said, "but if Elder Perla is willing, I will allow it."

Elder Perla nodded and stepped forward, reaching out a hand. One of the guards led Gaeren to the elder, and both of their faces went slack, their eyes blank for the span of a few moments. What exactly was Gaeren showing him? He'd given the briefest summary to the others in their travels, but she sensed there was more to his story. Would it condemn them or save them?

When Elder Perla stepped away, he frowned, his gaze troubled, but he said nothing and strode to his fellow elders. Giving memories must have been his primary spoke, because it didn't take long for all of their faces to reflect a deeper understanding of the situation.

That sliver of hope widened inside Aeliana as guilt and confusion flitted across Elder Gerot's and Elder Kraken's faces. They all eyed each other, but when Elder Algaen spoke, his face was still hard, his decision unchangeable.

"We do not expect kindness from the sprites," he said. "They owe us nothing, for they created us."

"But they didn't create me," Gaeren said. The crowd gasped, even though they had to know his words were true. "I may not understand your worship of them, but I respect it. Even so, they are not my creator, and they threatened my sister's life and my own life. Riveran's actions were to save me and in turn himself. Do you not have allowances for acting when threatened?"

The crowd grew louder, and Elder Algaen scanned the people, clearly recognizing he was losing his audience. His gaze landed on Nori, and she tucked herself further back under her hood. His lips pursed, and Aeliana debated how much trouble she was going to be in for requesting a public trial.

"Our verdict still stands," Elder Algaen called out, trying to regain control of the crowd. "Our first vote was to determine the guilt of the individual members of the party. The elders unanimously determined that Riveran was guilty of murdering the sprite."

Every one of the elders lifted their right hand as if replaying their deliberation before the crowd. Riveran's face took on a greenish tinge.

"We then determined if Prince Gaeren was guilty by association for his presence during the sprite's murder." At this, Elder Algaen, Elder Perla, and Elder Gerot raised their hands, the latter far slower.

"What does that mean?" Aeliana whispered, wondering if in their judicial system guilt for murder could be determined by majority or if it had to be unanimous. But the guards were too invested in the drama to shush or answer her.

"We then determined the guilt by association for the remainder of the prisoners." At this, only Elder Algaen and Elder Perla raised their hands. Aeliana pressed her fingers against her temple, trying to process what this might mean.

"As a result, Riveran and Gaeren will be hanged on the gallows. Aeliana and Velden will be given the opportunity to return to Vendaras, provided they take two of our people as ambassadors, who will then return alone so the silver fish is placed back under our control."

Several in the crowd nodded emphatically, but here and there people's brows furrowed.

"And what about the rest of us?" Kendalyhn asked.

"If our ambassadors return unharmed, we will deliver the remaining prisoners to Vendaras." Elder Algaen didn't need to explain what would happen if they did not.

The silence rang out until it was a deafening hum in Aeliana's ears. She expected Gaeren to protest, but his shock was as thick as Riveran's. He'd been prepared to defend his friend, but it seemed as though he hadn't been prepared to defend himself.

Aeliana's entire body shook with the conviction that she needed to do something. If only she could reach Durriken, if he could cross the barriers. The risk they'd taken in coming here had been far too great and the price too high, especially considering they wouldn't even see Lady Merinnia or learn anything to save her mother.

The solution came so swiftly it terrified her, but she still stood, placing a hand on Velden's shoulder to keep herself from toppling over. "I wish to invoke my right to receive judgment from the Seer."

Another collective gasp spread through the crowd, followed by a few titters.

Nori pulled her hood back, her face pale, her lips parted in horror. The elders showed equal surprise but schooled their features much faster than the crowd.

Elder Perla even laughed. "You're not Sayhleen. You have no right to call upon Lady Merinnia for judgment."

"After speaking with Sylmar, you determined that Gaeren and I held positions of authority. Does that not allow us the right to defend our people? To seek justice to protect them?"

"Not when your authority has been corrupted by murder." Elder Algaen's scowl shifted to Gaeren.

"What about me?" Velden stood as well. "Am I not owed anything for being Rhoda's son?"

The elders leaned in to whisper, and Aeliana closed her eyes, praying they might agree, then feeling guilty that the idea of him going to the Seer instead of her left her far too relieved.

But it didn't matter. Elder Algaen shook his head. "You have forfeited that right by associating with murderers. We are grateful that you returned your mother to our waters, but you are no longer welcome here."

The clear rejection of Velden seemed to pain him more than the refusal to let him see Lady Merinnia.

But then, from the corner of her eye, Aeliana caught Nori rising. The young woman stepped on stage, drawing everyone else's gaze.

"What are you doing?" her father hissed, which only made her stand straighter and raise her chin higher.

This time the crowd hushed of their own volition.

"They may not have any right to request judgment from Lady Merinnia, but I do." Nori faced her father, the brilliant orange scales flickering on her cheeks the only evidence of her fear, or maybe anger. "I have one chance to go to the Seer—one opportunity to request her guidance in my life—and I choose to use it now."

CHAPTER 47

THIS TIME the crowd's reaction became too loud for anyone to hush them. Aeliana scanned the sea of faces, the mix of confusion, shock, and even excitement giving her little confidence over whether this was a good or bad thing.

Elder Algaen's face screwed up into a murderous glare, his aqua scales surfacing, but Nori remained calm and collected.

"Do not waste your one opportunity," her father said.

Or at least, Aeliana thought that was what he said. As the crowd's reaction crescendoed, she was forced to read his lips more than listen. By this time, Nori's mother had reached the dais, her face as white as a sheet, and Aeliana stepped closer to catch their conversation, surprised the guards let her.

"Please don't do this," Aquana said, grabbing her daughter's hands. "They're not worth it."

"Who would be worth it, Mother?" Nori asked. "I've asked to use it for my own question this last year, and each time you refused. I'm tired of waiting for your approval. This time I know it needs to be done. We are doing a disservice to people who have sought sanctuary in our midst."

Elder Algaen wrapped a protective arm around his wife. "Retract your offer now, before it's too late. The elders will understand that you made a rash and emotional decision. They won't force you to follow through."

Nori lifted her chin. "I am of age to make this request. And as my elder, you are obligated to honor it." Her confidence faltered. "As my father, I understand why you might advise against it. But this is something I must do."

The scales on Elder Algaen's cheeks faded, his face drooping in a representation of something much deeper inside him breaking apart. "Very well."

He turned back to the elders, who argued in hushed voices, ignoring the crowd's demand for a response. Nori stepped back until her arm brushed against Aeliana.

"You certainly know how to make a splash." Velden grinned at Nori, who turned to face them. "I'm starting to see how we might be related."

Her laugh came out choked.

"Is this why you wanted a public trial?" Aeliana asked.

"I didn't expect it to come to this," Nori admitted. "I actually used the opportunity to search for the starbridges. I figured if everyone was here, no one would be home to see me. But then your request gave me the idea."

"So you have them?" Velden asked.

She shook her head. "They must have moved them. There was only a shell in the box Gaeren showed me. After hearing their verdict, I suspect my father has them in his pocket."

Finally the elders pulled apart, their stoic faces giving away nothing. Elder Algaen raised his hands. It did little at first, but when he started talking, people were quick to quiet down for fear of missing something important.

"As you have all witnessed, Nori Algaen has requested to use her visit to the Seer. As she has requested it on behalf of the foreigners, she will be expected to travel with the foreigners to the Seer's sanctuary, where all of them will receive judgment."

A gasp went through the crowd, and Nori's eyes widened.

"What does that mean?" Aeliana asked. "Why is he giving us what we wanted after he said we couldn't see her?"

Nori swallowed hard. "He's not doing it for you. He's doing it for me."

"Take them back to the hut." Elder Algaen waved a hand at the guards surrounding the prisoners, cutting off any more questions Aeliana might have had.

Her knees grew weak as the truth sank in, making her trip as the guards dragged them away. They were going to see Lady Merinnia after all. It was what they had wanted from the beginning. But now the only thing she could feel was terror. Would the Seer judge them fairly? Would she still give them answers about the curse if they came seeking to have their names cleared?

The trek back to the hut was quicker than it had been coming to the village center. The guards whispered amongst themselves, and Aeliana caught optimistic phrases proving that Nori's unprecedented request was binding. When they were deposited in the hut, their stomachs still growled, but this time her companions' faces held hope.

Holm pulled Iris into a tight hug, pressing a kiss to the crown of her head. Lukai hesitated, as if he might try to do something similar for Aeliana, but instead he sat alone, keeping his distance from both Aeliana and Kendalyhn.

Even Sylmar's teeth showed under his beard and mustache. "Not only did she gain us access to Lady Merinnia, but she bought us time," he said. "We owe her much."

"We owe her our lives," Gaeren corrected.

Velden patted him on the back with a squishy, webbed hand. "Well, you and Riveran do, that's for certain."

Gaeren and Riveran let out nervous laughs, the stress of the afternoon coming through.

"Nori said they weren't letting us go to the Seer for our sakes, but for hers," Aeliana said as they all found places to sit. "Does anyone know what that means?"

Velden shrugged. "My guess is that her father didn't want her losing her chance for her own answer. If she went by herself only seeking our judgment, she'd lose out on her opportunity. If the rest of us go, we get answers for our actions and questions and she can get answers for hers."

"Then why did her mother look terrified?" Cyrus asked.

"Because she expects Nori will see her own death?" Gaeren suggested.

Aeliana shuddered. "But she can avoid it, right? By marrying Gellen?"

"Oh, I hope so." Iris leaned against Holm, her face stricken.

"I saw a memory within a memory." Gaeren raised his hands in surrender. "I don't know how it works."

"And none of us really knows how a visit to the Seer works," Velden said. "The crowd's reaction is a good reminder of how little we know and that we might not like what we find."

The joyful atmosphere shifted a hair as he pointed out the truth they'd all been ignoring.

"That was *my* pessimistic line," Sylmar muttered, attempting to settle on his side for a nap. "You're supposed to tell a joke here."

The entire room stilled until Velden chuckled. "No, I think the uncharacteristic role reversal was much better."

It felt like ages, but the Sun still hadn't gone to sleep when Nori arrived accompanied by Gellen and a few others, bringing a feast in comparison to the paltry food they'd previously been served. Aeliana's mouth swung open when she also saw blankets and pillows tied on packs on their backs.

Kendalyhn raised her eyebrows. "Are we being fattened before we're served up on a platter?"

Nori snorted. "It's a three-day journey to Seer's Sanctuary, two across land and one across the water. They want you to be rested and well fed before we leave in the morning."

Gellen scowled, his eyes constantly following Nori, making it difficult for Aeliana to ask any questions. When they'd all eaten, Aeliana managed to pull Nori back for the briefest moment.

"Why did the people react that way? When your father offered for all of us to go?"

Nori gave a guilty glance to the hut door, where Gellen had bent to collect some spoons he'd dropped. "Lady Merinnia prefers to see people alone. It's not that she can't assist us all at once—it's that it leaves her agitated. It's disrespectful for us to ask so much of her."

Aeliana frowned. "Would the elders do that just to make sure you get your questions answered too? That was Velden's theory, but it feels weak if it's disrespectful."

"It could be that my father pushed for it. But the others likely agreed because they no longer trust me. I might be on trial just as much as you are." Her smile held a sorrow that made Aeliana's heart ache with regret.

"I wish we'd never come. You could have gone on with your life—"

"No." Nori cut her off, her hand slicing the air. "For years I have been waiting to start my life. Waiting for the signal that it was time. My life would have remained that way without you. This was always our path."

"Nori?" Gellen called.

"Coming." Nori turned to leave, but Aeliana snatched her wrist.

"Does he know you're helping us? Has he tuned in to your mind for our intentions?"

Nori recoiled. "Never. He would never do that without my permission." But then understanding dawned on her face. "He freely tuned in to yours because it was an assignment. But he's not all that bad." A few scales popped up on her cheeks. Perhaps an arranged marriage between the two wouldn't be as hated as Aeliana had feared.

As Nori left with Gellen and the extra guards, the Sun slipped behind the village to the west, reminding the prisoners they needed to sleep as well.

They spread out the pillows and blankets that now felt luxurious, but despite a full belly and knowing she needed sleep, Aeliana couldn't find rest. She shoved the blanket off, feeling suffocated instead of warm.

"It works better when you wrap it around you," Velden whispered from beside her.

"I'm sorry," she said. "Am I keeping you up?"

"No." It was too dark to see him in the hut, but she could hear the smile in his voice. "That would be my mind, which seems to be swimming across all of Paelen's Waters without my permission."

She held back laughter that might wake up the others. "Will it be hard going back to Vendaras after experiencing your home?"

"I'm not sure I'm meant to have a home," he said. "I can never be fully Sayhleen. Coming here and spending time with these people has shown me that. I relish learning their culture and applying what I can, but I could never live underwater like they do, and so I will always be an outsider. And in Vendaras, I'm a freak of nature. I can never fully fit in there either."

His words resonated deep within her, voicing things she hadn't been able to share. Just like him, she straddled two continents, two cultures. "Do you think maybe I'm not meant to be Vendaran either?" she asked.

He took his time answering, and her anxiety built with the silence.

"I think you are meant to be Aeliana, daughter to the high priestess, wielder of powerful magic. Wearing trousers or dresses and having short or long hair is irrelevant because there is so much more to you than your identity as a Vendaran or Lorvandan. If you stop trying to be one or the other, you might discover who you really are."

She toyed with a loose thread on her pillow. "It feels like I need to focus on being just Vendaran if I'm ever supposed to belong there, though. Kendalyhn hasn't been training me in history or culture for a while, not since… well, not since we found my magic shifted." Saying the words out loud made her wonder if they were really true. Was the magic training what took up her time? Or was it the awkwardness over the revelation that Kendalyhn and Lukai had been—or maybe still were—in love? "I suspect Sylmar will want me learning it all again once things go back to normal."

Velden snorted, which startled Holm out of his snore with a choke. The larger man rolled in his sleep, starting a round of everyone shifting their positions in the cramped space. Aeliana and Velden smothered their laughter in their pillows.

"I don't think there ever will be a normal," Velden finally said. "Even if we find this curse and help your mother. Even if we find all the starbridges and save the world in whatever mysterious way Orra wants. You don't need to try to fit in to whatever expectation Sylmar has. Your mother is destined to lead, and you are, too.

"But a leader brings many experiences to the table. If you try to get rid of your human side, if you try to be less Lorvandan, you're shoving down all the things you have to offer the people in Vendaras. Maybe they need a different perspective. Maybe they need exactly who you are. Today you offered yourself as sacrifice for your people. The kings and queens of Elanesse would never do that. That's the kind of leadership Vendaras is craving."

Aeliana stared at the faint traces of the hut's ceiling, the bits of twine she could make out in the darkness. "Are you giving yourself this same speech?"

He sighed. "I suppose I should. At least the bit about trying to meet expectations. The problem is when we try to fit in one culture or the other. We're not meant to."

She considered his words, wondering how they might change her approach. Instead of rejecting the potential role of leader, instead of denying whatever authority she might have as the high priestess' daughter, perhaps she could use it for good. Perhaps she could accept it on her own terms like she had today, when it gave her a chance to stand up for those she cared about.

"I always thought my mother was waiting for me to be ready to come to Sayhla Island," Velden added, "but now I think she always knew they wouldn't accept me. She was trying to get me to find my own way."

"I'm sorry, Velden. I didn't realize how far back or how painful your secrets were when you told me you had them."

"And that's not even the half of them," he muttered.

His words surprised Aeliana, and for a moment she was tempted to place a hand on his arm, to try using the noetic skills Gaeren had been teaching her to tune in to his memories. It likely wouldn't work with Durriken being so far away.

"I might not have dark secrets like Sylmar or Mayvus," Velden added, "but there are parts of my history I keep to myself. Not out of shame or fear, but to hold them close. Keeping them safe feels like a way to honor them."

"You don't have to explain." All temptation to tune in to his past receded, leaving the initial thought like bile in the back of her throat. Aeliana had had enough secrets of her own over the years; she wasn't about to pry any from Velden. "I'm so sorry for all you've lost, including the things you keep secret and safe."

"Thank you," he murmured.

As Velden's breathing shifted, Aeliana tried to fall asleep too, but the things he'd said swirled in her mind, mixing with her fears and doubts over their plans to see Lady Merinnia. Orra had said she didn't have to ask Lady Merinnia a question, that she could choose to remain ignorant.

Now it was less a matter of whether or not she'd ask the Seer a question and more a matter of which question she'd ask.

CHAPTER 48

Most everyone in the fortress was asleep, but Orra sat out on the northern keep's balcony, her eyes to the Stars. Her habits were almost as nocturnal as the winex, which was why she'd waited until this evening to approach them. Their numbers had dwindled this cycle. Even though they'd mated and buried their eggs in the eastern garden, several had left. More chose to return to their natural, nomadic ways than maintain the domesticated farce in the fortress.

But Felk, Lilik, and their small faithful clan remained.

Orra suspected this final bit of rejection might be too much for them, and her heart ached over what that might mean for Felk and Aeliana and the bridges they'd crossed between two seemingly rival species.

She folded up the letter she'd written, unsure in its wisdom, then made her way down the steep tower steps and through the halls to the eastern garden. When she first arrived, the winex were out, likely hunting for their evening meal. The guards were always more than eager to let them go, but they were more hesitant to let them back in.

She waited near the eggs they'd recently laid, placing a hand on the smooth surface and imagining the tiny creature growing inside. It was a wonder how the winex were designed. She wasn't surprised that Mayvus had been intrigued by their rebirth process. She would love to understand it as well. But not because she wanted to use it like Mayvus did.

"What are you doing?" Lilik's voice came out sharp and wary.

Orra turned slowly with a smile, not wanting to distress the winex further. "I'm simply marveling at your species. It's a blessing from the Sun to be born again the way you are."

Lilik's eyes narrowed, and the tension in her shoulders didn't ease until Orra removed her hand from the egg. "Why are you here?"

"I've come to see Felk," Orra said. "But I admit my news affects you all."

Lilik dropped to all fours and slunk across the room toward the eggs. Her eyes hardly blinked as she assessed Orra. "What sort of news?" Once she reached the eggs, she stood, placing her palms on the eggs as if testing all of them for the life inside.

"I would prefer to share the news with Felk, but I don't mind if you all listen together."

"All six of us?" Lilik muttered.

Orra faltered. "There are only six of you now?"

"The others all left. Said they felt stifled by this confined space."

"But you stayed…" Orra let the words hang.

Lilik sighed. "I stayed for Felk. But I want to leave. In my next life, I might not be able to stay. It makes me sad for him."

"The connection you have across lives is beautiful," Orra said.

Lilik eyed her strangely as if questioning whether or not it was truly a compliment. "He'll come soon. The smallest in our group hadn't made a catch yet." She turned back to the eggs. "I was worried about the eggs. He let me return alone."

Orra smiled in an effort to hide her pain for this creature who seemed to know the eggs had been in danger in the past, even though that had been a previous lifetime, something Emeris hadn't bothered sharing with them. It reminded her of Marnok and the way his memories seemed to be in there somewhere, just inaccessible.

She and Lilik awkwardly shared the space in silence until the light gallop of the other winex was heard. Sure enough, only five entered the room, including Felk.

For the first time, Orra suspected her news might be better received than she'd anticipated.

"Orra?" Felk asked. "You're awake late." He glanced up at the moon, barely visible through the garden's open roof.

"I'm leaving in the morning." Orra adopted their preferred direct approach.

A few of them stood a little taller, raising their noses as if sniffing out the danger in her words.

"Why?" Felk cocked his head.

"We've learned that Mayvus is bringing people from Ahmranas. She's building another army."

A few of the winex snarled, dropping to all fours.

"So you're running," Felk said.

Orra weighed his words, not quite sure she could say yes or no to the accusation. "We're traveling to warn Aeliana. But yes, we don't want to be here when she returns."

Felk and Lilik exchanged a glance, both reflexively leaning in closer to the eggs. "You're all leaving?" he asked.

Orra shook her head. "The army is staying behind. I suspect General Nels will give each soldier the option, and many might go home to protect their families and avoid a worse fate."

"But some will stay," Felk said.

Orra nodded. "However, they have not invited you to stay with them."

A flash of pain crossed Felk's face, but he quickly schooled his features. "They never wanted us here."

"Some of us did," Orra corrected softly.

"It's not our way." Lilik placed a hand on Felk's arm, her serenity crossing through to him until he visibly drooped.

"I understand," he said. "I wanted to meet Aeliana. The memories... confused me. I think she would have wanted to say goodbye."

Orra hesitated, then pulled the paper from her pocket. "I know you've worked on your letters in past cycles, but this one, we didn't spend enough time on them. I wrote this for you in case it helped."

Felk took the parchment, opening it and scanning the words. He'd maintained the ability to read ever since the first time Aeliana had taught him, but each cycle he had to regain the dexterity of forming the letters himself. It was one more way in which their rebirth each moon fascinated Orra.

"It will be your choice," she said. "You can place the letter in your nest on your last night and retain a connection to us, or you can throw the letter in the sea and move on. Aeliana will not blame you for living the life the Sun created you for. You were not meant for these walls." She glanced at the minimal trees around them, the atmosphere they'd hoped would be enough like the woods to appease the winex. But it hadn't been enough, and the winex could not be forced to be something they were not.

"The decision I make on my last night might not be the decision I make next cycle." Felk dug his toe in the dirt at their feet, looking far younger than one week shy of his rebirth.

Lilik wrapped an arm around his shoulders.

"It's not fair to my future self if I make the wrong choice," he added.

Orra smiled. "I could say the same of each of my lifetimes. It doesn't matter that I remember my past experiences. I still make different decisions, and I still have to live with the consequences. We each have to make the best of what we're given. I know you'll make the right choice, because neither choice is wrong, Felk. It's less about which choice you make in this moment and more about who you are in each of your lifetimes." She stepped forward, tapping him on the chest. "Aeliana sensed something in you that has carried through every lifetime she's known you. That's what matters."

His face flickered through a number of emotions as he and Lilik exchanged a glance. When he regained control of his mask, Orra stepped back, clasping her empty hands behind her.

"If you'd like to say goodbye to the others, we'll be gathered at the gates in the morning. But if you choose to leave during the night, I'll understand. Regardless of which choice you make, may the Sun's light always guide you."

Felk nodded but didn't return the farewell. It wasn't his way, and she didn't expect him to.

The next morning, when the soldiers gathered at the gates to send her off with Rildan, Emeris, and Marnok, the winex were nowhere to be found.

CHAPTER 49

THE TWO DAYS spent walking across Sayhla Island felt endless to Gaeren. The misty plateaus and valleys were easy enough to cross with their web of creeks and soft grass fields pockmarked with candlenut and breadfruit trees. But the unnatural silence that fell over the group was both daunting and exhausting.

Whenever the Vendarans tried asking the Sayhleens about the Seer's Sanctuary, they were met with distrustful, monosyllabic answers. Even Nori, who occasionally attempted to give answers, was often cut off by her peers' glares.

Gaeren hadn't expected all the elders to travel with them. But according to Nori, during one of her rare slips, it was tradition for at least one elder to accompany someone who had invoked their right to visit the Seer. They made it sound like they'd all come because of Nori's unique position as the daughter of an elder. But Gaeren suspected it was more to keep an eye on the Vendarans.

Gellen and six soldiers came along with the elders and their wives, making Gaeren feel like they'd come to ensure his and Riveran's doom.

"If we weren't with you, would it have been faster for you to swim?" Gaeren asked the second day, hoping if he didn't directly mention the Seer, his questions might seem harmless enough.

Nori glanced at her father, who walked ahead with his wife, their heads bent in conversation. She shook her head. "If we swam, we'd have to go all the way around the island. Tideholm is on the southern side of Sayhla Island, and the Seer's Sanctuary is across the northern coast. This is the narrowest part of the island, and it's a two-day walk from south to north. We'll travel by water up the channel to the east to enter the Seer's Sanctuary on the third day. I suspect it will be slower with all of you in tow, but we do have some small boats to help you along."

He pulled up the memory of the maps he'd seen in Orra's copy of *The Sins of the Stars*, wondering if any of the cities labeled on her map were still around one thousand years later. "Is Tideholm your capital?"

She frowned. "All the villages are equal in Paelen's waters, regardless of their size. Most have fewer elders than ours, but a couple of them have more. For every thousand people, one elder is chosen."

He raised his brows in surprise. He'd thought there'd been more than five thousand people in Tideholm, but that meant their population in general was a fraction the size of Vendaras or Lorvandas. But perhaps it had always been that way, since they had such unique physical features that required certain living conditions.

Before he could ask more questions, Gellen came and took Nori away, making it clear Gaeren had already gotten more information than he should have.

By the time they reached the northern shore, everyone was eager to switch to the boats. The Sayhleens put the Vendarans to work paddling with oars two by two while they transformed and swam alongside them, sometimes disappearing for long lengths of time. The brief respite from their cold looks allowed Gaeren to momentarily pretend things weren't so bleak.

As they left the coast of the island, it didn't take long to spot the coast of another island, its shores far more rocky with hardly any vegetation. They passed a few buildings cut into the rocks, where minimal trees and greenery created a tiny oasis in the otherwise uninhabitable coastline.

Nori surfaced near Gaeren and Riveran's boat, playing with the rope as if the tie had come loose. But it was clear the knot remained perfect. "That's the school for progenies," she murmured.

"Do all the progenies go there to train?" Gaeren asked.

She nodded. "And most stay on as teachers. In a village our size, the only remaining progenies are the elders and a few close to them. They mostly ensure they have access to all the spokes and nothing more."

Elder Algaen studied her from his place near Aeliana and Cyrus' boat. His stare sharpened enough to make her dive beneath the water once more.

Something about the way she explained their progenies left Gaeren uneasy. It was almost like Sayhleens kept control over them so they couldn't rise up and gain power over the people. Maybe that was a good thing. Or maybe it was just a different form of corruption in a different form of government.

Their third and final day dragged on as they paddled past the barren land, until Gaeren questioned if they were being brought to the Seer after all. Maybe the Sayhleens had some sort of sacrificial post where they left food for krakens.

The other Vendarans showed similar unease, especially when they were instructed to bring their boats to shore without anything but rock in sight.

"Where exactly are we going?" Gaeren asked.

Nori pointed to a dark space at the edge of the water. "The Seer's Sanctuary is a cavern deep within these rocks. It's only accessible from the water. In many ways, the island is like a tree, its trunk rooted deeply in the water and its branches flowing out in a wide circumference. But when you travel underneath the branches, you'll find empty pockets for nests. It's a space with little light and little to stimulate Lady Merinnia's highly tuned senses."

Gaeren could barely make out where the water lapped underneath the overhanging cliff. "Can we fit under there?" he asked.

Nori hesitated. "We don't usually take boats. I'm guessing it would be easier to reach it during low tide."

"When is low tide?" Gaeren asked.

"This time of year..." Nori glanced at the Sun's descent. "We missed it by a few hours."

"Of course we did," Gaeren muttered.

The Vendarans continued paddling, warily watching the rock wall grow near. At times, it seemed as though they would crash against it and be smashed to pieces. But the closer they got, the larger the space seemed, and soon it became apparent that if they bent down, they would fit under the rock while remaining in their boats. However, they would be at the mercy of the Sayhleens to pull them in the right direction without their oars for guidance.

Gaeren shivered, imagining the Sayhleens abandoning them and trapping them. It would be easy for them to do. Velden was the only one who seemed completely at ease with their position, and Gaeren vowed to follow the other man if boats were tipped. Just in case his amphibious instincts gave him a leg up.

After they'd been pulled under the rock for a few feet, darkness encompassed them, leaving flickering luminescent algae beneath the water as their guide. It reminded Gaeren of his walk through the sprites' cavern, and he grew more tense.

The claustrophobic paranoia settled to discomfort as the rock above them rose, allowing them space to sit up a little taller and look out a little farther. The cavern remained dark, but more luminescent algae, and possibly sea creatures, left bright imprints along the cavern walls, like a rainbow's reflection on the rock. It showed the cavern they entered was far larger than Gaeren had imagined.

The pool of water they slid across led to rocky steps that the Sayhleens began ascending, their scales and fins falling away for skin and limbs. Just beyond the steps rested a dais with as much headroom above it as any chamber in his parents' home. Stalagmites rose from the pool's edge in crystal formations, beckoning them closer to the dais, where at least eight women stood, their statuesque stances more intimidating than soldiers at arms.

As the Sayhleens pulled the boats the remainder of the way to the stairs, the women continued staring straight ahead, their long white dresses eerily reflecting the luminescent glow. Their bare feet were covered in scales, the water lapping at their toes. Each one wore a necklace, their starlocks in plain view for all to see. The unusual transparency left Gaeren uncomfortable, like they were partially undressed, and he avoided looking at each starlock's individual shape.

As if they'd been instructed to do so, everyone kept silent—even Cyrus. But their eyes wandered the entire length of the room, taking in the way it felt intentionally arranged even though everything appeared to be natural formations. Stalactites hung in mirrored patterns, and plants Gaeren couldn't identify rose from the water to line the cavern walls, their blossoms seeming to defy nature without the Sun's light.

When all the Vendarans stood on the dais, surreptitiously stretching out sore muscles from their cramped ride in the boats, the women turned as one, leading them to the back of the cavern. The glow from their dresses seemed to grow, likely a trick of their magic. But it allowed their guests to see a hall leading to another cavern.

The sanctuary seemed to grow in opulence the deeper they went, making questions build up in Gaeren, fueled by the fact that he knew he couldn't ask them. It was as magnificent as his parents' palace, but in some ways it felt like far more, because it seemed to be formed by the Sun's own hands rather than by the people.

When they reached the next cavern, it was far smaller, barely fitting their twenty-eight travelers and the eight women. Chairs and refreshments were given to all, but the elders remained standing, speaking in hushed tones with the women.

Nori sat near Aeliana at a table, and Gaeren found a chair across from them, leaning in to hear what Nori might be explaining.

"But who are they?" Aeliana was asking.

"They're the acolytes of the Seer. Each one of them is a possible replacement for her, but they don't expect it. There's no method to the madness of a new Seer being chosen. It's simply seen by the former Seer and decided. Sometimes it comes after mere moons of one Seer being in place; other times it's years. Lady Merinnia has been in this position since before some of the elders were born, so we all expect her to pass it on in the near future."

The acolytes kept glancing at Gaeren and the others, their sharp gazes intimidating as he wondered how much they could see. If each of these women were trained to be the future Seer, were they sifting the visitors' futures even now?

"What happens next?" Gaeren asked.

"From what my mother told me, this is where only one of us moves forward. I suspect they'll take us one at a time to see her until her patience wears out. We could be here for days getting through everyone." Nori's face grew troubled. "I don't know of any instance where this many have come to see her at once. I thought it was forbidden, but it seems it was tradition for it to be an individual's journey."

Gaeren took a sip of the fresh water they'd laid out, then grabbed some sort of seaweed roll that looked more edible than the other things on the table. Despite his practice at multiple ambassador meetings with strange customs and foods, he still made a face and set the roll down on an empty plate, desperate for a place to spit out the little he'd eaten.

"You don't care for the octopus intestine rolls?" Velden asked, slapping Gaeren on the back and making him choke on the slimy substance. Velden picked up the remainder of the roll and shoved half of it in his mouth in a single bite. "My mother made these for me when I was a boy. I'll have to get the recipe before we leave."

Gaeren felt sick watching the other man eat, but he was saved from responding by the elders and the acolytes turning to face the group, their gazes solemn. For the first time, the elders seemed nervous, and Elder Algaen sought Nori out with his eyes, his expression pained.

One of the acolytes stepped forward to address the group. "Lady Merinnia saw your approach. She is unhappy with your decision to come with so many, but she has seen that the result is good. She is willing to sacrifice her comfort to see all of you for the sake of the people. Once you have had your fill, we will take you all to her chamber."

Nori and Gellen both balked. "All of us?" Nori asked. "At once?"

The acolyte turned her way. "It has been foreseen."

CHAPTER 50

GAEREN GLANCED AT SYLMAR, whose grip tightened on his staff.

Something was very wrong. He would have suspected foul play from the Sayhleens if it weren't for their equal surprise. But now his distrust in the acolytes grew, as if they'd manufactured this entire visit. But how could they have? Even if they'd foreseen some way to use this to their benefit, they hadn't sent the Vendarans across the barriers. They hadn't pushed the elders to make it such a large affair.

His fear came full circle, reminding him of all the times Orra's ominous predictions had left him uneasy. If she were standing here, she would smile serenely and say it had all been arranged by the Sun. And who were they to question the Sun's decision?

No one else spoke up, and the food and drinks remained untouched for several long moments, their appetites stolen by their fear.

The acolyte who'd addressed them gave a sharp nod. "Very well, your guards can remain as well as your elders, but anyone who has called upon their right to see Lady Merinnia may step forward. It's important that you understand you do not need to state your individual requests. Her power is pervasive. Most come seeking answers to the future, but some come seeking judgment about the past. Her skills fall along the full length of the pneumatic spoke, so she will sift the thing you wish to know most, whether it be in your past, present, or future. If it's the future you wish to know, she will show you the possible paths, likely only three at most, sometimes only one."

Gaeren winced, unsure he would trust a single path shown. It seemed impossible. And what was it he wished to see anyway? He was supposed to be proving his innocence, but they'd come to find a cure for the curse. Except he wanted that for Aeliana. Deep down he knew that wasn't what Lady Merinnia would show him, not if she sifted through what they each truly wanted the most.

The acolyte raised her chin. "You will not all like what you see. You may not all leave here alive or sane. The things you learn may haunt you for years to come. Anyone who steps into her chambers comes with that understanding. You are choosing this knowledge. She is not forcing it on you, though it may feel that way in the moment, depending on what you see."

Riveran snagged the hem of Gaeren's tunic. "I don't like this," he whispered. "It's too much like the sprites."

"It makes me wonder if their source of power is the same," Gaeren murmured, "if the Seer's power really originates from the Sun after all."

Their conversation was cut short as the head acolyte's gaze rested on them. "Do you all accept this warning and agree to proceed?"

Everyone nodded.

"And do you agree not to hold Lady Merinnia accountable for seeing and sharing the truth, for she is but a messenger?"

The nods were slower to come this time.

"But you said she told you the outcome was good?" Aeliana clarified.

The head acolyte hesitated. "It is for the good of all people. I don't know if it is good for each one of you."

"We agree." Nori's voice rang out with confidence.

"Then so be it." The acolyte turned to head down another small cavern hall. Three of the women followed her, but the other four gestured for those seeking Lady Merinnia's judgment to walk before them so they could take up the rear. Gaeren and a few others were forced to hunch inside the cavern as the ceiling sloped downward, their growing discomfort representative of their growing fear. When the hall that had become more like a narrow tube let out into a larger cavern, Gaeren had to blink several times for his eyes to adjust to the new source of light. It came from deep within the pool of water at their feet, an unmoving cerulean glow that cast them all in a somber blue sheen.

The path they walked led around the circumference of the pool to an open area with a single chair carved from the same rock they walked on. A woman with long kelp-like hair and scaly skin sat so still on its seat that Gaeren questioned if he was looking at a statue of one of the first Seers or the current Seer herself. When they reached the platform, she turned ever so slightly, opening eyes that were milky white to stare unseeing at them.

Gaeren couldn't help recoiling, and a few others around him gasped, but the woman made no sign of offense.

"Take your spots along the ring," she instructed.

The acolytes led their group to a perfect circle cut from the rock surrounding the chair, placing each of them a few feet apart until they surrounded the Seer. Gaeren, Riveran, Aeliana, and Cyrus had all been stuck behind the chair, but Gaeren didn't mind not seeing Lady Merinnia's creepy eyes.

Nori, the only one in their eleven who had an inkling of what might be to come, stood directly across from them and in front of the Seer. To her left were Iris and Holm, their hands shaking with apprehension. On her right stood Sylmar and Velden, and even the half-Sayhleen looked a bit overwhelmed, his mother clearly not having given him details about her own visit to Lady Merinnia. Lukai and Kendalyhn were across from each other on Lady Merinnia's right and left, each maintaining a defensive stance.

Nori stepped forward. "We come asking for your judgment, guidance, and wisdom. We ask that you bring clarity on our existence and our purpose. Show us what you will so that we may move forward with a better understanding." The speech was given like some sort of poem the Sayhleens had all learned in childhood, a recitation that had been drilled into them along with their letters and numbers.

Nori then dropped to one knee and bowed in deference, so Gaeren did the same, and in a slow wave the others all joined them. Cyrus was the last, the indecision written on his face, and Gaeren suspected he was uneasy bowing before anyone other than the Stars.

When all eleven of them had copied Nori's posture, Lady Merinnia rose from her chair, her movements stiff as though she'd been sitting there since the last person had come seeking her skills.

"And so you shall," she said, her murmuring voice mirroring Orra's in the moments when Orra seemed to almost separate from her body as she sifted for truth.

Gaeren felt a brief moment of panic, a desire to take back the request and run from the room. But then he was no longer in the room and no longer able to run.

He found himself standing on a balcony, the wind blowing in the trees around him. Beyond that, he heard a strange hum, like the background noises of a dozen other rooms and settings were filtering through his senses. Lady Merinnia's voice echoed through his mind as he studied his surroundings.

You wish to know how to keep both Aeliana and Enla safe.

Guilt flooded through him as she cut to the heart of the matter. She wasn't going to show him anything that helped Aeliana or their group. But a strange flicker of hope wormed its way through his guilt. Was it possible to keep them both safe?

If you try to protect both, you will fail.

He winced, but there was no way for him to question her within this vision.

There are only two paths in your future. The first holds both women. As her voice faded from his mind, Riveran stepped out onto the balcony, pushing a chair on wheels. Enla slumped in the chair, her hands limp in her lap and her gaze unfocused. She looked far older, the lines on her face evidence of many years having passed, but Riveran had hardly changed. He wheeled her to a table inlaid with jewels and locked her wheels in place before patting her arm and stepping away.

In the distance, Gaeren heard the distracting cacophony grow louder, with Lady Merinnia's voice overlapping the sounds. It was as if he could hear remnants of every one of his comrades' judgments and visions as well. It left him anxious that he'd miss something in his own vision because of the chaos.

But very little happened as Enla sat there, unmoving and seemingly unaware of her surroundings. He wanted to call out to her, but like the memories he tuned in to, he had no control over this.

The vision faded, and similar to when he crossed the barriers with the starbridges, he felt out of time and place without the grounding sensation of the floor beneath him. Until he settled once more on a shoreline, the waves coasting in and out to compete with the other sounds echoing in the cavern where he sensed his body still stood.

Down the coast, a woman ran with two toddlers trailing behind her. She bent forward to scoop up water, splashing them to make them giggle. He held his breath, recognizing the long brown waves and slim form, daring to hope it might be her. When she drew close enough for him to catch the jade glint in her eyes, he recognized the same full lips and brown locks on the girl running beside her, just before Aeliana pulled both children beneath the waves, their laughter cut short by both the water and the vision fading.

The other path only holds one woman. Lady Merinnia's voice startled him as he tumbled through the emptiness again before the vision settled once more into the all-too-familiar throne room of his parents' home. Enla sat ramrod straight, the crown on her head glinting in the Sun's light streaming through the windows. A room full of people bowed before her, and she nodded at them, her face as stubbornly stoic as their father's often was.

I find it fascinating that your desire is to see their safety. Lady Merinnia's voice blocked out any of the conversation occurring around the room. *Do you have no care for your own safety?* He was tempted to ask the clarifying question she teased him with, but he sensed it wasn't an option. She had filtered through what he wanted to know most, and that was what she'd given him.

He had no second chance.

I would have thought that added information would have helped you choose which path to seek. I wonder if—

Her words cut off as a scream echoed through the cavern, pulling Gaeren from the vision. The disorientation hit hard as he reached for his empty weapons belt, and his eyes attempted to adjust to the far darker cavern before him. Many of his comrades stood, dazed expressions on their faces as they took in whatever vision Lady Merinnia still showed them, but Iris and Holm had stepped back from the circle, their eyes blazing with equal determination.

Iris held a dagger, but Gaeren wasn't sure where it had come from. Tears poured down her cheeks. "Please, Holm, don't make me do this."

But then Holm lunged for her.

CHAPTER 51

AELIANA'S EYESIGHT BLURRED, and a chill swept over her arms. The friends surrounding her faded slightly, replaced by a vision. The scene overlaid around her, leaving her companions as wisps behind the vision, which grew stronger as she watched it unfold.

The Seer's voice broke through her mind. *Most come seeking their future, but your future starts with your past. The full story is documented in the archives of the Dehvlonian Oracles. But here, you can witness the origins of your mother's curse.*

A young woman kneeled in a dark cave, her head bowed and hands splayed out on the earth as if in worship. Her hands were covered in tattoos that seemed strangely familiar. Details of the cave eluded Aeliana, but with a sharp gasp she recognized the other occupant. Bulbous black eyes and ruby wings. A nearly human form curled in on itself, and a mouthless face. It was the same sprite who had spoken with Aeliana at Lovers' Falls. Was this the cavern Gaeren and Riveran had reached?

The sprite flapped its wings to lean forward and raise the woman's chin with its long fingers and claws.

So… Malvinia, you seek revenge. The sprite's voice carried through Aeliana's mind without a mouth to project its words.

"My sister died at the hand of a Wyndren priestess," the young woman said. "I took my last breath with her. Now my bones rot, and by the light of the moon, poison breeds in my blood. I spread my poison and let it brew until I can repay the debt."

The sprite gave its awful slow blink, leaving a film behind that still made Aeliana cringe even though she knew it was only a vision of the distant past. The creature cocked its head but made no response, so the woman continued.

"The time for that revenge has come." She pressed her face to the earth once more and waited several long moments.

The sprite hummed its interest, its voice carrying through the cavern. *So you wish us to curse the family? That is a significant request.*

"My life is already forfeit." The woman's voice came out muffled but certain. "Take it as your price."

The sprite blinked once more, the film receding. Aeliana grew tense as the silence wore on, a part of her hoping the sprite might refuse, even though this is what she had come to hear.

A scream echoed in the distance, but neither the woman nor the sprite reacted, making Aeliana realize it was coming from the Seer's Sanctuary. She resisted the urge to leave the vision, knowing this was the information she needed most.

The sprite's words dripped with its pleasure. *Very well. A curse of the moon. A shadow of the Sun's light. Death bought by lifeblood.* The sprite's wings beat faster, and Aeliana's heart sped up with them. *For the loss of your sister, the Wyndren sisters will pay. Each—*

The roar of a battle cry erupted around Aeliana, nearly pulling her from Lady Merinnia's vision. She fought to ignore it, wincing as critical words from the curse were lost to whatever danger was unfolding in the room.

—cursed for their crime. A love, born of blood, doomed to wither by unfounded contempt. Where love might triumph, pride will prevail. Pain will be shared, heartache doubled. The relief of death will evade them, for their destiny is to watch the light leave each other's eyes. Until—

Screams erupted around Aeliana and her vision flickered, the dim outline of the sanctuary walls replacing the darkness of the sprite's cavern. Chaos ensued as her friends turned on each other with confusion and mistrust in their eyes.

"No," she whispered, closing her eyes. "Show me the rest."

She sensed Lady Merinnia's pleasure as the vision returned, but the sprite was no longer speaking. Instead, a flutter of wings filled Aeliana's ears, and dozens of sprites came forward as if they'd been embedded in the cavern's very walls. Their hands reached out, clawing at the dirt near the woman's feet, the ground opening up unnaturally fast until a grave lay before her.

The blood-red sprite's cheeks lifted with its invisible smile, and Aeliana shuddered along with the young woman. *You've made your choice and received your prize. Now for the price.* To the young woman's credit, she sat straighter, closing her eyes but lifting her chin as though offering her neck to the sprite.

"I am ready," she whispered.

A chorus of hums rang out before the woman was shoved in the hole. She cried out as dirt rained down on her, then fell silent as the sprites buried her alive. The soft dirt grew hard as they patted it down, and a small patch of flowers rose from the grave's center, just like Aeliana's daisies so often did.

She shrank away from it.

As the vision faded, a small emerald sprite materialized before the ruby one who'd made the deal. The green sprite held out its hands in wonder, and the red gave it a regal nod.

So be it.

This time when the sanctuary walls came into focus, Aeliana knew her chance for the truth was over.

From the center of the circle, Lady Merinnia collapsed against the chair, her head falling into her hands as she let out a moan. Aeliana blinked in confusion as her friends all seemed to turn on one another. Cries rang out as Sylmar and Velden rushed forward, attempting to separate Iris and Holm, who wrestled on the rock floor, blood spilling between them. But Iris gave one last thrust, and Holm let out a pained final gasp.

Aeliana thought she caught an apology on his lips before his eyes turned glassy.

"No," Aeliana cried, rushing forward. The magic in her blood stirred in response, pulling in power from her starlock, preparing to heal. But her healing skills had weakened, and he looked far too still.

Gaeren grabbed her waist and pulled her back against his chest. "It's too late, Daisy," he whispered, his voice hoarse.

Velden yanked Iris back, knocking the dagger from her hands. She made no effort to resist, her own sobs echoing throughout the cavern, her blubbering indistinguishable.

"Where did you even get a weapon?" Velden asked, his voice cold with accusation.

"It's mine," Nori whispered. "She must have pulled it off me when I was receiving my vision."

The battle that had seemed to encompass everyone was over, and Aeliana realized it had only ever been between Iris and Holm. Everyone else's faces held the same shock she felt. Gaeren loosened his hold, likely sensing she'd come to terms with the futility of her efforts to save their friend.

"What happened?" Sylmar demanded.

"I don't know." Gaeren ran a hand through his hair, his gaze stuck on Holm's body. "She screamed and then said, 'don't make me do this.' And then they were on the floor, each trying to kill the other."

"What did they see?" Nori's eyes held a haunted sorrow. "It's because of the vision they received. That's the only explanation for it. Something they saw made them enemies."

Aeliana knew everyone was asking the same question in their minds. How could they go from lovers to enemies because of a vision? A small part of her realized it was a double blow. This meant they hadn't all seen the curse that she'd seen. If no one else had seen it, she might not ever discover which words she'd missed.

"We can't ever know what Holm saw," Sylmar said, his face grave.

The only sounds left in the room were Lady Merinnia's groans and Iris' sobs, which turned to muffled screams as she brought her palm to her mouth. The place that had once held her bond mark showed a jagged pink scar, which she nursed as Velden lowered her to the cavern floor.

"Take her memory, Gaeren," Sylmar said.

Gaeren flinched. What had he seen in his vision? Did it make him afraid to see what Iris had learned?

"I want to see it too," Aeliana admitted. "I want to know for myself." She didn't know if she could this far from Durriken, but it was worth trying.

She and Gaeren each placed a hand on Iris' shoulder. Despite her pain, Iris must have wanted the vision to be seen, because it came through, disjointed at first, but clearer as it went on, perhaps fueled by Gaeren's magic as well.

The memory of the vision held a vaguely familiar cliffside. Once Aeliana recognized the scorched remnants of a campfire within a cave, it became clear it was the place Holm had found what he thought was Mayvus' body. But instead, Mayvus stood there, surrounded by half a dozen soldiers.

They wrestled Holm to the ground and took his blood, forcing a brand on him, making Aeliana's stomach churn. When the process was complete, he stood, no longer resisting. And Mayvus stepped forward, placing a glove over his hand. Her gait was unsteady and she nursed a wound at her waist, but she was clearly alive.

"You'll tell them you saw my remains. You'll convince them I'm dead. Send them on wild searches to waste their time while I build my army."

He nodded.

"You'll only remember this when I check in on you. You will continue among their company as though nothing has changed. When the brand heals, you will remove your glove, and I will mask it for you."

He nodded again, and the vision faded, pierced by Iris' mournful howl both in the memory and in the present.

Aeliana and Gaeren gasped, stepping away in horror.

"Holm betrayed us all," Iris cried. "I knew he'd been keeping something from me. But I never thought it would be something like this." Her sobs rent the air once more. "I couldn't cut it out before he attacked. It was the only way to stop him."

Her words became unintelligible again, and Aeliana bent forward, wrapping her arms around the woman who had taken care of her like a mother over the last several months, crying with her. Nothing could fix what she'd been forced to do.

"Holm was branded," Gaeren told the others, his voice raw. "He's been feeding information to Mayvus since he first found her in Durriken's cave—alive."

Iris' sobs grew louder, and Aeliana hugged her tighter. The faithful maidservant had been forced to kill her bondmate. It didn't matter that he'd been branded. She'd had to look him in the eye while she'd shoved a dagger in his chest. She'd had to watch the man she loved die by her own hand. It was a cruel trick, like something the sprites would have done.

Aeliana turned to glare at the Seer, who still hunched in her chair. "You said it would be good!"

Lady Merinnia's hands went to her ears and she moaned louder, hunching farther.

"Aeliana," Nori warned.

"How is this good?" Aeliana stood, but the acolytes came forward, blocking her path.

A few brought food and drink for the Seer, applying ministrations that were likely ritualistic after every visit.

"Why did you tell us it would be good?" Aeliana cried out again as the other acolytes dragged them back down the path around the circumference of the room. Gaeren and Velden hefted Holm's body between them, each clearly enhancing their strength to hold a man of his size.

It left Aeliana sick to see the man she'd loved and respected jostled about like a sack of potatoes. She turned Iris away so the other woman wouldn't have to witness the consequences of her actions, and Iris cradled her hand against her chest, her cries holding not just the sorrow of her actions but the pain of her broken bond.

When Holm was practically dragged through to the room where the elders and guards waited, a new round of chaos ensued. Each of the Vendarans was shackled once more with the same seaweed-like rope that had been used before. Nori cried out in their defense, begging her parents to have mercy and to recognize the loss they'd just experienced.

"Loss?" Elder Algaen, asked, gesturing at Iris' bloody hands. "Tell me, how did he die?"

Nori hesitated, her eyes seeking out Aeliana.

"We had an enemy in our midst, and we were unaware," Aeliana said. "Iris protected both our people and yours with her actions."

Iris broke out into sobs again, making the elders hesitate.

"What was their judgment?" Elder Perla asked.

Nori shook her head. "I wasn't shown their judgment."

A strange hope flashed in her mother's eyes, and a grim smile crossed Elder Algaen's face. "What did the rest of you see?" he asked.

Silence filled the room until Velden broke it. "I was under the impression that was meant to be a private affair. I don't believe we're under any obligation to share our visions with you, unless you would like to share the visions you saw when you came in return?" He raised his eyebrows.

Elder Algaen narrowed his eyes. "Then how are we to know if your judgment was guilt or innocence?"

"I think it's clear that Holm was the only one guilty in our party," Aeliana said, hating the way the words sounded like a lie. He hadn't been guilty by choice. "Lady Merinnia said the outcome would be good. Do you not trust her word in this?" That statement tasted even more bitter. She would never trust the Seer, even if she was forced to trust the woman's visions the same way she'd seen the sprite's predictions come true.

"Of course we trust her," Elder Mishkel said. "It's you we don't trust."

The glares around the room only intensified, no one ready to concede to the other group.

"It's late," the head acolyte said. "We respectfully ask that you withdraw from the sanctuary and carry on your discussion elsewhere. Your needs have been met in the only way we know how. We can no longer aid you. It is time for you to move on."

The elders and guards inclined their heads, and the heat of the argument was set aside, like water boiling in the background until the meat was ready for the stew.

They allowed the acolytes to usher them all back to the first cavern, where their boats remained tied up to the rocky staircase. A numbness enveloped Aeliana so that she didn't even realize she'd boarded the boat until Cyrus reached back to squeeze her hand, pulling her from her dazed shock.

"You're bleeding." Cyrus opened her hand, revealing a cut on her palm.

She frowned at it, then tried pulling energy from her starlock to heal it. Whether her energy was too depleted or her somatic skills too muted, her efforts failed. Instead, she tore fabric from the hem of her shirt, wrapping it around her palm.

"It will all work out," he whispered. "Not today. But eventually."

She nodded mutely even though he couldn't see as he faced forward and grabbed an oar.

"Did you at least get the information you sought?" he asked.

"I discovered part of the curse. I don't think I heard enough to be able to break it. Did you get it all?"

At first he said nothing, attempting to paddle until they were forced to crouch and be pulled by the Sayhleens. "I didn't see the curse," he whispered. "I'm sorry. I tried to make it my focus. But she found a deeper question in my mind. One that had a stronger hold. I'm so sorry."

She couldn't be mad at him, and yet she didn't know how to forgive him. This was what they'd come for. But now, because the Seer was too good at seeing, they'd all seen different things that had been weighing on them. She was likely the only one who had seen the curse, but it had been cut off by Iris killing Holm.

She buried her face in her palms as she bent over beneath the low ceiling, allowing the awkward posture to hide the sorrow that finally surfaced. Holm had been a gentle giant, one she trusted implicitly more than many others in their party. How could he have been betraying them? And yet no one was immune to Mayvus' magic.

Aeliana's own mother had been branded and unable to resist her sister's control. Perhaps that was what the curse meant by "a love, born of blood, doomed to wither by unfounded contempt."

Sylmar had warned them that anyone could be affected, but for some reason they'd all thought they'd be safe. They'd all thought they would know if one of their own had been turned.

And that was when it hit her.

If Holm had been serving Mayvus, his deepest desire from the Seer would have been to see what Mayvus wanted to see. Which meant Mayvus had likely heard the curse. Had she heard as much as Aeliana? Had she heard more? Or was there something else she'd sought? Perhaps the key to immortality through the winex's eggs?

Regardless, they had to assume that by seeing Lady Merinnia, they'd given Mayvus exactly what she'd wanted.

CHAPTER 52

THE RETURN TRIP to Tideholm felt even longer to Aeliana than the way to the Seer's Sanctuary. They were forced to bury Holm on a small island with no grave marker and no ability for Iris to ever come back to pay her respects. The Sayhleens watched as they mourned him, the confusion evident in their eyes. Only Nori seemed to find their grief understandable, perhaps because she was the only one willing to listen to Aeliana's full explanation of the branding done by Mayvus.

The wedge Aeliana had noticed between Nori and her parents seemed to grow wider after their visit to the sanctuary, making Aeliana wonder what Nori had seen and if she'd told her parents. But Aeliana wasn't ready to share her own vision with her new friend, so she couldn't expect the same in return.

That first night, hardly anyone slept, and Iris grew feverish from her bond having been broken, requiring them to carry her on a hastily constructed litter the following day. Paddling down the channel became a foggy test of willpower until they were back on the main island for the night. Thankfully the Sayhleens had finally acquiesced and removed the seaweed shackles—not because they'd regained any trust, despite Nori continually fighting to clear the visitors' names, but to allow faster travel.

Most of the Vendarans went to bed, exhausted after their day of paddling and their night of grieving, but the Sayhleens settled by a fire, and Aeliana and Sylmar sat a short way away, halfway between their sleeping comrades and Cyrus, who'd found his own space to kneel before the Stars.

"I want to focus on my somatic spoke again," Aeliana said.

Sylmar's eyebrows rose. "What brought this on?"

Aeliana's face heated, and she glanced back at the tent, picturing Iris and the way Aeliana had failed her in the Seer's Sanctuary. "The noetic skills are interesting, and clearly they're valuable for Gaeren and others who have developed them, but they feel like a distraction to me. I want to be able to heal and protect again. I don't want to come away from battles wondering if I could have saved someone if I'd only spent more time training." Her voice shook, and she closed her eyes, trying to regain control. But she hated what she had to say next even more. "And if those skills can't return to their full power because of my brand on Durriken, I want to remove it."

The murmur of the Sayhleens by the fire filled the silence, but Aeliana still felt too exposed as she laid her vulnerable remorse out before Sylmar.

"I'm not going to complain or argue if you ask to learn your magic."

She glanced at the older man, catching a proud glint in his eyes.

"Have you discussed this option with Durriken?"

She shook her head. "I can't reach him on this side of the barrier. I won't do it until I talk to him. I'm hoping I won't need to do it at all if we train hard enough."

His eyes narrowed as he rubbed at his beard. "You like your connection with him."

Aeliana hesitated. "I don't like that it's through a brand, but yes, I look forward to checking on him. I care about him the same way I care about Felk. I feel a responsibility for him."

He hummed, but Aeliana couldn't tell if he found that news good or bad. "It's interesting that you can't reach him. It suggests that brands weaken significantly when a barrier is between them. It makes me wonder if it's Mayvus who's crossing the barrier after all. Could she still control her brands if she did?"

"If not her, then who?"

He shrugged. "Your guess is as good as mine."

"What about the curse?" Aeliana asked. "Did you hear it in your vision from Lady Merinnia? I'm guessing out of all of us, you're the only other person who might want to know it more than me."

Sylmar hesitated. "I realize now that the Seer is not as simple as we would have hoped."

Aeliana's heart sank. "So you didn't see the same vision as me?"

He shook his head. "No. You want to break the curse more than anything. And while I want that too, my desires go beyond that. I want Mayvus brought to justice. I want to see her power end, whether that's through ending the curse or some other means."

Aeliana squeezed her eyes shut. "And because breaking the curse doesn't actually bring about that justice, that's not what you saw."

He sighed. "I'm sorry. Can you tell me what you did see in your vision?"

She started from the beginning, surprised she was still able to tap into enough of her noetic skills to recall the details with perfection. When she described the woman in the sprites' cavern, Sylmar sat straighter.

"She had tattoos on her hands?"

"Yes," she said. "They were similar to Marnok's."

Sylmar frowned. "Just one more way in which that man's past seems to matter."

"What do you mean, 'one more way'?" she asked.

"Your mother implied his past connected him to us. But she wouldn't reveal any details. I suppose the tattoos could be the same thing that connects him to us. Either way, he has some explaining to do when he shows up again."

Aeliana winced, imagining the interrogation Marnok had coming. "The sprite said, 'for the loss of your sister, the Wyndren sisters will pay. Each—' and then it was cut off by a scream."

"Iris," Sylmar said.

"Yes." Aeliana glanced at the bedrolls, wondering if Iris was sleeping any better that night. "I don't think I missed much because then it picked up with '—cursed for their crime.' So maybe each of them cursed for their crime?"

Sylmar stroked his beard, his gaze on the distant fire. "Were they each responsible for the death of her sister though? I can't imagine Emeris being involved."

Aeliana frowned, running the memory back again in her mind. "No. She said her sister died at the hands of *a* Wyndren priestess."

"That could still be what you missed. They may both be considered guilty for reasons we don't know. What came next?"

"Um, 'a love, born of blood, doomed to wither by unfounded contempt.' I thought maybe that's the deterioration of their sisterhood. Why they're enemies now instead of friends?"

He nodded but gestured for her to keep going.

"Then, 'where love might triumph, pride will prevail. Pain will be shared, heartache doubled.'"

"That explains all their strange mirrored injuries." Sylmar's face grew grim, as if hearing the curse made it more real. He'd probably been hoping this trip would prove Emeris' theory wrong. Aeliana would be lying if she said she hadn't also hoped that might be true. Then they'd be free to go after Mayvus without fear of what it might do to her mother.

"Then it said, 'the relief of death will evade them, for their destiny is to watch the light leave each other's eyes. Until—' and... that's where it cut out. I feel as if that last portion is what we need the most. It sounds like the thing that will take the curse away."

He nodded slowly, but she sensed he wasn't listening anymore.

"What do you make of it?" she asked.

"I think you're right about the things you pulled out, but the thing that concerns me most is the idea that death evades them and that they must see the light leave each other's eyes."

"What does it mean?" she asked.

"I'm not sure we can really know, but it suggests that they must be together when they die."

Aeliana froze. "Like, as long as they're apart, they're immortal?"

A strangled laugh escaped his lips before turning into a cough. "I wouldn't be surprised if that's how Mayvus interprets it. Especially after they both survived a dragon carrying her to a cave."

Then his face grew pensive, as if even *he* considered the possibility.

It was insanity to think a curse could be that powerful, but it *would* explain how they'd survived something so deadly.

"It doesn't make any sense though," Sylmar said. "In that scenario, I could cut off Mayvus' head and she'd survive as long as Emeris wasn't with her. How could that ever be possible?"

Aeliana shuddered at the image. "Maybe the sprites don't actually change things. Maybe they sift through the future and use that knowledge to make deals and accurate predictions. What if this curse is more like that? Maybe they knew how my mother and aunt would die and they used that to create a curse."

Sylmar considered her words, staring into the sky as though it might hold the answers. "While that may be true, the sprites do have magic. We can't ever underestimate them by thinking they can't impact the future."

She sat back as the hopelessness left her drained. "I don't know what to do with this information. I'd hoped we'd come away with answers and clear direction. Even the acolytes made it sound like what we'd come away with would be good. And now I'm just more confused." She closed her eyes, hating the way her mind dredged up a perfect memory of Iris stabbing Holm. "And angry."

Sylmar's grip tightened on his staff. "She did tell you the full story is documented in the archives of the Dehvlonian Oracles. Who knows who they are, but it gives us a new place to look."

"Across the barrier." Aeliana sighed. "It just feels like we're wasting so much time chasing down starbridges instead of trying to defeat Mayvus once and for all."

"But if the curse you heard is right," Sylmar pointed out, "it confirms your mother's intuition. Going after Mayvus now would end both of their lives. I assume you don't want that."

She shook her head. "Of course not."

"Then the only option we have is to seek out more answers. We'll have to be careful. Perhaps Holm wasn't the only one branded. Or perhaps she'll brand more of us. Trust was already hard to come by, but now it will be even easier to lose."

Aeliana glanced at her sleeping friends, hating that Sylmar was right. Even if they were all completely trustworthy, the smallest change in behavior might start making someone seem suspect. But this was the time they needed to be able to trust each other the most.

"We'll also need to let your mother know what you found. See if she has any insight."

"Could we bring her back here? Give her a chance to see Lady Merinnia?"

Sylmar glanced at the Sayhleen guards and elders. "First we need to figure out how to get out of here before we can even consider bringing someone back. It might take a miracle for each of those, and I would never count on more than one."

Aeliana glanced at Cyrus, knowing he would tell Sylmar to have more faith. But something in his posture looked different. His shoulders slumped, as if he was confessing instead of praising the Stars. "Has Cyrus seemed quieter to you today?"

Sylmar grunted. "Any day that Cyrus seems quieter is a good day. But he was in your boat, not mine. I expect you know best."

"I'm going to check on him before I relieve Lukai from watching over Iris." She stood, and Sylmar leaned heavily on his staff to rise with her. "Sylmar, if you didn't see the curse, what did you see?"

He hesitated, unable to hold her gaze. "I saw two paths. One in which I killed Mayvus, and one in which Mayvus killed me." The grim line of his lips disappeared beneath his mustache and beard as he pressed them even tighter, then he nodded good night and headed toward the bedrolls.

She watched him go, torn over his morbid revelation but unsure how to help him. He hadn't seemed as surprised as she felt. Maybe he'd had time to come to terms with it. But she also suspected he'd imagined those two paths himself long ago, and he'd come to terms with it before Lady Merinnia had ever revealed the detail of the visions.

She made her way to Cyrus' temporary worship circle, making enough noise to ensure she didn't surprise him. Then she waited a respectful distance, allowing him whatever time he needed to finish his worship.

"I'm sorry I didn't ask about the curse," he called over to her. It was as good an invitation as any.

She stepped closer, then kneeled beside him. "I don't think you had any control over it. I was frustrated at first, but no more with you than with Lady Merinnia. The system feels flawed, like some sort of sadistic way for her to use her power." She frowned down at the grass. "But maybe I only feel that way because we lost Holm."

He nodded, his pained expression returning to the Stars.

"Do you want to share about what you did see?" she asked.

He waited for so long she thought the answer must be no, but then his eyes grew red rimmed and his face turned a shade of pink in the moonlight. "I saw so much in such a short period of time. It sounds like others saw moments, and I saw centuries."

Her eyes widened as she saw the weight of this truth reflected in his face. "What did you see?" she whispered.

"I saw Orra, created by the Sun."

"What?" Aeliana couldn't mask her disbelief, but he went on as if he hadn't heard her.

"I saw her lead a rebellion. Not from a cruel heart or malicious intent, but out of love. She misunderstood what the Sun wanted her to do. And she led several Stars astray. I even saw the starbridges formed." He shuddered, then rubbed his palms over his eyes as if wishing to claw out the memory. "But I saw the Sun, forgiving and correcting over and over and over. I understand now what Orra was trying to explain. None of us have had it right. The Sun is a loving creator. Not some judgmental eye in the sky waiting for us to fail. And the Stars are no different than us. They're like the Sayhleens, only the sky is their sea. They reflect the Sun's glory in ways we can't. But they're still as weak as we are. They still need the Sun's forgiveness and guidance."

"This doesn't line up with anything we've been taught," Aeliana said slowly. "Not what your grandparents would have taught in the Stargazer, and not what my mother would have taught in the Sungazers."

"That's what I'm saying." He turned to her in earnest, placing his hands on her upper arms and gripping them tightly as if he wanted to shake the answers into her. And in some ways, he did, because her noetic skills latched on to his desire to share his memory. The vision that transferred to her was infinitesimal and incomplete. More of a feeling and an overwhelming, blinding light. But it gave her a brief understanding that the things he told her were true. It tore apart everything he'd believed all his life, everything his family had shared with generations of Lorvandans, everything her family had probably shared with generations of Vendarans.

She sucked in a breath as he pulled away, angling his head once more toward the Stars.

"What will you do?" she asked.

"This is my calling from the Sun," he said. "It's my burden to share this with the world."

"You're one person, Cyrus. That's too much for one person to bear."

"Maybe." He shrugged. "But many others will feel burdened as well. Maybe the truth will spread like fire." The passion in his eyes was contagious.

"For your sake, I hope it does," she said.

"For the Sun's sake," he corrected.

"Why do you sit out here and worship the Stars, then?"

He laughed, and she saw a brief glimpse of the carefree young man she'd met all those months ago in Gahldric Valley's Stargazer. She missed that man, the one who filled every silence with the thoughts he couldn't contain, the one who saw everyone as good, the one who made her feel like she had something to offer the world.

"I've been out here apologizing to them," he said. "I suspect they can still hear and see me the way I've always imagined, and now I'm embarrassed for the ways that I worshiped them."

"Oh, Cyrus," she said.

"Don't worry," he added. "I spent all day asking the Sun for forgiveness as well."

This time she laughed. "If the Sun is as forgiving as you say, I think once was enough."

He smiled. "I think I have my first convert."

"Are you two offering to take first watch?" Elder Algaen interrupted them, his stern face making them sober. "Or are you going to keep disturbing the rest of us who wish to sleep?"

"We're heading for bed now," Aeliana said, knowing the elders would keep their own watch whether Aeliana and Cyrus slept or not.

After taking a shift watching over Iris' shallow breathing, Aeliana thought she would be up late. She assumed she'd let the curse roll over in her mind again and again like she had the night before, if nothing else to keep the image of Iris stabbing Holm from running through her mind over and over. But something about discussing it all with Sylmar and Cyrus left her at peace. The Sun had likely known this would be the outcome when they came to see Lady Merinnia. The Seer had even declared it was a good outcome.

Aeliana had thought it was a terrible thing when she'd gone to Gahldric Valley's Stargazer and her presence had been the cause of Della's death. And it had been terrible. But so much more good had come from it, and it allowed her to see that sometimes there could be a good outcome despite terrible circumstances.

It would take faith like Cyrus' for her to believe this could all turn out well. But perhaps her faith was growing. Perhaps like him, she was meant to bring something new to Vendaras. Not faith in a forgiving Sun, but a mix of cultures. A leadership born out of trying circumstances instead of family feuds and royal traditions.

Perhaps Velden had been right, and she didn't need to become more Vendaran or less Lorvandan. Perhaps she needed to embrace the combination she'd been given and use it to bring change to all of Rhystahn.

It was a daunting thought, but for some reason she fell asleep more easily than she had in a long time.

CHAPTER 53

ARRIVING BACK in Tideholm felt like a step in the right direction to Gaeren—until the Sayhleens threw the Vendarans back in the hut. Extra guards were placed outside the walls as if they suspected the prisoners were more dangerous after seeing Lady Merinnia.

Nori brought them food the next morning, but the guards watched her like a hawk and little was said.

"I suspect they'll revert to their original verdict," she whispered as she passed Gaeren bread. "But I can help you escape."

"What about the starbridges?" Aeliana whispered.

Gaeren tensed as one of the guards leaned over Nori's shoulder with a frown. She never was able to reply.

That night, when she brought dinner, she spent more time flirting with the guards than trying to speak with the prisoners. It left several of the Vendarans irritated, but after she left, Velden chuckled and shook his head.

"Can't you see what she was doing?" he asked.

The others frowned and glanced toward the closed hut door.

"I guarantee she just poisoned them."

Aeliana's jaw dropped, and Gaeren echoed Velden's laugh, remembering all the times he and Riveran had snuck sleeping herbs into Enla's food. It required sleight of hand and distraction. Velden was right.

"I suggest we all be ready for something to happen tonight," Velden said, then settled against the wall as if taking a nap.

Sure enough, near the moon's reign, there was a tap, tap, tap on the back of the hut opposite the door. Gaeren leaned over, attempting to see between the slits of the thatched walls.

"I think they're all asleep," Nori said.

"Valerian root?" he asked.

"A different herb. One that will be missed by our medicine woman. So I suggest we do this quickly."

From inside, they dug through the thatch, widening a hole until the largest in their group could fit, while on the outside, Nori used a different seaweed to soften the net surrounding the hut.

"I don't suppose you'll send some of that home with us?" Velden asked as they all took turns crawling out. "Could be handy the next time we're here."

"I can't imagine you'll be back. It would mean your deaths." Nori grabbed a sack from beside her feet, throwing it over her shoulder.

"And what about you?" Aeliana asked. "Are you coming with us or staying here?"

Nori bit her lip, glancing back at the homes in the distance. "I don't think I have a choice."

Before they could ask what she meant, a shout rang out from the heart of the village, and her eyes widened. "Quickly, come!"

She ushered them into the forest.

"What about the starbridges?" Sylmar asked.

She shook her head. "My mother hardly left her room all day. I couldn't get them. But she should be in the town square by now. We can check the box, but if they're not there... well, I might need a couple of people to help me find them."

"I'll go," Gaeren offered. If there was any memory of where the starbridges had been placed, he was the one who could find it.

"Me too," Aeliana said.

Nori pulled the sack off her back and laid it out. "At least I found your weapons."

Eyes lit up all around as everyone scrambled to find their preferred swords and bows. But Iris' eyes filled with tears as she lifted Holm's sword. She sheathed her own dagger and knife, then hugged the sword that was far too big for her against her chest. At this point, they wouldn't be able to pry it from her, even if it cost her her life.

To Gaeren's dismay, Aeliana passed her dagger off to Velden. He knew it would allow the other man to find them after being separated, but he didn't like her giving up her best weapon. Though, when she pulled out a bow and arrow, he supposed it might not be her best after all.

"Come on." Nori led the group to the perimeter of the forest. "If the rest of you hide in the woods, we can meet there after we find the star-bridges. If they sound an alarm, you may want to take to the water. They won't expect that from you."

They all nodded their understanding, but before parting ways, Lukai caught Gaeren's eye. He hesitated, rubbing his palm and glancing at Aeliana, who was hugging Iris goodbye.

"I'll take care of her," Gaeren said.

"I know," Lukai said, then he turned back to the group, finding his place beside Kendalyhn.

Nori, Gaeren, and Aeliana crept around the edge of the village until they were lined up with the center.

"Most of the village is waiting in the square to hear the elders announce what happened at Seer's Sanctuary," Nori said. "They've all noticed we returned with one less. The rumors have gotten out of hand, and my father will have to give some sort of update or risk the people revolting out of fear. In many ways, a decision to stick with his original verdict would be an effort to protect the rest of you."

She shot Gaeren an apologetic look, but he shrugged. "It's something my parents would do in Elanesse. Everything for the greater good and all that, right?"

She nodded, then pointed toward a section of homes that looked a bit familiar. Probably the ones they'd used to clean up the week before, which now felt like ages ago.

"Our house is the third in from the left. My father has a guard stationed in the front and back, but I've already drugged the one in the back. I'll go first to make sure it's taken effect and then you can join me."

They crept across the village, keeping to the shadows, and Gaeren wished he had darker clothing so he could hide better. When Nori left them hiding in some bushes near her home, he reached out to tuck Aeliana's hair under her hood, remembering the way she'd grown it out again in the future Lady Merinnia had shown him. She smiled at him before tugging the hood down lower to cover her eyes.

The vision he'd seen of her running on the beach with what he assumed were her children came back to him, filling him with a strange mix of warmth and a twinge of longing. He wanted that future for her, but he didn't want the future that came with it for Enla. How could he choose? And what actions would lead to one path versus the other?

Nori waved them into the garden, then led them through the back door. "Come on," she whispered. "Theirs is the last bedroom upstairs."

They ran with her, following her steps to avoid any squeaky stairs. When they entered the room, the vision he'd seen of her mother hiding the starbridges felt closer, like he could overlay it with their present surroundings. He almost expected her mother to follow them through the door and pry up the loose board.

Instead, Nori did, reaching for the box. "Please be here," she whispered. But when she opened the box, it only held the pink shell. Gaeren swore and ran a hand through his hair, but Nori went still, staring at the shell. She lifted it from the box as though in a trance. "I'd forgotten this was here," she murmured.

"What?" Gaeren asked.

"I didn't think anything of it when I first saw it. But now..." She trailed off, her gaze slowly scanning the room as if she was seeing someplace else. "She knows."

"Knows what?" Aeliana asked.

Nori's gaze snapped to focus on them. "Nothing." She gripped the shell, then shoved it in her pocket. "Let's go."

"Go where?" Gaeren asked.

"I'm guessing the starbridges are in my father's pocket."

They followed her down the stairs, but as they rounded through the back door, she stopped short, making Gaeren and Aeliana run into her. Over her shoulder, Gaeren caught sight of Gellen leaning over to check the guard's pulse. They had no time to hide before he glanced up. His dagger came loose, its three trident spokes gleaming sharp in the moonlight.

"What are you doing?" The question was directed at Nori, but Gaeren sensed the other man tuning in to his thoughts.

He did his best to leave his guard down, knowing that letting the man assess the truth was more helpful than concerning at this point.

"Why would you help them?" Gellen asked.

"Because they're innocent," Nori said.

"They killed a sprite," he hissed.

"If a sprite threatened me, what would you do?" she asked.

His face crumpled. "That's not a fair question, and you know it."

Her tone came out fiercely protective. "And yet that's the position they were in. It wasn't fair. Who's to say what they did was right or wrong? We weren't there." Her voice softened. "They just want to go home. Just let them go home."

His gaze snapped to Aeliana and Gaeren, the indecision on his face giving Gaeren hope.

"We don't want to hurt anyone," Gaeren said. "We really do just want to go home."

But as he said the words, Gellen stepped back, his face slack with horror as he turned to Nori. "Why would you go with them?"

Nori stiffened. "You promised to never read my thoughts."

"I never thought you would betray your people," he threw back at her.

"I'm not betraying my people. I'm protecting a different set of people who wish no harm on our people."

"But you want to go with them? That's not possible. That would ruin everything."

Her eyes narrowed. "What does that even mean? Your plans for us?"

"I don't want anything to happen to you," he said.

The entire situation suddenly shifted as Gaeren felt a surge of empathy for this man trying to protect the woman he loved. "I think he's right, Nori. You should stay."

This time three pairs of eyes stared at him in surprise, then Nori stepped back, eyes wide. "For all the sprites," she muttered. "You know too, don't you?"

Gaeren's face heated.

"Did you see it from this?" She held up the pink shell. "Did you see the same two paths as my mother?"

Gaeren's mouth swung open, but he had no idea what to say.

"He did," Gellen said. "And I've seen it too. Or at least your mother told me what she saw. Please, Nori." He tucked his trident away, his pleading eyes like those of a child. "Please let me protect you." He reached a hand for her, but she slapped it away.

"That's all it's ever been to you," she hissed. "Protecting me for my father, offering to marry me for the sake of the people. I would have gone with you willingly if you had just—" She cut off, and suddenly the space they occupied felt small even though they were outside.

"Let's go." Gaeren tugged on Aeliana's arm.

"Go where?" she whispered. "We have no idea where the star-bridges are."

"Anywhere but here," he hissed back.

"It's fine," Nori said. "We can talk about this later."

"What if you don't have a 'later'?" Gellen's voice broke. "I saw you."

"I saw my future too," she said, "and I know which path is right. It's my choice."

She ran around the side of the house, and Gaeren and Aeliana followed. "Which one is it?" Gellen yelled after them.

Nori didn't answer. She led them through a maze of streets, hugging the shadows along the walls as they got closer to the center of the village. When they were near enough to catch voices on the wind, she pulled them aside.

"My father will expect to see me there. What he hasn't told you is that he has plans for the starbridges. Remember how they wanted to send ambassadors back with you?"

"You mean back with Aeliana," Gaeren said, "because I'm supposed to be dead."

She grimaced. "Yes, that plan. He wants our ambassadors to discover what's happening to the starlocks, why we're receiving so few. He wants to know if somehow your people are stealing them from ours. He wants to know if there's a way to restore the magic in our land. It's fading, and they're afraid Lady Merinnia hasn't picked another Seer because there isn't one."

"That's—" Aeliana broke off. "But we have fewer progenies in Vendaras, too."

Nori faltered. "Are you certain?"

"We have the same questions," Gaeren said. "We have one among our company who couldn't come. She's a grounded Star. We could ask her. She might know."

Nori's mouth swung open. "You what?"

"Her name is Orra, but she used to be called Sheen. I don't know about the Sayhleen account of the Great Divide, but ours tells of a Star who convinced the others to divide the lands to protect the people from each other. Orra was that Star, and her punishment was to remain grounded."

"Our story is similar." Nori's voice came out breathy. "But it's said the sprites herded us here for our protection from the Stars' plans to destroy all the lands and start over."

"I don't think Orra will know much more," Aeliana said. "She's been grounded for a thousand years. She doesn't know why there are fewer progenies any more than the rest of us."

"But she spoke to a Star on the northern keep," Gaeren said.

Aeliana hesitated. "That's true. And she's not always very forthcoming with what she knows."

"I'm coming with you." Nori's voice held a firmness, like she was convincing herself as much as them. "I want to meet her, and I want to bring back news for my father. If I offer myself as the one to go, perhaps he'll give me the starbridges. We wouldn't even have to make a scene or fight for them."

Gaeren and Aeliana exchanged a glance, and Gaeren recalled the bright light and Nori's glassy eyes. "I don't think he will," Gaeren admitted. "We needed your help getting out of your seaweed prison, but if it comes to a fight, most of us have magic. I think it would be better to leave you out of all of it."

Nori rolled her eyes. "I need everyone to stop trying to make decisions for me and to stop trying to protect me. Have you ever considered if maybe I saw something more than what the Seer showed my mother? If maybe I know more about my future than you all think you know?"

"What *did* you see?" Aeliana asked.

Nori pressed her lips together. "I saw my Awakening."

A smile bloomed on Aeliana's face that made Gaeren's breath hitch. "You received a starlock in your vision," Aeliana said.

Nori nodded, then glanced away. "What if there's a third path for me? One my mother's too afraid to consider, not because it's dangerous for me, but because it seems too impossible to be real? One that takes me across the barrier? Let me choose my future."

Gaeren's lips lifted. He couldn't help but appreciate her courage. "All right, lead the way."

When they reached the town square, Nori found a spot at the edge for them to hide, allowing them a view of the dais. Sure enough, the elders had gathered and were explaining their plans to the people. Before Nori even had a chance to step out of the shadows and offer her assistance, Elder Algaen pulled the starbridges from his pocket, lifting them high for the villagers to see.

Aeliana grabbed Gaeren's arm, squeezing it tight. He rested his hand on hers, unsure if it was to comfort her or himself.

"It's going to work," he whispered.

Nori strode into the crowd, and the closer she got to the dais, the more people parted for her. "I volunteer to take the Vendarans back."

Murmurs spread through the crowd, making it difficult to catch the elders' initial reaction.

"They've confided in me." Nori's voice rose. "And they have resources that can give us answers."

By the time she reached the dais, every eye was on her, and Gaeren felt less concern over how noticeable he and Aeliana might be in the mouth of the alley.

"They will help me get answers, but not if they're threatened—not if they're forced to leave loved ones behind. They've already had to bury one of their own on our lands, and it has broken them. Let me take them home, and they will help me find answers." Her chin rose with the declaration. If she had any doubt in her success, she hid it well.

"We'd never send you by yourself," her father said.

"We won't send her at all," her mother argued from her place at the stage's edge.

"She won't be going alone," a familiar voice from the back of the crowd called, "because I'll be going with her."

Once again the crowd parted, but this time it was for Gellen. As he made his way to the dais, Nori's face grew blotchy with scales. She shook her head but didn't say anything, perhaps taking her own advice to let people choose their future. Or perhaps she saw the way his offer gave them an edge.

Elder Algaen exchanged a look with his wife, and Gaeren could imagine what they were wondering. If Nori and Gellen went together, would that solidify their future as a couple? Was that worth the risk of sending her across the barrier? Even Gaeren wondered if this could be the solution.

No matter what Nori had said, he didn't think there was a third path. Her mother would have remembered any other path that left Nori alive. But maybe this could create a different version of the second vision. A version that allowed Nori time to earn her Awakening and to be with Gellen.

Nori pursed her lips, watching Gellen's approach as though calculating his demise.

They were a good match.

When Gellen reached the stage, he gripped Nori's hands in his. "Please let me go with you. Not because I want to protect you, but because I love you."

A wave of lovesick gasps tore through the crowd. But the loudest reaction came next to Gaeren's ear from Aeliana.

"Oh, it's about time," she murmured.

Gaeren laughed. "You're one to talk."

She glared at him. "What's that supposed to mean?"

"I haven't seen you declaring your love for Lukai."

She frowned. "You know very well why." Then she leaned closer to him to get a better vantage point, and he began to wonder… did he know? He reached under his sleeve to tug at the braid still on his wrist, as if it might remind him his focus was on protecting her and nothing more. But the heat of her pressed up against him became far too distracting.

"Give it up already," he muttered at his bond mark, which twitched incessantly.

"What?" Aeliana asked.

"Nothing." He turned his attention back to the dais, where the elders had finished deliberating.

"All those in favor of letting them go?" Elder Algaen asked.

Four of the five elders raised their hands, including Nori's father, and Gaeren's heart beat faster. Had Nori actually done it?

"Very well," Elder Algaen said. "In an hour's time, once we've raised the gallows again, we will hang those responsible for murdering the sprites, then let the others return to Vendaras."

CHAPTER 54

NORI'S GAZE sought out the corner where Aeliana and Gaeren hid, panic flashing across her face before she could school her features.

"No," Aeliana whispered. "They can't do that." She glanced at Gaeren, whose face had gone white. "There's still time to fix this. She'll have the starbridges. We can stop it."

He swallowed hard.

She reached for his chin, forcing him to look at her. "Do you hear me? We will fix this."

He nodded, then licked his lips. A strange urge to kiss them swept over her, and she shook it away as her bond mark throbbed painfully. It was only her fear that this was his last night propelling her to do something so ridiculous. He would have many more nights and many more chances to kiss his bondmate, not her. She rubbed her palm against her tunic to scratch away the itch.

As if the elders had instructed everyone to return home, the crowd started dispersing, and Aeliana pulled Gaeren down the street. "We need to get back. They can't know we left the hut."

"What about the others?" he asked, even as he followed her. "They're out in the woods and there's a big hole in the hut. The soldiers will realize they've been drugged."

Aeliana had no answers, so she kept running. They had to at least try. If the hut was found empty, they'd never be allowed to leave.

When they reached the woods, they ran even faster until they heard their names shouted in the wind. Velden stuck a webbed hand out to wave them down, then guided them through a copse of trees to a small clearing where the others waited.

Despite their exertion, Gaeren's face was still pale, so Aeliana filled them in on everything that had happened as quickly as she could.

"I might be able to hide the hole," Sylmar said. "Melt together some of the thatch so it's not so noticeable."

"You think that would be best?" Riveran asked.

Aeliana wrung her hands, understanding his hesitation. It was his and Gaeren's lives that were on the line, not the rest of theirs. "Nori will make sure she has the starbridges. She'll make sure you're able to cross with us."

Riveran nodded but blinked rapidly and looked away.

"And if something goes wrong," she added, "we'll use our magic— resort to Sylmar's original plan."

"We should have gone with Sylmar's plan when we first got here," Kendalyhn mumbled.

Aeliana wanted to argue. If they'd escaped from the beginning, they never would have had the chance to see Lady Merinnia. But what had they really learned from her? And at what cost? She glanced at Iris, who'd hardly said a word since Holm's death. Her physical sickness had mostly abated, but her soul still needed healing—healing that might not be possible in this life.

"I wish we had too," Aeliana whispered. "I'm sorry."

"Nothing we can do about it now." Riveran stood, and his acceptance seemed to propel the others into action.

They all rushed back to the hut and filed through the same hole they'd escaped through. It felt backward to return to their prison, but Aeliana had to trust their plan would work. It was the only way to get close enough to the starbridges, whether to use them with Nori or to steal them from the elders and escape.

Sylmar and Velden did their best to hide the hole in the thatch, but with the hole facing the forest, they just had to hope no one would notice the seaweed broken on the exterior. They'd barely finished when voices could be heard in the distance, followed by light steps on the dirt.

Aeliana leaned against the thatch, trying to find a decent view of their visitors, and she sagged with relief at the sight of Nori and Gellen—even though they brought four more guards with them. They nudged the sleeping guards, then made fun of them, threatening to expose their laziness to the elders, but eventually they opened the prison door and beckoned the Vendarans out.

"There are more of you," Velden quipped, drawing attention to himself to keep eyes off the strangely melted thatch behind them. "Have we gotten more dangerous as the days wore on?"

None of the guards responded, but they fell in line to escort them all right back to the same square Aeliana and Gaeren had just run from. Nori latched her arm through Aeliana's.

"How are you going to get the starbridges from your father before they're hanged?" Aeliana whispered.

Nori shook her head, the lack of an answer making Aeliana even more nervous when the gallows came into view. The crowd seemed to have multiplied since she last left; news about the hangings must have traveled fast.

At first, they put all the prisoners on the north side of the dais. Aeliana found herself gripping Gaeren's hand as if holding on to him might physically keep him there. But then she realized they should all be holding hands just in case there ever was a chance to use the starbridge. She nudged Cyrus and grabbed his other hand, gesturing for others to do the same until suddenly they were a unified front before the Sayhleens, probably appearing more defiant than they intended.

Just when her confidence rose, two guards yanked Gaeren and Riveran from their line.

"No!" She tried grabbing Gaeren's hand back, but a trident blocked her path, angled right at her neck.

"You can't take them," she shouted. "You'd be starting a war."

This made the elders pause. "A war against whom?" Elder Algaen asked.

"The Vendarans." She licked her lips, peering around the trident still a handsbreadth from her face. "What do you think will happen when we show up without their beloved prince?" She could practically hear Gaeren scoffing in her mind that he was no more beloved than Mayvus was.

The elders exchanged glances. Elder Perla cleared his throat. "Our ambassadors will bring back the starbridge. I don't see how a war can be started if you don't have access to our lands."

"Please," she said. "He's done nothing wrong." She didn't even care that she sounded like a petulant child. At this point she was merely stalling, hoping one of the elders might reveal the starbridges. Maybe Velden would even be able to sift out their location. Once they had the starbridges, they could leave.

"She's right," Riveran called out. "I'm the one who killed the sprite."

The people around the dais gasped, some stepping back as if his presence might taint them.

"Kill me, but let him live," Riveran said.

"No." Gaeren shook his head. "Neither one of us needs to die tonight." But their words were cut off as they were manhandled into nooses before the crowd.

Aeliana sought out Nori, whose face had broken out into bluish-purple scales. Nori tugged on her father's arm. "I don't know if they'll help me if it ends this way."

"Then there's no need for you to go." He turned back to the audience and began reciting the judgment placed earlier on Riveran and Gaeren by the elders.

Aeliana looked to Gaeren and Riveran. The faithful friend's eyes were closed, his lips moving in a silent prayer, but Gaeren's gaze rested on her like a fire that burned from the inside out. He gave her a solemn nod, and she wished more than anything that she had kissed him in the alley.

It couldn't end like this.

Lady Merinnia had said good would come from their visit, but Aeliana hadn't seen anything good yet. They would have to use their magic and fight now, then find the starbridges later. They were out of time.

Just when she was about to kick her guard and pull out her hidden dagger, Nori stepped forward, slicing at her father's trousers with her own dagger, and the starbridges fell to the dais. At first, no one moved, but as confusion and surprise spread, Nori snatched the starbridges from the wooden planks and raced toward Riveran to saw his rope with her dagger.

The guard manning Gaeren's noose was quick to pull the rope to raise Gaeren up, cutting off his air supply. His face turned red as he clawed at the rope, and the guard reached for his arms. Aeliana wrested her dagger from beneath her sleeve and flung it at the guard, pinning his arm to the wall and freeing Gaeren's hands, but the rope still pulled tight, and Aeliana ran for him.

A guard tackled her to the hard wood of the dais, and she lashed out with a light shield. But he was already too close, his grip already too tight, and her shield was pitifully weak. She kicked him away, remembering all of the combat skills Lukai had ingrained in her, allowing her starlock to build her energy even higher. Velden and Sylmar joined the fray, and she prayed they were all careful not to kill any of the Sayhleens, or they'd end up right back where they started: in the gallows.

When she finally fought off her guard, she caught sight of Gellen freeing Gaeren, and all their obstacles suddenly seemed surmountable. She built up her light shield around them, drawing her comrades into a tight circle. It flickered, her confidence wavering with it. Why was her magic so weak after it had been so powerful? Especially now, when she was far enough from Durriken that the brand shouldn't override her somatic skills.

It didn't take long for her comrades to form a defensive ring, their hidden weapons revealed along with the larger ones Gellen had retrieved. Aeliana even saw her bow on Lukai's back, a sight that brought her an unreasonable amount of relief. But the Sayhleen soldiers also had their weapons drawn, arrows nocked for whenever Aeliana's shield fully faltered.

At this rate, it wouldn't take long.

"It should be clear to you now that we could have escaped at any time," she called out. "We've done everything in our power to be workable. As we've said before, we don't want to harm anyone. We just want to go home."

She turned to Nori, who stood near the gallows with Gellen, the Sayhleen soldiers hesitating over whether to incapacitate their own people. Nori still held the starbridges tight in her grip. They were the Vendarans' only way home, and they rested outside Aeliana's circle of safety, a circle that was quickly growing smaller and dimmer. Her shield flickered long enough that one of the Sayhleens fired an arrow. It struck the shield just as the light flickered back into position, but all the Vendarans stood a little straighter, recognizing their time was limited.

"If you and Gellen still wish to return with us as ambassadors," Aeliana said to Nori, "you are welcome. But we are not kidnapping you or taking you against your will. It has to be your choice. I can't guarantee you'll be able to return soon. We've promised the star-bridges to Orra, the grounded Star we told you about."

Nori's eyes lit up, and even Gellen's interest seemed piqued. The two exchanged a glance, and when Gellen nodded, Aeliana caught a flash of hope in Nori's eyes that held more than just gratitude. Gellen reached for Nori's hands, and together they stepped toward Aeliana's light shield, the guards too shocked to stop them.

Aeliana tucked her dagger in her belt as sweat dripped down her forehead. Her starlock had faded to lukewarm, and she knew she couldn't hold the shield much longer. She gripped Gaeren's hand, then reached for Iris', urging the others to follow suit.

Nori and Gellen stopped before Aeliana with the starbridges, but then Nori dropped Gellen's hand, bringing hers to his cheek. Her eyes filled with tears, and as Aeliana dropped the shield to let them in, she barely caught Nori's whisper. "You'll understand someday."

When Nori shoved Gellen to the dais floor, Aeliana was too stunned to notice Nori coming for her next. When the other woman launched herself at Aeliana, the whistle and thud of an arrow met Aeliana's ears just before the weight of Nori knocked them both to the wooden planks. Bright light flashed all around them. Had someone used a starbridge without them?

"Nori?" she called out, her eyes shut against the blinding white-ness, but her voice was lost in the sea of shouts and confusion.

Nori still huddled over her, surprisingly heavy for her small frame, but she made no move to harm Aeliana or defend herself, which just left Aeliana more confused. Had the other woman been attacking her? Or…?

Realization dawned as her memory recalled the sound of an arrow. "Oh, no. No, please."

She blinked away the white spots, rolling Nori off her to find wide vacant eyes staring back at her.

"No!" she screamed again before tearing at Nori's tunic, looking for the wound. "I can heal you." The arrow had pierced deep through Nori's chest, the location and lack of blood registering in the back of Aeliana's mind as bad signs, but still she tried drawing the last vestiges of her starlock's power from her own body and out through to Nori's. But it was like throwing energy at a brick wall until it bounced back at her.

Scaly webbed hands joined hers, but instead of trying to save Nori, they cradled her, pulling her away from Aeliana, who stubbornly refused to let go.

"I healed Marnok," she murmured. "I can heal her too."

A new set of arms pulled from behind, and Gaeren's voice was at her ear. "That was Marnok's magic. He gave you his magic. It's too late now. Nori's already gone."

She still resisted, but Gellen's grip was stronger, and as he sobbed and pulled Nori into his arms, a small object fell from Nori's hand, a golden shell that looked identical to the pink one Nori had found in her mother's box.

A starlock.

"Go." Gellen's voice came out raw. "The others won't understand. But she sacrificed herself for you." He wouldn't look them in the eye, but he shoved both starbridges across the planks toward them, along with a familiar clamshell—the one holding the gemstone gifted to Aeliana after their underwater visit to the Coral Cove. His face contorted with his grief, and greyish scales surfaced. "She had a reason, and that alone is proof that you need to return. All of you." Then he turned away from them, burying his face in Nori's neck.

The dismissal brought Aeliana's pinpoint focus wider, making her realize the people around them were still in shock, the soldier whose bow was still raised turning white with his horror.

"I'm so sorry," Aeliana whispered, her gaze catching Elder Algaen, who held his hysterical wife, his own tears evident on his scale-blotched face.

She snatched up the starbridges and shell, then turned her back on people she feared had become enemies as she passed the golden arrow to Gaeren and the silver fish to Cyrus. Gaeren and Iris gripped her hands once more, and if Cyrus said the words, Aeliana didn't hear them. She gratefully let the bright light and the shift from solid ground to nothingness envelop her.

CHAPTER 55

ORRA STOOD on the boat's prow, closing her eyes against the wind and letting her fingers lightly rest on the braid at her wrist. She soaked in the way it hummed with life, an echo of what the starbridges had formerly been. She found herself holding her breath, relishing the strength of it.

Despite the silver fish being farther away now than the onyx stone had been when she'd last sensed it, she sensed the fish more clearly, a sign that her power was returning. She'd feared it wouldn't, even though she'd been conserving it.

Still, something about the thrum of her power felt off.

Just before, she'd sensed a Star's presence in Rhystahn and wondered at the connection. But her ability to sense the pinpricks of starlocks being delivered and removed had diminished over the years, and she no longer trusted it. Especially now that the Stars were communing again.

Had she instead sensed one of her own approaching a half-light to commune? An Ahmranan? Or Mayvus?

She shuddered, wishing she could ask Andreas or Reyna. But she'd lost the privilege of that sort of knowledge long ago. And now she no longer knew which of them she could trust.

"Everything all right?" Emeris asked.

Orra opened her eyes at the gentle question, at the reminder that they were berthed in Seaglass Port for the night, almost halfway to Andel. She was not a thousand years in the past, begging for one last chance to reverse her wrongs.

Emeris peeked out from her hooded cloak, which thankfully gave no one pause now that Winter Solstice approached and the weather was so much cooler.

Rildan and Marnok had found passage for them with some fishermen and traders. But Emeris had needed to keep herself hidden, from both Recreants and Loyalists alike since any attention would slow their progress.

"I'll be fine." Orra cradled her wrist against her chest as if holding the braid closer to her heart could somehow bring Bryton closer once more. "But I think the others have already returned from Sayhla Island."

"Isn't that good?" Emeris craned her neck, looking for Marnok and Rildan. "We should tell the men."

"We're still a week outside of Andel," Orra said. "We're on the complete opposite side of Vendaras. We could spend the next moon chasing Aeliana's group all the way back around if Larkos takes them north. They won't know to avoid the Ahmranans at Ahmranan's Viewpoint."

Emeris wilted. "So it's not good."

"Perhaps they've returned sooner than Larkos expects, and we'll catch him in Andel." Orra patted Emeris' shoulder. "Never lose hope."

Emeris nodded, then angled her head toward the waning moon. "That will be a new moon in the morning."

"A fresh start," Orra murmured.

Had Felk kept the letter? Would he place it in his nest for his next life? Breaking tradition after hundreds of years was difficult. And yet that was the only way things could change.

And it was time for a change. Orra sensed it in every part of her bones. She knew they were on the cusp of finding the starbridges, not just because she hoped to finally reunite them, but because she sensed the Sun working all around her. It made it harder to ignore the Sun's presence, harder to hide behind her own guilt and shame.

Her reckoning was coming, and she hoped she was ready.

She hoped all of Rhystahn would be ready for what was about to come.

CHAPTER 56

GAEREN HAD NEVER BEEN SO relieved to feel solid ground beneath his feet. As his senses recovered from the shift, waves broke on a shoreline and the salty scent of the sea brought him a nostalgic comfort. He dropped to the ground and buried his hands in the sand, shocked that he had survived and grateful that he had yet one more day to live.

But next to him, Aeliana fell to her knees with a shuddering sob. He wrapped his arms around her, and she clung to him as though his presence was the only thing still anchoring her. The image of Nori's blank eyes came back to him, and his heart broke right alongside Aeliana's.

Lukai approached, his eyes rimmed red, and Gaeren felt an odd sense of possession. But his bond mark twinged, and he released his hold on Aeliana, allowing Lukai to step in and comfort her in his place. He clenched his jaw and looked away, his chest burning with all they'd been through in the last hours.

He'd thought he was going to die for her. He'd thought it was his moment to sacrifice for all of Rhystahn, that his death would somehow eventually bring about peace for both Enla and Aeliana. But now that the moment had passed and he was here and alive, he was no longer sure what any of Lady Merinnia's visions had meant or how they connected to the sprite's deal.

The others seemed just as lost. Iris took herself to the edge of the water and sat, burying her face in her hands, Holm's sword tucked against her side. Sylmar and Velden approached the tree line, likely to guard from any unwanted visitors and assess their surroundings.

Without the Sun's light, it was difficult to get a sense of direction, but with the moon closer inland than to the shore, Gaeren suspected they were on the western side of Vendaras. The landscape even looked familiar enough that he suspected they might be near Rykarn.

Cyrus and Kendalyhn awkwardly sat together, her eyes not leaving Lukai and Aeliana while Cyrus attempted to engage her in conversation. It left Riveran and Gaeren alone for the first time since they'd traveled to Sayhla Island.

"She knew it would happen," Riveran said, "and she chose it anyway." There was a strange glint in his eyes that made Gaeren suspect he might not actually be talking about Nori.

"What did the Seer show you?" Gaeren asked.

Riveran blinked. "What did she show any of us?" he muttered, then shoved his hands in his pockets and looked to the moon. "I thought her visions were ridiculous until proven true by Iris and Holm." He dropped to a heated whisper as though afraid Iris might overhear them. "I have no claim on Enla, but she will always be mine to protect. And yet the visions I saw make that seem impossible. They don't even seem realistic." He gave a short laugh.

Gaeren's heart pounded as a new fear overtook him. How did Riveran's visions match Gaeren's? If they combined their knowledge, would it improve their understanding? "What do you mean?"

"I saw two paths," Riveran said. "One where I handed her an egg, a dragon hatchling." He shook his head. "The absurdity of it made it impossible for me to take anything seriously. But now I don't know what to think."

"How old did she seem?" Gaeren asked.

Riveran squinted at him. "How old?"

"In my visions," Gaeren said, "she looked five years older, maybe ten in one, but far older and almost sickly in the other."

Riveran's face went slack. "You saw Enla too."

Gaeren hesitated. "The Seer knew I wanted to keep both Enla and Aeliana safe. Despite how crazy a dragon egg might seem, that woman's visions are frighteningly accurate." He glanced at Iris. "I don't think any of us can deny that now."

"She looked older to me," Riveran admitted, "but it was hard to say. She seemed… broken."

Gaeren nodded. "It was the same for me in one vision, but in the other, she was still young. Something still seemed off in that one though. She seemed cold and alone." He was hesitant to mention Riveran's presence in the first vision, knowing that might make it seem better to Riveran in some way. He would never wish that sort of brokenness on his sister, but in the other, she'd seemed so much like his father, and he wasn't sure he could wish that on her either. "In many ways, it was like one path showed me my family's continued domination, and another showed me their downfall."

Riveran's lips pursed, and he dug the toe of his boot into the sand. "Even so, neither future looked very promising for her."

"But she was alive," Gaeren whispered.

Riveran's gaze shot up to meet Gaeren's. "Was Aeliana not?"

Gaeren glanced at Lukai and Aeliana, taking small satisfaction in the way she seemed stiff at his side, his arm wrapped around her shoulder. Then he hated himself for it, because it meant she wasn't receiving the comfort she needed.

"She was alive in one path. Alive and happy."

"With you?" Riveran asked.

This time, Gaeren couldn't hide his shock. "Sun's fire, no. I mean, I don't know. Why would she be? She's bonded to Lukai."

Riveran rolled his eyes. "At first I thought you might be interested in her because of her low starblood concentration. Anything to defy the ways of the crown." Riveran pulled his hands from his pockets and studied the scar marring his palm, the evidence of the bond he'd once had with Enla. "Although after seeing Aeliana's magic, I don't even know if your parents would care that her father is Lorvandan."

"You're being ridiculous," Gaeren said, even though Riveran's words only echoed thoughts Gaeren had had throughout their journey to Andel and Sayhla Island.

"Then I think I was jealous that you were bucking the system," Riveran went on as if Gaeren hadn't said anything. "That despite the bonds, you were choosing who you wanted. And part of me hoped that Enla might do the same."

"Enla has never bucked any system," Gaeren muttered.

"Maybe not," Riveran said, "but she would encourage you to do this. She already has. She wanted you to break your bond, and yet you haven't done it."

Gaeren frowned and studied his bond mark, its edges faded and distorted. He suspected over time it would go away just like Enla had said. It was the easy way out. But what opportunities would he miss in the meantime?

"Even if I cut it out, she still has hers." It felt strangely close to an admission that maybe something else held him back.

"What if she's saying the exact same thing about you?" Riveran asked. "It seems like a neat enough solution to me. Kendalyhn loves Lukai. You love Aeliana."

The bold statement startled Gaeren. "I care about Aeliana, but she's like a sister." The words felt like a lie as they left Gaeren's lips.

Riveran's laugh rang out across the shoreline, drawing everyone's attention. He cut it short as though it was disrespectful in the wake of all they'd experienced. But he still shook his head and smiled. "You're in denial. Maybe it's the bond that does it to you; I don't know. Maybe you'll never really know until you break that bond and see what your heart does without its influence."

"What did your heart do?" Gaeren tried to keep the anger out of his voice, knowing it was his parents who had forced them to break their bond instead of it being Riveran's choice. But it was hard to forget the pain Enla had experienced, the pain he was likely to inflict on Lenda and maybe even himself.

"I hated her when it was broken, but I also loved her." Riveran frowned at the coastline, clearly seeing something else in his mind, tempting Gaeren to reach for his friend's memory. "I thought maybe I could stick around and work in the stables or in the aviary with Gullet. I think your father even considered it because of how easily I calmed the animals. But when he had Enla bond with Croft, everything got mixed up again. It took time for things to settle. It still probably isn't quite right."

Sylmar and Velden approached, cutting off their conversation.

"The Sun's rise will be coming soon," Sylmar said. "We can't remain on this beach. Are these western shores familiar to you?"

Gaeren and Riveran both nodded.

"We're likely two or three days from where we left Bayla, Rox, and Breeve's family," Riveran said, and as he did, the familiar coastline fell into place in the map in Gaeren's mind.

Sylmar's irritated frown disappeared in his relief. "Good. We'll find a place to rest for a spell, but we'll aim to get at least half a day's travel in. Any town nearby that might have supplies?"

Gaeren let Riveran and Sylmar hash out the details while Cyrus approached Velden and passed off the silver fish. It was fitting for the half-Sayhleen to be in charge of it, which made Gaeren wonder if he should pass the golden arrow off to Cyrus. But Orra had charged him with guarding it, and he'd promised the Recreants he'd use it to remove his family from the throne as a last resort. He'd hang on to it for now.

His mind and gaze still strayed to Aeliana and Lukai. Riveran's words left him on edge, almost angry at the potential for their truth.

He'd thought love would be quick and obvious. Thallahan had described it as being like an Awakening. But understanding dawned as Gaeren realized that didn't mean it had to happen in an instant.

That same triumphant fire that had woven through him as he'd first gripped his starlock now reared again in his belly, but it was muted by circumstance. The realization that he loved a woman he was supposed to have hated because of her bloodline—a woman who was not his bondmate—left him reeling. It almost made the idea of breaking his bond worse. Because that meant he was doing it for himself instead of to free Lenda, like Enla had suggested.

But it also filled him with a dangerous hope. And yet that hope was tempered by the fact that she was currently in another man's arms.

Iris took first watch, claiming she couldn't sleep anyway. The dark circles under her eyes made that feel like a lie, but no one argued.

Gaeren thought he wouldn't be able to fall asleep either. But instead, the entire morning passed in a blink. He didn't feel like he'd rested, and all his effort went to putting one foot in front of the other while they headed north along the coast.

He couldn't decide if Aeliana was avoiding him or if he was unusually in tune to her current connection to Lukai, but as they traveled, she stayed with Lukai, Cyrus, and Kendalyhn, and he fell back with Riveran.

They were all dragging when the Sun's sleep came that night. They shared the meager supplies they'd acquired at a seaside village and set out some semblance of bedrolls, but strangely no one seemed eager to leave the fire and turn in for the night.

"What now?" Aeliana asked. Everyone's stares were hollow as the fire's light reflected in their eyes.

"We return to the Myndren Mountains," Sylmar said.

"We have no more knowledge than before," Aeliana argued.

"We have more than you think." Sylmar balanced his staff across his knees. "We have proof that your mother is right, that their lives are bound. If one dies, so does the other. If one lives, so does the other."

Aeliana's gaze grew wary. "And what will you do with that information?"

"I'm not sure we should discuss it." The abrupt dismissal brought everyone's attention up from the flames. "After learning about Holm's brand, should any of us trust the other?"

"Oh, stop." Iris wiped her eyes, but her voice held a soft anger. "Holm wouldn't want this. He wouldn't want you breeding mistrust among our people. Check our hands." She held hers out, and Gaeren winced at the fresh scar of her broken bond.

One by one the others held out their palms, some with bond marks, some without. Gaeren held out his, surprised at the way the scar from his brief brand of Aeliana brought him more joy than the bond mark that remained intact but faded. Aeliana's hand held multiple scars, along with an intact brand mark and bond mark.

"I saw Holm's hands too," Sylmar said, "free of a brand mark. There was a week or two that he wore gloves after he found the cave. Claimed he burned himself. I didn't think anything of it, especially since he eventually took the gloves off. But she masked it with an illusion."

"How is that even possible?" Aeliana asked.

Sylmar's gravelly voice took on even more of a growl. "Just because she brands people to steal their magic doesn't mean she doesn't have the option of pushing her magic back through to them. It's just not something she's ever wanted to do before. She's always been one who takes, never one who gives, and yet she finally found an instance where giving magic was the way to take things away."

They all grew silent around the fire, an uneasiness that pained Gaeren settling between them. He trusted these people with the same intensity he trusted his men aboard his ship, and yet he'd trusted Holm too. What were they supposed to do now?

"Would you like me to sift everyone's soul again?" Kendalyhn offered.

Sylmar shrugged. "I'm not even sure I trust that anymore."

Kendalyhn's face pinched, but she said nothing.

"What else did you see, Sylmar?" Aeliana asked.

The others seemed just as confused as Gaeren, but Aeliana's gaze remained locked on Sylmar.

"Maybe it's time we all come clean with what we saw at the Seer's Sanctuary," she added.

Sylmar's brow furrowed, but he didn't answer her question.

"We need more information," Aeliana continued. "Why not return to Andel and seek out Pacran? Go to Dehvlon. The Seer told me the curse was written down by their Oracles."

"I'm not sure we're ready to pay the price for more information." Sylmar's gaze flicked to Iris, and indecision warred on Aeliana's face. "This venture was as disastrous as seeking out the sprites."

"But we're missing something." Aeliana's final argument came out weakly, making Gaeren want to defend her. But he suspected Sylmar was right. At the very least, they needed a break before hunting down another starbridge. They needed to warn Emeris that she was right, perhaps bring her with them for her safety. Surely she'd fully recovered by now.

Heading to the Myndren Mountains would likely include a stop in Elanesse, something Gaeren wasn't quite prepared for. He'd put off his debate over aiding Enla or Aeliana and which could do more for the people, knowing that for the time being, Aeliana needed him more. But would it always be that way? The visions of Enla and Aeliana swam in his memory, blocking out Aeliana's crestfallen face.

He had to do what was right for the people, not just what felt right in his heart. But the two were becoming inexplicably tied together, and he was no longer sure he could objectively differentiate. Especially now that Riveran had gotten him thinking about breaking his bond again. Could he really return to Elanesse without having done the one thing Enla asked? But how could he return to Elanesse and Lenda if he *had* broken it?

Sylmar stood, leaning heavily on his staff and interrupting Gaeren's brooding. "We have another long day of travel in the morning. Time we all got some rest."

CHAPTER 57

INSTEAD OF FALLING ASLEEP, Aeliana's agitation grew. It wasn't so much that she thought they shouldn't be returning to the Myndren Mountains. She wanted to check on her mother, and in some ways, she wanted to ensure that Sylmar didn't do anything rash.

But it was hard to ignore the feeling that she should be doing something more. They needed to break the curse. Instead of pursuing the one guaranteed answer with the Dehvlonian Oracles, they were stuck looking for Larkos and waiting for Marnok to return and answer their questions. She pulled out the clamshell and studied the gemstone in the moonlight, wishing it offered more answers than questions. Instead, it filled her mind with memories of Nori's still face and empty eyes. The little sleep she got came filled with nightmares of Nori and Holm.

The following morning found her even more exhausted, and the travel to Bayla's home left her feet dragging. Introductions were made all around, but outside of noting Riveran doting on the toddler Rox and hearing that Larkos hadn't arrived yet, little of the exchange stuck in her mind.

But when she lay down, it was like a switch turned on, some internal drive for answers that tapped at her mind and refused to let her sleep. The living space in Bayla's home was too small to house them all, so while a few had been given beds inside, most of them, including Aeliana, remained on their bedrolls, back under the Stars around a dying fire.

Aeliana rolled over, hating the silence around her and wishing for Holm's soft snores to lull her to sleep. She couldn't imagine how much worse it must be for Iris. She scratched at the brand mark on her palm, then frowned at it, wondering why it was irritating her so much when usually it was her bond mark that itched.

Her eyes widened. There *was* something she could do, something that might have even more impact than she'd realized before. Now that she was back in Vendaras, she could reach out to Durriken again, and not just to see how he fared.

He was an ancient beast with the wisdom of lifetimes—an untapped resource.

Unable to lie still any longer, she wrapped an extra blanket around her to ward off the early winter chill and stepped away from the circle of those sleeping. They were still far enough south that the temperatures hadn't dropped below freezing at night, but they would soon.

Her agitation brought her out to the forest's edge, where she settled on a stump and closed her eyes, reaching out for the string connecting her to Durriken, the one he called a tether. It came much easier this time, like a ship reeling in a tiny lifeboat. A strange sense of relief pervaded her entire being.

Where have you been? Durriken's panicked voice hit her before she even sensed his surroundings.

We crossed the barrier. Her answer felt both obvious and inadequate. Had he been… worried?

The forest surrounding him came into focus, his eyes more accustomed to the dark than her own, allowing her a unique perspective of the surrounding nightlife. Collections of critters ran along the forest floor and through the trees, and dozens of gleaming eyes met Durriken's gaze from within the tree branches.

You should have warned me. The admonition made Aeliana's conscience prickle.

I'm sorry. I didn't know we would lose our connection. I didn't think it would upset you.

Then you don't understand tethers. A hiss of steam escaped his mouth as the words crossed between them, and he curled up tighter, tucking his nose under his paw as though trying to shut her out by cutting off what she could sense through him.

You can't be angry with me for that. I didn't even know what they were until after you claimed we had one. I still don't really know what they are. Velden said they haven't been done since before the Great Divide.

Durriken snorted, and the heat of it reverberated through her own body. *Perhaps it should stay that way.*

Her hold on him receded, and the vision of his surrounding forest grew dim. The pain of all she'd lost in the last several days swept through her like a thick poison, bleeding into her response. *I'm sorry you don't find me worthy of a tether.*

At first, she thought he was pushing her away. But then she sensed a tug holding her in place, a tautness to the tether that bound them, and she realized it was she who was leaving.

He realized it too. *Wait.*

The tension remained, and Aeliana sensed she could return to Durriken and relieve the tension, or she could continue leaving and permanently snap whatever bound them. Perhaps not the brand, but the other thing that now tied them together.

Either direction would give her room to breathe, space to think. But she didn't want that. Sitting in this tension gave her an alertness, and this decision would require focus.

I don't know much about tethering either. Durriken's admission held a foreign humbleness. *I refused it long before the Great Divide, when I saw the corruption of men. There were none I wished to be tied to in that way. My family chose differently.*

Aeliana sensed the dragon go completely still, and she longed to sit with him and lean against him, because the pain that coursed through him now crossed the tether and poured into her. The tension abated as she subconsciously drew closer.

You lost them. She shouldn't have been surprised. He was the last dragon, but that didn't mean he'd always been the only dragon. *How did they die?*

They didn't all die. My father died in this last span of time. His tether snapped with the Great War, when his half-light died, and he was never the same after. My mate and hatchling… as far as I know, they could still be alive. At least, they were when I last saw them. The Stars put the barriers in place to punish their descendants. But the half-lights aren't the only ones who were sentenced to a prison that day.

Understanding left her more than just curious. The longing that coursed through him filled her as well, along with a frightening flicker of hope, one that felt too dangerous to fan.

Which side of the barrier are they on?

He growled in frustration. *My guess would be Dehvlon. That's where we nested. But it's a harsh land with little to sustain dragons. It's full of burrowers and caves that are not fit for creatures who fly.*

She wondered why a dragon would bother nesting in such a place, but as if he heard her question, the answer came.

It's also not fit for half-lights. It provided plenty of solitude.

She let him sit in his grief for a moment, but her need for knowledge eventually bubbled to the surface. *What else do you know about Dehvlon?*

With that question, a dozen others poured out of Aeliana. She told Durriken of their time on Sayhla Island, the emotions she'd felt through it all crossing through their connection the same way his had. The shared empathy somehow made their tether feel stronger, but also less constricting. Durriken told her of Adella and Ahndru, and how from a distance he'd seen their grandfather move them to another city, away from the beast that had murdered their parents. She took on his loneliness the same way he absorbed her sorrow.

Instead of feeling tied down to the dragon, she felt anchored, and she sensed the agitation she'd carried with her over the past several days slowly abating. Perhaps she hadn't really been so frustrated over her lack of options, but rather, subconsciously, she'd been growing agitated over her lack of contact with Durriken.

My knowledge holds no power. Durriken's admission dripped with regret. *I know nothing of a curse that binds lives. And the Dehvlonian Oracles are still out of my reach. The barriers rise above the highest distance I can fly.*

She'd suspected he'd attempted such a thing, but it was still disappointing to have him confirm it. *Can you travel across the barrier with the starbridge?*

I'm willing to try. Something in his voice made it clear he held no hope, and she couldn't blame him. The starbridges seemed to be connected to the people groups they'd been created for. It made her want to test one on Felk too. Perhaps if they landed across the barrier with a dragon and a winex, things would go better from the start.

We plan to cross that barrier next, Durriken. Her promise felt thin, but it was all she could offer. *If the starbridge can't take you there, I will find your family.*

Knowing they're safe would be good.

Aeliana sensed the half-truth in his words. *But not as good as being reunited with them?*

The hum of his agreement was like the purr of a kitten that she felt from her head to her toes.

The barriers need to come down. Durriken's thought was a whisper between them, an echo of Orra's premonition.

I think you're right. But in the meantime, can you check on my mother? Make sure the fortress is still secure?

Durriken rumbled his assent.

As Durriken took flight toward the Myndren Mountains, Aeliana let herself fade from his mind, loosening the tether but not fully letting it go. She blinked against the darkness at the forest's edge near Bayla's home, her eyes never quite adjusting because she no longer had Durriken's vision.

And still she sensed the tether, a tiny thing niggling at the back of her mind, always present like a safety net rather than an invasive brand. Was it possible the tether could grow strong enough that the brand wouldn't be needed? A warmth settled deep inside her, a strange peace that didn't abate even with the disappointing realization that she was back at square one, with no way of finding out how to break the curse.

As she rose, a strange whimper met her ears. She went still, glancing at the new moon. Were there baby winex nearby?

She followed the sound deeper into the woods, always wary of the distance behind her. The winex weren't dangerous at this point in their cycle, but that didn't mean there weren't other predators about looking to take advantage of their newborn state. But as the sound grew louder, she hesitated, recognizing it wasn't winex. In fact, she suspected it wasn't an animal at all.

It sounded like a person.

She picked up her pace while trying to mask her presence in the woods even more. But when she reached a tiny clearing and found Gaeren sitting on a fallen tree, she paused, her heart rising to her throat. His face was contorted with pain and concentration as he hunched over his palm, digging at it with a knife.

With the dim moonlight, it was difficult to see much, but something wet sparkled on his cheeks and it made her break a little inside.

"Gaeren," she called out softly.

He started, dropping the knife, but quickly recovered, showing complete ease at her presence. They'd come so far since the enemies they'd been told to be. She'd seen in his eyes how much he cared as he stood on the gallows platform, and now she saw a flicker of it return to his eyes as he gave a weak smile.

She had no idea where it left them, where she wanted it to leave them.

He grunted out a greeting while using his shoulder to swipe the wetness from his cheek, then bent to retrieve his knife.

"What are you doing?" she asked, even though it was obvious.

"Something I should have done a long time ago." His words came out more defeated than determined, and he stared at the bloody mess on his palm. "I just keep picturing her, curled up in a ball, crying over the loss. The agony festering deep inside."

Aeliana tried to picture it too. She hadn't ever met Lenda, so the image was too fuzzy and dull to create the empathy she knew she should have. Or perhaps it was her desire for him to be free that made the image of him sitting before her far more pitiful.

She stepped forward and sat on the log next to him, their nearness reminiscent of the morning they'd attacked Mayvus in the Myndren Mountains so long ago. She reached for his palm, which shook, and steadied it with her own hands on top of her knee.

"I don't think Enla would have instructed you to do it if it wasn't in

Lenda's best interests. It might hurt Lenda tonight. But it sounds like it's freeing her for something better." Something whispered in the back of her mind that it was better for him too. But she suspected he wouldn't want to hear that right now.

He laughed bitterly. "I'm not picturing Lenda. Maybe I should be. I'm picturing Enla. I can't get past what she went through, not enough to be able to do this. I want to, but I think even my memories have been tainted and twisted to something so grotesque that my own fears make it impossible."

She frowned. "Like your memories aren't accurate?"

He nodded. "When I tried taking those memories from her, I think I left her with the sweetness that lingered in the pain and gave myself only the horror of the experience."

"I thought you said your mentors fixed that."

He shook his head. "They kept me from killing us both. But some damage had already been done."

"How long did it set Enla back? What will it do to you if you cut it out now?"

He ran his clean hand through his hair. "Physically? A week, maybe less. Iris made it seem easy, but I think shock and circumstances altered her experience."

Aeliana winced.

"But mentally?" Gaeren added. "Enla's never recovered."

"Maybe it won't be the same for you."

"It doesn't matter. I still can't do it. I've barely lifted the edge." He held it up for her perusal before closing his fist to hide the mark. "My work will likely be healed in two days' time."

More blood trickled out as he squeezed it in his frustration. It called to Aeliana with the faintest ring—like a distant bell—but she ignored it, far more focused on the pain seeping off him in waves like a symphony. She opened his palm, using one hand to splay his fingers across her knee and the other to gently pry his knife from his other hand.

"Let me help you," she whispered.

His breath hitched, and she became far too aware of his nearness. The way she no longer felt the chill of the coming winter because the heat of his body warmed her. Her offer felt like it could never be enough, but it also felt like the exact right thing to do. Even so, fear washed over her that he would find her offer appalling because now she wanted to do it for him. She wanted to be the one to free him the way he had freed her from Mayvus.

"Please," he whispered back. Then he closed his eyes and clenched his jaw.

She bent over his palm and tucked the knife point under the bit of skin he'd already loosened.

He hissed before steeling himself further, and she hesitated.

There was an easier way to do this, a way that could free not just him but Lukai as well. It could even free her. She set the knife down on the log beside her, and this time it was her hands that shook. Daisies unfurled at their feet, spreading out in a wave around them, spurring her on.

His eyes remained squeezed shut, his focus so intent on bearing through the pain that he remained unaware of her change in tactic. She allowed herself a moment to study the defined lines of his clenched jaw, the curve of his lips. It made her face heat, but it also gave her certainty that this was the better way.

She brought her hand to his face, and his eyes flew open in surprise.

"We don't have to use the knife," she murmured letting her eyes drop to his lips. "Jasperus said it only takes a simple kiss." Vulnerability swept through her. Perhaps he would prefer having it cut out over a kiss from someone he thought of as a sister, from someone who held the bloodline of his supposed enemies. Perhaps that sort of kiss was far too detestable.

Surprise flickered in his eyes, but when he glanced at her lips too, something in her chest squeezed tight before releasing and offering a warmth that spread even faster than the heat of her starlock.

As she leaned forward, there was a brief hesitation in his eyes that made her want to retreat.

"I can't ask this of you." His breath was hot on her lips. "This would break more than just my bond."

"I know. That's why I offer it freely."

His hesitation remained, his face too close for her to read what emotion might play across it, but then he leaned in, and their lips brushed.

The slight tingling sensation stirred a longing within Aeliana that she hadn't ever felt in Lukai's presence. A small part of her wondered if that had been enough to do the damage, because her bond mark ached, the pain growing even as something else far more pleasant surged within her.

But another part of her hoped it hadn't been enough, and she let her hand slide to the back of his head, drawing him in to deepen the kiss. He didn't fight it, and in fact, his unmarred hand reached for her waist, sliding her closer on the log until their bodies were lined up, allowing her to wrap both arms around him.

The warmth of the kiss turned to a heat that left her heady, the pain in her hand a distant reminder that they'd had a purpose for this that went beyond the security and acceptance and love she felt swirling through her.

Did he feel it too? Or was this just a transactional activity for him?

She broke away with that thought, terrified that she would see the truth of it in his eyes. But instead, his gaze held something foreign, an intensity that made his pupils seem even larger with the lack of light. His hand came to her jaw and his thumb brushed across her lips, and he leaned in once more. Hope surged through her, and she bent forward to kiss him again.

Before she could reclaim the connection she'd felt, the pain in her palm finally turned too sharp.

She sucked in a breath and held it to her chest, catching her wince mirrored on his face. And then the sharp pain turned to a fire so encompassing it was like her hand had been set into burning oil, and a scream erupted from her lips.

CHAPTER 58

THE SOUND of dripping water met Gaeren's ears and the tepid touch of a rag hit his face, drawing him to a groggy awareness. He squinted up at Riveran, his gaze resting on the other man's smirk.

"You have a way of stirring up drama wherever you go," Riveran said.

Gaeren winced as even his friend's softly rumbled words pummeled his head. "Aeliana?" he grunted out.

Riveran's smirk transferred to a full grin. "Velden carried her to Bayla's room. She'll be fine eventually."

Gaeren's palm throbbed, but he refused to look at it, picturing the scars he'd always despised on Enla's hands, expecting that Aeliana's palm now looked the same. Instead, he reached for the braid under his sleeve, rubbing the smooth hair as if challenging the bond mark he'd once had to flair with its righteous indignation. His palm continued its dull throb, but the pain in his chest ran deeper, an ache of something lost. It was magnified by guilt when he realized he should be thinking about Lenda and all the ways she was likely suffering back in Elanesse.

Riveran tipped a cup of water against Gaeren's lips. As he drank, Gaeren took in their place in the small bedroom Bayla had reserved for visitors, its only furnishings the straw mattress Gaeren lay on, the wooden chair Riveran sat on, and the meager dresser with its two drawers. Sunlight streamed through the window, making it likely to be midday, and the door remained shut, offering them a bit of privacy for who knew how long.

"Sylmar was impressed that Aeliana was mostly able to heal both of you before the pain overtook her. There was just a barely bleeding scratch left on your palm." Riveran's eyebrows rose, the unspoken question hanging in the air.

"There was nothing more to heal," Gaeren murmured, remembering the way Aeliana had laid down the knife and offered a kiss instead.

Riveran snorted. "Well, that should probably stay between the two of us unless you want the women scheming."

Riveran's lack of surprise made Gaeren's guilt flare more. A strange ache overrode the hope he'd had mere moments before. Or had it been longer? How long had he been out?

"You and Velden scheme enough without the women," Gaeren said.

Riveran chuckled and crossed his arms over his chest, staring down at Gaeren. His smile faded, and his teasing tone was replaced by genuine concern. "What made you finally realize how you felt for her?"

Gaeren started to shake his head, but the pain transferred to a sharp stab between his eyes, and he closed them in an effort to hold it back.

"When she offered a kiss," he croaked out, thinking back on the innocence in her eyes, knowing she didn't even understand what she'd offered. Jasperus hadn't lied to her; a kiss *could* break a bond. But there had to be a depth of love behind it that could compete with the depth of the bond.

At first, he'd meant to tell her that detail, to explain that it wouldn't be enough. But as he'd stared into her eyes, a warmth had grown in his chest, a warmth that rivaled the joy he'd felt during his Awakening. He'd fallen for her despite the bond that had tried holding him back.

The emotions roared within him again, the guilt and horror over what he'd done threatening to suffocate the ray of hope brought on by the memory of not just the kiss but the understanding of what he felt for her.

"Does she even know?" Riveran asked.

Gaeren gave another slight shake of his head, wincing at the way stars exploded in his vision even though his eyes were closed.

Riveran placed the rag over Gaeren's forehead as if it could weigh down the pain threatening to surface. "It'll get easier."

"When?"

"A few more days maybe? It took me about a week to return to full strength, but Enla's and my bond was stronger." He hesitated. "But so was Iris' and Holm's, and she fought through the pain to travel. But ours also weren't broken with a kiss. I'm not sure there's any way to know for sure. Each situation is likely different."

It wasn't the answer Gaeren wanted. Did Aeliana felt the same way, or had the years away from Vendaran culture left her free from this burden? Or was it worse for both of them because their bonds had been broken by unfaithfulness?

And yet what had they been unfaithful to? Lukai and Aeliana's bond had never been more than the protection her parents had designed it to be. And Gaeren and Lenda's bond had been more of an idea than an actual connection.

Even his remorse felt fabricated, like a remnant of the bond still lingered to torture him with guilt he didn't truly deserve. But it was still strong. Strong enough that the love he'd felt for Aeliana now felt tainted, which made him even angrier.

He longed to jump out of bed and shove away the feelings, to work them out in the yard with Riveran and their swords. But his entire body felt feverish and his muscles ached.

"Now what?" Gaeren peeked through one cracked eyelid to catch Riveran's shrug.

"We wait? At least you had decent timing. If we're stuck here waiting for Larkos to show up, might as well get that task out of the way."

It felt like Larkos should have already been here, but despite all their obstacles on Sayhla Island, they'd only been gone two weeks. Two extremely long weeks. Gaeren shifted in the bed, fighting through the agony so he could turn on his side, away from his friend.

"Although Sylmar and the others are in an uproar," Riveran went on as though Gaeren hadn't rejected his presence. "Even Bayla is a bit put out because she and Rox had to move out to the campfire since Aeliana's cries were keeping the boy awake."

The fire in Gaeren's chest intensified, except he couldn't tell why. At first it seemed to be concern for Aeliana, a desire for her to be taken care of. But a small part of him had the strange sensation they were both getting what they deserved. The feeling didn't match with his head or even his heart, and it made him despise the bond once more. Could he never truly be free of it? Even after searing it off with a kiss, would he be tied down by his guilt instead?

"Lukai's in the main living area. Kendalyhn's been taking care of him, but his recovery seems to be easier than yours and Aeliana's." The confusion in Riveran's voice sent several questions to the tip of Gaeren's tongue. He'd forgotten that Lukai would also be affected, but wasn't that what he and Kendalyhn wanted? Was it easier for them because Lukai hadn't been the one to break it? Would Gaeren and Aeliana have been better off cutting out their bonds instead?

It would make ironic sense if the way that had seemed easier actually held more pain in the long run.

"Why has no one given us all herbs to sleep?" he muttered.

"Oh, we have," Riveran said. "You've been sleeping for the last two days. I've changed your soiled clothes and sheets enough that any debt between us better be forgiven."

Gaeren groaned in disgust even though Riveran's voice held amusement. This vulnerability was almost as painful as the effects of the bond. He tried to remind himself it was worth it, that this was something he and Aeliana had chosen, that it was a gift for Lukai and Kendalyhn as much as a way to free Lenda, Gaeren, and Aeliana. But if it was such a good thing, why did it feel so terrible?

"Once Sylmar hears you're awake, he'll be in to see you." Riveran's humor left, his tone turning wary. "That man has been unsettled ever since we left Sayhla Island."

"He's never been settled," Gaeren corrected, burying his face under his pillow to block out the Sun's light. "I suspect he never will be."

Riveran's short laugh made Gaeren wince again and bury his head deeper. Despite his pain, his stomach growled, and the whine of chair legs pushing against the wood floor gave evidence of Riveran rising.

"They made a stew for Aeliana and Lukai. There should be enough left to tide you over until the next time you wake. I'll add some of my valerian root to it."

"Thank you," Gaeren mumbled, but he suspected Riveran was already gone.

The next time Gaeren woke, the pain in his stomach warred with the pain in his chest and palm, which he took as a good sign. He'd need to fight through it to eat and rise, or he would grow sick in other ways. But all that was forgotten when he cracked open his eyes and found Sylmar glaring at him from the seat Riveran had previously occupied.

"You're awake." The old man's statement bit like an accusation.

Gaeren opened his mouth, but his tongue was too dry for the words to come. Sylmar grunted his irritation, then passed over a glass, clearly not eager to nurse Gaeren back to health in any way. Gaeren struggled to take it, nearly spilling it in his efforts to wet his lips and tongue. The little he managed to get down allowed him to speak once more.

"Riveran said you wanted to speak with me."

Sylmar grunted again, and Gaeren suspected this was how much of their conversation would go.

"Why did you do it?" The old man's grip tightened on his staff, as if the answer Gaeren gave might determine whether or not it needed to be used.

One of Orra's favorite phrases came to mind, making Gaeren choke out a laugh. "There are a number of reasons. Nothing is ever just one thing."

Sylmar scowled. "Then name at least one."

"My sister told me to."

This answer made Sylmar pause, a strange reward for Gaeren in the midst of his pain. "Why would your sister suggest such a thing?"

Gaeren tried to shrug, then winced as the room spun. "I've stopped expecting reasons from her. Her reasons are always good—they're based on what she sees in the future. Or at least, they always were. She's been confused lately."

The memory of her confusion left him uneasy. He'd never actually checked in with Lenda to verify that she agreed with Enla. What if Enla's request that he break the bond had stemmed from her confusion? What if he'd done exactly what Enla hadn't wanted him to do because she feared it enough that she brought it into reality?

Sylmar's scoff brought him back to the present.

"What did Aeliana say when you asked her?" Gaeren asked.

Sylmar's eyes narrowed as he contemplated the question. "She said it was to free Lukai."

The pain in Gaeren's chest intensified, even though it was the answer he'd expected. It wasn't like Aeliana was going to declare love for him to Sylmar, of all people.

"You realize her mother put that in place for her protection?" Sylmar asked. "That you removed one of magic's deepest forms of protection just to satisfy youthful lust?"

Gaeren rolled his eyes even as the words hammered the guilt more in his mind. Clearly rumors had spread about how the bonds had been broken. "Youthful lust wouldn't be enough to break a bond. Besides, her mother also sent her across the barrier for her protection, and look how well that turned out."

Sylmar gave his standard grunt, which made Gaeren even more certain there was no counterargument. The bond had been hurting Aeliana more than it had been protecting her. They'd done the right thing.

Gaeren closed his eyes and settled back against the pillow. For the first time since he'd broken his bond, he felt the steady and solid presence of hope unmarred by the guilt and pain he still carried. Freeing her from an unhealthy bond hadn't been his motivation in breaking the bonds, but recognizing this truth eased the suffering of it.

Aeliana was now free to lean into the protection she'd garnered by her own willpower. The protection of friends who cared for her. The protection of a dragon who'd chosen to tether to her. The protection of a mother and father whose love surpassed any bond mark they might have placed on her as a child.

The bond mark had merely been a symbol of their love for her, and her tie to Lukai a dim reflection of it. She no longer needed that bond. And being free of it now freed her to choose another.

Gaeren had no illusions that it would be him, not after breaking their bonds. If the love he'd grown to feel for her felt tainted by his actions, her friendship with him might barely remain intact. How could she trust him to be faithful when he'd been willing to break his bond with Lenda? It made him no better than the man he'd once thought Riveran to be. All the ways he'd hated Riveran shifted into a self-hatred—a recognition that whatever love he'd felt for Aeliana would now be tainted by the truth that he was unworthy of it.

"People love rumors," Sylmar said, the change in subject so jarring that Gaeren struggled to drag his thoughts out like boots stuck in mud. "Everyone has it in their head that you and Aeliana are in love. A ridiculous notion considering you were willing to kill her the night we attacked Mayvus' fortress."

Gaeren couldn't stop his eyebrows from rising.

"Aeliana told me of your deal back at the fortress—how she asked you to kill her and how you found a way around it." Sylmar's voice held a hint of warning.

Gaeren shifted in the bed, attempting to sit up, but only landed with his head oddly angled against the wall behind him. "What does that have to do with anything?"

Sylmar leaned forward. "I know the way your family works. Your duty to your sister goes beyond any feelings." He gestured toward Gaeren's palm. "After all, you were willing to break a bond on her word alone."

For the first time, Gaeren glanced at his left palm, at the fresh pink lines on his skin. They would eventually become white scars, ever-present reminders mirroring the scars on his right palm that were left from the brand he'd placed on Aeliana.

"I think it might be wise to let the rumors continue," Sylmar said.

Gaeren couldn't decide if his mind was too far gone from pain or if he wouldn't understand Sylmar on a normal day. "I'm not following."

Sylmar sat back and folded his arms over his chest, gripping his staff between his knees so it stayed upright. "If everyone continues talking as though you and Aeliana broke your bonds over feelings for each other, they won't suspect you if you try to get closer to Aeliana. But I want you to get closer. There are things I need you to find out from her."

The pain in Gaeren's chest flared as something cold slithered through his gut, the warning bells going off in his head loud enough to blur his vision. "What are you talking about?"

Sylmar sighed, and for the first time, Gaeren saw a flash of remorse in the older man's eyes. "Aeliana is like a daughter to me, but she is just as susceptible as Holm was. Maybe more so." He hesitated, then leaned forward with a heated whisper. "Magic shouldn't change. I thought maybe I was mistaken. She's been an exception to so many rules. Her magic showed so young. It came through so strong when she started healing, especially once Marnok helped. Now she shows a fascinating aptitude for tuning in to memories. My fatherly pride overrode my sense of danger and I agreed it was likely from Durriken. But now, after seeing what happened to Holm, I've had to reevaluate everything."

"You think—you think she's branded?" Gaeren asked.

"It's a possibility we have to consider," Sylmar said. "At this point, we have to assume everyone's a possible threat. If we don't, we're already letting Mayvus win." The paranoia leaking off Sylmar should have been laughable, but instead it was contagious.

Aeliana had wanted to break her bond, and she'd wanted to help him break his. But what had been her motivation? Was it really just to free Lukai and Kendalyhn? Or was it to free herself? Maybe so she could be more firmly attached to something or someone else? He tried to shake the thought away, hating how Sylmar's suspicions could so easily be planted in his own mind.

"I still think her skills come from her brand on Durriken," Gaeren said.

"Maybe," Sylmar conceded. "But using magic through the connection of a brand can be just as addictive as blood magic. I never should have encouraged it, and now I fear it's made her susceptible to far worse."

His regretful tone sank deep in Gaeren's chest, making the suspicions hold more weight than if they'd been based in paranoia alone. "What do you want me to do?"

"Make sure she trusts you," Sylmar said. "Then get her to cut out her brand on Durriken just like you got her to release her bond with Lukai. I thought her connection to the dragon was wise at the time, but now I think it should be removed. Except she's grown close with him. I don't think she'll agree if I suggest it. Once it's gone, find out where her magic is really coming from."

"And I suppose I then report back to you?" Gaeren asked, bitterness coloring his words.

Sylmar frowned. "I know you don't trust me. You don't even like me. You're probably the only one in this group who has remained reasonably cautious. And I applaud you for it." He glanced at his arms as if seeing his own scars for the first time. "No one comes away from a connection with Mayvus like I had without scars that impact their thinking. My methods aren't always good. I'm not even sure that one could say the end justifies my means."

Gaeren snorted at the understatement, but Sylmar went on, ignoring the sleight.

"I hope that if you can remain wary of my decisions, you can also recognize the truth that someone who's been kidnapped and tortured by Mayvus' servants could be in a similar position. We all want to trust Aeliana, which makes her the easiest person for Mayvus to use to fool us all. The possibility has to at least be considered."

Gaeren looked away, hating how Sylmar's words stirred up an understanding he didn't want to have.

"I broke my bond fourteen years ago," Sylmar said. "It's not quite as freeing as it seemed, is it?"

Gaeren went still. "What do you mean?"

"It sounded good. Severing ties to someone you no longer wanted to associate with. Freeing yourself to have the choice to remain alone or to bond with another. Giving yourself space to think freely without the influence of a bond—a magic we barely understand." Sylmar's eyebrows rose, twisting the scars on his face into an even more gruesome pattern. "But you're not truly free. The weight of that decision to reject your bond will sit with you permanently."

Gaeren swallowed hard. He already felt the weight of the decision, but he'd hoped it would fade with time like Riveran's had. Except Riveran hadn't made that decision. It had been forced on him. Gaeren clenched his jaw, not wanting to believe Sylmar but too aware of the fact that he and Sylmar now had this terrible thing in common.

"Let the pain keep you cautious. Love is its own kind of magic whether there's a bond or not. You don't want to spy on Aeliana for me? That's fine."

Gaeren winced at the harsh reality of Sylmar's words, of what the man admitted he was asking Gaeren to do.

Sylmar grabbed his staff as if readying to leave. "But you should still seek out the truth behind her magic before you fall under her spell —before we all wind up right back under Mayvus' thumb because we weren't willing to ask the tough questions." He stood, leaning heavily on his staff to bend closer to Gaeren. "And if you discover there's a reason we can't trust her, I hope you'll come to me. Not because you trust me or like me, but because you know I'll do whatever it takes to protect people from Mayvus. Because you value your duty over your feelings."

Gaeren couldn't hold Sylmar's gaze, but he gave a short nod, more to get rid of the man than to truly agree with the request. He needed time to think about it, away from Sylmar's overbearing presence.

Sylmar paused as he crossed the room, turning back toward Gaeren. "There might not always be a way to save Vendaras and Aeliana too. If that's not a choice you can make, allow someone else to do it for you."

CHAPTER 59

THE CROWDED HARBOR was every bit as agitating as Orra remembered. Ever since her days sailing, she'd avoided Andel for that exact reason. One benefit of life as Pirate Redwood had been the open waters—distance from the distractions and chaos of the world. Sailing might have separated her from the earth that grounded her, but it had still felt freeing. Now she was reminded of all the reasons she'd kept a reclusive lifestyle with most of her personas.

Marnok and Rildan found an inn, and while the women cleaned up, the men went out to hunt down anyone who might have news of Larkos. With a city this size, Orra feared they could be there for several days, ruining their odds of catching up to Aeliana and the others. She'd used minimal bits of her energy to sense Aeliana growing closer, which most likely meant Aeliana's group had stopped somewhere, and Orra and the others were the ones gaining ground.

A murmur of voices outside their shared room made it impossible for Orra to fall asleep, so she rose, wrapping a shawl around her shoulders in anticipation of the inn's drafty hall.

"Eight days?" Emeris asked as the door creaked open. Marnok, Rildan, and Emeris turned Orra's way, a small smile crossing Emeris' face even though her brows still pinched with concern.

"I take it you've heard news of Larkos?" Orra asked.

Marnok grimaced. "He left harbor eight days ago, heading west."

Orra nodded, unsurprised, but her chest tightened with the confirmation.

"Is Aeliana still on the west coast?" Rildan asked.

"I believe so," Orra said slowly. "It will be easier to trace her when she's closer, but Larkos will likely reach her soon. We could be chasing them all around the coast of the continent, wasting precious time."

Emeris' eyes narrowed. "Are you tracing Aeliana or the starbridge?"

Orra tensed, but Emeris' eyes clouded over.

Rildan wrapped an arm around Emeris' shoulder, his efforts to direct the conversation away from his wife's confusion also, thankfully, distracting everyone from Orra's lack of an answer to the priestess' question. "We'll continue west as well. Even if we can't catch up, we could reconsider our plan to warn the Elanesses. Maybe General Nels has already sent Gullet."

They all exchanged weary glances, the reality of the fortress's fate in the Myndren Mountains weighing heavily on them. Orra frowned, thinking of all the ships in the harbor and which ones might be faster than Larkos' borrowed galleon. "If we could convince a navy ship to take us, we could possibly beat Larkos to Elanesse."

"And pass by Aeliana and the others completely?" Marnok asked.

Orra nodded. "I suspect they would also stop in Elanesse for Gaeren's sake, if not for supplies, on their return to the fortress. It might be better to get ahead of them rather than continuing to trail behind."

"And how would we convince our enemy's navy to take us?" Rildan asked.

Orra pressed her lips in a thin line. "By proving they are no longer your enemy. By giving them the knowledge we carry, the warning we held back in an effort to save face on General Nels' recommendation. If we can assume General Nels has fallen, his advice no longer needs to be heeded."

While the men considered the idea, Orra contemplated all the ways this plan could fail and succeed without actually searching through the future to see how it might turn out. With her own presence on board the naval ship, she couldn't completely trust anything she saw to be true. It would be a waste of her magic anyway.

"It could work," Marnok said.

"And if it doesn't?" Rildan asked.

Orra sighed. "Then we could be chasing them as they head straight into Mayvus' trap at Ahmranan's Viewpoint."

CHAPTER 60

Even though Aeliana had initially found it more than pleasant to help Gaeren break their bonds, now all she felt was sick over how they'd hurt Lukai. She lay alone in the tiny room that served as Rox's nursery, but each time Iris opened the door, it set her on edge as she recalled memories of her former bondmate's moans during that first night.

"He's stopped crying out," Aeliana said. "Does that mean he's gotten better or worse?"

"Lukai's fine, love," Iris said dryly. "Better off than you and that whiny prince in the other room."

Aeliana bit her lip, her gaze on the door even though her stomach growled over the meal Iris had brought in. "I need to apologize. I should have asked first. I didn't think—"

"It's clear you and Lukai weren't a good match," Iris interrupted, passing her a slice of bread. "Ever since we reached the Myndren Mountains, we've been expecting this. No one's surprised that you broke your bond. We're just wondering why it took so long." The small lift of her lips made Aeliana squirm.

Did they know she and Gaeren had kissed? Or did they think the bond marks had been cut out? What did it matter if they knew anyway? It was just a kiss. It wasn't like anything else would come of it.

She slouched in the bed and took a bite of the bread, letting her gaze fall on Rox's bassinet. She needed to recover and give him back his room. "Will Sylmar take me out to train today?"

Iris clucked her tongue. "Yes, but I think he's planning to send Kendalyhn in to work with you a bit first."

"Kendalyhn?" Aeliana turned, hoping to see the older woman's teasing grin back in place.

"Sylmar's got it in his head that we're all suspect," Iris huffed out as she stirred one of Velden's seaweed concoctions with more force than necessary. "He's been sending Kendalyhn to sift everyone's souls. Thinks he's being so secretive about it. But we all know what he's doing."

"I thought he didn't even trust that," Aeliana said.

"Doesn't mean he won't still do it. That man will never be able to trust another person again. It's sad." Iris' eyes held a strange mix of empathy and hatred. "But it's also extremely frustrating."

As much as Aeliana trusted these people, even they had broken that at times in the past—always with the end goal of protecting her, but it had still left her wary. It made her understand Sylmar's reasoning. And she didn't like when her mind worked the same as his.

"Does she hate me?" Aeliana asked.

"Who?" Iris frowned. "Kendalyhn? Why would she hate you? Lukai might struggle to forgive you—that's the nature of bonds. But Kendalyhn? You just gave her the greatest gift she could have received. I don't even think she'll use it as an opportunity to criticize you over your interest in Gaeren." A sly smile spread on her face.

"Interest?" Aeliana's face heated. "It was just a kiss. We agreed to do it to break each other's bonds."

"Ah, so it was a pragmatic choice?" Iris snorted, and while it was good to see a brief reprieve from her grief, being the brunt of her teasing stung.

"Yes. That's all Jasperus said it would take. A kiss. We figured it would be less painful than cutting them."

This time Iris let out a small laugh. "Not just any kiss will work. The kiss needs to have love behind it. An emotion stronger and deeper than what the bonds already hold. Otherwise it wouldn't be strong enough to break it. So yes, a simple kiss can break it. But not just any kiss."

Iris' words made something in Aeliana burn, a dull pain that turned to a roar that held the heat of embarrassment and horror. Did everyone think she and Gaeren had had some sort of clandestine meeting in the woods the night before?

She felt sick knowing the hints of attraction she'd felt were exposed before the entire group as something much bigger than she was even ready to admit. She hadn't considered her feelings could be stronger than a bond, but now, without her bond to Lukai to cause confusion, her body seemed to react to the possibility without her permission, letting a sense of desire unfurl inside her. Except instead of growing into something beautiful, it seemed to wither with the vulnerable truth that everyone knew how she felt.

Including Gaeren.

Clearly he had known how the kiss worked. Had her interest been obvious enough that he'd known it would break the bond? Or had it been his way of testing her, and now he had proof that he was right? Her embarrassment shifted to anger as she let the memory of the moment unfold in her mind. He should have explained it before their kiss, given her a chance to change her mind.

"Your palm is bleeding, like it's a fresh wound." Iris clucked her disapproval, then placed a new poultice on her palm.

Aeliana flinched, hating the way the cuts on her palms reminded her of how Arvid and Vera had bled her for magic. The consistent unexplained cuts she continued finding left a niggling doubt in her mind that made her squirm.

Iris misinterpreted her movements. "I'm sorry, love. The pain should get better in another day or so."

"It already has," Aeliana mumbled. "I mostly only feel it on my palm." Even though the words were true, they felt like a lie as the pain in her heart threatened to engulf her.

"I suggest you get a little more rest," Iris said. "Once Kendalyhn clears you, Sylmar plans to take you out for a bit of training, and he won't go easy on you."

"Finally." Aeliana rolled on her side, not because she was tired, but to hide the tears she blinked away.

When Aeliana woke again, the Sun's light streamed through the western window, the only hint at the time that had passed. She felt no more rested than she had when she'd closed her eyes. The creak of steps on wood clued her in to the fact that someone else's presence had woken her.

She turned, wincing at the way the movement stirred up the familiar aches and pains, then froze as Kendalyhn's petite frame stood hesitantly at her bedside. Aeliana glanced at the closed door, sensing a moment of panic that they were alone.

But then Kendalyhn dropped to the chair beside her bed, her face crumpling. "I'm so sorry," she whispered, tears trickling down her cheeks.

Aeliana fought to sit up, ignoring the way her palm turned to fire as she placed her weight on it. "*You're* sorry? Whatever for?"

Kendalyhn shook her head, then placed shaking fingers over her face. "It was wrong of me to interfere with your bond."

"I always found the bond suffocating. You know that." Aeliana reached for the other woman's hand, hoping to comfort her, but Kendalyhn winced, and Aeliana let her hand drop. "I never would have held him to our bond. It didn't feel right."

"Still," Kendalyhn said, "you don't know everything."

Aeliana stilled. "What do you mean?"

"Do you remember when Gaeren joined us, and Sylmar had me sift his soul?"

"Yes." Aeliana drew the word out warily, not sure how that had anything to do with their discussion.

"His motives were mixed," Kendalyhn said. "He wanted to rescue you, but in his past, there was also a deep desire to rid Rhystahn of the Wyndren family line. It had been ingrained in him as a youth. Instead of protecting you, I told him you're a Wyndren. It changed something inside him, put him at war with himself. Just like I wanted it to."

Aeliana winced, imagining how perfectly that had played out. How her anger at Gaeren's attitude toward Durriken had probably fed the misconceptions Kendalyhn had planted.

"I thought he might rid me of your presence, of the problem of your existence." Kendalyhn's voice broke with the admission.

"It's all right, Kendalyhn. Things have changed since then. We're not the enemies we once—"

"No." Kendalyhn's face blanched. "You need to understand. I wanted you dead. Before I shot Marnok, I had my arrow pointed at you." She squeezed her eyes shut and whispered, "I wouldn't have really done it."

The half confession made a fresh wave of pain flutter through Aeliana's chest.

"In the moment, I let my arrow train on you. I wondered how it would change things if my finger slipped, but I swear I never would have done it. And then when he pounced on you, I was quick to let it loose on him out of remorse."

Aeliana gave a short nod, blinking away the sudden rush of loneliness the full truth brought on. Kendalyhn had hated her far more than she'd realized, but that was in the past.

"I'm sorry," Kendalyhn whispered.

This time when Aeliana reached for her hand, Kendalyhn held on, her grip like iron.

"Then," Kendalyhn rushed on, as if her previous confessions hadn't been enough, "when Gaeren returned from Elanesse and I sifted him again, his soul had shifted. In his past, there was still the desire to rid us of the Wyndrens, but the light that he felt from your presence outshone that of the darkness. His desire to protect you seemed fueled by something deeper than a childhood promise. I was relieved that maybe I could still get what I wanted without him killing you. I hid that part of what I'd sifted, hoping it would eventually interfere with your bond."

"That's why sifting his soul made you wonder if you might not always hate me," Aeliana mused. Their conversation back on the ship felt like ages ago, but it came back to Aeliana with fresh meaning.

"Considering the circumstances, no one can blame you for hoping something like this would happen."

"My job was to serve you the way my mother served yours." Kendalyhn squeezed Aeliana's hands. "But I was serving myself. Lukai and I even saw the possibility with Lady Merinnia, and we kept it to ourselves, afraid that it would change if we told you or Sylmar. Your mother gave you that bond as a child to protect you, and we threw it away. We didn't even have the courage to break it ourselves. We let you suffer the consequences of it. We used you to get what we wanted." A sob cut through Kendalyhn's throat, making the rest of her words garbled as she rushed on. "I hate what I've done, and I hate that I can't put it right, and I hate that there's a part of me that doesn't even want to, because I still love Lukai."

The admission carried an ugliness that could have planted bitterness in Aeliana's heart, but on the heels of breaking her bond, it felt far more relatable, like something Aeliana would have done if the roles were reversed.

"The bonds aren't natural." Aeliana placed her other hand over Kendalyhn's, hoping the other woman was truly listening even though she still shuddered with her tears. "Maybe some of them are. Iris and Holm's seemed to be something beautiful. My bond with Lukai…it held no love—only fabricated connections that carried more obligation than love." She pulled back, grabbing one of her clean bandages and passing it over for Kendalyhn to dry her tears and runny nose.

"Even so," Kendalyhn said, "my actions were selfish. At the very least, for my own happiness I was willing to rob you of the protection your parents had given you. Worst-case scenario, if Gaeren had been the horrible prince we'd all imagined him to be, I was ready to let him kill you."

Aeliana nodded, not sure how to absolve Kendalyhn of all her guilt. The woman likely needed to forgive herself more than she needed Aeliana's forgiveness. And Aeliana's own experiences proved that would take time and repeated attempts.

"I hold nothing against you," Aeliana said. "I hope you can forgive yourself as well."

The door opened, and Kendalyhn quickly wiped her face once more, tucking the bandage in her cloak pocket.

"Time to train," Sylmar said from the doorway, eyeing the two of them suspiciously. "Did you sift her soul?"

Kendalyhn nodded, and Aeliana raised her eyebrows, wondering if the other woman had just lied to Sylmar or if she'd been multi-tasking.

"I'm ready." Aeliana rose from the bed, and when the room spun before her, she placed a steadying hand on Kendalyhn's shoulder. Kendalyhn rose as well, slipping her arm through Aeliana's for additional support.

Sylmar's eyes narrowed, but Kendalyhn lifted her chin as if daring him to ask, and he grumbled something that suspiciously sounded like "women" when he turned back to the main living area.

Outside, several members of their party were engaged in sparring drills around the camp, their bodies holding sheens of sweat from their work. Aeliana already felt the sweat pouring down her neck from her walk, leaving her embarrassed at her weakened state, but then Lukai stood before her, his face paler than she'd ever seen it and his eyes rimmed with red. He glanced nervously between Kendalyhn and Aeliana, as if unsure which one to greet.

"I'm sorry, Lukai," Aeliana said, unable to hold his gaze.

His entire body sagged with her words, and he leaned forward, crushing her in a hug. "Part of me hates you for it," he whispered. "I don't know. I don't understand it. Because there's another part of me that will never be able to thank you enough."

When he pulled away, he wiped tears from his face and turned away. The abruptness left Aeliana feeling strangely rejected, even though she'd wanted to free him. She supposed this is what Iris meant about things taking time.

The others nearby watched him turn from Aeliana to Kendalyhn, their sparring matches fading to defensive stances. It was then that Aeliana finally noticed Gaeren near the forest's edge, his sword drawn and held out toward Riveran, who mirrored his stance. Gaeren's arm shook, and when he used his left hand to steady his grip, his scar stood out like blood poisoning snaking across his palm.

His gaze caught hers, and something strange passed between them.

Something like regret or maybe apprehension. She sensed a shared fear that what they'd done had changed things between them, and not necessarily for the better.

She dropped her eyes and turned back to Lukai, but he'd already looped his arm through Kendalyhn's, guiding her off to the edge of the clearing. Her bond mark should have stung, and when it didn't, she rubbed hard enough at the scab until it did for other reasons.

She attempted a smile when she found Sylmar at her side.

"Ready to train?" For once, his croaky question was welcome.

"Yes. I'm not willing to go another day with such weak light shields. And I want to practice healing again." She swallowed past the lump forming in her throat as images of wide eyes and blood stains stuck in her mind. "I should have been able to help Holm and Nori."

Sylmar studied her closely, making her wonder if there was something wrong with her request, but then his gaze flicked to Lukai and Kendalyhn, who sparred at half their normal speed, Kendalyhn clearly going easy on Lukai in his weakened state.

"I'm inclined to agree that your somatic skills have suffered," Sylmar said. "Maybe even more so as we've had Gaeren teaching you noetic skills. But I can only help you with that so much at this point. Focusing on your constructive somatic skills would be done best with Marnok or Lukai."

Aeliana drooped at the truth of his words.

"Marnok is inaccessible, and Lukai…well, I think we should give it a few days."

She nodded, gritting her teeth in frustration.

"In the meantime, it would be good for you and Gaeren to spar. Once you've each reached your full strength, you can branch out to new sparring partners and you can train under Lukai again."

A glance up at Gaeren made it clear he'd heard the older man's recommendation. He hesitated, then nodded, beckoning her over to his circle while Riveran stepped away. Aeliana pulled out her dagger, but even that brought a host of emotions she wasn't ready for as her thumb brushed the daisy on the pommel.

The corner of Gaeren's mouth lifted, reminding her of all the ways he'd teased her, except now it was tainted by the fact that he'd let her make a fool of herself, exposing her feelings for him to everyone.

She marched over to his side, taking deep breaths to keep the trees around them from spinning.

"You look about as exhausted as I feel," Gaeren said. He sheathed his sword and pulled out a dagger, a swap that might have seemed thoughtful in the past but now felt patronizing.

"Iris might have mentioned something about you whining." She widened her stance and bent her knees, balancing on the balls of her feet.

His eyebrows rose, and he matched her position, holding his dagger in front of him with his other arm out for balance. "And here I thought out of everyone you might have some sympathy."

She swiped at his waist while he spoke, forcing him to jump back and cut off their conversation. Spots danced in front of her eyes, so she drew energy from her starlock, willing it to strengthen her for the fight. She didn't want him to go easy on her, but she also didn't want him to best her. They circled the rim of their sparring ring, their eyes locked, each waiting for the other to make a move.

"I was too busy thinking about how I'd hurt Lukai to worry about how you'd been affected." Her words came out harsher than she meant, and he flinched.

"That's fair."

This time he lunged for her, not with his dagger, but with his free hand, twisting her arm until she dropped the dagger. Despite the energy she'd borrowed from her starlock, her muscles were too weak and her skills nowhere near a match for Gaeren's. He continued twisting until he'd spun her closer in his grip, his dagger now placed at her throat and both of her arms pinned beneath his as her back pressed against his chest.

"Next time," he instructed in her ear, "hold your weapon closer to your body until you're ready to use it so you're not vulnerable to attacks."

She huffed and stomped on his foot, but while that move had worked on Lukai in the past, the steel toes of the prince's boots left him protected, and he chuckled, the laughter thrumming in his chest against her back.

"It wasn't enough to make a fool of me with the kiss?" she hissed. "You had to best me in a single move the moment we were matched against each other?"

His arms dropped and he stepped away, the cool air rushing between them making Aeliana shiver. She turned around to find his face contorted with confusion.

"What are you talking about?"

A glance around revealed most everyone watching. Velden stopped sparring with Cyrus to raise a webbed hand in a wave, then waggled his eyebrows suggestively. Aeliana groaned and grabbed Gaeren's hand, dragging him across the forest line for them to get some modicum of privacy behind the trees. Then she spun to face him, keeping her voice low.

"You knew it took more than a kiss to break a bond. You could have told me before I—" She gestured between them, then flinched as the confusion in his eyes switched to understanding. She looked away, her face heating. "We should have just cut them out."

He stepped closer. "I almost did tell you. When you offered a kiss, I didn't think it would work."

Tears pricked her eyes. "Well, now you know it did. And so does everyone else." She placed a hand against his chest to push him away, but he grabbed her hand and brought her closer.

"But then I realized it would, not because I was confident you cared for me, but because I realized how much I cared about you."

She stilled, then dared risking a look at his eyes, which burned with an intensity—a desperation to be understood.

"Thallahan compared falling in love to an Awakening, something I couldn't imagine when I related it to my bond with Lenda. But the moment I considered your offer, I recognized the feeling he spoke of— an overwhelming and incomprehensible joy combined with a strange...desperation and responsibility. A gift that has to be used wisely."

He flipped his palm over and lined his scar up with hers. Like Iris had pointed out, Aeliana's looked new, blood trickling out of a few spots where the scabs had broken open.

"The truth is, my bond with Lenda never could have matched what I feel for you. I've felt it for moons now, but I've been afraid to admit it. If you'd offered before our time on Sayhla Island, I'm not sure I would have even recognized it. But that night, I understood."

She stared at the marks on their palms, afraid to hope that she'd heard him right. He lifted her hand to his cheek, drawing her gaze with it.

"Does your outburst and hateful regret mean you might possibly have a fraction of the same feelings for me?" His face shifted into a cheeky grin beneath her hand, one that made her want to smack him— or kiss him again.

"Why do you always tease me?" she whispered even as she smiled.

His gaze dropped to her lips. "Because you either smile like that and give it right back, or your cheeks turn a shade of pink I've only seen on the clamshells near Rykarn. Either way I'm rewarded." To her dismay, he stepped away and gestured at their feet, where daisies had sprung up at least two feet around them. "Or sometimes I get these."

This time she stepped closer and placed her hand back on his cheek, relishing the way he went still, as if he might possibly feel the same nervous vulnerability. "I may need another kiss to know exactly how I feel."

His smirk bloomed into a full grin. "That can easily be arranged."

As he bent down, a shout rang in the distance, startling them both. They ducked around the tree branches and back onto the land cleared by Bayla's home, and one of Breeve's brothers came running from the shoreline.

"They're here," he called. "Larkos and the others are here!"

CHAPTER 61

"I THOUGHT you'd be happier to see me," Larkos said, "or at the very least your boat. It's not easy chasing a man down in this country when I have no idea where he'll be."

Gaeren tried to smile but suspected it came out like a grimace. He scratched at the scar of his bond mark, picturing Aeliana in the woods, grinning up at him with that teasing glint in her eye. Why hadn't Larkos come just another day later?

"A lot has happened," he said.

"I have letters for you and Riveran. Enla must have seen our reunion because she sent them to me in Valorian, knowing I'd get them to you." He chuckled as he sat on Gaeren's desk, an action that previously would have made Gaeren threaten demerits. "In some ways, those letters gave me the confidence to keep sailing west, knowing I'd find you one way or another. It's handy having a sister who can see the future, eh?"

Gaeren laughed, but it held no humor. "Not sure that's the word I'd use to describe it." Had Enla seen all this? She must have if she'd pushed him to break his bond with Lenda. But what reason would she have for encouraging him to fall for Aeliana? Sure, she cared for his happiness, but everything always boiled down to the good of Vendaras.

Even as he pictured Aeliana waiting for him back in Bayla's home, the visions he'd seen of Enla's and Aeliana's futures revolved in his mind. By breaking his bond with Lenda, had he put Enla in danger? Or Aeliana?

Without meaning too, he'd followed Sylmar's request and solidified Aeliana's trust in him. Even though that hadn't been his intention, would it still put him on a path to find out Aeliana's true motives? Would he discover she was branded just like Sylmar suspected? He shook away the suspicion, trying to bring back the image of her asking him for a kiss.

"Well, since you've gone mute, I'll go ahead and give you the letter now and find Riveran to deliver his." Larkos tossed an envelope on the table, then stood, ambling his way toward the door out of Gaeren's quarters.

Gaeren stared at the familiar script, his longing for home warring for his hope in a new home, because what did his old home hold for him anymore? Parents who were losing their hold on this world. A sister who gave him conflicting advice every time she saw him, changing her instructions at the whim of every vision she happened to see. A class of noblemen and noblewomen he could never relate to.

He lifted the envelope, and despite knowing he would question everything she had to say in the letter, he ripped it open and pulled it out.

Dear Gaeren,

I have been so afraid of which future you might pick. It's my greatest hope that you've made good choices that have led you to a place to receive this letter. But I'm still afraid that you have not. That you've placed others' welfare before your own and my letter has no destination. Too many of your paths fade because your love grows too deep. Please don't forget how much you're needed. Please don't forget that sometimes the way you can save others is by saving yourself.

Mother and Father are still upset. I'm not going to sugarcoat that truth. But I have not marked you as a traitor. I know the heart behind your words. I know you desire the best for our people. Even if you and I have different ways of getting there, we have the same end goals in mind. Don't forget that either.

I've seen things. Things I can't put in writing, but things I need to tell you. I'm terrified of what's to come. Not just of the possibilities, but of the certainties. So many of the paths narrow and our options are too slim. If Larkos gave you this letter, you should be near Rykarn. Please come see me before you head off on any more adventures. I know your missions are important. I've seen your goals and I won't keep you from them. But you can't reach them without hearing what I have to say.

Please come see me.

Your loving sister,

Enla

The chill that had begun crawling down Gaeren's back settled over the base of his spine, leaving a dull ache that felt more threatening than the Sayhleens when they'd been at their worst. He didn't want to think of Enla as the enemy, but he had to consider the possibility that this was a trap placed by his own sister, sanctioned by his parents. And then he also had to consider the possibility that it wasn't.

What had she seen and how would it impact his ability to protect both Aeliana and Enla? The idea that their end goals were in line felt ignorant. He could call his sister many things, but ignorant was not one of them. Not when she could see all the possible paths of the future. Not when she sought them out to her own detriment. She sounded clear in the letter, but how much more had her mind failed since he'd last seen her? Was Croft keeping her from overusing her power?

A knock sounded on the door of his cabin, and without thought, he bade them to enter. Riveran stood in the doorway, the concern on his face twisting the X on his forehead. "What did your letter say?"

Gaeren frowned, having forgotten that there had been a letter for Riveran as well. It wasn't the first Enla had sent Riveran, and it seemed inappropriate now that she was married to Croft. Or perhaps it simply rubbed him wrong, knowing that she'd likely given Riveran instructions because she didn't trust Gaeren to follow hers.

"She wants me to come see her," Gaeren said.

Riveran nodded, then licked his lips, glancing down at the paper in his hand. "She insists I bring you to her," Riveran admitted.

Gaeren snorted. "Was her letter as cryptic to you, or does she spell things out more plainly to someone who's not her sibling?"

Riveran shook his head. "If this is her speaking more plainly, then I'm afraid for her."

That same chill in Gaeren's back broadened, reaching around like ice in his stomach. "What do you mean?"

Riveran hesitated, then passed the letter to Gaeren.

It started out much like the letter he'd received, urging Riveran to bring Gaeren home, insisting they were not in trouble and that she could deal with her parents. But there were times where her pen trailed off, as if she'd lost her thought midway through the sentence. There were even statements that held affection, proof that either her bond with Croft had never fully taken or that her mind was deteriorating and falling back into the past when she'd cared for Riveran so deeply.

"I wasn't sure if I was going to go," Gaeren said, "but I can't ignore this."

Riveran's face relaxed. "What about Aeliana and the others?"

Gaeren rubbed the scar on his palm, then slid his hand under his sleeve to touch the braid. Aeliana planned to return to the Myndren Mountains, but he couldn't go that far. Not if Enla needed him. And yet how could he leave Aeliana now? Especially if Sylmar suspected she was branded. He squeezed his eyes shut, unable to consider that possibility. If Aeliana was branded by Mayvus, she wouldn't express affection for him, would she? And yet how had Iris been fooled by Holm's brand for moons?

This decision went far deeper than his feelings for Aeliana or even for his need to protect his sister. Both women would want him to protect the Vendaran people. Staying with Aeliana could allow him to protect the Vendaran people's future leader if the Recreants had their way. But staying with Enla could help him pave the way for Aeliana to have that future while still protecting his sister.

"They don't need us right now," Gaeren said slowly. "In fact, the distance might be good for a time."

"It's all right for you to be with Aeliana," Riveran said. "Breaking your bond freed you from a connection you didn't willingly make."

"That's not why I want distance. But I'm glad she and I will at least be parting on good terms. It should be temporary." Even as he said the words, his heart ached over the idea of saying goodbye. "We were born in opposing families, but we're not destined to always be at odds. Not if I have any say in it. I just can't ignore Enla's plea for help. Not after—" He glanced at Riveran.

"The sprites?" Riveran asked.

Gaeren nodded, then clenched his teeth as he folded up Enla's letter.

"So you'll let them sail on without you? In your ship?"

"It was a gift from my parents to distract me and appease me. It served its purpose. Now, it's the Recreants' ship. *To the Deep and Back* was never truly mine. Larkos can use it as he sees fit."

Riveran's mouth swung open, but Gaeren strode past him and out onto the deck. Several of the sailors greeted him while they worked, including Brogdon, who seemed far more at ease than when Gaeren had last seen him before they'd crossed the barrier.

Erech gave him a grin and salute from where he swabbed the deck, looking taller and tanner than Gaeren remembered. He returned the boy's smile but didn't change course as he made his way to Larkos, who instructed several sailors where to put supplies being brought on board.

Larkos showed little surprise when Gaeren shared his plans, but his suspicions ran far deeper than Gaeren's own.

"Do you think she's always telling you the truth?" Larkos asked.

"No," Gaeren admitted. "I think she tells me whatever she thinks will get me going down the path she wants me on."

Larkos nodded. "Well, at least you're not as oblivious as you seem." The words came out on a huff that softened the barb.

"You asked me in Andel how I could best serve the Recreants, how I could make a difference for my people." Gaeren frowned, his gaze on the door, his mind conjuring Aeliana and all the ways he thought protecting her might be best for the people. But despite Lady Merinnia's warnings, he couldn't believe that protecting both Aeliana and his sister was impossible. "I still think Aeliana is key to the Recreants' success. I can't explain why. But things have changed, and I no longer have a role as her protector. Perhaps I was only meant to help her get through Sayhla Island. I don't know. But Enla calling me home is an opportunity I can't pass up. You and the southern Recreants were right. I can do more to thwart my family's power if I take my place as throne warden."

The decision left him uneasy even though he knew it was right. Going up against his family while pretending to support them was the deepest sort of lie he'd ever told. But it was for their own good. He patted the arrow in his pocket, remembering his rash promise to the southern Recreants. He didn't regret making it. Taking down their throne from within would be far less bloody than letting the Recreants take it down from outside. Besides, if he stayed with the Recreants, Sylmar would keep pushing him to spy on Aeliana, and that was a line he wasn't willing to cross.

"You don't think she knows you've switched sides? After all, she sees the future." Larkos' words held a hint of fear, one of those rare moments Gaeren was reminded the hardened sailor saw him as a son more than a prince.

"Whether or not she's seen my discussions with Recreants in the possible paths or whether she's seen this exact conversation, she's confident she and I have the same end goals. That's why she's called me home."

"Are you so sure?" Larkos asked. "Sylmar likes to keep his enemies close. How do you know your sister isn't doing the same?"

Gaeren shrugged. "I think if she saw me as a true enemy in the future, she would have already put an end to my path. As much as she loves me, she will always love Vendaras first."

Saying the words out loud was painful. He didn't want them to be true, but it was a reality he couldn't ignore. Not any longer. Enla put the future of Vendaras before her own health and safety, so he couldn't ever assume she would do any different for him.

"She's not evil," he added, feeling a need to defend her. "I think she means it when she says she's doing what's best for her people. I'm just not sure she knows what's truly best. Not anymore. She thinks we're both fighting for the same thing. She doesn't realize how little our paths align."

Larkos' eyebrows raised, shifting the tattoos lining his scalp. "Strange words about someone who can see possible paths in the future."

Gaeren winced, wondering if he'd underestimated his sister. Was he wrong? "Just because she can see the possible paths doesn't mean she interprets them well. She used to berate me for not trying hard enough with Lenda. Then she insisted I break my bond. She changes which path she wants me to take on a whim when she sees something new. When I return, she's probably going to tell me to mend things with Lenda. Her mind is breaking. I don't know that we can trust her visions anymore."

Larkos nodded. "Calia always feared as much for her. It's why she has a soft spot for her, even though she's destined to be queen. Calia's mother had a similar fate. She lived a long life, but the last twenty years were spent in her mind, living out some future path no one else could see. It was difficult to watch."

Gaeren's fear for his sister grew tenfold.

"Why have you never told me this?" he asked, even though he knew it wouldn't have made a difference. Enla's choices were her own, and he couldn't stop her from this path. Not if it was one she wanted to take.

"Because I still have hope for her." Larkos' smile held a strange sorrow. "Even Calia still has hope for her. Enla has something Calia's mother didn't. She has you."

CHAPTER 62

"You're going to stay in Elanesse?" Aeliana tried to hide her shock. It felt petty after the last several weeks. But it also felt warranted after she'd all but told Gaeren she loved him. They'd set sail two days ago, and now they finally had a chance to talk alone again, only this was his news.

He tugged on her hand and led her to the stern of the ship where words carried on the wind would get tossed to the sea instead of into sailors' ears. "It's not an easy decision, but I have to see things through with my sister. Then I'll rejoin you in your hunt for the curse and the starbridges."

He made it sound like each activity would take a month or two at most. "You're offering to take on your role as throne warden," she said. "Isn't that a lifelong commitment?"

He sighed and ran a hand through his hair, but the wind just flung it right back in his face. "Larkos and I are working with the Recreants. Not just these Recreants"—he gestured at their friends on the ship—"but the ones who want to take down the throne for a democracy."

"My mother wants a democracy too," Aeliana pointed out. "Some of the Recreants may want her to lead, but it would be more of a figurehead as a high priestess. The power would remain with the people."

He considered her words. "That might actually be a good way to explain it to the southern Recreants. It would help unify them." He shook his head. "The point is, I'll be working from the inside to help take down the throne. The idea is that there won't be a need for a throne warden in the near future."

Aeliana gnawed on her lip before answering. "That sounds dangerous. How do you know they won't take you down along with your role?"

"It's far less dangerous than you all taking on the icebergs in the Northern Sea this time of year. I can't believe Larkos even agreed to it." He wrapped his arms around her, enveloping her in a hug. "You're risking getting there just to have to turn around and take the Southern Horn."

"I'll ask Durriken to check on the icebergs if it makes you feel better." She leaned into him, relishing the way she felt no guilt or twinge on her palm. "But you're avoiding my question."

"I guess my safety isn't a guarantee," he admitted. "But I can't just let them kill my family. I'll protect my sister the same way you want to protect your mother."

She nodded against his chest, mostly because she didn't want to pull away to say anything more. He was right even if she didn't want to admit it. Finding Mayvus and figuring out how to destroy her power while protecting Emeris was her priority. Everything else was trivial. Most especially any feelings she'd developed for a prince who was supposed to be some sworn enemy.

"Sylmar doesn't trust you," he added, finally making her pull away to squint at him.

"What do you mean?"

He glanced back at the others. "When we were still sick, Sylmar asked me to gain your trust—to figure out your real motives. He's worried you're branded."

She laughed. "I'm not—" She held up her hands, studying all the scars. "Would I know if I was branded and she'd disguised it?"

"Probably. But I don't think you'd tell me." He took her hands in his. "My point is that he's watching you—he might even ask someone else to spy on you once he hears I'm staying in Elanesse. I admire his diligence, but..."

Aeliana tried to smile, but she couldn't help thinking about the way her scars seemed to form new cuts. "What if he's right, except I don't know it? I've had cuts I can't explain, all the way back since I came to Vendaras. What if she's doing blood magic through me?"

Gaeren hesitated, running his fingers along her scars. "I don't see how that's possible. The blood she had that night was her only vial. I'm more worried my parents could be branded again than you. Maybe the cuts are something you've done in your sleep, or maybe they come back because they're infected. Or just accidents. You're not the most graceful woman—"

His words cut off with a grunt as she jabbed him in the stomach. "I'll have Lukai take a look at my hands, I guess."

"Trying to drum up jealousy?" He grinned at her. "It won't work when he's smitten with Kendalyhn."

She smiled and wrapped her arms around Gaeren once more.

"Gaeren Elanesse!" Larkos' voice carried on the wind. "This ship won't sail itself and my shift is over!"

Over the next several days, Aeliana threw herself into training with Sylmar and Lukai, striving to get her constructive somatic skills back while neglecting the noetic skills she'd gained from Durriken. The harder she worked, the more progress she made, but deep down she knew it was nothing like she'd been able to do before they'd reached the Myndren Mountains.

Durriken reported that the Myndren Mountains seemed undisturbed, with soldiers still fortifying walls and additional ramparts being built. She was tempted to ask him to get close enough to check on her mother, but even if the soldiers let him, she didn't want to put him in that dangerous position—especially since he'd expressed interest in tearing the place down.

Before she knew it, the week it took to sail to Elanesse had passed. Saying goodbye to Gaeren was as hard as Aeliana had expected, and watching him voluntarily walk away and weave through the ranks for final farewells was even harder.

Across the ship, Gaeren ruffled Erech's hair, then gave Larkos a light punch, pointing at the wheel with a stern glance and probably a warning for the ship's safety. Then he hopped from the ship's plank to the dock with Thallahan and Riveran in tow.

Several of the sailors' demeanors shifted as Larkos gave the orders to set sail again. For some of them, it was a stop at home. One they weren't allowed to disembark for since no one was entirely certain how well this group of Recreants would be received regardless of the prince's presence aboard their ship. For others, it was enemy territory, and tension seemed to rise equally across the board.

As they pulled out of harbor, two fishermen stood in their boats, eyes on Aeliana as they touched three fingers to their foreheads and bowed their heads. She shrank away from the bulkhead of the ship and tugged the hood of her cloak over her hair, which had finally grown past her shoulders.

"Remember," Sylmar said from beside her, "it's an honor to receive their salute of tribute. They recognize you as Emeris' daughter. You shouldn't shy away from it."

"It's not the symbolism of the salute that bothers me," she said, surprised to find her words were true. "Not anymore. It's that strangers know who I am. With Mayvus loose, it can't be good to make my whereabouts known."

"That's wise." Pride leaked from his tone even as his eyes narrowed. "We should consider disguising you at future ports." He continued droning on about safety measures, but Aeliana grew distracted as Velden approached one of the younger sailors, gesturing with his normal emphatic flair by pointing to his eyes and then over to the water.

The sailor he spoke to frowned, his words making Velden let out a frustrated sigh. When the sailor sent a nervous glance at one of his comrades, Velden gave his back a good-natured slap, leaving a wet stain that made the younger man shudder. Velden turned to catch Aeliana's gaze, and he gave her a sheepish grin before heading her way.

"Can I steal Aeliana away for some training?" he interrupted Sylmar. "I could use some sparring."

Sylmar initially grumbled, but he was never one to turn down efforts to train her. "Hand-to-hand or dagger-to-sword?"

Velden grimaced at Aeliana. "It never feels fair when she just has a dagger."

"It's all I can carry at this point," Aeliana said. "Especially when I have my bow and arrow."

"Maybe you should start carrying a sword. You'll never get used to the weight unless you start sometime." He passed over his own, and while it was lighter than most of Sylmar's training swords, it still felt awkward in her hands.

"How about hand-to-hand," she said, passing it back. Sylmar stepped away and leaned against the bulkhead, folding his arms across his chest and pressing his lips together until they disappeared within his facial hair as he settled in to observe.

Velden muttered under his breath as he tucked the sword away.

"What's got you so riled up?" she asked. "What did that sailor tell you?"

At first, his face clouded over with irritation, a rare look for his normal jovial demeanor. But then his lip lifted and his head cocked to the left. "Best me and I'll tell you."

She snorted her disbelief, but her curiosity was piqued. So instead of starting with her normal defensive stance, she moved in with a jab at his ribs. He barely dodged her and briefly lost his balance before laughing and making his own swipe. They weren't evenly matched on Aeliana's best day, but Velden's distraction seemed to lengthen his response times.

Perhaps it was cheating, but Aeliana let her magic flood through her, desperate to win a chance at hearing whatever had upset him. He'd been understandably moody ever since Andel. But that moodiness had shifted to something more calculating. She'd thought releasing his mother to the sea in Paelen's waters would lighten his load, but now he almost seemed more distracted than before.

"It was Lady Merinnia, wasn't it?" Aeliana asked between lunges. Her words came out in a pant, but his eyes still widened in surprise, and she made another lunge for his legs. This time she caught one, and he toppled over, rolling away from her grasp and popping up with unnatural grace.

"You're using magic," she accused.

He laughed again. "And you aren't?"

Her face heated, and they eyed each other once more. A few of the sailors had stopped working to watch, egged on by Erech's and Cyrus' excitement over the sparring. She couldn't spare a glance back at Sylmar, but he was probably proud she'd used the magic since she rarely did in hand-to-hand combat. Lukai had always taught her to fight as if her magic had been drained because that should be the only time she was fighting in the first place.

Thinking of him made her think of Gaeren, which left her distracted and vulnerable. Too late, she sensed Velden dropping for a kick to her knee. She was even slower to catch that it was a feint so he could trip her up instead when she dodged.

She toppled to the deck, where he placed his hands at her throat, calling for the win.

"It's not a guaranteed win," she grumbled. "I could get out of your choke hold."

Velden shrugged and stood, holding out a hand to help her up. "Probably true."

After taking a long swig, he passed her his flask of water, and the tiny crowd of sailors dispersed when Larkos yelled at them. Sylmar still watched them, frowning, but he didn't come any closer.

"You've improved a lot since we left Bayla's house," Velden said.

The compliment warmed Aeliana. "I feel like I'm nearly back to normal, except for my magic." She glanced at the scar on her palm, the faint reminder of the choice she and Gaeren had made.

Velden held out his own palm, his mysterious broken bond drawing her gaze. "You were right about Lady Merinnia," he said.

She raised her eyebrows. "I didn't win."

He chuckled, then let his gaze stray out over the water. "Maybe not. But there is value in sharing one's burdens with another. And Sylmar isn't exactly looking to swap secrets late at night."

Aeliana smiled at the image. "It wasn't difficult to guess that much. You're the only one who hasn't talked about what you saw in the

Seer's Sanctuary. I thought you would have been at peace after putting your mother to rest. But if anything, you're more agitated." She pulled out the clamshell and flicked it open, eyeing the gemstone with its myriad colors. It remained both a mystery and a reminder that she couldn't possibly save everyone. "None of us came away from that encounter with the Seer unchanged."

"No, we did not." He leaned over and ran a finger over the gemstone. "My mother had one of these around her neck. I never saw her without it, but I never knew its significance."

"It was a gift from the Sayhleens—before we went to Lady Merinnia. Gellen kept it from me, but when he gave me the starbridges, he also gave this back. He didn't have time to explain it."

"Don't lose it, then. I can't imagine we'll go back, but if we do…" He snapped the shell shut and closed her fingers around it before letting his moody gaze settle on something distant across the waves.

"What did the Seer show you?" she probed.

"A bit of my past. I hope some of my future." His smile turned wistful. "Come to the stern with me and I'll tell you. Let's see what you make of it."

CHAPTER 63

Aeliana and Velden settled at the stern of the ship, away from prying eyes and ears. He leaned over the water and inhaled deeply. Aeliana copied him, breathing in the salty scent. It was one of the few things that made her feel like memories of the home she'd had with her parents still sat dormant inside her.

"When Sylmar found me," Velden said, "I was recovering from being a bitter and broken man."

She scoffed her disbelief, and he held up both webbed palms.

"No, no. Believe me, I was. I had just learned to let a lot of it go in order to move on and be intentional with my choices when he showed up. Even though Sylmar has the unusual gift of being able to hold on to bitterness," he added dryly, "he pushed me to channel my lingering anger into something productive."

"What were you bitter about?" she asked, even though the evidence of it stared back at her from his palm.

"I never expected to find a bondmate. Not many women were interested when they realized my heritage. The fear of bearing a child with such oddities kept most from considering me a viable option."

Aeliana bit her lip, thinking about the charming young man Velden must have been, and how deeply prejudices had to run in order to override that.

"Sariah was the exception. And that was all it took. I didn't need dozens of women fawning after me, not like Ludo. When it's the right woman, one is enough. Except her father didn't approve." His jaw tightened, and he rubbed at his eyes as if shoving away the anger he'd once held on to. "I'm no longer sure what's true and what's a lie, not after Lady Merinnia's visions. But whether he cut out her bond or convinced her to do it, our bond was broken."

"Then what happened?" Aeliana asked softly.

Velden tucked his hands in his trouser pockets. "They say when a bondmate dies, you feel their death with them."

Aeliana shuddered, glancing at Iris, whose face still seemed haunted.

"According to her father, Sariah died giving birth to our child." His jaw tightened with the admission. "He claims I killed her."

"No." The ship dipped, and Aeliana's stomach churned with it. "Even if the first half of that's true—"

"I know." Velden let out a strangled laugh. "But the funny thing is that I'm not even sure the first part is true. Lady Merinnia showed me so much of my past. It stirred up the same old frustrations, but she showed me other things too. Things I hadn't thought possible."

"Like what?"

"She showed me Sariah holding a child. Not even an infant newly born, but a toddler by the sea."

Aeliana stilled, the gravity of his revelation hitting her with more force than when the wind had been knocked out of her when she'd fallen to the deck. "You're going to find him?"

"Her," Velden said. "It was a girl. The Seer showed me Sariah raising a beautiful little girl. One who could hold her breath underwater for at least an hour." A smile slowly grew on his face, his eyes alight with wonder. "One who earned her starlock at the tender age of twelve. One who grew into a young woman who was rumored to be a green-eyed goddess. One who men were drawn to like a siren but feared, because her affinity for water was so great. She could best any of them in the progeny schools with her magic."

"She sounds like someone Sylmar would have recruited if she existed," Aeliana said slowly, not wanting to diminish Velden's hope but feeling certain that if anyone knew of this girl's existence, it would be Sylmar.

"I thought the same," Velden said eagerly, "which is why I went to him first. He said he'd heard of her but that she kept to herself. That she would never take a side in any war or disagreement. That going after her would be like chasing the wind and asking it to fuel our army. Sylmar is attracted to power, but he's also one who goes for the sure thing. He takes risks when they're the only options, not right from the start."

She frowned and glanced across the ship at the man who'd taken her under his wing, who'd been a mentor who taught with tough love. She'd hated him at times. And she still suspected the scars on his soul ran far deeper than the ones on his skin. Scars that might eventually affect his ability to make good decisions if they hadn't already. What would he do when they returned to her mother with no clear answer? She feared he'd side with Emeris and suggest the only way to defeat Mayvus was by taking them both down.

As if he sensed the direction of her thoughts, Sylmar's scowl deepened, and he shuffled below deck while leaning heavily on his staff.

"I wasn't a sure bet," Aeliana pointed out to Velden. "And he went after me."

Velden studied her closely enough that she squirmed under his gaze. "He made sure you were a sure bet. Don't you remember what Sylmar promised when we first met?" Velden asked. "About teaching you to get rid of your magic?"

She nodded even though it felt so long ago.

"He can't do that any more than I can teach you how to excrete water." Velden held out his slimy webbed hands, letting the water flow over like a burbling spring.

The admission should have made her angry. Somewhere deep down, the words struck a painful chord, but another part of her felt sad for the man aged beyond his years as he carried weight he couldn't get rid of.

"So he lied to make sure I'd stay?"

"He might seem like the cranky rule-follower, but he's more likely to cross lines than anyone here if he thinks it's for the right reason. You stayed, so he would say that had been the right choice. He values the outcome more than the motive or method. He trusts himself to make things happen more than he trusts the Sun."

"My mother would say the Sun can still use our shortcomings for a greater good."

"And Cyrus would say it's the Stars." He grinned, and she smiled with him even though it was no longer true. "The point is Sylmar didn't have information that could help me."

"So now you ask the sailors," she said, bringing the conversation back around to what had started her prying.

Velden nodded. "Sailors can be a seedy and yet loyal bunch. But they are also some of the worst gossips around. Almost every single one of them has heard of the green-eyed goddess. Even Gaeren claims he sought her out once thinking she might be you."

"Me," Aeliana said in surprise. Her gaze swung to the shoreline even though she could no longer make out individuals, let alone the prince who'd long ago left the docks.

"He's followed every lead imaginable for the last seven years, ever since he was gifted this ship. If you hadn't been on the other side of the barrier, he would have found you long ago between his determination and resources. You had no chance at hiding."

"I wasn't hiding." She closed her eyes, imagining a younger Gaeren chasing after every rumor to follow through on his promise to protect her.

"Fine. Arvid and Vera had no chance at hiding you. But Gaeren claims he saw this green-eyed goddess near Seaglass Port. Said she was surrounded by children she'd taken in, children she taught how to fish and care for sea creatures. They lived off the knowledge she gave them. But as soon as he saw she was at least five years your senior, he knew the lead was a dead end and he didn't pursue her further."

"We should have gone south instead of north," Aeliana said. "You could have looked for her. Maybe even found Sariah."

Velden shook his head. "I'll find her eventually. Maybe both of them. I won't give up. But Lady Merinnia showed me something else. She showed me all the things she showed my mother—all the things that would come of her using the starbridge." He closed his eyes and tilted his nose into the wind, inhaling the sea breeze as if it strengthened him.

"So your mother did know how she would die," Aeliana murmured.

Velden nodded. "But that wasn't the last thing she saw. The Seer showed my mother you."

"Me?" Aeliana squirmed. "That doesn't make any sense."

"It makes sense of everything for me." Velden opened his eyes, which shone bright as he blinked back tears. "My mother saw me aiding you. She saw us changing the world. And she knew her sacrifice would be worth it."

Aeliana bit her lip and glanced at her hands. She couldn't handle the confidence in his face—in his words. She clenched and unclenched her fists, feeling even more unworthy of his confidence as she stared at evidence of all the ways she'd failed.

"I will find my daughter someday." He patted her back, the sticky wetness soaking through to her skin and drawing the sea breeze in to make her shiver. "Maybe even Sariah. But in the meantime, my purpose is to help you. We'll figure out the curse and save all of Vendaras. I won't let my mother's sacrifice go to waste." His smile wobbled, but he wrapped an arm around Aeliana and drew her in for a hug. "Recently I've thought if I ever had a daughter, I'd want her to be like you. It's how I imagine her while I wait."

"She sounds far better," Aeliana whispered as she squeezed him back.

"Hopefully someday soon we both find out." He pulled back, patting her once more before squirting her in the face and threatening to ruin the sweet moment they'd shared. "Until then, we need to get you strong enough to wield a sword."

CHAPTER 64

Gaeren and Riveran dropped Thallahan off in town, teasing him about his upcoming marriage and whether or not Fay still waited for him. The rest of the ride to the palace was somber as each man considered their next steps.

"Are you sure you want to come with me?" Gaeren asked.

Riveran nodded. "I have nowhere else to go."

"I could send you off," Gaeren offered. "Get funds from the coffers before they decide what to do with me. You could start over. You've already sacrificed more than any man should have to for the sake of Vendaras. No one would judge you for wanting to live out the rest of your life in peace and quiet."

Riveran grunted but didn't respond, confirming Gaeren's suspicions that the other man still loved his sister. Living a life without knowing how she fared wouldn't be peaceful at all.

"How is it that you still love Enla after your bond's been broken?"

Riveran's eyes widened, but he didn't deny the claim. "It's not about the bond. It never was. The bond strengthened what was already there. But even breaking the bond couldn't weaken the love it stemmed from. Maybe for a time it did. But I'm more likely to stop breathing than I am to stop loving her."

The words came out with so little hope that Gaeren felt the first stirrings of anger that his sister had married Croft so quickly. Then he marveled at the way his thoughts toward Riveran had shifted over the last year.

"She's a fool," Gaeren muttered.

They passed their horses to the stable boys, but then Gaeren hesitated, eyeing the main entrance. "Let's go through the back gardens instead."

Riveran followed without question, smiling when Gaeren gave his traditional mocking bow to Queen Amaya's statue.

"Who does she look like to you?" Gaeren asked, and Riveran shrugged, squinting up at the porcelain face. "Doesn't she look a bit like Orra?"

Riveran frowned. "Maybe. Didn't Orra say she'd followed her descendants over the years? Could it be one of her daughters?"

Gaeren laughed. "I guess that would make us related."

"No more than you and Aeliana are related." Riveran elbowed him in the side, and Gaeren winced.

"It was a thousand years ago. It's not like she's my cousin."

Riveran chuckled, the sound reminiscent of his carefree days before he'd been sent away.

They climbed the lattice leading to Gaeren's balcony. Unsurprisingly, the door to his room was locked, but he found the pin he'd hidden in the railing years before and swiftly opened it, gesturing for Riveran to enter first.

The room smelled musty, like Enla had ordered it shut up, knowing Gaeren would never return. It remained just as he'd left it after the trip to Lorvandas, even though he'd sailed around the entire continent and crossed a second barrier to Sayhla Island since then.

"You should think about hiring new maids," Riveran joked as he wiped thick dust from the desk's surface.

Gaeren frowned. "Usually she foresees my return. She gets everything ready for me."

Riveran gave a mock pout. "Is Gaeren not the most important thing in the world to Enla anymore? Did she find matters more pressing to attend to than her baby brother's needs?"

Gaeren shoved Riveran half-heartedly, but his mind still raced.

Something was wrong. He could feel it. "Maybe you should go back to the ship," he said. "Catch them before they leave."

Riveran dropped onto the bed, sending up another cloud of dust. He folded his hands behind his head and leaned back against the pillow. "They're already well out of harbor. Sylmar wasn't even willing to do a supply run for fear of being recognized. Why? What's wrong?"

Gaeren shook his head. "I'm not sure. Isn't it odd that she told us to come but didn't get my room ready? Even if she hadn't foreseen it, she told us to come."

Now Riveran's face turned wary, and he glanced toward the door. "It was written in her hand, though. And I don't think anyone could fake the letter she wrote me."

Gaeren nodded. "True. Maybe she just forgot or miscalculated how close we were." Even as he said the words, they didn't sound quite right. By now, Enla should have come to his room. "What if she's sick? Or what if my parents are sick?"

"Your parents haven't been right for a while," Riveran said. "And after your dramatic exit last time, I don't think you should seek them out without first finding Enla."

Gaeren nodded slowly, studying the room more closely. He tuned in to the space around him, but the memories evaded him, all far too old to still be present. No one had been there in days if not moons.

"We need to go find her." He opened the door to the hall, tuning in as far as his starlock's power could reach. His parents and their soldiers had crossed through these halls, but there was nothing that gave him concern. They headed toward the main hall, creeping down the winding path until they drew close enough to the central quarters that Gaeren suspected they'd be caught.

He let his magic unfurl like the tendrils of a vine until it latched on to a soldier standing guard just outside the front entrance. He pushed his starlock's power to infiltrate the man's memories, speeding back through them until he recognized his sister.

Despite looking healthy, her eyes were vacant, like she remained lost in her visions while walking through the halls. He swore softly under his breath, wondering why Croft wasn't watching out for her. He was a bondmate. It was what he was supposed to do. And yet deep down, Gaeren knew. Her stubbornness likely prevented the other man from protecting her from herself.

"She's in her quarters," he whispered.

"In the middle of the day?" Riveran's brow furrowed. "That's not like her."

Gaeren nodded. "At least it will be easier to get to her."

"You think the guards will just let you waltz in there?"

Gaeren grinned. "Have you forgotten how we snuck in as children?"

This time Riveran's smile matched Gaeren's. "Are you saying that passageway still exists? I assumed your parents blocked it up when they discovered us using it."

Gaeren rolled his eyes. "Of course they did. But we have our own resources. Stone masonry can be broken down."

They headed back to Gaeren's quarters, where he shoved aside a bureau to reveal a small trap door only two feet tall.

"Hmm," Gaeren said. "It looks a bit smaller than I remember."

Riveran snorted. "There's no way you're fitting into that."

They opened the door, coughing as the hinges creaked and even more dust filled the air. But despite signs of the passage's abandonment, a note and parcel sat before them. Gaeren grinned, ripping the note open and scanning its contents. Enla's script stared back at him with a short but relieving message:

I'll come back here this evening. Keep to your rooms. There's enough food here for both of you.

"Oh, food," Riveran sighed, then nearly moaned in his relief as he unwrapped the package, revealing biscuits, cheese, fruits, and jerky. He tore off a biscuit and paired it with a slice of cheese.

"Do you think it could be a trap?" Gaeren asked, even though he'd told Larkos he was confident it wasn't.

"We came back once already. She has no new reason to trap us."

Gaeren winced, thinking of all the ways he'd betrayed the throne since finding Aeliana. Just because his sister claimed to have forgiven his departing words didn't mean she truly had. Since then, he'd met with the Recreants in Andel, promising them the moon when he didn't even have Stars to give. And now that he'd committed to helping Aeliana and the other Recreants, Enla was sure to have seen that possibility in his future. What did she think of it all?

These thoughts swirled through his mind as he and Riveran ate and waited for the Sun's sleep. Even then, they sat in the darkness for at least two more hours until the first hint of scuffling sounds was heard on the other side of the passageway. When Enla's blonde locks finally came into view, Gaeren and Riveran scooted back, allowing her space to crawl through and out the other side.

When Enla stood, even the dust clinging to her dress and hair couldn't detract from her regal grace. Gaeren saw the admiration in Riveran's gaze and wasn't sure if he should smack Riveran for forgetting she was married and bonded to someone else or smack Enla for prioritizing tradition instead of Riveran.

"I'm so glad you're here." While there was warmth in her voice, her eyes held the same vacancy they had in the soldier's memories, lending a coldness that made Gaeren shiver.

"I'm so glad you show your joy over my presence by welcoming me with a clean room and some sort of dinner affair," Gaeren teased.

A faint smile crossed her lips, but it was an echo of her usual mirth.

"What's wrong?" he asked.

"Nothing yet," she said. "Mother and Father might not welcome you, so I was hesitant to alert them to your presence. I figured this way you could be here without it being known you're here. For now."

Riveran hummed his understanding, accepting the explanation without question, but Gaeren frowned. "You're lucky I didn't come through the front gates."

"It's never about luck. I foresaw what you'd do." The words held a lightness, like their usual banter, but something made her teasing fall flat.

"What else is wrong?" he asked.

She sighed and looked away. "The others think I've become less reliable." The words fell off her lips like they tasted bitter.

"What others?" Gaeren asked.

"Mother and Father. Croft."

"Croft?" Riveran tensed.

Gaeren shot him a look. Just because Riveran didn't like the other man didn't mean they should jump to conclusions.

"A few of my visions have been wrong." She hesitated on the last word, like it wasn't accurate.

On a whim, he flipped over her hands, running his fingers along her pale skin in case he could feel through an illusion hiding a brand.

She made a face. "It's nothing like that. Tobias has been checking us all for brands daily—Mother and Father especially."

"So then you know Mayvus is alive?"

Enla hesitated. "Yes, although they're not sure they believe me now. I've just…mixed up some of the things I've seen. It's not a problem. I confused some of the minor details after seeing so many options."

"Enla," Gaeren said on a growl. "We've talked about—"

She held up a hand. "I know. I'm doing less searching."

Once again, her words didn't feel quite true, and Gaeren placed a hand on her arm, using his secondary spoke to assess the truth of her words while also tuning in to her memories. Some of them came through disjointed, reminding him of Marnok's broken mind. Even within her own memories, she wasn't sure which visions she'd seen as possibilities versus which things had truly happened.

"You're not trying at all," he said. "You're letting every possibility come to your mind."

"How else am I supposed to direct an entire nation?" she hissed, wrenching her arm away to break their touch. Her face held an anger he hadn't seen since they were children, her composure broken. But just as swiftly, she smoothed out her features and raised her chin. "Despite my confusion, we're moving forward in the right direction. Croft has brought the navy north to prepare a defense against the Recreants."

"The Recreants?"

"I've seen war coming to our doorstep."

Gaeren and Riveran exchanged a glance. They'd spoken with Velden's old friends. The navy was corrupt and full of Recreants. She'd likely just brought war to their doorstep.

"Just like you thought you'd seen me break my bond with Lenda?"

Her brow furrowed. "But you did."

He rolled his eyes and steered her toward the chair in his room, guiding her to sit down. "Now I did. But last time I was here, you thought I already had."

"It's good that you did." She ignored his concerns. "Lenda was sick for a while, but now she's free. If we announce your return, she'll come to thank you."

Gaeren hesitated. "Why would we announce my return if you think Mother and Father are still angry?"

"We won't." She looked up at him, but her eyes focused somewhere beyond him. "I'm just saying she would if we did."

Riveran's lips thinned as he pressed them together. "So you're saying you searched out a possibility you had no intention of pursuing."

"Yes." Enla frowned, somehow not seeing this as a problem when it had been strictly forbidden by her mentors for her sanity. "Seeking out those kinds of possibilities helps me understand where a person's heart is at in the present. I know that she's not angry with you because she would thank you if she could, which means I know for now she is safe to be considered an ally, not a threat."

Gaeren ran a hand through his hair, his frustration bleeding into his words. "When would Lenda have ever been a threat?"

Enla's gaze clouded over once more. "There was a time when I told you to lean into the bond, because if you hadn't, she would have gone public with your betrayal, making the entire family out to be untrustworthy."

Gaeren sat on the edge of his bed, placing his elbows on his knees and balancing his head in his palms. "What changed?"

Enla hummed in thought. "I'm not sure. It was something about your voyage to Rykarn. Something about that made her realize she didn't want to be tied to this family. I think she might have broken the bond herself if I hadn't told her to give it more time."

Gaeren shook his head in disbelief. "All while I was hoping she would do it."

"That's a coward's way out, Gaeren," Enla warned him. "It would have been far worse for her."

Even as Gaeren questioned his sister's sanity, he shrank under her chastising. "Well, it's done now," he muttered.

Enla's face brightened with a smile. "I think it helped Mother and Father see you as less of a threat and more of a nuisance again."

"Again?" Gaeren asked.

"Oh, stop," she said. "You preferred it that way. When Gullet returned, I think they suspected you might be coming. It's fortunate the guards didn't see you. I'll have to pay off the stable boys for their silence."

Riveran stood a little straighter. "Gullet's here? Did he have a message?"

"No message. Didn't you just send him home?"

Gaeren and Riveran traded looks. Why would Emeris have sent the bird without a message? What could that mean? Nothing good.

"I'd like to see Gullet," Gaeren said.

Enla's eyebrows rose, but she nodded. "I can fetch him in the morning."

"Why weren't you in meetings today?" Riveran asked.

Enla's face finally held the guilt Gaeren had wanted to see after all of her unauthorized sifting through the future. "I've been banned from council meetings for a week."

"A week?" Gaeren asked.

"Like a child being sent to her room," she added bitterly.

"What did you do?" Riveran winced.

"I was in the office. I suggested we pardon the dragon."

"Durriken?" Gaeren asked.

"They still hunt for him. He's been sighted outside of Islara. But he needs to live. Every path in which they kill him ends in darkness, in death." Her eyes darted left and right until Gaeren leaned forward and shook her back to the present.

"Stop sifting the future." He drew each word out, ensuring she heard him, insisting she focus.

She licked her lips and nodded. "It's just that it's constantly changing," she whispered. "I want what's best for the people. You know that, Gaeren. You know that everything I do is for the people. But there are so many variables. The paths I see shift and change, like the sands of the Bahlric Desert in the wind. I can't nail down what will really happen unless I keep sifting."

He shook her again. "You can't help anyone if you completely lose touch with the present reality."

She winced as his grip tightened, and Riveran pulled him away. "Leave her be for now."

"But she's killing herself," Gaeren argued.

Riveran held up a hand, and Gaeren finally noticed the way the other man's eyes had turned red. "I know, but you can't bully her into doing what's best for herself."

Gaeren clenched his jaw and sat back down on the bed, watching as Riveran kneeled before Enla and placed his hands on the sides of her face. "Enla," he murmured, "look at me." It was far too familiar a touch for an old bondmate when she was married and bonded to someone else. But where was Croft now? Playing war with the navy he'd procured from the south? What kind of navy could he stir up in this case anyway?

"Please take a break," Riveran said. "You're different from the last time I saw you. It's not healthy."

"You're different from the last time I saw you, too." Enla's eyes filled with tears, and she brushed a hand over the X on his forehead. "I'm so sorry," she whispered.

He dropped his hands and scooted back from her touch as if finally realizing how intimate it had been.

"Have Mother and Father regained their strength?" Gaeren asked.

Enla shrugged. "Not completely, but they have started participating in council meetings again. I think it's because they don't trust me anymore. They've been giving more authority to Croft too. And I suspect that when he returns, they'll have him take my place at many of the meetings."

"But he's only a prince consort," Gaeren argued. "He has no authority in his own right."

"He does if Mother and Father give it to him," Enla said.

Gaeren rubbed his eyes. "Is this why you asked us to come back? You made it sound like you saw visions of something. Something we needed to know."

"I did?" Enla asked. Her brow furrowed once more, and she looked around the room as if it might hold answers to his question. "Oh, yes. Emeris is coming."

"Emeris is coming here?" Gaeren couldn't hide the disbelief in his tone. There were probably a thousand possibilities for the future, and now she was latching on to the ones that seemed the most concerning, even if they were the least possible. "Emeris was too weak to leave the fortress. The soldiers were guarding her in case Mayvus returned."

"I don't—" She glanced at her hands, which she opened and closed, as if weighing the possibilities in her hands. "I think so. It felt so real. I saw her arrive with two men announcing themselves as ambassadors from the eastern province. When that happens, you need to show yourself—to vouch for them."

"I think it's time you tried taking your tonics again," Riveran said, swiping the wetness from his eyes, "the ones that help you sleep. See if you can take a break from sifting. You need to find a way to turn it off."

She shook her head. "This one was close to the surface. I didn't even have to dig far for it. I'm certain of it." She reached out a hand to squeeze Gaeren's arm, sending him a barrage of images that made his head ache.

He shook her off. "Fine. It's all right. I believe you. Emeris is coming with a delegation and I should vouch for her. Is that all?" At this point, the truth of her visions no longer mattered. They needed to figure out how to calm her down and settle her magic.

"Please take me seriously," she begged, her gaze clouding over. "If you don't vouch for her, everything changes."

"I said I'll do it." He wrapped his arms around her as if he could smother the visions out of her. "Now please—stop searching."

She relaxed under his grip. "I'll stop."

He glanced at Riveran, whose lips pursed while he blinked profusely.

Gaeren had been right to come. Enla needed him here. But now he worried he'd waited too long.

CHAPTER 65

Gaeren tried to watch Enla closely after that. She'd spewed so much chaos he no longer knew what to believe. But each possibility she'd mentioned held enough truth he had to at least consider them as possibilities. He and Riveran spent the next two days and nights hiding in Gaeren's room while Enla snuck them food. Gullet held no clues about his presence, meaning if any note had been sent, it had been lost in transit.

On the third day, their parents still kept Enla from the council meetings, but they let her return to the throne room in order to welcome the navy representatives arriving from Andel. Before she left, she crawled through the passageway, heedless of the way cobwebs clung to her braids and the way the loose boards snagged at her silk.

"Today you must come," she said to Gaeren. "Remember the alcove where we would watch as children?"

Gaeren nodded, picturing the small space at the edge of the throne room, most likely intended for servants to be ready at a moment's notice. They'd observed many of their parents' outbursts and questionable rulings from that vantage point, forever tainting Gaeren's impression of them.

"Be there to watch the naval officers return. They won't be alone."

He pinched her arm when her gaze wandered, forcing her to focus again on him. It was a cruel trick he'd used when they were young, but it was also effective. And he wasn't willing to let her fall back into her dangerous sifting. "I'll be there."

She nodded, then retreated through the passageway once more.

"Are you really going?" Riveran asked as Gaeren rifled through his drawers for fresh clothes.

"Of course I'm going. Why wouldn't I?"

"If she was wrong about what she sifted, you could be caught by your parents. All your efforts to hide from them would be wasted."

"And if she's right?" Gaeren asked, unwilling to hold Riveran's gaze. Neither one of them had wanted to consider that possibility. Not only did it mean that some of Enla's visions still rang with truth, but it meant things hadn't gone well in Myndren.

"If her vision was right, wouldn't Emeris come find you?"

Gaeren paused, considering Riveran's perspective. "Maybe. But I've learned things no one else has heard by eavesdropping in that alcove. There are things we might need to know, and this could be the only way to discover them."

Riveran winced, and a memory came to Gaeren with so much force that he took a step back. Riveran stood in the throne room, kneeling before Enla and the king and queen, offering out his hand while his head remained bowed. It was fleeting but strong, the precipice of time that had changed everything for Riveran and Enla. Everything for Gaeren as well.

As the memory cleared, Gaeren's breath came quick, like he'd just run to his hideout in the swamp and back. "I guess I didn't see everything that went on in the throne room," he murmured.

Riveran blinked rapidly and looked away.

"You can stay here," Gaeren offered. "In fact, it's better if you do. If I vouch for Emeris, but my parents disown me for my treasonous actions, it's better for you not to be found with me. If I don't return before the night's end, you should go back to the harbor. Take Gullet with you, and send word to Aeliana."

He pulled the star-shaped bead from his starlock's necklace and passed it to Riveran, whose face held all the conflict Gaeren felt stirring within his own soul.

"You know it's the best course of action," Gaeren said. "Even if you don't like it."

Riveran swallowed hard and nodded, taking the bead from Gaeren. "May the Sun's light always shine upon you," Riveran said.

"And may the Stars' light always guide you," Gaeren responded, the words holding less irritation than they usually did.

By the time he'd changed and made it down to the alcove without being seen, the throne room was full of servants and soldiers. His uncle Danton and Tobias, the healer, stood on the dais, partially blocking Gaeren's view of the thrones. He nearly missed his parents' entrance, followed by Enla's. She approached her throne with trepidation, almost like she nursed a wound or struggled to remember which seat was hers. He itched to go to her aid and offer her a hand, then despised the fact that Croft wasn't there to do that very thing.

In fact, where was Croft?

Gaeren scanned the members of the navy for his brother-in-law. Before he could pick him out amongst the sailors, his father's advisor announced that the king and queen and the queen-in-training would receive the navy and hear their commitment to protecting the throne.

Formal bows were made, along with dry statements about their loyalty to the crown. There was little to garner Gaeren's interest until one sailor stepped forward, sweat pouring down his temple as he bowed low and raised a hand. The entire room went still as he requested the right to address the throne, a move that was either very brave or very stupid.

"Rise and state your case," the king commanded, warning in his tone. This man would likely receive demerits for approaching the throne without good reason. But then Enla turned her gaze Gaeren's way, nodding slightly. If she was right, this sailor had a very good reason.

"Your Honor, while in Andel, we were approached by a small delegation from the Myndren Mountains."

The king's eyebrows rose, which seemed to bolster the sailor's courage.

"At first, we thought it was a trick meant to gain passage to Elanesse. One of them claimed to be Emeris Wyndren. She had with her two men, one who is her husband and the other the son of witches."

A gasp rose through the room. What had Emeris and Rildan been up to since they'd left if they were in the company of witches? Unless… had Marnok returned? Was his status as the son of witches some sort of ploy they'd come up with to get attention? Or was this a truth about Marnok's past that he'd discovered?

"The final woman is a mystery. Even our progenies could not ascertain her identity. And she refused to answer questions."

Gaeren grinned. So, Orra had come. He'd assumed she'd stay behind because Enla hadn't seen her in her visions. But now that he thought about it, no one's magic seemed to work on Orra. She was either too far above it or too far below it, a strange truth that set her apart once more, alienating her from the people she cared about.

"They wished to come north in search of a peace treaty," the sailor continued. "They wanted to work together with Elanesse to protect Vendaras from Mayvus Wyndren."

This time, the gasps rose to murmurs that drowned out anything else the sailor might have said. A few of the soldiers called for order, drawing weapons to silence those who did not immediately obey. Gaeren allowed a small groan to escape his lips, hidden by the chaos. What made Emeris think this was where she'd find aid? They would have been better off in Andel, hunting for help among the remaining Recreants.

"So you brought them here," Gaeren's father said.

The sailor nodded, looking less certain than he had before. "If they were lying, we knew you would find the truth in their words. And if they were telling the truth, it seemed something you would wish to hear for yourself." The sailor dropped to one knee again, lowering his head and holding out his hand in a request for mercy for his approach to the throne.

The entire room held its breath as they waited for the king's response until he lazily waved a hand, palm up, signifying the man could go free. "Bring me these travelers and send for the progenies."

Gaeren dared to creep to the edge of the alcove where the shadow met the light, getting as close as he possibly could to catch sight of

Emeris, Rildan, Marnok, and Orra entering the room. The rest of the soldiers and sailors were dismissed, but they all lingered, hoping to catch wind of what the strangers had come to say. Tobias poured some concoction in the queen's drink while a servant fanned her.

"I thought I would require my gifted progenies to assess your identity," the king said, leaning forward and narrowing his eyes at Emeris. "But I can see your resemblance to Mayvus from up here with my old eyes. What truly brings you to my doorstep after so many years in hiding?"

Emeris curtsied and left her head hanging low, the respective deference almost comical in light of her constant humility as a priestess. "I apologize, Your Grace. I have not been in hiding for the last fourteen years, but rather imprisoned by my sister. Although, if I had not been imprisoned, I would have remained in hiding. It was never my intent to fight for the throne. I merely wanted to lead people to the Sun as a priestess in Celanoft, where you sent your son for his dedication year."

Gaeren grinned at the veiled accusation. He'd thought Emeris a pushover. But here she was referencing the fact that his parents had sent a spy in her midst within her very first sentence.

The king seemed equally taken aback as his brow furrowed and his scowl returned. "I don't see any chains or shackles on you now. So I will ask you again, what brings you here?" His father said the words slowly, and the soldiers at the edge of the dais took their cue from Gaeren's uncle Danton, the throne warden, and they stood a little straighter, their palms tightening on the pommels of their swords.

Emeris raised her head enough for Gaeren to see a sweet smile cross her features. "I've come to warn you of Mayvus' power. It seems you're aware of her method of branding and her preference for blood magic, so it should be no surprise that she remains a threat. We thought she'd been destroyed by the dragon. But she has found some old magic to keep her alive."

"Old magic?" the king asked.

"We have yet to identify its source," Orra chimed in. She made no effort to bow before the king and queen. Instead, she raised her chin high and clenched her jaw, her gaze darting around the throne room with disdain.

Gaeren nearly laughed out loud.

Enla turned a sharp gaze in his direction and shook her head slightly.

He bit his lip to hold it back.

"The fact is, Your Majesty," Rildan said, bowing low like his wife, "General Nels has received word from his scouts that Mayvus is building an army near Ahmranan's Viewpoint. It seems that she's bringing soldiers from Ahmranas."

Silence permeated the air for the briefest of moments. Even Gaeren felt a ripple of shock, though it was what they'd suspected before setting out on their hunt for the Sayhleen starbridge. Having it confirmed by Nels' scouts brought a terrifying reality to the suspicion.

But then the king was laughing, nearly choking. "Bringing soldiers across the barrier?" he asked.

"Yes," Emeris confirmed. "It's likely the fortress at the Myndren Mountains has already fallen to her men. When we heard her numbers were in the thousands, we set sail, both to find the other members of our party and to warn you. She will not settle for the eastern province you gave her. She will settle for nothing less than all of Rhystahn."

Gaeren barely held back his panic. Her numbers were in the thousands? Aeliana and Larkos would be sailing right past Ahmranan's Viewpoint, assuming they could make it through the icebergs. Could they get past the crazy priestess undetected?

The king still chuckled, a strange noise that permeated the air as they all let Emeris' words sink in. "Are you asking for our aid?"

Gaeren winced. Perhaps his own ambivalence toward the throne had made Emeris and the others think his father would be easily persuaded. Whatever hope they'd clung to was a waste. They never should have come.

"Yes," Emeris said. "If we work together with the Recreants, we can defeat her."

"You thought a dragon defeated her, but her old magic prevented its success. What makes you think together we can do better than a dragon?"

"Perhaps it has more to do with our motivation," Orra said. "The dragon sought revenge. He'd been her brand, and he wanted to pay back the woman who freed him by destroying the woman who'd imprisoned them both. But you and us? We are motivated by freedom. If we don't band together to stop her, we will all become enslaved, just like the dragon had been as her brand. If we don't fight, we might as well march back to Myndren and offer up our blood to her."

The king scowled, likely remembering the fact that he and his wife had recently been branded by Mayvus, but unwilling to admit that truth before these strangers. "You expect me to take you at your word when I don't even know you?"

"I expect you to send scouts to verify the truth of our words," Emeris said. "But I also expect you to prepare for war, assuming them to be true."

Gaeren glanced at the navy men. His parents already prepared for war, but on a different front.

"And what if your word isn't enough?" the king asked. "What if I don't want to send scouts all the way to the Myndren Mountains? What if I'm content to let you work out your family feud on the other side of the country?"

Gaeren sensed the pull to step forward, as strongly as if Enla had tied a string around his finger and tugged. His boot made the barest of scuffs on the marble floor, and the light hit his princely uniform— something he'd sworn he'd never wear again but had slipped on in the hopes that it might soften his mother's perception. Though it would probably anger his father.

"I will vouch for their word," Gaeren said. "Will that change your mind in any way?" He held his father's gaze long enough to see the man's face turn a deep red, almost purple, before he unsheathed his sword and took to one knee, balancing the tip before him and leaning his forehead against the pommel.

"If these men and women say Mayvus is building an army from Ahmranas, then Mayvus is building an army from Ahmranas. I watched them cross a barrier. I have crossed two of them myself. The starbridges are real. The people crossing the barriers are real, and they are dangerous. If Mayvus is building an army, then we need to build one faster. Because if we don't take an army to her doorstep and deal with this problem before it's too big, she will bring an army to our doorstep, and it will be too late."

"It's good to see you, Gaeren," Emeris whispered from beside him, "safe and sound." There was an unspoken question in her greeting.

"Aeliana is fine as well," he said. "But we lost Holm." He glanced up to see her falter in her bow. She raised her eyes to meet his, tears spilling over her cheeks.

"And Iris?" she whispered.

"Recovering from the loss," he said.

She nodded, then swiped at her face and resumed her bow, her shoulders shaking.

"Did you mean to send Gullet? He had no note."

This time Emeris looked up sharply. "We left Gullet with General Nels. So he could send word if Myndren was captured."

Rildan and Marnok exchanged stricken looks, and Orra's eyes slid shut.

Gaeren's father cleared his throat, a reminder that his patience was never long-suffering.

"When you returned, we pardoned you from your defection." The king's words rang out with an edge that everyone else probably heard as authority. But Gaeren knew the simmering anger that laced his father's tone. "But then you left again with treasonous remarks about your sister's choices and ability to rule. Why should we welcome you back with open arms, let alone take your word for these people who are suspected of being rebels in our midst?"

There was little Gaeren could say to redeem himself. So he let the silence ring out, choosing his words carefully. "Because I'm your son. And before you are the king, you are my father. And before Enla is a queen, she will always be my sister, and I her brother. Because we are family." He said the words firmly, nailing the truth of them in his mind even if he didn't always feel them in his heart.

It was the closest he could come to forgiving his parents, especially his father's abusive ways. He didn't understand their choices or their methods. But the Sun had seen fit to place them in a position of power and authority, even if it was just so that authority could be stripped away by someone like Emeris or Aeliana. Or by the people his parents were supposed to be ruling. He wanted nothing to do with their way of leading the country.

But they were still his family. And he would give them that small measure of respect in the hopes that he might receive it in return.

His mother blinked rapidly before downing the drink Tobias passed her with an unladylike speed while avoiding his gaze. His father flicked his wrist until his palm faced down, a mirror image of his pardon for the sailor who'd spoken out of turn.

"Take them all to the dungeons."

CHAPTER 66

It wasn't the first time Orra had been in the Elanesse dungeons, but considering Gaeren's agitation, it was likely his.

"It doesn't make any sense," he muttered, his grip tightening on the bars as he leaned his forehead against them. He peered down the dank hall as if one of the guards might suddenly appear and let them free. Marnok and Rildan sat with Emeris on the sorry excuse for a mattress in the opposite corner.

"I find that very little makes sense without a broader perspective than we might find from within these walls," Orra said.

Gaeren snorted, but Orra shot out her hand and grabbed his wrist, turning his palm over to see the scar from his bond mark. He pulled away from the bars, watching her warily, waiting for her judgment. She pulled back his sleeve and ran a finger over the braid around his wrist, sensing Aeliana's essence in it, feeling how it reached through time, marking her identity in ways the others couldn't sense.

"Is there a significance to your bracelet?" Orra asked quietly so the others wouldn't hear.

Gaeren stiffened, and Orra knew his noetic skills were bringing back every detail of the moment he'd asked about her own braid.

"It wasn't a gift, if that's what you're asking," he said.

"That's not what I'm asking." Orra released his wrist, and he covered the braid before leaning his forehead against the bars once more. The little she could see of his face in the shadows was lined with concern. "There's no shame in admitting she's more than a bondmate."

"You said he was more like a brother." Gaeren glanced at Orra's own braid. "I can't see her as a sister. Not like I did when we were children."

"There's no shame in that either." Orra held back her smile, worried he might feel mocked. "She's your other half. Maybe because of your childhood. Maybe in spite of it. You have to figure out what it means. It might not mean the same thing for you as it means for me. Unfortunately, it also might not mean the same thing for her."

He reached under his sleeve and twisted the braid. "Our paths keep crossing, but it could be a long time before they fully align. What if it simply means I'm supposed to protect her?"

"There's no shame in that either," Orra said softly.

Disappointment flitted across the young man's face. He'd have to figure it out on his own. She turned away, leaving him to his brooding so she could face Rildan, Marnok, and Emeris instead, the plink of water from a drain in the corner the only sound carrying between them. It brought back memories of Orra's days in this prison as Captain Redwood, and she wrapped her cloak tighter around her, scanning the stone floor for rats.

"It'll be all right." She said the words for the others, but more for herself. "They can't ignore us in here forever."

"Will your father give us another hearing?" Emeris asked wearily. When Gaeren didn't answer, Orra turned to find his head angled their direction, brow furrowed as he studied a greenish puddle by his boot.

"He won't give you another hearing, but he's likely to hear me out. I suppose that's what Enla saw that made her tell me to vouch for you."

"There's some of that broader perspective," Orra murmured.

He let go of the bars to bang them with his fists instead, then flopped down on the ground. He immediately stood again with a grimace, wiping at the damp spots on the back of his trousers. "I didn't even think they used this place anymore."

"They probably don't," Orra said. "But then they've never captured a Wyndren before. Only a handful of kings and queens have used this place."

"It's probably been here since Queen Amaya ruled," Gaeren muttered.

"No," Orra corrected. "It was built at least a hundred years after."

He squinted over at her. "I suppose you would know. You were probably around when she ruled. Riveran and I wondered if she was a descendant of yours. Her statue looks like you."

Orra raised an eyebrow. "I don't remember the name of every persona I've taken on, but some are impossible to forget."

His face blanched and his mouth swung open. "You were Queen Amaya?"

The others gave startled gasps, making Orra regret the admission. How was it this group of Recreants managed to make her give up details of her past that she'd always preferred to keep hidden?

"I guess that makes you some sort of great-great-great—and then some—grandson of mine."

He ran a hand through his hair, his eyes darting wildly as he put the pieces of her past together. "And that's why the Elanesse line has so much magic. Not because your son killed a Star, but because he already had such a high concentration from you."

Orra lifted a shoulder. "Both factors played a role." She'd been newly grounded in those days, floundering in her grief. She'd felt old instead of ageless, but after hundreds more years stuck on the earth, she looked back, and her former self seemed so young and foolish.

Despite being lost, she'd risen in the ranks quickly, catching the eye of the sad and lonely king whose parents had expired in the War of the Great Divide. Ruling the people had been a way for her to maintain some of the authority she'd been stripped of. It had felt right, even though now she knew it wasn't. That authority had been removed for a reason.

"How does Aeliana fare?" Emeris' tentative question startled both Gaeren and Orra.

Gaeren pulled away from the bars and clenched his fists. Orra held back a smile, sensing the change in him, both physically and emotionally.

"She's well," he said, "but they're sailing north and east to head for the Myndren Mountains. I don't know how we'll keep them from falling right into Mayvus' trap. So Aeliana might not be well for long." He pounded on the prison bars once more. "I never should have left. Maybe Enla didn't reel me in to a trap, but I'm stuck all the same. I thought I could stand by Enla's side and serve the Recreants from a place of power. Actually do something to help them."

"We've all placed bets with our decisions," Marnok said. "And now we've lost the gamble."

"My parents can be… ruthless with their authority, but every decision they make is calculated with precision." Gaeren paced the small chamber. "I don't know why they wouldn't at least listen to you. The fact that you oppose Mayvus should be enough to convince them to listen. They hate her after having been branded by her."

Rildan leaned forward, his elbows on his knees. "I'd forgotten they were branded. A lot has happened to us in the last few moons. And I'm sure a lot has happened to you. Who's to say they haven't been through a lot as well? For all we know, they're branded again."

"Supposedly Tobias has been keeping watch over that," Gaeren muttered. "But now I wonder if he's up to something with all those tonics he gives Mother."

As the heaviness of their situation settled over all of them, their stories came out. Rildan and Marnok filled in most of the gaps for Gaeren when it came to Myndren's presumed fall and their premature escape, while Gaeren gave details about the others' time on Sayhla Island.

"The Sayhleens were always a proud people," Orra mused. "Not in a haughty way like the Ahmranans, but in an honorable way. They had to defend themselves against everyone else who saw them as inferior ever since they were cursed by the sprites. Although that was a thousand years ago. People groups change just as much as individuals."

Gaeren's brow furrowed, and she waited for him to finish his story, to tell of the way he and Aeliana had broken their bonds together. When she was stronger, she could have read his memories in a blink to learn the details for herself. Now… well, now she couldn't spare the magic.

But Gaeren had latched on to her words, picking them apart until he needed answers to his own questions. "Velden told us the Sayhleens worship the sprites, but it seems like they don't even know what they worship. If they met the sprites I met, they'd want nothing to do with them."

Orra hummed, letting her mind sift through the little she knew of the sprites. Like most of the Stars, she'd found them detestable because of their origins, but since being grounded, she'd merely avoided them. How much more could she offer if she'd taken the time to learn more about them?

"Perhaps they wouldn't want to worship them," she admitted. "But Aeliana and Cyrus were surprised that you could worship a Sun who seemed harsh and unforgiving. A Sun whose favor has to be earned when the Stars they worship freely give their love."

Emeris sat up straighter. "Surely Aeliana doesn't still worship the Stars? Not after all the ways I trained her back in Myndren?"

"You even told us they were wrong about the Stars," Gaeren added. "That the Sun was the creator."

Orra closed her eyes and sighed. "You heard the truth you wanted. Yes, the Sun is the creator. But its love far exceeds what the Lorvandans believe about the Stars. The benevolence Stars can give is a mere reflection of the love given by the Sun. Your perspective is also tainted."

"Are you suggesting some of what the Sayhleens believe is true?" Gaeren asked.

"I'm suggesting they are just as confused and biased as everyone else. And that they shouldn't be looked down upon for believing the parts they understand. We call them cursed by the sprites. They call themselves created by the sprites. So they worship their creator. They don't have to like the sprites in order to respect them. Fear can breed respect. Sometimes it's unhealthy. But it's still respect."

"If the sprites created the Sayhleens," Gaeren asked, "who created the sprites? I can't imagine the Sun, whom you describe as so loving, would create such terrible creatures." His words came out bitter, and Emeris flinched.

"Of course they were created by the Sun," the priestess said. "Everything was."

"What about creatures who become dark spirits when they die?" he asked.

Even Orra stilled at that. "The dark spirits," she murmured, piecing together things she'd seen over the years, truths she'd not taken the time to fully understand. "It's a progressive deterioration. And also a cyclical form of destruction."

"What are you talking about?" Gaeren asked.

"Haven't you noticed the way the sprites hold characteristics of people? They're obsessed with knowledge and power. A certain type of person is willing to do anything to seek out that power."

"Are we talking about Mayvus now?" Gaeren asked.

"Mayvus is a prime example," Orra admitted. "But she is one of many over the last thousand years. Really since the beginning of time. Sprites were created by the Sun in their original form, but they're a twisted version of their past. Some of them I recognize. But not all. My reclusive lifestyle has kept me from meeting everyone who chose that path over the years."

Gaeren's face paled. "Are you saying—? Are sprites people who once practiced blood magic?"

Orra nodded, her heart aching. "They can't obtain the ultimate power they seek, but they come just close enough that it's clear they've severed all hope of reconciliation with the Sun. They can't leave Rhystahn and join the Sun in death, so they take a new form. And again, as you've pointed out, when they die as sprites, they become wisps of darkness, bent on repeating the cycle with new people practicing blood magic."

Gaeren's mouth swung open in disbelief.

"They become even less of what they once were," Orra said. "Because at one time, they were all half-lights."

"Maybe Riveran had the right idea," Gaeren muttered. "Maybe we should kill them all."

"And yet the Sun finds ways to use them, even in their darkness." Orra blinked away the tears threatening to spill over and glanced at Marnok, whose cheeks turned pink.

The grind of metal on metal met their ears, and everyone turned to the hall. A soldier led a man, bent by age, in a slow, painful walk to their cell.

"Father Fernandus," Gaeren breathed out.

"May the Sun's light give you guidance in whatever troubles you," the old priest murmured, stumbling to his knees on the stone. The soldier looked like he might offer assistance, but the priest waved him off, then continued gesturing for the soldier to back up. "Let the boy speak his confessions in private."

The soldier hesitated but eventually stepped away.

"Enla sends her love," Fernandus whispered and winked.

"She has a funny way of showing it," Gaeren said. "She needs to give a message to Riveran. Tell him to use the bead. He needs to tell Aeliana that Mayvus gathers her army at Ahmranan's Viewpoint. Aeliana needs to turn back because Emeris is here."

"And what about you?" Fernandus asked. "How can I help you?"

Gaeren shook his head. "When my father decides I've learned some sort of lesson, he'll let me loose. It's these people you need to help." He gestured behind him, and Fernandus took in Orra, Emeris, Marnok, and Rildan.

The old man's gaze rested on Orra. "Sun help us all." His voice held awe. "You're here to fix everything."

Orra went still, then dropped to her knees, ignoring the way the stone jarred her bones. "What have you seen?"

He shook his head. "I've heard whispers. In the silence of the morning. When the Sun's rising in the east. A Star to guide us all." He reached out and placed a gnarled hand on her cheek. "Your burden is heavy. The Sun will make it light."

"You're not—" Gaeren started, then hesitated. "Only progenies can sift the future."

"But the Sun can speak when it pleases." Orra closed her eyes in relief. "Thank you, Father."

The soldier cleared his throat. "I think you've all had enough prayer for today."

"There's never enough," Orra said even as Father Fernandus accepted the soldier's hand to rise. A warmth rose in her, stirred up by the hope in the priest's words. It bled through to her skin, making it take on the faintest of glows.

The old man winked at them all again. "May the Sun's light always shine upon you," he called as he left.

"And may the Stars' light always…" Gaeren turned back to Orra, his voice softening. "May the Stars' light always guide you."

The others all stared at her, and she turned to the bars, taking up Gaeren's former position.

"We should take turns resting," Rildan finally said. "It's bound to be a long night."

"You all go ahead," Orra murmured. "I have no need for sleep. Just the Sun's light."

She closed her eyes and leaned against the cold metal, wondering when she'd next be graced by its rays.

CHAPTER 67

THE FARTHER they got from Elanesse, the less Aeliana felt at ease. It was hard leaving Gaeren behind, but something else nagged at her, a suspicion that they were going in the wrong direction or making a wrong decision.

The weather turned painfully cold as they approached the Western Horn. True to Gaeren's prediction, Larkos had insisted it was too dangerous to sail this far north in the winter while Sylmar had insisted it was a warmer year and could be done. In an effort to appease both men, Aeliana had asked Durriken to fly north and check on the icebergs in the Northern Sea—maybe even melt whichever ones seemed most troublesome.

The old dragon had grumbled but eventually agreed. He insisted it was only to ensure Aeliana's safety and not to aid any war efforts.

Sylmar continued training her, but she noticed him looking at her differently, eyeing her palms with suspicion. She wasn't sure if the cuts on her palms made him suspect her of blood magic or if he'd given in to his fear that she was branded and watched for evidence of that. Either way, he was no longer trying to hide his suspicion.

His paranoia spread not just to her but to the others aboard the ship as well. Holm had never seemed to be branded, so really anyone could be the enemy. A sense of despair clung to everyone aboard the ship like a cloud carrying the weight and preparing to dump it in a torrent of rain at a moment's notice.

"Everyone is clean," Kendalyhn insisted while she and Aeliana sparred. While Iris had quietly settled into her grief, the younger woman had begun spending more time with Aeliana, the broken bond having severed whatever distrust lay between them.

"I think Sylmar's response would be that maybe it's you who's branded or that maybe Mayvus erased their memories of it."

"Sifting the soul is different from tuning in to memories." Kendalyhn rolled her eyes.

Aeliana used the distraction to knock the other woman to the deck, holding her dagger under Kendalyhn's chin. "How so?"

Kendalyhn shoved her away before standing and tucking her dagger back into her belt. "Memories can be erased, but motivation can't be unlearned. The desire to serve a master who's branded you would still stand out when sifting your past."

"What did you see when you sifted Holm's soul?" Aeliana sheathed her own dagger and wiped the sweat from her forehead.

Kendalyhn hesitated. "His devotion to Iris. I suppose Mayvus found some way for that motivation to mask anything else I might see."

Aeliana flinched. "I suspect that's why Sylmar doesn't trust it. Not when lives depend on it."

"How is your somatic training going?"

"It still feels muted," Aeliana admitted. "Like the well of energy I once accessed has run dry." Except even that wasn't quite true. She still felt the power surging inside of her and through her starlock. But now it rejected her efforts to use those somatic skills. She'd reverted back to being able to heal minor cuts and injuries, but little else.

It shouldn't have frustrated her. Not after she'd wanted to be rid of her magic for so many years. But now that she'd seen the good it could do, she hated losing access to it. Nori's glassy eyes flashed in her mind again, a constant reminder of the cost of losing her magic.

"You should train extra with Lukai," Kendalyhn suggested. "He doesn't mind. Especially now that things have normalized between you two."

Aeliana nodded. Things had gone better the last time she'd trained with Lukai. Her skills seemed to improve faster now that they'd worked through the mess of their bond. But the sense of wrongness around her grew, and a pain started in her palm that felt strangely reminiscent of her old bond. But it was in her right hand instead of her left. She ran a finger over the brand mark connecting her to Durriken.

"I think I might go lie down instead," she said slowly.

"If you need to talk later, you know where to find me." Kendalyhn's offer was both encouraging and strange considering Aeliana knew she'd find the other woman with Lukai.

She made her way to the captain's quarters, which now had a distinct feminine flair after Iris, Kendalyhn, and Aeliana had filled it with seashells, hair pins, and clothing. Aeliana set aside the clean garments that needed folding and lay down on the bed, closing her eyes and doing her best to reach out through the brand instead of collapsing into an exhausted slumber.

The tether grew taut when she sensed Durriken's presence, then his memories came forward, revealing waters full of ships as well as icebergs.

Where are we? The question filled her mind more than it came out in words, but Durriken seemed to understand.

I came to the Northern Sea like you asked. But this is what I found. Their words carry on the wind. They speak as if they follow Mayvus' orders.

Panic surged in Aeliana, threatening to break her hold on her tether with Durriken. They wouldn't be able to pass a fleet like that and remain undetected. How could they possibly reach her parents?

Should I destroy the ships? His words came out in a growl, and Aeliana sensed the heat of the fire in his throat, eager to be released.

No. Mayvus could be aboard any of the ships.

All the more reason to get started. Durriken brought his stump against his chest, stroking it with his good set of talons. *I have a mind to take her apart piece by piece. Give her a taste of the pain she caused me. It's messier than fire. But far more satisfying.*

No. Aeliana tried to send the word through more firmly. *Her life is tied to my mother's. That's why she didn't die when you took her to the cave. Even if you could kill her, it might kill my mother.*

Sylmar's theories about the sisters needing to be together to die felt too impossible to trust. But even worse, if he was right, the curse would keep them both from dying. Any injuries inflicted on Mayvus would cause Emeris to suffer the same fate.

The conflict Aeliana sensed from Durriken left her uneasy. He didn't have the same affection or interest in Aeliana's mother's safety. The only thing holding him back was that he knew it would upset Aeliana. She had to hope that would be enough to stay his fire.

Can you tell what they're doing? Are they planning to sail to Myndren?

I'm not sure. A memory flashed through Durriken's mind and in turn Aeliana's. A time when Durriken's perch in a cave brought him close enough to the soldiers to catch bits and pieces of their conversations without his presence being known. They spoke mostly of the promises they'd been given by Mayvus, their certainty that they could leave the frigid land of Ahmranas and live comfortably under Mayvus' rule.

We can't travel through the Northern Sea to get to Myndren. We'll never get past them.

Aeliana felt more than heard Durriken's affirmation. *What if I just burn most of the boats?* His eager offer eased some of the tension that had been growing along their tether.

Not yet. I promise, if there's a need, you'll be the first dragon I let use his fire.

He harrumphed. *I'm the only dragon. And you couldn't stop me from burning them if you tried.*

But you'll wait? A strange mixture of remorse and hatred ran through her, feelings from Durriken that weren't her own.

I'm not eager to kill so many again. Not unless there's a true need. If you find a need, I will be there.

You're not a weapon for me to direct. It's your choice. The confusion she'd sensed gave way to peace.

I know. She let the tether slide through her as she loosened her hold, like a rope gliding through her hands as it lengthened the distance. When the view of the ships in the frigid waters receded to give way to the captain's quarters of *To the Deep and Back,* she took in an unsteady breath.

Something about the room felt different. The door was open and light flooded in. Had Iris or Kendalyhn been in?

"What did he see?" The gruff words startled her, and she sat up, whipping around to catch Sylmar sitting at the desk, his staff laid out before him.

"How long have you been here?" she asked.

"Not long."

"Why are you here?" She glanced between him and the door. She had no reason to fear Sylmar, but the surprise at his presence left her on edge, making her wish someone else was here for this conversation.

"It was time to work on your magic. When you didn't show, I thought maybe you were avoiding me."

She winced. "I'm not avoiding you. I'm just—my magic feels like it's fading."

"Perhaps it's finally normalizing," he muttered. "It's almost like your magic leeches off of those around you. Healing when you're near Lukai and Marnok. Tuning in to memories when you're with Gaeren. I wondered if maybe it would be different now, without Gaeren's presence."

"I thought you said the noetic skills came from Durriken." She frowned. "Leeching magic off others doesn't sound like any type of magic you've described."

He raised his eyebrows. "Doesn't it?" It felt like he was insinuating something. Instead of trying to figure out his cryptic comments, she changed the subject.

"We can't keep traveling this way."

He stiffened. "Why not?"

"Durriken showed me the Northern Sea. It has icebergs like we feared, but it also has something far worse. Dozens of ships. An entire fleet. They seem to be with Mayvus, although I didn't see her. We could never get past them. Not by water."

Sylmar frowned, and she imagined him weighing the few remaining possibilities.

"And this information came from Durriken?"

She nodded.

"Because you're tethered to him through your brand mark? Are there any other connections you have that we should know about?"

The full weight of his implication sank in, stinging deeper when she realized he suspected she was leeching others' magic through brands and blood magic.

Aeliana stood, eyes narrowed. "I'll go share my news with Velden and Kendalyhn. Don't ever forget that you're the one who asked me to maintain my brand with Durriken. You instructed me to learn about Vendaran culture and history so I can step up and lead. I'm doing my part, but if you won't fully trust me, you're setting me up to fail. I don't know what more you want from me." She turned to leave, but Sylmar grabbed her arm.

"I don't know either. I don't feel like I know anything anymore. Not after Holm." He sighed and scrubbed his free palm over his face.

His vulnerability gave Aeliana pause, making her soften her tone. "Iris is right. Holm wouldn't want us losing trust in each other because he fell prey to Mayvus' methods. The strangeness of my magic has nothing to do with Mayvus. Half of my blood is Lorvandan. I may never get all my magic back because of it. And yes, I was raised around blood magic, but don't ever assume that means I'd turn to it. I'm only using the connections I have the way you've taught me." She shrugged off his hand, but before she left the room, his voice rose once more.

"What if I'm the one who's branded?" His voice came out strained. "What if I don't even know it? She had access to my blood for years. Who's to say she hasn't pulled out some old vial and made herself privy to all our plans?"

Instead of turning, Aeliana stared at the doorframe, contemplating the possibility while running her finger along the pattern of the wood. "We beat her once. We can do it again." She glanced over her shoulder.

He nodded, then looked away. "I'll speak with Larkos about turning around. He was never keen on sailing through the Northern Sea in the winter anyway. Gave me all sorts of warnings about how we'd be forced back to land by icebergs and sea monsters."

"So what? We'll travel inland? Or go back around the Southern Horn?"

Sylmar's mouth pressed together in a grim line until it disappeared beneath his facial hair. "Perhaps. But if she's formed an army that large with ships, it's far worse than I imagined. It's too late for us to go to Myndren. She'll beat us there and tear it down."

If they couldn't return to Myndren, they were out of options. "So we do the reckless thing," she mused. "We go back and join forces with the royal family."

Sylmar's eyes widened in surprise. He opened his mouth as if to argue, then closed it, nodding his acceptance. "And hope we're not leaving the jaws of one enemy just to offer ourselves up to another."

Sailing back to Elanesse took longer thanks to the winds, but it still felt too short for Aeliana. Her plan to ask the royal family for help felt full of flaws. Even if the Loyalists did team up with the Recreants to fight against Mayvus, the curse still hadn't been broken. They needed to find the rest of it in Dehvlon before they could truly go after Mayvus. As long as the curse was intact, going after Mayvus was the same as going after her mother.

Her dread over the whole affair meant she was suddenly standing in the palace's main hall waiting to be received by the king and queen while desperately hoping to be greeted by Gaeren instead. She twisted her hands until Sylmar's slight shake of the head made her stand straighter and smooth out her shirt before forcing her hands to relax against her sides.

In case things didn't go well, most everyone else had stayed back on the ship, leaving Aeliana, Sylmar, and Velden to hopefully broker some sort of deal.

"You say you're friends of Prince Gaeren?" The royal guard standing before them looked skeptical as he took in their appearance.

"We've spent some time sailing with him," Aeliana said, and the guard relaxed a bit more, his eyes flashing with understanding.

"Prince Gaeren is currently indisposed and cannot take visitors."

Aeliana tensed at the vagueness of his words. A million questions rose to her mind, but they weren't likely to be answered.

"I can see about getting you on the schedule for when the king receives requests from the people."

"How long will that take?" Sylmar asked.

The guard lifted his chin and looked down his nose as though offended by the question. "He's generous enough to see people twice a moon. The last time was a few days ago."

Sylmar's grip tightened on his staff. "That's too late," he said. "We bring news of pending war from Mayvus in the east."

At this, the guard raised an eyebrow. He said nothing for so long that Aeliana wondered if that had been their dismissal. But then she noticed his starlock. Was he invading their minds? She squirmed, sensing her mind shuffling through all the things she thought should be kept secret before being replaced by random memories that held no value, thanks to Sylmar's training. Even so, she hadn't been trained enough to defend against that kind of magic and feared it would be their downfall.

Eventually the royal guard gave a short nod. "Very well, come with me."

He took them to a waiting room with several chairs and a long table. Trays of fruit and cheese were brought in as though they'd been expected. Then they waited for what seemed like hours before the guard returned, beckoning them down a long hall. Another set of guards flung open doors that led to a room ten times as wide as any stargazer and three times as high.

How had a room like this been hidden inside the palace?

Aeliana's mouth swung open as she examined the opulent floors and detailed tapestries. Images of past kings and queens lined the walls as she, Sylmar, and Velden stepped forward and walked along the length of a red and gold carpet, each portrait taking on more and more of Gaeren's features the closer she got to the dais. The guard's introduction of their party was lost to her as she took it all in, and her distraction by the finery made her late to catch the three ornate ivory chairs, their occupants crowned.

A moment later than was likely respectful, she gave a low curtsy, eyeing Sylmar's bow from the corner of her eye to determine when it was appropriate for her to rise.

Were those Gaeren's parents and sister? They had to be. Every bit of her longed to raise her eyes and study them, to see the sister he spoke so highly of, the sister he would give his life for. Morbid curiosity made her also want to study the parents who'd either abused or ignored him for so many years in favor of dictating a country and raising the next queen.

"You may rise and state your case," the king said.

Because she'd been a hair late with her curtsy, Aeliana remained lowered a bit longer than Velden and Sylmar. But when her chin rose, her gaze shot to the younger woman she suspected was Enla. Her golden hair was braided in the front and the rest curled under her chin. Her blue eyes were as deep as Gaeren's, making Aeliana smile at their familiarity. But they held an uncertainty, like Enla wasn't truly present in this room.

Aeliana inhaled sharply at the sight of a silver heart starlock pressed against Enla's forehead. She'd seen it before, but she couldn't quite recall where—either a dream or a memory. Perhaps one of the visions she'd received in her Awakening.

"Well?" The king's irritation bled through that one word, and Aeliana snapped her gaze back to him.

"We've come to warn you of troops in the east," Sylmar said. "Mayvus is gathering an army, and we suspect she will regain Myndren if she hasn't already."

"We are well aware of the possibility," the king said, making Sylmar's face grow slack. "If you have nothing else to tell us, then you can be on your way."

"Will you let her regain it?" Sylmar asked.

The king's eyes narrowed, and he leaned forward. "I have no need to explain my war tactics to you."

"And what if we come offering aid?" Aeliana asked.

Sylmar eyed her warily. They'd come asking for the king's aid, which seemed far different from offering their own. But she refused to leave without trying everything.

The king sat back, his expression still distrustful. "Go on."

"Perhaps you already know that it was a large faction of Recreants who eventually subdued her."

"For a time," the king corrected.

"For a time," Aeliana agreed. "It came at a high cost for the Recreants, making them eager to ensure her demise. They are motivated to help. Their numbers aren't as mighty as they once were, but they are still powerful. Inviting them to help defeat Mayvus again would be like taking a baby chick under your wing. Perhaps they can help you defend or retake the fortress at Myndren Mountains, but perhaps teaming up with them is simply a way to keep them content and confident you're looking out for their best interests instead of your own, making them less eager to wage war on you next."

The king stroked his beard, considering her words. "Another delegation came here mere days ago, offering similar information, but with far less compelling arguments."

Aeliana stilled. "Who?" She pressed her lips together, realizing she'd spoken out of turn, but it was as if the question awakened Enla, and the younger woman smiled benevolently.

"Your mother and father, along with two old friends."

"They're here?" Aeliana wrung her hands once more, no longer able to control her nerves.

Enla glanced pointedly at her father. "They *were* here." She let the words hang in the air, her gaze never leaving her father's face.

"Tell me," the king commanded, "where is Mayvus getting her army?"

"From Ahmranas," Aeliana admitted.

The king stiffened, and Aeliana waited for him to call her out for insanity. Instead, he gave a brisk nod. "Take them to the guest rooms and have their stories verified by the progenies. We'll reconvene in the morning."

Aeliana glanced at Sylmar, her nerves rising, but pride shone in his face as he gave her a nod.

CHAPTER 68

THE SCREECH of the hall door opening made everyone in the prison sit up straighter. Gaeren stood and gripped the bars, leaning against them to see as far down the hall as he possibly could. A ray of light shone as a door opened. It wasn't their normal time frame for food or personal needs. Maybe it was Fernandus again, but this time with news from Riveran.

Instead it was one of the guards, and a different sort of hope rose in Gaeren's chest.

"Prince Gaeren." The guard gave a stiff nod in his direction, the title acknowledgment making Gaeren close his eyes in relief.

Something had changed.

The guard shoved a key in the lock. "Your father has rescinded his temporary judgment on your treasonous acts as well as on our guests' possible collaboration. New evidence has led him to reconsider the news brought forth by Emeris Wyndren, and deliberations will be held for how to proceed with joint efforts to eradicate Mayvus Wyndren's power."

Now everyone in the prison stood alongside Gaeren, their faces all holding the same shock Gaeren felt.

"Did he actually send out scouts?" Gaeren asked.

The guard hesitated. "Not to my knowledge. A second delegation arrived confirming your words. You'll have to ask your father for any more details."

"I *will* ask him," Gaeren muttered. "He owes these people an apology."

Shock rippled across the guard's features before he shuttered his expression back to the silent escort. As he led them through the dank hall of the dungeon, a rat skittered across the floor, and Orra let out an uncharacteristic gasp as she scooted closer to Emeris.

"I assume we'll be given rooms and attendance along with ample food and rest before we're expected to participate in these deliberations?" The question felt pompous after Gaeren's shift in politics, making him wonder if guards and servants within his own palace were part of the Recreants' movement. Because who would want to be treated the way the royal family treated most of their staff?

But it was meant to be more of a slight on his father and the poor treatment they'd received after approaching the king for assistance, and the guard's misstep made Gaeren suspect he understood.

"Of course, sir."

As much as Gaeren longed for the guard to pick up his pace, he and the others dragged, their energy levels low from a lack of food, sleep, and the Sun's light over the last two days. When they reached a section of the palace that started to resemble less of the dungeon and more of the royal rooms, the Sun's light streamed through windows, and they all slowed to soak in its rays. Orra even raised her hands and closed her eyes, a shiver running through her body as she soaked it in.

His father should be ashamed of what he'd done to these people— people who hadn't even been confirmed enemies. Things had to change, and Gaeren steeled himself to face the truth that he was the one who had to do it.

But it still came back to the same old question. Could he do it and spare Enla? And now he had the added complication of whether or not he could do it and spare both Enla and Aeliana.

The guard took them first to Gaeren's room, but Gaeren refused to be settled until he saw where the others were staying. He wouldn't put it past his father to escort him to his room and then return the others to the dungeon, fabricating some lie that they'd chosen to leave while letting them rot behind bars.

"My friends are not to be allowed to leave without my approval," Gaeren told the guard as Orra, the last of them, was given a room two halls down from Gaeren's.

The guard lifted a single brow.

"They're not my prisoners," Gaeren said, "but I want to hear it from their lips if they choose to leave."

A flicker of understanding crossed the guard's face, followed by his lips parting in surprise. It was yet another show of distrust in his father, but Gaeren no longer cared. It was time Enla took her place at the throne regardless of her confusion. It was time for their parents to step down. And as throne warden, he would defend his sister's right to the throne even from their own parents.

Instead of waiting for the guard to escort him, he used the small bit of energy that had infused him from the Sun's light to march his way to his rooms, the guard rushing to keep up. When Gaeren entered, he was surprised to see the room freshly cleaned, and his heart seized with fear for Riveran. Had his friend been caught?

A steaming bath and its fragrant soaps beckoned him from the other room, but he shut the door and made sure he was alone before sliding aside the dresser and checking the secret passage. Only cobwebs remained, without any note or sign that Enla or Riveran had used it recently.

"It's about time."

Gaeren's neck cracked as he whipped his head around to find his friend crawling out from under the bed, his frame seeming comically large as his chest got stuck.

"Are you just going to watch me or give me a hand?" Riveran reached out an arm.

Gaeren grinned, doing his best to pull his friend out, but without proper food and rest, he was weak, and they both ended up on the floor laughing. He dragged Riveran a handsbreadth at a time until the other man's legs were free. They both sat up, breathing heavily.

"Enla's been trying to convince them to free you, insisting most of your future paths hold the loyalty expected of a throne warden."

Gaeren winced, hoping it was a lie she told rather than more fruitless searching to confuse her compromised mind. "That's not why they released me."

Riveran nodded. "It's because Aeliana came."

All thoughts of food, sleep, and bathing flew from Gaeren's mind. "She's here? Under the same roof as my father?"

"Enla asked that she be given her own guest quarters across the hall."

Gaeren ran a hand through his hair, realizing mere feet and a handful of walls separated him from Aeliana. "And she's all right?"

Riveran shrugged. "Enla says she is. The information they gave matched with what you and her parents said, finally convincing your father that the threat was true. He's willing to consider working with the Recreants against a greater threat."

Gaeren shook his head. "I find that hard to believe. With all the progenies he has on hand, he could have tested our words at any point in time and he chose not to. What makes him suddenly trust them? What would ever make him willing to work with the Recreants?"

"Enla said they were tested by his progenies. He didn't give you or her parents that same honor, but perhaps that's part of the upcoming deliberations he has planned."

Gaeren squinted at his friend, his mind racing as he tried to map out the inconsistencies of his father's behavior. "But they brought the navy north to fight the Recreants."

"You're saying you don't trust your father's change of heart?"

Gaeren snorted. "That should have been assumed long ago. Right now I'm saying his reason for dishonesty in this scenario has me worried. What does he know that he's keeping from us? And is he really willing to deliberate, or is this some sort of farce?"

"I suppose we'll have to hear your father out to know for sure," Riveran said.

The idea of playing his father's political games left him exhausted, especially after sitting in prison for two days, where he'd had far too much time to think about all the decisions he'd made, both good and bad, that had led him to this point. "I want to check their hands for brand marks."

"Enla said Tobias reassured her they have none."

"Enla and Tobias didn't see how we were fooled by Holm." Gaeren pressed his lips together in a grim line, regretting his sharp tone. "I want to check for myself. And I want to see what tonics Tobias is giving Mother."

"That's fair," Riveran said.

"First, I should check on Aeliana." Gaeren stood, but Riveran also jumped to his feet and held Gaeren back.

"First, you should take a bath." He wrinkled his nose and shoved Gaeren toward the bathing room. "Aeliana will appreciate the delay."

CHAPTER 69

Aeliana paced in her room, which was starting to feel more like a prison cell than guest quarters. She'd opened the door twice, making excuses and asking for water or refreshments. But really it was to test to see if the guards were still there.

Sylmar was likely throwing a fit after them being separated for hours, and the thought finally made her smile in the midst of her concern. She'd tried sleeping and had even explored the room looking for any clues as to why they might have left her there, but it seemed like a standard guest room in a palace—far fancier than anything she'd ever stayed in. Still, there were four walls, a window that led to an impossible drop, and a door guarded by two armed men.

She wasn't free.

The knock that sounded was brisk and formal and made her jump up from where she'd sat perched on the edge of the bed.

"Yes?" she called.

"Her Royal Highness is here to see you."

Aeliana's heart picked up its pace. Enla? It wouldn't be Gaeren's mother, would it? It had to be Enla. "Yes, please. Send her in."

She smoothed down her linen shirt, remembering the silky waves that had billowed around Enla on her throne. But when the door opened, Enla stood there in loose-fitting trousers and a thin sleeveless shirt, far more casual than Aeliana had ever expected her to appear.

The guards balked when Enla tried shutting the door behind her, and though she glared at them, she left it open and turned back to greet Aeliana with a surprisingly warm hug.

"My father imprisoned your family," Enla murmured.

Aeliana stiffened, the warmth leeching from their embrace, but Enla tightened her grip and kept up her furious whisper.

"They've been released because you came, but I wanted to warn you—they were not well cared for. That will change now. I promise." She pulled back and gave a light kiss to Aeliana's cheek. "We're practically sisters since Gaeren spent his dedication year with your family." Her smile was too wide, not matching the troubled look in her eyes.

Clearly it was meant to show the guards that all was well, so Aeliana did her best to match the other woman's false joy.

"If only I'd had a sister." She squeezed Enla's hands in hers. "So yes, I'll claim you as mine." Aeliana led the queen-in-training over to a set of chairs and small table, awkwardly inviting her to sit as though it were Aeliana's home instead of Enla's.

A host of women came in delivering plates, napkins, tea, and biscuits, as if Aeliana and Enla had rung a bell for service. The pile of fruit and cheese on the platter was far more than they'd given Aeliana at her request for refreshments, and it was far more than the two of them could ever eat.

Remembering Enla's words about the prisoners' treatment, Aeliana made sure to tuck a little of everything in the folds of her napkin while they stumbled through surface niceties, discussing the room, the weather, and how Enla's day in meetings had gone. When the guards retreated to the hall, sufficiently bored, Enla let her inane chatter and laughter ring out as she helped Aeliana gather the food in napkins, shoving it all under pillows on the extra chair.

Eventually Enla leaned forward in the pretense of taking another biscuit and whispered, "Sylmar and Velden are angry that they haven't seen you, but they're catching up with your mother and Rildan in their room. My parents have offered to let the other members of your party stay in the palace, and I'll ensure they're kept safe. My father will have people listening in on everything they say, but at least they can begin making plans."

"Plans for what?" Aeliana asked warily.

Enla frowned, and her eyes grew distant. "Ever since my brother arrived, the paths have multiplied. With your arrival, they've become impossibly branched. If I took the time to look at them all, we'd be past all the possibilities before I even saw them."

Aeliana reached for Enla's hand, squeezing it hard until the other woman looked her way. "I don't want to see every possibility. I want to know what you, as queen-in-training and daughter of the king, think your father is going to do. Will he help us? Send us on our way? Or are we prisoners here?"

Enla started to shake her head, but then her eyes glazed over once more. She didn't answer for so long that Aeliana wondered if she'd lost the other woman to the future. It seemed like something Gaeren wouldn't want, but what was the best way to pull someone from such a trance? If she shook her, the guards would have her tied up before she could blink.

"You should speak with the man you call Marnok," Enla murmured, then raised her voice to call for one of the guards.

When he entered the room, he gave a slight bow, awaiting her instructions.

"Please send for Marnok. Aeliana wishes to see him."

"Of course, Your Highness." He bowed once more before exiting the room.

Aeliana frowned. "I'd really rather see my mother. She was often confused when I left her. I want to make sure she's well."

"We are all a product of our pasts." Enla's smile held a sadness that left Aeliana anxious. "For some of us, that means our minds are forever altered. She is well, even if at times it seems she's not."

"Is that what Gaeren would say of you?" Aeliana asked.

Enla winced. "You know my brother well." They stared at each other for a long moment, a strange understanding passing between them. "Thank you for helping him break his bond."

Aeliana's face heated, but Enla ignored her discomfort.

"Now he's free from obligations, at least the ones imposed on him by our parents and our positions. He's free to make choices about whom he serves and how."

"And what about you?" Aeliana asked.

"I will never be free," Enla said. "But this is also my choice. It's one very few could understand, but I've taken it on willingly."

Aeliana nodded. She probably understood even less than others who knew Enla well. But after fighting through the question of whether she was Vendaran or Lorvandan, she felt a small sense of camaraderie with Enla's position.

"Sometimes in life we aren't given choices," Aeliana said, "and yet the path we're forced down is still the one we would have chosen."

Enla's eyes cleared, and the first real smile lit up her face. It reminded Aeliana of Gaeren, and her chest seized with a need to see him.

"Very well spoken," Enla said, a teasing tilt to her lips. "You must be the daughter of a high priestess."

Before Aeliana could turn the conversation back around to her questions about the plan Enla had spoken of, the guard announced Marnok's arrival. Both women turned, and Marnok hesitated in the doorway before giving a stiff bow toward Enla. She waved off the formality and patted the chair next to her before rising.

"It's time I go see my brother anyway, now that he's bathed and eaten. I suspect he won't wait long to visit you, Aeliana, so your reunion with Marnok will need to be brief." She glanced meaningfully at Marnok's hands, which currently tugged uncomfortably at his collar.

Aeliana tensed, realizing Enla had probably already seen how this conversation played out and that was why she wanted Aeliana to have it. It was unsettling to know that Enla was both aware of Aeliana's need for answers about the tattoos and that Enla already had them.

But the other woman smiled serenely and gave Aeliana one last kiss on the cheek before sauntering out the door, taking all but the original two guards with her. The door remained open, and Aeliana debated shutting it but figured the guards wouldn't let her. Besides, her questions for Marnok had nothing to do with the royal family or politics.

"Are you well?" Aeliana asked, suddenly shy as she remembered Marnok's discomfort with her when they'd last seen each other.

He shrugged. "Well enough. We've been imprisoned for two days, but your arrival changed that. It could be worse."

"Why were you imprisoned in the first place?" Aeliana asked.

Marnok glanced at the door where the sleeve and sword point of one of the guards was visible. "I believe it's because your mother is a Wyndren. They weren't ready to trust her. Even Gaeren was imprisoned with us."

Aeliana sucked in a breath. "What?"

Marnok pulled grapes off a cluster, his hands shaking and reminding her of how hungry he must be. "It seems he's on the outs with his parents, and even his sister's goodwill wasn't enough to save him. You, on the other hand—something about your arrival made the king reconsider."

Aeliana shrank back in her chair, not wanting to evaluate what that could be. Besides, that wasn't the conversation she needed to have with him.

"Marnok," she began, then hesitated. "I know my mother showed you some of your past."

His hands stilled over the cheese, but their shaking seemed to increase.

"I expect you're not ready to share it, and that's fine, but I wondered if she showed you anything that might explain the tattoos on your hands. If that might be something you could help me understand."

With a frown, he took a piece of cheese, then popped it into his mouth along with several grapes. As he chewed, Aeliana watched a number of emotions pass through his expression, settling on some sort of determined resignation.

"Apparently it's not a well-known fact, but some of the highest witches in the various covens use tattoos to mark their status on their hands." He splayed his palms in front of him, allowing Aeliana to catch how the intricate pattern appeared somewhat faded compared to the darker lines on the backs of his hands.

"So that's why you went to the witches?" Her mind raced with the implications.

"I come from one of the highest orders among the witches." His brow pinched with pain. "They live deeper in the Myndren Mountains, near Mt. Vescano. Other covens travel there to make sacrifices at the mouth of the volcano during the equinoxes and solstices."

"My mother said you went there," she said, "but she made it sound like you were looking into the possibility of a witch having cursed her and Mayvus."

He gave a short nod. "It served a dual purpose."

"And you found your family?" she pressed.

He gave another short nod. "They don't exactly try to hide themselves. If you find the volcano, you find the witches. But what does this have to do with my tattoos?"

Aeliana set down her biscuit, her appetite gone. "When we were on Sayhla Island, Lady Merinnia gave me a memory of a woman with tattooed hands cursing my mother. It seems you all had the right idea when you thought it was connected to the witches."

"Maybe," he said. "But if they cursed your mother, they didn't share that information with me. I have no more answers than you."

Her heart sank, but she didn't completely lose hope. "The important thing is there's a way to break it." She leaned forward to lower her voice, hating that, for all she knew, the guards might be using magic to pull all this information from her, whether she whispered or not. "The curse is documented in the archives of the Dehvlonian Oracles, but I doubt we have time to find the starbridge and go there before we have to face Mayvus again. But what if we went to the witches? Surely they've documented their curses. I might even be able to find the witch I saw in the vision Lady Merinnia showed me."

Marnok shuddered, and Aeliana's confidence faltered.

"You'll be hard-pressed to find your answers among them. They hold no love for the Wyndren family. If they cursed your mother, they're not going to give you what you want."

Aeliana let out a huff. "I didn't expect I'd be able to waltz in and ask them how to break it, but I have to at least try. Maybe there's some way we can barter with them, or—"

"No," he interrupted. "Never make a deal with a witch. It's far worse than making deals with sprites." The haunted look on his face left Aeliana silent, but she'd gotten all the information she needed.

As his story had unfolded, she'd thought maybe she could ask Marnok to take her to the witches and help her, but it was clear he wouldn't be up for the task. This was something she would have to do alone.

"You're right." She swallowed down her fears and frustrations, pasting a smile on her face. "If we can't find the answers among the witches, we'll need to find another way. In the meantime, I could use your help training. My healing skills aren't what they used to be."

He smiled, but before he could respond, a commotion came from the hall with raised familiar voices. As one, Aeliana and Marnok rose, peeking out the doorway to find Gaeren, chest puffed out as he glared down at Enla, who smiled sweetly up at him, arms delicately crossed over her chest.

Gaeren's hands balled into fists. "I'm not waiting—"

"You don't need to any longer." Enla angled her head in Aeliana's direction, and Gaeren followed her line of sight, leaving Aeliana suddenly self-conscious about her drab appearance next to an almost-queen.

But Gaeren took two strides in her direction before wrapping her in a less-than-gentle hug, his frustration still fueling his strength. She didn't even have time to enjoy his nearness or wonder what it meant before he pulled back and snarled at the guards, "Aeliana and I are taking a walk in the gardens, and you two are not invited."

CHAPTER 70

To Gaeren's surprise, Aeliana's guards listened and stayed rooted outside her bedroom door. But it was most likely because his own guards shadowed them through the halls and out into the moonlit garden. After Gaeren speared a single look in their direction, they kept a respectful distance, and Gaeren finally felt free to speak.

"Did my father do anything to you?"

Aeliana's brow furrowed. "To me? You're the one he put in prison."

Gaeren rolled his eyes. "He had far worse disciplinary measures when we were children. I was fairly certain he'd release me eventually and call it a lesson."

Her eyebrows arched, and he gave a sheepish shrug.

"I could have been wrong, but I wasn't."

She glanced back at the guards and lowered her voice. "Enla seems just as much a prisoner. It's no wonder you had to come back."

Gaeren steered her through a grove of magnolias, hoping to block out the guards even more. "I hated leaving, but you have dozens of people protecting you. Sometimes I feel like my sister only has me. Besides, I knew you couldn't really leave. Less than a week away and you're already back?"

A breathy laugh escaped her lips, bringing his mind back to the night they'd kissed and the way her lips had felt on his. "Somehow, I suspect Enla has plenty of people watching over her. But I understand what you mean. She's your sister. And I'm… not." The statement hung in the air more like a question.

He wanted to explore that answer with her but not with war looming on two fronts.

"Did you bring Gullet back with you?" he asked instead.

"Gullet?" She frowned. "Maybe he came with my mother, but I haven't seen him since we left Myndren."

Gaeren halted his steps, glancing back at the palace. "Gullet arrived before your mother, and I sent him to warn you. We suspect it means Myndren has fallen."

Aeliana pinched the bridge of her nose as if warding off tears. "If it's already fallen, why is she still gathering an army in the north?"

"How do you know Mayvus gathered an army if you didn't get my message??"

She glanced up, her answer coming out distracted. "Durriken went to check the icebergs in the Northern Sea. He showed me a fleet of her ships. We knew we couldn't pass her, so we had to turn back."

"A fleet?" Gaeren ran a hand through his hair. "Where is she getting all the ships? Is she able to bring those across the barrier as well?"

"Speaking of Durriken…" She hesitated, then pulled on his hand, leading him deeper into the grove beyond the guards.

He marveled at the way she gripped his hand and yet no twinge of pain crossed his bond mark's scar and no guilt pricked his conscience.

"I can't expect you to fly off on a whim, not when you've just returned to your sister, but I can't wait any longer." She bit her lip, holding in some internal struggle.

Sylmar's suspicions rose to the surface in the back of Gaeren's mind, but this time he successfully shoved them back down, unwilling to entertain the idea that Aeliana was a potential enemy. Just like when they'd been on the balcony and she'd been branded by Mayvus, he knew Aeliana could never truly be an enemy.

"Wait, did you say fly?"

She laughed again, and he joined in, curious to hear the joke.

"Just to Mt. Vescano and back. How long would that take?" Her brow rose in earnest, waiting for him to do the math.

"You're serious?" His heart pounded with the possibility, and for a fleeting moment he imagined the wind in his hair and the earth passing by in a blur. He supposed it would feel like sailing, only a hundred times faster. "You want to go flying with a dragon?"

She hushed him, then ducked under a branch, pulling him back to the path so they could pick up their pace while the guards were stuck in the grove. "When Lady Merinnia showed me the curse placed on my mother, it was done by a woman with tattoos on her hands." She frowned at her own scarred palms, turning her hands over to study their backs. "They reminded me of Marnok."

Understanding dawned. "You think the woman who cursed your mother was a witch."

Aeliana nodded. "Now that we know that's where he comes from."

"And you're going to ask Durriken to take you to them."

She grimaced, then nodded.

There were so many holes in her plan. Would Durriken even do it? Could she even find them? And would they help her?

"It would be out of character for me to stay at the palace for too long anyway," Gaeren said slowly.

Aeliana's lips twitched, her eyes holding a mirth that made him want to give her the moon.

"And Durriken probably flies pretty fast."

She nodded, her face unusually solemn. "Very fast, indeed."

"However, I did promise Thallahan I'd bring Fay a princely gift at their wedding."

She tapped her lips as if deep in thought. "That's only two days away. It might even take that long for Durriken to get here. While we're gone, Sylmar and Velden can hash out details with your father about how they want to work together to recapture Myndren."

"So I tell Enla I'm taking a short trip to Rykarn after the wedding. I send Larkos out with supplies for Bayla and the Recreants to make my story look good."

Aeliana held out her hands. "Even better. It serves a dual purpose. That should settle it."

They grinned at each other, and a new sense of hope stirred within him. Not just for them to find a cure for the curse that plagued Emeris.

And not even for him to protect Enla while still serving the Recreants. But hope that when this was all over, he and Aeliana might be able to figure out more of what they were to each other.

"I guess I'd better hold up my end of the deal and go check in with Durriken." Aeliana glanced back at the palace.

"If you ask one of my guards to escort you, that will make it easier for me to give the other the slip." A strange sense of regret sliced through him at the thought of parting ways.

"Are you going to the Recreants?"

He nodded. "I haven't been able to see them since I was imprisoned. Tonight I need to convince them to go up against Mayvus in exchange for me taking my parents off the throne."

Her eyes widened. "And how would you do that?"

"By placing Enla on it instead. That's step one toward the people's freedom. As long as my parents are on the throne, a violent and bloody war will be required to enact change. But if my sister is on the throne… there's a chance at peace."

She nodded slowly. "Is Enla…well?"

The fear that clawed up his throat made it difficult to answer. "No. But that's why placing her on the throne is the best way to shift the power. She's not a threat to the Recreants, so giving her power is the best move for them to start gaining their own."

"And what about for her?" Aeliana asked, but he could see she knew the answer.

"She won't last as queen," he admitted. "Partly because I'll see to it that she doesn't. That's the best thing for her health." His conviction grew with his words even as his guilt flared. It went against everything he'd been raised to do as a throne warden.

"And what if you can't save everyone you've set out to save?" Aeliana whispered.

He stilled as the memory of his deal with the sprites flashed through his mind, followed quickly by the visions from Lady Merinnia. "It may not look the way we expect, but I still think it's possible. The future is never set in stone."

She gave him an incredulous look, almost as if she could hear the words he left out. But his confidence rested in his willingness to pay the high cost demanded by the sprites. The cost Lady Merinnia seemed to confirm by pointing out his absence in those future visions.

The hope that had grown during their walk was immediately snuffed. He couldn't dream about a future with Aeliana, not if he might not live to see it. The truth sobered him into being prepared for the night's agenda.

"Go on," he said, angling his head toward the palace. "Ask one to take you back to your rooms so I can leave." His abrupt dismissal made her flinch. But in light of his recent thoughts, he didn't rescind his words.

With a stiff nod, she turned back to the palace, and Gaeren rushed through the gardens, eager to get away from the reminders of what he could almost have.

When Gaeren finally found the tavern where Riveran had arranged a meeting, he questioned his sanity. There were only half a dozen tables, all filled with seedy-looking men either lost in their drinks or snarling at their companions, as if a brawl might break out at any moment.

Riveran waved him down from the darkest corner where he sat with two other men, hooded cloaks deliberately hiding their faces. Gaeren tightened his own cloak around his shoulders, ensuring the hood stayed in place as he approached the table.

"You didn't mention *he* was your contact," one of the men muttered.

"Would you have come if I did?" Riveran said the words to the stranger but smiled at Gaeren, slapping his back and practically pushing him down into the last empty chair.

"How'd you even recognize me?" Gaeren asked.

The other men snorted, and this time the second spoke up, his voice oddly familiar behind his growl. "Your cloak and boots are evidence of your wealth, and your signature swagger could be recognized a mile away."

Gaeren frowned. He didn't have a swagger. He took in the intricate stitching of his cloak and the fine leather of his boots, unable to argue the first point.

"I'll pick up some ill-fitting clothing on my side of town for you," Riveran said. "As long as you're buying tonight's drinks." He waved over the barmaid, and the other two men chuckled.

Gaeren ignored their condescension and held out a hand. "I'm Gaeren Elanesse. And you are?"

The first man cocked his head, giving Gaeren a glimpse of green eyes and a heavy brown beard, but he ignored Gaeren's hand. "It's brave of you to come here and expect to leave."

"Smits." The second man drew the first's name out in warning.

"If you kill me, I can't help you," Gaeren said, maintaining an easy smile even as his heart beat faster and he dropped his hand. Riveran had made it sound like these men had wanted the meeting. Had something gone wrong?

"What? Just because his oldest friend and an old man trusts him doesn't mean I have to." Smits snarled the words at his friend, but Gaeren flinched as he felt the barb.

"Riveran told me about a Smits," Gaeren said. "Said he would be the hardest to convince, which makes me like you."

The man chuckled and crossed his arms over his chest. "You're still an Elanesse, and that makes me dislike you."

Gaeren raised an eyebrow. "I expected you to hate me. If you merely dislike me, we've already moved a step in the right direction."

"What do you possibly have to gain from working with us?" Smits asked.

"Freedom." Gaeren swept his hands out to encompass the whole room. Not that the men in this room were a good example of freedom. "You all feel enslaved by my family, but I have no more freedom than you."

Smits scoffed, but the second man, who still hadn't given his name, shifted uneasily.

"They forced me to bond at a young age," Gaeren went on. "Something I now see as one step lower than slavery when it's done without consent. Freeing both myself and my bondmate helped me understand that." He held up his palm, hoping the dim light would be enough to show off his ugly scar.

The second stranger sucked in a breath, and Smits leaned forward, letting out a hum that gave Gaeren fortitude to go on.

"For the past several moons, I've been working with Sylmar and Velden, who can vouch for my support of the Recreants. I fought alongside them against Mayvus in the Myndren Mountains, something my parents only approved of when they realized they were on the losing side."

"I won't kill you, then," Smits offered. "Doesn't mean I'm willing to work with you."

"He has a plan," Riveran said. "Something that requires help from the inside. Help that only he can give." His pointed gaze rested on the second stranger, making Gaeren more wary. Who was that man?

Smits leaned forward, giving Gaeren his first full glimpse of the Recreant's face. Deep, ugly lines pulled his brow into a frown, the hatred in his narrowed eyes palpable as his lips pursed in disgust. "Unless you plan to murder your own family, I don't see what you could offer us."

Gaeren repressed the shiver threatening to run through him. "My parents have been grooming Enla to take their place. She might have done it by now if I'd been around as her throne warden. I'm stepping into my role so I can help her step into hers."

The unnamed man shook his head, the glint of metal flashing from under his hood. An earring? "They won't step down. Not yet. Enla is losing her mind to her power as a pneumatic."

Gaeren sat back, stunned. That was the information he'd hoped to give them to prove he was truly defecting and to get them on board with fighting Mayvus in exchange for his help. "How do you know that?"

Riveran raised his eyebrows, his gaze never leaving the fourth man. The silence remained unbroken until Gaeren couldn't stand it.

"Does all of Elanesse know it?"

"Just the highest level of Recreants," Riveran reassured him. "Even Sylmar and Velden aren't privy to it, though they might be now after staying with you."

Gaeren ran a hand through his hair, letting his mind race through how this might change things. Except it didn't. "The point is that if I'm by her side, I can convince my parents she's improving. I can get her to back off on her magic so she actually does improve. And because my father has reigned for over twenty years, I can invoke my right as throne warden to demand he hand over the title."

Riveran frowned. "That's a thing?"

"It's an obscure right that's only been used twice in Vendaran history. It still keeps the throne in the Elanesse line, but it keeps a king or queen from ruling past their prime. It wouldn't have helped a year ago, but now Enla is malleable. I could convince her to step down."

The fourth man chuckled, drawing all their attention. It started out low and soft, then rose until Gaeren feared what sort of attention it might draw. But it also sent a familiar rush of despair through him. He'd heard that laugh before. And it was always followed by an embarrassing defeat in the training field.

The man pulled his hood back, and Gaeren gasped as Danton winked, his gold earring glinting in the light. "It appears you listened to some of my throne warden lessons after all."

"Uncle Danton?" Gaeren whispered, then glanced around nervously even though none of the drunken men could have heard, let alone paid attention. "What are you doing here?"

"Same as you, it seems." He leaned forward. "Fighting from within the palace."

Smits pulled back his hood as well, his smile wide enough to reveal several gaps. Gaeren had passed some sort of test, and while half of him knew that had to be good, the other half couldn't fathom his loyal uncle as a Recreant.

Gaeren nodded slowly. "And did some of that fight include grooming me to despise my parents?" As he looked back, he realized his lessons had always held double meaning. They served their sibling as throne warden because their sibling shouldn't do it alone. They protected them because the people rightfully despised them. They stood beside them so they could be in position when the time was right.

And that time was now.

It left Gaeren feeling like a pawn all over again.

Danton's eyes flashed with remorse. "Your parents made themselves unlikable. What I've done is no different from what Larkos, Riveran, or even Father Fernandus did to an extent."

"Father Fernandus is a Recreant?" Gaeren choked out.

Danton nodded. "We fed you information and watched as you dissected it, pulling it apart to find the truth. You may be a noetic, but you have the heart of a pneumatic."

Gaeren thought of all the times Danton had been alone with his parents over the years. "Why didn't you just take them out? You could have done it years ago."

"Hear, hear," Smits said, gaining an elbow in his side from Riveran.

"Could you take out Enla?" Danton asked softly, but his words left Gaeren convicted. "The man is still my brother. Even when he was branded by Mayvus, I held out hope that he could change. I thought he had when the brand was revealed and he was broken by his failures."

Gaeren let out a snort, remembering how quickly his father had returned to his old ways.

Danton leaned forward. "Like you said, the timing has to be right. Killing your parents might have been a quick solution. I won't argue that. But it was never a long-term plan. Even if we killed Enla too, the nobles would just put someone else in their place. A bloody war would ensue, and with finances on the nobles' side, it wouldn't end well. I never wanted Enla's mind to break, but I'll admit it will make it easier to convince her to step down."

Gaeren grimaced. "So the plan I thought to present you with has been your plan all along."

Danton sat back, his familiar grin putting Gaeren at ease even as Gaeren wondered if it should. "We've just been waiting for you to be on board."

"I have one condition," Gaeren said quickly, feeling his purpose spin wildly out of control. Was he playing into the Recreants' hands?

Smits frowned and muttered something incoherent.

Even Danton's eyes flashed with distrust. "Name it."

"Mayvus is still alive and after Emeris. She wants power even more than my father. When she comes for it, you'll be tempted to let her take out the royal family." He leaned forward earnestly. "But we need to work together to take her out first. That level of cooperation could even lend support to Enla giving authority over to the people."

"Or it could weaken us before we go up against the king," Smits said.

"You shouldn't need to go up against the king if Enla takes his place and steps down," Gaeren pointed out.

He and Smits stared at each other for a long moment, the other man's glare making Gaeren's hope drain as quickly as the mugs of ale in the room. It was time for his last boon.

"I've also promised the Southern Recreants that as a last resort, I'll take my family to Lorvandas."

Riveran choked on his ale. "You did—why did you do that?"

"To show my commitment to keeping my family from returning to the throne. To make sure I could keep Enla safe."

Riveran's eyes widened.

"Regardless," Danton said, "I'd rather we get Enla to step down from the throne before we fight Mayvus. The Recreants will fight against someone threatening their democracy with more passion than they would fight against someone threatening the royal family."

Gaeren flinched, knowing, thanks to his own men, it was true. "It sounds like she's already reclaimed the fortress in the Myndren Mountains. I don't know if we have time for that luxury."

Danton shrugged. "Then I guess you'd better get started."

CHAPTER 71

GAEREN STOOD outside the council room doors, Enla's arm wrapped through his. He always needed a moment to collect himself before facing his parents, but this time he took even longer.

"You could just listen to the results of their deliberation," Enla suggested.

He side-eyed her with a snort. "Do you see that happening in any of my future paths?"

When her expression glazed over, he squeezed her hand.

"I was joking. I don't want you sifting anything. You know I can't hold my tongue in our parents' presence."

"One of the many reasons why it was best for you to be out at sea." Her smile held a maternal wisdom that made her seem far older. What could their friendship have been like if they'd grown up as siblings without so much weight to bear?

"You're entering the room with me instead of with them, so I assume you're in favor of my reckless plan."

She sighed and looked away. "I agree our parents have gone too far. I want to rule with more justice and mercy than they have. I didn't trust myself to do it before now. I need you to balance me out."

He tried not to squirm at her words, wondering if she'd sifted the possibilities of him betraying her. Was it something she saw and thought too impossible?

"They'll fight it," he warned her. "They may have wanted you to rule before I left, but now they'll say terrible things about your sanity. It will help my case if you show an ability to stay in the present tonight."

"I'll hold back my visions if you can hold back your sarcasm." The smile she gave was nostalgically reminiscent of the many she'd teased him in childhood.

The guards opened the doors, forcing them to adopt identical serene expressions. They marched in and stood before the dais where their parents sat on their council room chairs overlooking everyone's tables, and they bowed in tandem. Gaeren held his hands out to his mother, who took them with tears in her eyes.

"Your father only did what he thought was best for you," she whispered. Gaeren hid his scowl, using the time to run his thumb along his mother's wrists and palms. Outside of the rough scars he'd seen from their old brands, he saw and felt nothing new.

He did the same when he greeted his father, unable to decide if he was relieved they weren't branded again or if he wished he'd been able to blame their treatment of him on Mayvus.

With the ceremonial greeting complete, Enla and Gaeren left the dais and took their seats at the table closest to the king and queen. Enla purposefully ignored her normal position beside her parents' council room chairs, and Gaeren couldn't help the pleasure rising in him at his parents' shock.

Gaeren's sadistic joy dampened slightly when his mother's face crumpled, as if the slight had been a personal rejection.

As the council room filled with royal advisors and progenies, Gaeren avoided catching his uncle Danton's gaze, unsure if he could keep the knowledge of the man's ongoing betrayal off his face. Instead, he focused on Tobias, wondering if he was yet another Recreant disguised as a Loyalist.

When his mother had trouble regaining her composure, Tobias bent over, adding something to her tea. Gaeren frowned, still bothered by the so-called healer's tonics but unsure why. If Tobias was a Recreant, wouldn't he have killed the queen by now? And if he wasn't, what could it be other than calming tonics?

One of the advisors stood, and Gaeren winced, remembering him for his uncanny ability to drone on with a single monotonous tone. "We gather today to discuss the veracity of claims made by Emeris Wyndren and company, as well as Gaeren Elanesse." He stuttered a bit over Gaeren's name as if he knew the person accused of treason could one day be in charge of his position in the palace.

The formal evaluation of the progenies' reports verifying the truth of Emeris' and Gaeren's testimonies grew long and dull. As Gaeren's mind wandered, he recited his planned speech, wondering how soon he could make it without being too disrespectful.

It wasn't until Enla nudged him awake that he realized he'd dozed off.

"Despite acknowledging the truthfulness of all their words," his father said, "it doesn't seem to be in the best interest of the Vendaran people to engage in war alongside these Recreants." The words felt final, making Gaeren realize he'd missed significantly more than he'd thought.

"And how many of these Recreants are Vendarans?" Gaeren called out.

The room stilled, and despite knowing he'd spoken out of turn, he felt confident his words were the exact right ones that needed to be said.

His father chuckled as if tolerating the questions of a child. "Every single one of them."

"So you would let your people be taken under the control of a woman known for using blood magic—a woman who recently enslaved you with it?"

His father's face took on a shade of pink that bordered purple, reminding Gaeren that not everyone in the room had been privy to that detail. But he held his ground, waiting for his mother's calming noetic skills to permeate the room. He warded them off, unwilling to let the peace she might give silence his words.

"Those same Recreants prepare a war on us," his father ground out. "I will protect and defend those who are loyal."

Gaeren leaned forward, tapping his chin as if contemplating a new idea even though he'd planned out every word. "I thought it was our role to protect and defend all Vendarans, regardless of loyalty. Wouldn't protecting and defending them allow us to potentially regain loyalty?"

The king frowned. "You would waste all the resources we've built on people who would reject Enla as queen. By doing that, you would be setting her up with minimal resources when it came time for her to take the throne."

Gaeren stood and shook his head.

While Enla closed her eyes, as if pained by his actions, she didn't move to stop him, and she knew exactly what he planned to do.

"No, Father," Gaeren said, making several around the room stiffen at his lack of formality in the council room. "I would utilize the resources you've built to stand behind these people while Enla is on the throne, so they in turn will stand behind her, allowing them all to work together to rebuild those resources. It's what Enla would choose to do too, which is why I'm invoking my right as throne warden to claim her rightful place on the throne."

The gasps and murmurs spreading through the room were expected, and Gaeren didn't drop his eyes from his father's. It could have been the small boy inside him longing for approval, but he thought he saw a hint of pride or maybe relief in his father's eyes before the king guffawed and turned to Uncle Danton.

"He spends all his time out at sea and then suddenly returns and expects us to step down from the throne."

Uncle Danton shifted uncomfortably. "Technically, he is within his rights. You can agree and save face, or you can contest the decision and potentially create a third battlefront. I will defend you to your death, but I cannot speak for the other soldiers faced with that decision."

The king scowled at his throne warden, and Gaeren winced on his uncle's behalf.

But then his father turned that glare on Gaeren. "You expect me to step down now, when you're showing signs of making decisions that will ruin our nation?"

"I expect you to stand down out of respect for the laws that have put you in your position of power."

"Where were you last summer when we offered it freely? Instead, you show up now, knowing the risk of putting Enla on the throne in her condition. You're her throne warden. You should be looking out for her interests."

"What do you say to this, Enla?" their mother asked.

Enla's eyes fluttered open, her gaze too unfocused to put Gaeren at ease. But then her voice rang out loud and clear. "I support his decision. With Gaeren by my side, I think it's the right move for the Vendaran people. You have both served this country well, and you've raised us to do the same. It would be an honor to take that burden from your shoulders and bear it on ours.

"Let me take your place with Croft. Enjoy the remainder of your life without the sorrows of leadership. Go to teas and parties. Spend time with your grandchildren." Her face reddened, making Gaeren wonder if there was some announcement he'd missed. "Spend the rest of your days free of the burdens of the crown. Spend the rest of your time in peace."

"And if we refuse?" the king asked, his anger no more abated by Enla's beautiful speech than by his wife's calming noetic skills.

"Then the council reviews the royal decrees presented by the historian." Danton hesitated before rushing on, unable to hold the king's gaze. "You will likely be removed by force unless you can convince your soldiers to remain loyal despite the laws of your monarchy."

The king stood, and the rest of the room scrambled to follow, all bowing in deference as he made his way to exit the room. "We'll reconvene in two days' time with the historian and council members," he called out. But as he passed by Gaeren's place at the table, he growled a few more words under his breath, just for his wayward son. "I hope you know what you're doing."

CHAPTER 72

Orra made her way through the palace halls, flanked by soldiers. She hesitated occasionally, as if having trouble finding her way to the Sungazer. But she was in the oldest section of the palace, and she knew the layout as well as she knew the limits of her dwindling power. Still, the soldiers didn't need to know either of those things.

It wasn't the first time she'd walked to the Sungazer since being released from the dungeons, so they gestured down the right hall now and then, ensuring she made it there without getting lost. Emeris had spent much of her time in the Sungazer as well, talking with Fernandus about all she'd missed as a priestess during her time as Mayvus' prisoner.

This time however, Orra ran into Cyrus, his eyes wet with tears as he kneeled on the stone. The Sun's rays were just beginning to move past the circumference of the Sungazer's open roof, leaving the young man half in shade and half in light, his soul bared with his transition from worshiping the Stars to worshiping the Sun. Fernandus hesitated at the edge of the room, but before he could offer assistance, Orra stepped forward and kneeled beside Cyrus, taking care to rest fully in the Sun's light. She needed it.

She placed a hand on his arm. "Having one's faith challenged can be as trying as any physical altercation."

He wiped his cheeks and nodded but didn't seem convinced. "Shouldn't it be easy for me to worship the Sun if a Star herself tells me it's the ultimate source of power?"

"It's a difficult switch to make," Orra conceded. "There's no shame in admitting that. Too often people need to discover the truth for themselves in order to truly believe it. Lorvandans struggle to believe the Sun created them because the Sun seems too distant and unreachable. Vendarans struggle with the idea of a Creator being like a parent, desiring affection and camaraderie. You each see different sides of the Stars and Sun. You simply need to see them from all angles and adjust your perception."

"I want the Sun and Stars to stay the same, the way they've always been in my mind," he admitted.

"They're not changing. You are. And that's not a bad thing. If I'd told you these things the night you met me, you never would have considered them. But now you weigh their truth, eager to know what's right even if you don't like it."

He frowned, his gaze on the tile where dark patches marked his fallen tears. "I told Aeliana parts of what Lady Merinnia showed me," he whispered, "but not everything. And no one else asked. I don't think anyone cared about my visions because I know nothing of the Vendaran world or its curses and prophecies."

Orra hummed as she considered his words. "Perhaps the unbiased outsider's view is the most helpful one. It was an oversight that no one asked you." She leaned her head to the side until he looked up and caught her gaze. "Will you tell me now?"

He nodded, but his hands started shaking. "I think she showed me my future. I was back on Sayhla Island, far older with greying hair. I instructed the chiefs, pointing out the flaws in their worship of the sprites. They seemed to listen, but I have no idea what I taught them."

Orra smiled. "So you'll find your own mission from the Sun, separate from the battles they fight here in Vendaras."

"The visions showed me again, surrounded by people in furs amongst snow and ice. There were hundreds of men and women, but again, I don't know what I said. I saw myself back in Gahldric Valley and Andel's harbor. There was a ruined city built with a craftsmanship I'd never seen—buildings that looked ancient and decrepit, but…glorious." His eyes shone with the memory, and he swept his hands out in front of him to emphasize the vastness of the place. "In each vision, men and women gathered to hear me speak. Me. As if I had something worthy to share." The shaking in his hands intensified, and he balled his hands into fists.

"You don't strike me as someone who would shy away from saying what needs to be said, even if it's to a large group of people. So what has you so nervous?"

He let out a short laugh. "Gams always said I talk too much."

"Sometimes our greatest weaknesses become our greatest strengths." Orra placed her hands over his, infusing them with warmth and comfort.

He sighed and closed his eyes. "What if I say the wrong things? What if I teach them what I think I know and it's wrong? Gams and Gamps spent their entire lives teaching people to worship the Stars. I did the same because it's what I knew. It's what I felt convicted to believe and share. How can I trust any new convictions when my old ones were wrong?"

Orra closed her eyes, finally understanding his predicament as she related it to her own. She'd been wrong about so many things. She'd led her peers astray, convincing them the way to fix the world was to break it apart—and they'd listened. "I can't promise you that you won't lead people astray, but I can promise you that you will never lead people to the truth if you hide it away in fear. It starts with you learning not just the truths about the Sun and the Stars but truths about the people. You'll have to learn to sift for the truth and understanding without magic, and then you'll have to learn how to share it."

He nodded, the crease in his brow only slightly smaller.

"You said you were older in those visions. Give yourself time. No one expects you to become a priest in a Sungazer the moment you determine it's the Sun who deserves your praise. I suspect by the time you are meant to be serving the Sayhleens, the Ahmranans, and the Dehvlonians in that way, you'll be ready for it, and your words will come with confidence."

His gaze shot up to hers. "Ahmranans and Dehvlonians?"

She smiled. "You know the Ahmranans live in the harshest of conditions. Were you not aware the Dehvlonians are master architects?" She closed her eyes, envisioning the homes made for simple families that were far more impressive than even this palace. She'd always enjoyed visiting the Dehvlonians, despite their distrust of magic.

"But in the visions, they worship the moon the same way the Sayhleens worship the sprites," Cyrus whispered.

Orra's eyes fluttered open. "Is that so? That's a change in the last thousand years. I wonder why…"

The serenity of the Sungazer was interrupted by heavy footsteps in the hall, followed by a panicked Gaeren peeking in. His face fell when he found Cyrus and Orra still kneeling in the center. "Have either of you seen Emeris?"

They shook their heads, but Fernandus chimed in from his place in the back. "She left almost two bells ago. Said her head hurt and thought she might lie down."

Gaeren's hair stuck up as he ruffled it in agitation. "I have to leave soon for Thallahan's wedding."

Orra and Cyrus exchanged a look.

"What does that have to do with Emeris?" Cyrus asked.

"I thought she might have an idea for a wedding gift." He shrugged. "Enla is sending money on behalf of the family, but Thallahan gave up his eye along with their original wedding date for me. I feel like I should have something… more."

Orra snorted. "I suspect Fay will be happy as long as you don't take him on any more of your adventures."

Gaeren grimaced. "Maybe. She also said she expected a princely gift."

"Give him the thing you would most want," Orra said, shifting to rise.

Gaeren stepped closer and held out a hand to pull her to a standing position.

"I heard about the deliberation yesterday." Orra studied Gaeren's reaction. "I'm sorry it was a difficult meeting. Hopefully your father will see reason before you meet again tomorrow."

"Yeah, thanks. It could get messy." He winced. "But first I have to get through this wedding." He shoved his hands in his pockets.

A shudder ran through Orra as his fingertips likely brushed the golden arrow within. He still carried it and guarded it well, just like Velden held on to the silver fish. They were halfway there.

"You sense me touching it, don't you?" He bent down to look her in the eyes. "Do you still sense Mayvus using the onyx stone to build her army?"

Orra shook her head. "I sense very little these days. I fear it will impair our ability to find them all."

"What happens when you find them all and reunite them? Will the barriers finally be broken down? Or will you destroy the only way for everyone to cross them?"

"Neither," she whispered, and Gaeren frowned.

"Then what will happen? What am I helping you do?"

The braid on her wrist hummed in anticipation as Gaeren tightened his grip on the golden arrow.

"I'm not even sure I know exactly what will happen," Orra admitted. "I know it will bring back Bryton. I know the Sun prophesied it would happen, and that's enough."

"Who's Bryton again?" Gaeren asked.

"A Star," Cyrus murmured. "That's one of the other things Lady Merinnia showed me."

Orra stiffened in surprise.

"Before the bundle of light could take human form," he said, "it was divided into four parts, one for each corner of the earth. A way to reach the people torn apart."

It had been a long time since Orra had cried in front of people, but the tightening of her throat risked exposing the way her past haunted her.

"Are you saying..." Gaeren's gaze volleyed between Orra and Cyrus. "Are the starbridges pieces of...a Star?"

She blinked the tears back as best she could as she nodded.

Gaeren's gaze swung to the braid on her wrist. "Your other half."

Her lips trembled as she smiled, and one of the tears fell. "It's the only way for me to right my wrongs."

Unwilling to let them see more of her pain, she swept past Gaeren and out the door, ignoring the soldiers as they trailed her back to her room.

CHAPTER 73

Aeliana sat at the dressing table in her room, still surprised that Kendalyhn was fussing over her hair with the same focus she used when sifting souls. Even Iris had perked up a bit to get Aeliana ready for Thallahan and Fay's wedding while Enla serenely watched on from her place at Aeliana's tea table.

"I thought Vendarans preferred trousers," Aeliana said, picking at some lint on the silk gown Enla had lent her.

"Not for a wedding." Kendalyhn's face held mock shock that made Aeliana laugh.

"There are too many rules in your culture."

"I agree," Enla said.

Kendalyhn side-eyed the future queen while finishing up the braids scattered throughout Aeliana's hair. The Recreants weren't ready to trust Enla, with good reason, but Aeliana couldn't help seeing all the ways she resembled Gaeren. It made it impossible to see her as an enemy.

"You wear a dress most every day," Aeliana pointed out. "So you either have a different set of rules, or you're above them."

"I would much rather wear trousers," Enla admitted. "But yes, I'm expected to dress differently because of my role. When my meetings are done, I always change. These tight shoes come off too." She frowned down at her dainty slippers.

Aeliana opened her mouth to ask another question, but Kendalyhn chose that moment to dust a powder on her face, making her cough.

"Hold still," Kendalyhn said sharply, reminding Aeliana of the days when they were always at odds.

True to form, Aeliana ignored the other woman's instruction, pulling the clamshell from her pocket and opening it to reveal the pea-sized gemstone. "Enla, do you know anything about this type of gem?"

Enla leaned forward, her head angling to study it. "It's beautiful. But I've never seen anything like it. And my father has many gems," she added dryly.

"It's from Sayhla Island," Aeliana murmured, turning it so light reflected off each perfect edge of the gem.

"Sayhla Island?" Enla's eyebrows rose and she looked again. "It could be a fabled Sayhleen pearl. They're said to be a source of power, one the old kings and queens enslaved the Sayhleens to procure. I didn't think they were real. If they were, my father would have one. In fact, don't let him see you have it."

Aeliana bit her lip and closed the shell before tucking it back in her pocket.

"I'm glad you and Gaeren worked things out, love." Iris gave Aeliana a knowing smile.

Aeliana glanced back at Enla, but the other woman's face had regained its passive, almost vacant, look. Was she sifting the future again? Seeing how the Sayhleen pearl might be of use? Or looking to see if Gaeren and Aeliana's friendship was destined to become something more?

"Yes." Aeliana drew the word out slowly. "It's good to have friendships to lean on when war is looming."

Kendalyhn snorted, and Aeliana was grateful when Enla's response cut off whatever Kendalyhn was about to say.

"After our council meeting tomorrow, I can officially begin preparations. Your fight is the same as ours, even if my parents can't see it."

Aeliana hesitated, no longer sure if Gaeren planned to fly to Mt. Vescano with her or if he'd stick around to see through Enla's shift into power. She wouldn't blame him for staying, but she couldn't delay her trip. Not when they had no idea what Mayvus planned to do.

"Can you see what Mayvus will do? Do you know how we can best defeat her?"

Enla shook her head apologetically. "Perhaps if I had something that belonged to her, I could sift her future. Definitely if she was here with us. I've seen you and Gaeren taking ships to fight her in the Northern Sea, and I've seen him defending you at the fortress in the Myndren Mountains. But those scenarios are dependent on his choices. Even if he was as predictable as the seasons, which he's not, Mayvus' choices will create new branches, and I'll have to sift them all over again."

Aeliana shuddered.

"You have choices to make too," Enla murmured, her eyes glazing over.

Aeliana squirmed until Kendalyhn told her to sit still while she painted her cheeks. The whole idea of dressing up for a wedding in the middle of everything going on felt silly. Tonight she'd leave with Durriken. She'd find a way to break the curse. And then they'd finally be prepared to face Mayvus on their own terms.

Was Enla seeing all that? Was she seeing Aeliana succeed?

"Close your eyes," Kendalyhn instructed, and Aeliana welcomed the ability to block everything out as Kendalyhn painted her eyes with Enla's kohl.

Enla's chair creaked, and Aeliana peeked to find the future queen standing. "Give my brother my regards. And tell him he'll regret his gift if he gives it, even though it's the right gift to give." Her gaze shifted and her face went slack. She sucked in her breath before focusing in on Aeliana again. "I wish you success," she whispered. "But few paths hold it. Don't let him get hurt."

As she slipped out the door, Aeliana's pounding heart felt deafening. Did that mean Gaeren would come with her despite the meeting tomorrow?

"What was that about?" Iris asked.

Aeliana shook her head, and Kendalyhn clucked her tongue, grabbing Aeliana's jaw and holding her face still.

"She's losing her mind," Kendalyhn said. "We can't trust anything she says to make sense."

Aeliana swallowed hard, letting her silence confirm Kendalyhn's words. She hadn't told anyone else about her plans to seek out the curse from its source. She wasn't sure anyone would let her go, and she wasn't looking for permission.

"Yesterday she told Lukai to study the herbs in the apothecary in case he had need of them soon," Kendalyhn went on. "He wasn't complaining about the tour—it's probably his new favorite place. But why would she say something so bizarre?"

A knock sounded on the door, and two of the guards answered it before announcing Gaeren's presence. Aeliana rubbed her sweaty palms on the green silk skirt, leaving damp marks that made Kendalyhn frown.

It was going to get tossed later anyway. She had leathers on underneath, because she couldn't exactly ride a dragon wearing layers of silk.

As the soldiers parted for her to leave the room, she caught sight of Gaeren standing in the hall, nervously tugging on the buttons of his jacket. Her jaw dropped as she took in his formal fitted attire and his stiffly styled hair.

Then she bit her lip to hold back a laugh.

"What?" he asked.

"You look very handsome," she said.

He rolled his eyes. "Don't lie. Enla would never let me attend a wedding in anything less than this ridiculous costume. And I figured I ought to butter her up."

"Why?" Kendalyhn stood at Aeliana's side, arms folded over her chest.

He grinned. "It never hurts to butter up a sibling. Especially when they have the power to do things for you."

Kendalyhn made a face. "You have the most dysfunctional family I've ever met."

"I don't disagree." He held out a hand to Aeliana.

She stared at it just long enough for it to be awkward, then looped her arm through his.

As he led her down the hallway, she glanced back at the ever-present guards. "I don't know how you stand all the formalities and constantly being followed and watched."

"Why do you think I escape so much?" he asked. "Speaking of escape…"

She sighed. "You have to stay."

"I was going to ask if everything is good for tonight." His eyebrows rose, and she grinned.

"What about the meeting tomorrow?"

"Uncle Danton has it under control. And Enla approved the trip… to Rykarn"—he added with a sly grin—"before Father gave the deadline. Riveran's promised to look after her since Croft's never around."

"I haven't met him yet," Aeliana admitted as they stepped out a side door and into the chilly breeze.

"He's too busy with the navy men," he said, then snorted. "Maybe they're converting him to a Recreant."

The carriage ride into town felt long with several people pointing them out, whether because they were surprised to see her or Gaeren, she didn't know.

"I wish I had Lukai's illusion skills," she admitted.

Gaeren chuckled. "It would be convenient at a time like this."

"Where's the princely gift you promised Thallahan?"

His grin turned sheepish. "I didn't realize how hard it would be to find one."

"You didn't bring one?"

"No, I did," he rushed to say, then dug into his pocket.

For a moment, Aeliana wondered if he would pull out the golden arrow he guarded for Orra. Instead, a crumpled slip of paper rested in his hand, and he smoothed it out across his knee.

"I guess maybe I should have put it in a card or something." He grimaced and passed it over to her.

"What is this?" She scanned the legal terms that made her already slow reading even slower.

"It's the deed to *Starspeed*."

For the second time that night, her jaw swung open. "Your ship? You're giving him your ship?"

He shrugged. "Larkos didn't want it. He said being captain was a young man's game. And I'll be stuck at the palace for a while. There's no sense in letting her go to waste."

Aeliana clamped her jaw down, trying to picture Gaeren staying in the palace day after day with his prince's garb and perfectly coiffed hair. She could imagine it, but it was bleak. She caught herself mourning the image of his hair and tunic blowing in the wind at the ship's helm, the carefree grin on his face unable to be matched with his current attire.

"It's very generous." She passed the paper back to Gaeren.

"Think Fay will approve?"

"I think she would have been happy with a little extra money to get them started. This goes far above what she expected."

He grinned. "Good. You know how much I like to surprise people."

She smiled back at him as the carriage slowed. "That reminds me. Enla says hello and that you'll regret giving the gift."

He snorted and hopped out from the carriage, holding out a hand for her to descend. "Having the chance to prove my sister wrong just makes it even more perfect."

The Sungazer before them was modest compared to the one at the palace, but a large group had already gathered and festive wreaths had been hung from every surface. She'd almost forgotten it was Winter Solstice on top of the wedding. The holiday was one she'd never had reason to celebrate, but she'd always enjoyed watching the villagers have their dancing and feasting from afar.

They were outside the city proper, near the edge of the woods, and the Sun's descent left a glorious glow across the grounds. Gaeren pulled her through the crowd, and as they made their way to seats for the ceremony, Aeliana had the impression attending this wedding served a dual purpose.

"You want people to see us together, don't you?" she said. "To see us getting along."

He grinned. "Is that so wrong? For us to get along?"

"No, I just didn't realize this was a political move. I thought you were just going to a friend's wedding."

He gave a mock frown. "Just because it helps establish mutual trust between the Recreants and the Loyalists doesn't mean it's a farce."

They sat near the front by Thallahan's and Fay's families—likely a spot of honor because of Gaeren's status. A few of the merchants around them grumbled, hoping the ceremony wouldn't last long because they'd seen several trade ships approaching the harbor. As the Sun sank lower in the sky, Thallahan finally came into view.

"He really does look handsome with the eye patch," Aeliana said. "I'm guessing Fay finds him even more attractive than before."

Gaeren hummed in consideration. "I can easily put an eye patch over my eye if you'd like."

She elbowed him and laughed, but it came out breathy and her face heated. A single daisy grew at her feet, and she slid her boot over it before Gaeren could tease her.

As beautiful as the ceremony was, Aeliana found herself watching the sky, waiting for the Sun to disappear and the moon to make its ascent. She hoped Durriken wouldn't make a scene and that he'd wait at their designated meeting place.

Fernandus had come down to perform the ceremony, which was another way the royal family had blessed Thallahan and Fay. Aeliana had never been to a wedding in Lorvandas, so she had no idea if the traditions crossed cultures. Either way, there was something beautiful about the way Fay and Thallahan were presented as individuals before being joined as one.

They had just sealed their promises with a kiss, and Fernandus had begun unwinding the ties that bound them, when a scream broke out from the back of the crowd. Several others followed, and chaos ensued as people scrambled to see the cause of distress as well as escape.

Gaeren placed a protective arm around Aeliana, but she shrugged it off so she could withdraw her dagger from under her skirt. She cursed inwardly that her bow and arrow were back at the palace. When Aeliana finally caught a silver glimpse among the crowd, her breath caught.

"Winex," she whispered.

Gaeren had his sword out, and they exchanged glances. Winex typically avoided cities and large gatherings of people. Attacks were expected out in the wild, but rarely in a setting like this, even if they were near the woods. Plus, it was fairly close to the new moon. They had to be five or six days old at most. Barely the size of a teenager with half the strength of a grown man. It was a foolish time to attack.

As the crowd scattered, Aeliana counted at least a dozen winex prowling through the remnants of the party, most almost flat on the ground. As they crawled and sniffed, several went for the food laid out on tables, while others hissed and growled at the few half-lights, including Thallahan, who'd stayed back in an attempt to defend the people.

Aeliana hated the idea of taking down the winex. They looked too much like Felk. It didn't matter that she'd already killed one in a battle before. That was before she'd befriended Felk. She wasn't sure she could do it again even if one attacked her.

As Gaeren's lips settled in a grim line, she realized he had no such qualms.

A dozen feet away, two attacked a man, scratching at his face before he could slice at them with his dagger. Gaeren ran to the man's rescue, but Aeliana hesitated.

Why were the winex here? It was so out of character it left her on edge.

Without warning, one howled and lumbered her way, its nose to the ground until it reached her skirts. She adjusted her grip on her dagger, knowing she'd have to defend herself if it came down to it, but dreading the idea of telling Felk what she'd done. When the winex looked up, cocking its head, hatred and distrust filled its eyes.

But Aeliana gasped as she took in a black teardrop on its cheek. "Felk?"

The winex stiffened, confirming the name was familiar. It had to be him.

Aeliana's relief dissipated as the winex snarled and lunged at her.

CHAPTER 74

THE WEIGHT of the winex took Aeliana down, and her legs got tangled in her skirts, which ripped beneath Felk's claws. She managed to keep hold of her dagger, but she couldn't bear to use it, so she let that hand drift to the side. Hot breath reeking of fish and spoiled fruit swept over her face, and sharp teeth filled her vision.

"It's me, Felk!"

The snarls turned to the low hum of a growl, more like a warning than the start of an attack. "Are you Aeliana?" he ground out, his eyes conflicted. But the sound of her name on his lips brought a rush of relief.

"Yes. I'm Aeliana."

He cocked his head once again and sniffed more deeply. Then he stepped back, allowing her room to sit up and catch her breath.

"Do you—do you remember me?" They'd been apart for three cycles. It wasn't possible.

He shook his head, baring his teeth. From the rags at his waist, he pulled out a crumpled piece of parchment, then smoothed it out on the ground between them.

She bent over to take in the perfect calligraphy she recognized as Orra's handwriting.

"Aeliana?" Gaeren called, drawing her attention back up. He and two other men were at a standstill with the remaining winex, who had taken their cue from Felk and backed off. Their bodies rippled with the anticipation of an attack, as if the moment Felk gave approval, they would finish off the half-lights before them.

"It's Felk," she reassured him. Even the other winex seemed surprised she knew his name, and she hoped it was enough to stay their anger.

She glanced back at the parchment.

You are Felk. You know this deep in your bones. You are a winex, but you are also a friend of half-lights. You were saved by Aeliana, who took care of you like you were a son. You saved her and loved her like she was a mother. An evil priestess named Mayvus wants to hurt Aeliana. Mayvus gathers troops at Ahmranan's Viewpoint and plans to attack Myndren. She will go after Aeliana next. Don't let her.

Beneath Orra's perfect handwriting was Felk's child-like scrawl.

Your friend Orra, the Star, wrote this letter. It is all true. Protect Aeliana.

Felk

"You don't remember me," Aeliana whispered around the lump in her throat. "But you came for me anyway. Just because of this note?"

Felk's growls intensified. "How do I understand? How can I copy this and it be the same?" He pointed at his signature and his voice rose in agitation. "And I know it was me. How can I know? My clan doesn't know it, but I do."

She smiled. "Because I taught you to read and write."

He winced, as though the idea pained him. "Why?"

"Because we're friends. Just like your letter says." She hadn't had the opportunity to practice the noetic skills she'd pulled from Durriken for several days. Hadn't wanted to since she needed to focus on regaining her somatic skills. But this seemed like a time worth testing them once more. "Can I show you?" She held out a hand near his arm.

He shrank back, snarling as he glanced between her hand and face. When she didn't move, his gaze flicked to the parchment once more. He didn't trust her, and she tried not to let that hurt. But at least he seemed willing to trust his former self enough to hear her out, because he eventually held his arm out for her to grasp.

The memories she pushed at him were messy. She recalled them out of order and knew they held more impressions than actual moments. But she felt his arm relax under hers as she continued feeding him shared experiences of her caring for him, training him, and laughing with him. Times where they cooked together, played together, and fought together. Moments where he defended her and where she defended him. It was difficult magic she wasn't yet used to, and as her starlock heated, she sensed the power draining too quickly.

So she pulled back, hoping he'd seen enough. The glazed look in his eyes cleared, and his jaw slackened, revealing the dozens of teeth she'd feared moments before.

"Not friends," he said, eyes misty. "Family."

She nodded. "Gaeren could show you more. His skill is far greater than mine." Felk glanced at Gaeren, then took in the sight of his clan still in their defensive positions. He stood to his full height and held his palms up before jerking them down in some sort of motion that signaled for his clan to stand down.

They skulked away, the disappointment evident as they glared at the people they'd been prepared to attack.

"How did you even find me?" Aeliana asked Felk as Gaeren approached. She rose and dusted off her ruined skirts, passing the letter Gaeren's way.

Felk pulled another wad from his loincloth, making Aeliana grimace.

"Your smell." He held the dingy blue cloth to his nose and inhaled.

Aeliana recognized it as a scrap from what had once been her skirt, one she'd left behind after replacing it with the traveling leathers she'd since grown to appreciate.

"Orra gave it to you?"

He shrugged. "It was in my nest. The letter too."

"That's still such a long way, with such a small scent," Aeliana mused, but then she let the mystery go and smiled. "I'm so glad you're here. It's so good to see you."

"Not good." Felk glanced back toward the busier parts of the city.

"Why not?" Aeliana asked.

"Oh, no," Gaeren murmured, passing the parchment back to Aeliana, except this time he showed her the back side, where the scribbles held little organization. A comment was left here or there, some upside down or facing left or right. Phrases like "Cycle two, day fifteen" or "Cycle one, day twenty-eight" labeled each comment, forcing Aeliana to spin the parchment around to try to piece the notes together in order.

But four words that she couldn't ignore stood out.

Mayvus sails to Elanesse.

"No," Aeliana murmured, turning the parchment faster and trying to make sense of the other phrases.

Count ships

IIIII IIIII IIIII II

Follow ships

~~Protect Myndren~~ Protect Elanesse

Mayvus bad

Aeliana good - Sylmar? Emeris?

Blue cloth - Aeliana

Mayvus sails west - not Myndren

Protect Elanesse

Protect Aeliana

"She didn't even go after Myndren," Aeliana murmured. "My mother could have stayed."

Felk leaned over her shoulder and pointed at a phrase. "Yesterday. In swamps." Then he pointed northwest of Elanesse, beyond the city's harbor. Aeliana looked back at the phrase, and her starlock grew cold against her chest.

See ships! Run!

"Yesterday? How much time do we have before she gets here?" Even as she asked the question, she knew the answer. The merchants attending the wedding had been excited to return to their shops and taverns because they'd seen dozens of trade ships arriving.

Except they weren't trade ships.

Felk whined like a dog holding back a howl. "None. She's here."

CHAPTER 75

GAEREN'S CHEST seized with panic, then he met Aeliana's eyes. All their plans to go after the witches were a waste. Even their efforts to convince his parents to fight alongside them were too little, too late. Mayvus wasn't on the other side of the country, hiding in the Myndren Mountains. She was here.

"Once they left Ahmranan's Viewpoint, we followed by land," Felk said. "Ships travel fast, but the swamps are shorter for us. We lost a day, maybe two, for this last cycle and rebirth. But we caught up. We found you."

Gaeren glanced toward the city, where the harbor was just out of sight. Were the Ahmranans already disembarking? Were they harassing the people and hurting them? Or riling them up to help fight against the royal family?

Then Gaeren turned north, where the top turrets of the palace could barely be made out where the Sun disappeared beyond the mangrove tree line. "We have to warn the others. My sister—" His voice broke.

"Of course," Aeliana said. "You should go."

"What about you?" he asked.

"I can't go to the witches. Not if it means abandoning everyone else."

The full implication of her words sank in. They wouldn't have answers about the curse before facing Mayvus again. They had no way to stop her without taking out Aeliana's mother.

"Maybe it's time my mother just ran."

"And what will that do to everyone left behind with Mayvus?" Gaeren asked. "Won't she be indestructible in your mother's absence?"

"We don't know for sure that's what the curse means." Aeliana closed her eyes, and he hated that his question brought her pain. "But my mother believes it after hearing the curse. She'll never agree to run."

"What do you need?" Felk asked.

"You've done enough." Aeliana squeezed his arm. "Take your clan and go. There's only death waiting in the palace walls. She'll come for us, and she'll kill anyone in her way."

Felk shuddered, then glanced at the parchment once more. "My people can choose. But I will go with you. Our loyalty crossed cycles. I have only heard of that happening with mates."

Gaeren glanced around. "Is Lilik still with you?"

He smiled. "She prepares nests in the forest. I think she'll help too."

Aeliana nodded. "Anyone who wishes to help can head for the harbor. Stop anyone trying to disembark the ships and tell anyone else to hide or help fight. Although they probably won't listen." She wrung her hands and bit her lip. "On second thought, just stop anyone trying to disembark."

He nodded, then hesitated. "You were a good mama." His face clouded over with confusion, then he loped away, taking the other winex with him.

Time slowed as Gaeren and Aeliana stared at each other, the magnitude of what was coming making the strained moment feel too heavy. Other attendees peeked out from behind buildings and tables. Even Fay came forward to loop her arm through Thallahan's, her face pinched with worry.

"Why were they here?" she asked.

"They came to warn us," Gaeren said.

"Warn?" One of the men who'd stayed with Thallahan scoffed. "They attacked us."

"No." Gaeren shook his head. "I mean, some of them did. But they brought us news of Mayvus. She's on her way to attack the palace." A couple of people exchanged glances, their looks holding something that almost looked pleased.

Gaeren stiffened, but Aeliana spoke up before he could.

"You think she'll take out the threat of the royal rule? You think that would be better than your current situation? Your reprieve will be brief. She might take down the royal family and temporarily free you. But then she will enslave you in ways the Elanesses never would have. She will brand those of you with magic and discard those of you who have nothing to offer her. You seek freedom, but it will not come from her. Fight alongside the Elanesses or sit back and solidify your own doom."

Her words made the other men pause, and Gaeren stood straighter, grateful for her defense of his family even if they didn't deserve it.

She didn't wait to see if she'd convinced them. Instead, she grabbed Gaeren's hand, and they ran for his carriage. Together they removed the harnesses so they could ride bareback, and Gaeren instructed the driver to find a safe place to hide.

After they mounted, Aeliana turned back to him, her face holding an apology. "I can't go with you."

Gaeren frowned, pulling back on the horse's reins until it pranced in position beside Aeliana's horse. "Why not?"

"I have to go to Durriken."

Relief rushed through Gaeren. "He can help us."

Aeliana winced. "It needs to be his choice."

Memories of that night on the northern keep of the Myndren Mountains' fortress swept over him, entirely too clear thanks to his noetic skills. "You're not going to free him, are you? What if Mayvus brands him again?"

Aeliana closed her eyes. "I'll leave the decision up to him. I don't think he'll want to be free unless Mayvus is truly powerless. Hopefully he'll fight with us so he can be freed after. But I will not force him." She opened her eyes and flinched when her gaze met Gaeren's. "Either way, I know he'll take me to meet you at the palace."

Gaeren nodded but couldn't quite say goodbye. "Now your mother needs your protection just as much as Enla needs mine."

Aeliana shivered. "She'll let the others kill her if her death can protect them from Mayvus. I'll need to find another way—without the witches."

They stared at each other as their horses pawed the ground in impatience. Gaeren knew they had to leave—that time was a commodity they couldn't waste. But the unknowns of when they might see each other again felt even heavier than before.

The intensity on Aeliana's face brought Gaeren back to the woods where they'd broken their bonds. "I'll be there when you face her again," he promised. "I won't let you do it alone."

The air between them felt just as charged as that night, the idea of a kiss even more appealing. He inwardly cursed the horses and distance between them.

"Just don't brand me this time," she said with a grin.

"Fine," he said, grateful for the way she'd lightened the moment. "I'll find some other way to save you."

She cocked her head. "Maybe this time I'll save you."

He laughed, then nudged his horse's side with his heel and took off toward the palace with a wave over his shoulder, all the while wondering if he raced to save the wrong woman.

CHAPTER 76

As hard as it was to leave Aeliana behind, the memory of the sprite's warning for Enla kept repeating in Gaeren's mind on a loop, driving him forward toward the palace. He rubbed a hand over his mare's withers, silently apologizing for pushing her so hard.

As he approached the stables, he let her slow just enough for him to slide off her back and toss her reins toward a stable boy. He nearly tripped over his own feet when he saw it was Erech, and instead of running toward the palace, he hesitated, glancing between Erech and the harbor.

"Why aren't you with Larkos at the ship? Or better yet, with your family?" His words came out panicked as visions of young Breeve's battered body being pulled from the ruins of the northern tower in Myndren plagued him. He didn't even let Erech answer. "Never mind. Just get the mare settled, but then get yourself home. Stay as far away from the palace as possible. Mayvus is coming."

Erech's face turned white, and flashes of images of Erech's siblings were pushed into Gaeren's mind, as if the boy's fears shouted so loudly Gaeren's noetic skills were forced to take them in. Erech froze, nearly losing the mare's reins as she gave her own nervous whinny.

Gaeren grabbed Erech's shoulders and shook him out of his shock. "Go on! Now!"

The boy rushed the mare into the stable, and Gaeren had to trust he'd remember the rest of his instructions.

He took off toward the palace even though it was the last place he wanted to be. His parents wouldn't welcome his presence so soon after his demand that they step down. They couldn't punish him for being within his rights, but would they listen to him?

He approached the front entrance at a run, making the guards break formation and draw their swords.

"Mayvus is in the harbor," he announced, ignoring their weapons. "Get word to Danton and your commander. They'll need to call in all the troops. Where are my parents and Enla?"

To the guards' credit, they obeyed immediately, three taking off in different directions inside the palace, while two others remained behind.

"The king and queen are in the council room," one said. "Danton should be there as well. And your sister should be resting in her quarters."

Gaeren frowned. What the guard really meant was that she'd been confined there by their parents. They were still determined to find a way to keep her from taking the throne. He debated where to go first, but once again, the memory of the sprite made the decision for him. He swept past the guards and up the stairs. On his way to Enla's room, he peeked out one of the balcony windows, then swore as the tranquil ocean view was broken up by dozens of ships, just like Felk had said.

They dotted the harbor with a terrifying pattern of perfection, like the strategy games Danton used to give Gaeren for warfare instruction. Except he had no pieces to lay on the board for a defensive strategy, and Gaeren suspected the people were currently suffering because of it. Would it be enough to bring them on board to fight with the Elanesses after they heard Gaeren's promises? Or would they simply step back and direct Mayvus toward the palace?

His father could command the navy Croft had brought up to attack, but it might already be too late if Mayvus' soldiers swarmed the harbor. If they'd had just a little more time, they might have gotten the Recreants on board. They might have gotten Enla in a higher position of authority.

Four guards stood outside Enla's room, and Gaeren brought them up to speed while pounding on her door. Two split off, probably to report to their commanders, while the other two drew weapons, their stances even more alert than before.

When Enla opened the door, her eyes were clouded over, her face stoic. "It's good to see you, Gaeren," she said flatly. Did she actually see him?

"Did you know?" His voice shook with a frustration he hadn't realized he'd been harboring. "Did you see this coming?"

She cocked her head, and her eyes flickered as if trying to focus on him instead of whatever visions she'd been seeing. He placed his hands on her shoulders and shook her the same way he'd done to Erech moments earlier.

"Enla, I need you here," he ground out. "I need you present now."

She gasped in a frightened breath, and her eyes cleared, the apathetic gaze replaced by anxiety. "Is Mayvus here?"

He nodded, but something inside him broke. "You knew all this time, didn't you? You knew she was coming and you didn't tell me."

She shook her head. "It was one of a dozen paths. They weren't always certain. Sometimes the winex overtook them. Sometimes she sailed past the harbor. But you and Aeliana were supposed to be gone. She came too quick."

He slammed his fist against the wall, and she shrank away from his anger.

"You should have told me," he said. "We could have been more prepared."

"All the paths merge," she whispered. "No matter what we do, it all ends the same."

Something cold slithered down his spine. She'd never said something with so much certainty. It reminded him of the way Lady Merinnia saw only one or two outcomes, and it left him terrified. If only one path remained, did anything they might do even matter?

"What happens?" he asked.

She shuddered. "So much death."

"Yours? Mine? Aeliana's?"

She shook her head, and her gaze clouded over once more.

"Enla." He shook her again as he shouted, but this time, she remained lost in the visions.

Her lips moved silently—whatever conversation she was having wasn't with him in present day.

"I don't have time for this," he muttered. "Please, Enla, please come back to me." He slapped her cheeks, then took a glass of water from her bedside table and sloshed it in her face. She flinched but remained stuck, searching their future.

He never should have asked what happened. How long would she be lost, searching to give him an answer he probably didn't want to hear?

He swept her up in his arms like a baby and carried her out of the room. The guards exchanged glances, unwilling to question his unusual behavior. He took off down the hallway, knowing they'd follow. When he passed the same balcony window, he paused, gesturing for the soldiers to look at the congregating ships. With the Sun's sleep, lantern and firelight lit up the town, but it felt like more than usual, like Mayvus might be lighting fire to things not meant to burn.

"That's what we're up against. A madwoman with ridiculous amounts of magic and a fleet of soldiers she's brought from Ahmranas. Do you understand?" He glared at the soldiers as if they were to blame, then felt remorse as their faces paled. "This is war. We need every troop, every soldier, every man and woman in this city to fight. I will take Enla to our parents. But we need to launch a counterattack."

"I'll go to the healers," the second soldier said. "Make sure the network of progenies is being included in the commander's tactics."

He sprinted away without waiting for approval, breaking protocol by leaving Enla with only one guard. The man's desperation actually gave Gaeren confidence that the threat was finally being taken seriously.

Gaeren pursed his lips, dreading the next step. "Let's go to my parents."

The other guard nodded, and they took off toward the council room. As Gaeren swept past the council room guards and through the door, chaos broke out. His mother paled and rushed to Enla's side, calling for healers and demanding that Gaeren lay her down. Tobias joined them, leaning over Enla and blocking Gaeren's view of his sister.

Against his better judgment, he turned away and let his gaze lock on his father, who remained seated in his council room chair on the dais. Gaeren shouted to be heard over the panicking council members. "Mayvus is here. We don't have time for you to step down and let Enla make her choice. We don't have time for you to evaluate how this will impact your authority or rule. If we don't fight her, we will all die. And your response in this moment will determine if the people you claim to serve will step up and fight alongside you. If they don't, you will die. Enla has seen it in almost every path."

He was taking liberties with Enla's visions, not having been able to see them for himself, not knowing what deaths she'd predicted. Perhaps by telling him their dire circumstances, she'd changed the outcome herself, sending him on this trajectory to stand up to their father. Perhaps this was the path that could change the outcome.

Because Gaeren had to believe there was at least one.

He refused to accept that death was in all of their immediate futures.

Gaeren was shoved to the side as healers came forward. Council members spread out in small clusters, gossiping and murmuring over the news Gaeren had just shared. His father, however, didn't move. He studied Gaeren, and time stilled. How could his father, the king, be so unfeeling as to sit there and take in that announcement without any reaction?

"Please, Father," he begged, "do the right thing."

They stared at each other long enough that all hope fled Gaeren. How could he get Enla out of here to safety? He would not let this be the end for her. He would not let the sprite's prediction be true.

"Leave us." His father's voice carried over the commotion. "All but Enla, Gaeren, and my wife."

Tobias hesitated, but Gaeren's mother shooed him out of the room. "There's nothing we can do for her anyway."

Gaeren frowned. It wasn't like his mother to turn away a healer. She was docile enough to obey anything his father said unless it involved the healers. The only other time she'd refused them had been last winter, when they'd been sick before Gaeren had left to hunt down Aeliana.

When she'd been branded.

Dread pooled inside of him as the room emptied. He bent down to the makeshift bed the healers had put together from tables and cushions and reached for Enla. They needed to leave.

His mother's hand shot out and gripped his wrist. "No, dear. She needs to stay here and rest." Confidence in his mother's words swept over him. A certainty that she was right and that all would be well if he simply let Enla rest. It hit him with such force that his starlock burned as his automatic defenses went up.

She was using her magic on him.

He pulled his hand away and shook his head to clear it, but the sensation that he agreed was far too strong.

Beneath his outward contentment, he sensed an inward turmoil trying to escape. He felt secure with his parents, like they would care for Enla and protect them both from the incoming danger, but deep down, he knew that wasn't true.

And if anything, the opposing sensation caused a crack in the peace enveloping him. His starlock burned as he latched on to that dissonance and pulled it forward to the surface. He shook off his mother's hand.

"Why are you doing this?" He squeezed his eyes shut, trying to separate out the emotions, to discern what was real and what was fabricated by her magic. But it left him sluggish.

When he opened his eyes, his father stood before him, the rage on his face far more than a father disciplining his son. Even a somatic progeny who had often let his anger get the best of him during Gaeren's childhood. This held a loathing that came from someone else.

"You've been branded again." Gaeren's ragged whisper held the weight of his defeat.

His father's lip lifted in a sneer. "You always were slow to catch on to the ways of the world." His father's hand rose, and Gaeren flinched from years of habit.

Whether it was an act of mercy or efficiency, Gaeren's mind went black before he felt the force of the blow.

CHAPTER 77

When Aeliana reached the swampy clearing she'd instructed Durriken to meet her in, she grew anxious at how empty it was. Scanning the skies for the dragon's large frame revealed nothing. She closed her eyes and reached out along the string connecting them until she sensed his approach from both her place in the clearing and from his place in the sky.

The powerful beat of his wings gave her hope and confidence as he neared. But when her presence in his mind eventually allowed her a glimpse of herself waiting in the swamp, the strangeness of it made her hold on their tether snap. She stepped back with the force of it, and her vision cleared until she saw Durriken headed straight for her. Surprised by her own trust, she stood firm as he landed beside her, even though the air that rushed from his wings knocked her to her backside.

It dawned on her that this was the first time they'd seen each other since that night in the Myndren Mountains. All their experiences had been through the brand that connected them, and the magnificence of both his size and beauty left her startled. But they didn't have time to relish their greeting.

You're afraid. The deep rumble that met her mind held concern and curiosity.

"Mayvus is back."

The growl that came held a fierceness that warmed Aeliana. She and Gaeren would not be facing Mayvus alone.

"We can't go to the witches like we planned. Not now. She'll be coming to the palace and going after my mother. Maybe the royal family." She thought of the strange note Felk had carried from Orra. "Maybe me."

Those last two words made Durriken stiffen.

Aeliana's fear and sorrow magnified as she sensed it flowing through Durriken and back again as he shared it with her.

Your mother should be safe. Mayvus won't harm her if their life forces are connected.

A bitter laugh crawled up Aeliana's throat but got choked out by the tears she held back. "Others will take my mother's life if it's a last resort to save all of Rhystahn. She'll probably offer it to them."

The same way you offered yours?

She flinched. "It's different."

Durriken's hum held clear disagreement.

Aeliana ignored it. "I'd like you to take me to the palace. I want your help finding a way to defeat Mayvus while keeping my mother alive. But I want it to be your choice, not something you feel obligated to do because of a brand."

Durriken sat back on his haunches and pawed at the earth beneath him with his single front paw, the mud squelching between his claws. *You want to remove my brand. Do you not want to be tethered?* A strange emotion emanated from him, almost like the thought caused him pain.

She hesitated. "You said your ancestors were tethered to half-lights. Can't we remain tethered without the brand? Would it be strong enough to protect you from Mayvus trying to rebrand you?"

Durriken paused, studying where the mud hid his brand. *Perhaps if Orra seals it. Then it might be strong enough.*

"Orra?" Aeliana's breath caught. "She can do that?"

It's how it was done for my father and his father before him. Our tether has formed, but until a Star seals it, it's strength might not be enough to override the blood magic of a brand. But a sealed tether is a permanent connection, severed only by death. In many ways, it could be considered worse than a brand if it's not something both of us desire. The vulnerability returned to his words, making Aeliana's throat tighten.

She let his meaning sink in, making sure her decision was not made lightly. She hadn't wanted her bond with Lukai, and clearly she hadn't wanted to be branded by Mayvus or even Gaeren. She'd constantly been looking for a way out of her brand on Durriken because it hadn't ever felt right. But a tether held give and take with mutual understanding.

From the moment she'd met Durriken, she'd wanted the world to be wrong about him. He was grumpy and could be vicious, but he was also hurting—and had been for a long time. Maybe the others were right and she had a weakness for defenseless creatures, one that might come back to hurt her down the line. But Durriken had become far more than an animal to save.

"I would gladly bind myself to you with a tether." A ripple of pleasure crossed the air between them, and his nose dipped to the ground in acceptance. He lowered his entire body, offering his back for her to ride. She hesitated, then used her dagger to split her already torn skirt, grateful she'd worn the leathers underneath.

As she climbed up behind his neck, his scales flattened instead of flaring, giving her safe passage to the leathery place that held one of his only vulnerable spots. It made her realize that for a dragon to allow a rider, it had to make itself vulnerable. There was a two-way trust, as she expected him to safely carry her through the skies and he expected that she wouldn't stab him in the back.

As his three paws lumbered across the swampy ground and the power of his hind legs lifted them into the air, the sensation was both frighteningly unfamiliar and strangely nostalgic. When she'd flown in his mind, it had been smooth and consistent. But now his muscles rippled beneath her and forced her to learn the rhythm of gripping his neck and anticipating the pattern of the beat of his wings.

After a while, she grew used to it, but she knew she'd be sore in the morning—if she made it to the morning. Her stomach grew queasy, but she wasn't sure if it was a result of the rise and fall through the air or her nerves at approaching the palace.

"Orra will likely be at the Sungazer," she shouted to Durriken, pointing at the building on the eastern end of the palace. When she realized he couldn't see her arm behind his head, she fed the image through their tether. Her subconscious use of his noetic skills left her all too aware of how this might change things. Losing the brand would likely make her lose the noetic skills Sylmar had encouraged her to learn.

But it would be worth it to give Durriken his freedom.

He adjusted his trajectory, and with the descent, Aeliana's stomach grew even more unsettled. As he landed, a figure emerged from the Sungazer, and Aeliana recognized the statuesque frame of Orra patiently waiting for them as if she'd expected them.

Perhaps she had.

"I should have known the two of you were involved," Orra said as Aeliana leaped off Durriken's back.

"Involved in what?" Aeliana asked.

Orra spread out a hand, gesturing toward the palace. "All the commotion. Dozens of soldiers being called into the palace. Are they gearing up to face a dragon? Or is this more than a simple misunderstanding?"

Orra's question left a hollow ache in Aeliana's chest. Six months ago, Orra would have been telling them what would transpire. But now she had just as many questions as Aeliana. Was her power that weak? Or was her restraint that strong?

"Felk showed up at the wedding," Aeliana said.

Orra's eyebrows rose. "He followed my note, then." A small smile crossed her face. "It was a gamble, but they refused to let the winex stay at the fortress. So I gave him the choice of ignorance and freedom or following a trail that might lead to you. His loyalty goes deep, and that is not something to take for granted."

"Well, his trail also led him to Mayvus and her fleet of ships, which are currently arriving at the harbor."

Orra's face paled, and she reached out to grip the stone wall of the Sungazer. "She's come here?"

Aeliana nodded. "She never even went to Myndren."

Orra's eyes fluttered closed, and Aeliana suspected the other woman felt debilitated by her pneumatic blindness.

"We need to get my mother to safety. But we also need to keep Durriken from being branded again. If Mayvus has his blood…" Aeliana trailed off, thinking of the way Mayvus had branded Durriken a second time. It hadn't been as strong as the first since Mayvus hadn't waited for Summer Solstice, but that only gave Aeliana more concern that Mayvus wouldn't wait for the perfect time if she had more of his blood again.

Orra frowned. "Isn't that why you kept the brand?"

Aeliana glanced at Durriken, who gave his rumble of assent before lowering himself to the ground and resting his head on his paw. "We'd like to have our tether sealed instead."

Orra's eyes widened, and she reached for Aeliana's arm, placing her other hand on Durriken's wing. "You've started growing a tether?" She closed her eyes and let out a rush of air. "Oh, yes—and it's already strong."

The lingering nausea from their flight was replaced by a warmth in Aeliana's stomach that spread out to her limbs.

"And you want me to seal it." Orra opened her eyes, the smile on her face oddly bright despite the tension spreading out from the palace.

"Do you have the strength for it?" Aeliana asked.

Orra hesitated, then nodded. "I've been holding back my power for a moment like this. A moment when only my power could change the outcome. I didn't know what it would look like, but I suspect this is what I've been saving it for."

Aeliana sensed Durriken's relief alongside her own.

"Quick," Orra instructed. "Cut out the brand."

Aeliana wasted no time using her dagger to peel off the layer of her skin that held the inky blackness she despised. As blood trickled out, she was reminded of her past and the blood magic she'd been used for, but for once there wasn't even any pull she needed to resist.

Even though Aeliana healed herself while she worked, her vision blurred with the pain, and the task became too difficult to complete on her own. Orra took over, ignoring Durriken's grunts and growls filling the air as he dropped to the ground. He licked his remaining front paw even though no visible wound was present, merely a fading mark.

This time, when the brand was gone, Aeliana didn't feel the same sense of loss that she'd felt with Gaeren, because the faint tether that joined them remained, like a string waiting to be plucked to ring out a note of hope.

She placed her freshly scarred palm over Durriken's paw and closed her eyes, relishing the way the small string connecting them held a purity that had previously been tainted by the brand. The longer she stood there, the thicker the string seemed to grow, and the more stable their connection.

Orra placed her hands on each of them once more, and a light laugh escaped her lips. "Perhaps sealing your tether won't drain as much magic as I thought. Its roots grow deeper. Its foundation is already stronger without the brand."

Even so, Aeliana sensed the heat of Orra's power rushing through her soul—a burning sensation that gave her a new appreciation for Orra's identity as a Star. The other woman might not consider herself to be one anymore, but this kind of power could only come from something beyond this world. Tears poured down Aeliana's cheeks at the honor of being given this gift from the Stars she'd once worshiped. She supposed it was a gift from the Sun being given through Orra, but that was something she would have to ponder later, when her mother's life wasn't hanging in the balance.

With the heat came flashes of understanding, the hint of a lonely and lengthy existence, waiting and losing hope for its end. The love of her own family grew tenfold as she sensed Durriken's love for his, a taste of what a family bond could be. As she pictured the ruby and onyx scales of his mate and the golden hues of his hatchling, she felt like she'd known them all her life, which now felt tiny and insignificant in the shadow of his hundreds of years. She'd thought him ageless, but now she sensed he was not just old in half-light years—he was old for a dragon. Maybe even dying without his family.

A coolness followed on the heels of the burn, and a thick rope seemed to replace the tiny thread joining her to Durriken. When her vision cleared, Durriken's fiery eye stared back at her with a wisdom and understanding she felt reflected from her soul. She sensed a closeness to him that surpassed friendship or even the bonds of family.

Something undefinable that made her want to wrap her arms around him, despite his terrifying maw.

Instead, she bent her forehead to the tip of his nose, and he huffed out the slightest puff of warm air that enveloped her like a hug. Daisies bloomed all around them, and her laugh came out as carefree as a child's.

"The tether might be too strong at first," Orra murmured, her voice sounding frail. "But it will settle as you grow into it. It's not ideal to have a new one just before confronting Mayvus. But it's better than having none at all."

"Can she still brand him?" Aeliana asked.

Orra hesitated. "She can try. But he should still be able to resist even without your brand." Orra stepped back, almost tripping over her own feet. Her face paled as Aeliana reached out to steady her, but even more startling were the fresh age lines on her face.

"Are you sick, Orra? Was it too much for you?"

Orra shook her head. "I've been fading for a thousand years. It's a natural decline. One that I brought upon myself." She turned and stumbled back toward the main building of the palace.

"Where are you going?" Aeliana called after her.

"I have to prepare. If Mayvus is coming, so are the Stars."

CHAPTER 78

Aeliana placed a hand on Durriken's snout. "I have to go find my mother."

His rumble of assent held concern.

"Can you do a sweep and see where Mayvus and her soldiers are? Maybe see how much time we have or what exactly we're up against?"

He rumbled again, then nudged her gently, still nearly knocking her over, before turning around and taking a running leap. She watched in awe as his wings beat the air, undisturbed by how it knocked her to her backside once more. He was her dragon, and she was his half-light. She felt it in her bones the same way she felt the magic coursing through her blood.

Even Sylmar couldn't have anticipated this. He probably wouldn't even know how to use it to their advantage, and Aeliana decided she liked that. She didn't want anyone using Durriken. She wanted his choices to be his own. Now, they finally were.

His freedom gave her a sense of power that left her fueled for what she had to do next. She cut away the remaining rags of her green skirt as she raced toward the palace doors. The lack of soldiers at its entrance left her disturbed. Where had they all gone?

"Mother?" she shouted through the halls. "Sylmar? Iris? Where is everyone?" Concerned maids peered out of the rooms they cleaned, probably never having heard anything shouted in these formal quarters.

"They should be in their rooms, miss," one of the women said.

"Where are all the soldiers?" Aeliana asked.

The women frowned and glanced down the halls, surprise flitting across their features.

"They wouldn't be able to help, anyway," Aeliana muttered. "Never mind. Thank you." She took off down the hall and up the stairs, counting off the rooms until she came to her mother's quarters. This time, soldiers stood at the door, the sight strange after all the empty halls. She hesitated, wondering why, out of all the places the soldiers should be, they happened to be here.

But they'd seen her, so they ushered her through, and she found most everyone gathered together. Despite her relief over finding her mother, the soft click of a lock behind her felt ominous.

Emeris ran over and cupped Aeliana's cheeks between her hands. "You're all right. I was so worried."

"Then you know about Mayvus?" Aeliana asked.

"What about Mayvus?" Sylmar stood, thumping his staff against the floor to make his way over to Aeliana with a speed she hadn't seen in months.

"She's here—in the harbor," Aeliana said. "Maybe even closer now."

Gasps spread through the room.

"If you didn't know she was here, then why were you worried?" Aeliana scanned everyone in the room, counting them off.

Lukai and Kendalyhn sat on the bed, arms wrapped around each other in a way that would have made her bond mark twinge if she still had it. Her father and Iris stood at the window where her mother had originally been, and Iris searched the night sky.

Velden and Marnok played a game of cards at a table, their relaxed stance almost offensive in light of everything happening. Cyrus and Brogdon sat together, the sight of Mayvus' former soldier making Aeliana unfairly uncertain. He'd stayed on the ship when they'd crossed the barrier, and she hadn't seen him leave it before now. He'd wanted nothing more to do with being a soldier after his experiences, so why was he here tonight? Could Mayvus have branded him again?

"They gathered us all together and said our status as guests of the royal family was under review." Sylmar scowled. "We think something's happened with the king and queen."

Aeliana's concern heightened, and she checked the group once more. "Where are Gaeren and Enla? And Riveran?"

"We haven't seen them," her mother said.

"If Mayvus is here," Sylmar said, "we're out of time."

Everyone in the room dropped their gazes, unwilling to look at Aeliana or her mother.

"The trick will be getting the sisters in the same room to make it happen when they've locked us up in here."

"No," Aeliana growled out.

"It's the only way, dear," her mother said. "You've heard the curse. Mayvus is too powerful with me alive."

"Then we find a way to weaken her." Aeliana's voice rose with her desperation.

"As long as I'm strong, she will be too." Her mother gave an apologetic smile and held out her arms.

Aeliana accepted the embrace, but her mother's words echoed in her mind, as though they held a different meaning than she'd intended. The others formed some sort of line behind Aeliana in their acceptance, giving Emeris hugs and offering Rildan murmured condolences.

"No," Aeliana whispered, the words finally starting to click in her mind.

Everyone ignored her, writing off her words as grief.

"No." She said it again, louder. "We can find a way to weaken Mayvus. If you're weak, she's weak." She scanned the room, then stepped forward, tugging on Lukai's arm. "Didn't you tour the apothecary with the healers?"

"Yes." His brow bunched in confusion. "Marnok and I both did. It's in the west wing, on the third floor. They have hundreds of tonics, things I didn't know existed that can be used with or without magic.

Even the staff who aren't progenies can heal most anything." His voice held a bit of wonder.

"But aren't there things that could harm as well?"

He nodded warily. "Most anything in the wrong dosage can be harmful." His gaze flicked to Emeris. "Are you suggesting…"

"Yes." She turned to her mother. "Instead of killing you, let's just make you sick. Sick enough to weaken Mayvus and trap her, but not sick enough to kill either one of you. Then we heal you."

The room went quiet as the idea was considered, and Aeliana knew she'd found the solution. It was one they couldn't argue with, because trying anything was better than giving up and accepting Emeris' death.

"Moon's brew herb and valerian root could do the trick," Marnok said quietly, bolstering Aeliana's hope.

"Where would I find them? What do they look like?" she asked.

He described them both in detail, giving his best guess as to where they'd be in an apothecary, but the others started voicing their dissent.

"How will you get there?" Velden asked. "You may have walked in here free and clear, but they're not going to let you walk out."

She bit her lip, remembering the way the door had locked behind her, then glanced at the window where Iris still watched the skies.

"What do you see?" Aeliana asked.

Iris shook her head. "It's more what I don't see. The Stars— they're not dancing."

"The Stars?" Aeliana asked. "Orra thinks they're with Mayvus. She's going to look for them."

"If the Stars are on Mayvus' side, how can we possibly succeed?" Cyrus asked.

"Haven't you been listening to Orra?" Aeliana asked. "We can still succeed, because the Sun is on our side." She reached for her tether, finding it just beneath her consciousness—far easier to grasp than ever before. Without even closing her eyes, she was able to home in on Durriken's senses, to feel the cool air rushing around leathery and scaly skin, powerful wings flapping, and a keen mind scanning the ground.

They're much too close, Durriken told her. *I didn't have to go far.*

She felt her own sorrow pass through him. *Any sign of Felk?*

His lack of answer only made her sorrow grow.

Come back to me. Pick me up on the eastern wing. They've locked us all in my mother's room. She knew that just like she could see and feel through his eyes and body, he could do the same. And she trusted he would find her. *I need you to take me to the apothecary in the western wing.* She felt his assent more than she heard the rumble of his breath. Then she released the tether and bounced back to the room with a shudder.

"Are you all right?" Iris gripped Aeliana's shoulders. "You were gone"—she glanced nervously at Emeris—"like your mother."

"I was communicating with Durriken," Aeliana admitted.

Sylmar grabbed her wrist and held it up, his eyes narrowed. "Where's your brand?" Suspicion colored his tone, and Aeliana wondered if he would ever be able to trust anyone again.

"We're tethered. Orra sealed it. We don't need a brand." Her chin rose as she internally dared him to find something wrong with what she'd done. It hadn't been part of his plan, and that could be enough to make it wrong, but she would never regret this choice.

His eyes went wide, and another round of gasps spread through the room, but she didn't have time to explain more than that or wait for their shock to fade. She flung open the balcony doors and stood on the edge, sensing Durriken's nearness the same way she suspected Orra felt someone touching a starbridge. The internal awareness outmatched her other senses in a way that left her sight and hearing dulled.

"Don't try to escape. Instead, bar the doors. Make sure no one can come in."

She knew her actions would horrify everyone back in the room, but there was an absolute rightness to stepping on the edge of the balcony and leaping blindly.

CHAPTER 79

GAEREN'S STARLOCK heated against his chest, pulling him back to consciousness. It served as a warning as much as a comfort. He blinked slowly, taking in the way his body lay crumpled on the floor, his sister's limp hand hanging from the table above him.

"Some winex delayed them in the harbor," his father grunted in irritation from behind him, somewhere near the dais. "But they're on their way."

"I don't like that she had you hit him." The queen's cool fingers brushed the back of Gaeren's neck, and he focused all his energy on holding still, appearing unconscious, or maybe dead. Whichever would keep Mayvus happy when she checked in with her brands.

"She could have had me do worse." His father's response was barely audible and held a hint of confusion that reminded Gaeren of the broken man he'd found after returning from Lorvandas, the man who'd regretted the way he'd been used by Mayvus. It made him wonder if that man was accessible somewhere deep beneath the brand.

Maybe it was better if he didn't know. At this point, he would need to fight his parents to protect Enla. It was the only way he could get her out of here. His stomach roiled at the thought.

Then an even more detestable idea snuck through: he could escape without her. Despite being branded, his parents had aged in the last year, their status as Mayvus' pawns taking a toll on their physical bodies. His father might be able to kill him, but the king's reflexes would be too slow, and he wouldn't anticipate Gaeren leaving Enla.

But that was because Gaeren could never leave Enla. Not at the mercy of their parents. And definitely not at the mercy of Mayvus. Which meant he couldn't keep playing dead.

He slid away from his mother, who sucked in a breath, then kneeled, using Enla's table to pull himself to a standing position. The room swayed before him, but he blinked it back into focus.

"How did you hide it?" he asked. "I checked both of your hands."

"Illusion work," his mother said. "Just like she used on your friend Holm."

Gaeren scowled. "But I felt your hands."

His mother held out her palms, and the scar of her old brand slowly darkened until it held a fresh mark. "Funny how raised scars can feel an awful lot like a raised brand."

"This is madness." Gaeren tightened his grip on the table. "You really think serving the likes of Mayvus is better for your people?" He wasn't even sure what he was saying. He simply needed to stall and come up with a plan. What would Enla do in this situation? He almost laughed. She would look into the future and do whichever thing had the least negative consequences.

"It doesn't matter what I think," his father said. "I was a good ruler for a time, and I set the stage for her to take control. But she'll come in now and improve upon my failures."

This time Gaeren did laugh. "The father I knew never would have referenced failures. Not unless he was talking about me."

A flicker of remorse flashed across his father's face before his features hardened into the mask Mayvus had him wear. "The Elanesse family is full of failures."

His father choked a bit on the word as if a small part of him finally recognized that what he was saying went against everything he believed in. Somewhere beneath the facade Mayvus gave him, Gaeren's father remained. If anything, it made what Gaeren had to do even harder.

Typically, tuning in to memories didn't aid Gaeren much in battle. But fighting his parents with memories gave him the upper hand. Instead of pushing away his mother's calming hand, he welcomed it, allowing the contact to give him the opportunity to feed his own memories back into her mind. Memories of their horror and embarrassment when they admitted to Gaeren they'd been branded. Memories of their desire to set aside their rule in favor of Enla, and he now realized their change of heart likely had more to do with Mayvus than Enla's failing mind.

His mother cried out and dropped his hand as if he'd burned her. He pulled out his dagger and made a swipe at her palm, not quite ready to cut off her hand, but not able to get at the brand either. She pulled back and her eyes narrowed, her scowl far harsher than any expression he'd ever seen on her face.

"Is that how you're going to play it, boy?" she hissed, her voice almost feral. She hunched over and took a defensive stance, blocking his access to her hands and making him regret not going for it when he'd had the chance. Surely she would have forgiven him when all was said and done.

Gaeren's father roared his frustration, and Gaeren's throat tightened, closing off his air supply. His eyes widened, both with surprise and his body's panic to find more air. His father had never been one to shy away from lessons with physical consequences, but he'd never threatened to take Gaeren's life. The realization made him wonder if his father's harsh treatment had still come from a place of love, even if it was twisted.

But even if that was true, it didn't matter. Mayvus would still have him kill Gaeren.

His hands came to his neck, searching for the invisible vise tightening to cut off his air supply. But the damage was being done internally, and his noetic magic could do nothing to stop it. Instead, he crawled to his father, ignoring his mother's sobs because she stood rooted to the ground, unable to help as she watched her nightmares come alive.

His father's face held a blankness, and maybe it was selfish of Gaeren, but he refused to let his father kill him without knowing exactly what he was doing. He placed his hand on his father's shins. At first the old man sneered, well aware that Gaeren's magic couldn't stop this onslaught. But then Gaeren no longer saw his father's face. It was replaced by childhood memories.

There were very few positive ones, but Gaeren reached deep for them, focusing mostly on his time with Enla and the friendship they shared as siblings. Because despite the fact that he'd never had that connection with his parents, they'd given him his sister. And he would always be grateful for that.

He pushed memory after memory on his father of the times he and Enla had spent together. Of the times he and Enla had escaped their parents' wrath. The times they'd comforted each other after having been disciplined. And the times they'd challenged each other to do what was right despite their parents' influence. All the ways that their parents' efforts to mold them into ruthless leaders had actually driven them together and pushed them to seek compassion. Their parents' failures had made Enla the Recreants' greatest hope.

When the memories started to fade, he thought maybe he'd disrupted the control of Mayvus' brand, but somewhere in his dim awareness he realized it was that he was running out of air.

He was fading from the world.

At the center of the dimness a bright light appeared, an appealing glimmer in the midst of the darkness that called to him. But a sharp squawk followed by a sickening thud kept Gaeren from reaching for the light. He sucked in air, then choked on it like he was drowning, twisting to the side to cough and gasp. As his vision returned, he found himself bent beside his father's crumpled form. Scratches marred his father's forehead, and Gaeren turned to find Gullet's beady eyes staring down at him from the armrest of his father's council room chair.

For the first time, the bird's haughty glare held more pride than hatred, and Gaeren had never been so happy to see the smelly creature. "Gullet? Did you really just save my life?"

"I'd like to take some credit," Riveran said from behind him.

Gaeren's laugh burned his throat, but he welcomed the pain. It signified life.

"I thought you were dead, old bird. Did you just get lost tracking down Aeliana?" Gaeren stroked the hawk's head, but it still nipped at his finger.

Riveran stood with nearly a dozen winex, including Felk, who held down Gaeren's mother with Lilik's help. The look on their faces held more animosity than Gaeren liked, so he stumbled to their side with his dagger. "Thank you for your help, but I can cut her brand out."

Felk twitched as if holding back his desire to chew the mark out himself. "And then you win?"

Gaeren shrugged. "Something like that."

His mother fought as Gaeren sliced, and he winced, wishing he had Lukai's or Aeliana's ability to heal. But when the brand was removed and his mother had stopped fighting, she sobbed and begged him to do the same for his father. The winex were quick to obey, slinking over to the king to hold him down.

A few leaned in to sniff him, reminding Gaeren they were in a precarious balance of power.

"How did you find us?" Gaeren asked.

The winex didn't answer, which wasn't a surprise, but Riveran's silence made Gaeren glance up.

Riveran's face was troubled, and his gaze rested on Enla's still form. "She left me a note. Told me exactly where you would be and exactly what you would need."

Gaeren's stomach turned, and he wondered if he might actually throw up after all he'd been through. "Then that means I didn't change anything by coming here," he murmured.

"What?" Riveran asked.

"How could she know?" Gaeren continued, louder this time. "I tried to do something she couldn't have seen. Something that changed after she told me what would happen."

"Her visions of the future have gotten stronger," Riveran admitted. "She's been telling me things no one should know." He ran a hand over his hair, making Gaeren realize his X was almost completely hidden now.

Felk and Lilik tightened their grips, their nails digging into the king in a way that likely roused him more than held him down. Wasting no more time, Gaeren sliced at the brand on his father's palm, bringing the king fully awake. Gaeren winced, trying to block out his father's raving insults and threats until the skin was finally gone and his father went limp in Felk's and Lilik's grasp.

His father's face had grown deathly pale, making Gaeren wonder if the intensity of it all had been too much. But shallow breaths made the king's chest rise and fall, and to Gaeren's surprise, he felt a sense of relief. His parents both looked even older than they had the last time he'd seen them lost in their remorse.

"Thank you," Gaeren said to Felk and Lilik, gently tugging their hands from his father's arms. They resisted for a moment, but then they released their hold and slunk to the side of the room, crouching together in a strange huddle with the rest of their clan.

"You're too weak to fight Mayvus," Gaeren said. "I need to get you and Enla out of here."

"We should have handed our rule to Enla long ago," his father murmured.

Gaeren couldn't argue, especially since the last time they'd said that, Gaeren had been the one to refuse taking on the throne warden role.

"Can you make it to the hidden pass?"

His father shook his head. "Even if I could, your mother never would, and I doubt Enla would be willing to leave."

Gaeren frowned, glancing back at his sister's still form. "Riveran, can you get her awake?"

Riveran bent over and jostled her shoulders before shaking his head. "I've never seen her like this. I'm scared waking her could be dangerous. It might be something she needs to choose to come out of on her own."

"Where is Croft?" Gaeren grumbled.

"He and Danton are organizing the troops," his father said, then hesitated, as if unable to trust his memory from his time under the brand. "I think Danton might be working with the Recreants. Mayvus seemed to want me watching him. Whereas Croft was too gullible and malleable to concern her." His face twisted in a scowl usually reserved for Gaeren. "I don't think he's branded, but perhaps that's worse."

"You think he's working with Mayvus?"

The king hesitated. "I instructed him to let Mayvus and her army in the palace walls and he obeyed without question."

Gaeren winced. "How long ago was that?"

The king's confidence faded. "Too long ago. Our troops won't resist her people. They consider them allies at this point."

As if to prove his words, Gaeren heard shouts from beyond the council room, and he rushed to the nearest window, angling his head to see beyond the courtyard to the palace walls. Their home wasn't as secure as the fortress in the Myndren Mountains, and it wasn't the first time he'd wished they had enough humility to heighten their security. But their rule had remained uncontested for nearly a thousand years, outside of the rogue Wyndrens attempting to take what they thought was their rightful place.

Even the Recreants hadn't been enough of a threat for his parents to prioritize a stronger perimeter.

Hordes of Ahmranans approached, like a sea of half-lights riding a wave to the shore. Even if their father had attempted to defend the palace, it would have been futile against so many soldiers.

Had Mayvus brought all of the Ahmranans over?

He ran back to Enla, slapping her cheeks despite Riveran's protests. "Please, Enla, I need you awake. I need you to tell me what to do."

A soft moan escaped her lips, bringing him hope that maybe she could still hear him.

"Enla, how many Stars are there? Count them with me."

Her eyelids flickered, like when someone transitioned out of a deep sleep.

"I told you fifty-two, but I was wrong. Did you ever think I would admit that?" He chuckled even though he grew more tense as the outside crowd's murmur grew louder and the Ahmranans drew closer. "There were a hundred, Enla. Can you believe it? Orra—no, Sheen— told me herself. Did you know I've been spending time with a Star? One of the most important in history."

Her eyelids ceased their rapid movement, forming a slit as her weary gaze seemed to settle on him.

"Now only ninety-seven can take to the skies. That means I missed forty-five every time I counted."

Her lips moved slightly, and he had to bend his ear toward her mouth to catch the question she gasped out. "What about...the other three?"

Relief at her words and focus made him giddy, and a grin split his face. "Lucien was killed, and Orra—or Sheen—was grounded..." He trailed off, distracted as he pulled her to a sitting position to test her strength, which was utterly lacking. The answer he'd just discovered had actually been there all along if he'd bother to do the math. "The third one is Bryton, Orra's other half—someone who'd been more than a bondmate."

"What happened?" She fought to stand, but he shook his head.

"It sounds like Bryton... well, I think he'll take to the skies again when Orra reunites the starbridges."

The clink of gates rising outside brought a new sense of panic that overrode Gaeren's curiosity. Enla couldn't be moved, even if they had time to escape. His parents could never make it to the secret pass, and Mayvus would have no qualms about killing them all, considering they'd evaded her brands twice now.

"The starbridges," he murmured, reaching into his pocket to feel the warm, vibrating metal of the golden arrow. He'd promised to protect it for Orra, but he hadn't promised he'd never use it again. And he hadn't promised that he wouldn't give that task to someone else. He couldn't have promised that. Not when he'd known his time was likely limited.

Instead, he could make good on his promise to the Recreants. He could send his family to a place where they couldn't return to the throne.

Saving Enla with the starbridge could very well get him killed. But hadn't he always known that was the likeliest outcome? He laid her back down on the table, then leaned over the tug Riveran closer.

"I need you to promise me something." He pressed the arrow into his friend's palm, wrapping Riveran's fingers around its shaft. "When you come back, you need to give this arrow to Orra."

"When he comes back?" Enla's voice came out groggy, and her gaze clouded over once more. "There's only one path...in the future. So... much...death. It's the only path that takes us through."

The eerie finality of her voice sent a shiver down Gaeren's spine. He returned his focus to Riveran. "Can you take them?"

He fed the memory of Cyrus reciting the words through to Riveran, who scowled. "What about you?"

"I have to find Aeliana," he said. "I can't let her face Mayvus alone."

"And what if she's already gone? Then you'll face Mayvus alone."

Gaeren shook his head. "She wouldn't leave her mother, and her mother will gladly prepare to sacrifice herself for the Vendaran people. They're still here."

Riveran hesitated.

"We've always known this was in my future," Gaeren whispered. He didn't need to feed the memory to Riveran for the other man to know he spoke of the sprite's prediction.

"I promised her I wouldn't let it happen," Riveran admitted, his gaze falling back on Enla, who once again seemed lost in time. "I promised to let her take the fall." The love in his eyes was painful to see, compounded by the realization that the two of them had been conspiring against Gaeren. Maybe for his good, but still behind his back.

"We can't keep all of our promises," Gaeren said. "Not when we're making impossible ones."

Riveran stood a little taller, masking his face once more. "Which is why you ask the impossible of me." He whistled, and Gullet flew to his shoulder. "I'll take them, but I expect you here when I return."

Gaeren nodded slowly. "Should I make that a promise?"

Riveran snorted.

Gaeren let go of Riveran's hand, feeling a sense of loss as he gave up contact with both the starbridge and his friend. Then he pulled his parents over to Riveran and Enla, instructing them all to hold each other tightly.

"Try not to throw up on my sister when you land." He grinned at Riveran, who couldn't seem to return the smile as he swallowed hard and nodded.

Riveran would take care of Enla no matter what happened to

Gaeren. He knew that, and not just because Lady Merinnia had seen a path where things played out that way. It was just who Riveran was.

Gaeren stepped back, but before Riveran could recite the words, the doors flew open hard enough to hit the walls and pop off their hinges, sending dust and debris flying through the room. Riveran ducked while bracing himself over Enla, but Gaeren's parents fell back to the stone floor with groans, a cut blooming blood on the king's face. Gaeren tugged on their arms, attempting to pull them back to Riveran and Enla, but his mother cried out, favoring her left wrist and ankle.

The winex snarled, forming a protective ring, but boots stomped on the floor as the strange people with darker skin, golden tattoos, and piercings at their collar bones surrounded them, making the dust pick up even more.

"Gaeren?" Riveran called out before coughing. "Do I wait?"

"You need to go," Gaeren hissed at his mother as the room filled with Ahmranans. "Now!"

Her cries turned to sobs and she reached for her husband, who cradled her in his arms, where Gaeren noticed another cut bleeding heavily.

"I don't want to hide anymore." His father's voice held regal pride despite his humble position. "I would rather she killed me than made me her brand again."

Gaeren swore and pulled on his father harder. "She'll do exactly that. I'm the throne warden. My role is to protect the throne. There's no throne without you in it." But the stubborn man stayed put with his wife, their strangely calm acceptance of their fate making Gaeren more panicked.

But then his father smiled and placed a hand on Gaeren, feeding him energy he didn't know the old man had in his reserves. "You're Enla's throne warden, not mine." His voice grew ragged. "Protect her."

Gaeren hesitated for a breath to let the peace on his parents' faces drill into his memory, then he turned his back on them.

"Take her, Riveran! Now!"

Riveran recited the words on the arrow, and bright white light enveloped the two of them just as Mayvus entered the room.

CHAPTER 80

Orra stood in the courtyard as hordes of Ahmranans ran past her. A few paused occasionally as if debating whether they should engage her. But after being in the presence of Stars for several moons, it seemed they'd developed a recognition for what she was or what she'd been. They passed her by, clearly deciding it wasn't worth the risk.

Their high cheekbones and golden tattoos brought back memories of life before the Great Divide. The Ahmranans were a prideful people, but not without reason. They held more starblood than most half-lights, partly because they'd intentionally bred themselves that way, the same way the royal family verified starblood concentration before bonding their children.

But the Ahmranans had taken it to a different level, often turning those without magic into slaves. Perhaps they'd changed in the last thousand years, but if her experience with Lance and Victor during her days as Pirate Redwood was any indication, they were just as harsh as they'd always been.

"Have you seen Reyna?" she asked a few people passing by.

One woman side-eyed her. "She's with the other Stars," she said noncommittally before continuing on.

Orra scanned the people, looking for someone who might have more authority. The crowd grew thicker, forcing everyone's progress to slow, which worked in Orra's favor.

A tall lanky man stood out with twice as many tattoos as the others, his chest strapped with dozens of daggers and his starlock held in place at his collarbone with a bright red piercing meant to draw the eye to his power. She placed her hand on his arm to stop him, then sucked in a gasp as a familiar darkness welled in him.

"Victor," she murmured. He shared blood with the despicable Ahmranan pirate from her past, whether he was a direct descendant or some distant offshoot, she couldn't say. But it left her troubled. Why had Reyna and the others chosen to commune with these people?

The man's eyes narrowed. "How do you know my name?"

She shook her head and pulled her hand away, her fingertips feeling seared. "I didn't—you share his name?"

He pulled a dagger from his chest straps and angled it up toward her chin. "Who are you?"

The challenge brought back memories of her years with Captain Moss, along with a remembered response. The smirk that spread across her face was a welcome shift after so many lost years.

She knew exactly how to handle this sort of man.

"I believe your history books would refer to me as the Fearsome Pirate Redwood. I bested your ancestors, and I'll gladly do it again."

An amusing mix of fear and disbelief crossed his face, but all that mattered to Orra was his hesitation, which she took full advantage of. As if mere moments had passed since her time aboard the pirate ship, she knocked the dagger from his hand, stole a second from his strap, and cut the remainder from his chest.

Blood spilled from his torn shirt, and she winced. "I apologize. I've grown rusty over the years. I never used to be so imprecise."

He backed away, his face turning a dusky grey.

"Wait!" This time it was she who held the dagger beneath his chin. "Where's Reyna?"

The people rushing past gave them a wider berth.

His gaze flicked to the tallest tower, then back again. "They took to the skies with the Sun's descent."

"There are no Stars out dancing tonight," Orra said flatly.

He shrugged sheepishly. "Maybe they're not in the mood to dance."

The crowd nearly slowed to a stop, her stance with the dagger becoming more noticeable as others around them whispered and frowned. She'd have to trust that his slip-up was genuine.

She feigned a lunge to make him flinch, then took off in the crowd, dropping the dagger in the grass. He'd follow, but her lithe form slipped easily between warriors, whereas his bulk would not.

Before she left the outer courtyard, she stopped another woman. "Are the Stars on the tallest tower yet?"

The woman grinned maliciously. "Hopefully they're well past that now. Seems like there's some sort of hold up at the main door. If they can open up more doors, we won't be so bottlenecked."

Orra grimaced, wondering how these people had been chosen by the Sun and gifted by the Stars. It went against everything she understood of the Sun's goodness and the Stars' honor. Even when she'd had the joy of delivering starlocks, she'd shied away from gifting hers to the Ahmranans.

She glanced at the woman's starlock, which lay nestled in her collarbone, held in place by a piercing not quite as ornate as Victor's had been. She placed a finger on the sphere-like charm, far more interested in what lay inside than its shape. The woman stiffened, but before she could push Orra away, Orra let go.

"Telnar," Orra murmured.

The woman's eyes lit up. "Is he your Star as well?" she asked in awe.

Orra smiled softly. "I have no Star. Stars are not owned or assigned to people. He is not your Star either. Your starlock simply holds his essence."

The woman's gaze shifted to fear. "You're one of them?" She bowed her head and made to kneel, but Orra stopped her.

"Do not worship those who sin the same as you. And that includes Telnar." Orra stepped away, not bothering to see if the woman took her words to heart. If the Stars had been accepting these people's worship, things were far worse than she'd realized. Still, she would wait to get answers from Reyna.

She fought her way against the flow of traffic to reach a side door hidden just outside the gate. It blended well enough into the stone wall that she wasn't sure the current royal family was even aware of its existence. And when it took far too much of her energy to shift it out of place, that theory was confirmed.

Thankfully, the Ahmranans were all too focused on getting through the main gate to notice her slip in and shut the door behind her. Dust filled the air as she made her way from the derelict passage to the main floor, where she was forced to use another ridiculous amount of her reserves to push through to the main hall.

Each path she took was eerily quiet, the soldiers having been called to defend the king and queen. And yet they hadn't been out in the courtyard fending off the gathering Ahmranans, who'd easily entered through the gates. The deeper she went into the palace without any signs of fighting, the more she had to assume the Ahmranans had been welcomed, or at the very least expected. Were they secretly allies of the royal family? Or had the Recreants aided them in some way?

She sensed the presence of several half-lights in a room above her, one of them likely Emeris, if her internal map of the palace was still accurate. She hesitated, wondering if she should aid them in any way, but the warmth in her gut urged her forward like the rays of the Sun pulling on a string at her navel.

Her friends knew how to take care of themselves, but she was the only one who could speak to the Stars, maybe make sense of their actions or challenge them to reconsider.

When she finally approached the highest turret, she nearly doubled over as she sensed their presence growing nearer. It had been so long since she'd communed with her brothers and sisters. The brief taste of Reyna's presence on Summer Solstice had been a painful tease.

Tears spilled onto her cheeks. She wasn't sure she could survive if she lost access to them again.

When she left the stairwell for the open night air, it was Andreas who saw her first, and this time an audible sob left Orra's lips. She gripped the wall for support and reached out her other hand, longing to reassure herself he was real but also terrified he would reject her.

Instead, he ran to her and wrapped his arms around her, his welcoming touch so different from Reyna's judgmental hatred on the north tower's balcony all those moons ago. Over his shoulder, she saw at least a dozen Stars with more arriving as they shot from the sky and shed their reflective fire for human forms.

"I wondered if you might come." He moved to pull back, but Orra held him tighter, relishing the feel of arms around her, acceptance from her own kind.

"Forgive me," she whispered.

"It's not my forgiveness you should seek," he said. "I gave that long ago."

"I don't think Reyna will forgive me."

His laugh spread through her, the warmth as inviting as the Sun spilling over a mountain's ridge. "Reyna forgives no one."

This time when he pulled away, she didn't resist but kept her eyes downcast, unable to see his pity or distrust. "When I reunite the starbridges, I will ask Bryton's forgiveness."

"I'm not talking about Bryton either." He bent down and tilted her chin up, raising his eyebrows. His full meaning hit her.

"I don't deserve the Sun's forgive—"

"And yet," he interrupted quietly, "the Sun offers it."

She nodded, knowing he was right but still not ready to face all that she'd done. She couldn't earn that forgiveness by reuniting the starbridges, but it was difficult to imagine asking before having at least accomplished that task. The advice she'd given to so many others over thousands of years was now too difficult for her to take herself.

"I thought you'd all given up on me. That you didn't want anything to do with me."

"Not all of us." Beyond Andreas' understanding smile, Reyna's scowl came into focus.

"Joining us won't allow you to return to the skies," she said.

Orra stepped away from Andreas, not wanting to implicate him in the confrontation that was to come. Wind whipped her hair into her eyes while the other Stars' long locks ruffled near their knees—another reminder of the sacrifices she'd made for all the wrong reasons.

"I'm not asking to join you. I'm asking you to stop."

Reyna laughed, and a few of the other Stars around her echoed her titter. "Does it not fit with your plans?"

"You're doing what I did so many years ago," Orra said. "You're interfering in ways that the Sun would not approve."

Uncertainty flickered across Andreas' face, and he turned to Reyna. "Perhaps we should listen."

"The same way you listened to my doubts all those years ago?" Reyna asked.

He flinched and hung his head.

"I doubted your ideas." Reyna stepped forward, chin raised as she approached Orra. "I sensed your actions would not be approved by the Sun. Even as I began to split the earth for you, I felt the wrongness of it."

"And so you backed away," Orra said. "I don't blame you for that. You made the right choice then, but I think you're making the wrong choice now."

"And why should I trust your judgment after all your failings?"

Orra hesitated, knowing the question was a good one. The number of Stars staring back at her had grown to at least fifty, with more still landing on the turret, their glow receding until they resembled familiar forms from her past. She had to get them to reconsider.

She raised her voice, ensuring all would hear. "Tell me, has the Sun approved this endeavor? Has the Sun chosen the Ahmranans to receive some sort of additional gift like I hear you've promised?"

Reyna frowned. "All of these Ahmranans have starlocks. They've been chosen by the Sun and blessed by the Stars. What more do you need?"

"The king and queen were also chosen and blessed by the Stars. If my guess is correct from the time I've been with them, they were gifted by Lumina and Andreas."

One of the Stars near Andreas shifted uncomfortably. Moonlight revealed the worry in her eyes as she exchanged a glance with him, confirming Orra's suspicions.

"If you let Mayvus win, the king and queen will join the Sun tonight and you'll receive your locks of hair back."

"It's the nature of life for these mortals," Reyna said. "There's nothing wrong with them dying and being relieved of their starlocks. They join the Sun. We're giving them a gift."

A bitter huff escaped from Orra's lips. "A gift? And what gift are you promising the Ahmranans? What is the benefit to you if they come over here and take over the Vendaran lands?"

Reyna folded her arms across her chest. "I know it's hard for you to have perspective when you've been grounded all this time. But even you should have noticed there are fewer starlocks being given out. The Sun recognizes that the people are failing again. They continue to fight. They continue to value the wrong things. They need strong leadership."

"They need the Sun," Orra said softly. "That's all they've ever needed."

Reyna's eyebrows rose. "You seemed to think they needed barriers."

Orra's face heated. "I will always be the first to admit my sins. But that is what they are. Sins. I was wrong. Don't make the same mistakes I did."

Reyna huffed. "This is the Sun's doing, not mine."

At that, Orra stepped back, confused. Why would the Sun elevate a group of people bent on enslaving their own? "The people down there are power hungry, looking to kill and defeat, not love or unite. They can't possibly represent the Sun's will."

Andreas' brow furrowed in consideration.

"I don't expect to understand the Sun in its glory," Reyna said. "And I surely don't expect you to understand it, or even worse, disagree with it."

"I'm not questioning the Sun," Orra said. "I'm questioning you."

Reyna's face reddened with her rage.

"It's true. I went against the Sun's will. But I never claimed to be doing the Sun's will. I simply never asked what the Sun would have me do. It's far more concerning to me that you claim to have asked and gotten this answer. Whom exactly were you speaking to? Are you certain it was the Sun?"

Reyna's face grew even darker. "I will not listen to a grounded Star make accusations against me. The Sun has passed judgment on you."

"She's not asking you anything the rest of us haven't," Andreas said, drawing both women's surprised attention. "Several of us have not received the same vision from the Sun. It's difficult to move forward on your word alone when it seems to go against who the Sun is."

"I gave you the opportunity to go your own way moons ago." Reyna's skin took on a glow as the energy within her built up. "And with each revolution, you've grown more and more disgruntled. If you wish to side with the grounded Star, so be it. But just like she is not welcome back in the skies, you will not be either."

Everyone around them gasped, a strange hush filling the empty spaces in the room.

Orra shook her head. "That is not your call to make. The Sun grounded me. Not you. I have seen the depravity of Mayvus. If you are aligned with her, you are not aligned with the Sun."

"We're not aligned with Mayvus." Reyna muttered her name like a curse. "She's a means to an end. The Ahmranans used her to cross the barrier. Once she's done uniting all the people, we'll put an end to her power, paving the way for our strongest descendants to rule the rest. There will be no more need for starlocks. That is what we've promised the Ahmranans."

Orra backed away in horror. "Do you hear yourself?" she whispered. Then she turned to Andreas. "Are you in favor of elevating an entire race to oppress the others? You're taking away the Sun's right to bless the people. This is madness. You've turned your back on the Sun if you've turned your back on the majority of its creation."

Several of the Stars glowed, the burn of their anger palpable. Within moments, the division could be seen across the stone roof as well as felt between the Stars—half burning with anger alongside Reyna and half cold with fear beside Andreas.

"Says the Star who has been rejected by the Sun," Reyna spat out, her words hissing with steam.

Orra expected her to take to the skies any moment, the heat of her current state too intense for her earthly body. She would burn up and fly to the static stars, soaking in the blessings offered by the Sun. Orra's longing for the same brought her tears back once more. "I used to think it was better to do nothing, to not interfere," she murmured. "But inaction can still be the wrong action."

"What are you babbling about?" Reyna's rise in volume seemed to startle even some of the Stars reflecting her fire.

Orra stood taller, well aware that her dregs of magic could never stand against Reyna. "I can't let you do this. Not to the people, not to the Sun, and not to yourself."

Reyna's glow intensified, the whiteness blinding Orra until it matched the ringing in her ears. She had a sliver of hope that this would finally send her to the Sun, but then everything went black.

CHAPTER 81

AELIANA'S LANDING on Durriken's back wasn't gentle or graceful, but there was a rightness deep in her soul as she found her grip and wrapped her arms around his leathery neck. He flew her to the opposite wing of the palace, giving her a bird's-eye view of the hundreds of Ahmranans below. Shouts rose as they caught sight of Durriken, who then dove low on the north side of the palace, out of view. Once again she wasn't sure if her stomach turned because of the unfamiliar sensation of flight or because of nerves.

"They're already here," she murmured.

Had Gaeren found his parents and Enla? Had he gotten them to safety? She scanned the skies, not sure where to look for Orra and the other Stars, but bright glows on the highest turret made her suspect Orra had finally found them. Hopefully that was a good thing.

Focus on our task. Durriken's reminder rumbled through her mind.

She nodded, more for herself than in response to him, then ran through the names of the different herbs and roots Marnok and Lukai had instructed her to find. She relished the opportunity to finally take action and do something to protect her mother, but she also hated the fact that it all depended on her success at finding these herbs in time for them to be used correctly.

Her mother's life was in her hands, and it terrified her.

They didn't even understand the curse well enough to guarantee this could work. For all she knew, by poisoning her mother to weaken Mayvus, Aeliana would still be condemning her mother to die—perhaps a more painful death than the one Sylmar would have offered.

She shook her mind free of her spiraling thoughts as Durriken slowed by the apothecary. Despite the palace's southeast entrance being overrun by Ahmranans, none seemed interested in what the apothecary had to offer. In fact, they hadn't seemed interested in fighting their way into any part of the palace. They'd stood there, content to wait, as if someone might let them in. Were they all under Mayvus' branded spell?

Her gut clenched at the scarier question. Why weren't the royal soldiers fighting them back outside the gates? Were they attempting some sort of delegation with peaceful terms? Or had Gaeren's parents always planned to welcome the enemy with open arms?

Durriken's landing made Aeliana's teeth rattle as she fell more than jumped off his back. He took to the skies far faster than she thought he was able, and she felt his absence even though she knew he would only attract unwanted attention. Even now he might have brought dozens of soldiers headed in her direction. The Ahmranans probably knew Durriken was Mayvus' enemy, whether or not they suspected he was tied to the Recreants. If they served Mayvus, they would want to take him down.

She rushed through the doors Marnok had described. The front rooms of the apothecary were neatly organized with displays for members of the palace to come make purchases. But Marnok had warned her none of these items would have what she truly needed. They were all simple fixes for everyday problems. The valerian root and moon's brew herbs would be hidden in the back for use only by progenies of the crown. And of course they were behind a thick locked door.

At first she used her starlock, attempting to shift the lock mechanism inside the door, but without ever practicing that sort of magic and without understanding the locking mechanism, she felt too pressed for time. Instead, she found a mallet and swung hard at the knob. After three hits, the knob broke off and the door swung open with a faint creak.

Her chest rose and fell with the effort, and she sensed that Sylmar would be disappointed in her weakness. She promised him in her mind that she would redouble her efforts to train when this was all over, then flung open the door and entered a chaotic brewery and hatchery.

Animals in cages stared back at her with wide eyes, and potions burbled on back burners, making her wonder how this place didn't burn down at least once a year. A desperate need to free each of the creatures crawled up her spine, but that agenda would have to wait for another day.

For now, she hunted for the red fibrous roots and the light silver herbs. "Please, please, please," she murmured, unsure if she begged the Stars or the Sun to show her where to find what she needed. The only response she received was the whine of a black and white creature that might have been a raccoon. She hoped it wasn't a skunk.

"What do you think you're doing?" a voice demanded from behind her.

She froze, then turned slowly, examining the room for other escape options. But it was a closet she stood in, and the only way out was blocked by an elderly progeny. She'd seen him before, assisting Gaeren's uncle and parents. Trenton? Tobin?

"I need valerian root and moon's brew. My mother is very ill."

He snorted. "Are you looking to put her out of her misery?" He shuffled over to a table and pulled a single vial from a rack of dozens. "This will reduce her pain without harming her. Perhaps she'll recover, and then you'll have to live with the guilt that you almost killed her."

Her face heated, even though she didn't care what this man thought of her. "I don't need"— she paused, taking in the name of what he'd given her—"willow bark. I need valerian root and moon's brew."

His eyebrows rose, but his glance at the drawer to her right gave her a clue for at least one of their locations. "Then you aren't looking to heal your mother."

Pain shot through her shoulder, like lightning firing up the nerves in her hand, forcing her hand open to drop the vial, which then shattered on the stone floor. The noise sent several animals scurrying in their cages.

"Who are you setting out to kill?" His voice dropped, and she knew her life depended on her giving the right answer, but she didn't know what the right answer might be. He should be loyal to the king and queen, to Gaeren. But what if he'd been planted here by Mayvus?

She reached behind her, fumbling for anything on the table that might give her the upper hand. But the old man was both sharper and faster than she'd given him credit for, and the pain that tore through both arms this time made her cry out.

"Were you sent to kill the king?" he asked. "The king and queen have seemed sicker again lately. Is that because of you? They're not branded again. I've been watching for that. I've even been strengthening the queen's stamina to ward off susceptibility. Unless… is that what you came for? Are you taking their blood to brand them?"

Aeliana shook her head, but then she finally put the memory of him together. He was the king and queen's primary healer, Tobias. The sting of his magic lessened, and she changed the direction for her flailing arms to the drawer he'd looked at.

"I see the Ahmranan soldiers coming," he went on, "but maybe they're a distraction. You came with a dragon, and you look for the silent weapons of an assassin. That alone is enough for me to find you guilty."

"I'm not an assassin." Her hand found a grip on the drawer's handle. "I've been here for several days. Haven't you seen me with the prince?"

Tobias' eyes narrowed, and she realized it was a mistake to make that connection. "I suspected you all were here for an inside job. I'm surprised you didn't take the whole family out before bringing that witch into our presence."

She tried to defend herself, but the magic he employed rose higher with his suspicions, cutting off her words. She closed her eyes, begging for Durriken to come, not knowing if there was even anything he could do. As she reached through the tether, she sensed his panic and feared he might tear down the entire wing in his efforts to free her from this mad progeny.

Tobias released his hold, and she dropped to the ground, her legs giving out with the sudden relief from the pain.

"Please," she gasped out. "I'm trying to kill Mayvus."

"Of course you would say that now," he grumbled.

Aeliana's desperation grew as spots formed in front of her eyes. She scrambled for something to hold on to, to find purchase to stand and defend herself. Her starlock heated against her chest, reminding her she had far more arsenal than the dagger at her waist that she couldn't seem to grasp.

It was futile after the way her light shields had been sputtering, but in desperation, she let the magic of her starlock and starblood flow through her arms and into her fingertips, begging the Sun and Stars to give her something strong enough to defend herself.

Blinding white light filled the room, and the shield that formed before her forced the older man back against the wall, where he tripped over the mess of supplies scattered across the floor.

Aeliana's surprise matched his. This time, when the light shield flickered, she knew it was her emotions impacting its success rather than her skill.

Had breaking her brand with Durriken freed up her somatic spoke? Or was something else at play? She didn't have time to think on it further. And despite the light shield giving her room to breathe, Tobias still blocked her exit, and she needed a way out. Stalling, she inched to the right, picking through the now open drawer for the red vine-like bundle of valerian root and the shiny grey bulbs of the moon's brew herb the old healer had unknowingly pointed her to. She tucked them into her belt, missing the deep pockets of her skirts.

"What will you do?" Tobias asked, eyes wide.

"I already told you," she snapped. "I'm going after Mayvus."

He shook his head in disbelief. "How can I trust you won't kill my king?" As he cowered from her light shield, he seemed a decade older, his face holding fear and pain that made her ease up on the force of her light's glow.

"I suppose you can't," she said. "But maybe after this is all over, you'll be willing to trust me, because by then I'll have proven to be true to my word."

He hesitated, then barred the door, taking one last stand to force Aeliana's hand. She didn't have time for this.

The squeak of a ferret in a cage near her elbow reminded her they weren't completely alone. As the sounds turned to a bark that was picked up by the other caged animals, it dawned on her that the animals weren't necessarily afraid of her light shield. It was almost like they were rallying behind her. She scanned each of the cages, noting the mechanisms to open the doors required no key, just opposable thumbs.

When she glanced back at Tobias, his eyes held the same understanding, and they shifted to fear.

"How long have you been torturing these animals?" she asked.

"We don't torture them," he said quickly. "We extract only what we need to create the remedies the royalty require."

Aeliana snorted and reached for the cage door. "Then they give it up freely, and you won't mind if I let them loose." She opened the nearest cage, and as soon as the animal bolted from its prison, she let her shield drop. Three more cages were open before she sensed the full force of Tobias' magic crushing her chest.

She tried summoning another light shield, but it was an uphill battle with his somatic skills already on her, and she gasped as her power merely held off death from his energy targeted at her heart.

But then the onslaught suddenly ceased, and her light shield flared. Tobias' cries echoed in the cavernous room, and Aeliana was thankful her shield blocked her view of the animals' retribution. She rushed past the snarling forms surrounding the progeny and winced as their whimpers joined the fray. She might have just sentenced these creatures to death in order to defend herself. Hopefully they would have sense to escape, and hopefully the distraction would buy her enough time to escape as well.

She patted down her belt, reassured to find the herbs and roots still there, before rushing out of the apothecary and into the frigid night air. She scanned the skies, the lack of dancing Stars ominous in the night. At least it made it easier to spot Durriken's dark form gliding in the glint of the moon.

He landed and skidded to a stop beside her, his frustration thick in the air around them. She ran up his tail to find purchase at his neck once more.

That was too close. His rumble held a disapproval that Aeliana felt in her core, and as much as she hated disappointing him, she couldn't regret her actions. As they flew, he dodged stray arrows from a handful of Ahmranans, who'd left the eastern gate to hunt for the dragon they'd spotted. Aeliana winced as she felt the sharp pains along with Durriken from a few arrows hitting his side.

They're like splinters. His reassurance only went so far when she felt it too. Even so, his flight remained uninterrupted. He made a wide berth around the north side of the palace, finally angling in close when he reached Emeris' room. Aeliana's leap to her mother's balcony felt reckless, the timing of such a small window of opportunity too precise for how little experience she had riding and dismounting a dragon. Sure enough, she slammed into the wall with the grace of an elephant.

Thankfully, Lukai and Marnok had been watching for her, and their hands reached out to keep her from sliding down the palace wall's surface to her death. They pulled her across the balcony's ridge before collapsing in a heap of three, and then Velden was grinning from above her. "I wish Gaeren had been here to see that."

She shoved his face out from in front of hers with a laugh. "Why?"

"Because then he could feed that memory back to me over and over again." His chuckle was cut off by Kendalyhn's elbow in his gut.

"I think they know we're up to something," she said. "They're trying to get in the room now."

Aeliana stood, dusting off her trousers and pulling out the root and herbs. "I'm guessing the sight of a dragon flying around the palace tipped them off."

The others ushered her into the room, where her mother sat serenely at the tea table. Marnok sat with a steaming kettle and teacups while Lukai held a knife. Aeliana passed the valerian root and moon's brew over, not trusting herself to know accurate measurements for steeping herbs. The room grew somber as the reality of what they were about to do sank in.

"Are you sure you're all right with this?" Aeliana asked her mother.

Emeris nodded. "It's worth a try."

Aeliana winced, hating the implication that if it didn't work, her mother would die. Or if it worked too well, her mother would also die. There was too little margin for error in this plan.

Her father wrapped an arm around her mother, unwilling to leave her side through this trial. Cyrus kneeled in the corner, fighting their battle the best way he knew how. Even Brogdon's lips moved with silent prayer along with him while Iris and Kendalyhn stood behind Marnok and Lukai, hovering as if desperate to help.

Marnok crushed the dried herbs and placed them in a pouch, his hands steady. Lukai mashed the valerian root until a pus-like substance oozed from it, which he then mixed with a paste.

"She has to eat that?" Aeliana asked.

"The moon's brew infusion she can drink," Marnok explained while he worked. "That's what will make her feel sick and reduce her focus and strength, counteracting her magic as well. The valerian root can be dried and made into a powder to add to food and drink, but if she ingests both, the combination could be lethal. Smearing the paste on her skin will allow her body to absorb it in a different way."

"A paste sounds too slow," Aeliana said.

Marnok shrugged. "That's why we're tripling the concentration."

Unlike Marnok, Lukai's hands shook as he measured more of the valerian root and combined it with the paste.

"And it won't kill her?" Aeliana asked.

"One dollop on her wrist will make her sleepy," Marnok said. "Two will make her unconscious. A hair more will slow her heart enough to appear dead. But three full dollops will kill her."

Pounding came from the hallway door, and the crack of wood splintered the air.

Everyone's eyes widened, and Sylmar and Velden rushed to check on the security of the furniture blocking the door, fortifying it with their starlocks' strength as well.

"Hurry, Marnok," Aeliana murmured.

"If I don't steep the moon's brew long enough," he said, "it won't be strong enough to make her sick. Or if I put too much in to compensate for the lost time, it could be too strong."

She bit her lip. Too strong and not strong enough both meant too deadly. She tried to rein in her impatience, but the pounding picked up again, and this time the shouts sounded louder.

"Marnok?" Sylmar drew out his name in warning.

"I can't make it go any faster." The strain in Marnok's voice matched Sylmar's.

Aeliana's gaze volleyed between the steeping tea and the doorway, where she could only make out Velden's and Sylmar's cloaks as they strengthened the barricade of the door. Another crack splintered the air.

"There," Marnok said, pouring the tea into a cup and blowing on it.

"Don't be ridiculous." Emeris grabbed the cup from his hand. "A burnt tongue is the least of my concerns right now." She chugged it without hesitation. Her eyes watered as she set the cup down, and she beckoned for the water pitcher before drinking directly out of it in an undignified manner.

"Not too much," Marnok said. "You don't want to dilute the effects."

She slowed her swallows and set the pitcher back, pressing her hands against her red cheeks.

"What about the paste?" Aeliana asked.

Marnok frowned. "We take it with us and hope we don't have to use it. Incapacitating Mayvus with the moon's brew might be enough."

Lukai scooped the paste into a small container, careful not to let it touch his skin. After securing the lid, he passed it over to Aeliana. She hesitated, then shoved it in her trouser pocket with a shiver.

"I don't feel well," Emeris said, her eyes glazing over.

"That's good, love," Iris said while Rildan stroked Emeris' brow.

Then a final crack rent the air, and Velden and Sylmar were thrown back in a cloud of dust.

CHAPTER 82

GAEREN TRIED to blink past the bright spots in his vision left by Riveran's use of the golden arrow. But they were merely replaced by dozens of Ahmranans marching into the council room. The ease with which Mayvus took over the room left Gaeren baffled. Thanks to his parents' orders while branded, their soldiers hadn't put up a fight. Now, as they were ushered in as prisoners along with the king and queen, their training kicked in to defend the royal family, but it was too little, too late.

As if sensing her own role in Mayvus' success, his mother whimpered, and his father held her tighter, whispering words of comfort. In that moment, they looked weak and tired, and all of Gaeren's frustrations with them fled. They'd done terrible things. His father especially hadn't done right by him as a child.

But right now, they were also victims.

He toyed with the dagger at his belt, wondering if Mayvus was still weak from her time with Durriken. Could he hurl it in her direction and end all this? Or would she stop it the same way she'd stopped Sylmar's molten blades? If it worked, it might also kill Emeris, and that would kill something in Aeliana.

"It's been too long," Mayvus crooned, sidling up to Gaeren as if they were old friends. "I'd hoped we'd meet on better terms than we parted, but it seems you're already working hard against me."

She gestured toward his parents, and for the first time, Gaeren noted the bloody mess left in the wake of cutting out their brands. Even his hands had splashes of it, though he'd wiped most of it on his trousers.

"We talked about this last time," he said evenly. "You should really be enticing people to work alongside you instead of forcing them. It has a better retention rate."

She smiled, and without warning, she reached for his starlock, snapping the cord from his neck. He made a grab for it, even though he knew it was pointless. If he weren't so unevenly matched, he might have even fought her for it. But he'd be dead before he could do any real damage.

Even though his parents held no threat in their current state, two of her soldiers took their starlocks as well.

"I'm thinking about starting a collection," Mayvus said. "There are a few loyal soldiers in my crew who weren't blessed by the Sun. It's a bit unfair for a Creator to pick and choose, don't you think?" She tapped a finger against her lips. "Perhaps that's why the Sun is stepping back from choosing any of us at all."

Gaeren narrowed his eyes, trying to parse out her meaning in this poorly timed riddle while also evaluating his dwindling options to escape. "That's strange coming from you. I would think you'd be grateful to be chosen. Isn't that how you got your power to begin with?"

Her smile held the wicked glint of someone with a secret. "We're on the brink of a new age. Instead of individuals, the Sun has chosen a group of people."

Gaeren glanced around the room at the Ahmranans. "So the Sun is choosing a group you're not a part of."

She peered down her nose at him in the haughty way he remembered from her visits during council meetings. "I've been chosen to lead the people."

He rolled his eyes, knowing he was flirting with disaster but unable to stop himself. "I think I'd have to hear that from the Sun myself before I believed it."

Her hand gripped his upper arms, her nails digging in until he winced, wondering if she was drawing blood. But a coldness seeped through them that drove deep to his bones, and he feared she was doing something far worse than breaking his skin with her nails.

"I'd heard of your rebellious nature and thought maybe there was something there, something I could work with. But you've grown as soft as the other rumors say. I have little use for you as is. And do you know what I do with people I have little use for?"

He hadn't intended to search for her memories. He didn't expect he'd be able to without his starlock. But she pushed them on him with such clarity that he wondered where his magic ended and hers began.

Uncle Danton's broken body lay before him with too much blood to distinguish actual injuries and glassy eyes staring up at him. From Mayvus' perspective, he watched her booted foot toe the body and tsk over its lifeless state. The image was replaced by Croft, or what was left of him. His body had grown brittle and blue, like he'd been turned to ice and then cracked apart.

Gaeren gasped and tried wrenching free from Mayvus' grasp, but she held tight, letting the coolness of her touch turn to a freezing burn that made him panic. The vision faded, and she leaned in until her face was all he could see, her long nose and brown eyes so similar to Emeris', but full of a contempt her sister had never exuded.

"If controlling someone doesn't give me more power, I don't have time to waste on them." The hatred pouring off her was so visceral he felt certain these were his last moments. But then she released her grip and turned away.

As he rubbed the feeling back into his numb arms, she shifted her attention to his parents.

"Twice branded and twice thwarted," Mayvus said. "I don't usually give second chances, but their position of power made me show mercy."

She let the word hang in the air as she glided toward them.

"They're worth more alive," Gaeren said quickly.

Her laugh was high and screeching, like an iceberg scraping against the hull of his ship. "I didn't expect you to defend them."

As his parents huddled tighter, he rushed after Mayvus, not sure what he could do to stop her but desperate to try. But before he could reach her, his mother's scream met his ears. The skin of his parents' faces turned pale, almost white, before taking on the same blue tinge as Croft's. His mother's scream cut off, but both of their eyes went wide, the fear as frozen on their faces as the sweat on their skin.

Gaeren choked on a sob and stepped back, his hands balling into fists in his hair, the need to attack Mayvus warring with the need to be rational, to find a solution that wouldn't involve him throwing his life away for nothing.

Gasps rose around him as the soldiers of Elanesse all took in the death of their sovereign rulers along with the realization that they'd allowed it to happen. Cries filled the air as a few rushed to avenge their king and queen the same way Gaeren had wanted to, but with a flick of Mayvus' hand, their weapons clattered to the floor and their own bodies turned blue. The show of force riled up the winex and several more soldiers, but the sheer number of Ahmranans made it impossible for them to rally against Mayvus.

"Last time we met, I was too patient and generous." Mayvus turned her back on the frozen bodies and faced Gaeren once more. "It made me vulnerable."

"Patient? Or prideful? You'd think surviving Durriken's death wish might have humbled you. Made you want to change your ways." He tried to ignore the way his parents' bodies became brittle in his periphery, the way small chunks broke apart and tumbled down the dais stairs. At least it had been quick, perhaps less painful than what some of Mayvus' other methods might have been.

She snorted and grabbed his hand. "Regardless, I will not make the same mistake again." She yanked back his tunic's sleeve, exposing the braid on his wrist, then hesitated, raising her eyebrows. "You might be an even better catch than I thought."

Without warning, she sliced open his palm with a dagger, spilling his blood into a glass vial. His resistance was like a child against a warrior, and when she had enough blood, she shoved him to the stone floor.

"Controlling you is almost as good as controlling Enla would be.

She's evaded me so far, but I suspect she'll come for you. And now I wonder if someone else might too. Someone else I'm eager to get back. Except this time I won't be so greedy as to wait for Summer Solstice. I learned my lesson. Half the power of a brand is better than no brand at all."

Her words sent a different spike of fear through him, and his fear of dying by her hand suddenly felt welcome when compared to being controlled. When Enla returned, she'd have no idea he wasn't himself, just like Iris had had no idea Holm was acting under Mayvus' control.

Still, something else niggled at the back of his mind. If Enla had been evading Mayvus, did that mean Enla knew Mayvus had been controlling their parents? Enla had told him she'd seen all these deaths. She'd seen them and done nothing about them. Had she allowed this to happen for her own reasons? Or had this really been where all the paths led? He couldn't imagine her seeing their parents, Uncle Danton, and Croft all dying and deciding it didn't matter. Not unless there was something bigger that mattered in the future.

Or… maybe he could no longer trust her.

He shook the thought away, hating the disloyalty behind it.

When Mayvus used the same dagger to cut a mark on her shoulder, a sharp pain knifed through the cut on his palm. He lunged for her, preferring death over her successfully branding him. Her hand latched on to his arm, holding him at bay with an iron grip, but at least it kept that hand from being free to use his blood to form the brand mark.

They were at an impasse, one she could easily overcome by killing him, but something she seemed surprisingly hesitant to do.

"Restrain him," she murmured.

Within moments, two burly Ahmranans pulled him away, holding his arms behind his back.

A smile curled across her face, and she lifted the vial to her shoulder. Before she could follow through, a commotion in the doorway to the council room brought everyone turning that way.

At first Gaeren felt a sense of relief at the sight of familiar faces, but they all appeared beaten and weary, their own starlocks missing from their necks. He counted off his friends, watching as Sylmar and Velden were led to the dais, followed by Marnok, Rildan, Cyrus, Iris, Kenda-lyhn, and Lukai.

Mayvus capped off the vial of blood and tucked it in her left cloak pocket.

Tension rolled off Gaeren's shoulders, and a sliver of hope wormed through his gut.

One of the soldiers handed Mayvus a tangled mess of leather cords and starlocks, which she eagerly counted and tucked away in her other pocket, which housed Gaeren's and his parents' starlocks. Then she frowned and scanned the prisoners before stepping toward Velden, squinting at his cheeky grin. "I've heard of you." She yanked the earrings out of his ears, making him howl as the flesh ripped. "There, now we have them all."

Brogdon came in near the end of the line, and despite no longer having a starlock, he made a rush for Mayvus, showing a bravery and stupidity that Gaeren hadn't expected from him. He got several scratches in on her face before her magic brushed him aside, the force of her blow so powerful he flew against the dais' edge. He went still, hopefully just unconscious.

"I really hoped we'd all be able to be civilized adults for this meet-ing," Mayvus said, but then she stumbled, placing a hand over her stomach and reaching out to steady herself on the arm of his father's council room throne. Her face paled, and she glanced around the room. "Where's Emeris?"

The guards brought her forward, and for the first time Gaeren caught a glimpse of Aeliana supporting her mother. Fear lined her face, and a dozen regrets flooded his mind. When her eyes met his, her features smoothed over a hair, raising his determination to get them out of this mess.

Emeris tripped, drawing his attention to the way her pale features mirrored Mayvus'. Actually, the closer he looked, the more her face had a greenish tinge, like after Riveran crossed the barriers. Mayvus bent double, her face holding a similar sickly quality. Any disbelief he had over the curse's validity faded as he watched their mirrored reactions.

"What did you give her?" Mayvus moaned, her authority wavering with her voice.

A slow smile spread on Gaeren's face as he realized what they'd done.

"If you're going to depend on a curse," Sylmar said, "you might want to consider all the possible consequences of that curse."

She turned to glare at him. "What are you talking about?"

He stepped forward, his staff thumping on the wooden dais, making Gaeren wonder if he could still transform the weapon without his starlock. Could any of them stand against her in her weakened state? Could they combine efforts with the winex and the Elanesse soldiers to fight against her? And if they did, would her soldiers turn on her too?

"You saw the curse as an opportunity to extend your life, but you forget that its original intention was to weaken it. You are tied to Emeris in life...*and* in death."

"You are even more of a fool than I realized," Mayvus spat out, "if you think that's my only path to immortality." She fished a flask from her cloak pocket and took a swig from it.

"The winex," Aeliana murmured, her eyes narrowing.

Mayvus paused, then her malicious smile returned. "Some of my men told me you were partial to the beasts."

Gaeren felt the heat of Aeliana's glare from across the room even though it wasn't directed at him.

"You drained their eggs. All so you could test out a theory and sentence your soldiers to death."

"And yet"—she raised the flask as if to toast Aeliana—"it's keeping me alive."

The winex held at bay by the soldiers snarled, and Gaeren silently applauded Aeliana for riling them up. The sliver of hope grew. They might have a chance if they could line up all of their defenses just right.

If they could get Mayvus just a little bit more out of commission, Gaeren could get the starlocks she'd stolen. His parents' starlocks wouldn't be as effective as they'd been for their owners, but they could still boost a progeny's power. With half of them gaining back at least some of their power and the winex being primed for a fight, would the soldiers lose heart if they saw she'd been defeated?

"The concoction you've brewed still isn't enough to make you immortal," Gaeren pointed out.

Mayvus raised her eyebrows. "Oh, I know. I'm not depending on the winex fluid for immortality either." A sickening smile grew on her face. "I have something far better planned for that."

CHAPTER 83

Aeliana froze, the implication of Mayvus' words rolling through her with a horror far worse than she'd felt for the winex alone.

"What do you mean?" Sylmar asked.

Mayvus took another swig from her flask, and Aeliana wanted to knock it from the woman's hands. As Mayvus' health slowly improved, so did her mother's. It would be impossible to give her mother more of the moon's brew tea with the soldiers so close and watching. But what if she smeared the valerian root cream on her mother's wrists? She let Marnok's instructions roll through her mind. One dollop for sleep, two for unconscious, three for death.

What if she killed her mother in her efforts to thwart Mayvus?

"It's the Stars, isn't it?" Cyrus surprised everyone by speaking up. "You're using the Stars to gain immortality."

Aeliana frowned. "How would that even be possible?"

Mayvus laughed and stepped closer to him, making Aeliana even more tense. It didn't matter that they were all as defenseless as he was. The fact that he had no magic made him seem too vulnerable, like Mayvus preyed on a child. "I shouldn't be surprised that a human who worships the Stars would be the one to see the significance of my plans."

"What I don't understand," Cyrus said, "is why they're working with you. They have to know you plan to kill one for its power, like King Melchinek did."

Mayvus stiffened. "My, my, you really are bright for a Lorvandan."

"No," Aeliana murmured. "The Stars wouldn't work with you if that was your plan."

Mayvus turned her way with eyebrows raised, and Aeliana regretted her outburst. With Mayvus' attention on her, it would be impossible to give her mother the valerian.

"You would be surprised at the influential state of the Stars. They've watched this world break even further over the last thousand years. Their efforts to save the people with the Great Divide failed, and they are eager to reverse their mistakes."

"It was a punishment from the Sun," Emeris murmured.

"That's where you're wrong, little sister," Mayvus said, stepping forward and cupping Emeris' cheeks in her hands. "It's where I was wrong, too. All of us have been wrong. The Stars went rogue and tried to take matters into their own hands. The starbridges were the Sun's way of tempering the Stars' mistake, but even that won't be enough forever, and the Stars know it. Their desperation has them lining up as sacrifices for the promise of breaking down the barriers and reuniting the lands."

"How can you promise that?" Sylmar asked.

"Haven't I already united the Ahmranans and the Vendarans?" She gestured around the room. "Fewer and fewer starlocks are being given —not because they don't have locks of hair to give, but because that method is no longer working. It's putting power into too many hands and causing division as people seek to grow their power."

Sylmar snorted. "So they're trying to stop people like you. Again, I don't understand why they would work with you."

"They'd already chosen the Ahmranans, but without the stone, they had no way of reuniting the Ahmranans with the rest of the people. When I showed up, all of that changed. I desire power to make this world a better place. They see that, and they wish to reward it."

"How could they be so blind?" Cyrus murmured.

Aeliana's heart broke for him as his last bit of respect for the Stars was crushed.

"They knew that by coming here," Mayvus said, "we'd gain access to the golden arrow. And I suspect from the rumors I've heard that they'll also gain access to the silver fish. All that's left is the iron cutlass and we can bring down the barriers for good. Reuniting all of Rhystahn once more." Her words echoed things Orra had said over the last several months, but there was a wrongness to them that left Aeliana anxious.

She kept silent though, letting the others express their disbelief and frustration, and as Mayvus' gaze took in their disgruntled reactions, Aeliana pulled out the bottle of cream Marnok had made. The imprecise definition of a dollop made Aeliana break into a sweat, but she used her dagger to scoop out what she hoped was a dollop and placed it against her mother's wrist.

"Good job, dear," her mother murmured, her eyes already starting to flutter.

Mayvus stumbled once more, then glanced back at Emeris. She narrowed her eyes and took another swig from her flask, her grip tightening on the queen's council chair beside her. "I wanted you all to witness the city's downfall, to see me take the throne before having you hung as an example to the rest of the nation. But now I wonder if I'm better off ridding the world of you now, before you can do something foolish and try to save the people you claim to love. Like you did back in Myndren."

She took another swig, and Aeliana's mother blinked again, frowning. It wasn't working because the winex fluid was counteracting it, which meant a dollop or two wasn't going to be enough.

But how much would be too much?

Mayvus turned back to her soldiers, giving instructions to bind them all and take them to the dungeons. They were out of time.

"I'm sorry," she whispered, before using her dagger to smear two more dollops on her mother's wrist. She prayed it wasn't too much, and she prayed it was enough. When her mother fell limp against one of the guards, Aeliana bent forward, frantically checking for a pulse.

This time, when a moan escaped Mayvus' lips, she fell into the chair she'd used for balance. She nearly dropped the flask as she lifted it to her lips, and her words came out garbled. "Take her to the apothecary. Empty her stomach. I don't care how. They've given her something, and you need to get rid of it."

The soldier nearest gathered Emeris up in his arms to carry her from the room, and Aeliana saw all their hopes being carried out with her. Chaos broke out as the others attempted resisting capture without their starlocks. They were dependent on their combat training, and Aeliana knew they couldn't last against the progeny soldiers. But it was enough to force the soldier carrying Emeris to set her down to defend himself. On a whim, she kept out the valerian cream and dipped her dagger in it, smearing large portions on the soldiers who tried to capture her. They dropped like flies, and she had no time to wonder if she was killing them or merely incapacitating them.

A burst of light flashed through the room, the familiar shield shocking Aeliana because it hadn't come from her hands. As her eyes adjusted, she saw Marnok rushing toward her, then pulling her into the safety of his light shield's circumference.

"How are you—?" She didn't bother finishing her question. They'd never understood where Marnok's power came from because they'd never been able to find a starlock on him. And yet here he was, a master of the magic she thought she'd lost. His ability to create a light shield was no more or less confusing than her own ability to create one in the apothecary.

"When did you discover you could do this?"

"Your mother's memories showed me I could do a lot more than I remembered." He pulled her through the crowd, attempting to grab their friends along the way. But he was just as likely to bring Mayvus' soldiers into the sphere. They were halfway to the exit by the time they'd collected Sylmar and Iris, along with two soldiers Aeliana dispatched using the valerian cream.

"It's not enough," Marnok said, even as they added Cyrus and Gaeren to their protective barrier. "I can't save them all. At some point, we need to cut our losses and leave." His voice broke with the admission.

How would they know when to stop? Who would be the last person they saved and the first person they abandoned?

Gaeren placed his hand on Aeliana's arm, and a memory rushed through her mind at double speed, showing Mayvus placing his blood in her left pocket and all the starlocks in her right. When the memory cut off, he raised his eyebrows, angling his head toward Mayvus, whose eyes fluttered as she slumped in her chair.

"It's not worth the risk," Cyrus said, following their gazes.

Tears streamed down Aeliana's cheeks as she watched Lukai and Kendalyhn fighting for their lives outside Marnok's light shield. She couldn't even see her father or Brogdon in the fray. How could she stay in the safety of Marnok's magic and hope Mayvus would show mercy on the others?

"You have to go get my mother," she told Marnok. Even though saving her mother could potentially save the others, right now the request felt selfish. She just wanted him to keep her mother safe.

"She's right," Sylmar said, lessening some of Aeliana's guilt, and as one, those in the light shield began inching their way toward her mother's limp form.

Except for Aeliana. She grabbed Gaeren's hand and nodded toward Mayvus. He grinned, accepting the challenge, and together they dove out from the safety of Marnok's light shield, ignoring the other's protests. They wasted no time cutting Ahmranans down, Gaeren with his sword and Aeliana with her poisoned dagger, but the dais felt impossibly far, and it would only take one progeny to best them both.

"How can we get through the line?" Aeliana shouted, drawing Gaeren's attention to the soldiers guarding the dais.

Before he could respond, a rumble filled the air, making the entire room pause. Glass shattered from one of the windows, revealing leathery skin and claws. When the paw receded, a fiery eye replaced it.

"Durriken," Aeliana breathed out, then grinned as panic ensued.

The soldiers before them all crouched, as if the dragon's fire might go over them.

Gaeren slid across the floor on his knees, then placed his hands on the ground. "Jump, Daisy!"

She obeyed without thought, running to leap on his back and then over the heads of the soldiers. A sword flashed near her feet, but she cleared the line, practically falling on top of Mayvus, whose eyelids fluttered. Aeliana shoved her hand into Mayvus' pocket, triumphantly pulling out all the starlocks.

She didn't hunt for her own. Instead, she tucked them all against her chest, letting her starlock find her and heat against her tunic. She let her light shield spread out brighter and farther than ever before, like a wave that rippled through the room. It knocked the nearest soldiers to the ground, allowing Gaeren to leap onto the dais with her.

As he grabbed his blood from Mayvus' other pocket, Aeliana glanced across the room, where Velden's spurts of water fended off soldiers near Emeris. They were more like pathetic showers compared to his normal power, evidence that the water he wielded was part Sayhleen heritage and part starblood magic.

When Sylmar pulled Emeris into Marnok's light shield, Aeliana felt a burst of hope, but her mother grabbed the front of Sylmar's shirt, whispering something in his ear.

He pulled away, his eyes softening with regret. Time slowed as he pulled a dagger from Marnok's belt.

"No!" Aeliana screamed, but she was too far away to stop him from plunging the dagger into Emeris' chest.

Beside her, Mayvus gasped, her eyes opening wide with shock. Blood burbled from her chest, and her hands fought to bring the flask of her winex tonic to her lips. "Please," she murmured.

A sob broke from Aeliana's throat as she helped Mayvus lift the flask to her lips, forcing it between her teeth to pour it in. When it was empty, she threw it to the side, placing the collection of starlocks over Mayvus' chest. Her aunt's gaze lost focus somewhere over Aeliana's shoulder, as if she sought the eyes of her dying sister.

"Heal her!" Her voice came out hoarse with her tears, but her starlock obeyed, heating up as Aeliana envisioned the severed flesh being fused together. But the damage was deep, and blood still seeped between her fingers.

"It's over," Gaeren said, pulling on her arms.

"No!" She tightened her grip on her aunt's body.

"We have to help the others now," he insisted, his voice breaking with his tears. "They need their starlocks." He gripped her bloody hands. "Look at her face, Daisy."

Aeliana's vision blurred with her tears, but she rubbed them away with her shoulder. Mayvus' eyes held the same glassy gaze she'd seen on Nori and Holm. It didn't matter that Aeliana had had her starlock. It didn't matter that she'd had her light shields and healing powers back.

A piercing howl filled the room as Durriken felt the pain breaking open her chest.

She still hadn't been able to save Mayvus. She hadn't been able to save her mother.

They were both dead. And Sylmar had killed them.

CHAPTER 84

THE BLACKNESS that engulfed Orra came with silence. But then it faded to a dull gray, and muffled sound returned. With it came awareness of Andreas' arms surrounding her. The suffocating heat of his partially shifted human form—the cause of her blacking out.

"I'm sorry," he murmured, wincing, but she knew his back was taking the brunt of Reyna's anger.

"Let her take me," Orra offered. "She's partway right, you know. If you want to bring the barriers down, that's the final step."

He frowned but didn't move. "I suspect there are several other steps that need to come first. I won't let her rush things." But even as he said the words, he fell against Orra as Reyna's blows became too much. She welcomed the burn of his skin but still backed away, knowing her grounded form couldn't take it.

Reyna shoved him away from Orra. "It's time we're no longer weighed down by what you did." She released her glow enough to grab Orra's wrist without burning her to a crisp but then dragged her forward, turning her around to face the other Stars on the balcony. "We've all watched as Sheen has continued interfering while here on the earth. She has no respect for the Sun's authority, and she acts on her own will."

"And what is it that you're doing?" Orra murmured in Reyna's ear. "You can't tell me that working with the likes of Mayvus is the Sun's will, even if you plan to betray her. Maybe especially if that's your plan."

Reyna ignored her accusations. "It's time we sent Sheen to the Sun to receive her judgment."

"I was judged a thousand years ago," Orra added. "And the Sun chose to keep me here." Even as she said the words to counteract Reyna's, the truth of them hit her.

The Sun had left her here to do something. The Sun had still given her a purpose, despite all she'd done wrong. The Sun still wanted a relationship with her and still desired for her to do its will.

Something in her heart shifted, a crack mending, something frozen thawing. She'd been trying to listen to the Sun, to make decisions based on what the Sun would have her do. And while that was right, it came from the wrong place. "Everything we do should come from a place of love, not guilt."

Reyna frowned at her, the words not lining up with the lies she'd spewed to the other Stars. But Orra didn't care. She didn't need to prove anything to Reyna or the other Stars.

"The Sun's light exposes the darkness within us," Orra murmured. "Forces it out until none remains. It's not that we have no darkness— it's that the Sun removes it."

Reyna's light flickered, but Orra couldn't tell if it was from anger or if the Star was considering her words.

Orra turned to the rest of the Stars. "The Sun does not want you aiding Mayvus," she shouted. "Even if it's temporary."

The Stars with Andreas all exchanged nervous glances.

"And what would you know of what the Sun wants?" Reyna shouted back, those behind her calling out their assent. She pulled on Orra's short hair, forcing her head back and chin up. "You've disgraced yourself in a number of ways, the least of all shearing a source of the power given to you by the Sun. You're an embarrassment to the Stars."

Tears filled Orra's eyes as Reyna pulled harder, the reminder of why she'd cut her hair stinging far more than the pain of Reyna's grip.

"Give her to Mayvus," one of the Stars shouted. It sounded like Telnar, but Orra couldn't turn to look.

"Yes," another shouted. "We've offered our sacrifice, but giving up Sheen would be better."

The heat of Reyna's presence suddenly burned hotter as Orra's skin grew cold and clammy.

"Sacrifice?" Orra whispered. "You're going to gift her with your power? With a Star's death?" Orra's calm nature gave way to a panic she hadn't felt since the day she'd been grounded. "You said you weren't truly working with her. Have you already done this?"

"Of course not," Reyna said. "Have you seen us fast from the skies? Not that we would do that for the likes of you."

Orra shuddered, her horror slightly tempered by this bit of relief. With Lucian's death, they'd all remained grounded for a night, fasting from the Sun's light as they mourned their fallen brother. "Why would you give her the power of a Star if you're not working with her?"

"She's uniting the people," Reyna hissed. "We're willing to do anything if it means we can return the world to its unified state."

A moan rose from one of the Stars on Orra's right, catching Reyna's attention as well.

"Emeris," the Star murmured, and Orra went still.

"What about her?" Orra strained to see the Star's face, finally catching Excelsus' wide eyes and slack jaw. "What happened?" A new sense of urgency bled through her tone.

"She's dead."

Another cry broke out from Telnar. "Mayvus is dead too."

Every form on the balcony went still. Even the wind calmed beside them.

"No," Orra murmured. But she knew they were right. The Stars who had gifted them with starlocks would have sensed it. It wasn't like the starbridges being used. Orra was blind out here, but they were not.

"How?" she murmured, not really expecting an answer.

Reyna slapped her cheek. Orra's head flew back with a sharp crack before snapping back, her hair still in Reyna's grip.

"This was all a ruse just to distract us, to keep us from aiding her in her need," Reyna said. "How could you? You've ruined everything."

"The Ahmranans retreat," another Star called out. "We must guide them."

Several took to the skies while others made partial transfers to leap from the turret down to the courtyard. Orra closed her eyes, waiting to take whatever punishment Reyna offered. When the silence continued, Orra let her eyes flutter open.

Reyna dropped Orra's hair, letting the grounded Star fall to her knees beside her.

"Now what?" Reyna murmured.

"Now we turn to the Sun," Orra whispered. "Something I suspect you haven't done for a while."

Reyna snarled but backed away, letting her body burn brighter and brighter until she was like a flame burning Orra's eyes. When she leaped to the skies, Orra watched the trail of her fire fade into the night before closing her eyes in defeat.

She knew she shouldn't waste her power, but she used the dregs of her energy to reach out to Aeliana, to use the connection of their blood to sense the other woman's well-being. And while she sensed life in Aeliana's soul, it was full of grief and sorrow, and Orra fell down to cry with her.

CHAPTER 85

Gaeren pulled Aeliana against his chest, turning her away from Mayvus. The battle that had raged around them halted as chaos replaced determination. Several men and women cried out and cradled their hands. Some broke down in relief amidst their pain, while others fled the room.

Durriken let out another howl that drew everyone's attention to the dais.

Gaeren tensed, wondering if the sight of their dead leader would ignite the Ahmranans' ire, but instead it seemed to make them panic. The room they'd used as a trap for the royal family quickly became their own prison.

"How could he?" Aeliana murmured. Then she pushed against Gaeren, making a rush for Sylmar and Marnok, who lowered Emeris to the ground.

Gaeren swore under his breath and jumped from the dais after her, dodging those still fighting and rushing through those who'd decided the fight was already over. Aeliana lunged for Sylmar, but instead of railing against him, she wrenched her mother from his arms.

Gaeren quickly untangled the starlocks, placing his own around his neck. Then he passed the rest over to Velden, keeping hold of Aeliana's and Emeris'. "Can you make sure everyone gets theirs back?"

"That's music to my ears," Velden said, picking his fish hooks out from the pile. He held them up to the torn flesh of his lobes, then frowned. "Maybe Marnok can heal them."

They both watched as Marnok struggled to keep his light shield intact around Aeliana and Emeris, his face red and blotchy as he allowed her this chance to grieve.

"I can wait," Velden said. "He's needed more here." The half-Sayhleen's lips pressed together in an uncharacteristic grim line as he tucked the earrings in his vest pocket and headed for Brogdon, hunting for the axe-shaped starlock that belonged to the other man.

At Gaeren's feet, Aeliana half screamed at her mother to live and half yelled at Sylmar, her words becoming unintelligible. Except Sylmar was no longer beside them. He made his way toward the dais, his steps slow and heavy.

The state of confusion in the room stirred something in Gaeren, perhaps a sense of self-preservation, but also a bit of his royal blood and training. A part of him waited for his parents to command the room and take control of the situation, but their bodies remained broken, tossed to the side of the room. His faithful uncle Danton was also gone, and Enla—his safety and security despite her being so confused—wasn't here either.

Half the people in this room didn't respect the authority of the Elanesse family, but for those who did, he was the highest rank in the room. And yet the woman he loved was falling apart as she grieved the mother she'd only just found. He couldn't bear to leave her in such a state.

He scanned the royal soldiers, who gaped at the Ahmranans and Recreants filling the room. Their swords were drawn, but their faces held uncertainty over who was enemy and who was a temporary ally.

He took five steps to grab one of their collars. "Don't let any of the Ahmranans get away. Some were coerced into serving her, but some followed by choice. Take them all to the dungeons until we can parse out the difference."

The soldier licked his lips and nodded once, his eyes frantically scanning the room.

Gaeren sensed the other man's resolve as he stood straighter and turned to his comrades to relay the orders. Then Gaeren turned back to

Aeliana, hating what he had to do. Instead of pulling her away from Emeris, he wrapped his arms around her, bringing both of them into a tight hold.

"She's gone," he whispered.

"No." Aeliana's muffled cry against his shoulder was weaker than it had been.

"Please," Gaeren said. "Let's have Orra sing her to the Sun." The words got through to Aeliana in a way he hadn't expected, and she went completely still.

"She's with the Sun," she murmured. This time, when she pushed Gaeren away, he let her. She gently slid her mother's body back to the stone, closing her lids and straightening her limbs. He'd just lost his own mother and father, but this seemed far different.

The hardness on Aeliana's face left Gaeren on edge, and realization of her intentions came a moment too late. She jumped to her feet and ran across the room, aiming for Sylmar, who now kneeled next to Mayvus' abandoned body. In death, none of her people mourned her. They simply fled. Some mourned the loss of power, and some clearly celebrated their freedom.

But it was Sylmar who had tears dripping into his beard. Pain twisted the older man's features, his body shaking. His hands curled into tight fists, and heat rolled off him in waves like his magic held no control.

Aeliana had no respect for whatever grieving process Sylmar was going through. She launched herself on top of him, forgetting all the skills he'd taught her to incapacitate someone, and instead simply pounded his back with her fists, railing at him.

"You killed her. How could you kill her? We were getting away. We could have won." She repeated the words over and over, and rather than defend himself, he turned, letting her beat him until Gaeren feared there would be another death.

He pulled Aeliana back, grateful when Lukai joined him to stop her flailing arms from catching Gaeren's own jaw.

"You are a disgrace to the Recreants," she shouted. "You killed the high priestess they all loved. Everything you ever taught me, everything you've said has been a lie. You waited for this moment when you could exact your revenge."

For the first time, he spoke, shaking his head no. "It's what she wanted. She asked me to—"

"It was still your choice," Aeliana hissed. "Tell me the truth. Did Lady Merinnia show you killing Mayvus or my mother?"

He hesitated. "Your mother, which I knew would result in Mayvus' death."

She broke free from Lukai's and Gaeren's hold, letting her fists swing wildly in Sylmar's direction. "You liar! You lied to me! You knew all this time!"

Sylmar took the blows without fighting back until Gaeren and Lukai got her back under control. His face hardened once more, his familiar scowl returning, but he nodded. "I accept whatever punishment is due." He held out his hands, and the fire fueling Aeliana's anger seemed to abate.

"Lock him up," she murmured.

When no one moved to do her bidding, she wrenched herself free from Gaeren's and Lukai's grasp once more and stood tall, straightening her shirt. Her regal bearing was so much like Enla's that Gaeren felt himself stand a little taller too.

"He must be tried for his crimes," Aeliana said, "for treason against Emeris Wyndren, High Priestess. Lock him up in the dungeons with the Ahmranans until we're able to sort out his punishment. Take his staff and starlock, and don't let him have any visitors."

Lukai and Gaeren exchanged a glance. She had no authority in the Elanesse palace, but Gaeren suspected the people in this room would enact her requests before they would bother with his.

"I suppose you think you've done us all a favor," Aeliana went on, sneering in Sylmar's face. "You've rid us of Mayvus, and now we don't have to hunt down the curse."

Sylmar's face paled. "You still need to find the origin of the curse. You still need to—"

"Stop." She cut him off, her voice colder than Gaeren had ever heard it. "I've wasted the last year listening to you. We all defended your behavior, secretly seeing you as broken by your past. But you killed her." Her voice broke, and her shoulders slumped. "I don't ever want to hear your advice again. I hate that I've depended on you for as long as I have, and I refuse to listen to another word."

She strode away without a single glance for Mayvus' body, and returned to her mother's still form, kneeling beside it. By this time, Rildan had found Emeris, and along with Marnok, the three formed a strange huddle as they mourned her together.

It left Gaeren feeling like an outsider, especially since part of him wondered if she'd been too harsh. Had Emeris asked Sylmar to sacrifice her? Hadn't Aeliana asked Gaeren to do the same to her that night on the Myndren Mountains' balcony? If he'd followed through on her request, the others likely would have responded the same way she did now. But he would have done it because she'd asked him, and it would have felt like a loving way to free her, even if he despised himself for it.

He stared at Sylmar, hating that he continued to find ways he and this man were alike. It terrified him enough that he pulled a soldier from the ranks and demanded he lock the older man up along with the Ahmranans, just like Aeliana had requested.

Around them, the battle that had barely begun was over, and yet the room remained flooded with people unsure where to go from here. The winex slunk from the room, carrying out their dead without anyone trying to stop them. Felk nodded his farewell before he left, his face long as he took in Aeliana's anguish.

Gaeren watched her a moment longer too, wishing he had something to offer, but right now she needed her father more.

He turned away. And then he did something he hadn't expected to do for at least a decade or more. Something he hadn't thought he'd have to face without Enla. He gathered his father's broken body in his arms and headed for the highest tower. It was time to take the king to the Stars. It was time for them to release him to the Sun.

CHAPTER 86

Time passed in a strange haze that Orra couldn't hold on to. She kneeled on the balcony until every last Star had taken to the skies, leaving her shivering in the night air. Even Andreas had left her, but with the deaths that had occurred this night, it wouldn't be for long.

She imagined them all reflecting the Sun's brilliance. If she opened her eyes, she might see them dancing in the sky, but she suspected their anger and grief might hold their dance at bay. Even so, she waited, knowing they would return.

While waiting, she imagined the fullness of the Sun's glory hitting her celestial body. The way it had always felt like a fire that cocooned her in the Sun's embrace. She longed to share in that sensation with her brothers and sisters now, but it was lost to her. And she didn't know if she could ever gain it back.

She knew she was undeserving, but after seeing the other Stars making the same mistakes, carrying out decisions that would have as equally disastrous consequences as her own, she couldn't help wondering why they still received the blessing she'd lost.

It felt like days or years had passed until the sounds of footsteps coming up the stairway met her ears, and then it felt like mere moments. Had the people she'd grown to love aged and withered away like all the rest while she lay lost in her misery? Or had her sorrow been a cage for her mind that stretched out time?

The figure that emerged from the stairway looked wrong—the shadows too wide with too many appendages. When he stepped from the darkness into the moon's light, the single figure became two. An aged man being carried by his son, who had somehow aged himself a fair amount since the last time she'd seen him.

Her fear of time passing rushed through her once more, but as Gaeren drew closer, she saw it was a trick of the light, along with sorrow marring his features. It was his soul that had aged, not his body. Gaeren lay the brittle blue shell of his father down on the cold slab of stone, his pinched features looking almost angry. If Orra hadn't known him, she might have thought he hated the man before him. But she'd sensed the conflicting emotions in Gaeren in the past, the way love warred with hatred and anger fought with sadness.

"When we love well," she whispered, "we can be cut deeply."

He blinked over at her as if just now noticing her presence. "Will you sing him to the Sun?" he rasped out.

She nodded, then began her hum. She thought he might stay, but he backed away before lumbering down the stairs. By the time her song grew words, he'd come back with the body of his mother, as well as several frozen pieces that had broken off each of them, and he laid them side by side, placing his palms on their cheeks.

He whispered words Orra caught only because she knew how to listen for those final prayers. His regrets joined with laments, a desire to look and remember the good even if little had been there. A promise to do more, to be better.

As her song faded, so did his tears. He stood, wiping the remains of them with the back of his hand.

"Thank you." His eyes never left their bodies as he spoke. Then he laid out their starlocks on each of their chests.

The sorrowful empathy that had filled Orra was quickly replaced by a renewed hope. This was what she'd been waiting for. Her eyes shot to the heavens, and while she couldn't see the light of her fellow Stars, she sensed a growing nearness.

"Quick," she warned. "Get below. The time is near."

"But there are others." He gestured toward the door leading to the rooms below.

She shook her head. "Take them to a different tower. Now go." She didn't watch his retreat. Instead, she closed her eyes and held out her arms, beckoning for Andreas to return. He would come for the king's starlock, and Lumina would come for the queen's.

The heat grew to a burning fire that should have made her afraid. But she trusted Andreas. As he approached, the heat faded to a dull warmth, signifying they were taking on their human forms. Before she could fully recover, Andreas was wrapping her in a hug.

"You shouldn't be here," he whispered, his words harsh with fear.

The tears that sprang to her eyes came from relief, from the reminder that she wasn't as fully outcast as she'd thought—that someone still cared. Over his shoulder, Lumina looked on warily, arms folded over her chest and tangled in the black tresses reaching her knees. Orra couldn't remember if the other Star had sided with Reyna in the end or if she'd backed up Andreas.

She pulled back to study Andreas' face. Weariness lined his features. "What's going on with the Stars?"

He sighed and looked away. "Reyna and some of the others are making decisions and plans we don't all agree with. When you led us astray"—she flinched at his words even as she appreciated his straight-forward manner—"we were in the minority. We acted alone, and the others refused to help. But now, Reyna's not in the minority, and I fear her actions will have consequences that reach even further than yours."

"So there's a war among the Stars?"

Andreas glanced back at Lumina, and Orra sensed the wave of guilt flowing through them both. Lumina turned her back on Orra and kneeled before the king and queen. A hum resonated from her that would soon grow into a song, guiding the king and queen to the Sun.

"You're not fighting her." She realized the truth even as the words left her lips.

"We're waiting for the Sun to intervene."

"Why?" Orra asked. "You have the ability to stop her—or at least to try. Why would you not do that?"

Andreas frowned and stepped away. "You were punished for your choice. Reyna hasn't lost her status, which leaves us all wondering if perhaps she's right, and perhaps her methods are blessed by the Sun."

Orra shook her head. "You cannot presume to know how the Sun works. I don't understand it either. But you know what's right and wrong. We always need to stand in the light, even if the Sun is silent. Reyna was working with Mayvus. Half-lights might overemphasize the abhorrence of blood magic. They don't understand it's not the blood that makes it wrong." She pointed back in the direction of the council room where Mayvus' body likely lay. "But every time that woman spilled blood, she was working against the Sun. She welcomed the dark spirits. Now that she's dead, where do you think her own spirit went?"

"To the sprites," Andreas whispered. "She's joined their ranks, and now her destiny is to never become more than a dark spirit."

Orra rubbed her palms over her face. "I should have spent more time studying the sprites. I should have tried to understand if there was a way for them to change."

Andreas shook his head. "They made their decisions in their lifetimes. Their time as sprites is an echo of their existence. They're merely creatures between worlds fighting to remain alive a bit longer."

Orra shuddered. "And yet Reyna was serving a woman who became one."

Andreas rubbed the back of his neck, his face twisted in indecision. "Reyna told you the truth. We didn't intend to work with Mayvus. But one thing led to another, and some of the Stars have been…distracted."

Orra kneeled beside the bodies of the king and queen, letting Lumina's song comfort her along with the royal spirits.

Andreas joined her. "I agree with you though. We've begun interfering too much. Which is why I wait for the Sun to intervene."

"It's not about not interfering," Orra murmured. "It's about interfering in ways blessed by the Sun." She stared down at the king and queen, not understanding how the Stars could have let it go this far. She placed a hand on an arm of each of the deceased. "And this? Is this blessed by the Sun?"

Lumina's song broke off, and Orra stood, backing away. Just

because she was angry with her fellow Stars didn't mean she should interrupt their song.

Andreas' warm hand rested on her back, and she closed her eyes, absorbing its comfort.

"If the Sun doesn't stop Reyna," he said, "I can't rally the other Stars to do it. As long as her way is not blocked, they believe her actions are blessed." His voice shifted to a whisper, maybe to tune out Lumina or maybe to emphasize his point. "But you can still change things. Break down the barriers and bring back Bryton. It might be the only thing that makes the other Stars reconsider."

The weight of his suggestion added to the pain she already carried. "Where is the iron cutlass?"

"With Pacran, just like your people assumed."

She turned an accusing glare on him. "You've been watching us."

Andreas squeezed her hands in his. "I have been rooting for you, even if I must do it in secret."

"Thank you," she whispered. "And the onyx stone? Where did Mayvus leave it?"

He shook his head and pulled his hands away. "Mayvus wasn't the only one who used the stone. She's no longer its keeper."

Orra's eyebrows rose in question.

"Anara has it."

Orra didn't have magic to waste on searching out the truth. "Who is Anara?"

Andreas glanced back at Lumina, whose song had come to an end. "Reyna will say I'm interfering too much."

"Please, Andreas." She grabbed his hands once more. "Don't you want me to take down the barriers and bring Bryton back?"

He hesitated, but Lumina began glowing, signifying their time was up. "Ask Sylmar." He gently released her hands and matched Lumina's glow. "I think you're right, Orra. I think we misunderstood the Sun."

She blinked back tears, overcome by their brightness even as she strained to catch his words.

"The Sun left you here for a purpose. I'm sorry we've abandoned you to face it alone. But I suspect that too was part of the Sun's plan."

She crouched and shielded her face, unsure if she could hear the last of his words correctly.

"You'll succeed, Orra. If the Sun wills it, you'll succeed when the time is right."

The heat and light disappeared so fast Orra gasped and fell back, her gaze resting on the static stars above. Cold air made goosebumps rise as she shivered and crawled to the king's and queen's ashes.

"Thank you, Andreas," she whispered, laying her head on the hot stones where he'd been.

CHAPTER 87

"Aeliana?" someone murmured in her ear. "It's time to take your mother to the Stars."

She held tighter to her mother's arm, refusing to leave her body. Marnok and Rildan had stepped away a while ago, either because they needed less time or to give her privacy. But Aeliana couldn't imagine any instance in which she would abandon her mother to be burned up by the Stars.

"It's time, love." The voice came again, and Aeliana struggled to focus on Iris, who sat beside her.

"Maybe there's a way to bring her back," Aeliana said, turning to her mother so she didn't have to acknowledge the pity on Iris' face. She pulled the clamshell from her pocket, discovering it was cracked and damaged beyond repair. The gemstone within remained free of scratches, its glitter giving her a strange surge of hope. Enla had suggested it held power, but how could she unlock it? And could it ever be enough?

Her father swapped out with Iris, placing an arm around Aeliana. "Bringing her back from the dead is something that Mayvus would try to do. Even if it worked, would your mother want that? Would she ever be the same? She's caught a glimpse of the Sun by now. She will long for that more than she will long to be here with us. Let the Stars send her the rest of the way."

A fresh wave of tears streamed down Aeliana's cheeks, and she shook her head, even though she knew her father was right. She sat there longer, stubbornly refusing to leave until a foreign tug pulled on her heart. She rubbed at her chest, warding it away even as the feeling grew—the sense of someone suffering alongside her, sharing her burden in an effort to make it lighter.

Finally, the pull grew too strong, and she stood, tucking the Sayhleen pearl back in her pocket and taking in the full picture of blood seeping from her mother's chest. Sylmar had kept it quick and clean. But even that realization wasn't enough to let her forgive him. She let her gaze rise to the others around her, even the Recreants beyond, each one paused for her to give some sort of instruction.

She swallowed hard. Without her mother, they waited to see if she would step up. Without Sylmar, she had to decide if she truly wanted this. She caught Kendalyhn's eye from across the room, and the other woman gave an encouraging nod, placing three fingers on her forehead and giving a slight bow in Aeliana's direction.

If she did this, it would have to be on her own terms. The tug on her heart sharpened, as if confirming her choice.

"Take my mother to one of the towers," she conceded. "I'll come when I'm ready." As she turned away, Iris protested.

"Where are you going, love? It's not safe out there. Not until we sort the branded from the followers."

Others chimed in with their concern, but she ignored them, and the tug in her chest grew stronger, stealing away her breath. Through the broken window, she could only see the black of night, so she went through the door instead. As she walked through the chaotic halls, her presence brought a hush that followed her through to the gates.

"I know you're out here," she murmured, picking up her pace until she reached a large enough clearing. Several soldiers still occupied it, but they would run quickly enough when they saw Durriken approach. She closed her eyes, homing in on how close he might be.

Sure enough, shouts filled the air, bringing her eyes open to see the dragon she sensed coming in to land. As the terrified soldiers dispersed, Aeliana raised her arms, signaling Durriken in. When he landed, she held her ground for the first time before rushing to lean in and wrap her arms around the smooth portion of his neck.

A thrum of sorrow reverberated through his throat, echoing the cry in her heart. No words needed to be exchanged, whether out loud or in their minds. They stood in silence, the loss of Emeris melding with memories of Durriken's own family losses. Even as their individual pain deepened, it softened as they shared the weight between them.

"The Stars will come to take her," Aeliana finally said. "I wish to watch."

He lowered his only foreleg, allowing her to climb up his scales and take her place behind his neck. And together they rose into the night sky.

CHAPTER 88

As Gaeren leaned against the door separating him from Orra and whatever Stars she spoke with, a second round of heat came, forcing him away. He hadn't been able to hear anything more than murmurs out on the tower anyway.

The realization that his parents' bodies were now burned up, their starlocks taken by the Stars, distracted him from any eavesdropping efforts. He trudged down the steps, warding off anyone headed up the tower, then locked the door from the main hall, deciding Orra probably had ways of getting around something as trivial as a man-made lock.

In his absence, the council room had emptied far quicker than he'd expected. He'd only given a few commands to his parents' soldiers, but they'd been followed with precision and efficiency—something that made him feel oddly more connected to his family's throne. His parents hadn't been perfect. Far from it. But they'd done some things well enough to garner that kind of loyalty.

Sylmar, several of the soldiers, and all of the Ahmranans who hadn't escaped had been put in prison until their stories could be sorted out. Those remaining aided the injured or removed bodies, starting with the progenies, who were taken to the towers. Several of the dead were soldiers he'd probably known all his life, even trained with under his uncle's tutelage. He scanned the group, verifying

Cyrus, Brogdon, Lukai, and Kendalyhn were all accounted for. Hopefully the sailors had remained safe enough in town, warning the people.

The one person he sought most was absent.

A familiar shorn head stuck out in the corner, the lanky vest-clad form bent over an injured soldier. Gaeren made his way to Velden's side and kneeled next to him. "Where's Aeliana?"

Velden glanced up, his eyes haunted. "Rildan and Marnok carried Emeris' body to one of the towers. I think she and Iris followed."

"Where did they take Mayvus' body?"

"Who cares?" Velden muttered, turning back to his patient and slathering his seaweed mixture on the man's leg. The soldier's moan turned into a pained sigh.

"I care to verify that she's really dead this time."

Velden glanced up at Gaeren's sharp tone, his irritation softening. "I think they took her to the same tower. Someone blocked off the closest one, so they've all had to go to the turret in the western wing."

Gaeren didn't bother admitting it was he who'd blocked it off. He clapped Velden on the shoulder as he stood. "Thank you for giving the same care to the Loyalists as the Recreants."

The ghost of a grin fluttered on Velden's face. "I don't fault them for their loyalty, just who they choose to be loyal to."

"And if they choose to be loyal to Enla?" Gaeren murmured, posing the question more for himself. Riveran would bring her back, and then everything would change. But for the better or worse? How would it affect the Recreants? And how would it affect Aeliana?

If Velden answered, Gaeren didn't hear it as he stormed off to the western wing and the stairs leading to its tower. This turret was typically used by one or two soldiers as a lookout for ships, so when Gaeren stepped out on the balcony, it felt overcrowded.

Several bodies were laid out alongside Emeris'. Some he recognized as his parents' men; others were less familiar in their humble Recreant clothing. Even a few winex had been given the honor of being burned up by the Stars despite the fact they held no starblood. He suspected that had been Aeliana's doing, but as he scanned the terrace, he didn't see her.

"Iris?" He bent over the woman grieving alongside Rildan and Marnok.

She turned with a sniffle, confusion in her eyes.

"Do you know where Aeliana is?"

She shook her head. "She said she'd come when she was ready." She turned back to the woman she'd served most of her life.

Her answer made Gaeren uneasy, and he weaved his way through the mourners, asking again if anyone knew where she might be. Before he found a definitive answer, a woman came through the door from the palace, her white dressed singed and covered in black ashes.

"Orra?" Gaeren rushed to her side, checking her over for burns or cuts. Was it possible for the Stars to burn her even though she was one of them? Despite the state of her clothing, her body seemed unharmed. "What happened?"

"Where's Sylmar?" she rasped out.

He shook his head. "They're taking him to the prisons, but they won't let you in. Aeliana and I gave strict instructions that he shouldn't be seen."

She tightened a hand around his arm. "Please, Gaeren. He knows where the onyx stone is."

Gaeren hesitated. "It's too soon, Orra. He just killed Emeris. Can we even trust anything he says?"

She huffed in frustration, then closed her eyes. "When the timing is right..." she mumbled.

Before he could ask what she meant, a rumble carried across the skies as if an unseen storm rolled in. Everyone glanced up, fear in their eyes. Gaeren turned to take in the sight of Durriken soaring across his view of the moon.

Another eerie cry escaped the beast, followed by a blast of flame that lit up the sky, revealing a lone figure on his back, sitting tall and proud. Gaeren held his breath, the moment bringing him back to the first time he'd seen her all grown up, reaching out to touch a deadly dragon with her hair billowing in the wind. He brought his wrist to his lips, letting them graze the soft hairs of her braid.

She'd always been fierce. Even in her toddler days when she'd demanded he catch tadpoles or string together daisy chains. The people around him all stood, placing three fingers to their foreheads before inclining their heads in a bow.

She may not have been eager to take on a leadership role, but he suspected her current show of power and authority meant she'd come to terms with it. A smile slowly spread on his face, even though she'd further established herself as an enemy to his family's throne.

Now everyone could see her the way he always had.

He placed three fingers to his forehead and bowed his head.

CHAPTER 89

THE FOLLOWING DAY, the Sun rose like usual, mocking Aeliana with its bright glow. Her mother was dead. And all she'd been working toward for the last several months had been wiped away in one night—by Sylmar of all people.

She worked alongside the Loyalists and Recreants to care for the injured and prepare the dead for burial, then helped clean up all the mess left behind from the brief battle. Kendalyhn stood by her side as faithfully as Iris had stood by her mother's, her presence surprisingly comforting in the wake of all Aeliana had lost. She'd known she'd accepted her role as a Wyndren the night before, but it surprised her when others seemed to realize it too, bringing questions and information her way that normally would have gone to Sylmar and her mother.

Many of the same questions and information were delivered to Gaeren, forcing—or perhaps allowing—them to work together to find solutions that would please everyone. It helped that he seemed just as uncomfortable with a position of power he hadn't meant to take. At least his rule was temporary, and he could pass it back to Enla when she returned with Riveran.

Aeliana smiled at his clever way of protecting his sister and scrubbed harder at the blood staining the stone floor. She wished she'd thought to get the fish from Velden to do the same for her mother.

"If you're smiling," Gaeren said, "maybe this time I can get you to say yes." He winced when she glanced up, then held up both hands defensively. "Don't shoot the messenger."

Her smile fell. "Don't tell me you want me to go see Sylmar." She sat back on her heels and shoved the brush aside, grabbing a washcloth to clean off her stained hands.

"I understand why you don't want to see him. I don't want to either. But this time it's not just Sylmar asking to see you."

She folded her arms across her chest. "What do you mean?"

"Orra is asking to see him."

Aeliana frowned. "Why?"

"Something about him knowing where the onyx stone is."

"How would he know? He never even talked to Mayvus. He just killed my mother." Aeliana's words came out curtly, and while she regretted taking it out on Gaeren, she felt no guilt over her hatred for her mother's murderer.

"I didn't think he knew anything either. Which is why I let her go see him."

Aeliana's hands balled into fists. "You shouldn't have done that without talking to me. I don't want anyone listening to him spew his lies."

Gaeren hesitated, and Aeliana narrowed her eyes.

"You went with her, didn't you?"

He glanced at the door as if looking for an escape. "I might have."

She huffed and stood, dragging her bucket of water to the window and dumping it outside.

"I'm sorry. I thought nothing would come of it and that it would get Orra off my back, but here's the thing." He placed a hand on her arm. "He's telling the truth. I can't always sense it since it's my secondary spoke, but he was eager to prove himself. I gripped his forearm while he spoke, and every word he said was true."

"What did he say?" she asked against her will.

"He thinks there's more to the curse and that it's not over with their deaths. He wants you to keep searching for answers."

She stilled, hating the way it piqued her curiosity. "What, like something can bring them back?"

Gaeren hesitated. "I don't know. I don't want to get your hopes up. But I also don't think we can ignore him."

"What does this have to do with Orra's stone?"

Gaeren shrugged. "Apparently one of the Stars told her to ask him, but he wouldn't tell her unless you and Iris were present."

Aeliana nearly choked on her scoff because her throat was clogged with tears. "How can I face my mother's murderer?" She pressed her palms against her eyes. "And what does Iris have to do with anything?"

"You won't be doing it alone." Gaeren placed his hands on her shoulders. When she moved her hands, he was crouched before her, looking her in the eye. "I will be with you the entire time. And anytime you don't want to listen to him anymore, you can leave. But if he has something to say that can change the course of our plans—of our lives—we need to hear him out."

Aeliana closed her eyes, trying to think of her mother and what she would do in this situation. As much as it burned to admit it, her mother would have let Sylmar talk, even if it was just so she could discard his words the moment she left the room. She would never turn down information that could potentially help them. The job of a leader was to filter through that information.

And now that she knew Sylmar harbored some secret, could she really sail to the other side of the continent and forget about it?

"Fine," she whispered. "I'll go." She lifted Gaeren's hands off her shoulders and shoved him aside. "But you can't blame me if I use my light shield against him now that I have it back."

<hr>

Traveling to the prison cells was hard enough as Aeliana imagined her mother and father here with Marnok, Orra, and Gaeren.

"How did you stand it?" she asked Gaeren, squeezing his hand tighter as he led her through the tight hallway. Orra and Iris trailed behind them, the maidservant as clueless as Aeliana about why she'd been summoned.

The foul smells of body odor and waste infiltrated her nose, and dirty hands gripped the bars they walked past. So many voices called out, asking for mercy, until they blended together and she could no longer distinguish one plea from another.

"It wasn't this crowded when we were here," Gaeren said, "but it still stank, and we still grew restless."

Orra calmly hummed her agreement from behind them, but Aeliana noticed her scanning the ground and lifting her skirts as if ready to run.

"Has anyone started hearing their cases?" Aeliana asked.

"Ah, well, typically that would be the king's job. I'm not willing to wait for Enla's return, so I requested that various men be brought in as judges, but first we'll need to vet their honor."

"What will we do with the Ahmranans?"

Gaeren shrugged. "If we find the onyx stone Orra is so keen on, maybe we'll send them back. I'm not sure yet. It also depends on how many of them willingly fought alongside her and how many were victims of branding."

They reached a door at the end of the hall, and when they stepped through, they came across four more cells. Only one was occupied. The hairs on Aeliana's arm stood on end beneath her cloak, and she shivered as she stepped closer to Gaeren.

Orra strode past them, right up to the bars. "Both women agreed to come. So now you need to hold up your end of the bargain. Tell us where the onyx stone is."

Sylmar's gnarled hands wrapped around the bars. He looked oddly frail without his staff, yet his eyes held an intensity that made it difficult for Aeliana to maintain his gaze. She'd railed at him the night before, and while she no longer felt violent enough to harm him herself, she hoped when Enla returned, justice would involve full retribution.

"Thank you for coming," he said.

"We didn't come for you," Aeliana shot back.

He nodded. "I'm no broken dragon or lost winex. I can no longer earn your sympathy."

Aeliana frowned. "What is it you want to say?"

Sylmar closed his eyes and leaned against the bars. "There is one thing I've kept secret from you."

"Just one?" Aeliana scoffed.

"Just one left," he clarified, opening his eyes. "At first I thought it didn't matter. It would only cause you more pain to know it. When that message came on your skin after you first arrived, I didn't want to consider it was possible."

"What message?" Orra asked.

"My guardians—"

"Kidnappers," Iris cut in.

"Yes, kidnappers," Aeliana agreed, "carved words on my back to communicate with Mayvus. She used blood magic to send messages back, even across the barrier."

Gaeren shuddered beside her, and this time Aeliana stepped closer to comfort him.

"I don't think it was blood magic." Sylmar's grip tightened on the bars, making his fingers turn white. "The longer it went without her using it again, the more I was able to write it off as a fluke. Maybe it really had been blood magic. But when your mother's talk of a curse held merit, I saw things differently. I knew I had to consider the possibility."

"What possibility?" Gaeren's tone held warning.

"I had to consider that whatever joined Emeris and Mayvus could be connecting you to someone else too. Not blood magic, but something like a curse. When we first thought it could be Mayvus' own doing, it made sense. She wasn't one to do things halfway. If she'd found a way to bind her life force to Emeris, she was surely willing to use you in the same way."

"Who? Who would she bother binding me to?"

Sylmar's gaze turned pained, and he slumped against the cell bars. "After hearing your vision from Lady Merinnia, I know it wasn't Mayvus. I think the whole Wyndren line was doomed ages ago. Perhaps Mayvus never even had a chance at goodness."

"What are you talking about?" Aeliana's starlock burned against her chest with her impatience.

"You won't believe me, which is why I need Iris to show you her memory."

They all turned toward Iris, whose expression held confusion. "My memory of what?"

"Show her the night Anara was born."

Orra straightened, but Iris paled, her hand pulling at her collar. "How do you know that name?"

"Who is she?" Aeliana asked, recognizing the name but unable to place it.

"Anara has the stone," Orra said. "Where is she?"

"I don't know where she is," Sylmar admitted, "but if Iris shows Aeliana the memory, I think she can figure it out."

"You're not making any sense." Aeliana tried to recall where she'd heard the name. Memories cycled through her mind as if her noetic skills had returned despite losing them with her brand on Durriken—until one finally clicked. "There was a girl mentioned in Mayvus' journals. A girl Mayvus had tested the winex fluid on without any results listed. A girl who'd been young when you left Mayvus."

Iris gasped. "Anara's alive?"

Sylmar squeezed his eyes shut.

Aeliana glanced between them. "Did Sylmar and Mayvus have a daughter?"

The noise that came from his mouth might have been a laugh. "No."

"Iris? Did you and Holm have a daughter?" she asked.

Iris shook her head. "I wish," she murmured.

"Show her the memory," Sylmar insisted.

"I can't take memories anymore. I cut out Durriken's brand."

"And you tested it?" he asked. "Made sure the skill was gone?"

"My light shields came back. Isn't that enough?" She swallowed hard, hating the way she sensed herself looking for his approval even now.

"No," he grunted. "It's never enough to assume. Test it. If that skill is truly gone, have Gaeren get the memory for you."

Aeliana scowled and turned her back on Sylmar. Iris shrank away, and Aeliana tried to soften her features as she held out her hands. "Just think of the memory, and when I can't access it, Gaeren can instead."

Iris licked her lips and glanced between Gaeren and Orra. "I didn't know she was alive. I never would have…" She trailed off, then whispered. "Please don't make me show you."

Aeliana's chest tightened. She hadn't cared about Sylmar's babbling, but seeing Iris' response made fear pierce her soul. "I probably can't see it anyway. Just try."

Iris raised trembling fingers to Aeliana's hand, and the moment they touched, Aeliana fell into Iris' memory.

CHAPTER 90

AELIANA STOOD at her mother's bedside, the curtains and quilt looking oddly familiar. She'd seen them before in her mother's memories of their time in Celanoft. A scream echoed through the room, and Aeliana bent over her mother.

"Hush now, love." Her voice came out with Iris' soft lilt. "On this next one I want no screaming, just pushing. It's time."

Her hands pressed a washcloth against Emeris' brow before a strange calm overtook the room, allowing Aeliana the chance to catch her mother's swollen belly and her father pacing in the corner.

Her mother stirred once more, then gripped Iris' hand.

"Push now!" Iris instructed, even as Emeris strained and groaned, her face turning red with the effort.

It took several more contractions, but eventually a tiny head of dark hair emerged, and Iris pulled the baby out and lifted her onto Emeris' belly. "It's another girl," she announced, and Rildan came over, his face beaming with pride.

Iris kept busy, rubbing the baby dry and then cleaning up Emeris, not allowing Aeliana time to process what she'd witnessed.

"Shouldn't she be crying more?" Emeris asked.

"Every baby's different. I wouldn't complain if she was quieter than Aeliana."

Rildan chuckled. "I'm sure Anara will catch up to her."

Her parents beamed at each other, making Aeliana's chest ache. The memory flickered, and for a moment she saw Gaeren and Orra watching her near the prison cell.

When she returned to the memory, Iris was carrying the baby down the hall, choking on sobs. She bumped into someone exiting a room, then gasped as Mayvus turned, her face far less lined but just as calculating.

"What do we have here?" Mayvus peered down at the blanket.

"Anara didn't make it," Iris choked out.

"Hmm." Mayvus leaned closer. "You're certain she's dead?"

Iris shuddered. "She's cold and limp. We hear no breaths or heartbeats." She scooted around Mayvus before continuing her near run to the back door of the priestess' quarters, which opened up to a garden in the Sungazer's perimeter.

Her tears came faster as she found a spot to lay the baby before hunting down a shovel. As the last handful of dirt dropped down over the buried child, the memory seized around Aeliana, drawing her back to her place at Iris' side.

Orra and Gaeren watched her with curiosity and concern. Beyond the bars, Sylmar sat hunched over, wetness on his cheeks dripping into his beard.

"I'm so sorry," Iris whispered. "I should have told you about her. I should have told your mother that Mayvus was there. I never thought she could be alive."

Aeliana dropped the maidservant's hands, unable to process the apology. The memory couldn't be accurate. Because that would mean Aeliana had a…

"What's wrong?" Gaeren asked. "Did you see the memory?"

She blinked up at him, the added confusion over how she could still tune in to memories warring with the far bigger revelation.

There was only one way to truly test Sylmar's theory, to verify Iris' memory.

She pulled the daisy dagger from her belt and held it over her arm. The wrongness of what she was about to do flooded through her, but that was shame from her past, not conviction for the present. It wasn't blood magic. Not if what Sylmar said was true.

Even if his words could be believed, the connection she was about to test might be just as sinister.

But she had to know.

"Aeliana?" Gaeren whispered, suddenly at her elbow.

She let the blade slice into the skin of her forearm, the pain a dull echo of all the times Arvid had carved his messages into her back. The others gasped, but no one moved to stop her. The words were crudely drawn, blood trailing from the lines like tears.

Who are you?

She set the dagger down on the ground and closed her eyes, taking deep breaths while waiting. The others probably thought she'd gone mad. She hoped that was closer to the truth than this other possibility.

With each moment that passed, hope grew that it had all been a lie. That Sylmar had yet one more agenda even from behind his cell door. They could pass off Iris' memory as faulty. Lukai or Marnok could heal her arm, and they could all awkwardly laugh over how they'd been fooled by Sylmar.

When the first twinge came, Aeliana couldn't help burying her face in her shaking hands. She'd felt these twinges before. Strange pains and cuts that appeared from nowhere. Slices on her palm that had come and gone. She'd thought it was clumsiness. She thought it was madness left from her time being used by Arvid and Vera. She'd thought it was visions she'd had of her fears coming true.

But it had always been more than that. It had been the echo of those things happening somewhere else, *to* someone else. Someone else bleeding themselves for blood magic. Gaeren wrapped his arms around her, and she leaned into his comfort, hating that she would have to be the one to tell them all that their horrors were just beginning.

When the sharp pain faded to a distant throb, she knew her time was up. She couldn't bear the weight of it alone any longer. She stepped back and held out her arm.

Tears blurred her vision, but not before she caught sight of the confirmation she'd dreaded.

HELLO, DEAR SISTER. I'M ANARA.

AUTHOR'S NOTE

Do you have a minute to leave a rating or review?

Leave a review with this code!

Reviews and ratings are a huge help to indie authors. It only takes a minute to leave a line or two (seconds for a rating), but it makes my day! You can leave a review with this QR code.

Reviews are especially helpful on Amazon, Goodreads, and Bookbub, but don't feel like you have to leave a review on all three!

Looking for the next book?

You can find the rest of the short stories, novellas, and full length novels in the series on Karyne's website, as well as a suggested reading order.

Find the series with this code!

Still want more?

Find the extras here!

If the 600+ pages of *Salt in the Seas* were not enough, I have some extra goodies to tie you over! You can find free short stories, an audio glossary, high-resolution maps, coloring pages, and a fun magic quiz at www.kary nenorton.com/extras or by using this QR code.

GLOSSARY

This glossary of terms is not exhaustive, but should address the pronunciation and importance of any names/terms used multiple times in this book. Some explanations and terms are missing or left intentionally vague to reduce the risk of spoilers. Some terms may be spoilers for earlier books. For the audio glossary, check the bonus content available at www.karynenorton.com/extras.

Aeliana (a-lee-AH-nuh) - a young Vendaran woman with unusual magic who was stolen across the barrier to Lorvandas as a child and raised by two Vendarans who use blood magic

Ahmranan's Viewpoint - (ahm-RAHN-uns) - a point on the northern coast of Vendaras where Ahmranas can be viewed across the barrier on a clear day

Ahmranas (ahm-RAHN-us) - the country/continent north of Lorvandas and Vendaras with people who value physical strength over intelligence

Andel (an-DELL) - a large seaport on the southern coast of Vendaras

Awakening - an event that reveals if a half-light is deserving of a starlock; if the half-light survives their Awakening, they receive a starlock and will begin training in magic

Bamboo Island - a small island off the western coast of Vendaras;

it's the drop-off point for the starbridge that connects Lorvandas to Vendaras

Barny (BAHR-nee) - an old navy friend of Velden's

Barrier - a shimmering barrier between all the continents that was put in place by the Stars during the Great Divide

Bartholem (bar-THALL-em) - Cyrus' grandfather, the priest

Bayla (BAY-luh) - the woman Riveran pretended to marry

Bond mark - a raised red mark on the left palm that indicates someone is bonded to someone else; typically between couples

Bondmate - the person someone is bonded to; typically a spouse or betrothed

Brand - a raised black mark on either palm that indicates someone is being controlled by the person who branded them

Brogdon (BRAHG-dun) - the son of Jasperus, a former brand of Mayvus'

Calia (Kuh—LEE-uh) Larkos' wife, who has doted on Gaeren for the past several years

Celanoft (SELL-uh-nahft) - a city on the east coast of Vendaras where Emeris served as a priestess; the city where Gaeren went for his dedication year; the city where Aeliana lived before being stolen away

Croft (CRAHFT)- Enla's current bondmate

Cyrus (SY-ruhss) - a priest-in-training who befriends Aeliana

Daisy - Gaeren's nickname for Aeliana

Danton (DAN-tun) - Gaeren's uncle and the current throne warden for the king

Dark spirits - mysterious beings that are attracted to blood magic and can fuse with someone who uses blood magic to give them more power

Deep - slang for the afterlife apart from the Sun/Stars

Dehvlon (DEV-lawn) - the country/continent east of Vendaras with people who value intelligence over physical strength

Della (DEL-uh) - Cyrus' grandmother, the priestess

Dirk - (DERK) - an old friend of Velden's who recently died at sea

Dreyfus - (DRAY-fuss) - a conman who charges money for people to see all the treasures on his ship

Durriken (DUR-ih-kin) - the dragon

Elanesse (el-uh-NESS) - the capital of Vendaras on the northwest coast near the swamps; Gaeren's family name

Elder Algaen (al-GEE-ehn) - an elder of Tideholm on Sayhla Island; Nori's father

Elder Corantun (core-ANN-ton) - an elder of Tideholm on Sayhla Island

Elder Gerot (GARE—ut) - an elder of Tideholm on Sayhla Island; his wife is a sister of Elder Perla's wife

Elder Kraken (CRACK-en) - an elder of Tideholm on Sayhla Island

Elder Mishkel (MISH-kell) - an elder of Tideholm on Sayhla Island who proudly shows off his rainbow fin

Elder Perla (PURR—luh) - an elder of Tideholm on Sayhla Island; Gellen's father; his wife is a sister of Elder Gerot's wife

Emeris (EM-er-iss) - Aeliana's mother; a priestess who is well loved by the people

Enla (EN-luh) - Gaeren's sister and next-in-line for the throne

Erech (AIR-ick) - stableboy / cabin boy

Fay - the woman Thallahan wants to marry

Felk - the winex Aeliana befriends

Fernandus (fur-NAN-dus) - the Elanesse family priest

Gaeren (GAIR-en) - the prince of Elanesse and eventual throne warden to his sister who will be queen

Gellen (GELL-un) - a Sayhleen guard with noetic skills

General Nels - the head of the Recreant army

Great Divide - an event that took place a thousand years ago, when the Stars split the land and divided people groups by waters and barriers in order to prevent fighting

Gullet - the hawk that's always with Riveran

Half-light - a descendant of the Stars; someone with starblood in their veins, a person born of a human and a Star

Holm - Iris' bondmate; he spied for Aeliana's parents years ago; he's part of Sylmar's rescue team; a Vendaran half-light with no magic

Iris - Holm's bondmate; she was a maidservant for Emeris years ago; she's part of Sylmar's rescue team; a Vendaran half-light with no magic

Islara (Iz-LAHR-uh) - city near the heart of Vendaras

Kendalyhn (KEN-duh-lin) - parents were killed by Mayvus; now she's part of Sylmar's rescue team; a destructive pneumatic progeny

Lady Merinnia (Muh-RIN-ee-uh) - a Seer on Sayhla Island

Larkos (LAR-cohs) Gaeren's first mate; he has been feeding Gaeren Recreant political ideas for years; he is loyal to his captain, but not the crown

Lenda (LEN-duh) - Gaeren's bondmate

Lilik (LIL-ick) - Felk's mate

Lorvandas (Lor-VAHN-dus) - the country/continent where humans live

Lovers' Falls - a significant waterfall near the heart of Vendaras where the sprites live

Loyalists - people who support the royal family of Elanesse

Ludo (LOO-doh) - an old navy friend of Velden's

Lukai (LOO-ki) - Aeliana's bondmate; he's part of Sylmar's rescue team; a constructive somatic progeny

Marnok (MAHR-nock) - a man found with no memories or allegiances, but who joins Sylmar's rescue team

Mayvus - Emeris' sister and Aeliana's aunt; a high priestess who has risen to power on the eastern side of Vendaras

Mt. Vescano (Veh-SCAH-no) - a volcano at the southern tip of the Myndren Mountains

Myndren Mountains (MIN-drin) - the large mountain range running through Vendaras

Noetic - progenies who are able to tune into the mind

Nori (NOR-ee) - a Sayhleen eager to help the visiting half-lights; daughter of Elder Algaen

Orra (OR-uh) - a woman with mysterious magic who asks Gaeren to help her find a starbridge

Paelen's Waters (PAY-lehn) - the sea surrounding Sayhla Island

Pneumatic - progenies who are able to sift through the soul

Progeny - a half-light who has survived their Awakening and received a starlock; someone training in magic

Recreants - people who are opposed to the royal family of Elanesse and wish for democracy

Reyna (RAY-nuh) - a Star

Rhodasepha (row-duh-SEHF-uh) - Velden's Sayhleen mother

Rhystahn (RIH-stahn) - the known world that contains the countries/continents of Dehvlon, Ahmranas, Vendaras, Lorvandas, and Sayhla Island, and was a single continent prior to the Great Divide

Rildan (Rihl-dahn) - Aeliana's father

Riveran (RIH-vur-ehn) - Gaeren's best friend from childhood turned enemy and Enla's former bondmate

Rox (rocks) - Bayla's son; the baby Riveran pretended was his son

Sariah (suh-RYE-uh) - Velden's former bondmate

Sayhla Island (SAY-luh) - the country/continent south of Lorvandas where people live who have been cursed by the sprites to be bound to the water

Seaglass Port - a city on the east coast of Vendaras

Seer's Sanctuary - the place where Lady Merinnia stays to reduce stimulation for her pneumatic skills

The Sins of the Stars - a book accounting the Great Divide

Smits - a Recreant in Elanesse

Somatic - progenies who are able to adjust the body

Sprites - large winged creatures who live in Lovers' Falls and grant wishes for a high price

Starblood - blood that can house magic; comes from someone who is half-human and half-Star

Starbridge - an object that can transport people across the barriers

Stargazer - a tower with an open roof built to worship the Stars

Starlock - the conduit for a progeny's magic that allows them to develop stronger magic along one of the spokes

Stars - different from the static stars in the sky; they can take human form; they are worshiped by Lorvandans as loving creators

Stubs - an old navy friend of Velden's

Sun - worshiped by Vendarans as a distant and fearful creator

Sungazer - a tower with an open roof built to worship the Sun

Sylmar (SIHL-mahr) - a progeny with advanced power who's leading a mission to rescue Emeris; a destructive somatic progeny who has accessed metal on the rim of the Wheel of Magic

Thallahan (Thal-uh-han) - Gaeren's second-mate who is hoping to get married after this voyage

Tideholm - a Sayhleen city on the southern coast of the island; the place where the half-lights end up after crossing the barrier

To the Deep and Back - Gaeren's ship, formerly known as *Starspeed*

Tobias (toe-BY-us) - primary healer for the king and queen of Elanesse

Valorian (Vuh-LORE-ee-ehn) - a city in south Vendaras

Velden (VEHL-dehn) - a man with webbed fingers/toes whose mother was Sayhleen and whose father was Vendaran; a constructive pneumatic progeny who has accessed water on the rim of the Wheel of Magic

Vendaras (Vehn-DAHR-us) - the central country/continent in Rhystahn whose people are all half-lights

Wheel of Magic - the way magic is explained and defined, with the basic magic starting at the hub of the wheel before expanding to the spokes and eventually the rim; please see diagram in front of book for more details

Winex (WIHN-ex) - creatures that wax and wane with the moon

Wyndren (WIHN-drehn) - Aeliana's family name, descending from Valyn and thought (by some) to be the right rulers of Vendaras

Zealots - people who believe Mayvus should be on the throne

Kickstarter Acknowledgments

The following people are among the 354 generous backers who contributed to this book's creation and success by being among the first to buy it during the Kickstarter. I'm so thankful for both the new and returning readers alike.

Adam David Collings
Aimee Marie Sokol
Alex Grade
Alex Harlequin
Aly Benoit
Amanda Balter
Amanda Thompson
Amanda VanHoose
Amber Lloyd
Amelia Wickersham
Amy Mathew
Amy McKeever
Angelita Garcia
Anna Mykkeltvedt Havlik
Annarose Willhite
Anthony Kozak
April Choate
Ashlee Olds
Ashley Heinzke
Ashton Reynwood

AslansCompass
Bethany Aich
Billye Herndon
Bowden Jones
Brenna Greenfield
Brianna
Brittney Anderson
C.J. Milacci
Caitlin Millsaps
Caleb Friesen
Camy Tang
Carly Arave
Carly Hunt
Cheyenne H.
Chris Mobley
Chris-André Pedersen
Christopher Wesselstam
Corinne Brucks
David DeHaan
David Leighton

David W. Sanderson
Deann Fox
Derrick SMythe
Dona Watson
Dylan Lusk & Malia Jenks
Edina Hunter
EJB
EL
Elizabeth Grace Tresslar
Emilie Garneau
Eris
Erisnyx
Etta D.
Franchesca Caram
Gordon Sturgeon
Grace Ward
Hannah Abbott
Harrison tu
Helen J Roberts
Hermans
In loving memory
of Basil Martin
J.L. Hendricks
Jean Sitkei
Jenelle Schmidt
Jenna Levitski
Jessica A. Tanner
Jessica Meuth
Jessica Snoots

John Powell
Jonah Pavlicek
Jordan Edwards
Josiah DeGraaf
Justin Burgess
Kaitlyn Hess
Kandi J Wyatt
Karen Chong
Kate McGovern
Katelyn Gray
Katherine Malloy
Kathy Brasby
Kelsey Stenberg
Kent M. Smith
Kevin J Norton
Kiki C
Kimberly Werntz
Kristina Raine
Krystal Markham
Kyle Sullivan
L. Nabeta
Lark Cunningham
Lee Alexander
Lisa A. Moore
Lisa Heiser
Liza Clarke
Lorrianne Joseph
M.H. Woodscourt
Madge Watson

MadiJoy
Madison Pegram
Marena Callahan
Margaret
Mariah L. Rosewood
Matthea W. Ross
Matthew M.
Megan Malicoat
Megan N. Quinn
Melissa T
Michael Simko
Michelle Coffey
Mike from Arkansas
NeonPixxius
Nicola M Wilkinson
Nicole Sanders
Niki Kuhlman
Nikki Gibson
Noemi Hernandez
Or-El
Paul Horvath
Persephone Amloth Hernandez
Rachel F.
Rachel Lowe
Ray Xu
René Nobelen
Ricardo Monascal
Ringmaster

Sara Lawson
Sara Ontiveros
Sara Wilde
Sarah Henne
Sean Gray
Sherry Cammer
Stacey Markle
Stefanie Martin
Stephanie Fischer
Stephanie Price
Stephanie Roy
Stephen Ballentine
Steven "Waffles" Lane
Sue Still
Suz Rodgers
Tana Reeve
Terissa Chalmers
Terri Schwomeyer
Terry Mitchell Hulett
Terry Steinke
Tiffany Goldman
Tiffany Noble
Trenton Nash
Tyler Cheek
Vicki DeVico
Winston Crutchfield
Winter Dorr
Z
Z.R. McCormick

AUTHOR'S ACKNOWLEDGMENTS

I thought book two would be easier to write. Many of the scenes in these pages were in my head long before the first book was finished. But it ended up being so much harder. For the first time while writing, I knew people (like you) were waiting to read it. On top of that pressure, I had to write it while learning how to publish, print, and market the first book. And of course I had the bright idea to narrate it as well.

Even though it's scarier putting a book out in the world on the heels of the first one being so well received, I'm especially thankful for all of your excitement. It fueled my motivation and turned my self-imposed deadlines into shared goals. So thank you, readers, for both challenging and motivating me to make this book better than the first.

On the more practical side of things, I want to say thanks to St. Jupiter for knocking another cover out of the park and thanks to Rachael, for making equally gorgeous maps that are a million times better than the pencil scratched versions I send her.

A big thanks to Kelly and Janine for their encouraging words and eagle eyes during the beta reading stage. I hope you both enjoy the book even more after all the changes I've made.

Laura - I'm so grateful for your patience with all my misplaced commas and grammar failures. I don't know that I'm truly proud of my books until you've cleaned them up and I see them the way others might.

Thank you Constance and Janice for putting up with my incredibly long-winded book and for finding all its flaws. I'm so grateful for our friendships and chats about everything under the sun (and for finally meeting each of you in person!).

Carli - I can't wait to branch out to my sci-fi arm so I have more books to swap with you, but even if we never exchange more manuscripts, the support I have felt from you over this last year has meant the world to me. I wish we weren't on opposite sides of the country, but I'm so excited for all the author adventures we have yet to share in the coming years.

At least twenty-five percent (if not more) of this book was written in a beautiful cabin in Pinetop, where my in-laws graciously let me hole up and write. Thank you, Kevin and Trudy, for sharing that space with me and with my writer friends.

Holly, thank you for patiently listening to hours and hours of Paeter and me narrating not just these books, but the podcast episodes as well. I'm so grateful Paeter picked you all those years ago, and that I can call you my sister as well as my friend.

Thank you, Paeter, for all our years watching sci-fi and fantasy movies, for all our conversations about the highs and lows in life, and for all your support in this season of life. I never imagined our interests would someday converge into projects we could collaborate on. Having you put your time and energy into creating the audiobooks that bring my stories to life is a huge gift and I love that I can tell people I get to do that with my brother. Not many people have that kind of friendship with their adult siblings, and I don't ever want to take it for granted.

Silas, Garrison, Lydia, and Charlotte - I'm so grateful I waited until all of you were in school to start publishing. I thought it was so I'd have more time to write, but now I realize it was so I could have more life experience to bring to my writing. It's so fun to have all of you cheering me on.

And to my husband, Jon, goes the biggest thanks of all. Looking back on our almost twenty years of marriage, I'm amazed at all the ways we've gotten to live life together, and I'm so thankful I get to live it all with you. Thank you for putting up with my weird stories and anti-social habits. Thank you for being strong where I'm weak and for challenging me to grow. I look forward to balancing each other out for many more decades to come.

Thank you, Jesus, for all of the above. May the words I write be pleasing to you, O Lord, my rock, and my redeemer.

ABOUT THE AUTHOR

Karyne Norton hasn't found the key to time travel, immortality, or infinite lives, so she's taking a break from nursing and photography to focus on raising four human beings and writing fantasy and science fiction. When she's not writing, she's reading, which is why she's also the host of the Finding Fantasy Reads podcast, where she reads a new short story every week from a variety of fantasy authors. Her first novel, *Blood of the Stars*, is an epic fantasy that released March 2024.

instagram.com/karynenorton

amazon.com/~/e/B07JNDZ86M

bookbub.com/profile/karyne-norton

youtube.com/@findingfantasyreads

facebook.com/karynenortonauthor

goodreads.com/karynelnorton

9 781962 136068